When *Suburban Souls* was first published in 1901 by Charles Carrington, an active publisher of erotica in England and France, its sexual frankness and autobiographical disclosures quickly made it as sought after as *My Secret Life*. The first edition was strictly limited and did not become widely available until 1968, when Grove Press published the work in the United States.

The author identifies himself only as Jacky S., a 43-year-old broker with the Paris stock exchange. His memoir tells of his five-year love affair with 19-year-old Lilian Arvel. At the beginning of their romance, Lilian seemed to reciprocate Jacky's passion and willingly joined in mutual "exploration games," fondly calling Jacky her "Papa" and submitting to his strangest whims. Jacky's intentions toward Lilian were honorable, and while she lasciviously encouraged him to debase her, he did not object when she refused to give up her virginity. Gradually, however, their affair developed into a strange standoff, then came apart after the signs of infidelity became unmistakable—Lilian had lost her virginity to someone else and entered into a peculiar relationship with her stepfather.

Jacky occasionally digresses to tell of various light-hearted sexual interludes with others. But for five years Lilian controlled Jacky's destiny, even though she could not return his love. This edition also includes 20 appendices, among them the complete text of another novel, *The Yellow Room*, referred to in *Suburban Souls* as having been edited by Jacky S.

Suburban Souls

Suburban Souls

The Erotic Psychology of a Man and a Maid

BOOK-OF-THE-MONTH CLUB
NEW YORK

INTRODUCTION

❖

by Richard Manton and Barney Rosset

Charles Carrington was without a doubt the most famous and greatest of the publishers of erotic literature in the early 1900s, both in England and in France, whence he fled for refuge from the English authorities. And his greatest achievement was his publication of *Suburban Souls*—a book he may also have written.

The novel is more French than English. As with so many of Carrington's publications, it has the style of a book written in another language and then translated literally. There are such verbal oddities as a reference to the "Eastern Station" in Paris; even an Englishman would be more likely to recognize it as the *Gare de l'Est*.

Suburban Souls is a novel of sex and jealousy, as obsessive in its way as the self-consuming passion of the narrator for Albertine in *A la Recherche du Temps Perdu*. A decade before the first volume of Proust's great novel, *Suburban Souls* dwells on the true nature of erotic jealousy.

And although its sexual descriptions are more explicit, the novel has far more in common with the naturalism of Zola or Maupassant than with the pipe dreams of Edwardian erotica. The Parisian world of the 1890s, its cafes and railway stations, its metropolitan avenues and semi-rural suburbs of brokers and entrepreneurs, are evoked by a suggestive impressionism appropriate to the age.

The course of true love is far from smooth in

Suburban Souls. The strange and growing involvement of Jacky S. with young Lilian Arvel is meticulously and yet vividly observed by the victim himself. For Lilian is not the innocent Little Nell or Little Em'ly of Victorian family reading. She is eager to be morally corrupted, her passion woken with a perverseness that unnerves her middle-aged seducer. *Suburban Souls* sees this girl-child by the new light of Freudian theory rather than the comforting glow of Dickensian sentiment.

Ultimately, the book becomes far more an account of the mental state of Jacky S. than a study of Lilian and her depravity. One of the novel's most exciting incidents, in its effect on the narrator, is one in which he has no direct part—a young law student's vigorous attempt to rape Lilian. Hearings of the young man's assault on the girl he himself loves acts as a powerful aphrodisiac—to use his own term—and he makes her repeat the story to him often; thus we see his emotions of jealousy begin their pathological development. He presents Lilian with a copy of Sade's *Justine*, urging her to pay particular attention to Saint Fond's account of the pleasure to be derived from seeing one's mistress in the arms of another man. Later the relationship between Jacky and Lilian changes from that of an older lover and an adolescent girl to the contract of a whore and her paymaster. He calls her his whore for the first time while they make love and later on makes her masturbate him by the street railings as a common prostitute would. "Oh, yes, I am your little whore!" she whispers as she does so. "And would you do anything for me?" he asks. "Anything, no matter how dirty or disgusting?" Her answer is false, but it is the one he longs to hear—"Anything, as long as it is you!"

Inevitably, his reward for reducing her to the level of a prostitute in their fantasies is that she begins to act like one in reality. In his account of their relationship, Jacky complains increasingly of the motives that seem to drive Lilian toward him. His heart grows full of the "uneasy feeling of repulsion that her broad mercenary hints were beginning to cause in me." His first revenge is in cruel language, which he uses toward her both in their meetings and in his letters. But this style is entirely apt in their new relationship. "The more cynically and brutally I wrote," he says, "the better she liked it."

For Lilian to be mercenary was not the worst that might happen. After all, plenty of kept women in 1890s Paris lived on easy terms with their keepers. Soon, however, Jacky guesses that Lilian is a confirmed liar in the area of sexual relations. Her expertise in bed, so engaging at first, merely serves to convince him that "other hands and other male organs had been in contact with Lily Arvel's body."

Suburban Souls is never more purely the story of Jacky's own obsessions than in his analysis of Lilian the moral delinquent. Convinced that he has caught her out in lies about letters that she claims to have written but then lost, he gets out the packet of her correspondence to him. In this way, he subjects her *in absentia* to a psychiatric examination in the terms of the day. Like Proust's narrator, it is the man rather than the girl who makes the better subject for this. However, he concludes that "she suffers from anaemia or chlorosis. There is evidently psychopathic deterioration and she is a neurotic subject . . . . Masturbation and unnatural practices before the age of puberty have produced neurasthenia with its attendant symptoms. It is a clear case of hysteria."

Such passages serve to remind us that, whether or not 1901 was the publication year of *Suburban Souls*, it saw the appearance of a far more famous work: Sigmund Freud's *The Psychopathology of Everyday Life*. By a natural progression, the hero's abhorrence of Lilian's greed for money and his conviction that she is dishonest ripen at last into an all-consuming sexual jealousy. "She inspired disgust and excited desire," he confesses toward the end of the novel. "In a word she troubled the brain of whoever took an interest in her."

Their relationship had begun with Lilian addressing him as "Beloved Master." Before the end, she is calling him "My Own Slave." The links of the chain binding them are forged from a self-tormenting jealousy that consumes him like a wasting sickness. So, in the story of Jacky, the play must continue. Though the curtain has been rung down, the universal spectacle of love and hate goes on all the same.

I

DEDICATE

THIS STORY OF SORDID SENSUALITY

TO

MY HEROINE

ONE OF THE WICKEDEST WOMEN IN THE WORLD

THIS HOMAGE IS DUE TO HER,
FOR HAS SHE NOT WRITTEN
A GREAT PART OF THE
BOOK HERSELF?

I

1

Her father loved me, oft invited me.
SHAKESPEARE.

HEART. Why did you not ravish her?
. . . .
CONST. Not I, truly; my talent lies to softer exercises.
SIR JOHN VANBRUGH.

My great fear in setting forth this simple adventure of love and passion is that I shall not be able to carry home to my reader's mind the feelings, the hopes, the doubts and fears that so long racked my soul and stirred up all that was good and bad in the heart and brain of the writer—a very ordinary man.

I have always been a great reader of amatory literature and all books and novels relating to sexual matters, whether wilfully obscene or cunningly veiled; whether written by medical authorities, novelists, or even issued from the secret presses of Belgium and Holland. I often remarked that such tales were far from true to nature. I do not speak of lewd works, where impossibilities are presented merely to augment the sale of the volumes, but of the few which impress us with an idea of truth, being incidents, which, although highly coloured, might perhaps have happened all the same. Such are some of the best French novels. But most of them are written by men who misjudge women, and when lady novelists write about love they seldom show us a woman as she really is, their sympathy for their own sex guiding their partial pens in spite of themselves. Really true tales of sensuality are thus rare, and I come forward to give you mine, where I have carefully endeavoured to keep my imagination within bounds and tell nothing but what did really happen.

It will hurt me, and drag open smarting, half-healed wounds, but I mean to do it and go through it as an expiation.

I am the hero. I cannot help smiling as I write that word. I guess my readers will think I am going to praise myself, and with excuses lead up to an eventual conversion. Do not be led away. I am not a good man. Some may call me vile. You must not put me down as a professional romance-writer. No, I am plain Jacky S—, of the Paris Bourse, writing plain facts, and if I were to see the error of my ways and retire to a monastery at the end of the story, it would be feeble-minded and contrary to human nature. So pity me, and do not crush me beneath the weight of your righteous self-satisfaction. Had I been my own maker, and had I, as a baby, possessed the knowledge of the world I have now, I should have been a good man, without voluptuous longings or abnormal passions, and I should not be writing this vicious book. I know some men get more pleasure out of one Sunday's church-going than I have ever done in a year's enjoyment of wine, women, and gambling. I know not how they do it. I should like to be as they are, but I cannot change my nature, and I shall go to my death as I was born.

Let all young men who read my story, and who will spit out their pitiable contempt for me, the unworthy author, wallowing in the slime of sensuality, take a scribbling diary and jot down their secret longings for a few months. Truthfully, mind you. At the end of a quarter's record, just hark back and see if the chronicle agrees or disagrees with my acts.

Why are we as we are? Hereditary influences, education, surroundings—Heaven knows what. Conclusion: some men are bad, a few are good, most of us are betwixt and between.

I am at the top of the sinners' class and my only excuse is

that somehow I manage to be intensely wicked on an honourable, chivalrous basis of my own. You shall find out my style of villany as you read on.

I have spoken the prologue. Let me now try and introduce the actors in this miniature drama of lust.

Eric Arvel was a correspondent of the financial press. His duties brought him to the Bourse nearly every day, and he used to watch the market and send off long columns of criticism on the rise and fall of stocks and shares to newspapers in England, Germany, and Russia. He was a man of many languages and I never knew his precise nationality. I expect he was born of English and Continental parents and had been brought up in Great Britain. But his business and birth have very little to do with the present memoirs, although I often thought he was of Jewish extraction and the German strain seemed to predominate. Besides his financial elucubrations, he wrote letters of Parisian gossip for many newspapers, and had other strings to his bow. I think he was often employed by houses of business in London to travel and collect debts, or help to get evidence for solicitors in Great Britain. He journeyed greatly at one time all over Europe, and once had a mission that took him to China and Japan, returning from those countries with heaps of curiosities, such as quaint idols, dainty porcelain, and beautifully embroidered silk gowns, wherewith to delight the females of his household. I never troubled about his writings or his doings. It was no concern of mine what money he had or how he accumulated it. I had known him for years, how many I cannot now remember. I am 47, as I write now, and I am nearly sure we must have been acquainted twenty years before. I occupied a good position on the French Stock Exchange, and earned and spent money like water. When plying his avocation, he frequently fell across me and other members of my family, who were in the same line of business, and he knew all my parents at home. He was perfectly straightforward in all his monetary transactions, which is paying him a great compliment, as journalists are generally shifty paymasters. We seemed to have a little sympathy for each other, as we had many tastes in common, and so we got drawn together, although I think he was about twelve years my senior. I do not know his precise age, but we will say he is about sixty. He was fond of tales of scandal, liked gossiping about people, and was pleased to know how much money they possessed and if they were in good circumstances or not. I used to feed his curiosity and chop funny stories about all sorts and conditions of men with him. I would furnish him with what information I could for his articles, and he in return gave me a cunningly worded advertisement as often as possible. He liked reading as I do and I lent him books. One or two were of a spicy sort. I furnished him with reviews and magazines for years, sending him packets of papers twice and thrice a month. His tastes seemed to lead him towards lechery. I was always fond of women and so our conversation was often of the most lascivious kind. He was a great smoker and was seldom without the Englishman's briar in his mouth. I am also a votary of the weed, and we would swop tobaccos and have many a long chat together about the scandals of the Exchange, the amours of our circle of financiers and the latest echoes of the London clubs, for I am an Englishman, although my life has been passed in Paris. I never was much of a scandalmonger myself, being too indifferent to the wagging of the world, but I used to collect little stories to please my friend. I do not think he was very liberal-minded, nor very particular to a lie or two, especially when he fell to boasting about how he had succeeded in one thing or another, but I took good care never to contradict him. He possessed the usual vanity of ordinary middle-class folk, and gave his opinion on current topics boldly, albeit I could often see he had never studied the subject he was talking about. He was very fond of money, but careful and saving withal. One trait that always grated upon me was that he seemed pleased to hear of the downfall of anybody, even when the victim of circumstances was a perfect stranger to him and had never been in his way. So I suppose there was a little envy and a great deal of jealousy in his composition. In appearance, he was tall, corpulent, and a trifle weak at the knees. He was far from ill-looking and must have been handsome in his youth. He was fair, with a thick moustache and no beard; bald, with a fine-shaped Roman nose and open nostrils. He was shortsighted and wore a pince-nez. His eyes were blue and he bit his nails to the quick. Some ten years ago he had suffered from a mysterious malady, and he wasted to a skeleton, so that everybody thought he was not long for this world. He spoke vaguely of some kidney trouble, and then he rallied, miraculously as I thought, and grew quite stout.

During all these years I had only met him as one man of the world meets another and cared nothing about his private life. He had frequently begged me to come and see him at his suburban dwelling at Sonis-sur-Marne, which, as all the world knows, is about twenty minutes ride by train from the Eastern station of Paris, but I had always refused, or put him off on some specious pretext, as I was very diffident about making fresh acquaintances, and if there was one thing I hated more than another it was pushing myself into people's houses. But in 1895, having been bitten by a mania for possessing and rearing dogs, I happened to have a very fine litter of fox terriers, and I asked Mr. Arvel if he would care to accept a bitch six months old, who promised to make a nice animal. He seemed very pleased at the offer, telling me that he wanted a dog who would be watchful and give the alarm down in the country, and he asked me to come to lunch and bring the puppy, who I had christened Lili. Oddly enough, I found that my friend's house was called Villa Lilian, and this name was cut into the stone at the side of the gate. The name of Lilian or Lily is destined to play a great part in my life, as my mistress—for I have a mistress, as every Parisian has—was also named Lily. This latter lady plays but an insignificant part in this narrative, and so I pass her by for the present.

But the story is of my love and I will introduce her at once, as I am dying to write her description. My pen moved slowly as I tried to conjure up the heavy, sullen, dull figure of my host and now it runs fast; my pulse quickens and my heart beats, as I endeavour to give a faint idea of the lineaments and bearing of the girl who was destined to offer me a little pleasure and cause me plenty of pain.

And her name was Lilian too. She was a pronounced brunette, and at first sight you could scarcely call her handsome. But she was full of expression, and when pleased, and her face lighted up in the heat of conversation, was very pretty. Her visage might be compared to an unfinished sketch; the features were good, taken one by one, but they lacked completion and rounding off. Her eyes were beautiful, of a rich brown, large and liquid, like those of an intelligent hound, with long lashes, and symmetrical, bushy, black eyebrows overshadowed them. The sign of jealousy was unmistakeably there, for the brows met above the bridge of a sharply cut nose, which was perhaps a trifle too long. There was an air of decision about the pointed chin, but this singular young girl possessed a remarkable mouth, which could not fail to attract a masculine observer and which was in perfect harmony with her other features. It was long and large and the fleshy lips seemed to be never still. All her emotions, all the secret inward movements of her mind betrayed themselves by the ever-changing unrest of these two rosy cushions. Sometimes the corners rose up, unveiling a chaplet of pretty, white teeth, as pointed as those of a young wolf, and their pearly enamel contrasted with the brilliant carmine of the lips, which she was always biting and licking with the end of her tongue. Her sensual mouth resembled a brutal red wound across the dark olive tint of her face. Sometimes these strange lips pursed themselves together in a rapid pout; or half-opened, appeared to be drinking in a delightful draught of air, or better still, imploring the white heat of a lascivious lover's scalding kiss. When out of temper, she was positively ugly: two black circles appeared round the eyes, which became gloomy; a dull, bluish tinge overcast her skin and the mysterious lips turned positively violet. She possessed an admirable forest of splendid blue-black hair and needed but a blood rose behind her ear and a lace mantilla on her shapely head to be the living picture of a cigarmaker of Seville, and this was not to be wondered at, as she had Spanish blood in her veins. She was of middle height; thin, with no bust, and the lines of her figure were perfect, there being nothing angular about her. Her waist was naturally small, while her hips and the lower part of her frame were well developed. She was quick, deft in her manner, with a pleasing voice, and possessed the gift of being at ease in society, thus making those who approached her happy to be in her company. She spoke English with a slight accent, which was an additional charm, and was fairly well educated, writing both English and French with very few faults. She was domesticated, and knew how to sew, cut out and make dresses, and cook a little, but thanks be to Heaven, she was no musician and although the Villa Lilian boasted a piano when I first knew her she could only teaze it with one tapering finger. Her Papa had some peculiar theories about the necessity for a young lady to be able to earn her own living, and he had placed her for some years at Myrio's, in the Rue de la Paix, a celebrated house for making ladies' head-coverings. So Lilian was a milliner, and she made hats and bonnets for the wealthy little *bourgeoises* of Sonis, and the wives of the retired tradespeople, who inhabited the mansions and châteaux in the sleepy village during the summer, so Lilian had several workgirls in a kiosque in the garden, and was supposed to be lucratively employed in her leisure hours until such time as the proverbial Mr. Right should come along and take her away to bear him a strictly limited number of children and become a staid married lady. But this was not to be.

On my first visit to the Villa Lilian, in the middle of May, 1895, I was received with great cordiality. The little bitch seemed to please Monsieur, Madame, and Mademoiselle.

I must say at once that Mr. Arvel was not married and the lady who was at the head of his household was not his wife. She was a short, stout, little Frenchwoman, about 45 years of age, as far as I could judge, with the fine eyes, black hair, and pearly teeth that she had handed down to her daughter Lilian. She was very vulgar and quite uneducated but was a fine specimen of the French middle-class housewife, having all the qualities and faults of the Gallic peasantess. She was very frugal, avaricious, a foe to dusty corners and untidiness, and an excellent cook. I think Eric Arvel, who was a tremendous eater, loved her for the dainty dishes she used to set before him. Her greatest pleasure was to see him gorge and all her guests were bound to overeat themselves to please her. She seemed tolerably artful, cunning and hot-tempered. Besides her daughter Lilian, there was a son, two years younger, Raoul, but he was being brought up in England and I was not destined to meet him until three years later.

I already had a slight bowing acquaintance with Madame Adèle, Arvel's mistress, and I knew he had lived with her as her husband for about sixteen or seventeen years when this story opens. He told me frankly of his position, and how everybody at Sonis believed them to be married, and I found that he had brought up the boy and girl, his mistress being left a widow only three years after the birth of the children, and they had lived together ever since. He intended to marry her eventually and although they quarrelled now and again, she was evidently fond of her lord and master, but he, very hasty, obstinate and despotic, did not seem to care much for her. He liked his house, his garden, his dogs, his pipe and his bicycle, and when his routine work was done, dashed off with sufficient facility, his pleasure consisted of a heavy meal, a pipe, and desultory reading.

His house was a pretty one, and had been bought cheaply with the economies of Madame, to whom it belonged. A year after I knew him, some adjoining ground being in the market, he bought it, enlarged the garden and improved the house. I must not forget that Adèle's mother occasionally appeared on the scene, but she was a silly old lady, slightly eccentric, inasmuch as she tried to doctor everybody with mysterious herb medecines and was a general nuisance. Eventually, Mr. Arvel pensioned her off, to stop her coming to the house. He was the breadwinner, and I could see that his mistress and the girl did all they could to make him a comfortable home, as they were entirely dependent on him. He spent plenty of money on the villa and garden, meaning it as a little piece of property for Adèle, if anything should happen to him.

After this first day spent with the family, I did not mean to return, as Arvel's boasting conversation was trite and commonplace, and the mother was a cypher, once away from her housework or the kitchen. But I fell in love with Lilian at first sight. When I say I fell in love with her, I hardly know how to analyse my own feelings. I can only say that I desired her. But she was 19, and I was 43, and I tried to put this new passion out of my mind. There was my Lily too, in a pretty little home I had put together for her, bit by bit, and I had an idea that it would be a scurvy trick to make love to the young lady, who I may call the stepdaughter of my host. I made myself agreeable to the two ladies and was invited down to their pleasant little country house over and over again. Sometimes my faithful companion, my dog Smike, was invited too, to be petted and made much of by Lilian, and so was his mate, the mother of the bitch Lili, good old Sally Brass. I never came empty-handed, and brought them presents of perfumery, flowers, sweets, and such trifles as please the female mind. Lilian took no particular notice of me, treating me with politeness and nothing more. The little bitch grew apace, and Papa, who was very hard to convince, got into his head that in-and-in breeding was good for fox terriers and borrowed its father to cover the daughter, Lili. He got a tolerable litter, but they were all more or less faulty. An outside cross was wanted, but they doted on their pets and kept several bitches of the litter, and one dog, Blackamoor, who became the special pet of Mademoiselle. They already had one dog, a tremendous Bordeaux hound, very good to his masters, but ferocious with strangers. All this brought me continually to the cottage and no doubt I pleased the women, or else they would have taken good care not to have had me at their house so often.

I remember meeting Mr. and Mrs. Arvel, I speak of them as if they were legally married, at Le Treport, in August, 1896, quite by accident. I joked freely with Adèle, as French matrons are very fond of loose talk, being alone with her for a short time, and chaffed her about this trip with her husband to the seaside. Lilian was at home, with her Granny to look after her. It was quite a honeymoon, I said. She answered me quietly that Mr. Arvel was far from loving, and that she suffered greatly from his neglect, being rather sensual. This startled me a little, and I drew back and kept out of the way, as I was thinking of the daughter and not of the mother.

But it made me open my eyes and I began to think that perhaps I was rather too scrupulous and there might be a chance for me with Lilian. Mr. Arvel's conversations too were very lewd, but he particularly impressed upon me how innocent Lilian was. She knew nothing of the relations of the sexes and was very frivolous, not caring for any serious pleasures.

He complained that he could not get her to read a book and

so form her mind. In fact, he spoke against her and ran her down continually, and his mistress came in also for a share of his disdain. I was a long time victim of this peculiar mania of his, but I found out afterwards that such backbiting is a common fault with little-minded people, and occurs in many families. The more such parents love their children, wives or relations, the more they speak against them. The principal motive is jealousy, lest you should think too much of them, to the detriment of their own vanity, and they seem to get annoyed with themselves to find that the person they are trying to lower in your estimation should take up so much of their own thoughts or yours. But I could see that he was very fond of Lilian and was always talking about her. He would teaze her and call her "Scraggy," and pinch her calves as she passed him. She would shriek, putting out her tongue at him, and appealing to Mamma for help, and Adèle would scold both her and Papa.

I used to try to get alone with Lilian in corners, but she did not want me, and when she stroked Blackamoor, I would caress him too and attempt to get my hand on hers, but she never took heed.

I remember one day she was indisposed, as she seemed to suffer from stomach troubles, and, in her dressing-gown, she came and sat next to me on a sofa. Her father, as I call him to prevent useless reiteration, was seated opposite us. She was quite close to me and I could feel the warmth and pressure of her body through the light fabric of what was evidently her only garment. A thrill of sensual longing stirred me, but she felt nothing. I mentioned the circumstance to her a year later, but she confessed that she had no recollection of this trifling incident, which I always remember.

So things went on until the summer of 1897, when I made up my mind to gradually drop the Arvel family. I loved the girl, although I had never betrayed myself and I could see I was nothing to her. I dared not speak out, as I still had the sentiment of honesty, which told me that I must not take a mean advantage of my friend's hospitality, especially as he appeared to be very fond of the girl, and they were for ever together, when she invariably sided with her Pa against her Mamma.

When I was invited to Sonis, Lilian would often write to me in obedience to Papa's wishes, and I would answer her as prettily as I dared. I was quite surprised and delighted to find that in July or August, 1897, her letters seemed to get more cordial and one day she asked me to accompany her to the post-office alone. I went with great pleasure, especially as up to now Papa had always accompanied us, and the only liberty I had ever taken was a little mild chaff about marriage, when she would retort that she never intended to wed, but would always remain with her Papa. I was pleased to find that Lilian was as near as possible making love to me and I could see that I had very little work to do to make myself thoroughly liked.

The first few letters, which were merely invitations by her parents' orders, I have destroyed, but some of them now contained very gracious hints to encourage me to carry on what was fast growing into a real flirtation. We had many such walks and talks, but I was too flushed with my triumph to remember dates or take notes, and I must try to sum up all our conversations together and so get on rapidly, as I mean to endeavour to stick to plain facts, making my confessions as concise as possible. I have carefully avoided all reference to extraneous events (except in one or two notable instances), passing guests I met at Sonis, or indeed anything that has no bearing upon the loves of Jacky and Lilian.

Our talk began to run into very loose channels, as Lilian, in answer to an insidious question of mine, told me that one of her lady customers had made love to her, and much to her disgust had kissed her on the mouth. I explained that there was something masculine about her—she was wearing a boy's straw hat—and soon led her to talk about lovers. She told me that she had never had one, but had flirted a little. She did not like young fellows, but preferred men of mature age. Upon this I followed suit and put myself forward, to be, of course, agreeably received. This was our first important chat, as far as I can recollect, and I was soon in receipt of another note, begging me to come and spend the day and asking after the health of my dog Smike. She added that she sent a kiss to him, as she did not dare to offer one to his master, although she would dearly like to do so.

Our next interview, during another quiet ramble in the streets and lanes of Sonis, was more to the point. I took her hand in mine and caressed her bare neck as I made a bold declaration of love, but she spoke of danger. I explained that I was not a youth and that a man of the world like myself could give pleasure without fear of disagreeable consequences. I offered, in one word, caresses without danger.

"I should want more than that," she answered.

I thought immediately that she had already been in the arms of a real lover, and that she was alluding to the male's approach in its entirety, and resolved to let my pent-up desire have full vent. So I told her how I had long since yearned for her and reminded her of my little attempts to approach her. She quite understood that if I had returned to Sonis again and again, it was for her and her only. So I soon extracted from her a half-promise that she would come to me one day in Paris, and I was to correspond with her in a feigned lady's handwriting, as neither Papa nor Mamma tampered with her letters, as long as the envelopes seemed to betray a female correspondent, who might be a customer. I then asked for the promised kiss, but explained that I did not want a silly, grand-motherly pressure of the lips.

"I want a real French kiss," I said.

She laughed. I guessed she understood.

I simply thought that here was a young person fresh from the workroom of a milliner of the Rue de la Paix, who probably had already been enjoyed by a man, without counting possible Lesbian approaches of her companions, and thus I grew bolder and bolder. We returned home, and nearing the kitchen, which was in the basement, we passed through a lobby where there was hardly any light.

"How dark it is here!" whispered Lilian, and I immediately turned round and clasped her in my arms. My lips were on her mouth at once—the mouth I had longed for two years and more —and to my delight I felt her cool and moist, pointed tongue slowly insert itself between my willing lips and join mine. It was an enchanting embrace. I felt such a shudder of longing lust rush through my veins as I have never felt before or since, and I believe I shall never forget Lilian's first kiss.

LILIAN TO JACKY.

Sonis-sur-Marne, October 20th. 1897.

My dear Mr. S ...,

You must think I am a little humbug by not having received an answer to your charming letter, but really it is no fault of mine.

I have much to do this week and in spite of my great desire, it has been impossible for me to get away for the whole of one afternoon.

When I meet you, I should wish to have enough time not to run away directly I arrive. I am certain that we shall have much to say to each other.

Will you let me come to you Thursday week? If yes, I shall be in Paris at 2:30. Do not wait for me at the Gare d l'Est, but tell me yourself the place where I am to find you. I am too ignorant to fix a *rendez-vous* myself.

I hope to have a word from you shortly. Awaiting a reply, please accept the assurance of my most lively sympathy,

LILIAN.

LILIAN TO JACKY.

Sonis-sur-Marne, October 26th. 1897.

As I know my dear Marie is very amiable,* I ask her to kindly await me next Thursday, so that I shall not have to ask the *concierge* about . . . you?

I can see you smile, but what would you have? . . . I cannot surmount a certain feeling of timidity.

I have to go to London, Friday or Saturday, but this will not prevent me keeping the appointment, for—must I confess it?—I await next Thursday with immense impatience!

Soon I shall have the pleasure of teazing you and listening to all the silly things you talk about in your last note,

LILIAN.

Lilian was acquainted with a young woman about her own age, whose Christian name was Charlotte, and who was employed in a

---

* My letters, written in violet ink in a feminine hand on fancy note-paper, quite different from my own, were supposed to be from a female and I always signed them: "Marie."

firm of some importance in Paris. They sold lace, and Charlotte's uncle was at the head of the firm, I think. Anyhow, Charlotte occupied a certain position in the business, and as a person of confidence was required to visit London yearly in the autumn, it had been arranged that Lilian should accompany Charlotte and talk the necessary English. Lilian had already done this journey the year before and the two families were friendly. All Mademoiselle Arvel's expenses were defrayed, and she received one hundred francs for each week she stopped in London. It was generally a fortnight or three weeks until all the customers had been visited. Lilian was delighted, as she could thus see her brother Raoul, of whom she appeared to be very fond.

Lilian to Jacky.

Sonis-sur-Marne, Thursday, October 27th. 1897.

Here are all our, or so to speak more correctly, all my beautiful castles in the air demolished. I am really unlucky, I, who was full of such great joy at the idea of seeing you to-morrow, to be able to tell you, perhaps even to prove to you that a certain person not only seems to like you and interests herself in all you do, but that she really loves you.

But to return to the real reason of this letter. I am kept a prisoner by a severe cold.* Impossible to go out. If you will allow me and if it does not worry you, I will give you an appointment for next week, unless I have to go to London on Saturday. In that case, I will write immediately I return. It seems as if everything was against me just now. I hope you will think of the poor little invalid, who is always thinking of you.

Lilian.

Lilian to Jacky.

London, November 2nd. 1897.

I am here since Saturday evening and I already wish to be back again. No, decidedly, I shall never get used to London! All is sad and dull. The women look like machines on springs and the men seem to

---

* Her monthly indisposition?

be running as if pursued. Nowhere is there to be seen the grace of true *Parisienne*. I hope you will not be vexed at my frankness. I ought not to say what I think of your fellow countrymen, and yet in my eyes you are so unlike most Englishmen. At any rate, you only have their qualities. Thus having all English and French qualities, you must consequently be perfect. Still I confess that my hope is that I shall not find you so. What a bore a man must be who possesses every virtue!

No, I really do not know what I ought to bring you back from London, but you have only to make a sign and if it will give you the least pleasure, I shall only be too happy to do it.

I hope to be at Sonis for the end of next week. It is useless for me to tell you that as soon as I am free I shall write to you to ask if you still have the same wish for me. I have not quite got over my cold. Thanks for kind advice.

This letter carries to you a kiss as soft and as sweet as you can possibly desire.

LILIAN.

Strange to say there was no address on this letter from London, so that I could not answer it.

LILIAN TO JACKY.

Sonis-sur-Marne, November 16th. 1897.

Once more I am near you. According to my promise, and for my own pleasure, I quickly write to you. I shall be free any day you like next week. To you, my dear confidant, I may tell the little trouble I had on the eve of my departure from London. I lost a five pound note. Am I not unlucky? But I weary you with all my stories, so I leave you, but expect a line in return.

Soon I hope to see you.

LILIAN.

I did not like this letter, and my growing passion, from fever heat fell to freezing point. Was this the missive to receive on the eve of a young girl's first appointment? It smacked of the professional. Did she want to sell herself? I resolved to have no more to do with her, and despite the agony of disillusion, I answered as follows:

JACKY TO LILIAN.

Paris, Thursday, November 18th. 1897.

My dear Lilian,

I am very pleased to hear you have safely returned from your journey and that you are in good health.

I was not able to answer your letter from London, for you forgot to give me your address.

You are very kind in letting me know that you can come and say "how d'ye do" to me next week, and I should like to fix a day, but unfortunately I am forced to go away on Monday, having something to do in another country.

I am very sorry to hear of your trouble, but I hope things will right themselves. We are neither of us very lucky.

Affectionate sympathy from your friend.

MARIE.

This last note crossed one from Papa, as follows:

ERIC ARVEL TO JACKY.

Sonis-sur-Marne, November 18th. 1897.

Dear Jacky,

If you have nothing better to do, the ladies would be glad to see you to-morrow at eleven, to give your valued opinion as to the merits of a turbot fresh from England and a hen pheasant. I shall be at my office in the Rue Vissot until 10:15 to-morrow morning, and then I shall take the train for home.

Hoping you are all well at home, and asking you to remember me to everybody, believe me to remain,

Yours very truly,
ERIC ARVEL.

NOVEMBER 19, 1897.

I kept the appointment with Papa and he informed me that he had been in the North of England, but had passed a few days in London with Lilian, Charlotte, and the boy, Raoul, for whom, it

appears, he had procured a situation in a big wine-merchants' establishment of the British metropolis. He was in a terrible rage against
Charlotte for she and Raoul were engaged to be married, much to
his disgust. Raoul was too young to think as yet of conjugal ties
and Charlotte was very silly, and had no money, earning only a
slight salary in her uncle's business. He was very angry to find she
had captured the youth by her blandishments, and he hinted
vaguely that the loving couple had stopped out late and left poor
Lilian alone in the lodgings, which annoyed him very much. He
swore that the erring girl should never darken his doors again or
corrupt his daughter.

The day passed as usual, but Lilian was cold towards me. She
had to go and see a lady from England, who stopped at a hotel in
the Rue de Rivoli and who always bought a few hats of her, whenever she passed through Paris. I asked to be allowed to accompany
Mademoiselle, as I too had an appointment for that afternoon, and
Pa and Ma being nothing loth, we started off together.

In the railway carriage, I once more clasped my Lilian in my
arms, and found to my great delight that she was what I should call
a natural kisser, revelling in long-drawn-out caresses of the mouth.
Her lips seemed to weld themselves to mine, and I am sure that my
dove-like osculation and the touch of my tongue round her throat,
ears, and eyes gave her as much pleasure as a girl could feel.

"Your kisses make me crazy!" or: "Your mouth drives me
mad!" were two of her favourite phrases as, when shivering with
lasciviousness, she would tear herself from my embrace, only to put
up her brilliant mouth over and over again a moment afterwards.

There was no doubt that she had no physical repugnance to
me, for it often occurs that a woman thinks she would like a man,
and when he at last takes her in his arms, something about him,
his odour, his skin, his manner of embracing, his breath, nay, the
merest trifle, sometimes rudely dispels all the feminine illusion.
Lilian freely yielded herself up to the delight of being clasped to
my breast, and my lips pleased her as hers did me.

She asked me what I meant by my voyage for the following
Monday. I replied that I had business at Amsterdam, which might
or might not be done by letter, but that I really felt great remorse

and shame at my dishonourable conduct in making clandestine love to a young lady under her parents' roof, and I said that I trembled to think what would happen if her mother and father found out how I was betraying the implicit confidence they had in me. She replied hotly that her so-called father was a lazy, selfish, bad-tempered man, who cared not a jot for her or her future. And her mother was wrapped up in him and herself. They forced her to contribute one hundred francs a month for her keep, whether she earned them or not, and she was not happy at home. She could not understand the change in my conduct. I took her tenderly in my arms and told her that all my scruples vanished now that I felt her clinging to me, and the kisses of her soft and voluptuous mouth made me forget duty, honour, everything, but the hope of making her mine.

My hands wandered all over her body, pressing her luxuriant posteriors, her thighs, which I found of proper size, her arms, hands and neck, and I exclaimed:

"I know that Lilian returns the love I have felt for her for two years, although I am twice her age. I am happy now and care for naught else!"

And it was true, I was drunk with love, desire, lust, passion, call it what you will.

I made her unfasten her jacket, and sought to press her breasts, but there were only two little, faintly-developed hillocks. Her cloth dress was closely fastened under her arm with hooks and eyes.

"You hurt me," she said, as I feverishly moulded her little bosom.

"I love to hurt you. I love to think that you are mine to do with as I choose, to make you suffer, if I so will it, and I'll squeeze your tiny breasts until you wince with pain."

"They are small," she retorted, laughingly, "but they are firm. Now I want to know what it was you asked me to bring you back from London?"

"I would have written in answer to your letter, but you forgot to give me your address. This is what I wanted you to carefully keep for me and bring back with you," and I pressed my hand between her swelling thighs, outside her dress.

She hid her face in my neck, whispering:

"It is yours. I am yours entirely!"

Luckily, we had arrived at the station, and I drove her to the hotel in the Rue de Rivoli. I had forgotten all about her letter. I was oblivious of everything and everybody. I could only clasp her to me and caress her and kiss her, and kiss her again, until her lips were on fire.

But I did not forget to give her an appointment for the 23rd. I was on good terms with the proprietress of a house in the Rue de Leipzig, where they let furnished apartments, and where there was a little *pavillon* at the bottom of the yard. Lilian had only to walk through, without speaking to the *concierge*, and come straight to me, who would be eagerly awaiting her arrival at half-past two. With a last luscious embrace, I saw her go into the hotel and I drove home.

NOVEMBER 23, 1897.

I have just left Lilian. The day was partially spoilt, but neither of us are to blame. I was punctually at my appointment and I had made the toilette of a bridegroom. I waited an hour, but there were no signs of her, so I left in a rage, pursued by the sardonic grin of the *bonne*. I returned home and took off my finery, when I received the following *petit bleu:*

LILIAN TO JACKY.

November 24th. 1897. 3:45 P.M.

Have just been to the Rue de L. I was one hour and a half late, but through no fault of mine. There has been an accident at the Gare de l'Est and all the trains are late.

I hope you will excuse me and believe that I am furious, especially when I was told that you had just gone.

I am longing to see you,

LILIAN.

I shall only take the 6:45, from the Gare de l'Est to-night.

Of course, I was at the station at the hour mentioned, and found that her story was true. There had been an accident and there was a thick fog. The entire service was disorganized. The station was full of a seething, roaring crowd, and Lilian telegraphed home, stating the case, saying she should go and dine with her grandmother, who lived near the Bourse, and return to the station later, or perhaps sleep with the old lady.

I drove her about in a cab for an hour, which was all the time I could spare, having disposed of my evening.

We were now thoroughly familiar, and in answer to my eager queries, she told me she was a virgin. I did not believe her for an instant, but I naturally said nothing. I told her how I had made an elaborate toilet in anticipation of full possession, and she confided to me that she was very fond of fine linen, and that she, too, had put on everything she had of the best, including a black satin petticoat she had made herself. I put my hand under her clothes to verify her statement, and she let me place my inquisitive fingers on her thigh above her knee, but she objected that my hands were like ice, and I desisted. But I took her hand and thrust it upon the rapidly rising sign of my virility, outside my trousers, and she offered no resistance. I told her, with many cunning periphrases, that my lips would kiss every part of her sweet little body and cause her ineffable delight.

"And I will give you back kiss for kiss. You must teach me to love you as you love me."

"You shall be my little slave of love. Everything I tell you, you must do. I shall exact obedience. And now you must *tutoyer* me."

"That I shall never dare to do. You must keep on saying your delicious *tu* to me, but I shall always be respectful to you."

"As you choose. Perhaps you are right. I am so much older than you. I will be your father, and you shall be my little daughter. You are my incestuous daughter. Do you like the idea of committing the infamous crime of incest with me?"

"Oh, yes! It is a very pretty idea. I love to hear you talk, and as you kiss, tell me what you are going to do to me. You shall be my Papa, my sweet Papa."

"Now let me ask you something. Has M. Arvel—do not be offended with what I am going to say—he is not your real father, but only your Mamma's lover, as he has told me himself. Has he ever taken liberties with you?"

"Oh no! He is very respectful to me and very severe in everything of that kind. The only time he ever said anything rude was after he had nursed me through a long illness, when I had inflammation of the bowels. He said, one day: 'Lily, what a big black forest you have got!' I was so angry!"

I forget now all the promises of voluptuous passion I poured into her willing ears, but I can well remember that she answered incessantly:

"Yes, yes! Tell me more! Tell me what you will do to me!"

And she sucked my mouth deliciously. I spoke vaguely of infinite delights, of unknown joys, but I was afraid to go too far. If she is a virgin, I thought, I may alarm her, and, if she is not, she knows already as much as I can tell her.

So I dropped her near her Granny's but not before we had made another appointment for the 26th.

She is profoundly vicious and deeply naïve, not knowing herself what she wants. If my diagnostic is wrong, then she is the most consummate actress ever seen, beating Sara Bernhardt and La Duse out of sight.

I had now begun to make a few notes in my diary concerning this bizarre maiden. The idea about her being a clever *comedienne*, I jotted down at the time. My souvenirs will now take a more tangible form, as nearly every date stated is correct, and I can manage to render an account of every important caress we ever gave or received. Her letters were generally in French, but a few are written in English, and others in both languages mixed. I have not altered a word, but have simply translated them as well as I could. I wrote in French. Papa's letters I also give, and in fact every scrap of documentary evidence bearing on the story. Some of my own letters I give *in extenso*, as I kept copies of a few. Unfortunately certain missives,—the best or the worst,—are in the hands of the heroine, and I can only give a brief summary when necessary, as memory serves, or omit them altogether. The greater part of this narrative was written day by day as the incidents occurred, especially the later portion, and events, serious to me, transpired, which in the hands of a craftsman ought perhaps to have modified earlier opinions, and caused a more harmonious resetting of the whole story. I prefer to leave my manuscript as it is. It may be full of faults and contradictions, but these defects will show the reader that this is not a novel composed on ordinary lines. It is a simple confession, where a man coldly performs the operation of vivisection on his own heart and brain, and my greatest reward will be if the reader, on finishing the memoir—supposing that he does finish it—exclaims: "I should think it is all true!" And if lady readers gibe bitterly at the author, and say it is a tissue of falsehood and utterly impossible, then my triumph will be complete.

NOVEMBER 26, 1897.

Everyone knows the feverish excitement experienced by an eager lover, when awaiting his mistress at the first appointment. I felt hot and excited, and gave a great sigh of relief, when Lilian slowly lifted the portière and advanced towards me in the tawdrily furnished bedroom of the mysterious pavillon of the Rue de Leipzig. I quickly bolted the door, and drew her to me, placing her on my knee, as I sat on the inevitable chaise-longue. She seemed worried and frightened, and told me that she had great trouble in getting away from home. There was a tremendous struggle to get her dress unfastened, and she studiously avoided looking towards the large curtained bed that occupied the middle of the room. She hoped I would not touch it, as if I did, people of the house would guess we had been using it! I tried by my kisses to warm her blood, and I think I succeeded, for she grew more and more bold, and I was able to undo her dress, and feast my eyes on her tiny breasts, which were like those of a girl of fifteen. Nevertheless, the size of the red and excited nipples proved her real rage. I sucked and nibbled them greedily, and her pretty ears and neck also came in for a share of attention from my eager lips and tongue. I begged her to let me take off all her garments, but she wanted me to be satisfied with her small, but beautifully made breast. I pretended to be deeply hurt and she excused herself. I must have patience. This was the first time. She would be more yielding when she knew me better. I replied by boldly throwing up her skirts, and after admiring her legs, in their black stockings, and her coquettish be-rib-boned drawers, I, at last, placed my hand on the mark of her sex. It was fully covered with a thick, black undergrowth and quite fleshy. The large outer lips were fatter and more developed than we generally find them among the women of France. Her legs, though slim, were well-made, and her thighs of fair proportions. I began to explore the grotto.

"You hurt me," she murmured.

And as far as I could tell, she seemed to be intact, or at any rate had not been often approached by a man. I could feel that my caresses delighted her greatly and she gave way a little. At last, I persuaded her to take off her petticoat and drawers. She con-sented, on condition that I would not look at her. I acquiesced and she dropped her skirt and took off her bodice, standing before me in her petticoat and stays. She wore a dainty cambric chemise, tied with cherry ribbons, and I enjoyed the sight of my love thus at last in my power. I gloated over her naked shoulders; the rosy nipples, stiff, and glistening with my saliva; and the luxuriant black tufts of hair beneath the armpits.

She consented now to drop her petticoat, and as I leant back on the sofa, she placed one soft, cool hand over my eyes, and with the other, undid everything, until she stood in her chemise. She would not go near the bed and struggled to get away from me. Indeed, she would not let me touch her, until I closed the window-curtains. We were in the dark. I placed her on the *chaise-longue*, and going on my knees, I tried to part her thighs and kiss her mossy cleft. With both hands, she tried to push me away.

"You hurt me!" she said again, but I licked her as well as I could, and feeling the warmth of my mouth, she opened her thighs a little, and I managed to perform my task. It was difficult, as she writhed about, uttered pretty little cries, and would not sufficiently keep her legs apart. But I was not to be dislodged. I was not com-fortably installed. My neck was wellnigh broken. The room too was very hot; but I remained busily licking, sucking, perspiring, and my member, bursting with desire, already let a few drops of the masculine essence escape from its burning top. I am certain she experienced a feeling of voluptuousness, by the shuddering of her frame at one moment, and by the peculiar taste that I could not mistake. At last, she thrust my head away. And I rose to my feet, greatly pleased at leaving the prison of her soft thighs. I got my handkerchief, wiped my mouth, and returning to her, as she still laid motionless and silent on the couch, I threw myself upon her without ceremony. I inserted the end of my turgescent weapon between the hairy lips of her lower mouth, and forgetting all prudence, I pushed on. She shrieks and dislodges me. I try to regain my position, but I cannot succeed. She was a virgin; there was no doubt about it.

Lilian is half-seated on the narrow sofa, and I have no way of getting to her, unless I pull her flat down on her back. I am tired too, and very hot. I have twisted my neck and it is painful. So I relent and give up active warfare for the present.

"Take it in your hand yourself," I say, "and do what you like with it."

She does so, and leaning over her, I find she lets the tip go a little way in. Now all was dry and far from agreeable. I suppose I had done wrong to suck her so long. She had no more feeling of lust. So I moved up to her face, as she reclined with her head on a cushion, and straddling across her, rubbed my arrow and the appendages gently on her face and mouth. She did not move. I took her hand and placed it on my staff of life. She started and roughly drew her hand away. Strange inconsistency. She had placed it herself at the entrance of her virgin cleft; she had allowed me to caress her lips and cheeks with it, but now she recoiled at the idea of grasping it.

So I resolved to overcome any disgust she might feel, and putting the end between her lips, I told her rather roughly to suck it at once. She tried to, timidly; I could see she did not know how.

"Tell me, show me, and I will do all you wish."

I took her hand, and sucked and licked one of her fingers by way of example.

She took to it readily, and I tried to excite her and keep her up to her work by talking to her as she sucked me awkwardly. But the soft warm caress of her capacious mouth and the clinging grasp of her luscious lips excited me to madness. I moved in and out, slowly, saying:

"Darling! Lilian! It is delicious! Not your teeth, Lily. You must not let your teeth touch it! So! Lick it nicely! Let me feel your tongue! Do not move! Do not go away. I am going to enjoy in your mouth, and you must remain as you are until I tell you."

With angelic docility, she continues the play of her lips and tongue, and to my great surprise and delight I feel her hands gently caressing my reservoirs. And the crisis comes too soon. The pleasure I had was beyond words. I had kept back the moment of joy as long as I could, but now the charge exploded with violence, and I could feel that a very large quantity gushed into her mouth. I thought I should never cease emitting. Lilian did not stir until I slowly withdrew, having exhausted the pleasure until there was not a throb left, and my organ had begun to soften. Then she sat up and uttered inarticulate cries.

I rushed to get her a pail or basin, and in the darkness, knocked down a screen. She empties her martyred mouth. I give her a glass of water, and she rinses her throat.

"What was that?" she asked, as I half-opened one of the window-curtains.

"Little babies," I replied. "Did you like me sucking you?"

I lit the lamp, kissed her, and we chatted as she dressed.

"Yes!"

"And when I spurted that stuff into your mouth—did you like that too?"

"Yes."

"I ought to have penetrated your pretty body. Why did you not let me? Has no one ever done so to you?"

"I am a virgin, I swear it!"

"Have you never given pleasure to yourself with your hand?"

"Never. It hurts. I don't like that. I love you. I shall never marry. I shall live for you. You seem to be vexed that I am a virgin? If I was not, why should I not say so? Tell me what you want."

"I can't tell to-day. My brain is in a whirl. Egotistically, I want to be inside my Lilian. With regard to your interests and future —I ought not to take your maidenhead. You must get married and your husband will do that for you."

"Yes. Mamma says a husband can always tell on the first night if his wife is a virgin or not."

"I have been too merciful to you. I ought to have fastened your hands with my trousers' strap."

"Why didn't you? You know you can do anything you like to me."

"Well, we will let things be until another day."

"You must not be angry if I have been silly or have not pleased you, as this is the first time, you know. I promise to be more obedient in future, and I will try not to struggle when you touch me."

"You are a little *demi-vierge*."

"I know what you mean. I have read that novel: *Les Demi-Vierges*."

"I think you like the idea of *mutual* caresses without the real approach of a man?"

"I think I do. Cannot we be happy like this?"

"Perhaps. There are other things we can do together. Do you know what we did just now?"

"Certainly I do. I am not going to pretend I don't. The girls at Myrio's often talked about it. It is called *mimi*. And it is very bad for the health, is it not?"

"Yes, if repeated too often."

I thought she was sensual but silly. Had she chosen me to gratify her curiosity, having confidence in me from my age, and probably Ma's and Pa's praise, as Lilian tells me they think a lot of Jacky? She promised to write to me shortly for another afternoon's fun, but she still refused to *tutoyer* me, and never did at all, during our *liaison*.

I drove her to the station, and in the *fiacre*, she was dull and ill at her ease. Her eyes had a faraway look in them. She seemed to be thinking deeply. About what?

At that time I believed she was reflecting on the novelty and obscenity of what we had done together.

But as I write nearly two years later, vile and horrible thoughts rise uppermost in my mind. Let the reader guess, or return to this chapter when he has finished the book.

2

> . . . . . . Most merciful God
> Thou hast revealed to me the agony
> And bloody sweat of dire Gethsemane,
> The scourging of the pillar, the crown of thorns,
> The cracking, splitting nerves, and racked joints
> Of three hours' crucifixion. Thine anguish
> I here do feel, O God! bound, crucified.
>
> GEORGE MOORE.

To my great surprise, I had no news of Lilian, but a few days before I saw her at the Rue de Leipzig, I had sent to Mr. Arvel a parcel of kippers, haddocks, and bloaters, which I had promised the household on my last visit. I had talked to Lilian about the packets of periodicals I sent her father, the little presents I gave her mother, and how I praised and flattered them in every way so as to be often invited and thus approach her. She urged me to continue, but I was to be very careful with her Papa, as he was of a most jealous nature. She told me that she always spoke against me, as if she were to appear pleased when I came, I should never be asked down to Sonis any more. They were all going to Nice shortly after New Year's Day for three weeks.

LILIAN TO JACKY.

Sonis-sur-Marne, December 2nd. 1897.

My dear Mr. S . . . ,

Papa was desirous of writing to you these last few days, but he could not get a moment to himself to do so. I take his place therefore, and thank you on behalf of everybody for your present. The fish were exquisite. There is only one fault; there were too many of them.

Mamma wants to know when you will do us the pleasure of lunching with us? The sooner the better, as we have not seen you for a century. It was Lili's birthday to-day and that of her three little ones yesterday. We await your visit to celebrate that event. All our darlings are well. A caress for your faithful Smike, and all your other spoilt pets.

In the hope of soon seeing you, I pray you to accept the assurance of my most devoted sentiments.

LILIAN ARVEL.

I found the note strange, cold, and mysterious. I suppose I wrote that any day would suit me, but I received no reply. So on the thirteenth, I sent the following ambiguous missive, supposed to be from the female friend, Marie.

JACKY TO LILIAN.

Paris, December 13, 1897.

My dear Lilian,

You know I do not like to trouble you, and I have always told you that although I feel great friendship for you, and you, I believe, have a little for me, I never intend to worry you. I know your time is occupied and that you are not always at liberty.

What does all this mean, you will say? Simply to tell you not to forget me the next time you come to Paris, and try to pay me a visit for a minute or two as you did before, that is to say if you have the desire to see me. That would give me the greatest pleasure.

At your last visit you let me hope that I should hear from you shortly.

Dare I add that I am a little grieved and wounded at your silence?

Come soon if you can, and later on if you cannot manage otherwise.

Anyhow, a word from you would rejoice the heart of your sincere friend,

MARIE.

This note crossed the following invitation:

LILIAN TO JACKY.

Sonis-sur-Marne, December 13th. 1897.

My dear Mr. S ...,

You must think we are all dead. Such is happily not the case. If we have not written sooner to fix the day when we should have the pleasure of your company at lunch, it is because we have been very much troubled. Our three puppies have been grievously ill. We do not know if we can save the little bitch. The other two are better. My Blackamoor is luckily almost out of danger. Can you come next Thursday, the 16th? We count upon you to pass the day with us. Do not bring any of your dogs, not even your big treasure Smike. We find that the distemper is contagious and it would be a pity to make your pets ill. We hope you are in good health and that your new venture is successful.

Awaiting the pleasure of seeing you, we pray you to accept the assurance of our sincere friendship and believe me,

Your entirely devoted,
LILIAN ARVEL.

The above was typewritten, as Miss Arvel was very quick with her Papa's Remington, but there was a little piece of paper in the letter, bearing the following words, in her own handwriting:

The little girl will frankly tell her Papa the reason why she has not written to him, although she had the utmost desire to do so.

DECEMBER 16, 1897.

In spite of my most earnest efforts of memory, I can find nothing to remember of great importance during this visit to Sonis. I had lunch and did not stop to dinner. The girl kept out of my way. In the afternoon, Papa, Lilian, and I went for a walk together, and I can see myself now, strolling sadly along, my ungloved hands clasped behind me. Lilian, unseen by her father, placed her fingers in my palm for a moment.

I dropped back, and as her stepfather went on in front, I whispered to her: "Is it all over between us already?"

"Yes!" she answered, laughingly.

I quickly walked away from her. She trotted after me, saying: "No, no!"

At this moment, Papa joined us, and I was no more alone with her. When leaving for the station with my host, she came to bid me good bye, and called out with deep meaning:

"A bientôt!"

I thought her conduct passing strange. And I began to reflect about many things I had noticed. She seemed frightened of Mr. Arvel and yet very fond of him. He frequently told me the same stories two or three times over, and she would make fun of him behind his back. Yet when he laid down the law at table. I could see her eyes fixed upon him with enraptured attention. He was always talking about her and her future. She was lazy and quarrelsome and unable to earn her own living. Her bonnet-building scheme was a farce. And still he romped with her. I noticed too that the best bedrooms were on the first floor, where there was a long wooden balcony. The largest room in the front had two windows, and was Mr. and Mrs. Arvel's, with one big bed. This opened into a smaller bedroom at the back, where Lilian slept. The door of communication had been taken down and there were only two flimsy, looped-up curtains in the opening, not even a portière. I thought this was a peculiar arrangement for the bedroom of a young person of 21.

In fact, I began to fancy that there was something between Lilian and her mother's lover. It seemed to me that he looked upon her with the eyes of a satyr. He was always playing with her and pinching her. And she was so careful to tell me to befriend him in every way.

"I alone get on with him beautifully," she would say, "as his temper is awful at times, and Mamma will contradict him, but I flatter all his manias."

I sent him some enormous parcels of books, novels and light literature, and listened patiently to all his talk.

I felt very unhappy about Lilian and things in general were going very badly with me; the new law of 1893 on Stock Exchange operations had dealt a deathblow to my business. I scarcely ever went to the Bourse now, so that I no longer met Mr. Arvel, and I was busily engaged in putting on the market a new chemical product I had invented.

To add to my worries, my own devoted Lilian at home was very ill indeed, and I was her nurse. And I must digress and tell a rather sad story, which, however, has some slight bearing on this tale of vice.

As far back as 1880, I made the acquaintance of a young girl, aged sixteen and a half, who was taking lessons at the Conservatoire, with a view to adopting the stage as a profession. She was divinely handsome; fair, with light blue eyes; as upright as a dart, and she had a figure that sculptors begged her all her life to let them copy. I fell in love with her, my first Lilian, and as she innocently reciprocated my affection, I am ashamed to say I profited by the influence I felt I had over her, and brutally ravished her.

As I rose from the couch, where my love lay swooning, in great pain, unable to realise as yet the wrong I had done her, I mechanically went up to a looking-glass, and stared at my own reflection in the mirror. I did not know myself. My face was livid, my lips were white and cold, and my teeth chattered. I trembled all over and two big tears rolled down my cheeks, now that my animal desire was assuaged.

In truth, I felt like a murderer, and I registered a solemn vow that never more, if I lived a hundred years, would I take advantage of a virgin's yielding tenderness.

Now you know the principal reason why I respected my friend's daughter. This secret I have never divulged. I never told Miss Arvel. She does not know it now, nor will not, unless she reads this book.

My Lilian forgave me because she loved me, and our mutual affection grew, until it became perfectly plain that she could not live without me. There were no spoken protestations of affection on either side. Naturally we sought each other continually; and simply joined our hearts, souls, and bodies in God's union of the sexes. There was no question of money between us, to speak plainly. In fact, at that moment I had none. I was a gambler. When in luck I spent my gold, and when reverses came I cut down my expenses, and waited until the blind lady came my way again. This is one of my motives for having remained a bachelor. I often fancied myself allied to a young damsel of the commercial world, accustomed to the steady tradesmen of her family. I could see myself, after a winning settlement, buying her, for instance, a pair of diamond earrings, and perhaps the very next month pawning them out of dire necessity.

So when I seduced Lilian, I was down on my luck considerably. Her family was an illustrious one, but her father was a spendthrift, and he dilapidated the fortune, driving his wife into an early grave. This lady was a sainted victim and freely forgave her erring daughter, never depriving her of her maternal affection and advice. But she died a few years later.

One evening, Lilian came to me in great grief, and covered with wounds and contusions. Our intrigue was discovered, and her father had beaten her unmercifully, being drunk with absinthe. He had knocked her down, jumped upon her ribs, and bodily cast her out.

I took her to live with me. I shall never forget our initial attempts at house-keeping. We hired a small, unfurnished apartment, and our first acquisition was a mattress stuffed with dried seaweed. This cost five francs. It was laid upon the floor, and one end propped up by a travelling bag, served as a bolster and pillow all combined. But circumstances improved, and from odds and ends of furniture, picked up in the lowest salerooms, I was able in time to make a pretty little home for Lilian, full of quaint curios, fine, ancient furniture, and pictures, which I routed out of strange holes and corners in my travels.

Every summer, we went away on a pleasure trip. I took her to England, Italy, and Switzerland, where together we climbed mountains and explored glaciers. Her health then gradually failed her, and I became a sick nurse. She was alone in the world now. Her mother was dead. Her sisters and brothers did not recognize her. From time to time, her drunken, dissolute father cropped up, and begged some old clothes and a little silver. Times out of number, has she saved the unworthy author of her being from ruin, dishonour and starvation.

She had no one but me to look after her. I passed one whole winter at her bedside, when she went through the acute sufferings of articular rheumatism, and she knew no one half the time. She would take nothing, but from my hand, and for three months, I never let the fire go out by night or day. I was perfectly happy in nursing her. My own health was good; I had never been ill in my life.

But in the summer of 1895, she developed signs of heart disease, inherited from her mother, and was a confirmed invalid ever since. I could see her great beauty leaving her by degrees; all changed for the worst. Her temper became soured. I never complained. I hoped against the doctors who gave me no hope. I tried to nurse her, and pet her, and spoil her, and make her forget how ill she was.

Such was my life in the winter of 1897; business at a standstill, my devoted mistress suffering from a mortal malady, nearly always in bed, and I casting about, ready to try anything to make money, and hard at work on my new chemicals.

ERIC ARVEL TO JACKY.

Sonis-sur-Marne, December 23rd. 1897.

My dear Jacky,

I have been so busy writing Christmas letters, that I have not had time to write and thank you for your magnificent donation of books, the majority of which are new to me, and will be read with the greatest interest. Lilian promises herself a treat with them, when she gets to Nice, so you see you have given pleasure to more than one.

I am pleased to inform you that mercury in the shape of blue pill, cascara and podophyllin have proved admirable remedies for the canine species, and if you like, I will give you all the details, which will enable you to cure distemper with lightning-like celerity.

We want to know if you have any particular engagement on Saturday next? If not, will you come and spend the day with us, as we are anxious that you should sample the Christmas pudding. We should not, however, like to interfere with any family arrangements.

Again thanking you, believe me to remain with every good and seasonable wish for you and yours,

Yours very truly,
ERIC ARVEL.

No news from Lilian privately, only this invitation to their Christmas dinner. I resolved not to go, although I was perfectly free to do so, and I wrote a polite letter of excuse. They were off to Nice all three of them and I supposed I should never "have" Lilian again. As for the reason why she did not communicate with me that winter, after our first meeting, I have never known from that day to this, but I can make a shrewd guess now.

I made up my mind not to trouble the girl, but on the 30th. of December, I took a present for the mother and daughter to Arvel's bureau in the Rue Vissot, and sent Mamma the following letter. In preceding years, I had only given *bonbons*.

JACKY TO MADAME ARVEL.

Paris, December 30th. 1897.

My dear Madam,

Let me be the first, or at any rate one of the first, to come and wish you health, prosperity, and all you can desire of happiness for yourself and all those you love, during the coming year, without counting numberless years afterwards.

In gratitude for your frank hospitality and to prove that I have not forgotten your good, little (big) dinners, I take the liberty of offering you a slight present—a little umbrella.

Mademoiselle, your charming daughter, has always been so kind to me every time I visited your house, that I wish to show the esteem I hold her in, by begging her to accept a smelling-bottle, which will come in useful when she breaks the bank at Monte-Carlo.

And I wish her a happy new year too, and the realisation of all her wishes in 1898.

If I have badly selected my gifts, please excuse me in favour of the intention.

Now I am sure you will pardon me for not having come on Christmas Day, but we have the habit of making a family day of it at home in Paris.

I shake hands with Monsieur Arvel, and wish him all the compliments of the season also, without saying more, as he knows the feelings of sympathy I have for him.

I have sent the two little articles to his bureau, Rue Vissot.

Yours devotedly,
JOHN S. . . .

Please let me know Mr. Arvel's address and the date of your return, so that I may send him his papers and magazines to Nice.

But I have forgotten the dogs! How could I forget the blood of Smike and Sally Brass—my own flesh and blood—I have no heart!

Therefore, gravely, I wish a happy new year to Lili, Blackamoor and all the others, on my behalf and on the part of my own kennel. So be it!

LILIAN TO JACKY.

Sonis-sur-Marne, January 2nd. 1898.

My dear Mr. S . . . ,

Mamma and I are delighted with the two pretty presents you have had the kindness to send to us.

I hope to have to use my silver smelling-salts for the purpose for which you have given it to me. I do not believe it will be wanted in this way, I am not lucky enough for that, and besides, I am no gambler.

We thank you from the bottom of our hearts, and also for your good wishes. We form such a quantity for your happiness, that I will not even seek to enumerate them. It would be vain trouble; all this sheet of paper would not suffice. Papa begs me to tell you that he does not yet know where we shall put up, but as soon as we arrive in the sunny South, he will wire to you. As for our return, we will write as soon as the date is fixed. Mamma begs you to accept a slice of her famous Christmas pudding, which she sends you this day.

Our doggies are all restored to health. They have begun the New Year well. They send their caresses to you as well as to their parents, relations and all the others.

My dear Mr. S . . . , I pray you to receive the assurance of all my friendship,

Yours very devotedly,
LILIAN ARVEL.

Why not a word of love or passion? I never knew, I tried not to think of her and sought refuge in hard work. My days were spent during this dull winter, with manufacturers and patent agents, and my nights were passed in the sick room of my poor ailing Lily.

A worthy Dutch bookseller, Mynheer Vanderpunk, who had frequently procured old and curious works for me, now wrote from his dusty old shop at Rotterdam, and begged me to be kind enough to correct the text and revise the proofs of a voluptuous volume he intended to bring out under the rose, and which he called: "The Horn Book; or, the Girl's Guide to Knowledge." The manuscript was amusing and the task not a displeasing one for me.

I got very little rest in the long winter nights, being continually awakened to care for my sick mistress. She would settle down to sleep as early as possible and I, in an adjoining room, would read, or smoke, or try to change the current of my ideas in furbishing up this most lascivious text-book.

I remember well one chapter, which spoke of "pleasures of man alone, by the aid of woman, but without her reciprocal participation." One paragraph recommended a kind of false copulation, between the tightly closed thighs of a female.

I added: "This position can be recommended to all having to do with very young girls or half-virgins. . . . Incestuous Papas please note." (Dialogue V. Chap. II.)

And I had in my mind the lecherous old man and the passionate, dissembling girl of Sonis.

No news came from her until a fortnight had passed, when she suddenly took it into her shapely head to send me the following letter:

LILIAN TO JACKY.

Hôtel Joli-Site, Monaco. January 17, 1898.

My own darling,

You must really think I have forgotten all about you, yet such is not the case. Ever since our arrival here, the weather has been so fine that we have been out all day long.

Mamma being ill in bed with influenza, I am her nurse, so I am free for a little while. She is asleep and my very first letter is for you. How is my sweet Papa? Well and happy, I hope. Very naughty?

Since the last few days I am in a nervous state which I am unable to describe. I do not know what to attribute it to, unless it be the warm weather. It acts upon me like the coming of spring. If my little Papa was like that, I should be very much annoyed, for I have not the confidence in his chastity that I have in mine, and as I am absent the results would be disastrous.

I have got my smelling-bottle with me. It is on my toilet-table, and every morning as I dress, I tell to it a heap of things about my Papa. Oh! such pretty things!

I have not been out on my bicycle yet, but I have been several times to the pigeon shooting, and last Friday to Nice races. I have played roulette too. I have lost, then won, and after all I am just as well off as the day I started, being quits.

I expect a letter from you as soon as possible. You can address it to me like this, of course in your feigned handwriting: Mademoiselle L. Arvel, Hôtel Joli-Site, Monaco.

But I won't have "Marie" to write to me any more, or sign. I tear up your letters as soon as read, for my sake as well as yours, which you can well understand.

I fret about my dogs, yearning especially for my Blackamoor. Yours are happier, as they do not leave you. I know a certain person who would often like to be in the place of Smike. You know who I mean as well as I do.

I send you a big, long, and passionate kiss.

Yours lovingly,
LILY.

LILIAN TO JACKY.

Paris. Wednesday, January 23, 1898.

My dear little girl,

Your pretty letter made me very happy. I venture to think that you hoped for that result. It does me good to think that I possess a little bit of your heart and that you have truly some tender feeling for me. All the rest is very nice, doubtless very intoxicating, but without sincere feeling, it has but little value for me.

I tell you frankly that I began to doubt you slightly. I had good reasons. Since the 26th. of last November, you have treated me in rather a peculiar manner. But I will not darken my letter by scolding you. The first time that I shall be alone with you, I will explain in a few words what I mean, and which, by the way, is without importance now, for your letter completely effaces all my doubts. You will understand me if I say that you are not "business-like" enough. Even in love, you should try and realise what torturing thoughts come over us, as we wait for some sparse news of her who has said: "I love you!"

You owed me a word of tenderness; a pretty thought scribbled hastily; a telegram; no matter what to make he who was waiting far away take patience, my darling.

How you forget all those little things which nevertheless are important in life! You wrote to me on the eve of your departure, promising your address in the South. I have not had that wire. I could not therefore send the papers and magazines to Mr. Arvel. Tell him that you have done it, and next Sunday I will post him a packet.

My beautiful Lily, your Papa has had a strong attack of influenza, short, but not sweet, and at this moment I am worthless. I am flabby, feverish, and stupid. I am a rag, an empty sack, and I could look without emotion and see every sofa in the world burnt before my eyes.

I am pleased that you are in good health and that you are amused. Be a good girl, don't let yourself be cajoled.

Often I think of you. Since we . . . I think of you always, and I hope you will write to me all the pretty things you tell your smelling-bottle. I think that the ideas that gallop through your little brain are the same as those I also have when I think of my daughter. Do you know, my child, that we have such a lot of pretty, nice little things to practise together? You can have no idea of them.

But we'll see about that when you return. Good luck when you gamble! You know the hackneyed saying: "Unlucky at play, lucky in love!" Try and make the proverb lie, by being happy in both. I will attend to my part of the contract. Such is what I wish you.

If you should have bad news of your dogs—or especially of Black-amoor,—quick, send me a telegram and I will go to Sonis. They shall have the best of care, the same as mine. This is serious.

My dogs are fit. Smike fought big curs twice this month and he has been well bitten.

He is like his master, his bark is worse than his bite. He is very loving, cannot live without caresses, and the only thing he detests is neglect from those he loves.

Write to me soon and often. I think I deserve a few nice letters. You, wicked one, do not deserve a long letter, such as this is.

I think I love you too much. Thank you for your loving kiss. But it is only one. I send you a heap, placed where you like them best.

And now, do not be lazy. Do not be too long without writing to ask me if I am better.

I squeeze you tightly against me, sweet, and ask nothing better than to always be

Your own darling.

(*Unsigned.*)

LILIAN TO JACKY.

Cercle des Etrangers de Monaco.
Salon de Lecture. Monte-Carlo.
January 21st. 1898.

My dear Mr. S . . . ,

Just two words to give our address here: Arvel, Hôtel Joli-Site, Monaco.

We are all in good health and we hope you are the same.

We beg you to accept the assurance of our good friendship.

LILIAN ARVEL.

LILIAN TO JACKY.

Cercle des Etrangers de Monaco.
Salon de Lecture. Monte-Carlo.
January 21st. 1898.

Dearest,

You are not "business-like" in love, you tell me, in your long and good letter. I did not know that to please you I had to be "business-like," above all in love. In future I will be as you wish!

You had doubts, but what doubts could you possibly have? That is an enigma for me. Have I not been always very frank with you; have I not always told you everything, down to the smallest stupidities which other girls less—how shall I say it?—less foolish than me, would have hidden from you? Unless I receive from you very ample and fully detailed explanations, your daughter will be quite angry.

Make haste then to write, and unveil your heart until it is naked before my eyes.

If you would be a real darling, you will go to Sonis and pay a little visit to your grandchildren . . . the bow-wows. That will please me greatly, and in this way you will insinuate yourself still farther into the good graces of Mamma, which is quite indispensable.

We have received your papers, which are vastly appreciated by Papa and myself. I thank you.

We intend to pass a month at Nice from next week onwards. Until Sunday, you can write to me here. As soon as I know my new address, I will let you know.

You say your dogs are in good health? I am happy to hear it. I send a loving caress to all, and particularly to my fat Smike.

I leave you. They are waiting for me to have tea. *Au revoir*. A million kisses.

LILY.

MADAME ARVEL TO JACKY.

Hôtel Joli-Site, Monaco. February 1st. 1898.

My dear Mr. S . . . ,

I wish to thank you for your kindness, but really when I spoke about you going to see my dogs during my absence, it was only a joke, and I should never have dared to give you that trouble. I am delighted nevertheless, as I am now quite reassured about them. It is not necessary to be in Paris to have the influenza, as my mother has told you. I have had it, and severely too, although I am in the land of the sun.

We intend to remain another three weeks here; we wished to go and live at Nice, but the Carnival is shortly about to begin and it will be too noisy for Mr. Arvel.

I am pleased to hear that my pudding had such success; had I known it, I should have sent you a bigger slice, but that will be for next year.

Mr. Arvel begs me to thank you for the very interesting newspapers you send him.

Lilian was very happy to hear you had seen Blackamoor and found him well. She charges me with her thanks, and says you must caress Smike and Sally Brass, and all the others for her.

We have magnificent weather here and yet I long to be home again; the hotel food is very bad.

We hope that on our return to Sonis, you will do us the pleasure to come and see us often, and in the meantime I pray you to accept the assurance of my good and sincere friendship.

ADÈLE ARVEL.

I remember visiting Sonis, reviewing the dogs, conversing with the grandmother, whose acquaintance I made for the first time, tipping the servant, hearing that Madame Arvel had the influenza, and returning to Paris, when I wrote to Nice.

I also wrote to Lilian, and gave her to understand that I was not an ordinary lover. I was not jealous, I put no check upon her liberty, nor did I venture to criticise her conduct in any way. I wished her to enjoy herself, to flirt, and do as she liked. I only wanted her love, as long as she chose to bestow it on me. I suppose I must have said that I was grieved by her long silence, and that I did not require long letters, only a line now and again to show that I was not forgotten.

Her allusions to her own frankness and stupidity I must now explain.

Before what I venture to call my first possession of her body, after a fashion, I had asked her who taught her to kiss so nicely. She frankly told me that she had carried on a strictly platonic intrigue when she was apprentice at Myrio's, with a young law-student, who she called Gaston, but more familiarly: "Baby." He used to wait for her when she left the workroom in the evening, and take the train with her to Sonis, going back to Paris alone. He had kissed her lips, she said, and that was all. She added that he was fond of talking very lewdly, and liked to tell her what he wished to do to her if he could get her in his power—"just like you," she added.

One evening, in the railway carriage, he suddenly seized her by the two wrists, and throwing her skirts up to her waist, tried to violate her. She struggled and got away from him, when he burst out crying and begged her pardon.

He was always writing to her and I saw one of his letters. Sometimes he wrote in very free terms. I have a distinct recollection of some long story, where he said his family were forcing him to marry a rich woman, and he intended to get divorced and come back to Lilian. It appears he had arrived at Sonis one night and made his way into the garden, intending to climb up to her window, but Papa had come out with a gun, and he had jumped over the wall and escaped.

All this seemed very strange and rather rambling, but I did not cross-examine her. I think she also added that "Baby" had sent his sister to negotiate a marriage, but she had turned traitor after a visit to Mr. Arvel, who frankly confessed that he had not a penny to give Lilian, and that her husband must take her in English fashion for better or worse.

How much of this story was false or true, I know not, but I wish to make an avowal at once which will show the reader what a perverted debauchee I was.

I loved to hear Lily tell me about her platonic lover, Gaston. Her story of the attempted rape acted upon my senses like an aphrodisiac, and I often made her repeat it.

I wanted all the details. I would ask her if he saw her sex, or only her drawers, and how high her skirts were up.

I felt that I should like to see her in the arms of a strange man, or I dreamt of causing her to be shamelessly exposed and outraged by a woman in my presence.

The idea that her mother's lover desired her, and I was sure he did, transported me with lust, and I used to watch them narrowly. I loved to see him romp with her, slap her posteriors outside her clothes, and putting his hand a little way up her petticoats, pinch her calves.

She always used to say she would never leave her Pa, and I used to agree with her in front of him, and tell her that she could not do better than to love and obey him blindly.

I knew that she would make a wonderful instrument of pleasure if properly attuned. I came to the conclusion that she had been caressed, handled and dandled, and mauled about, ever since her early infancy by her Papa and Gaston, without counting any other male and female playmates I knew not of, and that is why she so freely accepted all my ideas, and was not surprised at my retreat in front of the fortress of her virginity.

Although she excited my sensual longings to the fullest extent, I yet felt great tenderness for her. I took an interest in her, as I could see her mother was selfish and stupid, and that Mr. Arvel, for reasons best known to himself, was not giving her proper advice. I wanted to enjoy her artificial love, which was quite an enervating novelty for me, and yet teach her honesty, and I was always thinking of her interests and her future. I could not do much for her, but I wanted her to find a worthy husband and go to him a virgin. I told her so. I made her understand that on the day of her marriage I would retire from her life, and whatever I felt I would keep to myself. She always answered that I should be her lover. I also told her that without marriage she could always tell me frankly if she tired of our connection and I would go from her without a word. I tried to put her at her ease and above all not to lure her on with false promises or lying tales.

I said I was vile, but may I not timidly plead that I was honest in my lewd way?

LILY TO JACKY.

Sunday evening.
(No date. Received February 8, 1898.)

My beloved,

A word in haste on this wretched paper that I find by chance and with this atrocious pen. You demanded it, so much the worse for you!
I have hardly time to breathe here.
And see, now I must leave you. They are calling me!
I kiss you all over . . . madly!

LILY.

I was very busy and very ill. The sharp attack of influenza I had undergone, and which I caught from my Lily, who had it still very badly, had left me weak and depressed, and I felt pains in all my joints, such as I had never experienced before.

My mistress was dreadfully, dangerously ill. I shared her bed of agony, and her condition required that the heat of the room should be kept up over 70° F. We were at the fag-end of a disagreeable winter, and I often rose in the night to attend to her wants, and hurried into the other rooms, where the thermometer would be at freezing point.

I finished "The Horn Book," and sent the manuscript to my good friend Vanderpunk.

My new chemical invention was put on the market on the 9th. of February. I could scarcely stand, and it was all I could do to muffle myself up in a fur coat and go to my Lily's bedside.

After a night of torture, when I got up several times to do my duty as a nurse, with my aching limbs bathed in my own perspiration and that of my suffering companion, I got a little sleep in the small hours, but when I tried to leave the bed at eight o'clock in the morning, I found every limb locked; each joint racked, and I howled with pain. It must be remembered that up to then I did not know what bodily suffering was.

In my impotent rage, mad with the burning fever of rheumatism, I lost all manly feeling and so far forgot myself as to bitterly upbraid my poor sick Lily.

"I have sacrificed myself for you. You have had the best part of my life. I never refused you anything I could afford to give you, and now you have taken the only riches I had left—my health! I shall be a cripple, and then what will become of me? As long as I was hale and hearty, I never complained. I have endured fearful nights of unrest by your side, as you tossed your fevered body about, and I have tried to sleep bathed in your sweat, and rushed, reeking, suddenly into icy atmospheres, to fetch you your medicines, light fires, and attend to you as if you were a baby. Each night you found me with clockwork regularity at your bedside. And now I am a physical wreck! My health and strength gone from me by your fault! You have taken everything, even to my health! God knows how I shall come out of this hellish strait! And just when I wanted all my energies to retrieve my fallen fortunes!"

I am ashamed to write more of my ravings. I was mad. I cursed myself, I cursed the world and I cursed our bed, and spat upon the mattress and tumbled sheets all fuming with my sweat.

Poor Lily stood aghast in a corner, her eyes distended with horror, and convulsive sobs shaking her debilitated frame.

One day I will ask her forgiveness for what was delirious blasphemy. She will pardon me, for she always loved me and always will. She has proved her love. She possessed every quality we are supposed to find in a woman—tenderness, devotion, and truth.

Perhaps I have already asked her pardon? Who knows?

How I huddled on my clothes; how I crawled out, I cannot tell, but I managed to be hauled into a cab and drove to my aged mother's little cottage in the outskirts of Paris.

There I hung upon the railings until I was carried to bed; a helpless, groaning stiffened log, on the morning of February 10, 1898.

I now went through all the sufferings of muscular and articular rheumatism. I knew my malady well, as I had seen my mistress through it.

I felt my hands beginning to pain me, and made haste to scribble a few lines with a pencil, from my bed, to tell Lilian Arvel, at Monte-Carlo, how bad I was.

On the morning of the 20th. of February, I received the following undated letter.

My two hands were now attacked and they were shapeless, evil-smelling bundles of cotton wool. Nevertheless, I had Lilian's letter placed on my pillow, and waited until I was left alone. I took it between my two stumps, although it was untold agony to move my arms. With my teeth, I tore open the envelope, and read as follows:

LILIAN TO JACKY.

Friday. (No date or place.)

If my Papa would give great pleasure to his little daughter, he must send her two hundred francs by return of post. Figure to yourself that since I came here I have lost freely, so that I have not a halfpenny.

It is naturally impossible that I can remain like this, and I at once thought of you, knowing well that you would be delighted to render me this slight service, and by the same occasion prove to me that you really love me as much as you say you do.

For the last two days I have been very, very ill, and I pity you with all my heart being in bed, and suffering as you do lately. If I could only be near you, how happy I should be to care for you in every way, to pet you and thus be able to prove to you how much I love you.

I long to be back in Paris. I am horribly bored here. I am like those village girls who fret when they can no longer see the steeple of their village church. I am absolutely lost when I am so long away from my dear Paris.

Yes, I flirt, but out of patriotism; so you need not be jealous, for you alone possess my love.

You will ask how I manage to flirt patriotically, so I explain:

There is at this hotel a young German officer, who is absolutely, madly in love with me. I encourage him, and sometimes I laugh at him, just when he believes that I am beginning to let myself be persuaded. This plunges him into fits of melancholy, which it would be impossible to describe.

You see my darling Papa, how wicked your little daughter is!

But enough gossip, I shall finish by wearying you with all my stories. So I leave you, telling you that I await next month with impatience. You guess why?

LILY.

My head fell back on my pillow. I shut my eyes and groaned with mingled physical and moral pain.

3

. . . . Telle que la voilà
Sous les rideaux honteux de ce hideux repaire,
Dans cet infâme lit, elle donne à sa mère,
En rentrant au logis, ce qu'elle a gagné là.
                                ALFRED DE MUSSET.

BEL. . . . Sure it must feel very strange to go to bed
to a man!
    LADY BRUTE.—Um, it does feel a little odd at first,
but it will soon grow easy to you.
                                SIR JOHN VANBRUGH.

The next day came an illustrated postcard, bearing a view of
the Château of Monte-Carlo, with the words: "Souvenir de
Monaco."

Lily had written thereon: "Best and affectionate remembrance."

It is needless to say that I did not answer her letter. I was too
ill and too much worried on all sides.

ERIC ARVEL TO JACKY.

Paris. 10, Rue Vissot. 4th. March 1898.

My dear Jacky,

You must excuse my not having written sooner to thank you for all
the pleasant hours you procured for me in the midst of my stay at

55

Monte-Carlo, where I think I nearly qualified for a hospital nurse, with the influenza, which thinned the company at dinner and filled up all my spare time.

I had some news of you all from Colonel B . . . , who was down at Monte-Carlo, not precisely "picking it up," I am sorry to say.

I hope your people are all quite well. Remember me to all your family.

I am still reading some of the books you gave me and when you have time and "envie," remember that the cook is not dead yet at the Villa Lilian, which is on the point of being done up and made beautiful for ever.

With every good wish, in which both the ladies join, and hoping that "Mord Emly" will, for the sake of Lilian, turn out all right and not a "Pall Mall Tribute," I remain, very truly yours,

ERIC ARVEL.

"Mord Emly" was the title of a serial story, detailing the adventures of a cockney girl, and then running in the pages of a weekly magazine which I sent him regularly. The allusion to the virtue of the heroine in the novel that Mr. and Miss Arvel were reading together struck me as far from delicate.

I still continued to suffer greatly and I had several relapses. My mistress was very ill as well.

ERIC ARVEL TO JACKY.

Sonis-sur-Marne. 11th. March 1898.

My dear Jacky,

I am very sorry indeed to learn from your letter that you have been called on to experience what a sad thing it is to be laid up. I do hope that the second convalescence will be more serious than the first and that when I call on you some day in the next week I shall find that you are right again.

Do not trouble to send me any books or papers. Wait until I call for them and see you at the same time.

I saw J— at the Bourse last Saturday, and I met your brother P— yesterday, and in answer to my enquiries they told me everyone was well and hearty.

Do not come too soon in this damp, nasty weather. Stop in until we have a change, and then you will perhaps come down and put in a week with the dogs, and try the cooking of our *chef*, roosting in one of the bedrooms upstairs, which shall be fitted up as you like.

Remember me very kindly to everybody at your house, and with every good wish from Madame and Mademoiselle, as well as from myself for your complete and speedy recovery, I remain, hoping that you will consider the invitation to stay down here, not as a compliment, but in the genuine manner in which it is meant,

Yours very truly,
Eric Arvel.

I had the visit of Papa, as announced, and I was able to thank him cordially for his kind invitation, which I could not accept, as though I got up for a few hours each day, I was not yet able to do more than hobble from the bed to the window. The doctor refused to let me leave my bedchamber at present, where I was carefully surrounded by screens, and I was even forbidden to go into the rest of the house.

Mr. Arvel came and talked. No one spoke but he, which I was very grateful for, as I was not in a fit state to carry on a conversation. I only remember that the Zola trial was discussed, and I discovered that my friend was a rabid enemy of Dreyfus. He refused to hear a word spoken against any man wearing the uniform of the French army, and as usual with him, I soon saw that he knew nothing at all about the case.

Just before he left, I was alone with him for a few moments and I begged him to remember me to Madame, and Mademoiselle Lilian.

To my surprise, he accepted the message curtly and sulkily. He frowned and his face grew dull.

I must not make myself out too clever. This change of countenance when I spoke of his daughter struck me as strange at the time, but I did not attach the importance to it that I do now. In fact, I am certain that all through the year 1898, I was not as perspicacious as before. I suppose my illness must have dulled my brain. I am perfectly sure that at any other time of my life I should not have been so patient as I was with Miss Arvel, nor should I have continued my *liaison* with her.

I am certain now that I was blinded by my great desire for

her, and that my ordinary power of reasoning had been shaken by the severe trial I had undergone.

I did hunger for the girl, in spite of her mercenary disposition and I fancied that she had some sort of love for me. I ventured to think that there was a little affection for me in her selfish soul.

LILY TO JACKY.

Tuesday. (No date or place.
Received April 26th. 1898.)

My dear little Papa,

Two of my letters with no reply from you. I do not understand it. That my last from Monaco did not get an answer, I allow, but how about my second? You have been ill and to prove to you that I have a little heart more tender than yours, I send you this note, but I swear it will be the last, if it is not more successful than the others. Then I shall understand that you wish to forget the end of the year 1897.

I have been bitten by Blackamoor in trying to prevent him killing another dog. As my right hand is damaged, I am obliged to use the machine to write to you.

I am anxious to have news of your health, which is only given to me very imperfectly by Papa, from what he hears of your people at the Bourse.

Therefore I pray you to answer me as quickly as possible, if you care to make me forget your gross rudeness.

I suppose you will honour us with your presence soon. Perhaps that is asking too much?

I count absolutely upon a scribble as soon as possible,

LILIAN.

JACKY TO LILY.

Wednesday, April 27th. 1898.

My dear little girl,

I had much pleasure in receiving news of your dear self. I have been thinking about you for a long time. In my thoughts you possess a double personality. Firstly, you are my sweet little woman with an intoxicating mouth and then you change into an amiable and demure young lady. I have been asking myself which you were going to be for me in the future?

I see that you have not forgotten the end of November, any more than I have.

The two last communications I received from you from Monaco, were a letter, to hand February 20th., and a souvenir postcard on the 21st. Since then I have two letters from Mr. Arvel and that is all. Have you posted me another letter which I never received? That is surprising.

Yes, I was angry, I confess, when I received your last letter from Monaco. Ill, exhausted by pain, I wrote you a few words in pencil from my bed. You answer me quite coolly, without saying a word about me or my health. I lost my temper and wrote to you no more. I will tell you about this when I see you.

Since the 10th. of February up to Good Friday, I have been in bed, then confined to my room, with lots of ups and downs—more of the latter—and now I get out, but not yet at night. I think it is all over.

I hope your bite will be nothing. I will teach you how to separate two fighting dogs. I pose as a cunning professor, but nevertheless, I was bitten myself last September, through tearing Smike away from a big hound. I never told anybody, not knowing the strange cur. But I am not frightened of going mad. I am perhaps mad already, who knows?

My poor Sally Brass, the mother of your Lili, died Saturday night last. She took cold. There was congestion of the lungs. Friday, they put her on a mustard plaster; then another Saturday night, and she dropped down dead. It was impossible to foresee this. I've had enough of dumb animals. Never again, after those I have are gone. Smike is wonderfully well. My two little bitches also, except Sally's daughter. She is unhappy. She keeps seeking for her mother.

The closing sentence of your letter ". . . honour us with your presence—that is perhaps asking too much," is a pretty little piece of impertinence, which I certainly do not deserve. Our private petty quarrels have nothing to do with my visits to Sonis, I think. Have I not always been correct? You deserve to be severely punished. If you want to be chastised, come quickly to Paris, one afternoon when it is fine,—will you?

Little Lily, do you feel naughty and wicked? Answer me quickly and fix a day for your coming, no matter when. I will await you, as on the last occasion, to kiss you all over and make you enjoy as much as I can. It will be very lovely. Come! I want you—entirely.

You see that I am not very bad and that my anger does not last long, especially with you, my daughter treasure.

My lips on yours,

Your PAPA.

I can see now as I write, that either by the effect of my illness itself, or possibly on account of the enormous quantity of salicylate of soda I had absorbed, I did not see things as clearly as I ought to have done.

For instance, I reproached Lilian with not having mentioned my malady in the letter where she asked for the two hundred francs. This was quite wrong on my part, as the reader will have seen.

At the same time, I ought to have been more impressed with her story of the letter which was mislaid. I have received hundreds of letters in Paris at various addresses, business missives, and love-letters, either at my dwelling, wherever it may have been, or even at post-offices, during the course of my various intrigues, and I cannot remember that one single one was ever lost.

I have not the slightest doubt that Lilian told a lie. She never wrote to me on her return from the South. If she had, she would have shown some anxiety for the ultimate fate of her letter, and would have been uneasy lest it should have fallen into the hands of some of my numerous relatives, who were daily at my bedside, or been stolen by a servant. I shall allude to the lost letter mania later on in my narrative. And when I tell her that I never received the epistle she mentions, she takes it as a matter of course, as the reader will see in the ensuing translation:

LILIAN TO JACKY.

No date or place. (Received April 28th. 1898.)

Beloved little Papa,

Your note has poured some balm into my heart, although it caused me to shed two big tears. Yes, I must confess that the death of Sally Brass made me weep, when I think she was neglected during your illness! If I had had the care of her, how different it would have been. Happily, my big darling Smike is well, but then you look after him yourself.

The reproach you make to me about my last letter from Monaco is unmerited. If you had read it properly you would have seen that on the contrary it was full of allusions to your health. The only thing that might have wounded your feelings was the demand I made, for naturally you have now classed me in the ranks of mercenary females.

And yet if you knew me well you would never have dreamt of such a thing. I was in a fix and worried. I supposed that I could tell you my troubles and even ask you to help me. I see that I made a mistake; let us say no more about it!

One of my letters has gone astray. I wrote to you immediately on my return home.

My health is good. I am slightly unwell at present, but that is nothing.

I can only see you in some little time from now. At present, I have no customers in Paris. I must therefore find a plausible excuse. But you will lose nothing by waiting.

I send you my best caresses, grumbling Papa!

LILY.

This letter was useful to me, as by reason of the mention of her slight indisposition, which I took to be her menstrual derangement, it fixed for me certain monthly dates.

It is impossible for me to remember how I answered her, as I have no copy or recollection, but it could not have pleased her very much, as the next communication is from her stepfather, nearly a month later.

ERIC ARVEL TO JACKY.

Sonis-sur-Marne. May 23rd. 1898.

My dear Jacky,

We have had a rare time here since you came down to see us last. We have been successively turned out of every room and even now we are reduced to the kitchen. We want to see you and show you what we have done up to the present, but it is only fair to say that we are still living in the kitchen, reviving old times, and all the upstairs rooms are encumbered with those odds and ends a housewife likes to collect around her.

Do you mind taking pot-luck in the kitchen on Wednesday next? I have a day free, and we can go over the garden without wooden shoes, unless it rains; but at all events come down in your heaviest of shooting-

boots, or you will get your feet wet. If you are better engaged than visiting in the kitchen, let me know. I hope we shall see you fit and well
and with a forty horse-power appetite. The ladies send their kindest
regards and hope to see you.

With best and kindest regards to all your family,

Believe me to remain, yours very truly,

ERIC ARVEL.

MAY 25TH. 1898.

I think I was but a sorry sight as I dragged my aching limbs
up the gravel path that led through the pretty garden of the Villa
Lilian to the house, where my sweetheart and her mother greeted
me warmly, thanked me for the usual peace-offerings I brought
them, and soon put me at my ease, while the father, in the best of
humours, did all he could to make me as comfortable as possible.
While on the subject of their hospitality, I must render them
justice once for all by saying that no one could be received more
cordially or better treated than I was at Sonis-sur-Marne. Nothing
was too good for me. My advice was asked on all sorts of subjects
and I believe that they all had a kind of respect for me. I speak
calmly and without vanity, but I really fancy that at one time
they all liked me and looked up to me.

The house was greatly improved. The garden was double the
original size, through the acquisition of the adjacent property, and
there was a small house, with a little garden, to be sold exactly next
door. Mr. Arvel begged me to buy it, but it was impossible for
obvious reasons, despite Lilian seconding his proposition with
meaning looks.

The dark passage near the kitchen where I had enjoyed
Lilian's first kiss was gone, and in its place was a brand new dining-
room, as yet unfinished, so the meals were served in the kitchen. I
had lunch, and then they made me stop for dinner. This was, I think,
the first time I had ever spent the whole day with them. It was
my first outing after sunset since my illness.

Arch Lilian begged me to help her to lay the cloth for lunch
and we were alone. Can my readers understand that I was so de-

lighted at once more being near my love that I have now no recollection of what I said to her about her neglect of me since November, her request for money, and the missing (!) letter? I shrewdly
suspect that in my convalescent condition, boiling over with lust
for her, I said nothing at all. I was in the seventh heaven of delight.
Whenever she touched me, purposely or by accident, the voluptuous effect made itself felt at once, and her influence over my
sexual organs never failed all the time I knew her, until a certain
moment which shall be described in due course.

She was sweetness itself all day long, and nothing could equal
the grace and girlish abandon of her manner. Her caresses were
frequent. Whenever we could get behind a door or on a staircase,
no matter where, her lips were joined to mine, and she would
shudder with delight as my hands wandered freely all over her
lithe frame.

The great trouble in my mind was that I knew I did not see
her often enough. I was certain that after a few times that she
might have been with me, I could have done *anything* with her and
bent her to my will.

I am not boastful and do not think much of myself—if I did,
how could I write these cynical confessions?—but I could see that
when I talked to her, her whole soul was mine, that she experienced
the greatest pleasure a woman could have in being with me, in
feeling me near her.

She made me sit next to her at meals and took care to keep
my plate and glass replenished. Pa and Ma were beaming with joy.
I knew instinctively that I was looked upon as an admirer of Lilian.
The position was an enviable one, and I resolved to let things go
on without recrimination, nor trouble at present about the future.

Ma's attack of influenza was alluded to. Lilian had had it too.
I told the tale of my illness, but without mentioning the cause.
I never spoke of my mistress, nor did they. It was well-known in
Paris that my handsome Lily was always with me and what I may
call my "conjugal" address was engraved on all my dogs' collars.
But they never alluded to her, nor did Lilian Arvel.

With regard to Mamma's sickness at Monte-Carlo, Lilian, being alone with me for a few moments in the afternoon, casually let

drop how she had been miserable down in the South. She never meant to travel again with her parents if she could help it. Papa always wanted to go to bed early. Mamma had to obey him, so there was no fun for her at night. I chaffed her about the German officer, but she said it was only a flirtation of the hotel-corridor type, and the epidemic had spoilt the whole trip. She had nursed her mother with the help of Papa. They had two bedrooms, one for her and one for her parents, but one night when Ma was very bad, Pa had come and *slept in her bed with her.*

I purposely refrained from taking any notice of this slip of her tongue, but I should have been as a blind man, if I had not noticed the visible desire of Mr. Arvel for my Lilian, the daughter of his mistress. And instead of feeling disgust or jealousy, I am bound to confess the truth: it excited my lust in the most terrible manner to think he loved her, and I seemed to breathe an atmosphere of incest that aroused my passions to the utmost extent.

Lilian was not well. She drank milk with her meals and had no appetite. Her mother tried to tempt her to eat, but she would refuse the heaped-up plateful and ask for smaller morsels, saying: "Tiny! Tiny!" This expression of hers became a catchword at the villa.

Raoul, her brother, was also talked about at table. He was doing well in his situation in London, but his infatuation for Charlotte, or Lolotte, as they called her, worried his mother greatly and sent Papa into fits of rage. Lilian took her part in some slight degree, but she could not forgive her for what looked suspiciously like the seduction of her handsome brother, of whom she seemed inordinately fond. When she first went to London with Charlotte, Raoul met the two girls at the station, and after dinner they went for a walk. On returning to their lodging, Lolotte let Lilian get into bed, and then said she was going out for a few minutes. She went off and slept with Raoul at a hotel that night, leaving Lilian to tremble and worry alone until the morning.

This story was openly told before me; and Papa, fulminating, narrated how he forbade Lolotte ever to come to his house again, or face him. But she was still friends with Mamma and Lilian; and, when Pa was away, would come and stop many a week-end down at Sonis and share Miss Arvel's bed, an arrangement which was known to the master of the house. These sidelights of suburbia delighted my vice. I enjoyed the study of this family, but most of all, of course, Lilian's love for me. It flattered my pride. I was 46; she was 22; she had chosen me as her lover. Could anything be more flattering for a debauchee verging upon 50?

I pressed her to come to Paris. She said that her mother was very strict and kept a vigilant eye upon her movements. I think she did look sharply after her and appeared to be very artful. I often had little conversations with her, but she would not be drawn out concerning her daughter. I gave her up in despair. The father was more communicative, and I felt that I had only to wait and listen to him, if I wanted to hear about Lilian.

I gathered that if she had work for Paris, or customers there to attend to, I might be able to possess her. Of course, it was easy to see that money would get her to come to me. I should have had to invent buyers for her hats and bonnets in the gay capital, pay for the things ordered, which would never have been made, or some like scheme.

But I had no money to spare. What little my purse contained was to pay for my poor mistress's comforts in her incurable illness.

Lilian showed me a small and very pretty watch her father had given her; and in his presence, she said she wanted a true lover's knot in various little precious stones to hang it on to the bosom of her dress. I said that I should be pleased to get it for her, if her father would let me do so.

He replied frankly enough: "Well, Jacky, as far as I am concerned, I shouldn't mind a bit, but her mother would never let her take it. She would be awfully offended and give it back to you at once. So you must not do it. We are English you know, but the 'missus' is French."

Some months later, when alluding to this, Lilian shrugged her shoulders, and said: "You should have given it to me all the same; they would not have minded, after the first growl."

When I left them late at night, with Lilian's promise to come to me soon and her parents' flattering compliments and hearty good wishes, I could not help thinking that Papa's pretty gift of the watch to Lilian was in return for some slight pleasure he had experienced by her side and in her virginal bed, while nursing Mamma through the influenza at Monte-Carlo. And a wave of concupiscence swept over me at the thought.

LILY TO JACKY.

No date or place. (Received May 29th. 1898.)

The little daughter is thinking deeply about her darling little father. She adores him and hopes to see him soon.

A long and soft kiss,

LILY.

I tried to get her some customers among my friends' mistresses, talking to them of a cheap little *modiste* I knew down in the country, who would not object to do up their old hats or work with their own materials. I was promised some orders, and I wrote and told her about my negotiations. I suppose by her answer, I must have written a very voluptuous letter, although for the life of me, I cannot remember now what I said.

LILY TO JACKY.

No date or place. (Received June 1st. 1898.)

My own beloved,

What a naughty, wicked, cheeky, and yet delicious letter! Truly only you can write like that. But what effrontery to class me as a little *modiste*.

Know then, my beloved Papa, that here I am considered as the best bonnet-builder of the locality and for miles round my fame has spread. I am the Virot of the village. It is a very grave thing to try and destroy my good reputation, so that you will get one kiss and one caress less. That is how I serve you for being so rude.

But let us speak seriously:

It is quite immaterial to me who I work for. I do not care if they are the sort of women you mention. They already form the majority of my customers. The only trouble is that they would take up a lot of my time, whereas if I could get an order from a wholesale house, as

I told you, I should only have to give the necessary orders to set my workgirls going, and then I could escape and be a whole afternoon with my adored little Papa. Which would be very naughty, but very agreeable. You, who have plenty of time on your hands, why do you not go among the wholesale people and try and find something for me to do?

If you don't find a way to make me come to Paris, I can't answer for my virtue, for since last Wednesday, after the day you passed at our house, I have no wish to be a good girl, quite the contrary.

So search and you will find. You will see that you won't regret your trouble, for your little daughter knows well how to reward you for all your efforts in her favour.

I love you,

LILY.

LILY TO JACKY.

No date or place. (Received June 23rd. 1898.)

My very dirty, but well-beloved Papa,

It is absolutely charming of you to think of your little daughter. She, on her part, does not forget you, which is quite natural, is it not? I await with impatience these famous lady customers you write to me about, for then my adored master will have all his work cut out to content me!

I am as naughty as can be at this moment in imagination only, naturally. From the idea of the action nevertheless, there is but one step, I think?

Your little daughter is unhappy just now; her mother is as hard and unjust as possible towards her. Mr. A. . . tells me that it is her change of life that is beginning to upset her, and that I must not pay attention to what she says or does, but I assure you that very often my patience gives out, and twice this week I have been on the point of leaving the house, as this sudden change in her conduct where I am concerned, afflicts me awfully and makes me miserable. I cry nearly every day. If I were with my dear little Papa, how different all this would be! I want you more than ever. I hunger for that warm affection you show for me. I am discouraged.

I love you madly,

LILY.

I had indeed noticed that Lilian and her mother were at log-gerheads. It was not to be wondered at. Mr. Arvel's mistress was evidently jealous of the attention he paid to her daughter, and, I could see, did not like the way they played together. They always had sly jokes to crack together, on very lax subjects.

Papa would chaff Lilian about "going to the theatre." He would say: "You like going to the theatre, Lilian?" The girl would giggle, the mother frown, and my host laugh outright. I sat by like a fool, and had to wait my opportunity to ask Lilian what "the theatre" meant, especially as they were not playgoers. It appears they knew a gentleman who had stopped at their house some time and who hated the drama. He had said that playhouses were sinks of iniquity and that people only frequented them to indulge in sly caresses and pull each other about. So "going to the theatre," in the Arvel language, meant the action of a man and a woman tou-zling and libidinously romping. Lilian, it was easy to see, was on the road to become her stepfather's pleasure-tool, to say the least. And I liked to see the lickerish girl and the sensual old man to-gether. I was thus able to come to the conclusion that neither Mr. or Mrs. Arvel were capable of giving proper advice to the brother or the sister. How they were to behave in life; the duties that they owed to themselves or society; the future of the woman; or the honesty and honour of the man; nothing touching on the proper way to live had ever been told to them. And why? The mother and he who stood in the position of father were absolutely incapable of instructing them. There were no sentiments at the Villa Lilian—only appetites. All they knew was that they should try and earn money and save a little; eat and drink; and when they found any-body less cunning than themselves—take advantage of them.

I could see no real affection in Arvel's house at present. He liked Lilian in a lustful way; Mrs. Arvel was fond of her man because he kept the house a-going, but they all spoke against each other, as each turned their backs. And when their appetites were satisfied they started quarrelling, I suppose, as they quarrelled be-fore me without shame.

Papa had a rough, loud voice, and one masterbuilder, who was engaged on the house, refused to come any more, as he said he was not used to be bullied and holloaed at. Mrs. Arvel was a shrew, and could not keep a servant, and Lilian answered her mother impudently, because she felt that Papa was behind her.

Nevertheless, Mr. Arvel sometimes vented his wrath on saucy Lilian too. He had told her on my last visit that women were incapable of getting their living. She turned sullen, and the black cloud came over her face. Her lips were blue, as she answered: "I get mine. Don't I pay you for my board?"

"Yah!" snarled Arvel, "but you don't pay any rent or taxes!"

"That would be the last straw," snapped the damsel back at him, "ask me to give you money now for my rent and I'll be off!"

These rows generally took place just at the beginning of the meals, as all their nerves were unstrung by the pangs of hunger. As soon as they were warmed up by wine and meat, they all got amiable again, and Pa would pinch Lilian as she passed him, and bandy pet names with his mistress. I always sat by and said nothing, although Mrs. Arvel would appeal to me and say ironically: "Is he not polite?"

I often had the impression that I was lunching or dining in a pantry, and that the coachman and cook were having a tiff with their daughter, the lady's maid. But what cared I? I lusted for Lilian.

In answer to her missive, I told her to try and put up with her domestic troubles, as if she ventured to leave her home, she would be ruined for life. She could have no idea of the career of a young woman alone in the world. There was no possible happiness for her outside the pale of social conventions, and she must play the hypocrite in a good cause and put up with everything from her mother, who, after all, loved her and had brought her up and educated her. I tried to give her an idea of the position of women according to worldly notions, and that is how I saw that the young lady who wanted to be kept well in hand, had been allowed to drift into my arms, for the want of good advice. Why Arvel had never put her on the right road was obvious. He wanted her for himself, although perhaps at that time he did not know what he really desired, or was powerless to judge his own feelings. I fancy that could he have analysed the sensations that were springing up in his breast, he would have tried to curb what I felt was a fast-growing desire for his mistress's daughter. But he could not reason; he only knew that her contact warmed his sluggish blood; that he felt young again when he tickled her, or romped with her, and that was all he desired or cared about.

Her future, her interests, the ultimate end of such unnatural intercourse could never have occurred to him, or he would have behaved more decently and stopped low wrangling, besides refraining from discussing the mother's menopause with her. But he had gone still farther with the maiden, as she had told me in answer to a question as to whether Mr. Arvel loved her Mamma or not:

"Oh, not much! Ma tells me he never touches her now. He only proves his love now and again at rare irregular intervals."

I threw all scruples to the winds. If Lilian did not play with me, she would get somebody else and Papa will be sure to have his turn one of these fine days. I cannot save her.

I began to tell her that I should love her more if she would be very obedient to me. I wanted to be her master. She must submit to be my slave.

I could wait no longer. I wanted her, and the promised customers not coming forward as quickly as I wished, I, impatient to taste her sweet body once more, reflected, and thought that a little cash would facilitate matters. I wrote and asked her if it was possible for her to carry out this little comedy:

"Tell your people that you have heard of a bad debt—surely someone owes you a little bill?—and come up to Paris to fetch it. Meet me and I will give you a fifty-franc note. Go back and exhibit the money to your Mamma and give it to her if she wants it, saying that you have succeeded in getting that on account, and that you are promised the same amount again, to be given by the lady before she goes to the seaside. A fortnight later, up you come to Paris again and return home to your parents with a few louis more. Thus I buy the liberty of my slave from her mother!"

LILIAN TO JACKY.

Wednesday. (No date or place. Received June 15th. 1898.)

My only master,

This time I will try my hardest not to bore you with all my troubles; I will keep everything hidden in the very bottom of my heart and only when we shall be all alone, will I, in the costume of Mother Eve—since such is your will and pleasure—open the corner of my heart which holds all that causes my tears. Thank you for the promptitude with which you answered my last scrawl. I have found fresh strength in your good and long letter. As soon as mother begins to be unjust, I think of you, and I, who have no patience, find enough to let her do and say all she likes without answering, or saying what is on the tip of my tongue, which always brings on quarrels. It is very hard all the same, and in truth I must love you profoundly to restrain my temper as I do. Evidently you are right in all you tell me, and I have decided to follow your good advice.

Your idea is quite feasible, especially as I have a customer who owes me money and Papa knows it. There is only an "if" and a "but," however. The idea of accepting money from you is repugnant to me, since your feelings were wounded during my sojourn at Monte-Carlo.

I do not explain myself well, but you who understand me so well, will be able to read between the lines.

This customer I am telling you about is a certain Madame Helena Muller. She owes me nearly seven hundred francs and I shall never get a sou.

You must write me a word, telling me when I can see you. I will arrange to tell the story you suggest and all will be well.

I am free, excepting Friday, when I have got some ladies coming to try on some hats.

Soon I shall see, I hope, my too much beloved little Papa.

I send you no kisses; I keep them all for our next interview.

Your entirely submissive slave,

LILY.

ERIC ARVEL TO JACKY.

10, Rue Vissot. Paris, June 17th. 1898.

My dear Jacky,

You are overwhelming me. Many thanks for all your books. You are one of the best. Will you come and dine with us *sans cérémonie* on Monday night? M. is coming, and we can offer you a good dinner.

Remember me very kindly to your good parents and everybody else, and believe me to remain ever,

Yours very truly,
ERIC ARVEL.

LILIAN TO JACKY.

No date or place. (Received June 19th. 1898.)

Beloved Master,

To-morrow, Saturday, is the most busy day for me, as I have to send home all the work of the week, and as you can easily understand, I must be there in order to see that everything is properly finished off.

Monday, we have a gentleman coming to dinner and there is some talk of inviting a certain M. Jacky S . . . as well. I do not know him, but I want to make his acquaintance and as I wish to please him I must not go out that afternoon, or I shall not be pretty enough in the evening!

Miss Arvel will tell M. S . . . what day the little daughter can pass a few pleasant hours with her dear Papa.

In the meanwhile, I send you a long, long kiss and a thousand caresses each one sweeter than the other.

LILY.

JUNE 20, 1898.

Of the informal dinner-party, I have very little to say. I managed to get a few brief moments alone with my love and reminded her that I should expect and exact entire obedience from her. She would have to submit to the worst kind of caresses next time we met, and I should measure the depth of her love by the manner in which she put up with the most brutal conduct from me, if my caprices should lead me that way. She was mine and I could do as I chose with her body. It would be the height of voluptuousness to feel that she was in my power, that I was free to inflict pain upon her, and she was to support all suffering, buoying herself up with the thought that all she endured, however disagreeable, was conducive to her master's pleasure. So saying, I smartly slapped her face, and she positively cooed with delight like a turtledove.

"You hurt me!"

And emboldened, I pinched her arms. She longed to cry out, but dared not, as Papa was not far off, and murmuring: "Oh! You did hurt me!" melted away on my eager lips.

I explained to her again that although she was absolutely free in the eyes of the world and could get married to-morrow if she liked without a jealous word from me, when alone in tête-à-tête with me, she was to have no shame, and I intended to destroy in her all feelings of pudicity, by forcing her to do everything I wanted. I should teach her the pleasure of being humiliated and degraded by the man she loved, and she would gradually get to relish the idea of trampling on all laws of decency. The initial stage would produce a novel kind of peculiar pain and suffering that would heighten and prolong her sensual enjoyment, as the smarting hurt of my mischievous punishments would retard the moment of joy and these conflicting emotions plunge her finally into the wildest vortex of lubricity. She listened devoutly and said the idea pleased her greatly. I secretly resolved to make an expert whore of her. She should have no shame, and recoil from nothing a man's lechery could invent in the delirium of desire. I wanted— mad vision!—to fashion a harlot out of a virgin, and hand over to a husband a Messalina with a maidenhead. I knew that I could easily fashion her to my wishes.

Anybody can by hook or by crook get a girl to lie still and with the aid of a little force and fascination gradually establish complete connection, but moulding a virgin to one's wishes seemed to me something new, and soothing to the last few fragments of my tattered conscience. I hankered to enjoy the winsome lassie and I would at that moment have cut off my hand sooner than have harmed her, or dishonoured her. I thought, in my folly, that I was behaving honestly to her, and I took great credit to myself for my forbearance. How far was I right or wrong?

JUNE 22, 1898.

I hesitate before beginning to narrate how I at last was able to press my Lilian's unveiled form in my arms, because I have to make an avowal, which I am sure will not be fully understood by many of my readers.

I loved Lilian with all the strength of my black soul. I cannot help if my brain is incapable of jealousy. I had given her my heart. I thought of nothing but her night and day, but I cared not what she did or to whom she granted her favours, as long as she proved her love for me. Worse than all, I wanted her to have other adorers. I would have placed her myself in the arms of many men, if she only came back to me afterwards. And the idea that her mother's lover pursued her with his lascivious obsessions; that he was perhaps her real father, caused me to love her more. Am I not sufficiently vile? And yet at the same time—supreme contradiction, that I cannot understand myself, unless it was the remembrance of my first Lilian—I respected her virginal film. I looked upon her as a sacred trust, as something I must not harm or violate. She was to me an idol to be worshipped, that I venerated too much to shatter or spoil. Once for all, I must, since I have sworn to tell the truth, make a statement to which I shall not recur again.

Whenever I had an appointment with Lilian, I always took care to have had at least one emission, either the night before, or more frequently in the morning, as our meetings were in the afternoon, so as to be sufficiently cool and not too excited, thus remaining master of my passions and preventing myself being tempted to rob her of her virgin's crown.

My sweet girl came at last quite punctually. She sat by me, close to me, and chatted. She told me that an *employé* in the offices of the Gare de l'Est had been frequently pestering her with his attentions. He wanted to marry her. He had seen her father, who had bluntly told him that his daughter had no dowry, and that he would not give her to any man unless the suitor could prove that he possessed at least a fortune of ten thousand pounds. The poor clerk had retired crestfallen. If the story was true, it only proved that Mr. Arvel did not want her to be married. I hinted as much to her, but she laughed the matter off and kissed me passionately, and I returned her caresses, devouring her face and neck. And now she gave me a great deal of trouble. I could not get her clothes off or pull up her skirts. She struggled against me. I was vexed, tired, and hot. It was not a loving encounter, but a wrestling bout, and to every one of my efforts she kept on repeating:

"You hurt me! Oh! You hurt me!"

At last, I persuaded her to consent to undress and get into bed with me. After a deal of haggling and on condition that I closed the window curtains, she gave way. I think she saw I was getting disgusted at her prolonged resistance.

She made me undress first, go to bed, and await her. I agreed and soon afterwards she slipped under the coverlet by my side. I went to take her in my arms, when she pulled the sheet between us so that my body should not touch hers, and giggled hysterically. But I soon clasped her in my arms, and pulling up her chemise, enjoyed to the full the pleasure of feeling her flesh against my naked body.

I took her hand and put it on my member. She dragged her fingers away and turned her face from me. I asked her why she did so.

"Oh! I make such faces when I enjoy! You can't know how nervous I am!"

How did she know she was ugly in the moment of joy? Who had told her?

"You must take my thing in your hand, Lily!"

"No! No!" she exclaimed.

"But see, I touch you!" said I, as I deftly manipulated her little button.

"You hurt me!" she whined once more.

So I, out of temper, feeling inwardly that she was coquetting with me, grasped her round the waist, threw her light frame over on to her belly, and pulling down the sheets and blankets, fully exposed her posteriors. Her bottom was round, well-shaped, and larger than one would have expected from such a slightly made creature.

"You won't do what I want, will you? Well, I'll make you. I'll slap you until you obey me!"

Then, without sparing her, I held her tightly with my right arm, and my left hand rained down a succession of smart slaps on her buttocks.

She struggled, shrieked, and kept on her eternal complaint:

"You hurt me!"

I spanked her with all my strength, paying no heed to her cries, and I should think she suffered nearly five minutes; a long period when being punished.

At last, my fingers aching, and being out of breath, I was about to desist, when she gave in and begged for mercy, putting out her hand to caress my private parts. She was more tractable now and I masturbated her until she gave down her elixir, but she still complained of the pain my exploring finger caused her.

Perhaps I did go a little too far. Perhaps I wanted to see if the hymen had been ruptured between November and June. But no, she was still *virgo intacta*.

She was very wet with all these manœuvres, which I could see and feel she enjoyed. I got on top of her, made her open her thighs, and put the head of my instrument just beyond the outer lips of her grotto, which, by the way, were very large and hairy, and en-clined to be fat. I did not intend to follow up my advantage, but I enjoyed the feeling that the clasp of her lower mouth gave to the tip of my acorn.

When I got too far, or pushed forward as if to begin the work of penetration, she continued her parrot-cry:

"You hurt me!"

I rolled off her body, she turned on her side, and her bottom was against my dart, as I clasped her to me. I placed the bursting, swollen weapon between the robust hemispheres. She liked this. I imitated her eternal, plaintive: "You hurt me!"

I asked her if she was happy and whether she would like me to suck her now.

"I want you first!" she murmured.

So I, being rampant, in spite of my efforts to keep back the emission, started plunging and pushing as if I would sodomize her, and I am almost sure that the tip of my organ of virility was in her anus. She was very hairy, and unlike women in general, had a slight growth all round the little wrinkled hole of her beautiful bottom.

I soon exploded my cartridge and she remained in bed. The closeness of her posterior charms prevented a drop escaping. I asked her if I had penetrated a little way in behind, but she denied it.

Then a little more play, and once more I made her spend with my finger, the while I sucked her large and fiery nipples. This time, she herself asked me to masturbate her. She thoroughly appreciated this last bout and wanted nothing more.

She had got some sort of an idea vaguely into her head that she could get married, and not let her husband penetrate her. She seemed to have horror at the idea of a man's perforator piercing her body. She kept telling me to be careful how I tickled her clitoris, as she had heard a story of a girl being violated by a young lover's middle finger! There was an impression I had, that real coition with a husband or a lover did not tempt her.

I began to talk cautiously to her about a friend I had in England. He was a lord and was married. Being much older than his wife, and being blest or cursed with the same tolerant ideas as I had, he allowed his better half to have lovers and I wanted Lily to send her brother, who was working hard in London, to the easygoing couple. She refused to communicate with him on the subject.

I offered her other women if she cared to try a little tribadism. But she would not entertain the idea for a moment. I soon found out that she really liked men and would not object to "fun" with two men at once. I asked her if she would lunch with me and my friend from London. She would certainly, but would not go to him when she went to England in the autumn.

After all was over and she was dressed, seeing that I was rather quiet and cool towards her, she crept up to me and apologised spontaneously and prettily for all her shortcomings.

"I meant to be your slave, and coming up in the train I rehearsed all that I should do and how I would be quite unresisting in your arms. But when you took hold of me, I could not overcome my feelings of shame. Let me get used to you and I will really be your 'thing,' as devoted to you and even more obedient than Smike, but you don't know how difficult it is for me to summon up courage and come along this Rue de Leipzig to you."

And then she wanted to remake the bed, so that the people of the house should ignore that we had used it.

Her mixture of true or feigned innocence, with her natural perversity and coquetry, bewildered and delighted me. She aroused my lust completely, and I could not look at her without the most filthy ideas of refined enjoyment crowding into my mind.

We left the house, and I took her to a café where we had a pint bottle of dry champagne. While drinking it and talking on indifferent subjects I saw her eyes half closing, her nostrils began to quiver, and her carmine lips, all fiery from the recent touches of my moustache and teeth, were bedewed with saliva.

"Why, you're coming!" I exclaimed.

"Yes, darling, but how do you know?"

I explained the signs that had betrayed her, and asked her the reason.

"Only because I am seated here alone with you! Oh! I'm sopping!"

She would have returned to the Rue de Leipzig, but it was too late. I was fortunate enough, although it was the month of June, to secure a closed fiacre and was able, during the drive to the station, to verify the fact that she was really inundated.

I must not forget that I gave her a fifty-franc note, which she said she was bound to show to her Mamma, to account for her prolonged absence from home, and I regretfully left her, thinking on my way home of her handsome drawers, ornamented with lace, and the dainty chemise to match, with its little bows of pink ribbon, and I weaved new schemes of future orgies with her—my Lilian. I was in truth very far gone.

4

Trouver, dans une souffrance de degré très variable, tantôt
légère, tantôt grave ou d'un raffinement atroce, qu'on
fait infliger, qu'on voit infliger ou qu'on inflige enfin
soi-même à un être humain, la condition toujours néces-
saire, et parfois suffisante, de la jouissance sexuelle: telle
est la perversion de l'instinct génital qu'on désigne sous
le nom de sadisme.

L. THOINOT.

LILY TO JACKY.

No date or place. (Received June 24th. 1898.)

It is five o'clock in the morning, but as I cannot sleep, I get up
softly so as not to wake the slumbering household and quickly write a
line to my well-beloved master.

The most conflicting sentiments agitate me since yesterday. I feel
ashamed of my lewdness and yet I regret having been so reserved.

I adore you, the thought of you alone drives me absolutely mad. I
am eager to see you again. I thirst for you. I want to be yours, yours
entirely; to be your thing, your slave.

I have a prayer to offer up to you: Next time we meet, if now and
again, in spite of myself I refuse you the least favour, I must beg of you
only to repeat to me this simple sentence: "Do it to prove to me your
love!"

I know that I am very silly, but my dear and beloved little Papa, I only ask to learn, and I often say to myself that I am very foolish to reserve myself for some creature I shall certainly never love, since you alone possess my soul, my heart, my body.

How long the days will seem to me until the end of the month! And I fear already that I have wearied you by my ignorance and my timidity.

I remember your dear lips,

Your
LILY.

LILY TO JACKY.

Sunday. (No date. Received June 27th. 1898.)

Adored master,

Your little girl is suffering to-day. Have no fear. It is nothing serious; in three or four days it will be all over.

How good and generous you are! You possess the patience of an angel, but your little daughter will really become your slave in every sense of the word.

One of the reasons which as well as my wretched shame prevents me from being as submissive as I should wish, is that I do not esteem myself handsome enough for you. I have an awful fear lest I should dispel all your illusions, you who have known so many women. If I was formed like a real woman and not like a silly, awkward young girl, it would be quite different.

I am well-built, I know, but really too thin. I should like to be marvellously beautiful for you; for your sole joy and pleasure.

I have a heap of questions to put to you the next time I see you. There are certain things that I do not understand at all, and that I should dearly like to know!

When you want to see me, make a sign, and I'll fly to you, my love, but not until the end of the month as arranged.

I adore you,

Your
LILY.

Eric Arvel to Jacky.

Sonis-sur-Marne, 30th. June 1898.

My dear Jacky,

I am commissioned by Madame to tender you her very best thanks for the very handsome addition you have enabled her to make to her dressing-table. I cannot tell where you discovered such handsome cut-glass bottles, such as they do not make nowadays, and which I can assure you are highly appreciated. We cannot help looking at them and since they arrived last night they have been in our hands time after time. You are really too good, and you embitter our minds when we think how handsomely you are always inclined to recognise a hospitality which in your case it is to us a true pleasure to exercise. Can you come down on Saturday and spend a long day with us so that we may thank you personally for all your kindness? We will have some fresh fruit and vegetables, and with a bit of luck we can give you some peas such as you have rarely eaten. Give my very best wishes to all your good folks at home, who I trust are well.

Yours very truly,
Eric Arvel.

Lily to Jacky.

No date or place. (Received July 1st. 1898.)

My best beloved master,

Do come to-morrow, then we can settle about Monday if you wish. But I am longing to see your darling face.

Come as early as you can, and try to stay as late as possible if you wish to please your slave and make her very happy.

I should like to bite you,

Lily.

July 2, 1898.

This day was a long and happy one. The best part of the time I managed to be alone with my Lily. And she was mine then, if ever a woman was. She was quite changed, and I felt she was now entirely under my influence. She was sweet, tender, and confiding.

As before, she asked me to help her to lay the table for *déjeuner* and although Mamma kept coming in and out of the dining-room, we managed to exchange many a sly caress. Lily had pleasant touches of amiability peculiarly her own. One spontaneous approach of hers I shall never forget, as she never repeated it, and it happens that I do not remember any other woman having done the same thing to me. I was seated on a little sofa at the end of the room and she was busy at the table. I was supposed to assist her, but I never did anything but kiss her. She dropped the plate she held, and coming to me without a word, bent her head and placed her cheek against mine. I did not speak, neither did she. And there she remained for a moment. That is all.

I treated her with kindness, but I exacted obedience, and told her curtly to kiss me and touch me as my wayward fancy dictated, and being forced to be obedient to me pleased her greatly. She told me that she knew she had not a good temper, could not brook authority, and that neither her mother nor her father could get her to do what did not please her. And yet to me she willingly gave way.

What she wanted me to explain to her, according to her letter, was the entrancing mystery of manly erection. I told her briefly, and she said she thought that males were always stiff and hard. I asked her if she had never looked at her dogs. She replied that she did not like to, that she had never dared.

Papa had told me that Lilian hated reading books. He had tried to educate her mind a little by giving her a few healthy English novels to read. French romances, he would not have in his house. I thought of *Les Demi-Vierges*, but kept silent. I never spoke of the girl to him, never even mentioning her name; but we hardly ever conversed without he talked of her. I asked her if she cared for books and she confessed she adored reading. So I had brought with me "The Yellow Room," which I gave her, and she ran and hid it away.

This story is thoroughly obscene and relates to flagellation and torture practised erotically on two young girls by the uncle of one of them.

During the day, in her impatience, she managed to slip away and peep into it, and in the evening told me that she thought she would like to read how the heroine suffered. I put her on her guard against the exaggerated cruelty therein described. I tried to make her understand the pleasure of subjecting a loved woman to one's most salacious desires, and that submission had its joys. I laid stress again on the enjoyment I should have in degrading and humiliating her when we were alone together, and she freely said that the efforts she would have to make, to curb her own disobedient nature for the sake of my despotic pleasure, would exercise a most extraordinary emotional effect on her sensuality.

I cannot tell how we kissed and fondled each other. I taught her to lick my face, neck, and ears, and I frequently made her feel my stiffened spear outside my trousers.

I would make her put her hand on it and note its softness. Then I joined her mouth to mine, and taking her fingers, placed them once more on the now hardened standard. This lesson of turgescent virility greatly delighted her.

I now come to the principal novel experience of the day. The last time I was at Sonis, I told her that when I came to visit at her house, I ordered her to tie a string or riband to the hair of her "pussy," and let the end peep out of her frock. The colour was to be assorted to the hue of the dress-fabric, so that I could pull at it now and then, unsuspected by anyone. By the slight smart the tug would give, I could thus feel that I was in intimate communication with the most secret part of her body, and could test her devotion to me by being able to inflict pain upon her whenever I chose.

She would prove her love by supporting this teazing inconvenience and therefore show that she loved me greatly by such humble submission to all my most weird and voluptuous caprices. She tried to laugh at the idea, but I could see she listened attentively and liked the originality of my strange whim. She found extraordinary delight in being the slave of a "very dirty Papa," as she called me, and when I mentioned the word "incest," as I did frequently, her eyes closed, her nostrils quivered, and her mouth literally watered, the moisture of her saliva bedewing her sensual and expressive lips.

Just before lunch, I said:

"You pretend you will obey me and yet you have not done what I told you on my last visit."

She knew at once what I meant, gave me an arch look and said she would obey.

In the course of the afternoon, Mamma went up to Paris to fetch another new servant. Papa asked me to go out with him and give the dogs an airing, but I objected, complaining of pains in my ankles. It is true they did hurt me, but not as much as I made out. He begged me to remain on a bench in the garden, and called his daughter from the kiosque, where she was at work with her assistants, to keep me company, while he went out alone, and there was no one in the house, but Lily, her workgirls, and me. Lily showed me the end of a piece of tape which peeped out of the pocket-hole of her dress behind, she having fastened it to the hair on the left side of her mount, and brought it round her hip through the slit of her petticoat. She sat by my side and I pulled it frequently. She would wince, tell me I hurt her, and kiss me furtively, as she kept a sharp lookout, so that the girls should not see her. I told her that I did not believe she had really fastened it where I wanted, and putting my hand in this opening, I got it round to where it was tied, verifying her statement, and tickling the top of her furrow a little. I told her she had placed it badly, and another time it must come out over the top of her belt or waistband. She told me that could be done.

I informed her that my doctor was sending me away to Lamalou, to go through a treatment lasting twenty-one days, to get out of my system the remaining vestiges of the malady that still made me suffer. I could hardly walk or close my hands, but the protracted illness had not dulled my masculine energies.

She arranged to meet me on the 5th. of August, at two P.M., and as usual, I told her what I intended to do to her. I should have a small riding whip with me, and no doubt after she had received a few cuts with it, to avoid further punishment, she would be very docile, and not struggle against me, and thus in time I should succeed in breaking down the barriers of her shame, which I allowed without hesitation was excusable and natural.

I informed her that I meant to kiss every part of her frame, which she would have to lewdly expose to my bold gaze, and I would even thrust my tongue between the cheeks of her bottom and command her to do the same to me.

"Yes, darling! And what else—tell me?"

I taught her to take my fingers in her mouth and lick them, and suck them, and then I did the same to her.

"Gaston used to kiss my hands," she said.

"But did he not kiss your lips?"

"Never!" she retorted, unblushingly. "You are the first man who has put his mouth on mine."

She forgot she had told me that "Baby" was the man who had taught her pigeon kisses.

After this, we were not alone together, until she went off just before dinner to gather some herbs for the salad. I went strolling behind her and saw the fatal cord trailing round her feet. It had fallen from her hip to the ground. I told her of it in a whisper, as Pa and Ma were not far off, seated at table, for we dined in the open air. She got confused, and turning awkwardly round, trod on it herself and the sudden jerk made her jump with pain.

When dinner was over, her stepfather, accompanied by Lilian, saw me to the station by a round-about road, so as to walk the dogs a little, and we spoke of her business as a bonnet-builder.

"I suppose," I said, "when you make out the bills, you add a few francs here and there when the customer is one of the silly sort?"

"Never," she answered, "I wouldn't cheat one of my own weak sex. Robbing men, I understand, but not women."

I never forgot this unguarded statement of hers.

Our conversation now turned upon marriage, and she once more said that she could not think of leaving her Papa and she nestled closely up to my host. I answered that I quite understood that and she was quite right to stop by his side, while he would be a fool to let her go. I added that he spoilt her, but a husband would exercise authority over her. I, for instance, believed in corporal punishment. Young women needed the whip, and if I had a giddy damsel to look after, daughter or wife, I should always have a small riding-whip handy and use it unsparingly. He agreed with me and I could see that he enjoyed my risky talk amazingly. His face grew serious, and then he laughed. A voluptuous feeling had crept over him, I am sure, by the peculiar look in his eyes and the general dull-ness of his physiognomy. Real sensual desire is a serious thing. Man is always serious and sulky-looking when his lechery is aroused, which is a sign of his dormant animality. Lilian laughed, with many a sly look at me. She knew what I meant. On nearing the station, she lagged behind, and signed to me that she had rectified her blunder, and got the end of the string above the waistband, in front of her dress. In the dark, I was able to approach her and pull it. I got a low, "Ah! it hurts!" and then a squeeze of her hand, a hasty kiss, and a sigh of pleasure in return. I was off, and the mother and father thought I left on the 5th., but I had arranged to devote that afternoon to Lily and depart the next day.

"The Horn Book" was now ready and I promised Mr. Arvel I would send it to him at once, as he was always pleased to read a smutty novelty. I despatched it to him a day or two afterwards. He said he would be careful to keep it out of Lily's way and would read it at his office. This remark struck me as quite unnecessary on his part, and during my little journey back to Paris I vaguely dreamt of Arvel and Adèle's daughter, reading "The Yellow Room" and "The Horn Book" together. I began to think that I could understand his talk in general much better if I believed the contrary of all he said, above all when he brought up Lilian's name.

I told her that Papa was going to have an obscene work from me, and that she should also read it on the sly when I returned to Paris. I told her I wanted him to have this naughty book so that he might be excited and perhaps violate her when I was away. In Au-gust, she would be alone at home with her Granny, as Pa and Ma were going to Germany for a short time.

With many cordial wishes for renewed good health by my baths at Lamalou, and a request that my first visit on my return should be for the Villa Lilian, I got into the train and shut my eyes to think of the delights in store for me before my departure.

JULY 2, 1898.

On my way to the Rue de Leipzig, where I was to meet Lily, I bought a light bamboo switch or riding-stick, preferring this to walking through the streets with a whip.

When she arrived, as she did punctually, and coquettishly dressed, showing that she had taken great trouble with her toilette, her first words were:

"Where is your whip?"

I showed her my switch:

"This is for you, Lily, and my dogs afterwards."

She had in her hand "The Yellow Room," which she had understood I wanted back at once. I told her she could keep it as long as she liked and not hurry through it. She had been reading it in the train. She said she liked it. It had made her "naughty," and she had been obliged to finish herself with her finger. I replied that I thought she had told me she never did that.

"I do not as a rule, but now and again I can't help myself."

I warned her to beware and not give way to the habit. When I went on to inform her that habitual masturbation deprives the sexual organs of women of their tone and elasticity, causing the secret slit to gape, and the inner lips to become elongated, she thanked me for the advice and told me she would resist the temptation, so as not to wither that pretty part of her body.

"I like my pussy," she said, "I like to look at the hair on it. I love to play with my hairs."

I informed her that she had a very pretty one and it would be a pity to spoil it. The two large outer lips should close themselves naturally, but if Lily gives way to onanism they will do so no longer.

I asked her to show me the paragraph which had brought about this crisis. She did so:

"He inserted his enormous affair in her burning c . . ., etc."

It was not exactly that sentence alone which so unduly excited her, but what lead up to this termination. She did not understand certain words, but guessed them from the context. She thought that the extreme and bloodthirsty, long-drawn-out cruelty, described in the volume, was impossible, but thoroughly appreciated the idea of man's domination over a woman, and to bend her to his lewd will, a little brutality appealed to her imagination. She wanted more books later on, but not tales of Lesbianism. Anything, simple lust or cruelty, as long as it took place between men and women. She thought that everything and anything was possible and agreeable, if a male and a female were fond of each other. This was far from bad philosophy, springing naturally from a virgin of 22. How changed she was now with me!

During our conversation, I had made her sit by my side on the sofa, with her clothes well up, as I wanted to see and feel her legs, calves, and knees. I made her open and close her thighs, and cross and recross her legs, as I chose to command.

I kissed her passionately. My lips wandered all over her face. I kissed her eyes, and licked and gently nibbled her ears. This last caress pleased her very much.

I made her stand up in front of me, and by threats of ill-usage and pinching the fat part of her arms, I got her, after a little resistance, to let me put my hands up her clothes, lift her chemise out of her drawers, and put my hand between her thighs, entirely grasping her centre of love. In this manner, my hand still gripping her plump, hairy lips, I walked her round the room, in spite of her blushes and protestations. It was an agreeable sensation for both of us. I had great enjoyment in feeling the movement of her soft thighs as she walked, my hand clasping her furry retreat. I halted in front of the looking-glass of the wardrobe, and forced her to look at the strange group we thus formed. She hid her face on my shoulder and I could feel she was now quite wet, heated, and ready for anything.

I asked her if she could take off her drawers without undressing. She replied in the affirmative.

"An English girl could not, but my drawers are fastened to my stays."

I reclined on the sofa and told her to take them off slowly, without sitting down. She did so with docility, and I enjoyed the sight of seeing her get her legs out of her beribboned undergarments. I called her to me, and stood her up again in front of me and close to me, as I sat on the *chaise-longue*, while my hands, up her clothes, now for the first time roved without hindrance over her belly, bottom, thighs and nature's orifice. It was a delicious moment for me. I put the left index as far as possible up her crisp fundament, gradually forcing it up with a corkscrew motion, as I felt her pleasure in front increasing, for I was masturbating her scientifically the while, with the middle finger of the left hand. I had great difficulty in piercing her anus, but to my astonishment, she did not complain of pain. She afterwards told me that she liked the feeling of my finger in the posterior aperture. The crisis came quickly for her and she could no longer stand upright, but soon sank gradually to her knees, all in a heap, sighing with satisfied lust, her head pillowed on my breast. I kissed her sweet neck and finished her as quickly as my wrist would let me, until she tore herself from my grasp.

Now I tell her to disrobe before me, until she is entirely naked. She refuses indignantly. The moment has now arrived for me to take hold of my cane, and as she still refuses, I give her two or three stinging cuts over biceps and shoulders, and, smarting with pain, she consents to undress until she is in her shift. I kiss and lick again all the charms of the upper part of her frame, which is now quite bare, and I teach her how to suck my lips, and tickle my cheeks and forehead with the point of her tongue, not forgetting my neck and ears.

Sufficiently excited, I order the chemise to be taken off.

"Never!" she exclaims.

I get my stick again, and show her how silly she is to refuse, as it is already nearly down to her navel. But she still will not consent, and I cut her, not too severely, over her back, shoulders and arms. I love to see the dark stripes raised by the whistling bamboo. She hardly winces at each blow. I am certain she likes the chastisement of the male. Suddenly, I twist her round and tell her to remain quiet, and take three cuts on her naked bottom. I pull up her shift, fully exposing her plump posteriors and she is quiet on her knees, leaning over the sofa. I do not hurry, but count slowly: "One, two, three!"

And the poor little bottom receives three severe cuts, stretching across both posteriors and equalling, although I do not tell her so, six stinging blows. I have tamed her, for she rises with a wry face, and drops the offending chemise to her feet. She is naked at last before me, in the full light of a sunny summer day. I kiss her and caress her again, admiring her flat belly and her splendid bush, as black as night.

She seems uneasy, but I soon bring a smile to her face again, by telling her that I will never do anything to her by surprise.

"I will always let you know beforehand, what I want, and if what I propose to do displeases you, tell me and I will then see if your master should give way or not."

And now I make her plainly understand what I intend to do to her:

"I shall lick you all over and then suck you, and you shall suck me until I discharge boldly and without reserve in your mouth. But I want to tell you something which is very important. The first time I had you, you expectorated my elixir. That is an insult to the man who is loved by a woman. You must swallow all to the very last drop, and remain with your mouth on the instrument until told to go. If you cannot perform the operation as I describe, it shows you do not love me, as nothing, however seemingly dirty, can cause disgust in you coming from me."

"But I can't. I shan't be able. I shall perhaps be sick?"

"You must try, and if you really love me, you will succeed."

I now stripped quite naked, and took her in my arms, as if she was a baby. She was as light as a feather. I lifted her up, until her body was on a level with my chin, and threw her from me on the bed with all the strength I could muster. It was a pretty sight to see her naked body tumble down all in a heap.

We were soon entwined together, outside the bedclothes, and I cannot describe our mutual kisses, caresses and pressures. I licked her face all over and sucked her neck, her nipples, and waggled my tongue under her arms, while her belly, navel, and thighs came in for their share of the kisses of my eager mouth. She uttered little shrieks of pleasure, and anon cooed like a turtle-dove, or purred like the rutting kitten she was. I turned her round on to her belly, and the nape of her neck, her shoulders, spine, loins and bottom were soon wetted by my saliva. I wished to get my tongue between her round posteriors but she would not consent. I was now too feverish and unnerved to press the point. It was a very hot day. So I laid over her, and started pretending to copulate and the end of my dagger went in a little.

"Oh! you hurt down there. On the top it is nice."

"Take hold of it yourself and put it where you like."

She placed the head just on her sensitive button, and I moved gently, the swollen tip rubbing against her clitoris. This she approved of. I told her that a woman could be enjoyed in the hole of her bottom. Would she let me? She answered me affirmatively without hesitation. I warned her that it hurt the first time.

"What a pity it is that everything hurts the first time!"

She turned her posteriors to me, freely offering them with a loving look.

"I must lick you there to make it wet."

"No! no!"

So I wetted my arrow with my saliva, and began to push between her rotund cheeks.

"You are not right!" she exclaimed.

"Guide it yourself, Lily."

She did so, and I thrust home.

"Oh!" she shrieked, piteously. "It hurts! You do hurt me so, Papa!"

At these words, a wave of pity broke over me. It would be a cowardly trick, I thought, to sodomize my confiding sweetheart. So I desisted, and my organ grew limp.

"Try again," she said. And she seized my weapon.

"Oh! you are not excited enough now!"

I did not tell her what had crossed my mind. And I never did. I often thought since of warning her against ever yielding up her anus to a man, but the idea to speak of this escaped my memory. I am afraid it will be too late when she reads this book.

I was hot, tired, and perspiring, but still full of desire. I rested and gave her a little lesson in the art of manuelisation, teaching her how to hold the manly staff, the way to move the wrist, slowly or quickly, and so on. She was an apt pupil.

Then she got up to arrange her hair and taking out the combs and pins, let her long black tresses escape in freedom. They fell below her tiny waist.

She seized my bamboo switch and began to teaze me as I laid on the bed, giving me slight blows with it. I jumped up to catch it, but the task was an impossible one. I chased her round the room and I must have looked a ridiculous sight with my semi-erection, and my testicles dangling as I ran. When I was about to seize her, she would spring on the bed, and landing on the other side, always get the couch between us. So, I, panting, lie down again and say coolly:

"It is disgusting to see a young lady jumping about a room stark naked. Lily, are you not ashamed?"

She took my words literally and rushed to huddle on her chemise.

"Of course, I'm naked! I forgot that!"

And she sat on the sofa trying to hide her pussy. I soon laughed her out of her chemise again and she was in my arms once more.

Then I gamahuched her seriously, reversed over her sideways, while she felt my spear, and stroked the appendages, masturbating me as I had just taught her. I did not ask her to touch me thus while I sucked her. She did it of her own accord. I opened the big lips of her little shaded slit, and looked well at it and inside it. It was small and pink, rather tight and thin inside, but seemingly little. The vagina was clearly closed up. She was a perfect virgin. She spent, and we rested awhile.

"Now you!" she said.

"How?"

"As you like!"

I opened my legs, and placed her on her knees between my outstretched thighs. She bent her head and engulphed her play-fellow. After a few hints, she sucked me like a professional. Her large mouth and sensual thick lips proved that she was born to be a sucker of men's tools all her life. I took her cheeks in my two hands, and held her head still, as I moved slowly in and out of her mouth, telling that I was having connection with her in a vile, un-natural manner. I then took it out of her mouth, and made her suck the balls alone, and tickle the erect member up and down the shaft, with the pointed end of her tongue. While she was busily engaged on the little olives in their purse, I rubbed my organ, all wet as it was, on her flushed cheeks, and informed her I should emit one day on her face, and in her hair, and in fact all over her, until every part of her body had been sullied by me. She got very excited by listening to this filthy talk, as she performed her task, and worked fast and furiously. I put my thigh between her legs and rubbed it against her furrow. At last, I felt I could bear the touch of her tongue no longer. I held her head, and pushed up and down myself, talking to her in a most disgusting manner, as the storm burst, and she tickled my member with her tongue until I was forced to push her away.

She looked up, and talked to me very gravely and seriously.

"You see it is all gone!"

I praised her, and she asked me timidly to be allowed to drink a little water. That I graciously permitted, and the voluptuous vestal begged me to let her suck again! She liked doing it!

It was five o'clock. We had been in the room since a quarter to three. I was dead beat, and I had not yet packed up my things for my departure the next day. We kissed and said good bye effusively.

She showed great jealousy, and tried to get me to talk about other women, probably to hear about my mistress. She would not believe I was going alone to Lamalou. She told me that she would write to me every day to prevent me forgetting her. I was not to have any love-affair with a woman, but she allowed me a night with a female now and again, as she was sure I needed it. She did not care how many different women I had, but would brook no rival. She could not receive any answers to her letters at her house, as the postmark would betray her. So I arranged to reply under initials to the post-office, Rue de Strasbourg, next to the Gare de l'Est. She was not allowed to go to Paris alone without valid reasons, but often unawares her people sent her up to fetch something, but she had to return by the next train. On those occasions she could go to the post-office. She did not care much about the accommodation of the Rue de Leipzig. The little minx would have liked me to take a place of my own, where she could keep a *peignoir*, etc.

She was fully dressed again, and said that when she talked to me she got quite wet. I verified the fact. Inside the big lips, which were very large and hairy, there was an astonishing amount of moisture, but as they closed so perfectly, her cleft was dry outside.

I told her about French letters. She did not know what they were.

"Why don't you get some, and then you could have me entirely, without fear of getting me in the family way?"

"Why don't you . . ." was a favourite expression of Lily's, but I knew I could not rely upon it.

I made her feel outside my trousers how the knowledge that she was so wet excited me, and she wanted to get on the bed again.

I asked her if her stepfather looked like a man who might be reading "The Horn Book" on the sly? I told her I was certain that he was in love with her.

"Why do you think that?" she asked me, assuming a very innocent air.

"Because you are a girl, who must fatally excite men's lust, and I cannot understand how he can live under the same roof with you, and not want you, especially as I know he is of a very voluptuous nature and don't care much for your mother."

I watched her narrowly as I said this, but she did not turn a hair. There was no indignation, real or feigned, nor any disgust or astonishment.

"You should rub against him whenever you can, and let your cheek and hair touch his face while type-writing together, etc., and then look at his trousers and see if he is in erection. You will then know if he has the carnal desire for you that I suspect."

"The other day," she replied, "he came into my bedroom without knocking. I was in my chemise, doing my hair in front of the glass. He turned very red and looked so silly. He scolded me for not locking my door and I answered that he ought to have knocked."

But she forgot about the curtained opening between the two rooms.

She mentioned that her favourite Blackamoor had contracted the habit of getting on her chair behind her back, and sniffing under her armpits. I told her to wash that part frequently.

"I do, of course, every morning!"

"Then use a strongly perfumed toilet soap. Dogs hate perfumes of any kind."

"Mother says I must never use soap under my arms. It is very bad."

"If you want to catch the men by the odour of women; by all means do not use soap. But the advice of your mother is what might be given to a *cocotte*, not to a respectable girl, and surprises me very much. But I suppose she does not know."

And then I slipped the promised fifty francs into her hand, and put her in a fly. With many protestations of affection, she left me, quite an altered girl; loving, and all her shame gradually going from her. I thought that after a few more meetings like this one, I should have no more to teach her.

5

Heaven first taught letters for some wretch's aid,
Some banished lover, or some captive maid:
They live, they speak, they breathe what love inspires
Warm from the soul, and faithful to its fires.
The virgin's wish, without her fears, impart;
Excuse the blush, and pour out all the heart.

POPE.

The Right Honourable the Earl of Fontarcy was an old friend
of mine, and our acquaintanceship was of over fifteen years standing, as far as I can recollect. He was superior to me in every way, by
position, birth, wealth and education, and I looked up to him and
admired him, for he possessed all the solid qualities of the Anglo-
Saxon. He was a man of few words; undemonstrative, but strictly
honourable; shrewd, and farseeing. I was very proud of his friendship, and I tried to be as staunch as possible towards him. I never
cared to have friends who were beneath me in social position, nor
visit people of no education. If I could not go into the drawing-
room of the highest in the land, I preferred to stop away, or taste
the pleasures of solitude. Therefore, I felt proud and flattered that
Lord Fontarcy should seek my society. When I went to England,
he invited me to his mansion in London, or received me at his
castle in the country, and he never passed through Paris without

seeking me out. He is over 60 as I write, and is still active and energetic, masterful and born to command. He had the same unprejudiced ideas as I have, with regard to the relationships of the sexes, and, as two voluptuous men of the world, we had had some extraordinary adventures together, which, however, have no bearing on the little episode of my life that I am now narrating.

Lord Fontarcy was divorced from his wife, but he had formed a connection with a most charming lady, a distant relative of his, who he eventually married. His *liaison* was known and winked at, as is usual among the British aristocracy. When he was invited by friends to hunt or shoot, Lady Clara, as I shall call her, was always welcomed as well, and by strange hazards, their bedrooms, if they did not actually communicate, were never very far apart. And in the fashionable society papers, their names always jostled each other.

She was a very good woman, quiet, calm, and sensible; but she possessed an inward fire of passion, which did not obscure her sound judgment of men and things. She liked me and was very kind to me. I never made love to her, although I think had I desired her, Lord Fontarcy would have shut his eyes to any little escapade on her part with Jacky, but I did not wish to jeopardise our old friendship for the sake of a few moments of pleasure.

I had told my friends a few of my ideas concerning Lily, and they were very anxious to meet her. I promised them that I would introduce her, if I could get over her prejudice, and that we would have a little orgie, when my lord and my lady, and Jacky and Lily, should shamelessly empty together the loving cup of unrestrained lechery.

In the meantime, I asked Lady Clara to send me her opinion of Lily, and I offer it here as a curiosity. It is not often that one woman gives her unbiassed opinion of another. It must be noted that she had never seen her.

CLARA'S OPINION OF LILY.

"Your Lily is really a nice girl and carefully brought up, but she does not care to give herself away too easily.

"Clara thinks that when the opportunity occurs, that if a little force is used, after gentle persuasion, that Lily would be more pleased than offended.

"Clara thinks that Jacky should see more of Lily if possible, as he cannot expect her to be heart and soul with him, unless she feels his presence or caresses often. She thinks Lily is ready to love him, but is a little wavering, or not quite sure how it will end with her. Lily will be like herself, and give her whole being entirely to her lover, only feeling real pleasure when in his arms, making him take pleasure sheathed within her.

"Clara also thinks that although Lily's mother says 'No' to a present or two offered to the daughter, she does not mean what she says. Besides, every true woman likes gifts from the man she loves."

No better example of the nature of Lord Fontarcy's liberal ideas can be given than the following extract from one of Clara's letters to me:

". . . Perhaps Lily would be benefited by the experience Clara went through with an elderly admirer of hers. She met him at a country house and was left alone with him, her host returning to town in the evening. His feelings ran away with him, but servants coming into the room, kept his overflowing attentions in check.

"He asked her to meet him in town. An opportunity occured to take him to certain chambers, where Clara and another could have a little amusement out of him. Clara made up a little tale about an uncle having gone away and left his chambers to be looked after. The other (Lord Fontarcy) was locked in an inner room, with his eyes to a convenient hole to witness operations.

"Clara went out, met her senile suitor, and brought him to the rooms, feeling very loth to display herself before the one she loved with another man, but there was no drawing back, and she had to do violence to her own feelings.

"When he was in the room, he at once tried the locked door, and Clara had a fit in case he discovered who was inside.

"After his inspection of the premises, he produced a French letter and suggested that he should commence at once. He got on her, and pushed and poked about, but the more he did so, the smaller his affair began to get, when he thought that if Clara knelt up, he might do it by the back way—dog fashion—but alas! that did not succeed. Clara did not even feel the tip of his member.

"He then said the letter pinched all the stiffness out of him and that he was too excited. Finally, he got atop of her again, and working up his organ with his own hand, managed to spend all over Clara's new drawers, which she had put on for the occasion.

"At which she blessed him, and he went away with the idea that he had still a maidenhead to take on the morrow, when he suggested meeting again.

"Clara retired into the locked room, to find consolation, feeling as if she had taken part in a battle.

"Clara must end this long scrawl by saying that she hopes the reader will find in Lily all he wishes and would like to know his plans for her."

Lilian to Jacky.

No place or date. (Received at Lamalou, July 7th. 1898.)

My best beloved master,

I want you to have this scribble to-morrow evening when you arrive, but for that I should have to post it to-night and I cannot do so.

Anyhow, you will get it on Thursday morning for certain, and I hope you will feel less lonely. It is true you have your good and faithful Smike, but that is not the same thing as if your Lily was with you.

I am so sad at the idea of your departure. It seems as if you will forget me during these three weeks.

I hate your doctor who separates us thus cruelly. How I should like to be near you! Thus I should prove to you that I could never be dull at your side, because I love you.

I care naught for the pleasures that you tell me are necessary at my age, for all that is false and superfluous. True happiness, after all, is to love and be loved and naturally give proofs of affection.

If you choose to try me, I venture to say in advance that you will be tired before I shall, although I would do all in my power to sweeten your life.

Would it not be delicious, say, my sweet Daddy, to be always together, never to part?

But I am mad, for I am not lucky enough to have the supreme joy to feel myself yours, entirely belonging to you and to be able to say to myself that nothing in this world could ever separate us again.

You find yourself too old for me, but do you not know, my well-beloved, that if you are proud to have inspired a passion like mine, I, on my part, am doubly proud to have been chosen by a man who knows what life is, and has been able to appreciate it as you have.

I am a little fool, but I only ask to know all, to learn all from you. How stupid I must appear to you!

I see that to be loved, a woman should never let the love she feels be seen, but some unknown force within me drives me to tell all that passes through my brain like the silly thing that I am.

Now all marriage with another becomes impossible. It would be a martyrdom of every instant for me. Never could I make up my mind to be even brushed against by any other man. There now, see what you have done, my dear and adored master.

I kiss you everywhere where it will please you the most.

Your slave,
LILY.

A caress for Smike.

LILY TO JACKY.

(Received July 8th. 1898.)

Only just a line to let my own darling know that his slave is continually thinking about him. How I envy Smike, he is always with you and can by a thousand little ways prove his love for you.

Besides, I am sure you really love him, whilst I am not quite so sure that you care for your naughty girl.

As you are away for your health, do not trouble to write too often; you must not tire yourself, but simply take life easy, and come back to your Lily quite strong, never to leave her any more.

I hope you found everything as you wished it to be at the hotel. Is everyone very kind to you?

How I should love to be down there, nursing and taking care of you!

I am anxiously looking forward to the end of the month, when you will be back again quite well and strong.

We have nice weather here; I trust you also have it fine. Hotel life is so trying, it would be dreadful if you had to keep to your room on account of the weather.

If you are not too tired to write, tell me all you do and how you like everything.

A most passionate kiss for my master and a caress for lucky Smike.

LILY.

LILY TO JACKY.

(Received July 9th. 1898.)

My adored master,

I have not been able to go to Paris yet and nevertheless something tells me that there is a note awaiting me. I shall go to-morrow morning, for I have several little errands, and I shall profit by them to go and fetch what I am sure is there.

I am impatient to have news of you, to know what you are doing, if you are not too much bored and above all if your health is good.

In all my letters, I can only tell you and tell you again one simple thing: I am horribly wearied. At this moment, life is a burden; I feel so lonely and so sad. My existence is incomplete, something is wanting and that something is you.

We have beautiful weather still, a little stormy, which gives me very naughty ideas.

If my beloved little Papa were here, I know what his pet daughter would do to him.

I am dying to see your darling features again, your dear face that I dote to gaze upon, but I have still a long time to wait—nineteen interminable days. I think I shall devour you when we meet again.

Now I must leave you. My big Blackamoor is waiting to take his daily bath, and Father is calling.

I kiss you with mouth, tongue, and lips, as you love to be kissed.

LILY.

LILIAN TO JACKY.

Telegram, received July 10th. 1898.

Lily feels lovingly.

LILY.

LILIAN TO JACKY.

(Received July 11th. 1898.)

It is useless, well-beloved master, to try to dissuade me from the resolution I have taken with regard to marriage. After having seriously reflected on the consequences, I have taken this determination. If I get married, it will be with you and with no one else. Please note, however, that I do not wish in any way to make you think that it is your duty to marry me; my thoughts are quite different. I only want to make you understand once for all that any union where you are not concerned is impossible for me. Think what a martyrdom of every moment it would be, and then my nature is too loyal to allow me to play a part. In spite of myself, I always let my feelings be seen. Being thus, there is no remedy. One must take me or leave me. You, my only lover and adored Papa must decide my fate.

Now let us talk of less serious things. I thank you infinitely for your good letter that I found here yesterday. I am going to tell you all my adventures at the *poste restante*.

a) Sensational entrance, when I do not dare, before all the eyes that are fixed on me, to go at once to the grating. I buy some stamps.

b) Still fearing to go up to the department of the *bureau restant*, I buy a letter-card and write, and post it to the Louvre about a little purchase there.

c) Still being the silly goose you know so well, I take a telegraph form, and write thereon the initials you know, for despite the desire I had to read your letter, I still had not the courage to ask for your missive out loud.

There you have the confession of a very stupid little girl.

Next time, however, I think I shall be bolder, for after all I am not the only female who has letters sent to a post-office, am I?

I am still more jealous than ever of my big Smike, who I love so well. He has every happiness, while I am like a poor, little, neglected one. He never leaves you, and can see you all day and even all night. All this is clearly very unjust. I am bored to death. Really, if my life does not soon change, I believe I shall go mad.

You must have lots of amorous intrigues to write from one till six. It is frightful to think about. I should like to be able to make you love me so much that you would not be able to do without me, which is at present my position with regard to you.

I have finished reading "The Yellow Room." The effect produced by this book upon me was terrible. Nevertheless, there is one thing that I found rather grotesque; it is the way in which the future betrothed makes love to Alice. It is quite in the modern style, is it not?

I cover you with kisses, literally all over, and each one is longer and more passionate than the other.

Your slave,
LILY.

LILIAN TO JACKY.

(Received July 12th. 1898.)

Another day gone by, and I am delighted, for 'tis one day less without you. What a pity that you should be away at this moment; Papa and Mamma are off to-morrow until Sunday and I shall then be alone. If you were here I should be full of joy, but in this case I shall only feel myself a little more lonely.

You can write to me here this week, if you like. I hope your health gets better every day. I am still very well; my heart makes me suffer, and that is your fault. Everything bores me, nothing interests me. Life seems to me empty and commonplace. If I had my master, it would be quite different.

Your newspapers were received Saturday evening. Thank you for "Our Dogs."

I have still not caught sight of the famous book that you lent to Papa. I think he keeps it at the Rue Vissot. And for a very good reason! . . .

I drink you slowly, softly, but passionately. To you go all my thoughts, all my desires.

LILY.

LILY TO JACKY.

Telegram, received July 13th. 1898.

Sweetest remembrance, love.

LILY.

LILIAN TO JACKY.

(Received July 14th. 1898.)

You know perfectly well I am jealous, and it is always very wicked, just like a naughty Papa that you are to teaze your daughter with that silly little Yvonne of yours; and although she is only eight, it is nevertheless a little of the love that is mine which she steals from me.

I am not pleased with you, nor with Smike, who lets himself be fondled by anybody. When blest with a Papa as dirty as mine is, one can never be easy, even when it is a question of a child only eight years old.

The master may want his slave to make him naughty from a

distance, but his slave is not going to excite you, for others might get the benefit.

Yes, I went and spent Sunday afternoon in Paris at the house of one of my lady friends, but accompanied by the servant-girl.

I want you to hear from me every day; that is why, when I can't write to you, I send you a wire.

You can tell me whatever you like about your "wretched fat belly." That will not prevent me from loving you. It is therefore useless to continue in that strain. You hurt my feelings.

I should like to be near you, so as to be able to rub you myself with Eau de Cologne, and to be able to kiss you all over, and suck you as you love to be sucked, making you thrill with pleasure.

You simply make my mouth water and something else too, when you tell me about the little drop that escapes you when you write to me. What shameful waste!

Yes, sweetheart, I like the idea of you doing mimi to me while I should suck you; I should think that must be simply delicious. I like everything you have done so far, and am looking forward to your idea of the paint brush. Shall I be able to do so to you also?

LILY.

I had been quite surprised by her matrimonial projects and I considered that she was getting too fond of me. Of my own feelings I will not speak, but I considered it was my duty to check her rising passion. So I began to write her coarse and disgusting letters. What I said, what I proposed, can be guessed by her answers. I painted myself in the blackest colours and impressed upon her that I was too old; a man of 46 could not marry a girl of 22. Besides, was I not an invalid, cursed with rheumatism, which might return at any moment, and slightly obese into the bargain? To my great stupor, the more brutally crude and lewd I was, the more she seemed to like me.

LILY TO JACKY.

(Received July 15th. 1898.)

Really, Papa, you are not serious. Fancy throwing away a letter I ought to have had! It shows how careful you are and how much you love your daughter. Your slave is very, very cross indeed, and if you go on in that shameful way, she will have to look about for a better master.

Your incestuous daughter has no preference for any tongue, but she would very much prefer yours. But, as she cannot have it, she must, for the moment, put up with French or English, as you choose to write.

I am very glad to think the treatment agrees with you and above all that it does not weaken you. I will do that when you return.

You can write to me here up to Sunday, but afterwards we must make shift with the *poste restante* of the Rue de Strasbourg.

Yes, I had your letter. I went expressly to Paris to fetch it. I should have been so sad if I had not got one. Smike is really too much spoilt, but I understand that you cannot bring it over your heart to punish him when he gets up to his tricks. I am just the same with Blackamoor. He is a darling, and I tell him everything that passes through my mind about my dirty Papa.

Good night, dear love, I run to put this note in the post, for I want you to have it to-morrow.

I desire you,

LILY.

LILY TO JACKY.

(Received July 16th. 1898.)

Do not write here any more, my adored one, as my parents arrive this evening. We must once more make use of the *poste restante*, which is,—my faith!—very convenient.

I also prefer the word "daughter" to that of *fille*; it sounds more intimate, does it not?

Do you know, dear master, that if I spoil you as you say so prettily, I am also spoiling myself.

You deserve to be very severely punished and you shall be when you return, and this is what I shall do to you: I shall suck you twice running, for having dared to write this sentence: "above all, at my age." Whatever do you mean? Verily, one would think that you take a pleasure in making yourself look older than you are in my eyes. I repeat to you once more, you can do whatever you like, I shall love you in spite of all.

You know very well that I shall not tell anybody what we do together and I do not wish to please any other man. I don't care a straw for anybody but you. You are the only one who will ever possess me, since you are the only one I love.

To be your footstool, lying under your writing table, with your booted feet upon me, and to serve as your chamber utensil, since you say you will make water on my naked body, are two ideas that are far from being commonplace. You know you can do whatever you like to me; oh, dirty and very disgusting Papa!

Smike is as cheeky as his master; I send him a sweet caress, and as for his proprietor, I bite him all over.

LILY.

LILY TO JACKY.

Telegram, received July 17th. 1898.

Soft kiss from your Lily.

LILY.

LILY TO JACKY.

Telegram, received July 18th. 1898.

Sweetest remembrance; love, kisses.

LILY.

LILY TO JACKY.

Telegram, received July 19th. 1898.

Many happy returns of the day, that we may love each other a long time yet.

LILY.

LILY TO JACKY.

Telegram, received July 20th. 1898.

I am very busy. Write here. Father away. Love.

LILY.

LILY TO JACKY.

Telegram, received July 21st. 1898.

Naughty darling. Best love.

LILY.

LILY TO JACKY.

(Received July 22nd. 1898.)

Papa, master,

Since you desire it, your slave submits, and although it is late, and she is very tired, she writes you a simple scrawl, for the sandman has passed and I can hardly keep my eyes open.

I have a deal of work just now, but in spite of that have a great desire to be very naughty. It is so nice, say, darling little Papa?

Women are bores. No, decidedly I love them not. My weakness is always for the strongest sex. Am I not right? See, how badly I write and what mistakes I make. No, really, I must leave you, my little bed awaits me. Nevertheless, I believe that if you were in it, I should not be long waking up, and your pussy, which is yours only, would be wetter than ever.

Your slave adores you and pines for you,

LILY.

A kiss for Smike.

LILY TO JACKY.

(Received July 23rd. 1898.)

It seems to me that you are neglecting me in no slight degree. It is probably the treatment that you follow, which by fatiguing you beyond measure, makes you lose all count. That is a pity, you know, for I do not love a dirty Papa who forgets his daughter. You are a real monster.

As I told you, Father is absent and Mother goes on Tuesday to join him. I shall never have the happiness to be able to go and join you. But also you do not make a move towards me and really one would think that you do not particularly care about me. If such is the case, you would be wrong to trouble about me. A little frankness and you shall soon be rid of me. I will never hang after you against your will, I assure you. Why should I do so? Forced love is ever worthless and I am too young to know all the tricks that certain women make use of to force men to adore them.

Once more, my very loved one, I say there is no tie that binds me to you, therefore you are quite free, especially as I won't go to the Rue de Leipzig any more, and if you do not think I am worth more than that, so much the worse.

You never informed me before you started that the doctor had told you to rest and stop over Sunday, and I strongly suspect that this is only a pretext to remain absent a little longer.

Lily is vexed.

LILY TO JACKY.

Telegram, received July 25th. 1898.

Just one kiss. Naughty.

LILY.

LILY TO JACKY.

Telegram, received July 26th. 1898. (Morning.)

Are you living?

LILY.

LILY TO JACKY.

Telegram, received July 26th. 1898. (Evening.)

Am ill through you.

LILY.

LILY TO JACKY.

Villa Lilian, July 26th. 1898.

Beloved, but very bad Papa,

I ask myself why you wrote to the *poste restante* on Sunday, when I told you you could address your letters to me here? You had not Mamma's presence to fear, or I should not have asked you to write to our house. You might to know by this time that I am more than prudent.

I have not been to Paris for the last few days, and I did not suppose I should hear from you at the Rue de Strasbourg. Hence my annoyance, thinking you were neglecting me in such a brutal way.

I use the type-writer to-day, so as to punish you a little, and if I had a little pride, I would leave you without news of me, as you do so conscientiously. But where you are concerned, I lose my wits.

Mamma went away this morning, as I told you. I am all alone here with my dogs, like a poor, little, wretched Cinderella. I have very frisky ideas, but I shall not tell you what they are, as you are not kind enough to me.

Soon I shall see you, I hope, my only love; and in spite of all, I send you a million caresses, each one more passionate and more voluptuous than the other.

I hang on your dear, adored lips,

LILY.

LILY TO JACKY.

Telegram, received July 28th. 1898.

Am dying to see you.

LILY.

LILY TO JACKY.

(Received July 29th. 1898.)

My only, best, sweetest love,

When a Papa does not do what his daughter asks, what happens? He receives unmerited reproaches. I begged you to write to me here and I naturally supposed that I should not have news of you at the post-office. Thus I was furious to find myself neglected and abandoned by you. That is the reason of my famous letter of Sunday which so displeased you.

I love you too much, and every little hitch puts me out. I fancied at once that you loved some other woman. There you see the jealous daughter appears again.

What a love you are to have sent me your photograph! There is only one fault; I can see too much of Smike and not enough of you.

Since yesterday, I kiss your dear face every moment and my happiness increases when I think that I shall soon be able to do it in reality. What a scrawl, you will say, adored master, but I am so unnerved that I cannot hold my pen.

Shall I come and meet you at the station when you arrive?

I am alone, I can do so easily.

I await your coming with something more than impatience, but nevertheless, do not be imprudent, and do not leave Lamalou too early if the doctor tells you to stop.

I suck you violently,

LILY.

LILY TO JACKY.

(Received July 31st. 1898.)

My own sweetest, loved Papa,

How happy I am; one more lonely day, and then I am to see you again. I am quite silly with joy. Will you just drop your daughter a line to let her know where and at what time you wish to see her on Monday?

I notice that you do not really love me quite as much as I should like to be loved, without any afterthought.

You seem to be ashamed of your Lily. What if someone you know should see me with you at the station? They would only think what a lucky man you are to have such a nice young girl's love. You may not think so, but so it is nevertheless.

You see, darling master, there are little things I cannot fail to notice, and sometimes I am afraid you simply mean to use me as a toy.

I hope my frankness will not sadden you again. Such is not my intention, on the contrary. But I love you truly and sincerely, so much so, that I would abandon all at a sign from you and for your sole pleasure.

Yes, in one word, mother and father, and everything and everybody.

I think that such entire love deserves in return true and sincere affection.

Your daughter desires you ardently and awaits Monday with the greatest impatience.

LILY.

P.-S.—I have done what my master ordered. From six o'clock last night until this morning, I did not pee, although I was dying to do so in the night. So I slept very badly. I also thought constantly about my dear little Papa, who was also thinking of me.

Lady Clara seemed to take a great interest in my *liaison* with Lily, and she had frequently written to Lamalou asking me for news of her. She was perfectly disinterested, as she had no Lesbian tastes, but she told me that the whole story pleased her greatly, and so I now and again gave her news of my "daughter."

I cannot do better than copy here a few notes that I jotted down about Lily, shortly after my return to Paris, having derived full benefit and relief from my course of baths.

JACKY TO CLARA.

(NOTES ON LILY.)

While I was at Lamalou, I tried to disgust Lily, as I was afraid she was getting too fond of me, but the worse I made myself out, the more she seemed to love me.

I told her I would discuss the marriage question when I met her, but not by letter, as things that sometimes look harsh in writing, pass easily in conversation.

I spoke against myself, about my age, my rheumatism and my big belly. She was pained thereat.

I wrote to her that I should like to have her naked under the table, as a footstool, while I sat and wrote. Also, that I should seat her on the bidet, and straddling across it, void my urine on her belly and "pussy." She likes these ideas.

She shall have a good talking to, when I see her. I will not scold by letter. I have no reproaches to make myself, as I never told her a lie or tried to mislead her. Is she madly in love with me, or is she scheming?

I would dearly like to take her maidenhead. But no, I must not ruin the poor lustful lassie. I will try to keep out of my Lily's body. I will not harm her.

I try to make Lily understand that the passions and the heart are two different things. She may be unfaithful perchance, but if she keeps a corner in her heart for me, I shall be satisfied.

She is not shocked when I try to bring her mind to grasp that she is absolutely my own slave, that she must obey my most voluptuous caprices, however vile they may be.

She writes so ardently about marrying me, etc., that I thought I would try to prevent her loving me too much, by telling her what a filthy brute I was, and laying stress on the fact that other men loved more decently than I did.

I stood confessed on my own showing as a despotic, tyrannical beast, gloating over her degradation and humiliation.

The more cynically and brutally I wrote, the better she liked it.

She is evidently fond of me and I must let things go on.

Does she think I am very rich?

She is very impatient, very excitable, and has got a hot temper. She has addressed reproaches to me, but I sincerely think she is slightly in the wrong. I have never lost my temper yet with her, but I treat her like a child, and she comes round again.

There was a slight misunderstanding about our correspondence and she wrote a nasty letter, giving me back my liberty, and saying she would never return to the Rue de Leipzig, as it was not good enough for her. I took no notice, but wrote quietly and reproachfully, and at last punished her for having written such a letter, by ordering her not to pee from seven o'clock at night until seven the next morning. She wrote saying she had obeyed me, and had passed a bad night.

I told her to come to the Rue de Leipzig on August 1st., as she was alone with her grandmother. I waited until 3:30. She never appeared. I went away, and did not return home until 6:50.

She turned up at 3:40, it appears, and sent me two telegrams. She was waiting at the Eastern railway station to see me.

I had dinner at seven instead. She wrote a rather furious letter, saying her Mamma would be back on Thursday.

LILIAN TO JACKY.

First telegram, received August 1st. 1898 about 4:30. P.M.

Will be Eastern railway station.

LILY.

Second telegram, received about 6:30. P.M.

Am waiting Eastern railway station.

LILY.

LILIAN TO JACKY.

Villa Lilian. August 2nd. 1898. 11 P.M.

What you could have done from 3 o'clock until 6:30, I really can't tell, and I will not even seek to know. That will always be a mystery for me, since you could only wait a little more than an hour, and yet you know I cannot always do what I wish.

In spite of my being alone at home, I still have to content my customers, and I am therefore late.

You lost something by not waiting a little longer, I assure you, for I was just ripe for a refined *gourmet* such as you are.

No matter, don't let us say any more about it, only Mamma will be back on Thursday, and therefore—

By losing patience sometimes, we lose many good things.

Lily is as vexed as she can be with her Papa and will not pardon him in a hurry.

I answered calmly and curtly, and gave her a *rendez-vous* for Wednesday, August 3rd.

LILIAN TO JACKY.

Telegram, received August 3rd. 1898.

Four o'clock. Usual place.

LILY.

Lily appeared, very pleased to see me, and very penitent, in spite of her peppery note, at the famous Rue de Leipzig, where she had said she would never come again.

She looked very sweet in my eyes, and was dressed in a charming, simple costume of écru *coutil*, fitting closely over her well-made buttocks. She was very proud of her bottom, and I have seen her tighten her skirt over it, and show it to her stepfather, when her Mamma had left her with him and me, saying she was Venus Callipyge.

Lily pretended to be cross, but I bluntly told her what a little fool she was. She had been an hour late on the preceding occasion and if any one ought to have lost their temper it should have been me and not her. She was perfectly ridiculous, with her jealousy and irritation, and finally I forced her to humbly beg my pardon. Then we kissed, as lovers had never kissed before. I half undressed her, and partly for fun, partly in earnest, slapped her, and pinched her, and pulled the black fleece that shaded her sex, making her suffer just a little.

I told her to come to me on the day when she was late, with the ribbon fastened to the hair on her *mons Veneris*, and she was also to have a great desire to make water, as she was not to "make herself comfortable" from the hour of rising. All this foolery she had done, and that is what she meant when she had said that she was ripe for me. This time, she had done none of these things, as she was annoyed with me. So I slapped her face. I frequently did so. I loved to see the slight patch of colour follow the sting of my hand upon her cheek. After each smarting blow, I saw the light of lust in her eyes, and her ghoulish mouth cupped my lips, as if to thank me for the exquisite joy my chastisement aroused within her. I recurred to the idea of her being my footstool, and I threw her roughly on to her knees in front of me, as I sat on the sofa. Taking her head in my two hands, I pressed her laughing face between my trousered thighs and rubbed her nose and mouth brutally against the cloth, through which the eager staff seemed trying to escape. Then I let her drop full length on the carpet, lying on her back, her skirts all turned up, and disordered; her drawers open. I kicked her with my booted feet, and turned her over with the toe of my boots, gently trampling on her naked belly. Lying thus at my mercy, she giggled, purred, and cooed, like a naked, happy baby after its bath. In the romp, some hairpins and combs had fallen from her luxuriant tresses, and gathering them up, I stabbed her thighs with the fine points, until she begged for mercy.

Then I pulled her up and made her take off my Russian leather lace-up boots, ordering her to kiss the soles and uppers. She did all I told her, and was happy to obey. Then I made her undress me, and she awkwardly performed the duties of a valet. Each garment, as she took it off, I ordered her to take across the room, hang it up, and return to me.

I commanded her to unbotton my trousers, fish out my member, and go on her knees and suck it. She was quite unabashed and would not have the curtains drawn. In the open daylight, we went naked to the bed. At the foot of it was the mirror of the wardrobe, and to her astonishment there was a looking-glass in the ceiling of the couch. We both sated our sight with the view of both our bodies writhing on the bed, madly kissing and feeling each other, enjoying the sensation of the absolute contact of our sensual skins.

I asked her if she wanted to be licked, but she preferred me to masturbate her.

I did so, and when she had convulsively joined her thighs in the delicious agony of the spending spasm, and recovered from the shock, I laid upon her. I got the tip of my weapon between the moist lips of her toy.

She said, as she always did:

"It does hurt so! Oh, you hurt me!"

And then she exclaimed:

"How nice it would be if it did not hurt!"

I then obliged her to lick my testicles and my thighs, and lifting my legs high up in the air, I told her and taught her that infamous, entrancing caress, called: *feuille de rose*, when the tongue, made as pointed as possible, penetrates the anus. She was quite docile and performed her strange task in a most charming manner.

Then she sucked me, and I spent freely in her delicious mouth, keeping her head in my hands, until I was quite soft again. Without an effort, she swallowed every drop, and when I left her lips, the urethra was as dry as if I had never emitted. She dearly loved sucking, and called my virile organ her *poupée*, her dolly.

I told her as she licked me, that I had still one or two more dirty little tricks to try with her.

I gave her two vilely obscene books to read, both on the same subject: the entire subjugation of a woman to man's cruelty and lust. They were: "The Convent School," and "Colonel Spanker's Lecture."

I told her that I meant to make her absolutely shameless, and utterly degraded, by the continual humiliations she would have to undergo when with me, and I explained that I gloried in making her do the most disgusting things. The more unutterably depraved I am, the more she likes it, and calls me her dirty Papa. She enjoyed being knocked about, shaken, and roughly handled by me.

When we were both naked, I made her lick me under the arms and suck my nipples. She demurred at sucking beneath my armpits, but I made her do it.

She liked the penetration of my ruthless fingers in her fundament, and I found that she had a growth of hair between the posteriors. As she gets older, she will be very hairy.

There was no question of money this time, her parents being away, and she informed me that her father and mother would leave her at home on the 20th., as they go to Germany, so probably I should see a little more of her.

My villanously lecherous brain now began to be excited by a dreadful idea. I dearly desired to give her up to Lord Fontarcy and Clara. In my presence, the couple could do as they chose with her. I tried to drive the dream away, but it kept returning daily and nightly. I thought it would be a fearful effort and a real ordeal for her, and the knowledge that I was corrupting the virgin who seemed to adore me excited and delighted me immensely.

I did not dare broach the subject. I thought over it, and in the meantime I remember that in all the letters I wrote to her, I tried to make myself out the most abandoned debauchee in the world.

6

O my love come nearer to Lilith
(Eden's bower's in flower)
In thy sweet folds bind me and bend me,
And let me feel the shape thou shalt lend me!
. . . .
What more prize than love to impel thee?
Grip and lip my limbs as I tell thee!

DANTE G. ROSSETTI.

And so I lay all night with him, but he . . . rose up
and dressed him in the morning, and left me as innocent
for him as I was the day I was born.

I frequently lay with him, and he with me, and
altho' all the familiarities between man and wife were
common to us, yet he never once offered to go any farther,
and he valued himself much upon it.

DANIEL DEFOE.

LILIAN TO JACKY.

Sonis-sur-Marne. August 7th. 1898.

My best beloved in the world,

Excuse me for not having answered your letter, and for using the
type-writer to-day, but a mosquito has bitten my hand, and it is in such
a state that I cannot use it.

I profit by a momentary absence of Papa to use the machine.

117

You are very impudent to send me such an awful caricature sketch of my very beautiful and very adored Blackamoor.

I think he is growing up nicely and I love him, so do not laugh in future at the way he carries his ears, or we shall not be friends at all.

I am sad at the thought of being so long without seeing you, for my parents do not start till the 20th. or later.

Waiting does not suit me, for as you know, patience and I have nothing in common. Besides, I want to see you. It is a bore to remain a fortnight or three weeks without giving a good kiss to one's Papa.

You warn me not to recriminate, but I can't help it. I must rebel against my destiny, and ask you to share my trouble.

I am off. Here comes Papa, and I won't have him question me about what I am writing.

To your dear lips, without forgetting my pretty beloved dolly.

LILY.

I think I had been writing some very erotic letters to Lily. I remember that I sent her an extract from a very obscene book, turning upon inhuman delights, entitled, "The Pleasures of Cruelty." (See Appendix A.)

I had also told her in my last letter, that she must remind me herself when she saw me again of all I had asked her to do and suffer for my sake. She was to say:

"Master, I have the ribbon ready for you to pull, and I am dying to make water, as I have not done so for many hours. May I do so now?"

There may have been other filthy things that she was to tell me and ask me to do to her, but I cannot now call to my mind all my extravagant exigencies.

LILIAN TO JACKY.

Sonis-sur-Marne. Sunday, August 21st. 1898.

My love,

I waited to be free to write to you, so as to be able to tell you: "Lily awaits a sign from her beloved master to run into his arms."

My parents are off at last. I am therefore left entirely to myself, and consequently when my darling little Papa wishes, his daughter, who is displeased with him, will come and tell him so with her own lips.

I will bring you myself the extracts you sent me, and in that way it will be easier for me to give you an account of my impressions. It will be sweeter to tell you all I feel, having my mouth glued to yours. and my cheek caressed by your beard, which is so silky.

I do not forget the orders in your last letter and I will remind you of all you desire.

A word from you, and I come to try and drive away a little of that sadness you feel.

Very softly, Lily imprints a long kiss on the end of her doll's nose, and pushes the point of her very indiscreet tongue where her Papa likes it to go.

LILIAN TO JACKY.

Telegram received at noon,
August 22nd. 1898.

Wednesday. Half-past two.

LILY.

LILIAN TO JACKY.

Telegram received 11 A.M.
Wednesday, August 24th. 1898.

Unwell. To-morrow, if you wish.

LILY.

LILIAN TO JACKY.

Undated. Received August 24th. 1898.

Lily is indisposed to-day, and if she is no better to-morrow, she will be obliged to put off the appointment.

In any case, if you do not receive a wire from me to-morrow morning, you can be at the usual place and I will come there.

Certainly, dear little father, I am grieved to have caused you pain, if only for an instant, but if however you had reflected a little, you would have found my silence quite natural.

Mamma is off on her pleasure trip, to a part of the world where it appears everybody is very elegant. As I look after her toilettes, and have to make her a lot of hats, I have not had a moment to myself, especially as she is not at all easy to please.

But I do not mind begging your pardon for faults, which exist in reality only in your imagination. There is only one terrible thing which you have probably put in your letter to frighten me: "I will punish you by not kissing you."

That I must resist with all my strength. I rebel. To be deprived of your mouth? I will never submit to that. I could not support such torture.

To-morrow then, my most severe master. I adore you.

AUGUST 26, 1898.

Lilian's father and mother had left her alone with a servant and her maternal grandmother. They had gone to Homburg. I was surprised to find that her periodical indisposition should be over by the 25th., when it generally made its appearance about the 27th., or 28th. Therefore, it must have begun on the 21st. And as she had not written to me between the 7th. and the 21st., I began to have shrewd suspicions that something was wrong.

I had got into my head that there was almost a complete understanding between her and her mother's lover. He had taken such great trouble to impress upon me that Lilian should on no account be allowed to get a glimpse at the "Horn Book" I had lent him, that I began to smell a rat. It was quite unnecessary to repeat that to me so often. Then again, she had written to me that she had not seen the book; that Papa kept it at his bureau and did not bring it home to Sonis. She had got that obscene dialogue too. I had sufficient knowledge of the secret monthly miseries of women to know that a virgin is generally pretty regular, but I was resolved to wait, watch, and not say anything. Lily was not communicative. There was nothing to be got out of her by a direct question; I must keep my ears open and see what she would let drop in her chatter.

I had a rod in pickle for her, however. Worse than a rod; in fact, a whip. I had ordered a strange instrument, which I am certain I invented myself, as I never saw it before or since. I called it the "whip-stick." Everyone knows what a swordstick is—a hollow walking-cane, in which is concealed a sharp blade or dagger. I had one made, but instead of containing a sword, it held nothing more deadly than a light lady's riding-whip, or whalebone switch. I could thus walk through Paris without exciting any notice. It was impossible for me to carry a whip in the town, and a very thin bamboo also looked ridiculous in the afternoon, in the hands of a portly, middle-aged gentleman in frockcoat and high hat.

Lily arrived; pretty, coquettish and very amiable. I scolded her for not having written to me for twelve days, but I did not touch upon the growing intimacy that I suspected between her, and he who stood in the light of a stepfather towards her.

I unscrewed the top of my stick and showed the whip that was hidden within. To try it, I made her lift up her skirts, and gave her one cut across her bottom over her half-open drawers. She uttered a shriek and writhed in real pain. I was surprised, but I found that using a riding-whip was quite different to a lithe stick or the hand. I soothed her and petted her, but tears were in her eyes, and she complained bitterly of the smart. I examined her bottom and found a long weal across her left buttock. What was worse, her drawers being open, the end of the lash had by some means curled itself right between the posteriors, and just above the pinky-brown orifice was a little cut. The skin was broken and there was one spot of blood, like a small ruby.

I did not think it advisable to let her know how cruel I had unwittingly been, but I glossed the matter over, and resolved to have a light touch in future with my whip. In fact, I never used it at all after this afternoon, when I was careful not to hurt her much. I afterwards gave it to Clara, who took it to London and delighted all her friends with it. She has it still, and it is one of her most valued possessions.

By aid of this whip, with which I carefully touched up Lilian over the back and the fat part of her arms, I got her by force to undress slowly before me, but before I had made her walk about the room with my hand clasping the two hairy lips of her second mouth.

When she was undressed, and I had feasted my eyes and lips on the neat little body I loved so well, and which excited me so strangely, I forced her to stand with her shift lifted up with both hands, as high as her neck. It was a pretty sight to see her thus exposed. She grumbled and laughed in one breath. She could hide nothing, but writhed about as she stood, as if by her serpentine movements she could conceal some parts of her frame from my lecherous gaze. If she tried to drop her chemise, I flourished my whip over her head and she took up her position again. As she stood there, bending down a little, as if by leaning her body over she could hide the fleece that cast a black shadow at the bottom of her maiden, flat belly, I slowly undressed, looking at her all the time, and walking round her as if she was a lay figure, and so heightening her confusion; which I thoroughly enjoyed.

Then I gave her my garments, shirt, etc., to go and hang up, and she knelt down and took off my boots.

She had tied the ribbon to the hairs of her mount and I amused myself by pulling it, in spite of her sharp little cries of pain.

On entering the room, she had reminded me of the ribbon and said she had a great desire to pee. I refused to let her do so for the moment.

Now, as we were both undressed, I told her she could empty her bladder, and although she wanted to very badly, she swore she could not void her urine if I looked at her while she did so.

I made her stand up, by threatening her with the whip, and felt her belly. It was quite hard and distended and I pressed my two first fingers into it on both sides, just above the thighs. She begged me to desist, saying that if I continued to press her navel and belly, she would be unable to keep from emptying herself any longer.

At last, by the aid of threats of the "whip-stick," and after a few mild touches with it, I succeeded in getting her on the vase, and her long pent-up urine trickled loudly into the pot, as I stood over her. She was crimson with shame, but nevertheless highly pleased and lustfully excited.

We then got on the bed, both completely naked, and after our usual kisses and close embraces, I ordered her to masturbate herself. This she absolutely refused to do, but I was obdurate. Again the whip was brought forward, and I kept it by my side on the bed. Finally, she reluctantly laid her hand between her thighs and began awkwardly and slowly, making out as if she hardly knew how. It was very pretty for me to see and feel her graceful body reclining across my thighs and watch the play of her features. She was cross and merry by turns, but lust soon overcame her, as the required result was brought about in the following way. She was willing to do what I wanted if I kept my hand on hers, and tickled her round about the tender spot, while she manipulated her rosebud herself. By the united caress of her hand and mine, she soon emitted and then had a long bout of tongue and lip sucking.

I then got over her, pretending to penetrate her in the natural way, until we were both beside ourselves with desire. We were face to face, her thighs open and legs outstretched. My weapon was rubbing against the upper part of the openings of her furrow, our tongues joined, and the index of my right hand slowly penetrating her hot fundament.

Suddenly, she threw her arms around me and closing her thighs, pressed my organ between them, saying:

"It is nice like this!"

I pushed up and down in the imitation vulva thus formed, and rubbed against her pussy; she moved her bottom up to meet my strokes. Pleasure seized us both at the same moment; I felt the shudder of joy vibrate through her frame and I discharged copiously.

I turned over on to my back, and when we had recovered from the effects of our enervating sham fight, I showed her what a state her thighs were in, and her mount covered with my thick semen.

"Ah!" she exclaimed, in fright, her face and mouth distorted with fear. "Am I no longer a virgin?"

She seemed greatly alarmed, but I explained the difference between what we had done and genuine copulation. Reassured, she made me cuddle her tightly and fell asleep on my breast. I kept quiet so as not to awaken her and slept as well. When we both woke, it was six o'clock, and Lily had slobbered in her sleep on my hairy chest, like a little baby girl.

We had a long conversation, when she told me that she found the flagellation scene, between the father and daughter, which I had lent her to read "rather tame," and would have liked the couple to have enjoyed each other after the flogging, and she asked me if I had any new ideas of erotic slavery for her. I answered that I wanted to lick her private parts while she was bound down and her hands strapped together, and I promised to teach her a novel onanistic method. I would produce the spasm in her by tickling her clitoris with a camelhair paint brush, as I had written to her already from Lamalou.

All these lascivious projects she adored to talk over. I made her beg my pardon for not having written to me, and forced her to stand before me when she was dressed, holding up her clothes, showing both a front and back view, alternatively.

Her great dream was for me to be with her in her own bed at Sonis. I was to take the train on Saturday night, August 27th., at nine o'clock, the servant going to bed at that hour. Her old grandmother was silly, and incapable of seeing or hearing anything. My love would meet me, and we would go for a walk in the dark, as there was never a soul about at night in those parts. And then she would slip me into the house—the dogs all knew me, and would not bark—and I could take the latest train back, after we both thoroughly enjoyed ourselves.

I made her understand that although the newest way I had emitted with her between her thighs pleased me greatly, still I regretted her soft mouth.

"Rest a little," she said, "and I will suck you."

It was too late and I was exhausted. I did not tell her that I had passed the night with an expert Parisian matron. She recurred to the most infamous of kisses—*feuille de rose*—when her tongue had lovingly penetrated my anus, and confessed that she liked doing it.

I wanted to broach the question of meeting Lord Fontarcy and Clara, but could not summon up courage. I fancied it might be a hard nut to crack, and I determined to leave the difficult demand for another time.

There was also something else on the tip of my tongue, but it would not have been politic to mention it.

Her silence of a fortnight, followed by the change of date in her "monthlies," and the ready and expert way in which she clipped my swollen shaft between her thighs, made me certain that

Mr. Arvel had been playing with her before his departure. They had been reading "The Horn Book" together, and the incestuous Papa had clearly copied this artificial congress from the identical passage I had introduced into the text expressly for him and his daughter! Be that as it may, the coincidence was curious, and besides, this is a well-known form of pleasure, with all those who wish to emit with children.

I had not taught her this style of sensuality. She had learnt it recently, and had been up to all kinds of tricks, thus bringing on her menstrual flux in advance of the usual date. Virgins in fair health are very regular, but all women who abuse any kind of sensual pleasure find that their derangement is just as likely to be before its proper date as after. Very often, women suffer agonies of fright, because they are behind their time; and fancying themselves pregnant, take strange drugs, while this tardiness is only due to overindulgence in the delights of Venus.

AUGUST 27, 1898.

It seems but as yesterday that I arrived at Sonis-sur-Marne that hot summer's night, and saw my "daughter" waiting for me with her dogs. How happy was I to stroll with her, talk soft nonsense, and pet and kiss her in the dark, while she returned my caresses with passionate enjoyment, and I revelled in the knowledge that an hour later I should be naked in bed with her.

The time passed rapidly, and we returned to the villa, when I stepped gingerly within the gate and trod gently on the grass, while Lily walked noisily on the gravel path to hide the possible noise of my footsteps. She went indoors, but in obedience to her orders, I slipped up the staircase, on to the balcony which ran round the house. She had purposely left one of the windows of the best bedroom open, and I went in and sat down by the side of the parental bed, now without sheets or blankets, and I threw my hat, overcoat, and whip-stick upon it. The latter article I had no occasion to use.

I had not long to wait; Lilian came into her bedroom, and called me softly to her, through the curtained, open doorway which connected the two rooms.

Lily's bed was a pretty piece of modern furniture in Louis XVI style, with mirrored wardrobe to match. It was a gift of her stepfather, and was for her to take away when she got married.

I was happy to be in her room at night, and I kissed her pillow, trying to find the place where her head reposed, much to Lily's delighted amusement.

All was quiet. Granny was in bed on the second story, but Lily was vexed with her, as she was restless and disinclined to sleep. I hinted that another time, I would prepare a sleeping draught for the old lady.

I had brought with me a small strap, with which to fasten Lily's hands and a new paint brush to titillate her clitoris but I did not use either.

I was thirsty, but there was nothing to drink. Granny had the keys, and Lilly could not disturb her. She was thirsty too.

"We have only our urine to drink!" I said jokingly.

"I will drink some of yours!" said Lily seriously, putting her face near mine, and there was an eager look in her eyes, as if she would have liked me to force her to do so.

There was no more shame between us. I undressed slowly and with nothing but a light singlet, went to bed, and laid fully exposed, while Lily quickly disrobed, and quietly used the night vase like a married woman.

She came to bed, and her capricious fancy had already caused her to divine what was passing in my mind, for she asked me how I should behave if I was really married to her.

I took her gently in my arms, and kissing her chastely, bade her "good night," and turned my back to her as if settling down to sleep, making a slight snoring noise.

Lily remained quiet an instant and then put her hand on my neck.

"Now, my dear, you must really let me go to sleep. You know I have to get up very early to-morrow morning, and I think it is most unreasonable to expect that your husband can be always caressing you. My dear wife, I beg you to put out the light and let us both rest."

Lily said nothing, but took hold of my member, and in a

few moments, she had got it as stiff as she wanted, and I turned toward her, and took her in my arms to enjoy the luscious intoxication of her melting mouth.

We showered on each other's bodies the most voluptuous caresses, and at last I pushed my Lily down in the bed, and she reclined between my legs; her cheek on my left thigh, I made her kiss and lick my member and also the dangling purse, and while she was gently sucking my testicles, I rubbed the stiffening rod against her face and nose. Then I took her by the nape of the neck and closing my thighs, kept her face imprisoned, pressed as hard as I could against my privates, even to suffocation, and then relaxing my pressure a little, I moved her head about in all directions, and I was really masturbating myself with her darling face. A little more and I should have spent madly, with her features pressed to me to receive the spurting semen, but I think the state I was in warned my artful virgin of the impending danger; so she slid away and took me in her arms.

She told me that she wanted to see me spend; she was mad with the idea of looking at her "dolly," as the seed spurted forth. I turned upon my back, and pillowing her head upon my breast, allowed her to enjoy her latest whim.

She worked me well with her nervous fingers, and never took her eyes off my organ, while I talked to her as lewdly as possible, telling her how dirty and vile she was, evidently much to her enjoyment, which rose to fever heat, as her wish was gratified by the full view of the gushing seed.

While maddened by the deliberate masturbation of my sweetheart, towards the end, I said that immediately the splash of semen should cease, she was to take my member in her mouth and suck it, so as to extract the last drops.

When I had spent furiously, I forgot my ravings during the moments of uncontrollable lust, and was quite surprised to find Lily slowly approach her lips to her *poupée*, and engulph it in her hot mouth, not at all disgusted to swallow the last big clot that was slowly exuding from the urethra. But the gland was so sensitive that I could not endure the delicate touch of her tongue, and I pushed her head away.

"Ah!" quoth Lily, "you did not think I should do it."

We rested a little, and then Lily put her hand on my privates again.

"I'm done now, my darling," said I, "you've thoroughly exhausted me."

"I'm so sorry," answered pouting Lily, "I don't like it when it is soft!"

"Like this, I'm not dangerous. You need not fear lest I take your maidenhead."

"Oh, my darling, you are never dangerous. I would trust my life in your dear hands. You are so delicate in all you say and do. It is so strange to me to see how you always act with us all; as my parents are so coarse and vulgar."

I offered now to make her happy, in any way she liked. She refused to be sucked and preferred me to masturbate her. I did so, and I think she cared for my fingers more than anything. I made her lay hands on herself, but she soon drew her own digits away and left me to finish her.

I was very thirsty, and she went on a filibustering expedition and managed to find a bottle of Vichy water, which she poured out, and brought to me with many a sweet word and caress.

Then she settled down between my legs, and supporting herself on her elbow began to talk.

She looked most beautiful at that moment, as I gazed upon her face with partial eyes. The yellow light of the candle suited her Spanish complexion, and her liquid, magical eyes sparkled as she gazed at me, getting excited as she spoke, and her splendid black hair flowed over her naked shoulders, for she slept nightly in summer, as she did then, with simply a day chemise.

This picture has remained in my mind, for I loved her then, or rather I might have loved her, if she had shown some slight, womanly tenderness, but she made me very unhappy, although I hid my feelings, by calmly unfolding a mad plan.

She wanted to go into business in Paris, in a small apartment, and hinted that I was to take it for her, and I suppose furnish it. I was to be allowed to visit her there, whenever I chose, and she would have a little kitchen and cook for me. I could come and have meals with her, and we would dine together quite naked.

I hinted that I did not see how she could manage this at all, but she got out of temper because I disagreed with her. So I held my tongue and listened to her, half asleep, as her ceaseless chatter went in at one ear and out at the other.

I kept on admiring her, trying to impress her image on my poor brain, softened by the boiling baths of the previous month, as I felt inwardly, although I tried to drive away the sad thought, that she only cared for me because she fancied I should be able to give her money, and I was forced to say to myself that I should not have many nights with her.

I asked her to get my watch out of my waistcoat, knowing that it was now close upon midnight, and the last train went shortly afterwards.

And indeed, if I remember rightly, for all this took place two years ago and I have seen many women since, I got up to use the chamber, and was about to dress, when she told me that she intended all along for me to stop with her, as she was dying for me to remain one whole night by her side.

After a few moments' hesitation, I accepted, and came to her again, when, after a long kiss, we fell asleep in each other's arms.

It was about five o'clock, when Lily slowly woke me with the touch of her cunning fingers, searching for her plaything, which she found in the desired state, and she placed it between her thighs, turning her back to me, and inviting me by her lascivious movements, to push and move in this artificial coition.

I got very lustful, and found that these artful tricks by repetition produced a nervous effect that was far from pleasant, and I knew at last that if I slept with her again I should become brutal and try to violate her.

I kept these thoughts to myself, but in my mad rage, I grasped her tightly, and shook her roughly and brutally.

"You can hurt me if you like, master. I love you when you are just a little rough; but what have I done to displease?"

Her soft tones brought me to my senses. I did not know what to answer.

"It is hot and dry between your thighs. Make me wet."

"I have lots of moisture for you," said she with a laugh, and putting her fingers to her tight slit, she wetted them with the moisture of her "pussy," put some on my stiff anatomy, and rubbed the inside of her own thighs. I put my hand to her gap, and found she was indeed quite wet.

Then I turned her over and got atop of her, and she imprisoned me between her thighs, as she had done a couple of days previously.

I leant upon my elbows so as not to press her little body.

"No, no!" she cried, "let me feel your weight upon me. I like it. Lie upon me. Crush me beneath you!"

I let myself go and pressed her beneath the entire weight of my heavy frame, as I frantically pushed up and down, my organ in prison between her thighs, rubbing among her hairs, and against her clitoris.

I soon spent, and my wife of one night clasped me tightly to her, her tongue in my mouth, as I felt that unmistakable thrill, or shudder, go through her frame, which women, with all their cunning, have as yet not been able to imitate entirely.

The wish to be crushed by the weight of a man's heavy body in bed; the repeated tricky, teazing, thigh-clipping to imitate the real thing, convinced me that other hands and other male organs had been in contact with Lily Arvel's body.

I then arose, and took my leave of Miss Arvel. Charlotte was coming the next day (Sunday), to stop with her, and I was to come down again on Wednesday, the 31st., and pass another whole night with her.

She led me to the window of her mother's bedroom, and I stepped out on to the balcony, while, half-naked, she hid behind the shutter.

I crawled softly down and stepped lightly across the grass. It was half-past five, and broad daylight. I was bound to think that I was doing a very dangerous thing for Lilian's reputation, as the villa was surrounded by other houses, and some neighbour might find it strange to see a man unknown to the locality, creep stealthily out at that early hour.

At the corner of the road, not a stone's throw from the house, was a wineshop, and a girl belonging to the establishment stood at the door. She eyed me curiously.

Again I saw more danger for my Lily, and I went up to Paris reflecting on all these things in the train.

I wrote to Miss Arvel that day, and explained my fears to her, suggesting that on Wednesday, I had better leave her at midnight and take the last train. In the darkness, at night, there would be no danger of my compromising her.

I did not tell other reasons that made me disinclined to go to her bed again; the fear lest I try to make her mine by force, and the growing, uneasy feeling of repulsion that her broad, mercenary hints were beginning to cause in me.

Was I a fool?

7

... Would you not swear,
All you that see her, that she were a maid,
By these exterior shows?
. . . .
Yet a virgin, a most unspotted Lily. . . .

SHAKESPEARE.

Lilian's plans for the future seemed to me impracticable, even if I had had the necessary available capital to set her up as a milliner. It must not be forgotten that I still had onerous duties to perform with regard to my poor Lily at home, whose life hung upon a thread, being no wife to me, and I began to suspect vaguely that Mr. Arvel and Adèle must have instilled strange ideas into their girl's head, as she appeared to weave all her schemes without showing any fear of her Pa and Ma. Did it mean that they would shut their eyes to any intrigues with a moneyed lover, or had her father taken such liberties with her that she felt she could brave him? Or a mere declaration of passion on his part just now would have been sufficient to show her the power she had over him. These and similar thoughts occupied my mind as I received the following:

132

Lilian to Jacky.

Sonis-sur-Marne, August 31st. 1898.

As ever, you are right, and I bow down to your experience and wisdom that I do not possess. It is even preferable that you do not come down on Wednesday evening as we had arranged. I will go with Granny to the *fête*. That will make me forget my great disappointment a little, for I felt much joy at the idea of having you again with me for one whole night.

Do not say, my adored one, that I am never contented, but I wish to arrange things with you once for all.

The life I lead at present is absolutely intolerable. I can only see you now and again and then always running and hiding like a thief, while my dream would be to have you often all to myself and only for me. This dream can be realised in two ways. Here is the first:

We must take a small apartment in Paris: three rooms and a kitchen. I should go and live there in the manner I told you, that is to say with the full consent of my parents to carry on my trade. Thus I should be entirely free; you could come and breakfast and dine with me as often as you chose and I should have you nearly every day. This thought drives me crazy with delight. And you, adored master?

Now for the second plan:

You would take a shop to sell the perfumes you make so well. Naturally, you would want a young girl used to commercial ways and at the same time pleasing to look at, as a saleswoman. I should be that young girl and I can assure you that the business would flourish. In this wise also I could see you as often as we could wish. As you see, two methods offer themselves to us at this moment. You must choose one at once, as later on perhaps we may not have the same opportunity. I await a word from you giving me your decision. If you prefer the apartment, I can start off at once to hunt for one.

Tell me also what day I can see you in Paris, as you can no longer come here?

I think of your dear lips,

LILY.

I had been showing Lilian some specimens of perfumery I had made, and had manufactured expressly for her a highly concentrated preparation of musk, as she was fond of violent scents. My chemical studies had of late led me in that direction. She saw money to be made with these odorous extracts. She was fond of money.

I answered, giving an appointment at the usual place, Rue de Leipzig. I also informed her that she had a wrong idea of life and life's duties, which I would explain more fully by word of mouth.

LILIAN TO JACKY.

Sonis-sur-Marne, September 1st. 1898.

If you have not understood my letter it is because you do not want to, for it was quite explicit enough. I cannot see either how the perspective of being able to see me as often as you wish could make you unhappy. I cannot make you out at all. I will not go to the Rue de Leipzig any more.

Come here in preference one evening, if you have anything to say to me.

And I thought my letter would please you. I am quite perplexed.

She who loves you too much,

LILY.

My reply stated that I considered her very silly, very disobedient and very hard to get on with, but nevertheless I was ready to take the train about nine P.M. on Saturday, Sunday, or Monday night, to talk matters over, if she would kindly choose one of those evenings and let me know in time. I heard no more of her until getting home to dinner at 6:30 P.M. on Sunday, when I found this wire:

LILIAN TO JACKY.

Telegram. 4 P.M. September 4th. 1898.

Can you come at once?

LILY.

The telegram had been at my dwelling since half-past four. I had some guests to dinner and could not leave them. I had waited for a letter until Sunday morning, before inviting them, and I felt angry to think that Lilian should expect me to be literally at her beck and call. I wrote at once that I could not run about to odd appointments at uncertain times at my age. I could not be her puppet. That she knew I took my meals with my family, and owed a slight amount of politeness to my near relations and others who were ready to dine with me at prearranged fixed hours, etc. That I had kept open three nights for her and she had not answered me properly nor given me due notice. In fact, she was not acting in a straightforward manner and I was disgusted.

This elicited the following epistle, which is ironical, to say the least:

LILIAN TO JACKY.

Sonis-sur-Marne, September 5th. 1898.

As ever you are right, and I agree with you that you should not be a puppet, especially at your age. I do not wish to disgust you entirely and if I have done so already, I beg you to excuse me, for I did not mean to, I assure you.

You require a calm and tranquil life and I can only do one thing —trouble your existence.

I humbly beg your pardon for my rudeness, since you say I am impolite.

LILY.

JACKY TO LILIAN.

Paris, September 6th. 1898.

When one loves anybody it is always nicer to answer letters as quickly as possible. That is what I do this day in reply to your few lines received last night, though perhaps you did not expect me to write?

You ask my pardon? I bear no malice, I am not angry. The way you act has not failed to grieve me momentarily. That is all. Let us say no more about it. I have made up my mind for the worst.

But I forgive you willingly and from the bottom of my heart. And I find that this exchange of bitter-sweet letters is an essentially stupid thing. It is ridiculous to go in for essays of literary style instead of seeing each other and explaining matters. I accuse myself of this fault and this shall be my last letter.

Your conduct has greatly wounded me. I pity you sincerely, as I fully believe what I have often told you: that you are in a great measure a victim to your nerves.

Being so, you prepare for yourself a life of sad agitation for almost always, people like yourself possess the peculiar gift of rendering profoundly unhappy those they love the most.

JACKY.

ERIC ARVEL TO JACKY.

Sonis-sur-Marne, September 9th. 1898.

My dear Jacky,

We are just returned from the land of "wurst," and are anxious to know how it has fared with you at the place where you consented to bury yourself to get rid of every ache and pain to which you had to make so many concessions. I have to thank you for the manner in which, notwithstanding your absence, you have kept me supplied with papers, and no doubt when I get up to Paris to-morrow I shall find a lot awaiting me, as we have been away a little over three weeks. The garden has suffered considerably during our absence, from the dogs, but they are all looking well, so I suppose we must not complain. Lili is still on heat, she seems never to be off now. Blackamoor is, as you may imagine, very miserable at being compelled to play the part assigned to Abelard.

When shall we see you? It is so dreadfully warm that we are on the verge of starvation, as we can get nothing tender to eat unless we take to boiled meats.

I suppose your family are all enjoying themselves away from Paris? When you write, please remember me to everybody.

All here send their kindest regards and best wishes, in which I most cordially join, remaining ever,

Yours faithfully,
ERIC ARVEL.

ERIC ARVEL TO JACKY.

Sonis-sur-Marne, 16th. September, 1898.

My dear Jacky,

I was pleased to see you had returned home, but we all regret to find that you have joined the "Tiny-Tiny" division. I want to see you and have a chat with you, but this week I was unable to name a day having all my accounts to make out, as well as to prepare a long series of articles on the gold mines.

Name your own day this coming week, and come and tell us all your adventures by flood and field since we last saw you.

Believe me to remain, cordially and faithfully yours,

Eric Arvel.

Eric Arvel to Jacky.

Sonis-sur-Marne, 18th. September, 1898.

My dear Jacky,

I am very glad to find that you are coming down on Wednesday. We will keep to the "Tiny-Tiny" principles as far as possible, and you can do as you say, put on your oldest and shabbiest "dog-trousers," as long as you will let the bow-wows do as they like with you. I have managed to instil a certain amount of respect into them as far as I am personally concerned, but I have nevertheless had to copy your example and wear a "dog-costume."

Come down early, but if you want me to tell you the mot de la fin, do not increase the many obligations under which you have placed the ladies by bringing anything down with you.

Yours very truly,
Eric Arvel.

September 21, 1898.

Lord Fontarcy and Lady Clara had passed through Paris and intended to return towards the end of the month. They were very excited at the idea I had formed to introduce them to Lilian Arvel. I think Clara did not much care for her own sex, but she had some notion that Raoul would be a nice acquaintance for her, especially as her master would not be jealous.

I have said that I would paint myself in my true colours, and I must boldly confess that recently I had imagined a horrible project for my own sensual delectation. I tried to drive it from my mind, but it would keep returning in spite of all my efforts. I wanted to see my Lilian in the arms of another. I desired to give her over to the tender mercies of my two friends, I being present, and the salacious picture of this abandoned outrage excited my dormant desire to a point bordering on madness.

So I repaired to the hospitable Villa Lilian, determined to force my love to accept and play a part in this *partie carrée*.

I began to think also that Papa and Mamma had some slight inkling that we were lovers, and no doubt they thought me much richer than I was.

I was well received as usual, and I noticed that Papa was more tender than ever with his stepdaughter. She seemed to encourage him. I purposely refrained from paying any attention to my host's growing passion for the girl, as I was bent on the sole object of procuring her for my vile purpose. I gloated over this species of cold-blooded rape I was preparing.

The dogs were very troublesome, above all Lili, who Black-amoor, her son, was trying to get at all day.

Papa enjoyed this struggle of canine lust and I suddenly sur-mised that I saw a lurid glare of incestuous thought light up his ordinarily cloudy gaze.

The in-breeding craze, condemned by all true fanciers, seemed to agree with his passion for his mistress's daughter.

I must not omit a little circumstance that confirmed my views on this subject.

Three months before, Lili, the original bitch I had given them, had been on heat and by the neglect of a servant, said Mr. Arvel, the enormous Bordeaux watch-dog had managed to cover the poor little animal. No one had seen the act committed and yet it was known to them all. Two months later, she had a litter of mongrel pups, which were dragged into the world by Adèle, and the poor mother was only just saved from death by tender nursing. Such a thing had never happened to me with all my dogs. I had always studiously avoided any *mésalliance*. I was inwardly disgusted. They had risked the bitch's life by their carelessness and worse than all, pretty Lili, after suffering in vain, was spoilt for breeding purposes.

And then the horrible thought crossed my brain that Eric Arvel, in some wild fit of bestiality, had allowed the hulking hound to crush into the poor creature. He had perhaps, Nero-like, enjoyed the cruel sight of the disproportionate impregnation and in company of Lilian—who knows?

I feel these reflexions to be insane, but I have sworn to sketch myself as I was and am. I wallowed in a slough of lechery in this house of lies and lust.

Before lunch, I had a long talk with Lilian and told her that her plans were impossible. What would Papa and Mamma say? She could not answer, or rather I guessed she dared not. She replied that I was no doubt tired of her, as I had written that she disgusted me.

I drew her to me and boxed her ears. She laughed and purred, as she always did when I struck her, and she was happy, as her olive cheeks reddened beneath the loving smart of my hand. But I kissed her tenderly and told her that she was silly. I was not disgusted with her physically. She was the most charming creature a man could desire between the sheets, but as a woman trying to get on in life, I considered she was entirely lacking in common sense.

At this, she seemed contented and we went in to lunch. The day passed off as usual at Sonis. Pa quarrelled with Ma, and then romped with Lilian, and she lovingly caressed him, and I kissed her in corners whenever we could get alone together.

Raoul's name cropped up and I heard that he had received a summons to join a regiment of the line in November, to accomplish his period of military service as a Frenchman. Three years form the maximum, but he, as a son of a widow, would only pass one year under the tricolour flag. Mr. Arvel explained that this was one of the reasons why he had waited to marry his mistress. When the boy had accomplished his twelve months of military training he intended to lead Adèle to the altar.

Raoul's mother evidently adored him and she consulted me openly at dinner on a very delicate question. The lad was earning a good living at the wine-merchants in London and the heads of the firm had taken a great liking to him. They were very much annoyed to find that they were to be deprived of his services during a whole year and had coolly advised him to remain in England and become a deserter. Both Lilian and Adèle seemed to take this as a matter of course.

To my great wonder, my host did not join in the debate. His

face seemed a blank and I could see that he was perfectly indifferent as to whether the son of his mistress and the brother of her daughter, for whom, I intuitively felt, he nourished a passionate desire, was disgraced for life or not. The two women seemed to have no opinion on the matter.

My feelings were aroused to see the future of an intelligent youth thus liable to be inevitably and irretrievably spoilt, and although I did not know him, I spoke up boldly and excitedly, and pointed out the folly of allowing him to be thus ruined, banished, and jeered at all his life as a cowardly malingerer, for the sake of one short year's penance in a blue coat and red trousers.

To retrace my pleadings would be an insult to my reader's intelligence; suffice it to say that the ladies listened attentively and I won them over to the cause of right and reason.

Adèle seemed so struck by my remarks that she hoped I would soon meet Raoul and continue my good advice to him personally, for her sake. All this was in front of Arvel who never moved. He only grunted with hidden rage.

It was easy for me to divine that he hated Raoul as much as he evidently loved Lilian, and was, I presumed, jealous of the brother. He did not care if Raoul became that shameful wreck, a deserter, or not; but would rather have seen him disgraced than otherwise. Strange anomaly! if he desired the sister, who was perhaps his mistress already, for aught I knew. Inwardly he would perhaps have preferred Raoul to become an exile, so as not to be troubled with his presence in France.

I am proud to think now that I saved the lad from disgrace, as I am certain that if I had advised them to let Raoul evade his military obligation, they would have listened to me, and his mother's lover would not have lifted up a finger to save him, but would have chuckled to see him fall. Adèle was too fond of her son, and he stood between his two loves as well as being between him and Lilian in some mysterious way I could not fathom at that moment.

Just before dinner, I had an opportunity of being alone with Lilian, and I proposed to her to lunch with two friends of mine from England, a lady and gentleman. I did not give their names.

She began by refusing, but I pressed the point, saying that I had promised already. She quite understood that she was to be a voluptuous toy for all of us to play with, and I could see she liked the idea, though she pretended not to. She said she would join us at the meal, but not do anything that was indecent. I retorted that it was then no use coming. She was to let me do what I liked with her and give her over to both my friends, unreservedly for their lust.

"No!"

"Is it really: 'No'?"

"You will see!"

"I want a definite answer. Will you let us do whatever we like with you? After lunch we may perhaps all be naked. Say yes or no without prevarication."

"Well then, yes!" she exclaimed, with a frown, as the affirmation came snappishly and unwillingly from her lustful lips.

Papa told me he had read "The Horn Book," and liked it immensely. He asked me for some more, principally works on flagellation, and I promised to send him a parcel of books on that subject. I did so the next day.

Just before I left, Papa brought me "The Horn Book," carefully wrapped up for me to take away.

This work was to have remained hidden at his *bureau* in Paris. I now find it at his house!

Mamma had gone to bed, I was alone with the father and daughter. Quite unnecessarily, Lilian put on an air of candour and said very slowly, with an emphasis on each word:

"What-is-that-book-Papa-you-are-giving-back-to-Mr.-S . . . ?"

She spoke deliberately, looking steadfastly at Mr. Arvel the while. He seemed confused and did not answer.

"Is it 'Guinea Gold,' by Christie Murray? I have read that. It is very good," she continued.

I changed the subject, but I felt quite certain by her artificial tone and by the stupor depicted on Papa's face at her audacity that they had perused the voluptuous volume together. They were an incestuous couple, I could have sworn it!

They accompanied me to the station and on the way I lagged

behind and passed the parcel containing the book to Lilian. She was wearing a short tartan cloth cape, as the evening was chilly, so she slipped it under her arm. She was supposed not to have read it.

Now this was the first edition of "The Horn Book," and as such was issued in large octavo size, printed on thick paper, and made up into a parcel, formed quite a bulky packet. On their way back to the house, Papa must have noticed that she held something hidden under her scanty mantle, and he could not have failed to see that when I shook hands with them on the railway platform I no longer held the parcel, and the pockets of the scanty covert-coat I was wearing were empty.

I was firmly convinced of their complete complicity and resolved to keep a sharp eye on them, but to say nothing about my suspicions to Lilian at present. She, however, had tried to put me off the scent by complaining that Mr. Arvel did not like her brother, and she added that her stepfather's temper was unbearable.

"Did you notice his horrible finger stumps? Does he not bite his nails dreadfully? Are they not awful?" she added, with an expression of disgust.

I supposed this was only her low cunning to make me believe that she did not care for him physically. When we were all three together, in the absence of her mother, she would pat him, and admire his prominent paunch, saying that she liked fine stout men. He would never answer, nor even smile, but a dull, blank look overspread his gloomy features. He loved her ardently.

LILIAN TO JACKY.

Sonis-sur-Marne, September 26th. 1898.

My own dear Master,

Of course I shall be delighted to be introduced to your friends on Wednesday. The only drawback is the finding of an excuse. As you can very well imagine, I cannot go and lunch out without a plausible pretext. And I can only see this way. Write me a letter supposed to come from that famous Madame Muller, Rue Lafayette. Although she does not pay her debts, she is our mutual friend, as thanks to her we passed two delicious afternoons.

You must sign Helena Muller, for such is the name of that amiable lady. This is about what you ought to write. She has returned to Paris, and according to her promise, she wishes to give me something off the amount she still owes me, and as I have been kind enough to wait patiently so long, she begs me to come and lunch with her on Wednesday, when she has a friend passing the day at her house, who may perhaps become a good customer for me. Arrange all this according to your idea, for I do not know how to twist these little lies about, while you do so beautifully!

Thank you, my cherished little father, but my eye is not better. I hope, however, that it will be cured on Wednesday, for I am truly an ugly duckling with my swollen eyelid. I go to London probably next week, so that I am impatient to see you, as I shall remain absent about a fortnight.

I will do anything you desire Wednesday, as long as I can passionately suck my dolly. It is such a time since I have had that happiness, that I promise myself to exhaust it completely.

A kiss on the end of its pink nose,

LILY.

SEPTEMBER 28, 1898.

Lilian's slight stye was nearly gone when she came to the place of appointment I had given her, and it did not mar her appearance. I had written a letter in a disguised hand, purporting to come from Madame Helena Muller, and I appraised Lord Fontarcy and Clara, who were now in Paris, of my success in overcoming Lily's slight scruples.

Clara had had great hopes of being able to get Raoul for an hour or two in London during the next month, as I told her that Lily would be there with her handsome brother and Charlotte, as the annual commercial round of visits was to be made by the two girls. I had great misgivings on that head, as Lilian seemed to be of such a jealous nature that she would not allow Raoul to form any new female acquaintances if she could help it. He, too, was madly in love with Charlotte and Lily made out to me that she did not want her brother to know the little tricks she got up to with me. She alluded to Charlotte now, not as Lolotte, but as Charlot. When I enquired the reason of her name being used in a masculine fashion, she made no reply. My salacious, suspicious mind immediately evolved the idea of some Lesbian amusements between the two girls. I knew that Charlotte slept in Lily's bed when she visited Sonis, when Papa was absent. She had been there just after I had passed the night with my sweetheart. I supposed that Raoul, Lilian and Charlotte had all played "mothers and fathers" with each other when they were in London, and perhaps Papa had participated too. This would account for his great hatred towards the lad, now that he was affianced to Charlotte, and Arvel also roundly abused his stepson's betrothed and called her a whore to me, but permitted her to frequent Lilian! Such inconsistencies on the part of a staid man of the world of 60 years of age require little or no comment on my part. I could plainly see that the more I advanced into the secrets of this strange family, the more vice I discovered. But what cared I as long as I fancied that Lilian loved me?

The *partie carrée* was to take place in a hotel-restaurant, which is a very useful kind of establishment for lovers and all amorous couples.

In these places, where the business of a hotel is carried on jointly with that of a public restaurant, some of the private dining-rooms are fitted up with capacious beds, and on opening a desk or a mirrored cupboard, there is to be found every convenience for the toilette and a plentiful supply of clean linen. There is always a table laid out for meals; the desired electric light, and the proprietor and waiters evince no surprise if several people order a repast and stop many hours afterwards, leaving the bed and bedding in a state of disorder. Nor do they trouble about their paying guests in any way. A man may occupy the room with one or more women. Or several men with only one woman, and I have no doubt that the same reception would await parties of men together and women without men. In fact, I knew one Parisian gentleman whose peculiar pleasure was to take his mistress to dinner at one of these restaurants, and when the coffee was served, invite the waiter to violate his companion in front of him, while he enjoyed his post-prandial cigar.

I had arranged the meeting in one of the quiet squares near

the Trocadero, and after Lily had arrived and immediately made the conquest of my friends, we trotted to the convenient hostelry, which is situated about three hundred yards from the triumphal arch of the Etoile.

We were soon installed, and a good fire was lighted, for the day was cold, but Clara objected to the first room we inspected, because there was a bed there. And this English lady positively blushed. She was at present, not up to our Continental standard, although kind and charming. So we gave way to her prudery and chose a snug room with a large divan. One reason for her coldness on this occasion was explained by her informing us that her monthly "turn" had begun that very morning. Lord Fontarcy also said that he was worn-out as he had been "going it" lately with his mistress. They had been visiting the secret haunts of Parisian pleasure together, and while we ate, they gaily told us some of their adventures. Under the influence of the meal, all barriers of restraint were soon broken down, and the dessert was not on table before I had kissed Lady Clara and Lily's lips were eagerly glued to those of my old friend.

Then she glanced archly across the table at me and whispered: "Dirty Papa!"

But she enjoyed the situation. Her eyes glittered, and she passed her tongue over her carmine lips, like a cat in front of a milk jug.

We talked of her brother. She was careful not to destroy Lady Clara's hopes and promised to look up Lord Fontarcy herself during her stay in London and dine with him one evening.

When the coffee and liqueurs were served and the waiter had left us, I rose and bolted the door. Cigars were lit, and Lilian puffed away at a little cigarette, after having in obedience to my orders, bitten the end off my Havannah. Lord Fontarcy was seated at the head of the table and I faced him. On his left, on the divan, came Lilian, with Clara next to her, and consequently on my right.

Mutual caressing and kissing was the order of the day, but poor little blonde Clara was not at her ease. The experience was new to her. She was, I felt, very loving when alone with a man she liked, but venereal sport in common was seemingly out of her line. It must be remembered too that she was bandaged up to a certain extent.

Lilian soon rose from table, although she was now on the best of terms with his lordship, they having been whispering and kissing together, and came to where I was sitting. I drew her on my knee and after she had given me her warm lips, I told my friends what pretty drawers she wore, and boldly pulled up her skirts; all of us had a full view of her dainty knickers and black stockings.

The sight was such a pretty one that Fontarcy was soon forced to draw nearer and he took a chair in front of me and began to place his hands on her knees and thighs.

I explained that as Lilian wore her beautiful drawers in the French style, it was very easy for her to slip them off her stays, to which they were fastened. She did so at once and returned to her seat on my lap. I raised her petticoats again and placed my hand on her hot slit.

I had ordered her to fasten the famous little pink ribbon on the hair of her mount before she left home, and there I found it. She whispered in my ear, as she pretended to kiss me, to take it off, as she did not want her new friends to know about it. I got rid of it with the dexterity of a professional juggler. I have it still and treasure it exceedingly, as it is about all I have got to remember her by.

I have let the cat out of the bag. Yes, my story will have a sad ending.

Lord Fontarcy was not slow in placing his fingers near mine, but Lily demurred: a mere formality.

"Sit quiet, and let us have our own way with you! If you resist, I'll kill you, my pretty daughter!"

Undismayed by my threat, she kissed me.

"I love to degrade and humiliate my love," I exclaimed aloud. "One of these days I mean to have her violated by a woman."

Now, our four hands wandered all over her buttocks, thighs, and even dared to approach her mossy mount and moist cleft. In fact, she got quite confused at a little game I invented on the spur of the moment. I made her try and guess which of our hands was on a certain part of the body. She was never right, and when I said:

"It is I who am feeling your bottom and not my friend," she would refuse to believe me and we chopped and changed about so quickly that she gave up trying to find out who held the fort in front, or the secret passage behind. It was no wonder that she could not guess correctly, as our mauling had already began to act upon her senses and her eyes softened, while her head fell upon my shoulder.

I drew back my chair a little and while we were indulging in a long and passionate embrace, Lord Fontarcy dropped on his knees and pushed his head under her petticoats.

What he did, I leave the reader to guess. I could not see him, but I heard the "cluck, cluck," of his eager working tongue. It must have been a great treat to Lilian, if I may judge by her passionate utterances and the manner in which the whole of her mouth engulphed mine, while she thrust her hot tongue as far down as she could, and plunged and writhed in a paroxysm of passion.

Clara sat by with her lovely blue eyes wide open. This was all new to her.

I brought Lily to her and opened the front of her bodice, showing the Englishwoman the pretty French corset. She explained that she wore a pair of London-made stays, and unfastening her dress, showed us her high white corsets, which crushed and flattened her sweet, plump breasts, instead of simply supporting them and throwing them forward as in the Gallic style. I felt her warm bosom and kissed her neck and rosy nipples, making Lilian do the same, while she sucked my sweetheart's baby breasts. But my lady was very cold, and as far as the two women were concerned, my little experiment was a failure.

Lilian now paired off with Fontarcy, and I embraced Clara and talked to her, trying to find out for her amusement some kiss that she might not know. She was an adept at the art of osculation, until I proceeded to show her the ball-room kiss.

This, I explained, was performed in the following manner: the lady is in a low-necked dress, her arms bare. She bends up one arm, and her lover's tongue tries to insert itself in the fold of the forearm at the elbow joint. This is also a promise of *minette*. Clara was obliged to confess that I had taught her something she did not know.

I now turned to Lilian, and made her undress completely, even to making her take off her shift, and she stood before us with only her shoes and stockings on, and her beautiful black tresses hanging down to her waist. My friends admired her slight, well-built frame, and taking her arm, I walked her about the room. Then I posed her in various attitudes, and a pretty little statuette she made too. I next forced her to put her stays on over her naked body, and she turned round and gave us the view of her rounded posteriors. We admired her legs and Clara showed hers. They were splendidly shaped and Lilian praised and envied them. Her own, she said, were too thin. Clara was thus half-undressed, but she was very shy, as she sat in pleasant disorder, on the divan, never having left her seat.

"Isn't my Lily a naughty girl?" I said to my friend.

"Indeed she is," replied Fontarcy, "she ought to have her bottom slapped."

"And so she shall!"

I caught hold of her and slapped her face. Then I kissed her, and threw her face downwards on the couch, holding her firmly by her small waist, her bottom being higher than her head.

My lord approached, and boldly rained a storm of blows on both the rounded cheeks, spanking her with both hands at the same time. Lily never moved; she groaned a little, but I held her tightly and bade her lie still. I now begin to strike at her backside with all the strength of my palms and her flesh soon became crimson.

Fontarcy returned to the charge and smacked her vigorously. While he did so, my right hand kept her tightly pinned to the divan, and I slowly inserted my left middle finger in her fundament, until its whole length disappeared entirely within her tight little hole.

Clara was gazing at us with hushed curiosity.

"Look," said I, "I have got my finger right into her."

"Where?" asked my lady. "In front?"

"No!" I told her, laughingly. "In the wrong hole!"

We now let Lilian get up and she sat down and took breath.

She did not complain of her smarting bottom, nor of my digital sodomy.

I told Clara she was a virgin and Lady Fontarcy was quite astonished.

"Do you mean to tell me that he has never been up you?"

"Never," said Lilian.

"Why?" asked the simple-minded British lady, turning towards me.

"Because I did not wish to harm her. She will get married one day and her husband will have her maidenhead. Her Mamma has told her that men can easily perceive if their bride is a virgin or not."

"Nonsense," chimed in Lord Fontarcy. "Look here, Lily, don't you believe such a fairy tale. Lots of women get married and their husbands think they have got a maid, although the blushing bride has had many lovers. If the girl clips her thighs together and makes a great fuss, the man can't tell, especially as the wish is father to the thought, and he is full of infatuation, love and champagne. Of course, I speak of a real disinterested greenhorn who imagines he has got an angel. He is easy to work on. The other kind of bridegroom you need not bother about, as he is mating for money or some other unscrupulous motive and therefore does not care if he finds the little bit of skin there or not. So, Lily, there are only two kinds of husbands on a first night: those who do not know, and those who knowing are indifferent. The lady hides a blood-stained napkin or towel in the bed. In the morning, the new recruit of the universal regiment of cuckolds finds the crimsoned linen, thinks his wife has used it in the small hours, and is perfectly satisfied."

I was now mad with lust and taking out my swollen member I forced Lilian to play with it. She made me get up and go a few steps away from Lord and Lady Fontarcy, saying in a whisper:

"Don't let her see it! She will want it! It is mine! She must not see it! She must not have it!"

I threw her on the ground. She rose to her knees, and I stood up before her, my trousers open and my red rod exposed. She quickly hid it in her mouth, throwing her black hair forward to screen my sexual organ and testicles from the gaze of my friends.

This was not fair for the aristocratic couple, as I wanted them to see the operation, so moving away from her mad mouth, I sat on a chair near Clara, and motioning Lilian to kneel down between my legs, I took her head in my hands and made her suck me.

"Go on!" I said roughly to her, and withdrawing for a second, I struck her brutally on the face with my enraged staff, knowing full well how she liked being treated roughly and voluptuously. I was mad with desire. And I lost sight of the spectators as my head fell back, and I enjoyed the burning, moist mouth of my beloved Lilian and the eager, vivid touch of her electric tongue.

Lord Fontarcy had seated himself on the floor, and holding Lilian closely embraced, he kissed her cheek, licked her ears, and whispered as she sucked me:

"Suck him well! Make him spend! He'll soon come in your mouth! Swallow it all!"

His brazen talk infuriated her to madness, her lips worked convulsively and her tongue twisted itself all round my throbbing tool, as her pretty head moved quickly up and down.

I was not long approaching the crisis, and a great gush of semen burst from me. With many a throb, I lost all notion of where I was, but I felt thick clots of viscous sperm leave my delighted mark of manhood and disappear down her throat.

She then lifted up her head, much to Clara's surprise. Never had she performed her task so well. There was not a drop left in my canal and all had been swallowed with rare completeness.

Clara was still astounded to think I had been Lilian's lover just upon ten months and had never had connection with her. She seemed to doubt her virginity, and I think Lord Fontarcy was incredulous too.

"But I am a virgin!" exclaimed the naked Lily.

"Let us see," said Fontarcy.

"But you'll hurt me," answered my girl.

After a little trouble, Lilian took her seat just in front of the window and opened her legs.

Lord Fontarcy went on his knees before her and delicately taking the hairy, outer lips of her private parts in each hand, began to open them gently.

"You do hurt me," Lily complained.

My lord was bent on carrying out his investigation and I must confess that I was nothing loth. I lit a cigar and sat down in front of her.

"Now, Lily," he said, "open your legs wide and pull your lips aside yourself."

She did so, stretching herself open as she sat on the edge of a light cane chair, and Fontarcy carefully opened the little inner lips as far as he could. We had a full view of the pretty, rose-pink interior.

"Yes, she is certainly a virgin," said my lord, gloating over the view, while Lilian, her thighs well thrown back and holding her plump hairy lips apart herself, allows us to examine her carefully and quite complacently, as if proud of this parade of her maiden charms.

"Come, Clara, and look!"

Clara drew near and in the full light from the window gazed for a few seconds at the open cockleshell.

"Yes," she said, slowly and seriously, "I think she is a virgin!"

"Think indeed! I'm sure she is! See, here are the sweet inner lips, the clitoris above, and the vaginal passage is quite closed up!"

I took a long look at Lilian's vulvary vestibule and could see the hymen or membrane, the edges of which, facing each other, made a slight projection of a deep, violet-red tint, resembling in shape a half-moon or a rudimentary letter S.

We were all satisfied that Lilian's vulva was innocent of the penetration of the penis and this searching examination put an end to the miniature orgie.

We each rearranged our dress and tried to look like sober citizens once more. Lilian was soon dressed and her hair tidied up, after a visit to the mysterious regions of the ladies' cloakroom.

The evening was fine, and proceeding to a first class café, we took tea outside.

I conversed with my friend and the two women chatted together. At first, they talked toilettes and then their voices fell to a whisper. Evidently we men were being dissected by our two charmers in true feminine style.

We then parted, Lilian promising to look up her new friends in London shortly, and I walked with my mistress to the railway station, as we both felt a wish to take the air and stretch our legs, though Lilian's had been stretched enough already.

We talked merrily and lovingly together. Lily had enjoyed herself, but she said she would have liked better to have spent the afternoon alone with me. She did not care for Clara; women were nothing to her, but I fancied she was not displeased with Fontarcy. She told me that he wanted to see her alone without me. I told her I was not jealous, as I had just proved that fact beyond dispute and that I should be very pleased if she went to him when she was in England, during the month of October. Probably she was trying to teaze me or to find out what I really thought. She also essayed a true feminine trick upon me, as she declared that Clara had asked what I intended to do for my Lily in the future, and what was to be her social position by reason of my connection with her. I felt perfectly sure that Fontarcy's companion had never said anything of the kind, but that Lilian made use of her name in order to tell me things about herself that she dared not ask me boldly and frankly. I evaded these burning topics, and diplomatically fencing, we at last reached the Gare de l'Est.

In the station, Lilian asked me if I had the money to give her.

"What money?" was my surprised enquiry.

"You know I dare not go home to Mamma without giving her what Madame Muller has supposed to have paid me to-day."

"I am hard up, I have nothing!"

"What a fearful position you have put me in! Mother is already suspicious. She will go mad and drive Papa mad against me."

"But you can say you have got an order for some new hats. That will keep them quiet."

"And when the new hats are not paid for?"

"Then you'll say they do not suit, or so on. In time it will all be forgotten."

"No, it will not. If I had known, I would not have come. This is dreadful for me!"

"Do you mean to say you have not got fifty francs you can show as if you had received it and then put it back again? Do you really tell me that all your accounts are so closely examined by your parents? I could not guess that you really are absolutely forced to bring home a few louis. It seems very strange to me that you can't get out of this somehow without me giving you money."

"No! no! I feel that I should like to run away and not go home at all. And it is so late too! What shall I say? What can I do? If I only knew somebody near here I would go and borrow it. It is dreadful!"

She seemed very much annoyed and her features were distorted with rage and disappointment. I felt disgusted with her and myself. I really did not think she would have been so hard upon me. I was far from being at my ease and she did not spare me, but reproached me bitterly. The hour grew near for the departure of her train. She bid me good bye icily and I told her to write to me from London. She turned from me without a word.

And I went away to see my poor suffering Lilian, at my little apartment, and soon forgot mercenary Mademoiselle Arvel as I cast up my accounts and reckoned what money I should require for the coming winter: coals, wood, medecines and all the incidental heavy expenses of a little household where there is a confirmed invalid. The fifteenth of October, the French rent-day, was approaching with giant strides, and I had hardly enough to make both ends meet. Poverty and passion do not go together, and when misery knocks at the door, Cupid flies out of the window.

LILIAN TO JACKY.

Sonis-sur-Marne, Thursday. (September 29th. 1898.)

Dearest Papa,

I am still stunned by last night's storm. It is impossible for me to tell you all the disagreeable things that were said to me, for I should want tremendous space to write it all to you.

I only succeeded in calming Mamma by telling her that my famous customer was going to send me at least a hundred francs by post tomorrow or the next day.

So therefore I come to ask you to make a great effort to procure that sum between this and then. As I know you are not well off just now, I will arrange matters so as to give it back to you on my return from London, but I beg you not to leave me in this trouble which has come upon me.

I count absolutely upon you for this, the first service I ask you to do me, and I know you will not leave me in such a predicament. As in every other matter I have confidence in you.

I await an answer as soon as it is possible for you. I hope to see you soon, my darling little father.

I send you all the kisses that I should have given you yesterday had we been alone.

Your slave who adores you,
LILY.

LILIAN TO JACKY.

(Undated. Received September 30th. 1898.)

My beloved little Papa,

A word in haste to tell you that Mamma said this morning that if I did not have fresh news and receive the promised money, she would accompany me to-morrow to Madame Muller's and show her that she must not make fools of people in this manner.

I tried to point out to her that I should then lose the new customer that had been introduced to me. She replied that under no pretext would she allow me to work for anybody presented by this creature. What steps ought I to take? If you do not send me to-morrow what I have asked you for, I think the best thing will be for me to confess all; that will perhaps prevent a scandalous exposure. I cannot let her discover that I pretended having received money from that woman.

I pray you, answer me quickly. I leave for London on Tuesday or Wednesday only.

I love you, notwithstanding all the sufferings I endure through you for the last two days.

My lips on your dear mouth,
LILY.

In reply to these two short, threatening notes, I sent on October 1st., a letter of excuses purporting to come from Madame Helena Muller, and enclosing a fifty-franc note. I received no acknowledgement, nor did I hear from Lilian.

8

And thou art old; thy hairs are hoary grey,
As thou wouldst save thyself from death and hell,
Pity thy daughter; give her to some friend
In marriage; so that she may tempt thee not
To hatred,—or worse thoughts, if worse there be.
SHELLEY.

DAUGHTER. . . . To marry him is hopeless
To be his whore is witless.
BEN JONSON.

Wear this jewel for my sake, 'tis my picture;
Refuse it not; it hath no tongue to vex you.
SHAKESPEARE.

I passed a terrible month of October. As usual, every winter, my poor homely Lily was very ill. More new doctors, more demands on my half-empty purse, and to make matters worse, her temper, under the influence of her terrible, relentless malady, grew unbearable. She was jealous and querulous, and I always had to give in, as the slightest emotion might have proved fatal.

Miss Arvel had not acknowledged the receipt of the money I had sent her at the beginning of the month nor given any signs of her existence. I supposed she had gone to London, as she had told me, but I was not certain. Anyhow, she had not written and I did not know her address.

Lord Fontarcy asked me once or twice in his letters about her, as he and Clara expected her visit, she having promised to look them up if she went to England. But I could tell him nothing. Indeed, it was I who asked him for news of her.

He replied that she had not turned up, despite her promise, although she had his address. He could not understand her conduct, or perhaps he did not like to speak against her to me. All he wrote were these words: "Strange girl!" And Clara, discreetly, said nothing.

It was very odd that in the preceding year, when in London in the autumn, she had written to me, but had forgotten (?) to give me her address. Here again, she is silent. Evidently, I was not to know where my love was in the habit of stopping in London, when she was there with Charlotte and Raoul; and Papa, if in England, visiting the two girls daily. Did they think that I might take it into my head to cross the Channel? That contingency did not suit the party, or I should have been approached on the subject during the summer. I was not wanted when they were in England.

My *demi-vierge* was a puzzle to me just then. She had been a real enigma. I was very sorry I could not have her more often. She excited me dreadfully, as she never failed to do, whenever I involuntarily conjured up her image in my daydreams of lust. On the other hand, I was glad, as I could do nothing for her.

She wanted money and that money I had not got. Perhaps, thought I, my little lunch has caused a revulsion of feeling. I should have had very slight regret if she was disgusted with me, as even that might have been to my future advantage. But my passions called for her. In a sensual way I yearned for her. My common sense told me it was better for both of us not to meet again.

Her stepfather always asked after me at the Bourse, where I did not go any more. I supposed he would invite me if it suited him. I foolishly worried myself very much about Lilian and as time went on and no news came, I was, I confess it, weak enough to drop her a few lines on the 30th. of October, signed: "Marie." I do not know now what I said, but I suppose I expressed my surprise at not having heard from her. In my erotic cecity, for I can call it naught else, I had quite forgotten her last note, wherein she threatened me that she would confess all to her mother, unless I sent her the money purporting to come from the imaginary Madame Muller.

ERIC ARVEL TO JACKY.

Sonis-sur-Marne, 4th. November, 1898.

My dear Jacky,

When you know that I have had half-a-dozen painters in the house, several bricklayers and a carpenter and locksmith for the last three weeks, you will understand why I have remained so long without thanking you for the many hours of pleasant reading the books I returned to you afforded me. I wish that the feminine confessions had been written by a woman, but I suppose that the daughters of Eve can keep their secrets better than men, and if they do tell tales out of school, when among themselves, they never find them written down. Many thanks for the budget of papers and the two packets of photographic printing paper. I have just had a dark room built, and if I manage to pull through the winter I shall go in for photography as a paying amusement .

When will you come down and eat the "*côtelette d'amitié*"? What do you say to Tuesday next?

With every kind of wish for you and yours, and with united best wishes for yourself from the Villa Lilian, believe me to remain,

Cordially yours,
ERIC ARVEL.

ERIC ARVEL TO JACKY.

Sonis-sur-Marne, November 8th. 1898.

My dear Jacky,

Many thanks for your letter. I was sorry you could not come to-day but as we always want to see you *sans cérémonie* tell me what day will suit you best during the week save Saturday or Sunday. We shall be at home all Friday and probably Thursday, although on the latter day, I should be forced to leave you at two o'clock to go to Paris, to do some work due to appear in a Berlin paper on Saturday.

I am grateful for the offer of more books and I do not refuse, but I am going to London some time next week and I could not leave them about during my absence, so I will ask you again on my return.

Hoping that everyone at your house is well and that you have picked up again, I remain with every good wish for you and yours,

Most cordially,
ERIC ARVEL.

NOVEMBER 11, 1898.

When I arrived at the suburban paradise to spend a happy day, I was introduced to Raoul, who I saw for the first time. He was a tall, handsome youth of 21, with fine eyes, a nice black moustache and a thick head of hair to match. He very much resembled Lilian, and had she been dressed as a man and her upper lip slightly blackened they would have been as like as two peas. He spoke English very well with a strong French accent, and I found him to be a very agreeable young fellow, but I had few opportunities of judging him. He seemed very fond of his sister and she had evidently some authority over him at that time. His mother simply adored him and spoilt him as much as her old lover would let her. He, I could not mistake it, positively loathed the very sight of the boy, who, in return, did not care a straw for him. Raoul had a sly look in his eye and when he smiled, his lips curled scornfully and sarcastically. Like his sister, he had an expressive mouth. He had a splendid set of teeth, but I was disgusted to see that they had been greatly neglected, being quite green with accumulation of tartar. I told Lilian about this, and she thanked me warmly. When I met him again, they looked clean and wholesome, as a man's mouth should, especially when lucky enough to have a good set of teeth. Arvel was no father to him and his mother did not know. She was cunning, and sufficiently artful to pamper her old lover's stomach and put up with his tempers, but her intelligence was not above that of an ordinary domestic servant.

Raoul was in France for a year, and he was off to join a regiment of the line on the 15th. He was to be stationed at Belfort.

I talked to him and put him at his ease as much as I could, for Lilian's sake, and to my surprise, I saw that he had no idea of how to behave towards the officers who would command him, nor of the obligations and discipline of life in barracks. Arvel hardly spoke to him except to sneer visibly whenever he opened his mouth, and only Lilian's warning cough and intercession between him and Mamma kept him from quarrelling with everybody. Lilian was a power now in the household, I could see.

The house had been thoroughly done up and painted. I was shown the dark room, a very useful construction, near the garden gate, fitted with every convenience for Mr. Arvel's new hobby. He explained to me that he saw a future in taking photographs and writing articles round them for the illustrated newspapers, as that was now a new fashion in journalism. He had visited some old castles in Normandy already last month with a splendid detective camera he showed me. His negatives and the letterpress had been well received and an engagement on a newly started newspaper had followed. I knew a little about photography and gave him a few hints for which he was grateful.

Lilian was as cold as ice to me all day. She kept away from me in her workshop and I spent my time mostly with Papa, who talked against his stepson. According to him, he was a lazy, good-for-nothing fellow, fond of gadding about at nights, a silly fool to be betrothed to Charlotte—who was a little whore, though Lilian's friend—and utterly incapable. Luckily for Raoul, he said, his employers had taken a foolish fancy to him. His mother could see no faults in him and he had even got on the right side of Lilian. I tried to pour oil on the troubled waters, but nothing I said could stop my host growling when he felt inclined to growl.

Then I tried to interest the youth and draw him out, and Lilian would flit about a little in the background, with a cloud on her brow and two black crescents under her eyes. A neighbour, I think it was the wife of the village baker and pastrycook, came to see my little milliner and she had foolishly brought her black poodle with her, although she knew that the Arvel dogs were rather savage and jealous. The Bordeaux hound rushed at the intruder and began to worry him, and Blackamoor and the other dogs also attacked the poor little beast. Lilian, shrieking, appeared to get the big dog off, and everybody galloped to the scene of the affray. Eventually, all was made right, and the poodle, barring a little bit of flesh nipped off his loins, was none the worse for his encounter. But Lilian burst into a fit of hysterical weeping and though I tried to whisper a few words of comfort in her ear, she turned roughly away from me without speaking. What had I done to merit such rudeness from her?

Papa had engaged a waggonette and we were all to be driven a few miles off to the establishment of a horticulturist to buy fruit trees for an orchard and kitchen-garden, to be inaugurated next spring in the newly acquired ground.

We were all ready to start, but Lilian sent word she would not come, pretexting a lot of work, although Mamma asserted it would do her good. Lilian was far from well, she said, she had no appetite, did not sleep, and suffered from headache. So we started off without her, Raoul joining the coachman on the box.

As we jolted along, Madame Arvel told me what she evidently thought was greatly to her son's credit, as showing his love for his sister.

He was fearfully upset at seeing the dogfight, and witnessing the outburst of tears of Mademoiselle, and his anxiety grew into positive uneasy fear when his mother told him that it might be serious for his sister, as she was very unwell that day. Mamma chuckled at the brother's solicitude for the girl during her catamenial flow. I thought about the indelicacy of discussing such topics between mother, brother and sister, not to mention the master of the house and lastly myself.

So I sat to a-thinking as I felt awfully bored, listening and forcing myself to answer the commonplaces of Ma and Pa, and now and then my ears were delighted with fragmentary echoes of Raoul's remarks to the coachman. His every sentence began with the same words:

"In England we do so-and-so!"

My thoughts went back to the date of Lilian's menstruation. It generally began on the 27th. or 28th. In August, it was all over by the 25th., and in September also, as she had lunched with Lord and Lady Fontarcy on the 28th. of that month and now we were at the 11th. of a fresh period of thirty days, and she was menstruating freely. She was suffering from anæmia or chlorosis, I could plainly diagnose, though my medical knowledge was slight and empirical, and in such a state, sexual excitement and masturbation, alone or in company, would produce irregularity of her periodical loss of blood. She had been to London with Charlotte and had returned with her and Raoul. I did not know when she had left, nor how long she had been back. What had she been doing at the West End? How had they been living? Had she joined her handsome brother and Lolotte between the sheets? Was her friend in the lace trade a little Lesbian? Here was an explanation of Arvel's jealousy and hatred of the lad. Suppose that Lilian loved Raoul too well? Had they ever played carnally together as children, perhaps to amuse Arvel . . . perhaps at his instigation? That would be quite enough to make him jealous now that he loved Lilian, I imagined, not like a child, whose half-innocent caresses had warmed his blood before he joined Adèle in bed, but like a woman ripening gradually for sensual service at his fireside.

Time would show, I said to myself, and I drove those thoughts from me and wondered, poor fool that I was then, what Lilian meant by sulking with her wretched old Jacky!

Mamma and Papa bought about five hundred francs' worth of trees. Adèle was mad on gardening just then. She thought she could manage to have fruit enough to go into business the next year. I chatted with them all, and tried to be friendly with the brother.

I saw nothing of my charmer until a few moments before dinner, when we were all in the drawing-room. She arrived, nicely tidied up, with a dash of powder on her dark complexion. She immediately went to her Papa and sat on the arm of his chair, after having patted his face and told him how well he looked. She had a box of fancy note-paper in her hand and told me it was to write to her most intimate friends with.

"I am going to write some letters now," she said saucily. "When I don't care for the people, I send them type-written notes on Pa's business paper. Eh, Papa?"

He did not answer. He never responded to her advances or to her caresses before me. Whenever she rubbed against him, or tickled him, or caressed him in any way, his face grew dull; he frowned, and lost all expression. He loved her and a caress from the loved one was evidently a serious thing for him.

"You should never write letters. Never confess, never write and never reply. Such are the instructions of an old lawyer, a friend of mine."

And so we fenced for a quarter of an hour, Lily chaffing me to please her Pa, I supposed. She admired his clean-shaven chin and cheeks, and coolly told me that she hated men with hair on their faces. I wore my entire natural beard.

Then I was alone with her for a few moments just before we sat down to dinner. I took her in my arms. She struggled and got away. I slapped her face smartly, but she did not take it as usual, and complained I hurt her and was too brutal.

"Look how you have brought the blood into my cheeks, everybody will see."

She was very pale and my slap had caused a patch of crimson to overspread one cheek. This was a sure sign of poverty of the blood and deficient circulation. I asked her if she was cold. She shivered and said she was always chilly. I told her she ought to wear woollen stockings. She showed me her feet. She wore worsted socks under her black thread stockings. Here was every sign of anæmia and I inwardly thought that she must also suffer from that disagreeable affliction, vulgarly called the "whites." That would account for her occasional coyness with me, and also for her lack of sensual excitement the winter before. Anæmic girls are no use in winter; the circulation of the blood is deficient, and there is a discharge from the vagina generally accompanying the menses. At that time, if any attempt is made to worship at the altar of Venus or practise masturbation, there are ovarian pains and stomach cramps, such as Lilian complained about.

I need not say that I kept all these remarks to myself and being very much in love, I no doubt looked and behaved like a spoony swain, although I tried as I always did to be very gay and make everybody laugh, even if the joke was at my expense.

During the meal, Lilian thawed a little and slipped her foot under mine, letting it remain there all the time.

The Dreyfus affair came on the *tapis*. As was his wont, Arvel stuck up boldly for the heads of the French army. I ventured to say that whatever had occurred, there was no doubt that the alleged traitor had been illegally condemned, as pressure had been brought to bear on his judges in the council chamber by showing them secret documents, of which the prisoner and his lawyer ignored the existence, against all ideas of justice and fair play.

"But suppose they could not show them?" said Arvel.

At this answer, which I leave to my readers to appreciate, I could do no more than give up talking about the matter and I dropped the subject.

Raoul joined in, saying that he had only read English newspapers and knew very little about the case, and Adèle called across the table to me:

"Is he innocent?"

"Yes," I retorted.

"Then why don't they deliberate (sic) him?"

"They will in time," I answered, and Arvel shrugged his shoulders and talked a lot of nonsense about the luck of Dreyfus in being judged by his brother-officers and what more could any man want?—he added.

I did not reply. I amused myself looking at Lilian, who gazed on her Pa with undisguised admiration. Her eyes were fixed on his and her half-open mouth drank in every word he let fall. Once during the dinner, she touched my hand with hers. Usually when I dined at Sonis, she never forgot to peel and prepare some fruit for me. This night I was neglected. I remember too that the conversation turned—as it always did at Sonis—on some indecency, either in a Parisian newspaper or at a theatre, and Papa denounced the immorality of the Parisians.

"Londoners are no better!" blurted out Lilian, in a passion, "how about the massage establishments?"

I noted this peculiar remark and saw Papa drop his beak into his plate. When Lily was flooding, Lilian's temper was bad.

Mamma was at the head of the table. On her right, was Papa alone. On her left, Raoul was seated, and next to him Lilian. I was at the bottom of the table, facing Mamma, but luckily there was a big lamp in the middle and I could hardly see her.

I suppose Papa was thinking whether Lilian's "tootsies" were on mine or not, as there was a slight scuffle under the hospitable board and Papa called out to his daughter:

"Hullo! scraggy longshanks, where have your feet got to? Can't you tuck 'em under your chair?"

"Oh! its no use you trying to *faire le pied* with me, you know!"

This is a slang expression, and may be translated as "playing the foot game," *i.e.* lovers' wireless telegraphy by means of sly mutual pressures of the lower extremities.

Still more indications for me of the emancipation of my sweetheart. But I was too much concerned with my own troubles to bother about Lilian and her mother's old lover just then.

Having silenced her amorous Papa, she rose and said she was going to take the dogs out with her brother. To my surprise, she turned to me, and asked if I would accompany them and smoke, and digest my dinner. Of course I accepted, and all three, without counting the canine pets, we went out along the road. It was a fine night with a bright moon. Raoul was not troublesome. He knew the part he had to play, and walked on in front teazing Blackamoor, leaving Lilian and me practically alone together.

I broke out at once:

"What is the matter with you?"

"I am very vexed. You left me in the lurch, and so I resolved to try and forget you. That is why I did not write from London as I had promised, nor did I go to see your friends. I asked you to do me a slight favour and you abandoned me entirely in the hour of need."

"But, my darling, I sent you a note purporting to come from Madame Muller, containing fifty francs."

"*I never received that letter!*"

"Good God! It's true I never registered it! This is horrible. In spite of all I may say, you will always have an afterthought that I have invented this lie to save fifty francs! How could it have been lost? Letters rarely go astray like this."

"Oh! the postmen are such thieves down here!"

"I sent it. I forget what day it was, but I'll look up my diary when I get home. I am stunned. What fearful ill-luck! Why should just this very letter be lost when so many others I have written have always reached you safely?"

I could not say very much more, I had not much time, as we were due to get back to the house for my train and I was all abroad. I must have looked as stupid as I felt. It was a hard case for me and incidentally for my friends, Lord Fontarcy and Clara. I was very unlucky, that was certain.

Resuming my talk, I said to Lilian:

"As you did not get the fifty francs, how did you manage?"

"My mother went to Normandy with Pa to do some photography and write about some châteaux, and I told her in a letter that I had received some money from Madame Muller."

"But when she came back, did she not ask to see the cash? You say she sees and knows everything?"

"Yes, but I told her I had used it to pay a bill that was due."

If I had recovered from this crushing blow, I might have continued by wanting to know whether she had seen the bill and if I could be allowed to see it too, but I frankly confess that I could not reason properly at that moment. I could only keep thinking how unfortunate I was. Nevertheless, it slowly dawned upon me that Lilian was awfully mercenary, and I think my love for her began to shrink a trifle. She went on to complain that Papa had found a post-card in one of the books I had lent him. It was from my mistress's dressmaker, speaking about a price to be paid for embroidering a jacket. Mademoiselle was evidently jealous of her or pretended to be so, and she plainly said that a man who could spend such sums on fashionable attire, and holding the great position I did in Paris, should have been more liberal with her, who had done all I asked her, and she thought I was rather tightfisted and a scurvy fellow (pignouf).

I must have been looking very miserable up to this and I lifted up my face to hers in the moonlight.

I was choking with rage, disgust, and surprise. I was completely taken aback and could not find a word to say:

"Oh, Lilian!" was all I could gasp out.

I think she must have seen something in my face that frightened her, or perhaps she thought she had gone far enough. She put her arm through mine and told me that it did not much matter:

"I am very unhappy! We were so miserable in London, were we not, Raoul?"

And she called him to create a diversion.

"I was in bed each night at ten o'clock. We went to no theatres or music halls. We had no money. All three of us, Lolotte, Raoul, and myself would dine at a foreign restaurant, and fagged out, retire to rest."

Heaven knows how much of this was true. I could not analyse her talk then.

We returned home, and at the gate, Raoul asked me if I was going to sleep at their place.

Lilian chimed in gracefully:

"Oh no! We are too poor and common for him!"

And she bounced past us. After having bid Pa and Ma good night, and thanked them for their kind reception, etc., Raoul and Lilian escorted me to the station.

The brother obligingly disappeared in the trees and she gave me her mouth, and put her hand to see if my manly organ responded to the cunning thrust of her tongue between my lips, as it always had done. Satisfied with her examination, she became somewhat mollified.

But there was a barrier between us. I felt a strange uneasiness, and I really do think that this was the turning-point of my *liaison* with Lilian. From that moment my feelings underwent a change. I could not see for myself just then, but light did come and I was saved, as the reader will see.

She asked after Lord Fontarcy. I told her how he had called her, "a strange girl."

She said she did not like the couple, though she could at a pinch have put up with Fontarcy himself. She told me frankly that her brother would never have consented to go and see Clara, as he was madly, sentimentally in love with Charlotte, who had been three weeks in London with her. He was fully resolved to marry his mistress, although she was about three years his senior. And Lilian added that she was tired out, unhappy and felt very ill.

"You require care, Lily. Your health is not good. You are anæmic!"

At these words, which I had let drop harmlessly enough, Lilian started as if I had shot her.

"Anæmic? I? Anæmic!" she shrieked out, and her face was all black, and her mouth twisted awry. She was in a fit of mad passion. "I don't know what you mean. You've given yourself away fairly this time! You think you are talking to somebody else. You're quite mistaken, my dear fellow!"

I was surprised at this outbreak, but was cool enough in spite of my trouble to divine that if there was one thing Lilian hated more than another it was the truth.

I had pity on her too, because at that moment I still loved her in my vile, salacious way and my bowels yearned for her. I had not yet had time to think over the events of the day. But I knew enough of women to see that she was under the neurotic influence of difficult menstruation and as such must be spared for the nonce.

I do not remember if I spoke about seeing her again or not, or whether we made any plans for the future. I know I alluded to my beard. She shrugged her shoulders and told me that she was only running me down to please Papa and divert his suspicions, if he had any.

I never spoke of him nor of the numerous signs of illicit intercourse between them. I wanted to hold my tongue and learn more.

I told her I would write and I asked her to make a few discreet enquiries at the post-office at Sonis.

She did not reply, but with a cordial "adieu," Raoul and her saw me into the train and we parted good friends; not lovers, only friends.

I went back to Paris and dreamt that I was on my honeymoon with Lilian Arvel and that I was alone in a railway carriage with her, her skirts thrown up and my hands on her naked thighs.

I looked up my diary and found that I had posted the fifty-franc note on the first of October.

I composed a letter for Lily. I wanted to write a beautiful letter to her. I desired to make all my next letters kind and delicate, so that they should exactly delineate my thoughts and my state of mind as I wrote them. I kept altering a comma here, a word there, and often changed the order of sentences. This did not change the sense, but I flattered my wretched self that I made my prose lighter and clearer, with more tenderness, more kindness, more passionate love. Alas, poor Jacky!

JACKY TO LILIAN.

Paris, November 12th. 1898.

My dear Lilian,

As soon as I got home last night, I quickly looked at my diary and I find I sent the bank-note on Saturday, October 1st. The letter ought to have been delivered on Sunday morning, the 2nd.

In spite of all, I am as if stunned by a blow from a club, proving such atrocious ill-luck that I can hardly realise the fact of it being precisely that one particular letter which should have been lost or stolen.

What a misfortune for me and naturally for you too!

I have always tried to be so careful, to protect you, who I had so much joy in imagining to be my daughter; so that for once, neglecting prudence, I find myself in a pitiful position, for what causes me enormous grief, of which you cannot form the slightest idea, is that you have no longer confidence in me.

I am sad, weary, disgusted with life and all its defeats, illnesses and wounds. One has so little happiness in this world, and such, . . . oh! such trouble!

But you are young and you cannot understand at all what I feel. In a few short years, when you will have been able to appreciate life better; when you will have seen other things and other men, then you will think of me and render me justice. To-day, I hope for nothing.

I pray you, excuse the serious tone of this letter of complaint. There is nothing so silly as a man who groans and laments, but if I go mad with rage in front of this paper; if I choke in my throat as if I were about to be weak enough to weep, it is because I think that you have attributed to me: lies, villany and meanness. You have believed that my soul was base and paltry, as vilely low as that of a huckstering shopkeeper! But enough; perhaps I ought not to send you this sad scrawl?

Let me conclude with an effort to be gayer. I dreamt of you all night. Irony of the fates . . . we were on our honeymoon! I had just married you!

This was an effect of cerebral impression, caused by my conversation with you in the station, the railway ride, etc.

I thank you for your kiss, for your slight caress.

Do not forget to tell your brother, as I can see that he does not have all necessary advice given him, to cease having a will of his own directly he enters the barracks, and never to answer a superior even if a hundred times in the right. Let him become a machine—if I may venture to say so—and not a man.

Make him wear flannel, and woollen socks. It is impossible to walk with cotton hose; he would soon get blistered and bleeding feet.

Tell him also never to say: "In England we do this or that." He will find such conduct more prudent—at least for the moment.

He loves you well, that I saw. He will listen to this advice coming from you. Make out as if these were your own ideas.

And I love you also.

J. S.

LILIAN TO JACKY.

(No date or place.) Received November 15th. 1898.

My little Father,

I will not let you have a moment of sadness through any fault of mine, so I come quickly to tell you that I have no longer the least doubt about you, for a man who can have the kindliness and the delicacy to be able to understand all you have understood, cannot be base one instant.

Therefore all is forgotten and I am once more your loving "daughter."

I wish to believe that the wretched month I have just passed was only a nightmare, a bad dream.

I have suffered greatly. I found myself so lonely, so neglected. But all this is quite finished, is it not?

My brother left yesterday by the midnight train. I gave him all your advice and I thank you a thousand times.

Yes, you have guessed rightly. I love him very much. He is so gentle, so good, and then he loves me fondly too.

If you have dreamt truly when you supposed we were on our wedding trip, how proud and happy I should be; and I am certain that you would regret nothing, for I would make you so happy that the horrible sentence you write to me in your good letter would never enter your mind.

You are sad, fatigued, tired of life, say you? That is because you have no tie to make existence a pleasure. But if you had a good little wife, very loving, full of care for you; a pretty little household:—"home,"—in all the true sense of the word, your ideas would be quite different. And you have only a word to say to possess all this. Do not suppose that I speak lightly. I have reflected seriously and I am convinced that we should be mutually happy. Do you think it is so very amusing for me to see you only during a few short moments, now and again, and always with a little apprehension? And it will always be the same if we continue like this —but I will no longer.

I kiss you madly as on certain days,

LILY.

JACKY TO LILIAN.

Paris, November 16th. 1898.

My darling daughter,

I must hold my pen tight to-day so that it shall not escape and bolt away across the paper to express to you all the sweet joy your delicious letter, which I received yesterday, has given me. I can only see one thing: you love me!

That letter is you: my Lily, my daughter, my slave, my love, all mine; your heart to excuse me, to console me, and your body a hundred times offered for my pleasure, my lust, my enjoyment . . . and a little for yours, by the sole fact of the pleasure you bestow. For I often remarked that you found your pleasure in provoking mine. I would ask you: "What do you want now?" And you would answer: "You!"

When you are near me, you feel that movement which opens the sources of pleasure in your inmost being. I am proud to have been the first who produced in you that effect, and you always experience it when I am by your side; when I rub against you; when I look at you. I remember the first time I came to this conclusion; we were in that café where we drank some champagne. You looked at me, your nostrils quivered; you were spending and yet our conversation was commonplace. You were near me and you loved me as you loved me to-day. I never have understood your love and your passion better.

You talk of "certain days" and of your mad caresses.

Impudent girl! Do you wish to awaken in me all my lust, and excite and provoke all my desires—all the yearning I have for you? You make me remember my imaginations of slavery. I wish to call to you to come to my arms. I wish to command you to run to me, to execute all the voluptuousness of which I dream when my thoughts wander towards you —as it happens too often.

I have still a little virgin paint-brush in a corner of a drawer, wrapped in tissue paper. I would also teach you the bicycle race, when your saddle would be my mouth and face, and the handle-bar the head of the bed, or you could turn round and. . . . Will you, say Lily, my little incestuous daughter? . . .

But I stop and read over what I have just written. I ought not write thus to you. I am mad. So much the worse for me! . . . I send you my incoherent thoughts. Excuse me. I will try to be more cold and reasonable.

My dream, which was delicious, for you gave me your mouth in the railway carriage, and then your thighs and the rest, is impossible to realise for reasons which I will give you some day by word of mouth. It would be too long and useless to tell all here. I must be brutally frank and say that I can give you nothing that you deserve. You have come too late in my life. I am unfortunate—not by your fault, I hasten to say— and if I could have foreseen that our love would have become what it is to-day, I think I should have fled. Besides, you must remember how long I resisted? Yet I regret nothing, I shall always have the remembrance of the exquisite joys given and taken. But there is no future for us. All you write to me is just and sensible and when you say, "you will not continue like that," I have only to bow my head. I have nothing to say. You are right.

I ought to have been stronger and not have succumbed, but your eyes were too beautiful; your lips, rosy and moist, too sweet; your passion caused mine to grow. I took you and chanced it. It was so lovely. I say I took you. I do not say I hold you now, and yet you are mine, despite that I love you too religiously to profit by your delicious weakness and make you a woman. That word "religiously" may not match the rest of my letter, but you will understand what I mean—what passes through my brain. And if I am forced to disappear to-morrow from your life, even by your orders, you will always be mine for your whole life, in spite of yourself, free or married, by the sheer strength of the feelings I excite in you. Therefore; fly from me, for I have nothing to offer you but a little sensual pleasure and that is not enough. Leave me alone with my wasted life. It will be better for both of us.

This letter is vague. Will you be able to make head or tail of it? What is the "horrible sentence" of my poor letter? Have I said anything horrible to you . . . whose soul I martyrise?

Have you never guessed how I always struggled against your fascination? How many times have I regretted a night I refused at Sonis—do you recollect? I feared to compromise you. Yet had I been more selfish? That lost night! . . . what a fool I was!

You told me: "I often go to Paris now." Is that true, or only to teaze me? You often liked to vex me by telling me little things which were not true, to laugh at my amazement afterwards.

Can I see you? anywhere you like . . . to talk to you an hour or less, between two trains . . . if it is true that you often come to Paris. I ask nothing of you. I no longer speak as master. I am a wretch and a coward!

I have nothing of you as a souvenir, not even your photograph. Your letters are not mine, but your property. I want to give them back to you. I have nothing but a little bit of pink ribbon.

J. S.

The foregoing letter I have copied from some rough notes which I happened to keep. I think I wrote more than what is set down here. I alluded to my age and said that marriage was impossible between a man of 46 and a girl of 22. I also concluded very erotically, asking her to meet me at night in the darkness of the country lanes at Sonis, while her Pa was in London during the remainder of the month.

The general effect of my letter was to show her that I could not possibly carry on our connection any more, as I could see that she wanted something advantageous—money or marriage; and infatuated though I was, it slowly dawned upon me that Miss Arvel did not want Jacky, if Jacky was poor. At the same time, I was careful not to blame her in any way, but heaped reproaches on my own head.

I had no answer. I did not expect she would reply when I wrote. I bore up manfully against the blow, for which however, I was slightly prepared by her silence during the preceding month, and, being so much troubled in every way in Paris, I began to get used to the buffetings of the world. One wound more or less, what does it matter when you are fighting, and getting the worst of every round?

She could only have written in one way and that would have

been to say: "I want to see you at once," and she should have appeared and cried in my arms and proved her love for me in a thousand pretty ways. Luckily for me, she did nothing of the sort. She was not one of the crying kind, being too selfish and hard-hearted. She never wept for me.

I think as far as a man can judge himself, that I really felt an immense love for her, of an intensely sensual kind at that moment. I will not tell what thoughts filled my racked brain at this juncture, but had she sought me out, she might have done what she liked with me. But it must have been at once; every day took me farther from her. She did not know her power then, and I may as well say frankly that she never regained it. She did not really care for me, save as stepping-stone to get over part of the torrent of life dryshod.

On the 6th. of December, I received a small envelope, bearing the Sonis postmark. It contained a little portrait of Mademoiselle Arvel, about the size of a postage-stamp. This had been torn off her railway season ticket, which I suppose she was now renewing.

It was in answer to the last part of my letter of "adieu." I supposed that she wished to begin with me again, so I sent the following note which I candidly confess I wrote with great care and sincerity.

JACKY TO LILIAN.

Paris, December 7th. 1898.

My dear little Lilian,

I am very perplexed. I do not know if it will please you or not to receive a few lines from me, as I ignore what you may have thought of my last letter, written about the seventeenth of November.

As far as I can recollect . . . it is nearly a month ago! . . . and the time seems so long to me. . . . I wrote then a few sentences a little too lascivious. I do not ask you to excuse or to pardon me, for I sent that letter under the influence of a species of fever, combined with lust. And I am sure you have understood and if you are vexed with me it is not for that. Therefore I am going to be calm and reasonable, and as brief as possible. As you have not answered me, I think it may perhaps bore you to receive a letter from me, but I shall soon know that by this very simple sign: if you do not reply, that will mean that Miss Arvel informs me that my little daughter is dead. Indeed, when the 26th. of November passed without news of her, my heart went into mourning. It is true that I am so unhappy, covered with so many wounds, so to speak, that a new grief, a fresh wound, cannot increase my sufferings much. For me only the worst happens.

See what a wretched position I am in, in front of you. If I complain, that will seem to you perhaps ridiculous on the part of a man. If I show temper, you will say I am spiteful because you will not see or write to me. If I sulk and do not write to you, you will think (and rightly too), that we ought to be at least polite and always answer a note, especially when corresponding with those we love and esteem. But it is all over between us two. Our love has gone with the summer sun, with all that was joy and pleasure. Now the cold winds blow. All is frozen. Winter is here.

Let me get done: the real motive of my letter . . . which is probably tiresome for you . . . is to thank you a thousand times for having sent me the portrait of my little daughter, so adored, so desired, who will never come to my arms again, since she is no more. I can see her prettier than on that photograph, because I love to remember her features when she smiled, her mouth half open, her lips all moist, and her beautiful Spanish eyes lighted up and sparkling, laughing. Then she was truly beautiful. Poor child! I loved her well.

It is a good and charming movement coming from the bottom of your little heart that has made you send me that portrait, and I recognise your usual kindness.

I dare not ask you news of your health, nor of your brother, nor of Blackamoor, because I do not want you to think that I use tricky means to drag a few lines out of you.

I ask for nothing; I want nothing of you out of pity or charity.

I think I have already told you (an old foreign snob like me has the privilege of repeating himself a little), that I detested the idea of two persons who love each other, or who have loved, doing composition, or sending ironical letters, making bitter-sweet sentences, etc. If I write to you it is purely and simply without any after-thought to have the pleasure of chatting with you from afar.

A strange idea has just come into my brain . . . (you know my peculiar imagination? All this pleased you once. Why have you changed? Mystery!—which I shall try to clear up.)

"Mademoiselle Arvel had a little sister, Lily, who loved me. She is dead. I called her my daughter. When poor Lily died, her big sister, **who** knew of our *liaison*, found a photograph of her, and sent it to me. She died towards the end of September."

I assure you I loved her well.

J. S.

My bookselling friend in Rotterdam was evidently pleased with my efforts in correcting "The Horn Book," for he now took the liberty of sending me another long and very obscene manuscript to correct and send through the press for him.

It was called, "The Double Life of Cuthbert Cockerton," and strange to say, was principally about incestuous love between a father and daughter.

This book necessitated a lot of correction, and Vanderpunk insisted upon me adding a few words to the preface, and I did so, with the thought of my love Lily, now dead to me, running through my poor brain. (*See Appendix B.*)

END OF VOLUME I

II

1

Amour, fléau du monde, exécrable folie;
. . . .
Si jamais, par les yeux d'une femme sans cœur,
Tu peux m'entrer au ventre et m'empoisonner l'âme,
Ainsi que d'une plaie on arrache une lame,
Plutôt que comme un lâche on me voie en souffrir,
Je t'en arracherai, quand j'en devrais mourir.

ALFRED DE MUSSET.

I have already said that my health had been bad, and that I had great difficulty in getting over my sharp attack of rheumatism of the spring. The treatment at Lamalou had pulled me down exceedingly and after the course of baths of boiling water, I returned to Paris in a state of mental and bodily fatigue.

That is why I had fallen an easy prey to Lilian, and I had not struggled against the fearful longing I felt for her; nor had I troubled to reason with myself. My brain was dulled. In September, I had enjoyed long bicycle rides in the country, and I now began to experience the benefit of the waters I had taken. I was light and gay, without a pain, and my sweet invalid companion also had a brief respite, in this gloomy fag-end of November and beginning of December.

I carried on now a pretty intrigue with a new flame, and the lady in question was such a curious person that I think she deserves to be lightly sketched in this my little book, which, started in summer, sylvan retirement, as a rapid review of a love-affair, is fast growing into a stout work of salacious confessions.

THE STORY OF A SLAVE.

I dined at the house of a French friend, a married man. I was introduced to a lady, who I had never seen in that house before. She was rather goodlooking, but a trifle too stout, of Oriental style, like a fine, fat Jewess. She was about thirty, and had two children. Her husband was a manufacturer, and lived in the north of France. She was alone in Paris for a few days, I forget now for what reason. Louise, as I shall call her, seemed to like to laugh and joke with me, and sat down to the piano, and played for me and to me. She was a splendid performer and was very well educated. The little party broke up early, and as Madame Louise made out that she was not at her ease in Paris alone at night, I offered to be her cavalier and take her home to her hotel. I was accepted, and we left together. We were soon friends, and I prevailed upon her to walk with me instead of riding, and by dint of persuasion, got her to go to a café with me.

She talked of her home in the country and of the difficulty of getting good servants. I told her jokingly to whip them to make them obedient and that many women, whether domestics or ladies, liked to be chastised. It was a lucky hit of mine, as she would not let the subject of flagellation drop, and after a little fencing, I elicited from her that she dreamt daily and nightly of the joy of being a slave to a man she would love. Louise would never have gone so far if she did not want me to make love to her, and at last she promised to meet me in Paris the next afternoon.

Then she really became my chattel, a most docile toy, and she came to Paris every month or so, and scarcely ever failed to meet me. I hear from her now occasionally, and our adventures together would make a most entertaining volume. But I have only introduced her here, to give the translation of some of her letters, which will enable the reader to guess what Louise wanted, and which

I knew well how to manage. I need only add that she was perfectly disinterested, and it may be guessed that this peculiar passion cannot exist among professional beauties.

Master,

The day after I became your slave I wrote you a letter of twelve pages, telling you of my dreams of mad torture, which I made as I desired you to be a thousand times more cruel than you were with me.

Then I reflected, and tried to forget you, and never more return to this kind of voluptuousness. I burnt the letter, and I hoped that you would never write to me; that I might be strong.

But I cannot. I return to you. Do with my body as you will, but my dream is that you should only see in me a slave and naught else; that is to say a creature who you will always cause to suffer cruelly.

I see you now, as in a vision; your eyes with the same expression they had in the cab, forcing me to look at you; telling me so, roughly.

And then, when I come to Paris, you must not receive me in such a rich apartment—for a slave, the vilest place is too good—but at an ordinary hotel. Then you will lunch—I could get to you about eleven o'clock —and I would look on without eating, happy to accept on my knees what you would please to throw me.

You could exact anything from me, forcing me to reply at each command: "Yes, master!"

I must never be allowed to answer in any other manner, and if I forget myself, you will box my ears with great force. You will force me to caress you with my arms bound behind my back, and if I lick you awkwardly, you will flog me on any part of my body; and never, never will you allow me to show any other expression on my features but that of the most absolute tenderness and submission.

Afterwards, you will cause me to approach you, and look, by violently stretching open the lips of my private parts, if I desire you. Should I be wet, you will make me cross my legs, and brutally you will force your fist between my thighs. You will pull my hairs, force me to show you the sign of my sex, and if I am pouring with liquid lust, you will cut me with a riding whip. You will make me wash myself again with the water containing the lump of ice, and you will dip a towel in the frozen liquid and put it on my loins, so as to annihilate my desire.

Should you wish to ejaculate in my mouth, when you are in the bed, you will put me on my knees over you, my back towards you. Thus you will have the pleasure of pinching me, of biting me, or of lashing me, while I shall have your divine instrument in my mouth.

And if I am exhausted by unslacked lust, you will only give way to me when I have begged and prayed for coition, and you will possess me with my arms bound, tortured by a cruel belt that will compress my waist.

You will force your fingers into my slit, which will be thirsting to be filled up by you, and you will command me to fix my eyes upon yours, and with your other hand, you will pinch me, prick me, and scratch me with a needle, for the pleasure of seeing me suffer. I would that you were very, very cruel. Perhaps I shall be free one day next week. I will get to Paris in the morning and go back at six o'clock.

I await your orders, master, and on my knees, I kiss your feet.

Your submissive and devoted slave,

LOUISE.

———————

To-day I desire you madly, and your cruel eyes. Oh! to look at them on my knees, to see them plunged into mine, to feel your hands enter pitilessly into my flesh, hurting and bruising me; brutally taking hold of my leg, dragging down my stockings, and watching your joy increasing, as the needle's point sinks into my quivering body. At each painful stab, I would say: "Thank you, master!"

Oh! to be knocked about, pinched, humiliated and degraded; to see you smile cruelly at my sufferings and kiss you all over, while I should be dying with discomfort in the instruments of torture you showed me; to suffer for you, master,—oh! how I desire you!

I can no longer support the thoughts of you! If you were here I would prostrate myself at your feet and pray you to make me enjoy.

Oh! I will be continent, I promise you; I will do nothing alone. I will wait. I have no will but yours. You forbid masturbation; I will obey. It does me good to write you my insensate longings.

Make me suffer, even from afar. Send me something that I can wear next my skin that will hurt me.

Oh! for my mouth on your naked body, to kiss your feet, and let my tongue touch everywhere! I am mad with lust. My throat is dry, my heart beats and I am all wet. How I long for you! Pardon me, do, my master; I will be so submissive, so tender with you, so obedient to make you forget all my shortcomings. Write to me soon, I supplicate you.

With humility, I lie at your feet, you can walk on me. And I shall still say: "Thank you!" I kiss the darling feet that stamp upon me, and also your dear hands that hurt me.

I kiss your whole body, my respected master. Oh! if I could always be frightened of you, as I was the other day beneath the gaze of your cruel eyes.

I want to be frightened of you always; you must be wicked and cruel; your only joy must be to make me suffer without ceasing.

You must make me come myself as you order me on my knees, to receive a flogging, if you so desire it.

I am your thing, your bitch, your submissive slave.

LOUISE.

———————

You must do what you told me on my next visit to Paris: put me on my knees before you, my eyes turned to yours; the vase beneath my chin, and splash my face, my lips, my cheeks, with your hot urine, amusing yourself all the time by hurting me, and always exacting a tender and submissive look in my eyes.

It is so difficult for me to support your gaze, when it is hard and cruel, as it was last night beneath the glare of the electricity.

I wish to see your small hand gently prick my flesh with your scarf pin; and revel in your awful joy, as you see my blood, and then force me to pour vinegar upon the wound.

You will allow me, will you not, master, to suffer through you, and for you?

Pardon me for having tried to escape from your influence. I come back to you, more tender, more humble, more submissive than before. Do to me whatever you please.

You will see, master, all my efforts to satisfy you, so that your joy may be complete so that you may permit me to kiss your hand. The traces of your hands are still on my flesh, my arm is still black and blue.

Pardon me my bad writing. Next time, I will strive to make my writing more legible, but to-day I am too nervous, I hunger too much for you.

If you wish it, if it will please you that I read the books you told me about, I will do so with joy. But I should wish that all you do be for your desire and your caprice, and not to be agreeable to me.

The only reward of a slave is that her loved and respected master should find her worthy to suffer for him and for his pleasure.

I will try also not to think of myself when I talk to you. I will only think of making your pleasure slow and perfect.

I will try and support pain with a tender and submissive look, and my face shall show pleasure whatever I feel, so as to please you, and not have the hard and sulky expression, for which you so rightly whipped my bottom the other day.

You should be still more exacting; very severe, very cruel, to form me for your taste, and make me sweetly tender, docile, and obedient, punishing me each time I give way to my lust; and driving it out of my frame by dint of suffering.

Let me only think of you; only dream of you; let me only look at you; let my eyes, like those of a fawning, loving cur, never leave your eyes; let them never look elsewhere; nothing should make them turn away from you, when I am in your dear presence.

I am very sensitive about the hair. You must order me to let it down, and then comb it out, pulling it roughly, until the tears come in my eyes, and if I weep, punish me for my silly sensibility. You will do that, will you not? I wish to suffer for you, my desired master.

Have you not dreamt worse sufferings than these?

If so, will you kindly tell me of them, so that I may think of the suffering in reserve for me, and get my mind used to fresh divine torture.

Do not forget your little riding-whip. Shall I bring one myself?

If I had my own way, this letter would never be done, but it would end by wearying you. I finish here regretfully. To write to you is a great joy for me.

I place my head beneath your feet, which I feel on my face, crushing my cheeks with your boot heels. I feel your hand twisting and tearing my flesh; then you pinch me. I feel your hand smartly slapping both cheeks, while I am on my knees, my arms strapped tightly behind me. I feel the stinging lash of your whip cutting into my flesh at long intervals, so as to make your pleasure last longer, and tears roll down my cheeks, in spite of all my efforts, as, to punish me for loving you too much, you tear off the hair that hides my sex. Each time I must say to you: "Thank you, master!" If I forget, your dear hand shall slap my face, as hard as it can strike, and always my eyes are fixed on yours: softly, tenderly, and submissively. I am your enduring obedient slave,

LOUISE.

This new passion did not prevent me nursing my poor Lily at home, and working at my chemical inventions, while I took as much exercise as I could in the open air. I seemed to get younger and gayer, as I would leave my bed as early as possible, and stride merrily along, drunk with the lightness of the pure morning air, my good old Smike careering joyfully round me.

Good health means gaiety, and my greatest trouble was the beggarly lightness of my banking account, now that my poor invalid seemed a trifle better.

Now and again, I thought of the Lily of Sonis, and I felt that there was something very strange in her conduct.

I had said in my last letter to her that I would try to elucidate the mystery, and having, as I expected, no answer, I began to ask myself what steps I ought to take to unravel the puzzle. All my old powers of reasoning, that I thought I had left for ever in my bed of pain, came gradually back to me, and I saw that Mademoiselle Arvel had no real tenderness for me.

I had never read her letters over again, although I had often said to myself that I would do so. I had them all, as I have given them here, dated, and tied up in a bundle.

One afternoon, my new mistress, Louise, failed to keep an appointment, and having a moment to myself, I got the packet of Lilian's letters out of a drawer of my desk, and read them all carefully through, one by one.

Then I began to vaguely sketch in my mind all the little criticisms that I have spread over these pages, and I found the explanation of many things she had said to me and which I had let pass at the time.

When she told me that rigmarole story about the fifty francs, supposed to have come from Madame Muller, and how she wrote to her Mamma in Normandy, that she had got some money, and had paid a bill with it, without showing any papers to her vigilant parent, I had smelt a rat. But I was so stupid in my blind passion, that my suspicions did not take a proper shape, until I reflected upon the letter of the 26th. of April, wherein she said that she had written to me on her return to Paris from the South, and that the letter had been probably mislaid.

I jumped to the conclusion that when she denied having received the unregistered missive, containing the fifty-franc note, she was telling a deliberate lie.

When she came to lunch with Lord Fontarcy and myself in Paris, she expected more than she got. She evidently hoped for some present from my friend. When I sent the money, torn from me by a threat, she was disgusted at the smallness of the sum, and never acknowledged it, nor wrote to me from London.

Then, when I dropped her a line five weeks afterwards, which was weak on my part, she got me invited to Sonis, and to excuse her fault, she worked the missing letter dodge again.

Two missing letters in ten months! She lied.

When I first made love to her and offered her caresses without danger of pregnancy, she answered that she would want "something else," *i.e.* money.

After our first meeting in November, 1897, when she left me at the railway station, I noticed her uneasy look. She was thinking of the five pounds she said she had lost in London, and was no doubt saying to herself: "Is he not going to give me something?"

Laugh at me, kind reader, if it so please you, but at that time I should not have dared to have offered her money.

When I write and tell her my grief at being suspected of paltry mendacity, she replies immediately that she is ready to marry me. She would have no hesitation in linking her existence to a blackguard who would lie to a woman for two sovereigns.

I could only find one excuse for her. She suffers from anæmia or chlorosis. There is evidently psychopathic deterioration, and she is a neurotic subject.

Masturbation and unnatural practices before the age of puberty have produced neurasthenia with its attendant symptoms. It is a clear case of hysteria.

No doubt she had been often received in her mother's bed, and Arvel had played with her as a mere child. The mother shut her eyes to his behaviour, finding that his passion for her daughter kept him at home.

She cooked for him, and allowed her girl to romp with him. Here is the explanation of the door of communication being taken down between the two rooms.

Raoul has also had funny little games with his sister. As children, Arvel encouraged them. Now that Lilian is a woman, he becomes jealous of the lad. They were not always well off, and pigged together in one small lodging. And Charlotte, who sleeps with both sister and brother in turn? When they are all three in London, what barriers of shame can exist between them? and, to cap all, when Papa is in England with both girls and no mother by, what goes on then?

No wonder Mamma was jealous of her daughter at the beginning of the summer.

And Lilian's lie to me is easy to explain. On the eleventh of November she is in the heighth of her flow. She has a fit of weeping, a mental and emotional sign of irritability and instability, impairing her integrity, and rendering an unbalanced individual like this morbid girl, capable of any villany while in such an emotional state.

If she were still a virgin, she would not be long before she got penetrated by the male, and perhaps the work was being done as I wrote these lines, at the end of November, 1898.

All the best and most sacred part of my love was gone. Lust alone remained. The idea of her being the mistress of her mother's old lover still excited me. I bow my head, as I confess that the thought of this loathsome *liaison* stirred up my secret erotic longings, even as the plan of the visit to a brothel might inflame a man of tranquil spirit. He knows that he is going there to choose a mercenary, common female who will give him an imitation of love for a few coins. It is disgusting, and he is well aware of it, but he goes there all the same. He is sensually excited and that is enough for him.

So I felt with regard to Lily, but I was saved, as I began to judge her, and what was better, I judged myself.

I felt strong, and proof against her wiles, or any future lies, for what harm can come to a man from wicked, womanly intrigues, when he despises himself and has no vanity for the sirens to play upon?

But I never forgot this particular lie of Lilian's. I may pardon her perhaps some day, for who and what am I, that I should refuse to forgive a neurasthenic woman? but forget it—never!

Immediately before and immediately after the advent of her "courses," her sentiment of actual desire would doubtless increase, as she had caused me to be invited just on the day when she was menstruating. She was no longer unwell on the 25th. or 27th., but had jumped to the middle of the month.

Last year, I had sent Papa and Mamma a parcel of smoked fish. On the 8th. of December 1898, I repeated my little attention, and on the 12th., the post brought me this note, which is dated the 10th., and bears the postmark of the following day.

LILIAN TO JACKY.

Sonis-sur-Marne, December 10th. 1898.

My dear M. S . . . ,

We have just received a parcel of delicious fish. Naturally, we suppose that it is you, who according to your charming custom, have had that delicate attention, for nobody but you could show himself so amiable in everything.

Mamma begs me to be her interpreter with you, so as to thank you, and charges me to tell you that she would have been very happy to have you for lunch and dinner, but she will not bore you beyond measure with the society of two women, knowing well that it is preferable that Papa should be there to receive you better. Therefore, we put off the pleasure of having you amongst us until the return of Papa.

Mamma joins me in begging you to accept the assurance of our sincere friendship,

LILIAN ARVEL.

Here is news of her during menstruation, or when she is due; a sure sign of nervous, psychic trouble, for this note came exactly a month after her last "turn."

I did not write, as it would have been uncalled for, and I heard nothing of Lilian until the morning of Boxing Day.

LILIAN TO JACKY.

Sonis-sur-Marne, December 25th. 1898.

Dear Mr. S . . . ,

We hope you have spent a Merry Christmas and that the New Year may bring with it the realisation of your wishes.

We have Monsieur and Madame Poqui, "local residents," to dine with us to-morrow, Monday night. They are very simple people. The lady is an excellent pianist. Will you come down in the afternoon to go for a walk and dine with us? There will be no ceremony or dress. "Dog clothes" allowed.

Papa brought you over some tobacco and a thousand matches.

With every good wish, believe me to remain,

Yours very sincerely,
LOUISE ARVEL.

DECEMBER 26, 1898.

According to French custom, I was bound at this festive time of year to give presents down at the Villa Lilian, where I had partaken of so many meals, so I bought for Mamma: a jar, or tea-caddy, of Dresden porcelain, with a silver-gilt screw top, filled with tea, and for Lilian: a small, ancient looking-glass, or hand mirror, with solid silver frame and handle, of the Louis XV. epoch.

I went in answer to the invitation, carrying with me the presents, which comprised both Christmas and New Year's obligations.

I was affectionately greeted by Mamma, and Lilian soon appeared, called down by her parent to receive her present.

She was very pleased to see me, I was sure of it, as I watched her narrowly. She had taken a little trouble with her toilette, and her face was thickly powdered, while she had reddened her lips. This was new to me.

She looked older and bolder, but as I greeted her, she seemed very confused and turned red and white by turns. Her hands trembled a little. She did not speak very plainly, being all of a heap, and in her excitement, she said:

"What a long time it is since we have seen you! You never honour us with your presence now."

"I come when I am invited! Here is a little friend I have brought you."

"I want no little friends!"

"But this is a friend who will always tell you the truth, after a few moments' reflection. As I know you love truth, and detest lies —here is a mirror for you! And I wish you a happy new year!"

She reciprocated my wishes, and was delighted with my gift. But she said very little, and the more gay and lively I was, the duller she became.

I went for a walk with the father. When I returned, she fetched me, pretexting that she wanted me to come and help her to get linen out for the dinner-table from Mamma's cupboard in the best bedroom, and we were alone.

I was indifferent. I kept a watch on myself and found I did not have the same desire that I formerly felt whenever I was near her, breathing the same atmosphere.

Seeing me so *nonchalant*, she began to show a little temper, and in return to some cool remark of mine, made use of a very coarse exclamation, amounting to: "I don't care a damn!"

I replied that I had nothing to say in answer to such talk, and to annoy me, and probably excite my jealousy, she told me that she had a customer who was going to give her a ring.

"A customer, eh?" I replied. "Male or female?"

"A lady, of course! Customers often give presents. Lolotte had one given to her."

"I know such things are often done in the Rue de la Paix, but then the girls who get the presents are forced to suck the ladies who are so generous, or let themselves be licked and played with."

"You are a most awful, dirty man, and very impudent to talk to me like this!"

"What does it matter? You have nothing in common with me any more."

"Of course I have not! But I have got a new sweetheart!"

She paused for a reply. None came. I laughed.

"He is an officer—a lieutenant. And through him I shall get favours for my brother. My sweet officer has given me a silver *châtelaine*."

I congratulated her warmly, and with genuine pleasure. I really did not care for anything she might say to me, true or untrue. Did she think she could arouse the jealousy of the man who had himself handed her naked body over to his friend? Yes, I suppose so. I knew there were men who did not mind infidelities as long as they were committed in their presence. Otherwise, they were jealous. I use the word advisedly, as I can find no other under my pen. I, luckily, had no such mixed feelings. Before abandoning her to Fontarcy, I had put a severe question to myself: "Will you be jealous later? If so, beware, Jacky, of the green-eyed monster."

I answered the small voice of my conscience, as follows:

"Lilian is ambitious and mercenary. She had been perverted before you knew her. Nothing can save her. So amuse yourself with her as long as she lets you, without fear or remorse. She is a perfect toy, for a debauchee like yourself. All you can ask is that she should act honestly with you."

Finding I was not to be drawn out and that nothing she said had the slightest effect on me, she got a little more calm and a trifle kinder, and before going downstairs to the dining-room to lay the cloth with the linen she had got out, I asked her to kiss me. She refused, and then, grave for the first time, I told her I should never ask her again. So she gave me her mouth.

We had some more skirmishing talk in the dining-room, and I told her that it was no use to be so nasty-tempered, as I knew she could not live without me.

Here she pretended to turn up the lamp, and hid her face from me, not answering. I now noticed that whenever she was in a quandary as to what to reply to me, she said nothing. I always interpreted her silence as a hit for me.

"Somebody has been putting me away with you? Perhaps Charlotte has been speaking against me?"

"Oh no, the poor girl!" she replied.

I found that she was redolent with a very powerful, pungent scent, in which musk predominated. In answer to whether it was any of my making, she refused to give me satisfaction, but I at last elicited that it was a mixture of "Le Jardin de Mon Curé" and "ambre." The first-named coming from an expensive house in Paris, I guessed that her new lover or lovers had given it to her.

And as I watched her in the strong light of the two large petroleum lamps lit for dinner, she seemed greatly altered. She was a trifle stouter; her glance was more audacious; she was more womanly. I had not seen her for six weeks, and I could have sworn a great change had taken place.

I went to the cellar with her father, as he was in some difficulty with a padlock below, and wanted me to help him. As I was going down, she called out in French:

"Mr. S . . . , do you like going down to the cellar?"

Now this was a bawdy slang term for the lingual caress, as applied to a woman's private parts. "Going down to her": under her petticoats, or beneath the bedclothes. A similar phrase is: "doing the little photographer," in allusion to the disappearance of an operator's head under the black cloth of the camera. Recently the young men of Paris call it, "going down to the cream shop."

I was so astonished at hearing her say this quite loudly before her stepfather, that I could only turn round and stand stock-still on the steps, looking up at her, as I gasped out: "No!"

When I returned, I asked if she knew the meaning of what she had said.

"Of course I do!"

"Who taught you that? You never learnt it from me?"

"Never mind who it was!"

"Does he do it nicely?"

"Beautifully!"

"Then you are no longer a virgin?"

She fired up at this. The blue-black cloud overspread her features, and she looked ghastly through her powder.

"You are an insolent fellow. I certainly am, just the same as ever!"

Poor Lilian, I am afraid, betrayed herself by the expression of temper that always showed in her face when I was right. I felt certain that she was no longer a maid.

"Does your Papa know the meaning of what you said?" I continued.

"If he does, he will never dream I do. That is why I said it." And to change the conversation: "Do you know I am not going to Nice this year but shall remain here alone with Granny? Pa and Ma leave on the tenth of January."

I now began to use the same tactics as she did. When embarrassed, I found it easy not to speak, and so I let the statement of her being alone at home go by, without the observations that she doubtless thought it would bring forth.

After some more desultory chaff, she asked me:

"Do you want to sit next to me at dinner?"

"No!" I replied coolly.

But she placed me next to her all the same, and I told her during the soup to put her foot on mine and keep it there. She did so, and seemed pleased, merry, and happy to be with me.

The table was a square one, and we sat at the end, where there was just room for two. She was on my right. On her right was Papa. Whenever she could, she caught hold of my hand and made motions imitating the act of masturbation on my fingers, and I tried to follow her example by copying the same caress on her palm or between her digits. I was perfectly certain that Mr. Arvel saw part of our play. She was very excited and knocked my glass over.

She could not finish all her plum-pudding, and for fear of her mother, who had made it, asked her father to change plates with her. He refused, and finally I took her plate and finished her slice, under her father's eyes. In fact, we behaved like lovers, quite openly.

During the meal, Papa got into a towering rage with the servants, and bawled out his remonstrances in a strident voice, as he half rose from his chair, as if he would leave his place to go to them.

Lilian rose too, and placing her hand on his portly paunch, said to him in English:

"Don't be silly, darling!"

I thought this rather strange, as she had never addressed him in this way before me, especially as Mamma, so jealous, I was led to believe, knew what "darling" meant. I kept this to myself for many months.

Lilian distributed little bits of holly, fixing one in my button-hole herself, to bring luck during the next year. The withered remains of my sprig are stuck in an ornament on my mantelpiece.

As I write, I look up and see it, just upon a year afterwards. I have had no luck these twelve months. So I rise and throw the darkened, prickly leaves, and discoloured stalk and berries in the fire. They curl up and turn black, even as Lily's lips, when I aroused her anger; and then they disappear, even as Lily's lips.

After everyone has their holly, I produce a branch of mistletoe, and whisper to Lilian that I am going to kiss every woman at the table. I knew this coarse, commercial traveller's joke would be properly appreciated at Sonis.

Lily flies into a towering rage again, and under her breath tells me that if I kiss her mother, she will never speak to me again in her life. Strange jealousy! I do not insist. I did not wish to kiss her old grandmother, nor her Mamma, nor the lady guest.

During dessert, when she condescends to prepare me an orange, she again tries to make me jealous, by telling me that she had been a great deal to Paris lately, and had been to some theatres. I took all she said quite coolly and told her one or two plays I had seen. Then I asked her what pieces she had witnessed, but she dropped that subject quickly. I did not believe her. Her little trick was to try and invent stories that she thought would teaze and annoy me, and above all excite my jealousy.

I felt quite a different man with her. I was entirely at my ease and watched her well, listening calmly to all her statements. I had great command over myself now, and I could divine all her deceit, and began at last to study and know her, even as I knew myself. Analysis, alas! is death to sentiment.

When the guests were gone, she asked me to go out alone with her and the dogs. Her parents consented. This was absolutely the first time that she had left the villa alone with me at night. She spoke up boldly too, as if mistress of the house. I noticed all these changes, and made up my mind to get to the bottom of all the hidden vice of the villa, if I could. This resolution excited me strangely. I felt like a kind of sensual Sherlock Holmes.

We went out, and I walked with her in the lonely, frosty roads.

"Put your arm round me. And now hold me tight. Feel my back and shoulders. Pinch my arms. Take me. Be nice and rough."

I obeyed her behests and she pressed herself against me, cooing and purring, as in the old days. But I did not have the old sensation of pleasure. I felt some slight upheaval of my innate salacious being, but not as I once did. And a great feeling of bitterness came over me, as I thought of the lie of the lost letter, and what trouble I had had to gather the money together to keep my poor invalid in comfort in Paris, and how this black, lascivious lass had treated me for the last three months.

Lilian now broke the silence, by using the little phrase with which she had so often teazed me when we were together:

"You hurt me!"

"I adore hurting you. But if I hurt you, take it in your hand yourself, and stop it if it goes in too far."

She rubbed against me like a cat, with a little mewing laugh at this recollection.

The more caressing she got, the more my bitterness increased, and I spoke out, surprised at the sound of my own voice, hoarse with suppressed rage, which she did not guess at, astonished at the courage I had to talk so plainly. A few months ago, I should never have dared to be so veracious and categorical, whatever she might have done.

Jacky. But why do you treat me so strangely? Why didn't you write to me, or try to see me. You do not love me. No power on earth can stop a woman communicating with the man she really loves. Why even your fraternal love is stronger than the feeling you have for me. What could prevent you seeing or writing to your brother?

Lilian. Oh, I don't care for him.

Jacky. Then who do you love? No one? (No answer.) It is true you never said outright to me: "I love you!"

Lilian. But the other woman has everything, and I have nothing.

Jacky. Don't talk about her, please. She is very ill. Her heart is touched. She may live perhaps only a few months, perhaps years, no one can tell. But she is always suffering and sometimes—as you want me to tell you everything—her limbs are swollen until they are as big as yonder post. Do you want any more details? (No answer.) Do you want me to leave her?

Lilian. No, it is your duty to look after her. You have had her youth, as you would have mine.

An answer was on my lips. I could have asked her what she was doing with her youth, and to whom she had given her flower. I could have demanded details, concerning the mystery of her life, and what strange feeling of misplaced pride had caused her to give way to the senile passion of her mother's old love? But I resolved not to touch upon that topic as yet. I studiously avoided alluding to Mr. Arvel any more. I had something else to tell her before that. I was sensible enough to know that I should have had no satisfaction, but on the contrary, she would have been on her guard against me, and perhaps warned Papa that I was too far-seeing. More evidence was what I wanted, and I resolved to wait for it. I did not care if what I was going to say would widen the breach between us for ever. I was quite prepared for her to tell me that all was over between us, and I behaved and spoke as a man would when seeking the rupture of a *liaison*.

JACKY. I want to say something to you. I wish to speak plainly, and you must promise me that whatever I may say you will not be offended. And after all, if you are, what matters it? I shall then only be in the same position as I was this morning. In spite of all you have ever said or written to me, you do not love me. All you care for is money; the money you think I ought to give you. Whether I have got it or not, does not matter to you. You are mercenary. I told you I had nothing but my love, and that was clearly not enough for you, and so you never answered my last letters, proving that you did not want to see me, without I gave you money.

LILIAN. You only wrote a lot of foolishness. And if I did not write, it was because you told me not to.

JACKY. That is a lie! I said: "If you do not write, I shall know you have had enough of me." Read my letters again. And even if I had said so, I am going to be fool enough to tell you what you ought to have written—if you really loved me: "I want to see you. I don't care what you have written. Come to me, for I want to see you soon. Be of good heart, for I love you."

LILIAN. But you want everything and give nothing in return. I am not mercenary.

JACKY. That is not true. You are. I'll prove it. I could not fathom your conduct up to now, but I have just done so. Listen to me. I am not intelligent—

LILIAN. Yes, you are.

JACKY. No, I am not. I am slow at seeing things, but I remember, and think them over, and put two and two together; and by analysis and deduction I find out the truth, even as I have now got the key to your mysterious conduct of the past month. I know you now. That is why I brought you a looking-glass. I can see all, as though in a mirror. Every move you make has a motive of venality.

LILIAN. (*Quite off her balance now.*) You don't understand! You have wrong ideas of me! You are strange! You are unjust!

JACKY. Then tell me what you want. (*No answer.*) You would not come to Paris where we used to go any more. Shall I take a furnished apartment at about a hundred and fifty francs a month?

LILIAN. No.

JACKY. Will you come if I promise you five louis for every visit to me in Paris?

(*Here she did a thing I had never noticed in a woman before. She turned away from me and twisted her body as if I had a whip in my hand, writhing as if I had struck her.*)

LILIAN. Oh! no! no! I don't want that!

JACKY. Then tell me what you are driving at. Marriage? That you've asked me for twice. I'm 46, going on for 47. In four or five years I shall be used up, good for nothing. You'll be in your prime, and I shall be done for, perhaps a querulous, rheumatic invalid. I am a prisoner. Can't you see that? You should be kind to a man in prison.

LILIAN. All men are free, or should make themselves so. You have no consideration for me or my feelings.

JACKY. Untrue again. Whatever I may be, I have been loyal to you. You made the first advances. I have not seduced you. You set your cap at me. Is that a lie? (*No answer.*) You know that I should never have dared to take a liberty with the daughter of the house, where I was a guest, unless I had plainly seen that she wanted me. I have long since proved to you that I desired you two years before you thought of me, and I kept my lust hidden. Had I been the traitor you try to make me out, this is what I could have done, and take heed of what I am going to say, as it applies to all men. (*I caught hold of her by the arm and tried to see her face, but she kept her features averted from my searching gaze and bent her head upon her breast. To make her hear me, I had to bend my head too.*) This will be useful to you: beware of men who promise much. Let me suppose that this summer I had promised you all kinds of things for the end of the year—marriage, money, and God knows what! Then I could have said: "Now let me have you entirely." Believing in me as you do, and though you often lie to me you know I have always been truthful to you, have I not?

LILIAN. Yes.

JACKY. Well, I could have taken your maidenhead, perhaps got you in the family way, and gone away laughing at you and all your people. (*There was no reply to this. She bent her head still more, and dragged herself away from me, writhing strangely as she spoke.*)

LILIAN. But this is my position. I am a milliner. It is supposed down here that I am carrying on this trade merely as a pleasant occupation until I get married. I have talent and taste. I know I have. Here I hardly make headway. I can't get workgirls or fresh customers. I have to give a hundred francs a month to Father for my keep. (*The last time she told me this, the sum was a hundred and fifty. And Papa had just told me in the afternoon that he had given her a purse with silver mounts and five louis in it for a Christmas present. This did not look as if she was paying for her board now, whatever she may have done up to this winter. The word "darling" would not be so lovingly applied to a grasping Papa.*) He gives Mother only a hundred francs a week to keep house. It is not enough for five mouths and all the dogs. Besides, he is a great glutton and wants everything of the finest and well served. He does not care a straw for me or my future. I know I please men generally and I could marry to-morrow if I liked (?), but I could never act the part of a loving wife to a man I did not care about. My stomach rises at the very thought. I want to go and live in Paris, and start a millinery business in a little apartment of my own. My parents won't help me. When I came to Paris this summer to you, and brought back the money you gave me, supposed to be the bad debt coming in from Madame Muller, they received me with open arms, and asked no questions. But when I returned from you and your English friends empty-handed, there was an awful row, and Mother was going herself with me to see the lady I was supposed to have spent the day with.

JACKY. Which reminds me that I thoroughly believe you had that letter of mine with the money in it, but being angry at having to worry me for it, and thinking too that it was not enough, you never acknowledged it. Later, when I asked you about it, to get out of it all, you denied having received the letter. That was a lie.

She did not seem astonished at this accusation, but looked quite dazed and replied softly: "What ugly ideas you have of me!"

JACKY. But you can't go and live alone in Paris. You might perhaps carry on a business, if you were to go home and sleep at your mother's every night, but otherwise your reputation would be damned. People would talk, and ask your *concierge*, and he would say that you were all alone, and that there was an Englishman who often came and stopped late, and so on.

LILIAN. But I know a girl who is in business all alone, and no one speaks against her. I could not go backwards and forwards, as the work must be ready for the girls at seven A.M., and sometimes they work until eleven at night. You don't or won't understand me.

JACKY. All this sounds very fantastical to me. I don't understand it at all. And I can do nothing for you in this matter. I have nothing for you. It is all too strange.

LILIAN. It is you who are strange and unjust. I am very unhappy at vegetating down here and I worry and fret when I think of you!

JACKY. (*With surprise.*) What! Poor little Lily, does she really think about me sometimes?

LILIAN. I shall be in Paris to-morrow evening at five P.M. I have to see a customer. I have many customers in Paris now.

This was a lie to teaze me and make me jealous, and to confirm my opinion, I try the following proposition:

"I will come and meet you at the station."

LILIAN. (*Quickly.*) Suppose you do? How much better off will you be? What good will that do you?

JACKY. No good at all, but I should see you for a few minutes. As you don't care about it, I will not trouble you.

We were now home again, and nothing more definite had been said. I bade good bye to her mother, who gave me a lump of pudding to take away, and Lilian and her father accompanied me to the station. Mademoiselle was very quiet, and looked embarrassed, but caressed me furtively on the way. My plain words had evidently been a surprise for her. It was half-past twelve; time for the last train.

I can see myself now standing on top of the steep steps that led to the bridge conducting to the up platform. Papa and his Lilian looking up at me, as I wave my hand to them. She gazes at me with a look of wonder and puzzled wistfulness in her large eyes. I turn away with a feeling of pity and sadness for her. She does not know me, and does not possess any delicate feelings, and the advice that her Papa will give her will never be conducive to her benefit.

I returned home with the impression that she would no longer have any wish to see me again. I was glad I had found the courage to speak plainly. How many men would have dared to tell a woman they desired anything that might cause them to lose her? I supposed she would send for me, if she wanted me, and if she did not, so much the better for me; it would be a worry the less, for considering the slight amount of sensual satisfaction I got at rare intervals, it was not worth while associating with the semi-incestuous couple.

I had to write to Papa the next day about a bitch he had ready to whelp—more in-breeding!—and to send to his *bureau*, in the Rue Vissot, a box of writing-paper for Lilian, which I had promised her as far back as the famous 11th. of November, but which I could not get from the maker. I had two boxes made. One was for my Lilian at home. It was fancy dark blue note, with the name of Lilian in the corner, embossed in white.

Mr. Arvel knew about the paper and I think he knew a little more.

I determined I would not make the slightest move towards her.

My lady readers will be very angry with me, and tell me I expected too much, having been cruel, really quite too awfully cruel, morally, to a poor little girl, whose only crime was that she wanted to get on in the world, and how could she do that, unless she got somebody to help her—lover or husband?

To which I reply that had Miss Arvel been a poor little milliner, living alone in one small room, working truly for her daily bread, depending on the caprice of her employers, I should have befriended her to the utmost, and moved heaven and earth to make her comfortable. But she had a good home, and everything she wanted, with parents, who whatever their vices, did all they could to sweeten her life, and at any rate kept her off the streets.

I was to be the victim, it seemed. What beasts men are! There was my poor dying companion at home ready to deprive herself of the common necessaries of life if I so willed it; ready to do without her doctors and medecines—unfortunately useless—if my purse was empty, and I was neglecting her, and fencing with this little viper, a living lie, and bad all through, from her tapering heels to the ends of her black tresses.

I ought to have behaved with the same dignity as the year before, when I refused to go to their Christmas dinner, for what had I gleaned? That she was certainly no longer a virgin, and had become her "Papa's" plaything. In answer to my accusation of venality, she simply replied by a description of her commercial projects. There was not a word of womanly tenderness; being so taken by surprise, she had no time to invent any story. For a year, she had the reins loose on her neck. I suddenly woke up, and blurted out my real idea of her disposition. What a surprise it must have been for her!

Like many women of strong passions I have met, she is perfectly hysterical and readily anxious to try all kinds of strange joys, but they never have any idea of truth, or what is right or wrong, or of the flight of time. Everything is muddled in their brain, and they are only fit to be enjoyed, and avoided as much as possible out of bed, or they would lead you to hell. This theory explains her strange proposals: marriage, and going into business with me, etc.

I sent her the box of pretty writing-paper on the 30th. of December. I wrote inside the lid: "1899. A Happy New Year! Never answer any letters."

The same evening, I received a New Year's card, representing a sailor in a boat, with "1899" painted on the bow. In the distance, a brig is rapidly sinking, a perfect wreck, but flying a flag, whereon is inscribed: "1898." In the boat is a large bouquet of lilies. Underneath the picture are the words: "A Good and Happy New Year!" and my charmer had enclosed her father's card, and written thereon, with her own fair hand: "With Mr., Mrs., and Miss Arvel's best wishes."

I really think they would have allowed me to set the girl up in business, or marry her, or anything, as long as there was money hanging to it. I think they would have sold her to me, or shut their eyes, if she was a rich man's mistress. Anything for money. My eyes being open, I found all this very curious and amusing.

2

Even as a botanist only wants one leaf to determine the family to which a plant belongs, even as Cuvier would reconstruct an animal of which he had only a few bones, we can deduce the knowledge of the man in whom we have remarked one single trait of character, especially if the act be a trifling one.

Indeed, for important things, people take precautions, while in trifles, they act according to their natures, without taking the trouble to dissimulate.

SCHOPENHAUER.

ERIC ARVEL TO JACKY.

Sonis-sur-Marne, January 6th. 1899.

My dear Jacky,

Many thanks for your letter, and for all the good wishes it contained. They are heartily reciprocated for you and yours.

We had a funny commencement to our New Year. At about three in the morning, we were woke by our unruly Bordeaux hound, who barked without ceasing. I went downstairs, and found that he had wanted to give us notice that the little bitch put into the warm kitchen with him in a box of her own, had given birth to a litter of puppies to the credit of Blackamoor, who is unmistakably represented. There were six puppies, three of each—one male and one female—the very image of

203

their father. The latter pup is dead, but the male remains. The five which live are white, save one—the colour and marking of your Smike—and likely as a female to make a good match for him. Will you come down and see them on Sunday, taking breakfast with us?

Yours very truly,
ERIC ARVEL.

I began the New Year under the impression that Lilian Arvel would cease all communication with me after my frankly brutal speech of Boxing night, and would naturally, or rather, unnaturally, in this case, wean her father from me, as I was more and more convinced that she was the real mistress of the house.

I suppose I must have acknowledged the New Year's card, by a polite note of seasonable greetings, as the above letter shows, and I was quite surprised to guess by what I read that I was still in Lilian's good graces. Had she not told her Pa? or did they still think I was only an old miser; or at any rate, that I had enough for what they wanted, if I would only loosen my purse strings?

It mattered very little to me now. I looked upon the couple as a pleasing puzzle for my concupiscent curiosity to play with, and I resolved to follow up my quarry. I had nothing to lose. My great love was well-nigh dead. The lust still remained, although less. But I felt towards Lilian as a man feels towards any woman who pleases him; he desires her caresses, if he can get them, and if he cannot, he carries his manly cargo into another port.

I noted the success of the in-breeding mania. Here was a daughter of my Smike, covered by her father, and accidentally (?) coupled with her own brother, who is of course by her sire. To crown all, my genial friend wants Smike, the original Adam of the lot, to "line" one of the latest products of this incited canine incest.

It could not but desire to see what fresh developments awaited me out of such strange material as was to be found at the Villa Lilian.

I got the letter on Saturday morning, the 7th. of January. I could not accede to their demand and go to them the next day, Sunday; the weekly day of recreation being sacred to my invalid companion, since I had left her bed about a year ago. And I was agreeably flattered to be invited on a Sunday to Sonis, as I knew that was the day when Lilian was entirely at liberty, the little work-shop being shut.

I made up my mind to go at once and surprise them, as I knew they would be off to Nice in a few days. So I took the train after lunch and found no one at home, but Mamma and the puppies. The latter were really very fine, and I urged the old lady to keep them, until they were two months old, and then sell them.

One looked exceptionally good, as far as I could judge from a six day pup, and I was told that Lilian had said she intended to bring it up for Jacky. They were her litter, said Ma, and if they were sold, the money would be for her. My silly heart beat a trifle faster at this. So Lilian was not vexed. She rather admired my frankness, I guessed, and I felt certain she had some sort of respect for me and was fond of me in her own peculiar, hysterical way. I resolved in future not to spare her, but to treat her coolly and tell her, as near as possible, what I thought of her. If she liked to keep on with me, she could, but I did not want to play the languishing lover.

Lilian was in Paris, at her Father's bureau, helping him with some type-writing, which had to be done before his departure. It was arranged that Adèle was to go and fetch her daughter to do some shopping that afternoon. Would I go up to Paris with her? I agreed and we went together. Mamma's conversation was all about Lilian and what a good, obedient girl she was; a splendid housewife, and domesticated. She spoke of her as if she was blest with every virtue.

I tried to draw her out about the affection of Mr. Arvel for Lily, but she refused to follow me on that delicate ground, and I was too cautious to press it. Her talk was that of an old bawd, and I imagined that they all still had designs on Jacky. Mamma was very cunning. Under a veil of hearty maternal affection, she hid a deep, designing nature, and was difficult to get at.

I let her run on, agreeing politely with all she said, and cudgel my brains as I will, I cannot remember much of her conversation. It could not have been very important.

We soon arrived at the Rue Vissot, which is a few minutes

walk from the Eastern railway station, and found Lilian and her stepfather installed in the one room, which formed his Paris *bureau.*

At the type-writer sat Lilian, bolt upright, visibly ill at her ease, and at her side, Papa, quite surprised to see me walk in with his mistress.

To my mind, they looked as if they had been indulging in an eager discussion, or making love. There was some heavily-written manuscript in front of them, but the last lines had been dry some time.

I explained my visit to Sonis, by saying that I was not free next day, having to go and fetch my bicycle, which I had left in the country, on the Orléans line, and could not lunch with them, but I had taken the liberty to run down and view the pups before the departure of the family for Nice.

I thanked Lilian in suitable terms for her offer of the pup, which I accepted, and she was very cold and over polite. I was the same. I exaggerated my tone and watched Pa and Ma. They did not seem surprised, and according to their custom, they never interfered when Lily and I were talking.

I was invited to dinner. I hesitated, and then turning suddenly round to my sulky love, I boldly said to her:

"Shall I?"

She started with surprise at being thus audaciously consulted in the presence of her father and mother, and visibly embarrassed, replied:

"Certainly—that is, if you like!"

So I accepted, and from that moment, I treated her purposely before her parents as if she was no longer the daughter of the house, but something higher—or shall we say—lower? And I was familiar in my talk with her. More like a son-in-law, but these shades of conduct were thrown away on the people of Sonis. They did not know; did not understand; and did not care. Or perchance, they pretended not to notice? But I was greatly amused and delighted to find that I had regained such complete mastery over my own passion.

Lily and her mother went off to make their purchases, and it was arranged that I should pass the afternoon with Papa, and go down to Sonis with him at dinner-time.

He rapidly finished his work and to pass the time, began to show me some private photographs. My readers will guess what they were.

"You see I keep them carefully locked up. I am so frightened lest Lilian might see them."

I chuckled inwardly at this ever-recurring phrase. It was perfectly useless and in very bad taste to always try and impress upon me that she was so innocent and had never seen anything obscene. She was in her twenty-third year now, it must be remembered. It was unnecessary, I take it, to mention a daughter's name, while showing obscene photographs or books. Is it not perfectly well understood that a father, tutor, stepfather, or guardian would keep such things out of the sight and reach of young people? Why this exaggerated declaration of virtue? Then he got out a framed photograph of a Japanese beauty, and told me for the third or fourth time all about her. The story was briefly that when in Japan, he had a native girl on hire as his mistress. Here she was photographed with him. Again he told me how careful he was to hide and lock up this little picture, but when he spoke of his wife finding it, I saw he was frightened of her. She was truly, madly jealous, or had made him believe so.

I think I pitied the poor old chap a little that day. He was a slave to all his grosser passions. The soft blandishments of Lily and the excesses of the table—these were his delights. The two women had got him firmly fixed between them.

I felt certain, as he unrolled the very ordinary tale of his Japanese amours, that Lily had heard it too from his lips. He told the same stories always over and over again, and knew nothing of the world, as it moved daily. His brain had stopped ten years ago, and in a garrulous, purposeless way, he would talk to me of people we had known about that time, and so will you and I, reader; so will we babble on, when we get to live over threescore, and continue to indulge in wine, women, alcohol, and tobacco, until we are *sans* eyes, *sans* teeth, *sans* penis, *sans* everything.

We went to the station eventually, having first locked up the photographs, with great fuss and luxury of precaution, and got into a wrong train, which took us right on to Meaux. It was Papa's fault, and he was in a fearful funk. I noticed curiously enough that he dared not stop out after a certain hour, and he was dreadfully exercised lest the ladies should have arrived before us. Luckily, we caught a train back quickly enough, and there was not much time lost. We raced to the house, as fast as Papa could shuffle, for I noticed that during the repose of the winter, the pleasures of gastronomy had rendered him quite obese, and to his gasping relief, found that the entrancing fascination of the Louvre and the Bon Marché had made the ladies late. We were home first, but they soon arrived.

Lily did not come near me. I stopped with Pa; he showed me a small smoker's table, garnished with tobacco jar, ash-tray, cigarcutter, etc., that his two women had bought for him. He added that he hated receiving presents from them. He told me he had given Lily a purse with money in it, but he did not speak of any gift he had made to his wife. He took me upstairs to wash my hands. The bedrooms were no longer on the first floor.

It was too cold, I was told, and the second story was now used nightly, as there were three rooms, opening one into the other. The doors were left open, it appears, and one portable stove kept them all warm. One bedroom was occupied by Pa and Ma, another by Lilian, and the third by Granny, who was installed there, ready to take charge of the house when Mr. and Mrs. Arvel had left for the Riviera.

He pointed to one bed and I saw an expression in his face and a light in his eye that I had never seen before, as he said to me, with a devilish grin, and his mouth full of saliva:

"That's where Scraggy sleeps!"

And he stroked the pillow with an affectionate gesture of his stubby, nailless fingers. Then he showed me a suit of pyjamas on his bed, and told me that Lilian had made them for him.

The dinner passed off without notable incidents, but afterwards Lilian calmly asked me to go out with her and the dogs, in the dark, leaving Pa and Ma at home. It seemed to be a recognised thing now, that I could walk out with her at night. No doubt Mamma knew I could not hurt her now.

I must confess, with due shame, that I have no particular recollection of our chat, although it ought to have been important enough after what had passed at our last meeting.

My impression is that I waited to hear Lilian complain of having been accused of lying venality by me, and that she never alluded to anything, but seemed to want me to forget everything and start afresh. So I was bound to think that I had guessed aright; should I be forced to despise her now?

All I can find in my scribbling diary is one word: "Reconciliation." So we must have patched up a peace somehow or the other. Lily went so far as to repeat that she had tried to forget me and could not. She also said that the old couple, who had dined with us on the 26th. of December, had put me down as her fiancé. This was certainly one of Lily's little crammers to see what I would say, and she had placed her own thoughts, words, and ideas in the mouths of these strangers.

"I suppose, one day when I get down here, I shall be introduced to some nice young man, and Mamma will say: 'Mr. S . . . , allow me,—Mr. So-and-so,—Lilian's betrothed!' "

"Oh! that will never happen," she exclaimed, adding a peculiar half-sigh, half-groan, that I was fated to hear twice more later on, and which seemed to be the strongest expression of anguish to which she could give vent.

She told me that she was not going to Nice. That was no lie, at all events, and she said she would try and manage to see me while she was alone at the villa with her Granny. She was very impressive in informing me that she could not get to Paris without good and valid reasons, but I did not grumble about that. I knew she could do pretty much as she liked. I let her chatter as she chose, and was careful not to commit myself in any way. She could have no suspicion of what I thought. I almost lost my presence of mind, however, when she told me that she had broken off the marriage between Charlotte and Raoul. She said that they did not meet any more. How she managed it, she would not tell. I dared not press the point, but the sister slept with the lad's mistress and they were still friends, but Lolotte was not to see Adèle's son any more. What did it all mean? I jumped to the conclusion that Papa was now fairly ensconced in Lilian's heart and bed, and together they had jockeyed Raoul's sweetheart. Mamma spoke about the rupture of the marriage and hinted that Charlotte had too many lovers. Wicked Lily had betrayed her brother's betrothed, but was artful enough to still be friends with her. No wonder she called Charlotte a little goose.

Lilian was not well. She looked pale, worn, and worried. A doctor had been consulted, and she was taking cod-liver oil. I had guessed aright about her anæmia in November, but I held my tongue now, and did not recur to her fit of blind rage, when I had dared to say she was poor-blooded. I would not quarrel any more with her.

Lilian kissed me rapturously and promised to write to me soon.

"Not at all," I answered, "I want to see you as soon as possible."

"No, no; you must wait."

"Then you don't love me. All right, darling, let all be over between us."

"Oh! no, do not say that," and she showed great concern and alarm, as she always did when I spoke of a real farewell.

"When do your parents leave?" I asked.

"On Tuesday, the tenth."

"Then I shall take the nine o'clock train on Tuesday night. You can bring the dogs out at a quarter past nine, and I'll walk about the Avenue de la Gare up to the Place d'Armes, until I see you."

"Perhaps I'll come and perhaps I shan't."

"I'll bring you a pretty book I want you to read. It is all about cruelty, with pictures."

"Oh! I should like that!"

"And it is in French too. I have never lent you a French book yet. Now perhaps, you will come out to get the volume, which is quite decent and proper, and meant for young girls at school."

She laughed, and gave me her luscious mouth, as we finished our little walk. I wished her parents: bon voyage, and promised to keep Papa supplied with papers during his absence. Mamma said Lilian had such a lot of work to do that she could not go with them, which was a great pity.

I did not believe Mamma. They were leaving Lilian at home for a purpose. What was it? Was it for me? I began to think I was not of much importance. She had other lovers—real ones—who she did not want to stay away from, for interested motives. Or did Mamma, now knowing Lilian was on an equality with her, refuse to travel in her company? These were the little mysteries I never was able to solve, with many more, which I hope will not bother the reader as much as they did me. I rather liked getting on the track of this series of traps and pitfalls. I felt my sense of penetration growing very acute, and was as pleased as the schoolboy who deciphers a rebus, knowing that the year before, I had been totally unable to reason as I could then.

JANUARY 10, 1899.

I popped the first volume of the original edition of *Justine et Juliette* (by the notorious Marquis de Sade, in 10 parts, with 101 engravings,) in my pocket, and at 9 P.M., well wrapped up, with a good cigar in my mouth, I took the train to Sonis. I was scarcely out of the station when I met my charmer, who I noticed, without saying anything, had freshened herself up, and put on a very nice hat and cloak.

Lily began her old trick of trying to teaze me by asking me ironically why I took the trouble to come down and leave my warm fireside. She also made a fuss when I wished to kiss her. So I retorted, and told her that I found she lacked all true feminine tenderness and pleasing politeness.

"I do not mean the ordinary politeness of society, which is a kind of light varnish which cracks and peels off at the slightest scratch, but true politeness of the heart; that which is to be found in worldly manifestations, as well as in sentiment; and in sensual affairs, just the same as in social associations."

Lilian said I was too serious.

"And I find you are not serious enough. You must not think I only want your body. I am very fond of you; fonder than you think. I can have lots of women's bodies. I want something more, and that is why I am here. But I shall not get what I desire at

Sonis. Here I find only falsity, trickery and little villanies. And you are such an awful liar too!"

"I'll not have you call me a liar. I am not a liar!"

I begged her pardon ironically and asked her how she had got on with her lovers during the last three months.

"I have no lovers," she answered snappishly, "I have had a letter from Gaston and that's all."

"What did he say?"

"Oh! a lot of filth," she replied contemptuously.

"Do you mean to tell me that you have been twelve weeks without spending?"

There was no answer.

"I really thought you had somebody who had cut me out. Let me see, there's the lieutenant. And you have been all this time without a man's member to play with?"

"No, I haven't!" She was getting angry now.

"How many have you had?"

"Fifteen!" she exclaimed, in a nervous, staccato manner. The words came through her teeth, when she was in a passion, as if clicking automatically from a talking machine.

"A good many! And I had hoped to see you married shortly. I should have liked to have left you with a good husband."

"Who would have me without a dowry? And then we never see anybody down here. You are the only person we invite. But I have told you I could not play a part, or imitate with a man the love I did not feel."

"You want a man who you could love as you do your Papa. Oh! not me—Mr. Arvel, I mean." I paused for a reply. None came. "You do love him. How beautifully you made him that suit of flannel pyjamas. Did you really cut it out yourself?"

"Of course I did."

"You are very clever. You can make dresses, hats, and cook. I noticed how well the trousers were made. They were really trousers and not loose pyjamas. Did you take the measure of the trousers yourself?" She was silent. "How nice! I wish you would do that for me. I should like to feel your fingers fumbling with the tape between my legs."

"You are always the same; quite obscene."

"True, I am an obscene devil. I am a sadistic wretch. A disciple of the Marquis de Sade, whose masterpiece I am going to lend you to read. I have brought you the first volume. I glory in my shame, because women love us; we are dirty beasts, expert in every vile caress. We leave aside all mawkish sentiments. No birds, and flowers, and soft music with us. Am I not right, my darling daughter? Answer me, my child!"

"I'll not have you call me your daughter, nor your child. I do not like those terms of affection now. And I will not be your slave either. All that is over. I won't call you Papa any more!"

She said this rapidly and with genuine accents of rage. I drew my own inference from this strange outburst. Of late Papa had been using these words to her, and in my mouth they jarred on her nerves.

A strange thrill stirred me. I had frequently told her to seduce Arvel, so as to be mistress of the house, and I felt sure the thing was always in the mind of the stepfather. She had laughed at my vile imagination, as she called it. Had I been the indirect means of this guilty understanding? Had I driven her into his arms, only to lose her myself through my own bad advice? If so, I deserved my fate.

But no, the true reason why I had often persuaded her to give way to him, was because I always saw that it was bound to happen, even if the act had not been really consummated during the past winter; during the long evenings beneath the lamp, when Mamma had gone up to bed early, soon after dinner, leaving Pa and Lilian alone together. To sum up: I should think he had always had his hands under her petticoats, more or less, from childhood and her final fall would be insensible.

"I'll be your mistress, but not your slave, nor your daughter," she continued.

"Whatever you like, Lily, as long as you tell me that you love me. You do love me, do you not?"

"Of course I do!"

"Then say so. You have never said to me: 'I love you!' "

"I love you! I love you! I love you!" She said this with the same nervous clenching of the teeth. It was an effort for her, under a feeling of annoyance, to be forced to utter these words which she did not feel.

Decidedly, she did not care for me, and she started off once more to talk about her millinery business and how she wished to open in Paris. Each time I met her and heard her speak, I noticed more and more the emptiness of her heart. I allowed her to continue her discourse unchecked, and she always returned to a series of vague complaints, when she would make out that we could be much happier and see each other more often, if I could help her by finding a small capital. The more she asked, the more quiet and calm I became. I pointed out the folly of her projects. I also added that I had no money and without beating about the bush, informed her that I was heavily in debt as well.

"Really now? You have debts? Dear me!" she exclaimed, with surprise. "How unlucky we both are! And I am not at all well. Papa has made me some quinine wine, as I have been ordered it."

I asked her how he did it. She informed me that he put sulfate of quinine in sherry. I ventured to disagree with this formula, and told her that I thought the bark properly macerated in old Malaga would be better and she asked me to make some for her. I promised I would. She thanked me, and we talked about books. She alluded to "Flossie" which I had lent her in the summer, and believed it was incredible that a girl of fifteen, such as Flossie was, should have experienced pleasure at her age, in using her maiden mouth to quench men's lusts. And an English girl too! that was quite impossible.

I did not dispute, although I knew from experience that directly the crisis of puberty is past, a girl is ready for anything, if of warm temperament.

I asked her if Raoul was much cut up about breaking off his engagement. She answered in the negative and told me that he had written to her, and had finished up his letter by saying: "I kiss your sweet lips!"

"I sent it to Papa to let him see what Raoul had written to me," Lilian went on to say, "and told him not to let Mamma know. And of course, the first thing he did, was to translate this compliment to her and we have both got into an awful row. Papa is vexed with Raoul, and Ma is in a temper with me."

Now I could see more than ever why Papa was jealous of his stepson. Always shadowy signs of incest with Lily; and half-truths!

I verified the story of the purse with a fiver in it, given by Papa. I had greatly changed my estimate of Lily's veracity. I now did not believe one single word she might say.

I pressed her to come to me in Paris. She swore she could not get out. Granny had orders to telegraph to Nice, if she absented herself without a plausible excuse! This was an awful lie. She did not wish to get into bed with me. Had she wanted me, she would have arranged to meet me somewhere or somehow. Or more likely she was expecting me to offer her money. I did not push the point. What was the use? I had no money to spare, and if I had I do not think I should have given it. Any fool can buy women.

Without me asking her, she told me that it was not possible to get me into the house at night, as Granny and her slept in two rooms, with the doors open, so as to let the heat of the stove into both, and she would try and arrange something else for me, if she could. "But there is the dining-room," I asked. "The stove is perpetually alight in it?"

By this time we had reached the house and stood beneath a gas-lamp in front of the gate. Lilian put on an air of innocent candour, and said slowly, like a child repeating something learnt by heart:

"What can we do in a dining-room?"

"Nothing," I answered, roughly.

My face must have betrayed me. In my disgust, I forgot myself, and lost all control over my features. My mask dropped off. She kissed me warmly.

"You are all topsy-turvy. What is the matter with you?"

I did not answer.

"Well, good night," said Lilian.

"Good night, and adieu!" I angrily replied, turning on my heel and striding off to the station.

I was very vexed at the moment. But it soon wore off, as I could see through her so well. She was very coquettish and wicked, but shallow and superficial. Her great trick was to "work up" her man by all kinds of artifices and carefully watch the effect produced on him. If she found she had gone too far, she would come back with a kiss and a caress, until the next manœuvre, and so on *ad libitum*, as long as the amorous male would stand it. Is this the way cunning courtesans wheedle money out of men? Do their votaries offer gold to induce the intriguing female to put an end to their torment? I suppose so. It simply disgusted me. I had no experience with wicked women. And I found out why. I had never stopped long enough with a thoroughly bad, scheming woman. When such a one would start her tricks, I saw through her, and was off and away. Why did I have so much patience with my black magpie, Lilian? I cannot tell. I was never her dupe long, if ever I was at all. I suppose I had felt a great lust for her ever since four years ago, and this would take a little while to get out of the system. But I was gradually sickening. She was always begging. I must have been mad up to then. I wanted to be loved for myself alone, at the age of 47. Perhaps I was like a woman and my change of life was acting on my brain? I had only been the half-lover of a quarter-virgin, so there was nothing much to regret. After all, it was better that she should have treated me badly for the last two or three months. A few words of tenderness, one leap of her heart, if she possessed one, towards mine, and I should have continued to live in the belief of her love for me.

You have nothing to complain of, Jacky, I soliloquised, you have had a year's amusement with this trifling intrigue. Twelve months illusion: is not that enormous in the ordinary sadness of life?

And so saying, I put out my lamp and settled to sleep.

LILIAN TO JACKY.

(No date or place.) Received January 12th. 1899.

Dear naughty darling,

Here is what I wish to propose to you: if next Sunday you have nothing better to do, you can come here directly after lunch, under the pretext of asking me for one of the little dogs and you can choose it. We can then go and have a nice walk, both of us, or stay at home, as you choose, and you shall stop and have tea with your

LILY

JACKY TO LILIAN.

Paris, January 12, 1899.

Little Lily,

Your proposal is adorable; to pass a whole afternoon with you would be true happiness for me. And then I feel that I possess your thoughts and I see that you try to please me. I am very grateful.

Unfortunately, we do not live like characters in a novel and have to go through life in quite another way. We must show that we possess common sense and a practical spirit.

What would your parents say when they heard that I visited their house while they were absent and that I had passed several hours with you?

Reflect a little, and you will understand, I am sure, without wanting me to explain myself more fully.

If you desire more ample explanations on this subject, I am quite at your disposal, without any hidden thoughts, quite frankly, and in platonic fashion. To prove my good faith, I will take the nine o'clock train any evening you may point out, Friday, Saturday, or following days, no matter how the weather is, and I will only stop with you the necessary time to demonstrate to you the impossibility of your amiable project.

To sum up: visiting Mademoiselle alone with her Grandmother, in the absence of her parents, would be rude and incorrect, calculated to make them uneasy, and sufficing to close their house against me for ever.

Don't be wicked, jealous, nor in a temper.

Yours always, even in spite of yourself,

JACKY.

LILIAN TO JACKY.

(No date or place.) Received January 13th. 1899.

Having been brought up like an English girl, I am consequently more practical than romantic, and if I proposed to you to come here Sunday, under the pretext that I gave you, it is only after having carefully reflected on the consequences, and knowing all the ideas that my parents might form on that head. I was absolutely convinced of the solidity of my proposal.

You will not profit by my good intentions in your favour? Very well then—do as you like.

You cannot, however, prevent me from remarking that you are never free for me on a Sunday. You probably have to occupy yourself with your bicycle, as on Sunday last.

I am not wicked, nor jealous, nor out of temper. I only note simple facts.

(Unsigned.)

JACKY TO LILIAN.

Paris, Saturday, January 14th. 1899.

Dear Lily,

All last night and this morning I have reflected on the letter received yesterday evening. I can only repeat that I feel sincere gratitude for your good intention which delights me, but your starting-point is false. The more I think about it, the less I understand.

The aversion I have for the exchange of sour letters and which I have often expressed to you, grows stronger than ever, therefore I will be truly brief.

Since nearly three months, I suffer, I think, as much as a man can possibly suffer morally.

A new subject of discord now springs up between us.

This is atrocious!

JACKY.

She did not write, and I am ashamed to say that two days afterwards, I sent her the following letter:

JACKY TO LILIAN.

Paris, January 16, 1899.

My dear Lily,

You are vexed with me because I think that I ought not to enter your father's house when he is away. Do you not understand that?

I think that if I saw you I should find arguments to convince you, for the last letter that you wrote proves that you are very intelligent.

I have an immense desire to see you. It is a great joy for me to be at your side.

That is why I hasten to send you these few lines to tell you that I shall come to Sonis to-morrow, Tuesday night, by the nine o'clock train, and I will stroll about until ten.

If you can't or won't see me, you need but send me a wire, as follows: "Do not come."

I could have waited a few days before writing to you, but I do not wish you to believe me capable of sulking, or of watching to see who will come round first. Those are little, vulgar, stupid, mean artifices which are repugnant to me.

I love you and would like to see you to tell you so, and force you to say to me, your lips against mine, like the other night: "I love you, I love you, I love you!"

I come to you loyally, sincerely and frankly, without beating about the bush; without chicanery; ready to answer all your objections and to plead my cause with you, without lying, showing myself to you as I am. So much the worse for me if you will no longer love me. I shall always love you, good or bad, dead or alive, even if I may be forced to think no more of you as a mistress.

At all hazards, I shall put the second volume of that little book for young people in my pocket. If you do not want it, you will return me the first volume and all will be at an end.

Do not fear that you will meet a silly, whining lover, groaning, and scolding. To-morrow evening you will simply see your dirty Papa, and quickly you will offer him your pretty mouth, saying: "Good evening, Jacky!"

And we will begin to quarrel if you will.

But I want to see you.

JACKY.

A few months ago, I should have written, like the saucy wretch that I am: "Lily, don't forget to tie on your little pink ribbon." Now I no longer ask for anything.

JANUARY 17, 1899.

Lilian had invited me openly to spend Sunday with her in the absence of her parents. I refuse and she is vexed with me. What is the reason of this seeming imprudence? She is hand in glove with her Papa, and is now his mistress. Or she wishes to compromise us both. They must all have had a very mean idea of my intelligence to think I could not see through them.

These were my reflexions, as full of curiosity, a curiosity which bid fair to conquer my lust, I took the train after dinner. It was a dull and showery night, and with the fear of rheumatism still upon me, I put on my box-cloth overcoat and a pair of thick shooting-boots.

Lilian was already out on the warpath, received me as usual with tantalizing remarks, and showed great jealousy. My refusal to pass Sunday with her touched her to the quick, and I was obliged to tell her that I always spent the weekly day of rest with my poor invalid mistress. She retorted that I did not love her much, or else I would not mind a quarrel at my home for her sake. I tried to make her more reasonable, but all my trouble was in vain. I allowed that she should feel some pain at my apparent devotion to my mistress, although I made her understand that the doctors forbade her all excitement or worry, but I could not see why she should draw me on to behave so indelicately towards her stepfather. Here I watched her closely, as I said:

"I will not come openly to the villa, when the master of the house is away. I have behaved dishonestly enough as it is. Do you think it is the action of an honourable man to carry on an intrigue with the daughter of the house where he has been received with such confidence?"

I paused for a reply. None came. I continued:

"If your Papa was to know what I have done with you, he would be justified in kicking me all round Sonis, and I should have nothing to say."

She never answered me, and my heart leapt in my breast as I now knew perfectly well that Pa, Ma and Lilian formed an infamous Trinity of which I was to be a victim.

My home thrust caused her to hurriedly change the subject, and she talked of "Justine." She had read the first volume and I had the second in my pocket for her. It had created a great impression on her. The parts that pleased her most were those where there were men and women together.

"Oh! that book!" she exclaimed, "I have not slept for reading it. I roll about my bed, and bite my pillow, and I am forced to relieve myself with my finger. I could not help it. And then it is in French too. The other books I have of you are in English. I will return them to you to-night. This is the first French one I have read. I am going to be very good to you to-night. I will take you into the house. I have arranged with Granny by telling her that I am going to sit up and write some letters. She knows I received one from Papa to-day. By the way, I want you to do something for me in Paris. I do not want to go up to-morrow, as I have such a lot of work. I have got a lot of commissions from Papa."

And she drew out a type-written letter. I stepped back, out of delicacy, but she said I might take the letter, and read it, and keep it to do all that he requested. I did so, and at that moment had no idea of writing our story, or I should have copied the conclusion of the paternal missive. In guarded terms, Papa alluded to her health and begged her to take great care of herself. He said that she could count upon his great affection, and wished her to think of him as he was always thinking of her bodily health and her future welfare. It was not the letter of a guardian, but that of a lover.

Then we had our usual little quarrels. I was always reproaching her for her caprices and hard-heartedness, and she was ever jealous of my mistress, and hinted that I ought to work harder and try and make some money.

Then she would press closer to me, and make me kiss her and feel her all over, outside her clothes. I had a gold pin in my scarf, and as our conversation touched upon the pleasures of cruelty, I amused myself by slightly pricking her arms and thighs, as the sharp point was strong enough to penetrate her clothes, and she did not seem at all averse to this insane diversion.

I asked her why she was always so wicked to me in winter time. Last year she would hardly see me, and now again it was the same. I compared her to a dormouse, but she could only laugh, and as usual I had no satisfaction. I ventured to say that perhaps she had some animosity towards me for having given her over to Lord Fontarcy. But she scouted the idea and said she had enjoyed herself enormously.

I wanted to know her impression while being flagellated and sodomised by my finger before witnesses.

"I had a feeling of disgust to think that Clara was there, looking at me. I would do anything you might possibly think of with men, but I loathe women. I would not mind being alone with ten men."

"I love to degrade and humiliate you for my sensual pleasure, and there are lots of things I should like to do to you and with you. But I would not exercise real cruelty. I should always tell you beforehand what I was going to do, and if approved of by you, if you think you would like it, we could try it."

"I'll never come with you again if there are to be women present."

"Then if I asked you to join me alone with another woman?"

"I could not. I should refuse. I should be sick, or have a nervous attack. I hate women. If you and your friend want to amuse yourselves with women, don't invite me, but get some other girl that day."

"I will never ask you to meet a woman, as I quite understand that tastes differ. I, too, find no pleasure with my own sex, but I can quite understand that other men might."

"You are tolerant and are large-minded. I like you for that. I should be very pleased to meet Fontarcy again with you, but without Clara. It would be beautiful to be alone with you two. He likes me too."

"How do you know? You never saw his member. It is likely enough he never got an erection with you."

"Yes, he did. When I was being sucked, I saw it sticking out. It was stiff against my leg."

"That was while he was licking you."

"He never licked me. You did. But I saw his big, stiff machine."

Here were two hallucinations, or falsehoods. My readers will remember that Lord Fontarcy had produced her orgasm with his tongue, and not I, and I knew perfectly well that he did not open his trousers that day. I have since submitted this to him, and he agrees that Lily was mistaken. I take it that she was thinking of someone else.

"I am pleased you like all my mad imaginations," said I to Lily. "When Lord Fontarcy returns to Paris, if you could get out, no doubt he would be delighted to see you. I don't know anybody else well enough to offer you, as it is a ticklish thing to propose. All men do not understand such things. There is no danger with my friend. He lives in England and does not even know your name."

I asked her why she had never looked him up in London and she replied that she was frightened of her brother. She said she kept him in entire ignorance.

"And now," whispered Lily, nestling up to me, "tell me something nice and horrible, that you would like to do to me."

"I should like to have you naked—"

"Always naked!" she interrupted, with a sneer.

"Yes, for this diversion, most certainly, and then strap a broad leather belt round your loins as tight as you could bear it, so that you would not only be very uncomfortable, but I should enjoy the sight of your small pulled-in waist, and your bottom which would swell out bigger than ever in consequence."

She kissed me most voluptuously and asked me for some more "dreams" of mine.

"You are my slave, and you stand upright in front of me, not necessarily naked this time. Your legs are close together and with the same belt, I strap your thighs together, just above the knee, as tightly as I can. Then I would force my hand through your thighs just under your pussy, from the front, and then from behind, under your bottom, and the brutal passage of my hand would hurt you a little, but you would have pleasure, as I would tickle your slit. I should enjoy the delight of power and domination, without speaking of the soft contact of your skin, and the captivating manner in which my hand would be imprisoned between your thighs. And you would be ashamed to be thus exposed and humiliated. The combination of two such opposite sensations would be very pleasant indeed."

"Oh, I should like that!"

"I promise you we will do it. You always did enjoy being badly treated by me."

"Oh! I like all you do!"

"There are men who enjoy being ill-treated too."

"Yes, I know. One of my best customers, who lives down here, Madame Rosenblatt, married to a German Jew, has got a lover, as her husband don't give her enough money for her dress. Her friend possesses that mania. He has got a German grammar and studies it. He is about 40 years of age. He has a small apartment in Paris and he goes there first and begins to learn his lessons. Madame Rosenblatt soon appears and pretends to be in an awful passion with him. She boxes his ears, and makes him kneel down and say his verbs. Whether he knows them or not, he has to take down his breeches, and she beats him well. After that, he gets into bed with her and enjoys her. His birthday is soon due, and his mistress is going to give him a present: a little silk cushion for him to kneel on. I am making it and she is paying me well for it."

"Has she never asked you to see her pupil, or have you never evinced any curiosity to view this strange correction?"

"Oh, no! But she wanted me to go with her one day. She told me he would like to be whipped and humiliated in front of a strange young woman, but I shall not go. I would not do such a thing."

I am obliged to confess that this story excited me very much, and although I had never allowed a woman to domineer over me as yet, I almost thought that I should have no objection to play the unruly pupil, if the governess pleased me, just to see how it felt.

I held strong suspicions that Lily had seen this pupil-lover, and that the cushion would be paid for by the man himself.

I still continued to be as dumb as a fish, or I should never have heard or learnt anything.

According to Lily's calculations, Granny and the servant were now in bed and fast asleep, and it was safe for me to follow her into the house, I did so, stepping cautiously on the grass, so as not to let my footsteps be heard on the gravel, as I had done in August. It was raining hard. A pace or two to the right, and I was in the dark room, and waited there while Lily went to see if the coast was clear. She soon returned and taking me by the hand, guided me into the warm dining-room, where we sat down on a little sofa under the window.

I took her in my arms and embraced her with great tenderness, beginning to put my hand under her clothes. She repulsed me, and told me that she did not see why she should give way to me, as I showed no desire to do anything whatsoever to content her.

"When you try to please me you shall have all you want, but until then: nothing, nothing, nothing!"

I immediately withdrew my hand from her calves—she had not let me get any higher—and releasing her waist as well, I drew myself entirely away from her.

"I guess what you are up to. These are the tantalizing tricks of a coquette. Possibly Madame Rosenblatt"—I did not dare say Papa and Mamma—"has given you advice how to behave with me. I can hear her saying to you: 'Never give way to men too readily, or they will think nothing of you. Hold the carrot in front of the donkey's nose, but don't let the animal touch it until he obeys you. Keep the chaps away from you and they will run after you all the more!' I understand all your ways."

And I got up as if to go.

"Come and sit down by me," she said, as she looked at me strangely, with a wondering look in her eyes, astonished at being read so easily, "and I'll be good to you. You know I like you so much, that really I don't know what I am about when you are near me."

And she threw herself upon me, and kissed me as she had never kissed me before, begging me to suck her lips and tongue, and caress her in return.

She ruthlessly thrust my fumbling fingers from her, and told me she was "unwell." Her monthly courses were now on.

I at once made a little mental calculation. She had begun her menstruation on the 11th. of November, that was the last date I had been able to note and she was therefore due again on the 12th. of December, or thereabouts. Here we were at the 17th. of January. Why so late? Now I understood Papa's letter regarding her health. No doubt there was the fear of being in the family way. Had he drugged her before his departure? Or was the old witch of a grandmother dosing her with her secret decoctions of herbs, so as to bring on her tardy "menses"? Is that why she is friends with me again? If she found herself really *enceinte*, did she intend to give way to me entirely, and declare all her trouble as of my making? There was some deep scheme, which I never got to the bottom of.

She took me in her arms and pillowed my head on her breast, as she sat at the end of the sofa, and her audacious hand pressed my stiff dagger outside my trousers. She pinched it.

"Do I hurt you, Jacky?"

"No!"

"And now," pressing it with all her strength.

"No! I like that!"

"It does hurt, but you won't say so. I'll try again," and she gripped the acorn top through the cloth.

"Ah! now you hurt me! But I like the pain coming from you, Lily!"

It was cosy in the pretty little room, and I was very comfortable in Lily's embrace! my head almost underneath her arm; my delighted nostrils enjoying the odour of her armpits; the true coppery, wild-beast fragrance of a brunette, who, during her menstrual period, puts no water on her body.

She now began to undo my trousers. I put out my hand to help her.

"No! Let me do it. I like to arrange it my way."

She unbuttoned the breeches, and drew out the little gentleman, who was as pleased as Punch to show himself and stood up bravely.

"Ah! here is my *poupée!* I love to see it and play with it! Are you happy, Jacky?"

"Yes, Lilian. I am so pleased to be caressed by you. I like you to see me thus, all shamelessly exposed to your gaze. Kiss me! Now look at it! Keep your eyes on it!"

She gently moved her hand up and down the shaft. She was more expert than when she had masturbated me in August.

"I want to see more of you," she said, and I opened my trousers as fully as I could, letting them down a little, and pulling out the testicles. These she caressed as well and passed her hand even lower down, tickling the neutral zone between the scrotum and the fundament. And then she closed her hand, manipulated me furiously for a few seconds, and when I moved convulsively, feeling that I was about to spend, she suddenly stopped.

"Why do you cease, darling?"

"I don't want to make you enjoy too soon. I am trying to make the pleasure last as long as I can!"

Lily had been taking lessons, I saw plainly.

"Well, do what you like with me. But don't hurt me. Would you like to hurt me? Or violate me, perhaps?"

"Oh no, dearest."

"I should like to be quite naked with you, all dressed as you are!"

She moulded my testicles, never taking her eyes from my weapon, and then once more firmly grasped it with her left hand, supporting me against her breast with her right arm.

For a little while longer, she continued her play, shaking it violently in her soft hand, and gradually going slower until her fingers became motionless. A wee caress of the wrinkled purse, an exploration of the perineum, and then back to the principal actor, who, no longer able to restrain himself, burst in delicious agony and sent a gush of semen on to my belly, followed by several thick clots, much to Lily's delight, as I distinctly felt a thrill run through her frame, the unmistakable shudder of voluptuous pleasure, that I knew so well.

"Why! You've come too, Lily!" I exclaimed, in delighted rapture, as soon as I regained my senses.

"Yes! How do you know?"

"I felt you spend!"

She was still under the influence of the feeling the onanistic play had excited in her, and she threw herself furiously upon me, and taking my head in her hands, thrust her mad tongue down my throat, and sucked my lips until she took my breath away.

She was a real woman at that moment of her life, inasmuch as she adored the male, with the true evidence of the force of his desire pointing to heaven and would have let a man do anything to her, and she would have done anything to his body.

She rose and fetched a clean dish-cloth from the adjoining kitchen, as she said she did not dare go upstairs to get a towel. She carefully wiped away all traces of the recent spermatic eruption, and we settled down for a talk, after she had got me some brandy and water.

She looked over the second volume of "Justine," and enjoyed the pictures. A little packet was ready for me, containing the first volume, and also "Flossie," "The Yellow Room," "Colonel Spanker's Lecture," "The Horn Book," and "The Convent School."

And then we spoke of marriage, and I talked about her virginity, narrowly watching her expressive face the while. I told her that our voluptuous games were all very well in their way, but if I lived beneath the same roof with her for a few days, I should most surely have complete connection.

"Indeed," I added, "you Lily would ask me yourself to make you a woman."

I saw again the troubled, puzzled look come into her eyes; there was an expression of pain in her face and she leant her cheek on her clenched hand, which was tightly clasped.

"Should I? Tell me more, Jacky. Talk to me. I like to hear you."

I told her how delicious the nuptial tie must be, when both man and wife really love each other, when there is no disgust, no repugnance. On the other hand, how horrible for a girl to be thrown into the arms of a brutal male, who violates her on the first night, and perhaps makes her hate the approach of a man ever afterwards.

"Yes, that must be horrible!"

A change came over her. She looked angry, worried, pained, and disgusted, and seemed full of regret. A confession was trembling on her lips. She looked at me with melting eyes, and then they flashed fire. As I spoke, she seemed angry with herself and with me. A pause, a sigh, and she regained her self-possession, entrusted me with Papa's commissions in Paris and gave me the money to get them done. She lost her temper, and began worrying me about the plan to spend Sunday with her. I refused once more, and complained vaguely of her conduct towards me during the past winter and how unreasonable she was even now.

"Would you have sent for me, if I had not written my last letter?"

She was turning over the pages of "Justine" as I spoke, and she looked up at me with a wondering, wandering look in her fine brown eyes, and these words dropped languidly from her fevered lips, tired by a long series of wet kisses:

"I don't know!"

"I read you so well. I know how bad you are, and yet I am here. It is a great struggle between this—" I touched my penis,— "and this—" I placed my hand to my forehead.

"But how about that?" and she put her hand on my heart.

"Never mind that, I won't tell you anything more. I'll say nothing."

"I suppose you think I am not worthy to listen to you? Or perhaps that I cannot understand?"

"Perhaps. Anyhow, you will find out one day how I loved you, and later on I shall have my revenge. Oh! not as you think; I shall never harm you. Other men will avenge me. When you shall have been jeered at, mocked, and sullied; forced to smile, when some syphilitic wretch shall have made you sick with his pestilential breath; crushed beneath the weight of a monster, covered perchance with eczema; sweating; stinking; you will retch with disgust, and between two fits of vomiting, softly in the night, you'll cry bitter tears, and despite yourself, my name will come from your lips, yet burning from the pressure of the hated mouth. You will call for me: 'Jacky! Jacky!' And he will not be there!"

"But I shall never have anything to do with monsters, so that can't happen to me!"

I looked at the clock. I just had time to catch the last train.

"Oh! of course, there you are looking at the time. You are tired of me already."

I sat down again and listened as she told me to see about some seats for the Opéra Comique, the new building which had only been inaugurated in December. She wished to go with her first workwoman, I think. I departed, and lamp in hand, she opened the door to me, but could come no farther, as a perfect storm of wind and rain was now raging.

"I shall look forward to your visit on Sunday."

"Not Sunday, please, Lily."

"Yes, or you will see how angry I shall be."

"Not Sunday, my darling."

"Yes! Yes! Yes!"

The glow of the lamp showed me her black and sullen, frowning face, as she closed the door angrily. Through the blinding rain, I ran to the station. The last train had left, just five minutes before and I was stranded about ten miles from Paris.

I turned back and tried two infamous inns, to see if I could get a bed for the night. The first one never answered, and at the second, a ferocious dog drove me away.

It was no use lamenting. I had half a mind to return to the villa, but I was fearful lest Lilian should be unable to hear me, or that I might wake the servant, or Granny; so I started to walk. The ten or eleven miles did not frighten me, but the road was far from being safe. To be stabbed, or thrown into a river or a canal, for a few pounds, is not very nice. I thought of this, as I stumbled along all in the dark, my little parcel of books in my hand, and Lily's money in my pocket. I lost my way, regained it, slipped and fell in the mud, and as I picked myself up, saw a carriage approaching. I had walked two or three miles. I asked for a lift to Paris. Luckily for me, it was an empty brougham going to Pantin only. I arranged to give the man five francs, and I jumped in and found a rug on the seat. I lit a cigar and made myself comfortable until I got to Pantin. The rain had ceased. I paid the man and gaily tramped through the silent streets.

Before getting into bed at about three in the morning, I opened the parcel and looked through the books. In "Flossie" and "The Yellow Room," I found several heavy, black thumbmarks. Papa, beyond a doubt, had read these volumes with Lily.

I laughed grimly to myself as I jumped into bed, and with a loud and merry: "Good night, Lily!" addressed to my solitary pillow, I turned on my side and was soon snoring. But at half-past eight, I was up and dressed, and with my faithful comrade Smike, was soon at the bedside of my sweet, suffering, unsuspicious mistress.

3

How now, how now? how go maidenheads? Here, you maid?

SHAKESPEARE.

. . . what opinion he must have of my modesty, that he could suppose, I should so much as entertain a thought of lying with two brothers?

DANIEL DEFOE.

LILIAN TO JACKY.

Thursday. (January 19th. 1899.)

My very own Jacky,

Are you? No, you are not. You do not love your little girl as she ought to be loved.

I almost had an idea of what would happen to you Thursday night, and I waited a good long time before going up to my room, supposing that if you had missed the train, you would have thought of returning here. I am truly sorry at what happened to you, without nevertheless being able to pardon you the affront you put upon me after all for next Sunday.

No, you are not a man, as you fear a few moments of bad temper or a scolding, for that is the only reason that prevents you coming on Sun-

231

day. I can plainly see that I shall never occupy anything else but the second place in everything and every way.

I thank you extremely for all the commissions which you have done deliciously well, therefore I will abuse your kindness and ask you to be so kind as to go to the Opéra Comique when you receive this note, and take the eight-franc seats you mention for Saturday evening.

We will settle up Sunday if I see you, or by letter if you do not come. I count upon your amiability for these tickets. Can you send them to me by post?

You will lose if you don't come. You would find something good, for I feel inclined for a little naughtiness. Those who wish to profit therefrom, please take notice!

I love you too much and I am unhappy.

LILY.

JANUARY 23, 1899.

I had executed all the commissions entrusted to me by Arvel's daughter, and had been able to obtain for her, or rather for her father, a very large percentage, such as he would probably not have succeeded in getting. And by the manner in which the little piece of business was done, he must have known that I had managed it. The seats for the theatre, I also bought, and sent by registered letter, to avoid the accident (?) of the preceding October, and I also wanted her to feel that I had never forgotten the lost bank-note. She was so careful not to allude to this when she saw me, that she no doubt felt the implied reproach. I have no recollection how I answered her last letter, but I think I sent her a statement of accounts, and once more impressed upon her that it was impossible for me to leave Paris on a Sunday. I added that I should come down to Sonis on Monday night, the 23rd. of January, by the usual train, with all the receipts for her Papa, and another volume of "Justine," ready in an envelope, and if I did not see her, I should slip everything in the letterbox of her villa, and return the way I had come.

So I went accordingly, and found my Lilian strolling in the dark with her dogs. To my great surprise, she was extremely gracious, and had evidently given up as a bad job all idea of trying to drag me away from my dominical duties. She had enjoyed herself very much at the opera, having gone with one of her workgirls. I replied that I had intended to go myself and see her at the play, and she said I ought to have done so. I could not very well answer that perhaps she had not gone with the girl, or that if she had, the latter might have told her parents that I was there. All this proved the hidden complicity of both mother and father, and had I opened my mouth on this topic, it would have lead to useless quarrels.

I told her during our walk that Lord Fontarcy was shortly coming to Paris again, and very probably he would show a desire to see her once more.

"You would have to be very kind to him this time, especially as Clara would not be there. You could not refuse giving him pleasure with your mouth, the same as you like to do with me."

"Oh no, I could never do that to *him!* I would use my hand, but nothing else. I have no idea of disgust with you. I would do anything for you!"

"We will see later how far your devotion will take you. I shall feel great excitement in forcing you into the arms of my friend, and I am sorry I do not know anybody else I can trust. You can have no idea how pleased I am to think that you love me well enough to prostitute yourself for my pleasure."

"Yes, I do love you and all your ideas."

She said this in a low voice, under the influence of an inward wave of voluptuousness, for I must not forget to remind the reader that our conversations, during these nocturnal rambles, were carried on to a running accompaniment of the most lewd kisses and reciprocal gropings and touchings.

"I have the vilest ideas with regard to you," I continued, "there is nothing revolting, degrading, or horrible between man and woman, but what I should like you to execute with me, and I will eventually force you to say that I have become a vile, repugnant brute in your eyes."

"Never, never! You don't know what you say. Have I not told you over and over again that everything you do in regard to the pleasures of love is perfection, and just what I like? I have enormous delight with you."

"I am afraid you would refuse many things when it came to a pinch. Look at all the horrors described in the book you are reading, and which no one should ever know you have perused. By the way, I have brought you down another volume. Well, you have noticed how the poor martyred heroine, Justine, is forced to go with nearly all her persecutors to the water-closet, and wait until they have evacuated, to cleanse their fundaments with her tongue. Would you do that with me?"

The answer came quickly, without hesitation:

"Certainly, I would! I'll go to the closet with you. But I won't let you go with me."

I now made her tell me the story of Gaston's attempted rape in the train again, and I could not help excusing him. She agreed with me that she had done wrong to lead him on, having never granted him the least favour, but now, knowing what she did about men and their desires, she would never have let him kiss her and play with her, to such an extent, if she had no intention of giving way.

This talk and a lot more of the same kind, that I cannot now remember, had made both of us most fearfully excited, and we must have formed a strange picture, if anyone had met us, on the dark road. Lily's hat was all awry, her hair disarranged, and her face, neck, and throat glistened with the saliva my delighted tongue had deposited on her warm flesh. We held each other closely embraced, and her arms must have been black and blue from the way I had pinched her, always much to her delight.

I desired her greatly that evening, and in my pocket was a leather belt, which I had bought that day, as I had hoped my wayward girl might take me into her house again. Of course, I did not tell her of my peculiar purchase.

I had noticed that she was much stouter, as I held her in my arms, and I told her so. She agreed that there was a slight increase of fat.

"That is because you are no longer a virgin," I explained.

"What makes you say that? I am a virgin, I assure you."

"You seem strangely altered in many little ways," I answered, "and your entire bearing, which last year was that of a young girl, is now to my idea more like that of a married woman."

She laughed. I continued:

"I can soon see if you are a virgin or not."

"How?"

"I have only to insert my finger gently, if you will let me."

"Certainly, I will. Why not?"

"Why not indeed? Come along, put your foot up!"

"What do you mean?" she asked, feigning surprise.

"You have only to place one of your little tootsies on yonder bench and I shall be able to tell you in a jiffey."

She laughed and began to walk a little bit faster, getting away from the bench, and complaining that she was afraid some one might see us. Why had she not found that out before? The silly girl was utterly mistaken in me, and believed she could make me digest the most transparent falsehoods. As I walked by her side, silent for a moment, I could not help asking myself if the game I was playing was worth the candle? Should I not do better to leave her alone entirely to rot in peace, entrenched in her laager of lies, with her mother's lover? The thought of the old gentleman made me inclined to take up my position again, as I wanted to be certain of what was at present mere conjecture. And I was very curious to see what would be Lily's next manœuvre. Why did she so wish to keep up the fable of her virginity? I had told her scores of times that she could do as she liked with her body. I was not jealous, nor did I expect fidelity; all I desired was a little love now and again, if she cared to grant it to me, and when she told me to leave her, I would do so without a word, and keep all my suffering to myself. This evidently did not suit her, as she must have wanted me to be jealous, so as to have some feeling to work on. At present, I was impregnable. I waited for her to speak, and as I thought, she tried to punish me for my suspicions anent her maidenhead, by trying to arouse my jealousy—which did not exist.

She had been invited to dine out the evening before (Sunday), by Madame Rosenblatt and her sister, together with some gentlemen friends; cousins, brothers-in-law, or what not. If memory serves me rightly, one of them was an officer. I candidly confess that I do not recollect the story properly, as it was rather muddled. In plain words, it was a lie. The only thing that was true, was that she had had what is vulgarly called a jolly good spree, and had dined in a private room with a merry party. I only asked her quite coolly how she managed to elude the vigilance (?) of the silly old grandmother. She replied that Madame Rosenblatt had sent her a false telegram, inviting her to dine with her at her house. The dinner had taken place at the Hôtel-Restaurant Narkola, which I knew from experience to afford bedroom accommodation, as well as meals. She had been so jolly, and drank so much wine, that she had lost a silver purse which hung on the silver *châtelaine* I never saw. She pretended to be very much put out about this loss, as she was frightened that her Mamma would notice it and ask her awkward questions. There were twenty francs in the purse too. I replied that there was a slight balance due to me on the commissions I had executed for her father, and I should be pleased to offer her that, and shortly I would give her a new silver purse, although it might not match the one that was gone.

"Oh! that would not matter, but I dare say you think I have told you this story to make you give me something."

"You should not say that. I only know that you say you have lost a purse with money in it. You therefore need not repay me for the two seats I got for the Opéra Comique, nor shall I claim of you the little sum due to me on your Pa's account. As for the purse—"

"Never mind about that. I thank you for the seats, but I am afraid you will think I expected you pay for them."

"I do not think anything. I only know that it gives me great pleasure to make you the smallest present in the world and you know very well that it would be impossible for me to accept money from you for theatre tickets."

She thanked me briefly, and looked up to me with surprise and timidity, as if trying to read me and utterly failing to do so.

I inwardly resolved never to allow her or her people to penetrate my thoughts. The only way was to change my conduct and humour every time I saw them or the daughter. I had no chance at Sonis unless I became a perfect comedian, or walked off altogether.

So I entered on my part at once, instead of showing my suspicions about her virginity, or the absurdity of the story of her dinner with Madame Rosenblatt. I was very gay, respectful and tender, during the finish of our long walk and we reached the door of the house. I gave her the accounts and receipts for her Papa and another volume of "Justine." I returned her the letter from Nice, but I kept the type-written envelope, on which was her name and address. Without asking her to let me into the house, I made as if to go, holding out my hand to say good bye. She broached the subject herself.

"I can't take you into the villa to-night, as Granny won't let me sit up. Even now, she is waiting for me to come to bed, and I shall be scolded for stopping out so late. There is another thing too, that I hardly like to tell you. I am unwell again. I thought it was all over and now I have got what is almost a *perte*, or flooding, which fatigues me very much."

"Anyhow you are not *enceinte!*"

"How amusing you are!" she replied, laughing.

"Poor little girl! I suppose you must suffer too from the 'whites'?"

"How strange you should have guessed that!" She spoke with feigned astonishment.

"I had some *fleurs blanches* for the first time in my life last Saturday. How ought I to cure them?"

"You must see a doctor and take a course of tonics, and some iron and quinine. I will make you some quinine wine. You should use a syringe with some astringent for the 'whites.' "

"You know I can't take injections!"

This was playing the game rather too strong, but I withheld a bitter laugh, as I bade her a loving farewell and saw her go into the house.

This had been an evening of revelations for me. Papa had left her at home to bring on her periodical flow by hook or by crook, and permission was granted to go with the paying friends and lovers at the accommodating Hôtel-Restaurant Narkola, where I could play the spy the next day if I wanted to know about the banquet. And there was the repeated lie of the maidenhead! Lily little knew that in habitual liars, persistent, obstinate denegation is equivalent in many cases to an avowal.

I stopped short in my stride on the way to the station, and although it was a frosty night, a heavy sweat broke out upon my brow, as I thought of what might have been. Up to last October, I was deeply struck with Miss Arvel, and had I been rich enough, I do not know where my weakness might have taken me. To think that I might have given my name to her, introduced her into my family, and one day found old Eric in my bed! My marriage would have broken the heart of my poor, sweet, devoted invalid at home. I should have pensioned her off, and sent her to some warm climate—had I been rich. Other men have put away wives and mistresses after years and years of cohabitation; why should not I have done the same—had I been rich? I could have refused nothing to Lilian Arvel, or her parents, and so should never have allowed myself time to analyse their motives—had I been rich.

And I wonder what the few passengers waiting on the platform of the station of Sonis that wintry night, thought of a mad Englishman, who suddenly lifted his head out of the depths of the broad, warm collar of his fur-lined pelisse, and, taking his pipe from between his lips, shrieked aloud:

"Thank God, I'm poor!"

I should not have been human if I had not been extremely annoyed at Lilian's conduct towards me. I was wounded in every way, and I felt there was a lack of confidence; she would tell me nothing of her inmost feelings. I was to be an ordinary victim to her wiles, and this being entirely repugnant to me, I resolved to let her run loose. I was getting tired of her tricky ways.

These thoughts crowded into my brain, as on the 24th. of January, I started making her some quinine wine. It was a great success and I manufactured several quarts, which met with the approval of everybody at the villa, as I gave them to her later on.

Lord Fontarcy now reappeared in Paris, and the day after I had made the first lot of wine, we had a quiet bit of luncheon together all alone, as Clara had not accompanied him this time. Naturally, after we had discussed serious matters, the talk reverted to Lilian, and in as few words as possible I stated the case, without seeking to spare my own poor self. His face showed great preoccupation and I could see that he was in point of fact, quite disgusted with her.

"Why can't she be frank and good to you quite simply, or else let you go in peace and never see you again?"

This was a plain, Anglo-Saxon way of putting things which a woman like Lilian was totally incapable of understanding, and had she been as he wished, this story would never have been written. I asked him if he cared to see her, adding that I knew she would be glad to join us in a little orgie, but he declined, and in a few cautiously worded sentences, led me to understand that he did not approve of her conduct in general, and having no faith or confidence in her, preferred to have nothing to do with her. He was, I think, vexed at her having broken her promise to Clara and him concerning the proposed visit to his place in London, being very sensitive on all such simple points of honour, if I may be permitted to use such a term here. What pleased me most about my good old friend was, that although inwardly disgusted with Lilian's stupid game of hide and seek, he studiously avoided saying anything that I might have construed as being against her. But I read his kindly thoughts:

"She is fooling thee, but that is your own lookout; if you like her calculating, capricious ways, who shall gainsay thee, surely not I, thy friend? But I will have nothing to do with her. She is too dishonest for me, and I fear her, and all such scheming maidens after her kind."

All the above he did *not* say, but I knew him well enough, after a friendship of twenty years, to be able to know exactly his great horror of deliberately wicked women.

On leaving him late in the afternoon, I stopped mechanically in front of a jeweller's shop, and my eye fell upon a row of silver purses. I remembered how Lilian had told me that she had lost hers from off her *châtelaine*, and I resolved to buy her one, and send it to her as a present, which would signify: "Good bye, sweetheart, good bye!"

I chose a pretty purse, with a separation in the middle to divide the gold from the silver, and going into the nearest post-office, I sent her a letter-card, couched, as well as I can recollect, in the following terms:

JACKY TO LILIAN.

Thursday, January 26th. 1899.

Little jade,

I have just had lunch with Fontarcy, who desires to be remembered to you. I have bought you a silver purse, with a separation.

"Purse—separation." How do those words strike you?

I will send it to you shortly, and also your quinine wine, which will be ready in ten days.

I hate you!

"PIGNOUF."

This short and rude note brought the following answer:

LILIAN TO JACKY.

No date or place. (Received January 28, 1899.)

For supreme elegance and refinement, commend me to the signature, with which you have embellished the note received last night. Nevertheless, I prefer the name, which I often catch myself murmuring under my breath; the name which for me possesses infinite sweetness— Jacky—and I assure you I will never answer any letter signed otherwise.

"Pignouf," signifies a mean cad. You are one perhaps, but I would pray you to forbear carrying your love of truth so far as to use that highly decorative word as a nom de plume.

I am in bed just now. There is no danger, but I suffer greatly. I will tell you all about it when I see you.

Amuse yourself well with your friend; but do not renew the little orgie of last year with anybody else but me. I shall know it; and I assure you that all would be finished for ever between us. On that subject, I do not possess your lofty and liberal ideas.

Give Lord Fontarcy a nice long kiss from little Lily. Tell him I should love to see him and that I hope to very soon. Is he quite well and happy? I really believe I am in love with him. Are you jealous, my poor, darling Papa? I am afraid your daughter is very naughty. She feels so anyhow.

Thank you for the quinine and also for the purse; how kind you are to have thought of that!

Your little puppy, Pip, grows more and more handsome every day.

He is the pick of the litter. He has got a funny, little, twisted tail; quite wonderful, but not as beautiful in my idea as that of Jacky. I speak to him of his future master, and he is very satisfied with his fate. But will he always remain with you, or share the life of all your others? This last idea does not please me at all.

As for me, I do not hate you—I adore you!

LILY.

JACKY TO LILIAN.

Paris, January 30, 1899.

My little Lily,

I need not explain to you the sweet joy that your last letter, received Saturday morning, has given me, since you wrote it with the firm intention to please me. That I perceive and feel completely. What has often vexed me was to see that you knew well how to make me love you when you chose, but you did not always choose.

If you would only use the tenth part of your malicious and natural cunning to bestow upon me a little of the inexhaustible kindness which is to be found, it is said, at the bottom of every woman's heart, how happy you would make me, by bringing a trifle of happiness into my life, which, already so sad, was about to become more desolate without you. For when I sent you that letter-card last Thursday, I was firmly resolved to break with you. Perhaps, as you are very intelligent, you read between the lines of silly and low joking, and, understanding my thoughts, you have had a leap of love towards me, and you wrote to me to console me and stop me in time. Is that right? No matter; the essential is that you wrote me the most beautiful letter I have received from you up to the present, I think, although you have sent me some very nice ones—especially those of Lamalou.

After leaving Lord F. . . , I saw some silver purses, and the idea struck me to buy one for you and make you a "good-bye" present. I love you too much to endure any longer your treatment of the last few months. Hideous nightmare! If you had been indifferent to me, I should not have noticed it. But the rôle of the suffering sweetheart, groaning, whimpering, swearing, supplicating, afflicted with the epistolary dysentery of unhappy lovers, juggling with the words: "sadness—wounded pride—broken heart," and other commonplace phrases, is not in my repertory. I saw myself continually the toy of a little shrew, with a heart of stone, wicked, teazing and bad-tempered, to say the least. It was too much. It was sickening, and I did not want to return to my vomit.

I wished never to see you more, and I had the intention to put off all invitations by pretexting a voyage. Two such refusals and I should never have been invited again. I should have passed for a boor, and should have felt great grief, but not much more than this winter; and time, I hope, would have closed my wound.

Am I right or wrong, my little daughter? Heaven only knows! But such was my firm intention. Ask Fontarcy.

Is he your new sweetheart? And Gaston, what will he say? How sweet you are! Oh, you are a real woman! What makes me split my sides, is that you take upon yourself the right to make me a cuckold before my eyes, or behind my back, and I must say nothing, and never stray from the path of virtue? Where is the little slave of bygone days? She has broken her chains.

But I will be avenged, and this is how: you say you want to renew the little saturnalia of last autumn? I am willing, but I condemn you to execute such horrors with your new lover, that you will be disgusted with him for ever. That will be your punishment.

I begin to see now what you like, and perhaps I may be able to satisfy you in a terribly exquisite and perverse way. But it is a very delicate matter. I must talk to you quietly about it. I am accomplishing a work of seduction just now for your future enjoyment.

And you, love, work for me. Think of everything that might please me in your house at Sonis, and out of doors when you can venture to escape.

Seriously, I should like to have news of your health. Are you perhaps more ill than you like to tell me? I am very uneasy about it. You do not say what it is, but I guess. I have already guessed lots of things about you! I have to—you are so wanting in frankness.

Poor little puppy Pip! You are very amiable! Only think, he was about to become an orphan; what an escape—and for me too—and for Lily too!

What you say about the name of Jacky delights me and tickles me agreeably. What happiness if, when I see you, you were to be as in your letter. You ought to—but no, I am not going to tell you what you ought to do to make me love you. If you have naught that is good in your soul for me, say so and let me go!

JACKY.

L<small>ILIAN</small> <small>TO</small> J<small>ACKY</small>.

Tuesday. (January 31st. 1899.)

Can you come to-morrow night by the nine o'clock train? I shall expect you and do my very best to secure an hour's *tête-à-tête* in the nasty little dining-room you know.

Is Lord Fontarcy still in Paris?

My parents will be back Saturday.

Kiss and love,

L<small>ILY</small>.

As I went to keep the above alluring appointment, I reflected on the mind and character of my charmer and the result was far from being complimentary to her. I was surprised to find that she had answered a letter, where I had the sinister audacity to say that "I did not wish to return to my vomit!" I was opening my eyes at last, and I did not care if she were to be offended with me or not. Still I could not have very deep love for a woman to write to her as I had just done.

Where she made her great mistake, as a trifler with men, and I beg my lady readers to make a note of this, was in not knowing her customers. She used the same bait for all her fish. It was easier for her, but such proceedings savour of narrow-mindedness. A woman is clever who alters her tactics with every lover. A true huntsman uses a different cartridge for each variety of game. Had I desired the complete favours of this hysterical, selfish creature, I should have had to pay a fearful price. And, in return for all my sacrifices, I must have suffered in the terrible bondage that would have held me—a sensitive man—tightly tied, by the links of my own lusts, to this fearful example of a wickedly neurotic female, without reason, without shame, without the slightest particle of self-respect. I was vile enough, in all conscience, and I have little right to judge her, but I had no wish to torture her; I wanted a little love, if it suited her to love me, and that was all. She could do whatever she liked, and enjoy a crowd of miscellaneous lovers, as long as she behaved honestly to me, and when she had enough of me, she was to say so, and I would walk out of her life without a murmur. But this was too simple and sincere for her. There was no money in this, nor any hold on a man. I was not jealous, I had never asked for her virginity. How could such a man be "worked"? It will also be noticed that I asked her in my letter to think of all that might please her in her house. I meant that she was to try and make her Papa like me exceedingly, so as to invite me often, and she accepted all my sly innuendoes on this subject as a matter of course. I wondered too why she called her dining-room: "nasty"? I had never said so, but it must have been because Papa had possessed her in that room, in the evening after dinner, when Mamma had gone up to bed. I also thought, as I sat in the train, that the principal reason for her kind invitation, was because I was bringing a little silver purse.

She was waiting for me with her dogs as I came out of the station, and greeted me kindly, affectionately, and with much rapid gossip, so as to prevent me recurring to the harsh part of my letter. I was quite satisfied to have produced my slight effect; I knew—alas!—that all my remonstrances would be soon forgotten.

After a short walk, she told me to keep a sharp eye on the dining-room wondow, which faced the road. When I saw the light go out, it would mean that she had gone upstairs with her lamp to Granny and would see that all was quiet for the night. I was to go for a little stroll, and when I saw the light reappear, come softly into the house, as that would mean she was back in the dining-room again, waiting for me, and supposed to be writing letters. Everything was arranged as she told me, and twenty minutes later, I was in her arms. She had nothing on but a dove-coloured dressing-gown, of some soft material, over her chemise, petticoat and drawers.

After a passionate bout of kissing, she sat on my knee and chatted gaily, and I frankly confess that I forgot all her wretched shilly-shallying in the joy of holding her loved form clasped in my arms.

Why she had been ill in bed was this: she had suffered agonies through toothache and after trying all the domestic remedies of her grandmother, and obtaining no relief, had fled to Paris alone, and rushed to a Dental Institute. There, a young dentist told her she had a very bad abscess of the gums and declared it must be operated at once. On her affirming that she feared suffering, he offered to administer some gas and produce insensibility. To this she had consented.

"Were you not frightened? He might have taken liberties with you and perhaps violated you? Had you no fear, as you say you were all alone with him?"

I watched her narrowly as I said this. She answered me coolly that she had no fear on that head, and I felt more certain than ever that I was right in thinking that her maidenhead had disappeared in October or November.

Duly put to sleep, she remembered nothing more, until she found herself half-undressed and quite dazed, with several windows open, and a crowd of people round her. It appears that the young doctor had administered an overdose, and as an older man, who was now in the room, told her, her life had been in danger. She had been accompanied to the railway station and was now, although out of bed, still under the care of a doctor.

I told her that she ought to have telegraphed for me, but I did not say how I felt inclined to disbelieve her entirely. Her troubles, to my thinking, might be connected with her womb, and I was afraid that the visit to a dentist meant some uterine exploration. There may have been an abcess as well, and I felt a movement of horror, as I thought of a contaminating contact. It is only just to say that these disgusting thoughts came into my mind later. Everything seemed to conspire against Lily, and drive me slowly from her: her own conduct and the dread secrets of her prostituted frame.

The operation had taken place during the past week, and Charlotte had spent Sunday with her, sleeping at Sonis, before the return of Lily's parents. While Lilian talked to me, I had my hand on her naked thighs, and toyed with the luxuriant growth of hair on her mount.

"Charlotte did like that to me the other night as I was falling off to sleep,—just the same as you are doing to me now."

"Did you spend with her finger?"

"Certainly not," answered Lily, indignantly, "I turned over, pushed her hand away, and went to sleep."

I have often noticed that if a woman is allowed to talk without being contradicted, she will tell a series of half-truths, relating to what occupies her mind at the time, and an attentive listener is thus often put on the track of secrets he would not otherwise be able to get at. Many men also possess this same grave defect, and lack the retentive power which should prevent them making the slightest allusion to anything they may wish to hide. So I gathered that Charlotte and Lily had plenty of tribadic fun together.

Still I kept my own counsel, and by laughing and joking, contrived to produce upon her the impression I wanted; that I was a love-sick loon, desiring her madly, full of strange sensual longings, and ready to believe anything she might tell me.

I now began to get rather lecherous and excited, having her half-naked body on my knee, and I made her stand up, while my hands wandered all over her lithe frame. She still kept up a slight show of resistance and I felt greatly irritated and lewd, as I knew that my angel was merely shamming, being by this time expert at every caress. But I played my part, and enjoyed the idea of passing for a fool, especially as I knew that all my sayings and doings would be reported to Papa and Mamma on their return. I opened her *peignoir* and was astonished to find that she had grown much fatter in every way and I told her what I thought. She agreed with me, but did not seem to suspect that I noticed she was now a woman. All her girlishness was gone.

As she stood in front of me, I took off her petticoat, and she, in obedience to my wishes, at once dropped her drawers and was naked, with the exception of her loose robe, chemise, shoes, and stockings. I will not weary my reader with an account of my ecstatic caresses, lickings, and feeling of that serpentine body I loved so well, and which I had not seen naked for four months, but I must describe how I fulfilled a strange longing I had felt for some time past.

I had in my pocket the leather belt of which I have already spoken, and she graciously permitted me to clasp it round her naked waist.

I drew it in as far as it would go, and unluckily found I had forgotten my penknife, or I would have made some fresh holes, to tighten it still more, as my idea was to hurt her a little. It excited my passion to a great extent to imagine that a woman could endure a little suffering for my sake. The circumference of her naked waist was about twenty inches, and I could have easily have gained a couple more had I persevered. She compained in a sweet way that she was not at her ease, and that she did not look pretty, as her little belly jutted out in front by the pressure of the girdle. Paying no heed to her peevish complaints, I drew another strap from my pocket, and fastened her legs securely together just above the knee.

Then I forced a passage through her legs from the front, and thoroughly enjoyed the sensation of roughly pushing my hand between her smooth thighs thus drawn together. She seemed to enjoy the fun, especially as I did not forget to caress her clitoris, ever moist, on the way. Now I altered my tactics, and keeping my right hand forced against her slit, my left tried to effect a passage through the strapped thighs from behind.

Directly I began to push my hand under her bottom, she gradually let herself fall to the ground, and with many a contortion, managed to dislodge my fingers. She swore I tickled her to such an extent that she could not bear it. I desisted, having long since made up my mind that I would allow myself to be made a fool of, until I should tire of the rôle of victim, and so I released her legs, but left the belt still round her waist. I then asked her what I should do to her, and she asked me to provoke her orgasm with my tongue and quickly installed herself upon the little sofa for that purpose. I was in a good humour and smiled to myself, as I thought what splendid control I had over my passions. Here was a woman, who swore continually that she adored me, exercising all her cunning to keep up the pretence of her virginity, and trying all she could do to present only a front view of her secret charms. She willingly stood up naked before me, but when I approached her from behind, when my fingers could have so easily slipped into an excited vagina, she artfully wriggled away. I ought perhaps have spoken, but I was curious to see what she meant, and where she was going. Did she know, poor fool that she was?

She reclined upon the couch, and I was soon on my knees, my tongue sucking and licking all her body, from her breasts to her knees.

I was very excited, albeit I never lost my presence of mind with her, and I told her I loved to lick her all over and I felt certain that at some time or another I had kissed every part of her body, except her feet.

"Oh! you kissed and licked my feet too once!" she exclaimed.

"Did I? When was that, darling?" I knew perfectly well that I had never done so to her.

"In August, when you slept all night with me."

What strange illusions, and what a quantity of lovers she must have had to so mix up their caresses! I grunted an answer that might have meant anything, as my mouth and tongue were busy at work upon her lively clitoris; and I found, being perfectly cool and collected, that her private parts were quite different beneath my lips, being fatter and more open, and my tongue seemed to slip more easily within and penetrate further. I now began to caress her with my hands, while I continued sucking her in the most artistic and elaborate way I could, and I tried to get hold of her two hairy lips and under pretence of caressing her, force a finger within. But she was too artful for me and taking my hands in hers, drew them away. She seemed to enjoy my efforts to please her, and kept me between her legs so hard at work, that I lost all desire and got quite tired. I remember now how I thought of Charlotte, and guessed she had pumped my Lilian dry on Sunday, and Monday morning too, and I grasped the difficulty of my task with Lilian, having to fight against Papa, Lolotte and her other lovers.

And so I sucked and sucked, my penis rising and falling, according as my thoughts led me, but Lilian laid with closed eyes, enjoying the sensation caused by my industrious tongue.

Now and then, she would murmur: "Enough! Enough!" and then, of course, I went on more ardently than ever. But the best of everything must come to an end and she at last pushed me away, I must have been at least an hour between her thighs, which I consider a record time for such a young woman.

She lay panting; breathing heavily, her eyes half-closed, her legs outstretched; all in voluptuous disorder, her shift rucked up to her navel and wide open in front, showing the ruby nipples on her baby breasts.

"Now I am going to see if you are still a virgin, as you agreed to let me do."

"All right," she said, dreamily, raising herself a little, "how will you do it?"

"With my finger," and I went to work and just placed my index at the entrance of her grotto. She started and drew herself up, out of my reach.

"Oh, it is so tender and sensitive so soon after spending!"

Here was yet another proof of the wrecked virginity, but I took not the slightest notice. I found this useless fencing very curious, but I wanted to ejaculate also and therefore resolved not to quarrel. I drew near to her head, as she reclined lazily on the couch, and I rubbed my weapon and my testicles all over her face for a few minutes, revelling in the fascinating contact.

"I shall spend on your face, dear."

"Oh, don't do that!" she cried out in alarm.

"Well then, take me in your mouth."

"I can't, I am still sore about the gums."

She was so indolent, tired, and worn, that I could see she was quite out of sorts, and would have thought it fine fun to let me depart as I had come. But I induced her royal highness to take it in her hand, and she gripped it tightly and manipulated it cleverly enough as I stood by the side of the sofa, my breeches down; while she still lay in the same position.

"Let me see it," she said, turning her face towards its scarlet head.

I was getting near the crisis now, under the influence of her soft hand, and I held her head up and said to her:

"Look at it! Keep your eyes on it!"

She fixed her gaze upon it for a second, and then turned her eyes away and released her hold. A tired expression came over her face; she had spent her fill and wished me to finish quickly, or not at all. How selfish she was! How she loved me!

"How shall I spend?"

"With my hand! Make haste!" And she accelerated her masturbating movements.

"Let me spend on you!" I exclaimed, panting with suppressed desire.

She laughed, but opened her *peignoir* and pulled up her chemise, exposing herself completely, as she guessed my wish. She gripped my bursting rod fast, and shaking it violently to and fro, I felt the most torturing pleasure as the floodgates opened, and the seed flew in the air, to my great delight and relief. She held the red knob well over her belly, but her grasp was so convulsive that the liquor escaped with difficulty and in tiny spurts and clots. As she felt the hot drops fall rapidly, one by one, on her hairy mount and stomach, she uttered a little cry of surprise and dismay at the fall of each one:

"Oh! Oh! Oh! What a lot! Will you never be done?"

At last the shower ceased, and she let go my dart. As I recovered my self-possession, I could not help smiling as I noticed that her black bush was covered with little spots of spending, as if snow had fallen. There was some too on her smooth belly and the edges of her dressing-gown were also soiled. It is astonishing how the seminal spurt goes far, and lands in all sorts of holes and corners, when allowed to escape in the open.

She arose with a sigh of relief and asked if she might take off her belt. I released her and gloated over the red marks its pressure had left upon her skin.

And now we sat down and talked awhile, as she lazily turned over the pages of "Justine," and explained to me what awful pleasure that infamous book had given her. She loved the disgusting pictures too, with which this terrible work is adorned. One character amused her greatly. She spoke quite seriously about it and I could see that this was a deep impression. I allude to Dorothée, or Madame d'Estreval, who appears in the third volume, possessing a clitoris three inches long. It was this malformation that had greatly excited the libertine imagination of my sphinx-like mistress.

Having spent, she once more began to worry about me and

show signs of jealousy, which increased as I told her that I was obliged to go to London shortly for a few days on a matter of business. Indeed, it was a wild-goose chase after some money that was owed me, and which I saw a chance of getting, if I went myself. At this tale, her temper increased, and I pulled out my little parcel, containing the silver purse, which she was artful enough not to have alluded to as yet, although she was no doubt waiting for it.

"Here it is," I said, "and I had a good mind to throw it in your face and say 'good bye' for ever, if you had not sent me that nice letter."

"It is a very pretty purse," she said, dreamily, but evading a direct reply.

"What a bad temper you are always in, directly you have spent!" I replied.

"And before, as well!"

"Yes, my darling, you are always out of sorts. You have got a devil's temper, you little whore!"

This was the first time I had ever dared to use such a word to her, or indeed to any woman. To my great surprise, she did not mind. I think she rather liked it; I was coming down to her level, she thought.

"If I am a whore, pray, sir, what are you?"

"A maquereau! Your Papa-maquereau!"

She started and looked at me strangely, as I had never spoken to her like this before, and I wondered at my own boldness, which arose from the flight of my illusions.

In obedience to her request, I explained to her what I meant when I said in my letter that I was preparing something new and terribly perverse for her special delectation. Knowing, or rather guessing, that she would like to renew the little orgie we had enjoyed with Lord Fontarcy; that is to say, allowing her to be with another man in my company, I had been casting about to find that second person, and, to attain my object, had begun to throw out hints to a gentleman in whom I had entire confidence, and whom I saw every day. Lilian was very eager to know who, and I did not teaze her long. The man in question was my own brother, who I was trying to seduce for her, without telling him who she really was. This vile scheme delighted Lily, and excited her greatly. She urged me on my work to debauch my brother's brain for her, and there is no doubt that the idea of belonging to two brothers acted in a powerfully lascivious way upon her seething, salacious imagination.

Promising to do my best, I took a tender leave of her, and told her I would write, as soon as I knew when I left for certain and where I stopped in London. She allowed me to write openly to her from England, although my letters would bear the British stamps and postmarks, showing a difference to the preceding year, when I was not allowed to correspond direct from Lamalou. And perhaps the parents always knew all along?

4

Alors, le souvenir excitant l'espérance,
l'attente d'être heureux devient une souffrance.

ALFRED DE MUSSET.

> PUT. Fear nothing, sweetheart: what though he be
> your brother? Your brother's a man, I hope; and I say
> still, if a young wench feel the fit upon her, let her take
> anybody, father or brother, all is one.
> ANN. I would not have it known for all the world.
> PUT. Nor I, indeed; for the speech of the people:
> else 'twere nothing.

JOHN FORD.

My journey to London became inevitable and I thought there was a chance for me to put my hand on a large sum of money. I dropped a line to Lily on February 4, and left the next day.

LILIAN TO JACKY.

Monday. (February 6, 1899.)

My adored Jacky,

I am not going to do like you—write without scolding. I must absolutely scold you. You went off to London without warning me of your exact departure, and without asking me if I would like to go with you. I would most certainly have gone if you had asked me, and how happy we

253

should have been and how I could have been "naughty" at my ease, without any fear, or afterthought.

You never imagine any combination which would allow us to be together. It seems to me that if I were a man and as much in love as you pretend to be, I should surely find some scheme, and be happy for a few days at least, at any cost. Life is so short that we must be truly in the wrong not to take a little pleasure when we can.

My parents have returned, and it will be no longer easy for me to get out now, otherwise I should have had much pleasure in lunching or dining with you and Lord Fontarcy, if that would please you.

Frankly, this is what I think, as you know well that I cannot love him, since I am silly enough to be madly gone on you. Nevertheless, if it amuses you, you can tell his lordship that I have a great passion for him. He will believe it or not; it will not matter in the least. Above all, no debauchery in London, if you please.

This is what I beg you to bring me from London: a husband, or a *miché sérieux*, of sufficiently refined taste to appreciate a good *taille de plume*,* etc. If you wish to please Mamma, bring her a little tea. I suppose I do right to tell you everything frankly. Need I stand on any ceremony with my dirty Papa? I am no longer your slave, I am your mistress, and I shall punish you on your return as you deserve. I desire a letter of you from London. You can write in perfect safety.

Au revoir, beloved Jacky, my dear love, my sweet little husband. My mouth is better, but Pussy frets after her little dolly. Good luck, sweetheart, and come back soon. Thanks for the quinine.

A most voluptuous kiss from

LILY.

P.S.—If you can imagine a combination, we can lunch and pass the afternoon together on your return. Another kiss.

---

* Literally: "the cutting of a pen." A universal slang term among French-speaking people, signifying labial pollution, as performed on the male. Derived from schoolboy vernacular, as when a pen or pencil is cut into a point, it is generally twisted round in the mouth before using. In all schools, there are a few boys who lend their lips for the accommodation of their comrades, and the expressions: "Shall I cut your pen?" or "Cut my pen!" are well understood, when preceding the buccal onanism. The collegians made use of their erotic *argot* beyond the walls of the universities, and added a new expression to the language.

My sweet Lily, as can be seen by the above letter, was now perfectly emancipated, and Papa and Mamma must have been quite *au courant*. She spoke freely about going away alone on a journey with me, and told me to get tea for her mother, besides writing boldly to her house.

My journey to London turned out an utter failure, and I told Lilian as much when I answered her at length by return of post. All her "combinations" simply meant payments, and it seemed to me that her parents, finding that her maidenhead was gone, given to Papa or a stranger, allowed her to have a few subscribers, on condition that she brought home some money every time she went out.

I told her that I could offer her a nice lunch, with lots of love and nothing else, but she could come out on a Friday, which was a day of mortification, and then all would be well. That I often thought of her in London, and imagined her running about with her madcap, lustful friend, Charlotte, to all the fashionable massage shops. I said that I did not expect an answer, as I knew the fate reserved by women for men who were "stone-broke." I added that she could understand my letters much better now, as her mind was more developed and *she was more open in every way*. Also, that I had focussed the X-rays upon her and now saw through her plainly. I said I was off again, back to Paris on the ninth.

ERIC ARVEL TO JACKY.

Sonis-sur-Marne, February 11th. 1899.

My dear Jacky,

I have been endowed with a fair share of laziness. Of this you must be convinced, since I have not written to you. I have been "going to" every day, but the sun in the South is so intimately connected with *dolce far niente*, that my good intentions have only added to the paved surface of another place. I must thank you very much indeed for your weekly instalment of papers, the last of which enabled me to return home without experiencing the tedium of the journey. I must confess a weakness in favour of "Pearson's," "Tit-Bits," and "Answers." The pups are in splendid condition, and Lilian is anxious to receive her first instalment as a breeder.

When will you come down and see the dogs, so as to advise about the advertisement, putting us on a par with the dukes and princes who ask the public if they want to "buy a dawg." How would Monday do for you? Lilian takes a holiday and would be free. With kindest regards to all at home, believe me to remain,

Yours very truly,
ERIC ARVEL.

MONDAY, FEBRUARY 13, 1899.

I was very pleased to visit the Arvel family again, but had I not still had some lingering lust for the daughter-mistress of the house, I ought to have broken off the connection there and then. The girl told me plainly enough that she wanted to be paid to come out to lunch, and when I coolly replied that I had no money for her, does not take the trouble to answer my letter, but gets me invited instead to come and see her at her house, and makes Papa write the letter and mention her name twice in it.

I arrived with all my little presents, as usual, and was cordially received, especially by Mamma, who was delighted with her tea, and was not surprised to find that I should bring her from London just the very thing she wanted!

Lilian was very gay and sprightly. She was dressed more coquettishly and with greater care than formerly, and her lips were artificially reddened, without counting a new beauty-spot on her cheek, made with a careful application of a caustic pencil. Liberal use had been made of her special musky mixture, and she perfumed the whole house with the delirious odour that now evaporated slowly from her redolent skin, puffing up mixed with her natural armpit scent. In fact, all her maiden grace had departed and she looked like a brazen strumpet. She spoke up boldly, and her mother seemed quite subdued now, albeit on good terms with her, but I may say at once, to save me alluding to it too often, that her behaviour with her Papa was perfectly free and outrageous, and she never left him a moment's peace. I could see he greatly enjoyed what appeared to me to be her complete seduction of him, and I, to my shame, am obliged to confess that her coquetry with the old man, had a most libidinous effect upon me, and I was in a fever of lust every time she mauled, and patted, and petted him in my presence. I think he liked to be cajoled in front of me. Very likely it excited him to think I was jealous, and no doubt Lilian had not yet told him that Jacky positively liked her to have as many men as it might suit her to enjoy.

Raoul was there, and he seemed to be getting on very well at Belfort, never having been punished yet. Papa was just as furious against him. They were at daggers drawn, and I was perfectly certain that if the elder man so hated him, there were some reasons connected with jealousy of the sister, for I could find no other cause for this bitter feeling against the lad.

Lilian had got into her head that she should go up to Paris with her brother the next day, and join in the riotous fun of the boulevards, watching the maskers, and revelling in confetti-throwing. She made out that her parents would not let her go alone with Raoul, and so she asked me at table if I would take care of her, and meet her and her brother in Paris, to spend the afternoon with them. Of course, I accepted, and after strong opposition by both Papa and Mamma, the motion was carried.

I did not get to speak privately with Lilian until after lunch, when she was in her workshop. Before I had hardly time to open my mouth, she exclaimed that all was false that I had written from London. I suppose she meant that I was wrong to throw doubts on her virginity, or dare to imagine that she knocked about London "on the loose," with Charlotte. And then she made herself so agreeable to me that I fell under the charm once more, as she informed me that she had been earnestly endeavouring to force her father to invite me often and to be great friends with me, so that we could meet more often. She also told me how I was to behave with her Mamma; how I was to praise all her cooking, and above all interest myself in the welfare of her son, who the old lady adored. Lilian was so good and kind and earnest that I forgot all my grievances, and gaily accepted the situation, which seemed as if I was to be the accomplice of Papa and Lilian. This crapulous alliance suited my debauched nature, and I took the liberty to add:

"I am a virgin as far as my own sex is concerned, but if your

Papa likes to violate me, he can do so. Anything to be near you!"

To my surprise, Lilian took this vile proposal as a matter of course, and coolly replied with a little laugh:

"No! No! I know he would not like that, and I should not care about it either!"

We then went for a walk in the garden, accompanied by her brother, and as ever, she began to teaze me. What it was about, I cannot now remember, but I told her that I could not put up with wickedness from her. Then, suddenly changing her tone, she swore she was not going to alter her nature for love of me. I replied that even in that case, I should find consolation, as if she was very bad to me, I should have less regrets when the end should come, as it surely would if she did not amend her ways with Jacky. At this, as whenever I spoke of leaving her, she came round again, and in the sweetest way in the world, promised that in future she would always be good to me. I was infinitely delighted at this kind word from her, and running to the new white wall near us, I took out a pencil and wrote up the date: February 13, 1899.

We had no more words that day, with the exception that I had occasion to tell her that I knew she sometimes said she had not received letters when she had, and that the trick of *billets doux* going astray was a very old one and quite worn out. She only laughed slyly at this, and did not mind it at all. And we were all very happy together. I had never been treated so kindly by them. Papa called me his dear Jacky, and affectionately tapped me on the shoulders, asking my advice on photography, with which he was very much taken up just then, and Lilian came and praised me as much as she could in front of him, saying how useful I should be to her fond Papa, and he proposed that I should become an effectual aid. He suggested that when there were great *fêtes* in Paris: reviews, state funerals and so on, he and I should go together with his fine detective camera. After taking as many views as possible, I was to start away to Sonis with the plates, and develop them rapidly, while he stopped in Paris to write the letterpress. As soon as I could manage, I was to return to Paris with the negatives finished, and manuscript and photographs could thus be sent off to London by the night mail, and in case of need I would take everything over myself. To do all this, it was necessary that I should learn the management of all his apparatus, and the recipes of his developers, etc., and so it was agreed that I was to come to the house much more often. I was swimming in an ocean of delight, and at each project for my collaboration with Papa, my Lilian appeared with a cunning smile on her rose-pomaded lips, and a side-glance at me, as if to say: "See what I am doing for you!" In the evening, she told me plainly that she was working her Papa in an underhand way for me, and in time I should be his secretary, if I liked. Even the mother took me on one side while I was busy at the south side of the garden with some printing frames, for we were hard at work already on some views of Sonis and the house and garden, and told me that her husband had too much to do and that he ought to have somebody to help him in his writing. I replied that I had some small amount of literary talent, and should be glad to do anything he wished, and she gravely said that I should have to work with him. Can it now be wondered that I fully believed all this, and felt grateful to Lilian, as this was her doing, and all for love of me? Disinterested love too, for she knew by this time how poor I was.

The kindness of the Arvel family and the sweet solicitude of Lilian extended all through the month of February, and I mention this fact, so as not to keep recurring to her parents' goodness or her caresses, as she never passed me without a gentle touch of her fairy hand, or she would give me a luscious kiss if there was no one in sight.

I believe the afternoon was rainy, for we passed much of our time in the drawing-room: Lilian, Raoul, and I. Papa was busy doing some press work and was shut up in his little library. Lily was very gay, and so was I. We frolicked and belaboured the piano in turn, laughing and singing like so many children. I was struck by the great love shown towards her brother by Lilian, now that for the first time I saw them together for a few hours. She would ask him to kiss her, and throw her arms round his neck, while their lips would meet in a long embrace, and Lily would heave a deep sigh of satisfaction and exclaim: "O-h-h-h, sweetheart!" I loved to see this voluptuous play between brother and sister, which confirmed all my suspicions, and the mere sight of their gambolling together in such a lewd way, quite unbefitting their consanguinity, caused me to have violent erections as I sat with them. The same madly voluptuous feeling would also overcome me when she approached her Papa, so the reader must not be astonished when I tell him that all my old desire for Lilian had returned and was stronger than ever from this moment. I think any man would have felt much the same in my place. I was in a delicious daydream of lust as I danced and waltzed with Lily that afternoon, and she gave her brother and myself a private view of some high-kicking, which was simply remarkable for a liberal display of black stockings and frilled drawers of more sober style than those she wore when she came to me in Paris. Whenever she lifted her leg, I did not fail to notice that she half turned her back to me, and Raoul had a full view of the mysteries of her *lingerie*, while I only saw as far as her garters. The whole concluded with a rapturous bout of osculation, as Lily threw herself on her handsome brother, and I sat by in an armchair, possibly looking as silly as any man must, when his virility threatens to continually burst through the cloth of his nether garments.

During our play, Lily spoke of tuition in dancing, and our talk drifted into speaking about lessons in deportment. Merrily taking up the suggestion, she put me through a kind of fantastical drill of her own, and made me sit down, remain motionless, with my legs apart, or joined together, and I had the greatest trouble to hide my lump of manhood from the brother's gaze, though perhaps he saw it all the same.

I am not ashamed to say that the idea of being ordered about by Lilian excited me to boiling point, and for the first time in my life I began to realise that there was really a bewitching kind of lascivious joy in becoming the slave of the woman we love, and I could now understand what was meant by Masochism.

Everybody seemed happy in that house, and the only blot upon the picture was the backbiting of Papa with regard to Raoul.

Lilian was anxious to sell her litter of pups, so I arranged to put an advertisement in a Parisian "dog paper" as soon as possible, and Papa declared that all the proceeds were to go to the fair daughter of the house.

Mamma was very gracious to me, and went so far as to consult me on the *menus* of the future meals I was to take at their hospitable dwelling. I begged her to be less generous in future, and not to put three rich dishes on the table at every *déjeuner*, as she had been in the habit of doing, but to treat me as a real member of the family, and cater for me in more sober style. She agreed, and bidding me good night, left with Raoul, going up to Paris to see *Cyrano de Bergerac*; Mamma was right glad to go abroad with her handsome son, who had really improved through his military training, and looked very well in his French military uniform, although it is not very pretty.

I was in the seventh heaven of delight, and saw a great erotic future before me at Lilian's house, being pleasantly aroused from my day-dream by Lilian whispering to me:

"By and bye, ask me before Papa to put on my Japanese dress!"

Before I had time to reflect, I heard her call over the top of the staircase:

"Papa! I am going to dine with Mr. S . . . , as a Japanese girl!"

He pretended to be annoyed, and said it was not *comme il faut*, and her mother would be vexed, but I, of course, smoothed him down, and said I had asked her, adding that we were in the thick of the carnival, and therefore a pretty disguise might be tolerated. He gave way, and I soon afterwards met Lilian on the stairs, coming out of her bedroom in full Japanese array, looking the very portrait of a fashionable "geisha." Her robe was adorned with large scarlet flowers and set off her dark complexion to great advantage. The loose gown was largely open in front, cut in V-shape, and I could not resist thrusting my hand into her *corsage*, but she rudely repulsed me, with an air of defiance. Lilian was full of these whimsical changes of mood. I let the matter pass, and complimented her on her beautiful appearance; for in truth, she looked weirdly fascinating.

She told us that she had had great difficulty in finding the key that fitted her Mamma's wardrobe, so as to get out her costume, and shortly afterwards, we sat down to dinner: Papa, Lilian, Granny, and myself. The old woman does not count in this narrative.

Lily took her Mamma's place at the head of the table, with Papa on her right; I facing him, and the grandmother at the end. I merely mention this meal to note that Lilian frequently placed her feet on mine, with many a loving pressure, and towards the end of the meal, I distinctly noticed that at one moment, withdrawing her feet, she made a decided lurch of her body towards Papa, and must have touched his boot. I saw the well-known change come over his face: a look of dumb bewilderment, which left his features without any expression, as he dropped his head in his plate, and insolent triumph lit up the bold countenance of his mistress's offspring.

After dinner the table was laid out with supper for Mamma and her boy, when they should return from the theatre, and Papa and I were seated on a broad divan, in the little vestibule giving on to the dining-room, and which was used as a kind of smoking corner. Granny had disappeared, and Lilian came and threw herself languidly on the sofa, pressed close against Papa, and placing her half-bared arm on his shoulder, she lightly caressed his shaven cheek with her fingers. He did not respond to her blandishments, but the same silly, dazed look came into his eyes and his lower jaw dropped. How ugly we are, when we are sensually excited!

Lilian said she was happy to be nice and quiet with her dear old Papa, and I asked her as usual when we three were alone together, when she was going to be married.

"Never!" she exclaimed, "I am going to be an old maid and stop with my poor dear old Papa and take care of him."

"And quite right too!" I heartily answered as I always did when this was said.

I was in the same state of sensual longing as before dinner, and I am sorry to say that my recollection of our conversation is slightly dim and confused. Lilian did most of the talk, and I kept the ball rolling as well as I could. I was panting with lust, and Papa seemed as if under the influence of some pleasant drug. Lilian was the embodied type of the bold, black temptress, as exemplified in modern cheap fiction, and I am certain now that she was quite cool, and revelled in the idea of sitting between her two elderly lovers, perhaps laughing in her sleeve at both of us.

Our broken chatter, as we smoked lazily, drifted to Papa's recollections of his travel in Japan, and he told us how the ladies of that sweet land of immodesty wore their light flowing garments and what they carried beneath them. This was an opportunity for Lilian to tell us that she had no stays or drawers on, and she rose, tightened her dress around her, and then turned about with her draperies pulled tight over her large and well-shaped posteriors. Humming a scrap of a tune, she waltzed in front of us two men, and after a few steps, again took her place next to Papa, patting and caressing him as before.

The conversation still turned upon the delights of Japan, and Papa said with a sly laugh, that he had been very dull all alone in that faraway country.

Lilian looked at me across her Papa and put out her tongue, not as a saucy girl might, but with a salacious wriggle of its rosy point, worthy of an experienced courtesan. I did not respond, as I was frightened lest Arvel might see me.

"If you were so virtuous in Japan, what is the meaning of that photograph at your *bureau?*" And Lily assumed her most innocent air, as she put this ticklish question.

I was delighted, as I always was when I found I had guessed aright, as I had done in January. There was an awkward pause, but I tried to save the situation by saying:

"The possession of photographs of women means nothing. I can buy pictures of actresses in Paris, but it does not follow that I know the ladies."

Papa seemed really confused and to teaze him, I suppose, or to excite him before me, Lily said:

"Oh, but the photograph I mean is not the portrait of a woman alone!"

Papa did the best thing he could do under the circumstances: he got up and left us, and as he rose, Lilian put her thumb to her nose, and "took a sight" at him, much to my inward disgust, as I felt sure she would also turn me into ridicule with him whenever she could, and such low cunning did not please me.

"Take care what you do. He might see you, as when you showed me your pretty tongue just now," I whispered to her.

"Oh, he is so short-sighted!" was her sneering rejoinder.

"I see you know all about his adventures in Japan!" I exclaimed.

She looked at me with well-acted astonishment.

"I don't know what you mean!" was her icy retort, and she leant across the still warm empty place, marked by the deep impression of her stepfather's body, and gave me a most luscious kiss, interrupted by the return of Mr. Arvel. He sat down again between us, and once more Lily's hand tickled and caressed him.

It was getting late, and I began to talk about departing, and looked round for my coat, and some newspapers I had in my pockets.

"I want 'Le Journal;' I used it to wrap round the bottle of quinine I brought. There is a story in it that I have not quite finished. It is very good."

"I've read it," said Lily, quickly, a smile playing on her lips.

"What is it?" said Papa, with a slight yawn.

I did not answer. I felt embarrassed and I wanted to hear what Lily would say. She looked saucily at me, and thus I was forced to break a nasty pause.

"It is about a father and daughter—"

"Oh, yes!" Lily interrupted me. "A father marries his own daughter!" And she looked at me with audacity, as she moved her fingers slowly on her Pa's cheek. I could not meet her glance, and I am certain that she was the coolest of the three of us. I felt most terribly lustful and would have given much to have taken her in my arms at that moment. To hide my voluptuous emotion, I busied myself in collecting my newspapers, gloves, hat and stick, etc.

The story, *Le Lien Factice*, is to be found in "Le Journal" of February 13, 1899, and relates how an old gentleman marries a young girl, and on the wedding-night, respectfully informs her that he is her father, having been her mother's lover, and he gives her proofs in her mother's handwriting. The girl's legal father had always been jealous of him, and had made the daughter unhappy besides, so, fearful lest he should be forced to quarrel with the widower, and therefore never see his daughter again, he had resolved to marry her. But he only wishes to make her happy, swears he will respect her, and as soon as she finds a lover, divorce from her, to let her marry the man of her choice.

"Let us hope that we may not find him too soon, Father!" exclaims the girl, and the story ends with that remark, leaving the readers to guess what they like as a conclusion.

Papa now made as if he was very fatigued and could not rise from the divan, and Lilian told him not to move and she would go and get him some matches he required to relight his pipe. She got up, and passed her hand lightly over his large stomach, her favourite caress to him; but this time her right palm descended swiftly, rapidly, and gently, and as she rose, her fingers passed over his private parts, which were distinctly to be seen, forming a vast protuberance in his trousers, which were tight and of a very light colour.

This was done quickly, her hand trailing behind her, on getting slowly up from the sofa, as if it was an accident.

I was glad she went out of the room at once, without turning round, as I felt an extraordinary wave of lust pass through me and I went red and white by turns. I knew I should have had the greatest pleasure in the world if I could have seen them in bed together, and I had an intuitive feeling that my presence excited Papa, and he would have allowed me to join him with Lily, if she chose.

She now returned, having renewed the powder and lip-paint, and told me it was time for my train. Evidently she wanted to get rid of me, to have a long series of caresses before Mamma returned, so she told Papa to get up.

He made out as before, laughingly, that he was too tired to move, and so Lily took hold of his left hand to pull him off the couch. He being too heavy, she could not move him and asked me to help her. I did so, by grasping his right hand, and together we dragged him to his feet. This was nothing, but after an evening passed in the society of the semi-incestuous couple, the touch of his warm and moist palm had a most peculiar effect upon me. My flesh had never been in contact with his, save in the hurried conventional grip, and the knowledge that Lily held one hand I the other, all three knowing our mutual relationships, irritated my desire to a most fearful extent. I was very thankful to my charmer for her efforts in my favour, as I thought she was endeavouring to do her best to let me into the secret of her *liaison* with the master of the house.

My brain was in such a whirl of lust from this day forward that I am sure I missed several signs and incidents that might have shown Eric Arvel and Adèle's daughter in closer connection perhaps, but I think anybody will now be satisfied that Papa and Lily were lovers.

My passions were excited immensely, and cudgel my brains as I will, I cannot call to mind whether the couple accompanied me to the station or not.

If this story was a novel, it would now be my duty to say that I was hurried out of the house and left to go to the train alone, and then I should say that I climbed over the wall, and creeping up to the window, saw Papa and the Japanese beauty joined in the closest copulation.

In the excitement of desire, and while emitting freely, as only heroines of bawdy books can, she cries out: "Oh, if Jacky were only with us, Papa!" At these words, I jump through the window, and am naked at once! We join in triple voluptuousness; we are surprised by the return of Mamma and Raoul, and they are also introduced into the tableau.

Unfortunately, this is a true story, and I remember now that Papa saw me to the station alone, while Lilian went probably up to bed to get undressed and wait for him to return, while I went quietly to Paris by the train.

What is perfectly sure, however, is that the continual state of erection I had been in all day, without satisfaction, left me with excruciating pains in my testicles, and I made up my mind not to let the presence of Lily and her sly caresses have such an effect on me in future.

On arriving at the Eastern railway station, I met Adèle and her soldier son going to take the train home, and I stopped and chatted with them for a few moments.

The spirit of mischief moved me to tell Mamma in a careless way that she would find her daughter at home in Japanese costume, and I added that Lilian had had hard work to find the key to get out the dress.

"Dear me!" replied Madame Arvel, innocently "I've got my key in my pocket. Lilian has her own costume in her bedroom wardrobe."

After hearty thanks for their cordial reception they went to their train, and I departed thinking over Lily's fib, which was to hide the fact that the Japanese dinner disguise was a pre-arranged project between her and Papa.

SHROVE TUESDAY, 1899.

Lord Fontarcy was on a flying visit to Paris alone, and we breakfasted together, while I excused myself for leaving him at two o'clock, as I told him that I had to meet Lilian and her brother and join the confetti fight. I asked him to come with me and told him how he could make use of the occasion to worm himself into Raoul's good graces and get him for Clara. He refused, as he did not see the fun of waiting until Raoul had finished his year of military service in September. Nor would he accompany me to see Lily, and I saw that my good old friend did not like her at all and appeared frightened of her and all her family. Without knowing the secret of Lilian's life, which discovery I kept to myself, his experience in matters of this kind, greater than mine, led him to go so far as to utter the sinister word, "blackmail," but I laughed at his well-meant warning and told him that I knew how to take care of myself.

I did not tell him that I knew how Lily, who had undoubtedly had some kind of carnal pleasure with her brother, was too jealous to let him make the acquaintance of Fontarcy and his wife. That was why she had broken off his engagement with Charlotte, meaning to keep him for herself.

He left me, and I went to the place of appointment, arranged with my Lily of Sonis, which was at the corner of the Place de l'Opéra, near the Café de la Guerre.

I was frightened I might miss her, as the crowd had already begun to thicken, and the tiny atoms of coloured paper were flying thickly, as the gay Parisians threw them into each other's faces, with many a merry laugh.

Lily now appeared, prettily dressed as usual, and powdered, scented, with her reddened lips, according to her latest fancy. Raoul had not arrived yet. She told me he had taken an earlier or later train, I forget which, as I was under the charm, and thought only of the happiness I felt at spending a whole afternoon with her. I suppose her brother had gone to see Charlotte, but it is of very little account.

Lily scolded me, as her Papa, she said, had informed her that I was not energetic, and did not try to get on in the world. As long as I could find time to get out with my dog, Smike, that was all I wanted, she said.

I told her of a certain number of projects I had formed and she gravely approved of them, but I could not help saying that I was unaware such interest was taken in me at the villa.

"Oh! we often speak of Jacky and we want you to get on. I do all I can for you with Papa and Mamma, as I am really very fond of you."

"Excepting in the winter."

"You must not complain, as Gaston, poor fellow, ran after me for years, and I never granted him *that!*" She clicked her thumb-nail against her teeth in true Parisian style.

During the conversation, we were walking round the Opéra, until at last I took her into the Café de la Guerre, and we sat down and had a glass of champagne, her beloved beverage, keeping our eyes on the door, so as not to miss her brother.

She now made me a kind of declaration of love and completed my sense of sensual intoxication, by telling me how she loved me and how she had tried to struggle against her inclination, but unable to forget me, she had now made up her mind to throw all scruples to the winds and let herself be mine without restraint, enjoy herself with me and see as much of me as she could. Life was too short to deprive oneself of love! Did I not believe her? Was she not doing all she could for me at Sonis?

"Doubtless you love me a little. If not, I should not be here to-day, as there is nothing to make you seek me out, unless you choose, but you are very ambitious and in your wordliness, lose all tender feelings. I know you would like me to be better off and join me in business if possible. But what would Papa and Mamma say to you being in partnership with me, or if I provided a sum of money to start you as a bonnet-builder in Paris, could I afford it?"

I never got an answer when I introduced her parents' names into the debate, and I judged it to be more prudent not to allude to Papa, or the fun on the divan of the preceding evening. Nor did I tell her that Fontarcy was in Paris. We drifted on to other subjects, and I repeated what I had always said and believed, that the only future for a woman in France was the married state, and that if I had always been fool enough to respect her, it was because I saw her with a loving husband in all my dreams of her future. I thought it best not to allude to the least thing that might hurt her feelings.

"You will pass happy nights in the arms of a husband, and will soon forget Jacky, his filthy caresses and his mad ideas of whips and belts. Don't forget, Lily, that husbands enjoy their wives in very sober fashion, without any fancy flourishes."

"Then I should not like it!" she exclaimed, with a disdainful toss of her pretty head.

Raoul now appeared on the scene and joined us in a glass of champagne; Lily told me I was to spend all day with them and return to dinner in their company at the villa, but I demurred, saying that I had already been there the day before, and such behaviour would savour intrusion. Lily told me to have confidence in her and not to prevent her bringing about our mutual happiness in her own way. I accepted, thinking in petto, she was the mistress of the house.

Raoul and his sister whispered together, and begging to be excused, both of them went off to see somebody, who was employed at the American bar, which is in another part of the building, and it struck me that Lily was well-known in the establishment. I knew it was frequented by many officers. She returned soon, with Raoul, giggling and whispering foolishly with him, and we began to talk about starting on our tour down the boulevards, to join in the paper war, which had already waxed fast and furious. Lily boldly said before her brother that she wanted to do a little "pee" first, and we waited until she came back, with a fresh dab of powder on the end of her insolent nose.

After loading ourselves with bags of confetti, we were soon lost in the fray, and I cannot now remember how much we used, but none of the ladies on the boulevards that day were more audacious than Lily. She attacked all good-looking young men, fighting till vanquished and surrounded, as she always was, by a crowd of lusty males, who, under pretence of covering her with confetti, popped their fingers down her neck, or pinched her posteriors. I am sure she liked the rough horseplay, although she would break away from her tormentors and throw herself in my arms, hiding her head in my breast, which ostrich-like proceeding dispersed the attacking party, and she drew breath until the next onslaught. I noticed that she rushed at all soldiers in uniform, especially young and handsome officers, and boldly making a stand in front of them, defied them, as it were, to mortal combat, and my suspicious mind, remembering her talk of Boxing-night, immediately gave her an officer as a lover.

The battle continued without interruption until nearly six o'clock, with only one or two interruptions, when seeking the shelter of a doorway, we extracted tiny fragments of paper from Lily's beautiful eyes.

I fully entered into the fun of the riotous public romp, and we gradually got away from the best part of the boulevards. As dusk came on, liberty degenerated into licence, and I amused myself by making Lily a little jealous by the sight of my vile behaviour to ladies in the crowd. I approached them with hands outstretched, as if to throw confetti, but I only put exploring digits down their necks, or even went to the extent of pressing their breasts, when the bust of an unknown beauty looked tempting. It was a rare treat to mark their cry of stupefaction, at being so imprudently outraged by a stranger, and before they could recover, I was off, seeking fresh game.

Tired out, dusty and with her luxuriant locks full of bits of coloured paper, Lily cried, "Enough!" and we made the best of our way to the Eastern railway station, where having a little time to spare, I treated the two young people to refreshment and supplied Raoul with cigars.

In due time we reached Sonis, Lily being very tender in the train, and Raoul turning out a model of discretion.

I found Papa reading some of my magazines and whether I was expected by him I know not; but Mamma had not been warned, as I caught her on my arrival in the kitchen, superintending the preparation of the dinner, and attired in a dirty old dressing-gown.

Everything passed off very agreeably, and everybody treated me with the utmost cordiality, while Lilian insisted on putting on her Japanese costume once more, and I made my appearance in the dining-room attired as a Jap as well, Lily having fished out for me a man's oriental gown, in which I looked as ridiculous as possible. Mamma set her face against Lily's masquerade, and said it was not *convenable*, especially before me.

At dinner, Lilian was seated next to her Papa. I was at the lower end of the table, on Lily's right, and she pulled her clothes halfway up her leg, and threw one over mine, keeping it there during the whole of the meal, without attempting any disguise.

After dinner, all the womenfolk went away with Raoul to prepare for his departure, as he had to return to his regiment by a late train that night, and a large basket of eatables was got ready for him.

During this time, I sat and smoked a pipe with Papa, and his talk as usual took an obscene turn. I promised to bring him a small parcel of books from my little collection, and mentioned "The Romance of Lust."

At this moment, he got up to fetch an ash-tray, and turned his back to the door, at which Lily appeared, and looking at me, without uttering a word, threw up her clothes, completely exposing her legs encased in black stockings, and her drawers, which, half-open in front—purposely, no doubt—showed a portion of the liberal growth of black hair which hid the mark of her sex. Papa turned round,—she was gone!

Resuming our confab, Papa asked me what "The Romance of Lust" was about, and I told him a few of the leading incidents, as far as I could remember. He expressed surprise, and I answered him very slowly and deliberately:

"I am never surprised at anything where passion is concerned!"

He did not reply, but I saw the same dull, blank expression

that always spread over his face when nonplussed, and neither of us spoke for a few seconds, until Papa rose, and making some excuse, left me alone.

Raoul now took an affectionate leave of his Mamma and Granny, who idolized him, and Lily, covering up her Japanese costume with an ample waterproof, accompanied Raoul and me to the station, Papa following us.

On the way, she told me that she had arranged for me to be invited on Friday, to have a long day's work at photography with Papa, and suddenly in a mock whisper, said, lovingly:

"I am going to tell you a secret!"

"Proceed, your story interests me!"

"You are a dirty pig!"

"That is no secret!"

"No, but this is: I love you, just because you are an adorable dirty pig. I should hate a man, if he was not horribly naughty, as you are!"

When we reached the platform, she managed to get me into a dark corner and give me one of those delirious, long, wet kisses which she knew how to make thoroughly enjoyable. It was only interrupted by the appearance of Papa, and if I did not know he was short-sighted, I should have thought he saw us.

"Papa! Mr. S . . . has been telling me about a book on photography he has got for you!"

Papa did not reply, but only grunted, and Lily continued, with a merry twinkle in her eye:

"Oh, Papa, he is such an awfully naughty man, and so vicious!"

There was another awkward pause, until I laughed, and made some joke or the other, and we all said good bye, but not until Papa had forced me to accept an invitation to spend the day of Friday and have a long spell of photography.

The dog Pip was mine now. I took it to Paris either Shrove Tuesday, or the day before, as near as I can now remember, and Lily seemed very affected at parting with the pretty little animal she had brought up with so much care for Jacky.

I concluded this eventful day for me, by a long conversation in the train with Raoul, when I tried all I knew to give him good advice, so that he should not get into any scrapes at Belfort, and seemed sensible and grateful for my counsel. I could not have said much more had he been my son, as I had been led to believe that Mr. Arvel never took the trouble to speak to him at all.

He went to catch his train to the eastern frontier, and I returned home in a state of wild delight, quite under the spell, and thoroughly convinced that Lily loved me and was duping her satyr Papa for and with me, or else he allowed her to have me as a lover. I did not take much trouble to fathom the arrangement exactly, as I was quite content to let things be as they were and trust to Lily.

FRIDAY, FEBRUARY 17, 1899.

Laden, as usual, with quinine wine, perfumery, books and papers for Papa, and a volume of "Justine" for Lily, I was again punctual at the train, but I anticipated a good scolding from the young lady, with whom I was over head and heels in love, having quite forgotten all her past whimsical treachery and deceit in favour of the lascivious sweetness of her present attitude towards me, as she seemed to allow me to become a sharer in the secret of the passion of her stepfather; and it appeared as if I should at some near period be admitted to their sports, a consummation I am abandoned enough to confess I prayed for with all my heart.

I had shown the pretty Pip to a veterinary surgeon, who was a good friend of mine and my mistress, and he, after extolling its beauty, declared it was afflicted with a shortness of breath, which would render its bringing-up very difficult, if not impossible. My poor Lily, who was passing through a most trying recrudesence of her old rheumatic symptoms, resolved to forgo the pleasure of keeping the little animal, especially as we had three dogs already, my particular Smike and two others; and only dog-fanciers know the trouble it takes to bring up a dog from puppyhood, Pip being, as it will be remembered, only six weeks old. So my devoted invalid covered him up in one of the little woollen shawls she knitted herself, and cried over him as she put him in my arms.

Upon the servant opening the gate of the Villa Lilian, I dropped Pip on to his paws, and he was right glad to scamper to his mother, who was disporting herself in the garden, with the four other puppies of the litter, his brothers and sisters.

I went to Papa's study and gave him a parcel of books, including the four volumes of "The Romance of Lust." I had also brought down for him, the copy of the first obscene work I had ever lent his daughter:—"The Yellow Room"—and to give it to him, I moved towards the window, under which stood a little table. I called to him to come and see this book, which I made as if I had forgotten. As I had shown him each of the others, he had made some remark on each, facetious or otherwise, and as he came towards the light, I put the book on the table and stepped back a pace or two, so that I have a good view of his face in the full noonday sun, and he could not see me. He took up the little volume, and bending down, slowly opened its pages, holding it close to his eyes, as shortsighted people do. All expression left his face; he knit his brows, opened his mouth, and did not speak for a second or two, as, visibly embarrassed, he slowly turned over the pages.

Then he closed it, without a word, and asked me to come out for a stroll, while the lunch was being prepared. I followed him, highly delighted at the success of my ruse, as I was now perfectly convinced that Lily and he had read my bawdy books together. I may say at once, that he afterwards returned me the volume without saying a word in favour of the work, or against it.

I noted that Lily never took me to help her to lay the cloth any more, but she asked me to accompany her in longish walks on all kinds of pretexts, such as doing commissions in the village, taking out the dogs, going to the post-office, etc., and Mamma beamed on us both. She had got the habit of retiring to rest immediately after dinner, leaving Lily with her Papa, and they were supposed to retire about midnight. Papa never got up before nine or ten o'clock, and Lily brought him his breakfast in bed. She was not in good health and took drops of nux vomica before meals to give her an appetite. She looked far from well, in spite of her coquettish toilettes, and rose lip-salve and face-powder, without counting her *grain de beauté*, which I could see was carefully renewed.

At the midday meal, she was in a towering rage with me for having brought back Pip, and her face was perfectly hideous, all dark and scowling, with blue lips, as was her wont when out of temper. I gave my motives, and said that I had braved her anger, sooner than sell the pup, which I could easily have done, or given it away and told some lie to her. She refused to listen to my reasons, and it was only when her mother took my part, and told her not to be rude to me, that she gave way and came back to her usual manner.

The advertisement for the sale of the dogs had appeared the day before for the first time, and they were delighted at my effort to put a few pounds in Lily's pocket. So much so, that she and her mother had ordered an ice-pudding for lunch for my special benefit.

All went merrily as a marriage bell, and Lily, alone with me, asked for news of the gentleman I had promised to seduce for her. I told her frankly that I had proposed to my brother to join me in a miniature orgie, saying that I would introduce him to a little brunette, but, of course, without telling him her name at present. After accepting in a half-hearted way, he had cried off when I asked him to tell me the day he would be ready, and I apologised to her for raising false hopes. It was not my fault if my brother was inclined to be a little sentimental and averse to sleeping with women who had been with me. Lily heaved a sigh of regret. The idea of being in the arms of a brother of mine had excited her greatly. I spoke of her plan to get to London in my company, but she did not seem to think there was anything out of the way in coming to England alone with me. It could be done by her making out that the employers of Charlotte would be supposed to send her to London on business, paying her expenses and giving four pounds a week, during her stay. There was no occasion to write any forged letters, or do anything except send her a first-class return ticket; her parents would believe her, whatever she might say. Now was the time to go, as she could say she was wanted for the fashions of the coming summer. I added that on the morning of her departure I could be at the Northern railway station, as if I were going to London alone, and affecting surprise, offer to chaperon her as far as Charing Cross. Lily could not guess that this was a little trap of mine to see if her Pa and Ma knew of our intrigue, and she agreed that my plan was perfectly feasible, always providing she came home after a fortnight or so with a ten-pound note of her own at least. I told her I would see about it and perhaps in a few days, I might be able to afford it. But inwardly I am forced to declare that I could only think of a certain poor ailing woman in Paris, and there were old bills owing to doctors, a long score at a chemist's and other little odds and ends.

Lily was very excited at the thought of being alone with me for a week or so, and I told her that she would have to be my slave, and we both got ourselves into an awful state of lust by imagining what we would do together. I remember she took such a fancy to a couple of very nasty fancies of mine that she made me repeat them.

At the word of command every morning, she was to rise, and stripping naked, seat herself on a toilet pail, after having prepared a tooth-tumbler, with tepid water and dentifrice. I would then rise and clean my teeth, expectorating on her body, she allowing me to rinse out my mouth and empty my throat all over her, so that the liquid would fall upon her and trickle down her breasts and belly, dripping into the receptacle. Then she would become the living chamber utensil of her beloved master—"a thing you often said you would do and never did"—she added regretfully, and I saw that she really enjoyed these filthy projects. She would then have to soap me in my bath and assist at my toilet, and when completed, Lily having put on my boots, etc., I would go out and leave her to get dressed herself.

The rest of the day passed off in the ordinary way; Papa and I were in the dark-room most of the time and even after dinner. Lily would escape from her workshop whenever she could, and come and pay us a visit. Then I would get a long kiss, and half of her wicked tongue would disappear down my throat, which I vastly enjoyed, although I knew I should pay for my fun in the evening, by testicular pains.

Mamma was rather against the photographing craze, as Papa passed too much time in the little house, which was very damp and cold, and he had taken Lily to assist him—I pricked up my ears at this—and the two had spent the whole of one evening shut up alone together, in the famous dark-room.

It was indeed very cold, despite the large petroleum lamp that was burning, most of the printing being done by artificial light, and being in there after dinner, Lily appeared, saying her hands were cold, and boldly stuck one paw into Papa's trouser pocket, while with the other hand stretched out behind her, she caught hold of my member. I immediately unbuttoned myself. She slid her hand inside, and gently tickled the top. She thus had one hand in her Papa's trouser pocket and the other was feeling me.

"Your hands are not cold," grunted Papa, with the dull, serious face of the lewdly excited man, that I now knew so well.

"But suppose I like to say they are?"

Finding now that Lily was always putting her hand between my legs, whenever we were in the dark-room with Papa, I never went to Sonis any more, without arranging my drawers in such a manner that my organ was at liberty, and I only had to undo two buttons to have it ready for her hand. Many a time, Papa would be developing, mixing, explaining, and I was not learning anything, but was caressing Lily; and she kept her hand on my naked weapon behind Papa's back and sometimes we were all three entirely in the dark, when a plate was being developed.

Just before dinner was served, Lily said that I ought to sleep at Sonis one or two nights now and again. I answered that I should be delighted to do so, that very night if she liked, but I should have to be up very early so as to see my mistress in the morning, as was my habit.

"I hate her! I hate her!" she cried, clenching her little fists.

I paid no attention to these ravings, but waited patiently until the storm subsided, and then I asked her if it would do any good for me to sleep at the house.

"You would not come to my room in the night?" I said, dubiously.

"Yes, I would. I would manage to worm myself in to you!"

I asked her how it would be for me to have a false attack of giddiness after dinner, which I could ascribe afterwards to indigestion, and I showed her exactly how I would act as a man utterly unable to stand upright without assistance. It was arranged that I should play that part, and she added that Mamma would never let me go to Paris in such an apparent state of weakness. Having arrranged with her not to laugh while I was acting, as I knew in that case I should laugh too, she left me and we dined shortly afterwards. But the first moment she could find to speak privately to me directly the dinner was over, she told me not to attempt my scheme of sham illness, as I looked too well and jolly after the meal. I did as she told me, but I still think that she consulted Papa and it was by his orders that she changed her mind.

I have no recollection of anything more particular taking place that day, but I find by a note in my diary that I was again a guest at the Villa Lilian on:

FEBRUARY 21, 1899.

Instead of taking a train at ten o'clock, as I usually did, I could not get to the station except for the 11:30, and while quietly seated in my compartment, I saw Lily running up and down the platform, peeping into every carriage. She was looking for me, hoping that I had taken the same train as she had. She had been up to Paris to go to market and was returning with her purchases, being accompanied by one of her workgirls. We carried on our conversation in English, and we spoke of a letter I had written her, wherein I had informed her that "all the schemes on which I had built to be able to take her to London, had fallen through, and I was very unhappy, but nevertheless I counted on the love of the daughter of the Mikado, and hoped she would intercede for me with the great chief and master of the house, over whom she possessed such *extraordinary influence*." I wished her to understand that I knew all that was going on between her mother's lover and herself, but that I was not jealous and could perfectly understand that a man could fall in love with a young girl, with whom he was in daily contact, especially as she resembled her mother in several little ways. Here was a man of strong animal instincts, linked to a vulgar, jealous woman, albeit devoted to him as the breadwinner, and I should think, incapable of disinterested affection. To keep him at home, she would voluntarily shut her eyes to any commerce he might have with Lily and the task would be easier if they had already, both of them, been too free with her as a child. Lilian never took offense at this moment when I recurred to the understanding that existed evidently between Mr. Arvel and herself, while I made my allusions in a most respectful manner and never let myself be betrayed into speaking against him, although Lily always alluded to him with a show of contempt, and I sometimes pitied him as whatever his faults, he slaved and worked for these two women, who after all only formed his little harem. He did sleep with the girl, but was it real incest? Was he her real father, or not? The idea could only be loathsome to the lascivious lass, but as long as she herself felt no disgust at the approach of the man whose lips had pressed her mother's for twenty years, and who had dandled her on his knee and brought her up, who had a right to feel indignant? She was a woman of strong passions, and if she was to become a whore, what mattered if the little man who was her natural guardian possessed her or not? As far as I was concerned, I was rather pleased to think that now she ran no risk of being driven to ordinary professional prostitution.

Lily was very lively and full of fun, and she got quite spoony over a handsome young officer who was seated in front of us, and who really looked very smart in his cavalry uniform. She turned red and white by turns as she furtively admired him and I chaffed her about her adoration for the military.

An exalted personage had just died in France, and all sorts of strange rumors were floating about concerning his death, as it was currently reported that he had died suddenly in a woman's arms, or rather had succumbed to the caresses of a complaisant mistress. He had died in erotic delirium, and this end, more frequent than many people might think, was only remarkable by reason of the great positions the unfortunate victim to his passions had occupied during his lifetime. His age was about 60, and I told Lily the peculiar story of his last moments and how he had while unconscious continually called upon his numerous concubines by name and cursed his weak organ of virility, because it refused to respond to the call of lust.

On arriving at Sonis, I went for a walk with Papa, and I recited to him the wonderful end of the great statesman. I looked at him out of the corner of my eye as I walked and talked with him on the pleasant country road, and I soon saw the dull, sullen look steal over his face again as I broached erotic subjects, which I saw interested him deeply, and now I was almost certain that I could produce that expression on his features whenever I chose.

Elated with the sense of my power of reading the thoughts of Lily's Papa, I took the liberty of asking him if it was true what I had heard concerning the genital strength of men of sixty years of age, more or less. I explained that it appeared to be a most unfortunate state of things when the desire of venereal diversion, centered in the brain, persisted years after the seminal flow had ceased, and I opined that it must be terrible for an old man to be tortured by lewd imaginations without having the natural means to gratify them, when driven by erotic dreams into a woman's arms. It was a fearful ending for a man to finish up like a mad eunuch. He pooh-poohed my theory, which I submitted to him with the greatest deference, as I always treated him with respect and politeness, and told me that desire ceased always when the virile power was dead, and though I did not believe him, I agreed with him all the same. I always enjoyed the suburban skill of the narrow-minded dwellers in villadom, as they possessed a wonderful knack of settling the most difficult problems in a moment. They always knew everything, and arranged political and social complications with a rapid coolness that would have seemed conceited in a Cavour. And they did not want a fine library, a staff of secretaries or a lot of expensive maps; they settled things offhand in a tramcar or a railway carriage.

I envied such men as these, and Mr. Arvel was of the same kidney, for they made life easy for themselves by the adoption of certain easy formulæ which did away at once with all useless discussions. With some, all women were prostitutes; another camp swore females were angels. It was the same with everything else: religion, the army, and the benighted inhabitants of any other nation. Their petty view of things in general betraying limited intelligence only inspired me with a desire to leave their society at once, but their principal fault was that, in their great desire to show their knowledge and talk at all hazards, they thought nothing of confiding to utter strangers the secrets of their wives' wombs, their daughters' constipation, and all possible sexual troubles. Arvel's pleasure was to talk against everybody, and he did not spare Lilian, her brother, or his wife.

But we were all very happy in spite of his grumbling and there was joy in the house of Arvel, and money too. All kinds of goods kept continually arriving from the big shops and stores of London and Paris during this month, and Arvel pulled out handfuls of gold to pay the bills. The garden too cost a lot of money, without counting the photographic requisites and the painting and decorating of the new part of the house, which was never done with and was sufficiently comfortable.

During the breakfast, which was most generously served, in spite of Mamma's promises of moderation, Lily's health was the topic discussed and Papa announced his intention of taking her away on a journey to give her a little change of air. Mamma did not object and Lily said nothing. I opened my ears as wide as I could, and as I was always ready in that house to agree with everybody, gravely said that it was the very best thing that could be done for the health of Mademoiselle. Papa mentioned the name of a seaport town and asked me what I thought of it. I replied that I did not think she would care much about the sea at this time of year and that there was not much to be seen in a small French port at any time. So Papa suggested Brussels or Berlin, and after a little conversation it was decided that Lily was to visit Brussels, where she had never been. It was on the tip of my tongue to ask Mamma if she was going too, but I thought better of it, and indeed the sprightly Lilian left me no time for reflexion, but kept me thoroughly enchanted with the frequency of her most audacious caresses and never passed her good Papa without touching and tickling him too.

I told her how excited I had been to see her in Japanese costume and asked if she could not manage, as she knew how to make a dress, to knock up a very low body and come to dinner one night in this very *décolleté* bodice, which I wanted to be quite low under the arms, so as to show the arm-pits, and was to be cut in the same V-shape as the Japanese costume, both front and back, as that shape suited her thin figure admirably. She replied that she dared not attempt such a thing, as Mamma had scolded her dreadfully about the Japanese disguise, and as for fancy dresses, at that moment: "she wasn't taking any!" I loved to hear her speak in English slang with her French accent.

We had a very nice long walk that afternoon together and she enchanted me by giving me a little present as a surprise. This was quite spontaneous, and formed the first and last present she ever gave me. And it was simply a little sachet about two inches square, of white silk, embroidered with the initials of our two Christian names. It smelt strongly of Lilian's aromatic scent, but the curious part of the matter was that she told me she kept the wadding it contained for two nights inside her virgin (?) furrow, in order that I should always be under the charm of the *odor di femina* which I loved so well, especially when I knew it was Lilian's. In spite of my blind lust for her, I am sorry to say that I did not believe her; I could not see Lily sleeping two nights with a little bit of wool inside her crack, for anybody. Still I was very pleased to think she should take the trouble to invent such a pretty lie for me, as the intention to make me happy was clearly there. I discovered that she carried her hatred of sentimentality so far as to be very delighted when I called her by the most opprobrious epithets and as I applied them to her, she would purr and lick her lips in a transport of delight, and rubbing herself against me, make me repeat the words: *salope, putain, vache,* etc., over and over again.

She also asked for more erotic dreams of cruelty and told me she kept most preciously the strap and the paint-brush I had left behind me at the end of August, when I had slept all night with her. I told her how I should like to spread-eagle her by tying her to the end of a bedstead, her arms and legs stretched out, forming with her body a kind of a Maltese cross, but she pulled a long face whenever I spoke of any position or diversion of passion which would force her to open her legs. I was more than ever sure that her little bird had flown, but I put on a most innocent air and asked her if she was not afraid to trust herself so much alone with me, because I might throw her down and violate her and I could do it easily here at Sonis, as she dare not cry out or make a movement that would disturb her dress.

"You need not take all that trouble, as I am keeping it for Jacky!"

I was so astounded at the coolness of her reply that I was suffocated for the moment, and she profited by my stupefaction to run on and tell me what happiness it would be for her to go on a journey with me to London and sleep with me several nights. I gathered from that proposition that she wanted to keep me from her until she could get me into a bed at night, and then she would make me believe I had seduced her. I was careful not to say too much, or she would have flown into a temper, been on her guard and I should never have known anything.

The same fun went on as before in the dark-room just as before dinner, and once being alone with Papa, he asked me if the authorities still allowed bawdy-houses to be carried on. I replied in the affirmative, and no more was said about the matter, but I thought it was just on the cards that Papa wanted to take Lily with him to one of those hospitable homes of free love.

Lily reappeared and put a stop to our conversation and we soon had to go in to dinner, for which we were late, much to Mamma's disgust, and we were treated to a long lecture from her as she pretended to make out that this photography was a folly and would never bring in a penny, while he and Lily would catch their death of rheumatism, if they passed their evenings in the damp little hut together as they were now doing nightly. This diatribe did not prevent Lily from following me to the tiny studio when I had to go in the middle of the dinner, or a plate would have been spoilt. We had a good bout of lip and tongue sucking and she put her fingers in the front of my trousers for a second, and then we returned through the dark garden as if nothing had occurred. Lily's lips were all chapped and feverish and she kept putting on the pink pomade. Both Papa and myself must have been licking her delicious lips this month, as they had never been licked before.

After dinner, Lily and I were quickly in the drawing-room, as Mamma had stopped all photography for the night, and getting rid of Granny, we kissed and caressed each other to such an extent that I begged her to finish me with her hand, or I should go mad. "What, really? You will enjoy in your trousers? You must not do that!"

Granny now returned, and speaking to me, drove my unsatisfied lust from my mind for a time, and then the pains came on again. I sat by her side as she tried to knock a tune out of the piano, but as her Papa said, "she couldn't play for nuts."

I talked to her in English and told her how I was suffering from what was called a "suppressed horn" and that I wished she had made me spend in my breeches just then. She said that would be disgusting. I retorted that there was nothing to be disgusted with when it is a man we are supposed to love, and she was very happy to have me tell her that if ever she slept with me again, she would have to lick my feet and under my arms, without counting other peculiar and strongly smelling parts of a man's body, at six o'clock in the morning, when all is hot and redolent of a rutting male. She agreed, and all was arranged in her mind to try and come to the station with me and masturbate me in a secluded spot, but nothing came of it. I think she played a deep part, promising me anything, and praising all I suggested, but I could not take any notice of what she said. I always guessed she would cry off at the last moment, and despite my great desire, I never believed much of all the stuff she told me, though at this moment I was ever head over heels in love with her.

Now came Papa to interrupt us, and he carefully installed his portly figure on an armchair, while Lily, as if obeying a sudden impulse, left the piano abruptly and took a footstool, which she placed at Papa's feet and then sat on it, pushing herself hard against his legs, as I could plainly see. Papa always maintained a dignified silence when Lily approached him in loving style before me. Mamma joined us and there was no peace until I had promised to come and spend the day on Monday, 27th. of February, as Raoul was to be there, having a holiday on account of the funeral of the illustrious personage I have referred to, and there was also to be present, a German friend of Mr. Arvel, of the Berlin financial papers.

FEBRUARY 27, 1899.

I started from Paris with a novel for Lilian, called *L'Anneau*, as the subject treated of a young girl who falls in love, but her sweetheart fights shy of her because she is a virgin. So she throws herself in the arms of a cool, debauched rake, who is quite surprised to find she is a maid, but he violates her speedily and, fearful of the responsibility, never sees her again, but the man for whom she has done this also discards her. Another lover now comes after her, but he is sentimental and proposes marriage. She accepts, hiding from him the fact that she is no longer intact. Through the boasting indiscretion of her seducer, as I call him out of politeness, the would-be bridegroom finds out her deceit and reproaches her bitterly. The curiosity of the novel is in the up-to-date manner in which it concludes. In the old sentimental days of my youth, the author would have rushed to suicide as a wind-up; here the young man takes the heroine to be his mistress and we leave him buttoning the girl's boots after a scene of sensuality in the middle of the day. I also kept Lilian supplied with the volumes of "Justine," and Papa and lynx-eyed Mamma must surely have seen the volumes sticking out of my pockets.

And another peculiar circumstance took place that very day. The advertisement about the dogs brought a number of answers and I may say at once that two were eventually sold for fifty francs each, out of the five that formed the litter; and all kinds of applicants wrote to ask about the pups. Mamma showed a post-card where most peculiar details were asked, the writer thinking that these were pedigree dogs, whose sire had won prizes at shows, etc. I told her to answer and say she did not know anything about pedigrees, but the dogs could be seen at any time.

"Sign your letter with a woman's name, and then you need not bother to give particulars. Any name will do,—Marguerite, Antoinette—"

"Or Justine!" exclaimed Mamma, interrupting me, while her

beautiful black eyes pierced me through and through, as she tried
to see what effect her bold mention of that name would have
upon me. I was taken aback and staggered for a second, but I made
no sign. Mamma and I were alone at the time, or else she would
not have been so bold. I debated with myself whether I should
tell Lilian or not, and after reflection decided to keep this queer
answer of Mamma to myself for the nonce. It was a useful bit of
information anyhow, as it enabled me to see that the mother was
an accomplice to Lilian's goings on, and as the afternoon grew
towards a close, another incident confirmed my theory and this
time it was of much greater importance.

We were all in the dining-room. I think the five o'clock tea
was being drunk, or had been served, when a ring was heard at the
gate of the villa. It was a gentleman who had come to see the
puppies, from the advertisement in the newspaper. Whenever anybody called, Lilian always rushed to the garden to see who it was,
and evinced great curiosity and a wish to show herself, and Arvel
generally followed suit, as he also liked to know what was going on.
But this time the couple never moved, and Papa told me to go
after his wife, who was already in the garden, and explain about
the dogs to the gentleman. I went, wondering at the attitude of
Lily and her Papa, who were standing up side by side, their backs
to the *buffet*, and both looking embarrassed and uneasy. Lilian
held her head down, and Papa looked quite shame-faced and also
seemed to be studying the pattern of the carpet. The visitor was an
officer in the French army, and he gave his name and address,
which I carefully noted, and he also mentioned that of another
officer, his friend, an amateur of the canine race, who I knew by
reputation as an *habitué* of the Café de la Guerre, where he used
to have his letters addressed. The visitor was a fine, tall, gentle-
manly, handsome fellow, about 35 years of age, with blue eyes
and a large fair moustache, but with no beard. I was very glad
to note this little detail, as I knew Lilian liked shaven chins, and
I wore all my beard, as I have already stated. He seemed very quiet
and subdued in his manner, and was visibly either ill at ease, or
very shy and nervous by nature. He asked a few unimportant questions about the little dogs and Mamma drew him away to see the

rest of them and their father and mother, in another part of the garden. I turned back to the house out of discretion. As I went strolling along, I saw the officer striding towards the gate, followed by Mamma, who had to trot to keep up with him. He was very tall, and little, paunchy Mamma was running by his side, talking earnestly and looking up at him, like a street-walker soliciting an unwilling stranger. She followed him out of the gate, and I went back into the dining-room, where I found Lilian and her Papa, who had not moved from their straitened position against the buffet.

Raoul, who was at home that day, on a special holiday on account of the funeral I have mentioned, now came running in to the dining-room and announced that Mamma had made a present of a pup to the officer, although he had not seemed surprised at first being asked sixty francs for the one he had chosen. Everybody seemed astonished except Lilian, who asked me what I thought. I answered that I could not understand it at all. I could not tell Lilian that I fancied he was her adorer, and that she was giving each of her lovers a pup, as I was to have had one. Papa, coarsely, as was his wont, said that if he had been a man and such a thing had happened to him, he would have thought that the woman who gave the animal, to him a perfect stranger, wanted him to sleep with her. Mamma took me on one side and in a greatly excited state, her voice, quite hoarse, and her lips white and trembling, excused herself to me, saying that she had done this to curry favour for her son. This was laughed at later by Raoul, who explained that he was in another part of France, and naturally this officer could do nothing for him. Altogether each one acted his or her part splendidly, including myself, who listened and looked at each and every one, saying never a word, nor betraying myself in any way. This is the man who took her virginity in November, I expect, and accounts for the story of the lieutenant, the silver châtelaine, and the late newly-developed love for officers in general. I kept my own counsel.

The German friend arrived after breakfast, but left before the officer came, I think, although he has but the place of a lay-figure in this story.

Papa had fainted away as from giddiness on Saturday and Sunday and was far from well.

After lunch he had a slight fit of vertigo and it was all he could do to keep on his legs. I offered to stop with him, but he refused and went to lie down, while Lilian, who I watched narrowly, never turned a hair. She seemed very hard-hearted, for although he was nothing to me, I suffered to see my big, strong friend grow white, and stagger like a drunken man, but the boy and girl were unmoved; and as it had been decided that Raoul, Lily, and I were to go out on bicycles, we did so, leaving Papa with his wife and Granny.

I must not forget that I had borrowed a Kodak and took everybody's portrait, but most of my films were monopolised by Lilian, and I got her in all sorts of positions, with her dogs and without, and I experienced sweet lustful emotion in ordering her to turn and twist in front of the lens, and make her pose in a variety of attitudes, merely so as to have the pleasure of commanding her to stand in such and such a way. She obeyed me with docility and was kind, loving, and tender to me all day, looking very bewitching both in front of my camera with her big, red, burning lips, and afterwards during our pleasant ride, in a bicycle costume, with a divided skirt.

When we returned from our ride, Papa was better, and I tried to diagnose his illness and reckoned it up as the result of a long winter's indulgence in the pleasures of the table, with no exercise; and living in a confined atmosphere, breathing the poisonous emanations of a slow-combustion stove in his sleeping apartment. There were the remains of the old mysterious illness of years ago and I began to ask myself if he were not syphilitic perhaps, but all this was in a very crude state in my brain at that moment, as my faculties were dulled by Lily's blandishments. Papa recovered enough to come and take some photographs of Lily with Raoul and me, and I tried to get Lily with her head pillowed on the broad breast of her handsome brother in uniform.

We dined late and Lily was seated next to me. She pulled her clothes up so as to expose her naked left thigh and signed to me to touch it. She remained like this all through the dinner, and I felt her thighs when I chose and when I could, without counting touches of her hands, and pressures of her feet. Add to this the kisses of the whole day and I think I had nothing to complain of.

The German friend had been invited to come and lunch on the first of March and go out for a bicycle ride afterwards with Miss Arvel, and I was told to come too. I consented, nothing loth, and returned to Paris with Lily's kisses wet on my lips and thoroughly convinced that despite Lilian's many lovers she still kept a corner in her heart for me. And I was ready to forget and forgive all, Papa and the others, past, present and future, if black Miss Arvel would keep her word with me.

MARCH 1st. 1899.

Papa had experienced difficulty in getting the requisite poisonous chemicals used in photography and I brought him what he wanted, some cyanide of potassium and bichloride of mercury, one ounce of each, together with some other trifles, measuring weights, samples of photographic papers and so on, to make myself agreeable to him, and I had, for the last year, taken subscriptions to the papers he liked and which I found inexpressibly silly: "Answers," "Tit-bits," "Pearson's Weekly," and a more serious publication, "Photography."

Soon after my arrival, and the most flattering welcome, Lily, who was ready dressed for the bicycle, gave me back the novel, *L'Anneau*, and when I asked her how she liked it, merely nodded her head, and ran away, leaving me alone. I had made a hit then? Something in that book had touched her to the quick. What was it? Had the man to whom she had given her virginity last winter left her after the sacrifice, or was she disinclined to talk about the rupture of the hymen? Should I ever know? What an amusing game of hide and seek she was playing, and what was her motive, if indeed she had one at all?

The Berlin gentleman I had already seen came to breakfast, and he spoke German nearly all the time with Papa, while Lily and I had it all to ourselves at the end of the table and a very pleasant meal it was, my lustful charmer being as amiable as it was possible to be.

In the middle of the repast, the wine ran short. Lily was sent to the cellar, and asked me to accompany her, which I did with delight, and we sucked each other's lips and tongue with rapture, Lily telling me to follow her into the dark-room immediately after breakfast, as she wanted to show me something there. We left Papa eagerly discussing the Dreyfus case in German, and as usual he was all in favour of the generals, as was the Teutonic guest. I had refused to join in the discussion, although Mamma, knowing my opinions, tried to get me to talk on the subject by telling the stranger that I held contrary views to his! I preferred to slip away with Lilian and we were no sooner inside the little cabin than after a long sweet kiss from her fevered lips, she plainly informed me that she wanted me to give her pleasure with my finger as she felt very "naughty." Nothing loth, I put my hand up her clothes, as she stood up, leaning against the sink, and my finger immediately touched the spot. I was very surprised to see her start and draw back, with a rapid movement, dislodging my hand completely. I saw at once what had happened. She knew, of course, that she was no longer a virgin, but her great preoccupation was to make me still believe in her virtue. In her excitement, she had presented herself in quite an easy position, the knees half-bent, eager to be manipulated, and I, full of lust and luncheon, had pushed my finger in too far, as I could tell by the soft warmth and moisture. I asked why she drew away from my touch.

"Oh, that is nothing. Don't be offended! Surely you can excuse an instinctive movement of shame?"

I was too clever, and at the same time too excited myself, to do anything but agree with her, and I was content to do my best to bring about the crisis, as she stood bolt upright now, her thighs pressed together. After the usual expressions of pleasure, she suddenly broke away from me, exclaiming that she had spent, and I said to myself that she had been remarkably quick about it. She now made a dive for my neglected organ, which she found quite ready to her hand, as it was all prepared, sticking out of the drawers, as I have explained. She caressed it a little, telling me to keep a sharp eye for fear any of the workgirls should come along, and bending down, took it in her hot mouth, rolling her agile tongue round its swollen head. She had not been sucking me for two seconds, when she got uneasy, and left off. I begged her to continue and finish me, as she stood by my side laughing and looking, and admiring my sign of virility, and she bent down again, once more popping it into the velvety seclusion of her warm mouth. But directly she felt that I was about to ejaculate, she left off suddenly, exclaimed that she heard footsteps, and fled rapidly from the tiny building, leaving me all alone with my stiff rod sticking up out of my trousers. The disappointment was so great that my erection soon passed off, and I was too much in love with the coquette to feel any anger with her.

With the same sensation of stupid passion, which is pleasing in its way, I started on my ride, with Lily and the German. Miss Arvel showed us the road, and she agreed to pilot us to a kind of tea-garden, about ten or twelve miles off. The German was not troublesome; he walked Miss Arvel's bicycle up all the steep hills, and there are many along the Marne, while we lagged behind and talked. I saw Lily did not want to work too hard, so as not to perspire, or tumble her hair. She wore a veil too, and was powdered, perfumed, and her lips well reddened, albeit they were swollen. Our conversation was very lewd. I showed her a lusty beggar on the road and admiring his rustic beauty, asked her if she would like to see his staff of life, adding that he would very likely show it for a few coppers.

"He would show it me for nothing," said Lily, with a merry laugh. "Charlotte would go and ask him, if she were here." And with a change of tone: "I can rub my little button in this divided dress, as I walk along," and the German being a long way off, she made all the requisite movements as far as I could see, and after a time announced that she had finished. I need not repeat how I talked to her; my readers will guess the state I was in.

"You don't think I've come like this?"

"Yes, I do! I know you are so awfully lewd. But soon you will be able to enjoy yourself immensely when you will be travelling alone with your Papa."

She feigned surprise and pretended not to know what I was talking about, but I saw she was not offended with my allusions to her Papa's love for her.

"You are going away on a nice little journey all alone with your Papa who loves you dearly, and you are very fond of him, which is not to be wondered at, as he adores you. It is a real honeymoon. Do not think I am jealous. I have noticed his love for you for a long time. It reminds me of a beautiful novel I have got, and which I must lend you, all about a father and daughter who go away together for a pleasure trip."

"Do you think that a daughter cannot misconduct herself with her Papa without travelling with him?"

"You are quite right, but it is much nicer to be entirely alone with the man one loves, amid fresh scenes."

She did not answer me, but laughed the matter off and changed the conversation. I think I chaffed her a little more that day, when the hazards of our ride brought us near to each other, out of hearing of the German gentleman, and she took it all in very good part, as if I was alluding to any ordinary flirtation. I am bold enough to say that she was proud to have made the conquest of her mother's old lover. What amused me most was the part played by the woman who was known as Mrs. Arvel. Did she know? As a jealous woman of ordinary intelligence in sexual matters, she must by this time have an inkling of what was going on, if she had not connived at it already by her policy of the open (bedroom) door. That was the one blot on the salacious picture, to my thinking, for having long since made up my mind that Lilian was one of those women of passion who were destined to have many lovers, a fact that excited my passions more than anything, it was a matter of perfect indifference to me who the man was, and how many we were to share her affection. I did not know whether to feel pity or disgust, when I thought of Lilian's mother. The latter sentiment carried the day, and I put her down as a selfish, calculating woman, who had given up her girl to serve her own ends. I felt a trifle horrified at that idea. All women have been tempted in their lives. Some fall, some few resist temptation, generally for the sake of the children, when there are any; and many a time I have seen and heard mothers, sometimes in a low station of life, shudder and weep at the idea that the little one, who had clung to their breast when an infant, and who they had seen grow up from an unsteady, tiny toddler to a graceful girl, might one day despise and blush for the woman who had carried her nine weary months in her womb, and whose lilliputian feet had kicked ever so gently within, as if to say: "Mummy, I am here!" How then can a woman who has ever "felt life," as it is called, in that way, prostitute her child surpasses even my understanding, all debauched and besmirched as I am. No, there was no excuse for Adèle; any woman is free to dispose of her own body, but not to debauch her children, her own flesh and blood. It is quite bad enough when they "go wrong" themselves. Lily's mother could not plead ignorance, as she had lived among harlots all her life and knew what went on behind the scenes in Paris and London.

I did not say very much more to Mademoiselle Arvel than is set down here. I, like all love-sick men, was afraid to put her out of temper, an easy task with wilful Lily, and I possessed a sentiment of delicacy with regard to her which was perfectly ridiculous. I hinted that she had done well to accept her Papa's love, and thus become the true mistress of the house. Her brow grew dark and serious as I spoke and she dropped into a brown study. To prevent her being too sad, I joked, and begged her not to forget poor Jacky, when she became "queen of the harem," and she allowed me to make all these silly quips and jokes. If I had not seen with my own eyes the recent passion of Papa and Lilian's seduction of him, my conversations with her would have sufficed to fix her guilt, as no girl, however debased, could have supported the strain of my lewd talk if there had not been something between them; something more than mere playing and romping.

Laughing gaily, we reached the garden and the inn to which it belonged. I called for a bottle of champagne which we soon finished, and Lily had her full share of her favourite wine.

We returned, and were late getting home at dark, Lilian having slipped us on the road and we two old fools lost our way. We had no lights and I was riding a hired machine, without a break, down steep hills in the dark. We struck the town at last, and I use the term advisedly, as I got my front wheel into a tramway rail and came down elegantly. And my reader must remember that I was 47 years of age.

We got back to the Villa Lilian, and were received like two prodigal sons, or rather two gay, old prodigal fathers, and as I told the story of how Lily had left us in the lurch, her Papa whispered gently to me that she was "yappy"; *i.e.* mad. (London slang of the East End.)

Lilian wished to know what we were making a mystery about, and I told her. I tried to improvise a "Limerick," and began:

> "Miss Arvel was a pretty young Jappy,
> "Who her Pa said was perfectly 'yappy' . . . "

And of course, I pretended to be unable to finish it.

Dinner was now served and Madame Arvel complained bitterly that she had prepared tea for all of us, including the gentleman from Berlin, and all the two big potfulls would be wasted.

"Not wasted, Mother," said Papa, with a saturnine grin, "it will do for Lilian!"

The remark being made in English, no one understood it but the speaker, Lilian and I, so Papa repeated it to Granny, laughing and chuckling to himself, as if he had made an excellent joke. I laughed inwardly, as by what he had said Papa had corroborated my suspicions extending over two months, concerning the virginity of his daughter. For the benefit of all young unmarried men, I must explain that tea is used as an astringent in cases of the "whites," the same as alum or walnut leaves, but such infusions are of no practical use, unless taken as an injection, and as injections cannot be taken by virgins, Papa was simply telling me that his bewitching Jappy was no longer a maid, and the tranquil way in which he said it, and the matter-of-fact manner in which Mamma, Granny, and Lily herself laughed at the witticism, proved that her maidenhead had gone some time back, sufficiently long enough ago for all her people to get used to her shame, if they knew what shame was.

I sat by as if I heard nothing, putting on the most innocent air I could assume, but nobody took any notice of me. No doubt, in years gone by I had let many strange remarks pass, without notice, so wrapped up was I in my love for Lilian, and they were all quite right to continue to treat me the same. I was not displeased at finding that I was supposed to be a fool, and I made up my mind to continue to play the part of one, which was the only chance I had of finding out the truth, without counting, and I hardly knew it myself then, I had a mortal dread of quarrelling with her I still foolishly called my Lily. So I suppose Papa thought Lilian had told me the truth, or that I had had connection with her, as he had, and she had not yet told him how I was a kind of a half-believer in her virginity.

When Papa had spoken, dinner was nearly over, and Lily jumped up and called me to come and help her to take the dogs out, and we promised to be back in time to say "good bye" to the German and accompany him to the station.

Lilian, finding that I had paid seemingly no attention to Papa's remark, made herself most agreeable to me, and I suspect the champagne and the day's outing had made her feel a wee bit jolly.

She told me point-blank that she wanted me badly and that she had formed a plan to get out on the day of Mi-Carême, which was Thursday, the 9th. of March, and spend the afternoon with me.

"What shall we do that day?" I asked, as I did not know but what I was wanted merely as an escort, as on Shrove Tuesday.

"Whatever you like, my darling, I shall be yours that day, and I will go anywhere and do anything you like."

I thanked her effusively, as I always was foolish enough to do every time she took it into her head to be like an ordinary tender woman to me, and our lips met in one of Lily's special, long, sucking kisses. There was not a soul to be seen, and we embraced and caressed each other madly; indeed I was rampant with lust, and made use of the most bawdy language, much to the wayward girl's apparent delight.

I cannot remember how it happened exactly, but I should fancy that I alluded to our masturbation of the morning.

"I owe you one!" said Lilly, "as you made me happy and I was too frightened to finish you, but I will now if you like!"

And before I knew where I was, I was walking along the

country road which led from the Villa Lilian to the Place d'Armes, with my person fully exposed, and Lilian gently manipulating me as I walked by her side. Whenever we caught sight of a rare passer-by, I drew my overcoat over my stiffened member, and Lily, with-drawing her fairy fingers, marched by my side like a nun going to chapel. Was it my fault or Lilian's that Papa's name was men-tioned? Lily always called him: "Mr. Arvel," when she spoke about him to me, and I talked once more about his love for her, she still pressing the sign of manhood in her warm hand, having taken off her glove for the purpose.

"It would be to your advantage to let him love you. Why don't you seduce him?"

"That would not be difficult!" was her swift rejoinder.

"I am a long time coming to-night," I said after a few moments' silence, during which I began to enjoy the touch of her clever hand on my private parts, for I could feel she was rapidly becoming an expert. "I suppose Papa is not so long coming as me?" I asked this question in a most quiet, offhand way.

"Oh, he is much longer than you," she replied quite naturally.

"How do you do it?" I answered, "with your hand or your mouth? Which does he like best?"

I thought I was getting on finely and had I had a proper reply this book would never have seen the light. Another moment per-haps, and I shall know all and as I spend she will confess her im-posture. But I had no experience with wicked women, as Lily dropped my weapon, which was about to go off, and ran away from me across the road. Like a fool; like a man burning to emit, I went after her, my miserable weapon sticking out in front of me at half-cock.

"What's the matter, Lily?"

"How dare you speak to me like that?"

That is what she said, or words to that effect, as she saw she had been too far. I only knew one thing at that moment; I wanted to spend, any way she liked, so I put my pride in my pocket, especially as I did not care whether Papa used her as a toy or not, if she would toy with me. I begged her pardon, making a very pretty little speech all about people who love each other never sulking or quarrelling together, but making the necessary complaint at once, and after discussing matters, the one in the wrong should freely beg the other's pardon and all be cleared up at once. Entirely mollified, my queen deigned to take me in her soft palm once more and kissed my lips, complaining how chapped and feverish her own were, while she continued to rub my stiff shaft.

We were standing on the pavement against the railings of a beautiful villa, and I told Lily that she was behaving like a common woman who made men spend in holes and corners at night time for a few pence.

"A common low prostitute that a man can do anything with, not like you, a wretched little cow . . . quicker now with your hand . . . who does not love me in spite of all she says!"

"Oh, don't say that! I do love you and would do anything for you!"

"Faster, love . . . faster, little whore!"

"Oh yes, I am your little whore!"

"And you would do anything for me? Anything, no matter how dirty or disgusting?"

"Anything, as long as it is you!"

"I take you at your word! I have a little biscuit in my pocket and when I have come, I will moisten it with my spendings and you will eat it!"

"Certainly, my darling, and I am ready to do anything else you may ask me!"

"All this time she kept on with her movements to make me enjoy, and I was so greatly excited that I knew I should be a little longer than usual in attaining the height of pleasure. It was a cold night; I was tired from my ride, and the champagne and the wine and liqueurs I had drunk had got into my head, for I am a water-drinker. I wanted to be finished before anybody came along the road to interrupt us, so I called out to Lilian:

"Faster, go faster still—and grip me tight! So! Hold it as tight as you can!"

"I can't press it tighter! I can't go faster! Oh, my wrist aches! I can't keep on! I shall let you go!"

"Beware if you do, little whore! I'll pay you well!! I'll give you a franc, two francs, if you do as I tell you!" She redoubled her efforts. "Now, I'm coming!"

Lilian shrieked, as if frightened, but she had sufficient *sang-froid* to direct the jet through the railings of the garden, against which we were standing, and I lost my head in the delicious agony of this onanistic diversion in the open air.

I took the biscuit and with it wiped away the drop that remained at the urethra, walking after my sweetheart, who had moved on a pace or two. I offered it to her. She refused to keep her word, as I thought, and I was in no way disappointed. I knew my own mania, common to many other men, if they would only confess it. It is that of imagining all kinds of horrors, or impossible tricks and schemes of lust when they are under the influence of extreme sexual excitement, but once they have discharged their elixir, all is generally forgotten. Women know this, and promise anything to the male while he is in this state. Beware then, my masculine readers, of what you tell your mistress during the long-drawn-out copulation of the morning, when, steadied by the work of the night before, the erection is constant, but the end is as yet far off. Ask your mistress at the moment to give up to you all her relations, masculine and feminine, to grant you the most filthy and unheard of favours. She will consent to all, and when you are satisfied, will laugh at your insensate longings. You, perchance, have betrayed your secrets, while talking as you lazily moved in and out of her hot gap, and now she knows that you want her sister, or would dearly love to have the little girl or boy who is asleep in the next room, in bed with you two. Perhaps the child you covet is of your own blood? So much the more voluptuous, but take heed of the awakening, when the delightful crisis is passed. Thus Lilian was debauched, I venture to think, when she came into the bed of her mother, between her and her lover, in the morning early.

I threw away the biscuit, laughing inwardly at my own folly, which I take a strange pleasure in unveiling here, and we began to turn towards her home.

She explained that she intended to go up to Paris on Thursday, the ninth of March, which was the day of Mi-Carême, under the pretext of visiting Charlotte, and her parents would let her, if she took her principal workwoman with her. She would leave her at the station, which would suit the girl too, and come to me, meeting the assistant in the evening to return home with her. I was delighted and thanked her a thousand times. Then she told me what to say to each of her parents in turn when I should see them at the station. I was to evince a lively interest in Raoul, and ask Mamma how I could send him some Eau de Cologne, since I myself had taught them that it was a sovereign remedy for tender feet. To Papa, I was to say that I hoped I should soon have the pleasure of a long, long day with him in his dark-room, without any gadding about, so as to become a real and efficient aid to him.

When we got to the station, the train had gone and the German too. We were both well scolded, and after due apologies on my part, I walked on with Mamma, as there was half-an-hour to wait for another train. I told her that I wished to send some Cologne water to her son, and she told me to arrange it with Lily, as Papa must not know, being too jealous of the lad.

During this, I watched Lily, who was eagerly and excitedly whispering to her Pa. Then I said good night to him as Lily moved away to let me recite my lesson, and he heard me out patiently. When I had finished, he frowned; and grunted, as was his habit, but never answered me at all. He was no dupe of our, or rather of Lily's petty intrigue, nor did he take the trouble to dissimulate.

After the usual effusive compliments at the end of such an amusing day, I took my departure, and went away to dream of the charming offer that my adored Lilian had made to me, all for love of me, for that glorious Thursday in eight days' time.

5

Virgin me no virgins!
. . . .
I must have you private—start not—I say, private;
If thou art my true daughter.

PHILIP MASSINGER.

Then, as to what she suffers from her father,
In all this there is much exaggeration.
Old men are testy, and will have their way.

SHELLEY.

LILIAN TO JACKY.

Sonis-sur-Marne. March 5, 1899.

My Jacky, who is mine alone,

My sweet dream for next Thursday, day of Mi-Carême, will not be realised, as I start for Brussels, Tuesday morning. I am very much annoyed. I should also have liked to have seen you before my departure, but in spite of all my insinuations, there has been no chance of arranging matters to have you invited. So I am in a rage, and I dare not insist too much for fear of exciting suspicion, which must not arise at any cost.

To-morrow is Papa's birthday. Do not forget to telegraph your best wishes on receipt of this note, which I write in haste, and in which I make the most monstrous faults; but you will excuse me, will you not?

I must have a line from you before I start, Monday evening or Tuesday morning.

I leave you; I hear someone coming upstairs.

I kiss you where it will please you most. I love you,

LILY.

JACKY TO ERIC ARVEL. (*Telegram.*)

Paris, March 6, 1899.

Many happy returns of the day.

JACKY.

As it will be seen, I sent the wire of birthday congratulations to my old friend, and I was highly delighted to do so, because I had no idea when his birthday fell, or what was his exact age, but I took it as proof that Lily was still at work for me, and in reward for my absence of jealousy, was doing all she could for me to remain in the best books of her elderly lover, for there was now no possible doubt concerning the illicit intercourse of the semi-incestuous couple, and once more the knowledge that he also knew about me from Lilian—as he could not be such a blind fool as to have ignored our connection—brought a glorious thrill of lust through my veins, as I conjured up a lascivious future at the Villa Lilian.

In obedience to my charmer's commands, I sat down and wrote her at once the letter she had ordered, which, as well as I can recollect, for I kept no copy, may be summarized as follows:

I thanked her for thoughts of me. I excused her not keeping her appointment, as it was not her fault; I told her to enjoy herself in every way and not to fret about me. She need not even trouble to write, if she could not find an opportunity. What did I care for a letter or so, more or less, since she had told me how she loved me? I was proud to be one of her troupe of marionettes, which she manœuvred with such skill, and she was so clever, I opined, that I took the liberty of calling her Mademoiselle Bismarck; and did not forget to put in a good word for the health of Papa. I told her that I should love her without stupid jealousy, and added some guarded maxims about women employing their natural cunning, talents, and beauty to entrap men for their own ends. "Seduce and give way, but propose your conditions beforehand, and remain sovereign mistress." I told her that I had been thinking over what she had said about an instinctive movement of shame when I had touched her between the legs. I wished to cure her of that feeling, desiring her to be absolutely without shame with me, and utterly perverted, if she cared to please me. I intended to punish her for that recoil from my middle finger, by making her stand before me, and with her clothes well raised, open her drawers and masturbate herself thoroughly, remaining as long as possible in this humiliating position, until thoroughly cured of all false shame with me. I concluded with all kinds of good wishes for her health and enjoyment, and recommended her to go to the Wiertz Museum, and the Zoological Gardens at Antwerp.

LILIAN TO JACKY.

Hotel des Grands Fabricants. Lille, March 8, 1899.

My best beloved,

We left yesterday morning, or rather yesterday afternoon, at 1:15 for Lille. We arrived at 5:30, took a little walk, and then had dinner. Then we went to a concert, where we assisted at a two hours' procession of the most grotesquely ugly women it is possible to imagine. After that, we returned to go quietly to bed in a large double-bedded room, as they told us there were no rooms communicating.

This morning, Papa had gone to Roubaix to see a friend. As for me, I told him that I did not care to go, so as to be able to write to my Jacky, for perhaps I shall not be able to do so before my return.

Now I am going to write to you very frankly. You are not mistaken; Mr. A. loves me and without quite knowing it himself. Nevertheless, he is and always will be respectful towards me. To begin with, I love Mamma too much to let things be otherwise and I do not love him at all! And then the bare idea disgusts me deeply, and is repugnant. Therefore, in future, I shall keep a watch over my most trifling words, and my most innocent gestures, as far as he is concerned, for I will not encourage this idiotic passion.

My dear adored one, you who are my only love, I hope that you will be able to understand completely what I am going to say. I am very unhappy here. I suffer and I should like to be home again already; firstly, to see you, to feel that you were near me, and also that you might support me by your counsel. I want to open my heart to you more than I have done up to the present. I feel so lonely and so sad. Mamma does not love me as before, and yet she has nothing to reproach me with, and I love her dearly. Mr. A. is so wicked towards my brother, that the poor woman thinks she ought to love him doubly. Note that I am not jealous, I love my brother too well for that, but I suffer to feel myself neglected by Mamma and I am too proud to let her see it.

But I fatigue you with all my lamentations; how can I help it? It seems to me that you alone understand me.

Love me well and tenderly, my beloved Jacky, my adoration. I swear to you that I require all your love and that I am worthy of it. Never have I loved any man before you, and never has any other man touched me.

I detest Mr. A., for it seems to me that it is his fault if Mamma is so changed towards me.

You . . . I *love*,

L<small>ILY</small>.

I am very good and shall always be so, where you are not concerned.

If ever I felt the lack of literary training, it is now. Oh! for the pen of a Thackeray, or the smallest modicum of his talent, to enable me to bring home to the reader in some slight degree the effect this letter had upon me. That it was entirely false from beginning to end, I was nearly inclined to believe; and although I did not mind her trying to conceal from me that she was now the official concubine of her mother's old lover, I felt a terrible pang of disgust and horror to think that Lily had pushed the deception so far as to try and render me unhappy and extort my pity by daring to say that she was suffering. I was always ready all my life to put myself in the wrong, so I confess I did for an instant have a little remorse, as I reproached myself for having given her bad advice. Had I debauched her? Had I ruined her young life? Had I, by my infamous training, nurtured those wrong ideas in her, which had driven her into the arms of a senile satyr, who had perhaps violated her, whipped her, kept her all night at work on his body, and disgusted her entirely? I got the letter in the evening. It was long; one of the longest letters I had ever had from her, and there was not an erasure in the whole of it. So, evidently, she had been at some pains to compose it and catch the post. She was fresh out of bed when she did so. I think the document may have been geniune up to a certain point, as far as the words "double-bedded room," and from there, all branches off confusedly, and she wanders and flounders about in her desperate attempts to hide the truth from me. And why write at all? Had I not told her a hundred times that I was not jealous and that she was free to dispose of her body as she listed? I wanted but a trifle of that love which she had always offered me herself from the onset, and as I have plainly stated in this wretched story, I never asked her for any favour that could possibly interfere with her young life, now devoted to the old man, who had shared her mother's bed for twenty years or more.

And why drag Adèle's jealousy into this pitiful writing, designed to trick and pain? She knew very well that her mother had naturally been jealous of her for years, and now she alone could form an idea how her mother looked and felt on the morning of her departure, and what she had said to her husband before God. There may have been some little disgust at the events of the night, although that is open to doubt, but any trace of physical repugnance would soon be gone after a nice déjeûner, when her Papa should return from Roubaix, if ever he went at all. Arvel's jealousy of Raoul I have already explained.

It is likely that the sexual act itself in its bare manifestation of penetration had no great charm for my ex-virgin, who cared much more for the preliminaries, and delicate caresses and attentions. Papa had probably never "had" her at his ease, nor quite freely, entirely naked in a bed in his arms; and the month of February had served as a sort of training for him, to get up his genital strength for this "honeymoon" trip. He was too fat and scant of breath, unable to stoop, and he would require time, warmth, and full commodity and space to enjoy a woman at his age.

It had long been arranged that she should give way to him. She had seduced him, partly from interested motives, partly through vice. She liked him; she was used to him. It was a great achievement for her to have triumphed over her mother, who in time would come round and accept the situation, if she had not done so already, and the two women would hold Papa between them and look after any money and property he might leave behind him when he died.

I took a great deal of trouble to try and analyse Lily's feelings from her horrible letter, with its depressing undercurrent of physical repulsion, showing the disillusion she experienced at the first night completely alone with him and at his mercy. In the morning, sick, tired, disgusted, full of regret and remorse; all her daydreams of tender voluptuousness rudely dispelled by the long and painful pushing efforts of the heavy-bodied and coarse stepfather, with his teazing semi-erections; ready to vomit; the cheap champagne, and bad drink and food of the provincial restaurant, and café-concert having produced their effect of nausea; her thoughts go out to me, and she starts a confession, which, like those of all hysterical females, is made up of equal parts of truth and lies. Lily is fearful lest I despise her; this tardy effort to stand well in my eyes is pitiful in the extreme, and to anyone unable to dissect the mobile brain of such abnormal creatures, the letter penned after this "first night" with Papa reads as the wailing cry of a violated, disappointed bride.

And perchance, all said and done, it may have been a vast and wicked hoax, arranged by the guilty pair to torture and trick a miserable lover, who must perforce, according to their petty ideas, be madly, wildly jealous, and at any rate, Lily, full of weak vanity, posing as a queen over men, and badly advised as usual by her Eric, would imagine that once a man has said, "I love you!" to a woman, he is her slave, bound by the chains of his passion, forged with his own hands, and therefore in a fit state to accept whatever stupid falsehoods his mistress would have him believe.

I am convinced that women are purely instinctive beings, inexplicable; continually changing and renewing their ideas and capable even—accidentally—of obstinate fidelity. They are to be pardoned or despised according to the degree of love we may feel for them. Arvel's mysterious daughter liked us both, but she wanted to keep her secret. Her treachery towards me and which she knew I had discovered, was a precise and plain fact which had upset her murky understanding.

She thought she was in duty bound to make me believe she had chosen between us two men, by saying that she must hate Arvel because she loved Jacky, not realising that I was quite ready to grasp the fact that a woman could be just as faithful to two men as to one.

LILIAN TO JACKY.

Hôtel des Trois Pigeons. Brussels, Wednesday, March 15th. 1899.

My love,

Just a word, in the greatest haste, to announce my return to you. We leave to-morrow, Thursday.

I am delighted, firstly because I hope to see you soon, and secondly, I am dreadfully bored here.

I must have a letter from you at Sonis for Friday, without fail.

To your dear lips,

LILY.

The foregoing was scribbled in pencil on the paper of the hotel, with its printed heading; the letter from Lille was also on the hotel paper, but in ink.

About this time, I had received news of Lady Clara, who was travelling in the south of France, and she never forgot to ask for news of Lilian. I had told as well as I dared that the course of my true love was far from running smoothly, and, without initiating her into the mystery of Lily's *liaison* with her Papa, I said enough to show her what a wicked little woman was my idol, and I told her that the history of Jacky and Lilian was as strange as a penny novelette.

"A novelette?" replied dear Clara, by return of post, "say rather a real three-volume novel! You write very nice letters, Jacky, why don't you put your adventures into a book?" I scouted the idea at first, but now smarting at the treachery of Lily, who was trying to turn me into a simple uxorious, paying customer of hers, I gradually got used to the thought of making the whole story of Lily, as far as I knew it, in book form. I counted my puppets. There were Papa, Mamma, Raoul, Charlotte, Lily and the author. A goodly troupe, by my faith! of which the first five formed as many links in a chain of vice; pleasant, alluring vice to a libertine like myself, but my gall was bursting to think that all was now changed, by reason of the news from Lilian. She had been talking to her Papa, and I was not to be admitted into the magic circle. The chain was stretched against me. Hence her change of attitude at present. I ought to have remembered that I was an Englishman, and have walked away quietly, without ever giving proofs of my existence down at Sonis, but long residence in France had made me as cunning as a monkey. I was tickled at the scheme of using my puppets to form a future novel, and I seemed to be doubling my personality, as I looked upon myself as an actor-author, playing the principal part in one of his own dramas. I wanted purely and simply to find out everything, with regard to Lilian, not for my own curiosity, but to be able later on to take her pretty head, and rub her sweet, pointed nose in her filth, shovelled up by her own hands. I knew perfectly well that Lilian was no longer a virgin, but up to now, I had pretended to believe her when she kept up the fiction to the contrary; I was fully convinced that she was the mistress of her mother's old lover. I wanted to show Lily that I knew all the lies she could invent; I should have the ferocious satisfaction of a Marquis de Sade, if I could only succeed in showing Miss Arvel that I saw through her, by placing before her eyes proofs of her own villany. How was that ambitious programme to be carried out?

It was a long time before I hit upon a scheme, or plan of campaign, which would enable me to show Lily and her parents, if necessary, that I not only knew, but possessed proofs, of three things: Lily's intimacy with Papa; the disappearance of her maiden-head; the evident complicity of all the inhabitants of the Villa Lilian to get money out of me, and let me have my sweetheart every day to myself if I would only "pay, pay, pay!"

How was I to go about my wild scheme? It did not come to

my mind all at once, but when it did creep into my brain, I fully grasped the idea, and it became an obsession, until I worked it out. To resume everything briefly, I intended to play "Hamlet" in private life, and pretend to go mad, if need be, to get Lily and any other inhabitants of her villa off their guard. Of course, should Lily prove true and tender to me, as she had promised before going to Brussels, I would drop my Shakespearean mask, and become my ordinary self once more. I knew I could hardly fail to succeed, as they were all so self-sufficient, that they would never dream that any man would sacrifice his own vanity, and coolly and calmly play the fool to try and find out a lying sweetheart's secrets.

To begin, I wrote the letter that Lily wanted to be at her house when she arrived home, and I kept a rough copy of it, which I am thus able to give here, and now all my love being well-nigh gone, and naught but a slight, forlorn hope of future lust remaining, I began to make notes and collect material for the volumes which are now in the hands of my patient reader.

JACKY TO LILIAN.

Paris, Thursday, March 16, 1899.

I love you, my Lily, and shall always love you whatever happens. I loved you first. I love you faithful or unfaithful, good or bad. Present or absent, I shall love you the same. You are my only love; the last love of my life.

Is not this the best answer I can give to your letter from Lille,—the cry of a troubled soul?

You can understand that I have great difficulty in composing this letter. I have so much to say to you; so many things which cannot be written, I think.

I have been truly full of anguish. I have worried my brain and passed through every kind of moral torture. I reproached myself many things, and felt remorse for certain advice I gave you. I accused myself of not having loved you as I ought to have done.

What greatly pained me was a sentence where you spoke of not being worthy of my love. But, little darling Lily, if one of us is unworthy, it is certainly not you.

You spoke of lamentations? I could complain all day, and I shall only be happy when I shall have seen you and consoled you. I will not let you suffer, darling.

The love I feel for you is quite devoid of all jealousy or mean afterthought. You have only to tell me, as you do now, that you love me and I shall be the happiest man in the world. I believe in you, because I feel that you adore me truly, and that you are always trying to find out how to give me pleasure. You are always thinking of me.

Certainly, I adore your caresses, your hands, your mouth and all your body—your childlike breast, your little black and pink thing, the other callipygean side, and your thighs, and all I have pressed, pinched, struck, felt, licked, sucked and moistened with my seed. But if you were to offer me all that, giving me to understand that you love me no more, that you give yourself to me solely for my pleasure,—I would refuse everything.

I appreciate with tender joy your true and entire love, with your heart coming at last to me with all your confidence. How good you are now! and I am worried, as I think that you have perhaps sacrificed yourself for your Jacky and I am responsible for the pain I cannot help seeing in your letter.

I must remind you that you promise me for the future absolute frankness; you pledge yourself to open your heart to me. You tell me that I alone understand you.

Then the mania I have for turning over every word you say in your letters, and for scrutinising and analysing all that comes from you does not displease you? Do I see clearly when I observe you, my angel?

There are moments when I curse my clairvoyance and I envy the grocer who is neither perverted nor vicious. But I have one consoling thought—if Jacky was not so *cochon*, you would not love him.

For the advice you ask, I am forced to tell you at once, until I can better make you understand my thoughts by word of mouth, that we should have no pride or haughtiness with our mother. You must absolutely go to her as if you were a little girl. Do you not know that we are always little children for our mothers? And a mother is never astonished to see her children come back to her at any age, as they used to do when they were ten years old.

Already a year ago you asked me the same thing, and my counsel was identical. The beginning of the reconciliation will be hard for you, perhaps, but you must persevere and make yourself caressing, tender and full of prayer to her. I cannot develop my idea more fully here.

This letter may seem to you stupid and incoherent. You must excuse the writer. I grope in the dark.

Since the 8th., I am as a madman. Only Smike understands me. The other day he did as follows for the first time in his life. We were alone. I felt all "topsy-turvy"—your word when you put on your air of innocence. Softly, he came to me and licked my face, my eyes. Then he left me, and went and laid down sadly.

Last Friday, at three o'clock in the morning, you were with me. I felt myself seized in a close embrace and a hand seemed to touch my face. In the trouble of the dream I said to myself: "Ah! 'tis Lily,—that is why Smike does not bark." I called you and woke bathed in sweat, crying out your name.

If I let you catch sight of a little corner of my heart, so sensitive when you are concerned, you must not think that I have become a poet since your departure. No, in spite of myself, I am always thinking of some delicious follies to execute with you, my adored little woman, and I have added a few holes to your leather girdle. You will give yourself freely up to this game of teazing pain and imitation of torture, will you not? I love it so much, because I know you give way for love of me.

I mean to inflict supreme shame upon you. I will have you in front of me in your drawers, and you shall come to me, opening them yourself, as I shall order you, and pushing away the chemise to show me your "pussy." I shall leave you thus for some minutes, happy at the slight humiliation you will undergo in exposing your nakedness yourself. Next, you will open your little slit yourself, with your two hands, so as to show me the inside quite fully. And I shall be quite naked, having undressed myself at once before you, so that you may judge yourself of the effect you produce upon me. It will be an extraordinary lewd delight for me to be naked as I was born, and keep you a little while with me, you being completely dressed.

I have developed the photographs I took of you and your brother, etc. There are only six good ones out of the twelve negatives. Bad work, that. But at last I have a photograph of you, taken by me, for me. I have half a mind not to show it to anyone, not even to you. It is indeed my Lily, who twisted and turned with such docility before me. I have the effrontery to adore you when you obey all my caprices at once.

One day in my life, I should like to have you quite humble and tender, saying: "Yes, Jacky,—if you wish it, Jacky,—certainly, Jacky, as long as it pleases you," etc. I should like to box your ears, and you say to me: "Thank you, Jacky." That is impossible; it is not in your nature.

I hope that the end of your journey was better than the commencement, and that your health has been good.

What would I not give for an hour or two of quiet chat with you! I will not read over these pages; if I do, I shall not have the courage to post them. But this will not prevent me when I see you, from treating you like the lowest woman in the world, and covering you with insults, as I call you by the filthiest and most infamous names,—since you have told me that to be insulted by Jacky makes you spend.

To both your wet mouths!

JACKY.

LILIAN TO JACKY.

Sonis-sur-Marne, March 18, 1899. My Birthday.

My own Jacky,

At last here I am back again, and I find your good, long letter. Have no fear about our correspondence, as never any of my letters are opened; you can therefore rest easy on that point. I was awfully bored during the whole week we remained in Brussels; in a word, this trip has been more of a task than a pleasure. I have many things to tell you, but I cannot describe them, as it is impossible to develop my thoughts on paper. So I shall do my best to have you invited.

I love you.

LILY.

P.S. Mind and amuse yourself well to-morrow, Sunday. I know that it is a day that you would not sacrifice and give up to me for anything in the world. This is a pity, as I shall be free to-morrow.

In my letter, to which this was an answer, I had put a postscript expressing fears lest my letters to her might fall into the hands of her parents, which was part of my scheme to prevent her thinking that I suspected her collusion with her Papa and Mamma.

What I had said in my long epistle had evidently worried her not a little, as I plainly let her see that I suspected something, and that I pitied her not a little for having been forced (?) to give way. And it was perfectly natural that I should sympathise with her, since she had apprised me of her suffering. My tenderness for her supposed trouble annoyed her, because she was lying. She tells me that she is going to get me invited to her home, and in her little, venomous P.S. teazes me for devoting my Sunday to the sick woman, as I had told her. I received Lily's note on Sunday morning early, as I was just rushing off to the country to spend the day with some relations of my poor mistress. I did not like them, but I went with the sick woman, who always thanked me for my slight sacrifice; she knew and appreciated it, as being done for her. So I sat down and nearly missed my train, in scribbling a hasty word to Lily, entirely forgetting in my temper the precious part I was playing, albeit it fitted itself in all the same. The evil intent was plain. She knew I was not free, so she said she was. She was also cognizant of the fact that at such short notice I could not come and storm her Villa, or telegraph boldly to her to meet me in Paris, in the face of her parents. I was very angry, and I told her, after the usual compliments for her birthday, of which I had hitherto ignored the date, of my rage, something after this style:

"Your P.S. was bad. I am deeply hurt. It is a useless, insulting sting. You are silly, and that makes me understand the word 'task' in your note. Beware then, lest you become too foolish; too kind; too good and easy with those who are not quite so loyal as Jacky. If you give them all the kindness that is so conspicuous by its absence in your P. S. you may just as well be dead. Do not be a slave, but try and make slaves; I will teach you how.

"Do you remember that night last winter when I missed the train, and I said to you: 'Some time in your young life you will be crushed beneath the rank, stinking, sweating body of some brutal monster? Then you will call out for your Jacky in the horror of the night; but he will not be there!' I did not think my prophecy would come true so soon, nor that I should be such a truthful soothsayer."

Next day I reflected how foolish I had been to write so harshly, just at this juncture when I wanted to get as near the truth as the Arvels would let me. But I soon found a means to repair my error and turn it to account, as the changes of mood that I was now going to simulate would make Lily and her father believe that I was going mad, and nothing is so flattering for a woman, as to suppose that she has such power over an infatuated male.

I am very intimate with a manufacturing jeweller, and to him I repaired without loss of time, and ordered, from my own design, a very pretty lady's ring, consisting of a turquoise, with a diamond on each side, and when made up, it formed a very handsome present.

I chose a turquoise, as that stone is symbolical of the month of November. Many of my readers may not know that there is a stone for each of the twelve signs of the Zodiac, and the last month but one in the year, governed by Sagittarius, has for gems, the blue stone I had chosen, and also the carbuncle, and in occultism they are lucky, and bring inheritances, gains, and fortune to the wearer. I chose the turquoise, because I had first had Lily in my arms in that foggy division of the calendar, and I had another reason, which the reader will see in due course, but I carefully refrained from letting her know, until it should suit my purpose to tell her.

After ordering the ring, I went to a post-office, and wrote a most designedly foolish letter to my own sweet Lily. I announced my present, and asked how I should offer it to her. Should I slip it into her hand on the quiet, or give it openly as coming from Mr. S . . . ? If she cared to say it came from a lady-customer, she could do so, as I did not wish to show off before her parents. It was quite enough for me to know that she had it from me. I said it was merely a trifle, but that I could not unfortunately afford to give her what she really ought to have.

I was very saucy to conclude with, saying that when I saw the word "birthday" on the top of her note, I immediately thought of a present for her, but I resolved not to give her anything, because of the insulting venom of her wicked P.S., and I think I added something about her want of delicacy at such a moment as the present, when her duty was to spare my feelings and be as considerate as I was. She knew that I was condemned to the weekly agony of a sickroom, and that if she loved me, she would write one word of regret, that little word the truly loving woman utters, when she hears the voice of her sweetheart change, as his eyes grow dim, and she hastens to cry to him: "You were wrong, dear, to say those cutting things to me, but I was wrong too. Let us forgive and make it up!" I added that she would never say those words, and I did not care if she did not. I was utterly indifferent and expected nothing but evil from her.

On Wednesday, 22nd. of March, I was confined to my room with a slight attack of influenza, the prevailing epidemic at that moment, and which I had caught from my poor mistress, who was always sure to become a victim to any contagion. Having nothing to do, I continued my work of posing as a mad lover by sending the following letter to Lily, which I devoutly hoped she would show to her Papa, and as I wrote it, I fancied I could see her running up the gravel path, after having taken her correspondence from the box, as I had seen her do, but this time, she would wave my letter over her head, exclaiming: "I've got him, Papa! I've got him!"

JACKY TO LILIAN.

Paris, Wednesday, March 22, 1899.

My nerves have been shattered these last few days for many reasons, but principally because you gave me to understand that you were unhappy, disappointed, and something had happened to cause you a great disillusion. I suffer too from pangs of remorse, as I think I am perhaps the cause.

I was about leaving for the country on Sunday, to put on a good face in front of people I loathe. The little bit of wickedness in your letter (which was otherwise delicious for me, although, poor little Lily, you still spoke of your misfortunes), fell exactly at the proper moment and on the right day to drive me beside myself.

It was stupid, for at an ordinary time, if I had been a little gay, I should not probably have paid much attention to it.

Therefore in my stupid rage, I answered too hastily, and in a coarse, cruel and impolite manner. I am not ashamed to confess that I bitterly regret all I said, especially as it is not my habit to write in such a manner, and above all to you, who I love more than anybody in the world.

Besides, I have not waited long to repair my wrong-doings, as my letter of Monday shows. Therein I offered you with a good heart a birthday present, proving that I tried all by myself, without waiting for a reproach from you, to mend my ridiculous ways, for which I blush.

You once said to me: "You don't know how I am worried and annoyed when I think of you!"

Fancy then, what I feel to-day, my adored Lily, and you will find a thousand excuses for me. I ask you simply to bring things back to the point they were at on Sunday morning. I ask you in the name of our love.

Oh! this correspondence, these sterile letters! I curse the deplorable facility for writing which I possess. It always makes me say something I should have left unsaid.

Here my rough notes break off abruptly, but, if my memory serves me rightly, I terminated by an abject apology, and declared that the fear of losing Lily had made me so ill that I could not sleep, and was obliged to take large doses of chloral, although I can truly say that I never was forced to fly to a narcotic in my life, and I added that if she would send a kind word by telegram on receipt of my letter, I felt almost sure I should regain my power of normal sleep. And I signed, "poor Jacky."

LILIAN TO JACKY. (*Telegram.*)

Sonis-sur-Marne. March 23, 1899, 9:50 A.M.

Sleep well, sweetheart.

LILIAN TO JACKY.

(No date or place.)
Postmark: Sonis-sur-Marne. March 23, 1899.

My very Own,

You had the scent of a detective to write to me yesterday, as I confess that I felt disposed to never more give you the slightest sign of life after your letter of Sunday.

Papa is in bed with the influenza, and I myself am only just a little better.

You are absolutely in the wrong and you do not understand what

I write to you concerning Mr. A. There is positively nothing and there will never be anything between us, but a great desire on his part, which manifests itself openly each time that he finds himself alone with me, which is horribly wearying in every way, and even rather more repugnant than anything else.

I suffer greatly from this state of things, but how can you fancy yourself responsible for it? It is no more your fault than it is mine, I suppose?

Thank you for the ring. I shall wear it with all the more happiness, knowing that it comes from you. It is preferable that it should be Mr. S . . . , who gives it me openly, as one of my lady customers is going to offer me one, and two would be too many.

You will soon be invited, but the indisposition of Papa alone puts off this happy moment.

I am impatient to see you, for we have a multitude of things to say to each other, and then I wish to see you for the sole pleasure of feeling that you are near me.

To your dear lips,

LILY.

The effect of my insane correspondence was now beginning to make itself felt; and my young lady was quite bereft of all prudence, or the atmosphere in which she lived had caused a total eclipse of all moral sense. Here was a young woman declaring coolly that her mother's old lover pursued her daily with his infamous passion; she living under the same roof as him, and this desire manifested itself openly whenever they were alone together. Which possibly meant that he opened his trousers whenever he caught her on the stairs, or coming out of the W.C. To write so coolly concerning a stepfather, with whom she had just travelled all alone, added to her letter from Lille, would, I thought, have been sufficient circumstantial evidence in a divorce-court, but I was still dissatisfied, and the more she tried to keep me off the track of her incestuous secret, the more I wanted to know.

Seriously speaking, no woman could live in the manner Lily wanted to make out to me. The loathsome disgust she would feel at the approach of the lips of her beloved mother's paramour, at

the touch of his gouty, nailless hands fumbling round her petticoats; could drive her to flight or suicide, if she really was the
right-minded girl she now wished to make herself out to me.
Where were the dreams of collaboration and photography with
Papa? How about the appointment for the day of Mi-Carême?
She talked vaguely of inviting me to her house, but there were no
signs of sensual longing. The ring and my show of rage, followed
by an unasked-for apology, had quite fogged Lily, and she took no
trouble with me, thinking evidently that I was in a condition to digest the rawest falsehoods, and I could not divest myself of the
notion that Papa was amusing himself by reading all my letters,
and that he was now her lover, pander, and father-confessor rolled
into one, so I locked myself up in my little den, and wrote the
following extraordinary concoction destined to throw such a cloud
of dust in their eyes, that in their vanity, she like all shallow, crafty,
vain women believing that my love or passion for her was so great,
that I could be easily rendered blind, and forget all teachings of
experience and common sense; while Papa loving darkness, rather
than light because his deeds were evil, kept advising her to stick
to the lie she had written to me in that vile elucubration from
Lille, which I am almost inclined to think was composed by the
pair together, or at his dictation, over the *café complet* in the
morning, in the double-bedded room. And why double-bedded?
I had only Lily's word for that. Since she had been imprudent
enough to write to me, probably because I expressly told her not
to, on the printed paper of the hotel at Lille, what was there to
prevent me taking the train and passing one night in the same
hotel, perhaps in the same room? My lust was sufficiently cooled
now to enable me to shrug my shoulders, as this thought came
over me. And I am sorry to say, I declared that they were not
worth the trouble, and I preferred to stop at home in Paris and
nurse my influenza, which was troubling me considerably. Moral:
Be careful how you use the hotel note-paper. A good plan is to
write at a different hotel to that you are stopping at. You can
always get a sheet of their paper for the trouble of taking a cup
of coffee there, and if you know how to lie glibly, an answer can
easily be received there too.

JACKY TO LILIAN.

Night of 24/25 March, 1899.

Little Lily darling,

So you have been ill? Influenza? You say that you are only just getting better?

I asked for news of your health in the long letter I wrote to you on your return. I hope that when you receive these lines you will be quite reinstated.

I am better. Sleep has come back to me, a little. Your good telegram, followed by a still better letter, comforted me and made things easier.

Then, darling, I felt myself loved by you. In 1897, you loved me only a little; in 1898, much more; and in 1899, you love me passionately. After my letter of Sunday, I might add not at all.

Frankly, that letter was too insulting. I still blush for shame of it. You have pardoned me, my love, because you are "crazy on Jacky." You said that yourself, when you called me your little husband. A wrong done to a woman we love is only inexcusable when she no longer loves us.

I still feel the desire to excuse myself. I detest narrow-minded, obstinate, pigheaded, vain people who think themselves degraded to have to say: "Pardon me, I am wrong."

I know some of the middle classes, decorated with the Legion of Honour, who would let themselves be cut into a thousand pieces sooner than retract anything they have once said. How stupid! I am vicious, perverted, depraved, my intelligence is below ordinary standards. I am a very ordinary faulty, vulgar man, but I try to be delicate in my sentiments and when I have to reproach myself for having done wrong, I candidly confess it. My loyal avowal is my best justification. I know the folly of mankind, and that the loving heart is often the prey of error or weakness. I shall always acknowledge my mistakes without false shame, pride, or obstinacy, but with sincere regret.

Charming Lily, who is about soon to call me to her side! I shall be able to touch you, to feel you near me, to enjoy your perfume, living flower that you are; read my pardon in your beautiful eyes, and depart with the satisfaction that I am still loved by you.

For the ring, spare me, I pray you, sweet love, the annoyance of having to give it to you, before everybody. Be ready and dressed, as soon as I come. I will give it to you when we are alone. Then you can run and show it to your parents, to know if you are allowed to accept it, etc. You know the old tune better than I. It is only a trifle, and for that reason will pass as swiftly as my tongue in your mouth. I am not rich enough to give you what you deserve. I only fear that by its style, by the stones I have chosen, it may not perhaps please you. And you are so good for me that you will always say it delights you exceedingly. I should like to put it on your finger myself. I would that it were never off your hand, that you wore it at night; especially at night.

I go mad when I sit down to write to you. It is true that I see you so seldom. My letter takes the place of a chat with you.

I feel my light, little, pointed, perfidious whore of a pen which would like to spring from my hand, not to be "cut," but to wander across the paper, and touch upon a burning topic to which you alluded in a bold, albeit delicate manner in your letter. And the inkstand is there gaping wide, full of treacherous blackness.

Permit me, sweet little baby, to wait until I see you to talk to you about it. I am afraid of myself and am frightened of my own literary dysentery, I feel that in a tête-à-tête with you I could risk saying almost anything, but written words seem often hard and wounding; that is why I leave a portion of your letter without an answer.

You write well, you say much in a few words, just enough. That is rare in a woman, but I have remarked—I have told you so—that you possessed a little of the resolution and the firmness of a determined man. I think I am more tender and sensitive than you. A man has never made you cry, I am sure, and never for me—but halt!—little, dirty prostitute of a pen!

I have some Eau de Cologne, a pint, prepared in a tin travelling bottle. It is what I promised your mother for Raoul. I must really bring it, or else your Mamma will think that I am one of those idiots who promise heaven and earth, and never mean to keep their word.

Shall I bring another volume of that romance of sanguinary pleasure? And now, enough! I have worried you sufficiently for this once.

To my dear lips, say you? Those are charming words, and I answer: Take them, my Lily, take the whole mouth of your

JACKY.

Although I tell you in my letter that I would not mention the burning subject you allude to in your note, I cannot prevent myself from saying that I sincerely pity your lover of Sonis. I judge him a little from myself. One vicious, depraved man is much alike to another. You love me and I live in the hope of some little compensations now and again, and yet I am very unhappy by the great longing I feel to have you all naked and palpitating in my embrace. How then must he suffer, from what you tell me? For he sees you daily, hourly, and there is no hope for him. Nothing for him. That must be Hell upon earth. I can understand his recent illness, his vertigo. I feel for him. I have known him over twenty years. He knew me as a youth. Now I like him more and my heart goes out towards him, as you make me realise his state of continual desire. Such is cruel suffering. In writing this, I have to make a great effort not to send you a lot of erotic stuff about the dreams of lust you cause me. I make myself ill with imagining all the things I could do with you. Alas! my poor dreams of voluptuousness are fated never to be realised.

When I write to you all these nice, lewd, mad tricks, my brain whirls round, and one of the four following disgusting things is sure to happen:

I.—I cannot sleep and if I slumber a little, I dream of you, and I ejaculate spasmodically in erotic nightmares, which fatigue and exhaust me physically and morally. Hence my nerves are unstrung by the cerebral masturbation of those erotic letters. I take chloral. I lose my temper and thus nearly lost you; to sum up: rank stupidity!

II.—Or I master myself, and then I have frightful pains in my testicles and lower down, in consequence of these erections and partial erections that I overcome and drive away. That is what happens to me when I return from Sonis after a long, but never too long, happy day, passed with Lily. These are particularly sharp pains, especially as they begin by sweet, slow enjoyment of a teazing kind, provoked by your delicious secret touches, and your stolen kisses, my beloved.

III.—Or else, being alone by day and night, thinking of you in spite of myself, and of all I could do with you, my hand slides, without my knowing it, between my thighs and with a few movements of my wrist I discharge in my fingers. It is idiotic and sickens me as soon as the brief sensation of burning pleasure (?) is passed. Thus does one become disgusted with oneself. Once I spent in the train coming back from Sonis this winter, after you had said to me: "What can we do in a dining-room?"

Miserable mankind! What a dirty bundle of rags is our poor body, when excited by our sad monkey brain, boiling over with infamous lusts.

IV.—To conclude: the sole resource of salvation for he, who can still have an erection and emit, is to seek out natural, complaisant pleasure for cash on delivery, but I think that disgusts me as much as my hand. All my life I have hated mechanical delights. I never had any taste for the joys of love without some sympathy; if only for an hour; without a little reciprocal passion; or, let us say a small quantity of affectionate illusion on both sides, in default of true love.

What confessions! You will soon know the male in all his ugliness. Perhaps you will be disgusted with me?

If it pleases you to answer me in a few lines you will make me very happy. I chiefly beg news of your health, and of your Papa.

I should wish you to give serious attention to what I am going to tell you. When you announced your departure, you said to me: "I must have a letter Tuesday morning." Then, from Brussels you wrote: "I must," again. Those orders expressed by you gave me a new sensation, that I had never tasted or desired with any other woman up to now.

The first revealing shudder of this new form of passion which comes from you to me, because it is you, shook my frame when I was with you and your brother in the drawing-room, where, laughingly, you gave me a kind of little lesson of discipline. I have already spoken to you of the effect produced, as well as of the strange excitement caused in me by your recital of the tale of Madame Rosenblatt's pupil. You are cunning enough to guess the meaning of my new thoughts. If this is repugnant to you, if you think I am ridiculous in trying to see if we cannot both find a novel and real pleasure, I, being your slave in every way, in the true sense of the word, and you, by holding me beneath your severe yoke, to be punished when you shall judge that I deserve it,—I promise never to speak to you about it.

I must confess frankly that this desire, although a little vague at present, thrills me and makes me tremble deliciously. I am agitated voluptuously by a movement that I have never yet experienced until this day. I am quite overcome by this change which has taken place in my being.

It rests with you to do with your Jacky whatever pleases you in this direction, or to forbid him to have such ideas.

In either case, this is the only indication that I shall give you. To teach you your part practically would cool me completely. I could not do it; I should not have the courage; I give you the broad lines, hoping that as I dare to say that my *poupée* rises at that idea, you, as you say you love me, ought to be wet as you read these words.

I will not tender you the homage of my obedience, unless you also get a glimpse of a new incarnation of sweet, loving delights.

I offer you the virginity of my humiliation. I shall understand that you accept with transport the abandonment that Jacky makes to you of himself, and of his so-called manly rights, but I should also comprehend without surprise that you would perhaps like to remain as we are, instead of reversing our positions to see what would come of it.

I tell you also frankly that, although taken up by this strange longing, ever since the day I told you, it may happen that once tried I may be the first to mock at myself. That remains to be seen.

It is an experiment to be tried, if you smile favourably on my ideas. With my wide tolerance for every manifestation of sexual passion, whatever it may be, I should not be surprised either to see you accept with enthusiasm, or refuse with mirth. As you please, Lily. All you do is right.

I have faith in your imagination, if you accept the command of your lover as freely as he gives it.

In the meantime, whatever you decide, I give up to you the direction of our correspondence, and will only take the liberty to write to you when you desire a letter, telling me the day, etc., as you did when travelling.

I have serious reasons for asking you to accept the entire direction of our *liaison* in the future.

I feel that I want to believe in you, to see events with your eyes, and feel in everything as you do; as you shall kindly direct my mind, by your firm will.

You have seen, I confess it humbly, that I have dared to doubt your word, though plainly written, as I rebelled idiotically against you last Sunday, when I began to lose the faith I had in you. I actually dared to form absurd theories about your conduct, instead of dutifully, and religiously believing in you, as I had done up to the present.

Take me therefore quickly and knead my brain,—the unbelieving brain of a man madly fond of you,—as you will, so that I may look at things as you desire and direct. Let me only have the ideas that you may dictate to me. I want to believe in you blindly. You shall be my religion; my holy, persecuted virgin.

Save me from my thoughts, and come and direct my soul with my body for your caprices, for your wants.

I await the pleasure of your answer with anguish. My eyes will be dim as I shall open your letter, if you deign to write to me shortly, to signify my salvation to me, and the peace of my tortured heart brought to me by the blind worship I dedicate to you.

But directly I see that in your great kindness you accept to *tutoyer* me,—while I shall return to the true respectful formula I ought never have abandoned,—I shall know that I am at last worthy of being fashioned and moulded by you, as you may wish.

I hold at your disposal all straps, belts, pins, whips, and all instruments, which I confess, to my shame, I meant to use with Lily.

Your humble slave,

JACKY.

I felt sure that the foregoing letter would convince Lily that I was mad with uncontrollable lust for her, and I also wanted to know if her Papa saw my letters to her. That is why I had added the paragraph concerning the unfortunate lover. The only danger I ran was that Lilian should see through my artifices, and feign indignation at my bold insinuations. But no, I had had in my life a tremendous experience of liars, and I have found that habitual falsehood-mongers are exceedingly credulous themselves, and Lily and her father would be sure to fall into the trap I had set for them. That a man should so degrade himself as to boldly set himself down in writing as a convert to the doctrines of Sacher-Masoch, and parade his sexual inversion, proves that he is entirely under the charm of the enchantress, and by apparently throwing aside all vanity, I hoped to arouse all that of my infamous couple.

The girl would be proud to show her old man how desirable she must be to so fuddle my brain, and her elderly lover would be elated to know that he was making a fool of me.

How lucky it is that women are not truly intelligent. All they really have is their natural charm and the power to draw us in their net by reason of their possessing that which our genital instinct forces us to covet: the little, furry money-box. Put a coin in the slit, and the figure will work, but as our lust is soon satisfied: to keep us enthralled, women's cunning is called into play, and their principal weapons—lying and craft—are furbished up to supplement the influence produced by their beauty and our own infatuation. If, added to their sexual sorcery, they were able to get the true range and direct their fire; without exaggeration of mendacity and diabolically distorted fables, then would all men be slaves without exception.

In my case, Lily was so sharp in her jugglery, as witness her recent letters and principally the missive sent after the night at Lille, that she would never credit that I might fathom her deceit and take to sending Machiavelic manuscript as well.

The study of this strange creature became quite absorbing, and I left myself no rest. I thought about my old flame by day and by night. It was well I did so, as I suddenly remembered that I possessed a very old friend, who lived in Brussels, whither he had retired to end his days, after a long and brilliant career at the English bar. He had been a criminal lawyer, and his name, Augustus Mallandyne, was well-known in the divorce-court. He would seize the situation at once, so this was what I wrote to him.

JACKY TO AUGUSTUS MALLANDYNE.

Paris. Wednesday, March 29, 1899.

My dear Mr. Mallandyne,

I want you to do something for me, which is very easy, but it is confidential, delicate work, such as only a man of the world like yourself can undertake for another man of the world like myself. Please note my subtle flattery, as I purposely refrain from speaking of your legal talent.

And after all, if you do not like the job—why do not do it. But if you can, you will be rendering me an immense service, at no cost or trouble to yourself.

I have no time to-day to tell you all the ins and outs of the story, but I will, and you will be delighted, later on. It is a charming love affair, and if you can get the information I want, I may be very happy.

A lady and gentleman stopped at the Hôtel des Trois Pigeons, 255, Avenue des Haricots Blancs, Brussels, for about a week, leaving for Paris, I believe, on or about Tuesday, the 16th. inst.

Description of gentleman:

Tall, any age over 50, bald-headed, aquiline nose, wears a *pince-nez*, talks loudly, with an English accent, dresses carelessly. A fair moustache, no beard or whiskers. Big belly.

Description of lady:

Young, about 23 or 24, looks older. Very dark, lots of black hair, good figure, although very thin. Long nose, not pretty, but pleasant; fine Spanish eyes, swarthy complexion, nice teeth. Coquettishly dressed.

Would probably register under the name of Arvel. Try for this name first. If not Arvel, what name?

Did they travel as Mr. and Mrs.? Or as father and daughter? Or uncle and niece? Or what?

IMPORTANT—What rooms did they occupy? What numbers? *Single bedded; double bedded; two rooms communicating; or two separate rooms?*

Did they seem loving and happy? Was the girl sad or gay? Did they go out at night, or go to bed early?

I want you to go at once about this, as soon as you get my letter. I shall look for details by return and expect a letter Good Friday morning—if you are in Brussels.

. If necessary, be generous to garçon *d'hôtel* or *femme de chambre,* and I will refund any *pourboires* you give. May I ask you also to send me back this letter? Not that I care much, but this is rather indiscreet, what I am doing.

The whole story when I have heard from you. Be quick, and accept beforehand my heartfelt thanks.

JOHN S...

P.S. To make things easier, I enclose a photograph of the lady, I have just got hold of. You must hurry, please, as the photograph has got to be put back in its place before its loss is discovered. So please return it with information, if you don't mind undertaking it.

To avert suspicion, go gently to work like this at first:

See visitors' book. If you find:

Arvel, Miss and Mr.

or,

Arvel, Mr. and Mrs., with dates and numbers of rooms, or number of room,—say nothing, but remember the figures, and under pretext of choosing a room for a friend who is coming, go up and find out the sleeping accommodation of the rooms occupied during their stay by the Arvel couple. Because if they registered as Arvel, I shall not want you to show portrait, or get other details, unless the servants should gossip easily.

LILIAN TO JACKY.

No date or place. Received March 30th. 1899. Postmark:
Sonis-sur-Marne.

My own Slave,

It is an understood thing. All you propose in your letter pleases me enormously, with but one exception. I want you to still continue to *tutoyer* me.

Enclosed you will find an article on fashions that you must translate literally into English, and as soon as it is done send it me with a long letter.

You will be invited for Easter Tuesday, if you do well the little work I give you now.

LILY.

I want a very passionate letter.

This note contained a long article on ladies' fashions, cut from a Parisian daily paper, and I was highly pleased, as I saw my vicious scheme was working well. The translation was wanted by Papa, there could be no doubt about it, and the fact of asking for a lustful letter proved that my mad effusion had amused and perhaps excited the lecherous stepfather. It is always a bad sign when a woman asks a man to write letters in a given key, and nearly in every such case, someone is waiting to laugh at the writer. It may only be a female friend, but of a surety the confidential character of the correspondence is gone. It is no longer the frank communion of two hearts that beat as one; a third party has been invited. I could not refrain from heaving a deep sigh of regret, despite all my scepticism. Lily had betrayed and sold me to her mother's lover; my letters served to make me a laughing-stock in his eyes, and I shuddered to think what a fearful fate awaited me if I had been possessed of less knowledge of the wickedness of the world.

The more I found that I was right in my awful conjectures, the more I was devoured by the feverish desire to carry on my endeavours to the bitter end, and know the worst. It was only thus that I could cure myself of any love I might still feel for the traitress of the villa.

Spurred on by the spirit of deceit, I tackled the translation and got it done and posted the same day. I did not forget the letter of lust, and dashed it off so quickly that I had no time to make a copy. But I made a few notes next day, as I was still thinking, and the thought assumed firmer proportions every day, of writing my romance that was growing fast out of the festering soil of the garden at Sonis.

Some of the photographs I had taken last month were tolerably good; one, representing Lily lifting up her skirt just a little, and smiling saucily, I had printed several times, and a copy was enclosed in my letter to Mallandyne, to aid in identifying the pretty little tourist. Another showed her reclining on her brother's breast. He was standing up in uniform and his arm encircled his sister, whose eyes were half-closed, her lips parted; and there was a smile on her features that gave her the appearance of a woman in the act of enjoyment, and there is no doubt in my mind but what she did feel a secret titillation of the vulva at that moment. I had rendered an ordinary sheet of note-paper fit to receive the impression of the negative, and I printed her head and bust on it, temporarily arranging the plate so that no other details appeared.

My letter was not very good, consisting of four pages of erotic twaddle, relating to the cruelty of women. I was careful only to speak very vaguely and I did not give her any details of what could be done to a man who might be really fond of being whipped or ill-treated by one of the weaker sex. I knew Papa was fond of books on flagellation, but I did not see my way clear to give him examples of torture. I told Lily that she knew how disgusted I always was when I had to write lascivious letters, as the effort aroused my passions uselessly, which was my real opinion, and it was downright cruelty on her part to force me to write voluptuous manuscript, being unable to see her as I should wish. Not content with making me suffer morally, she now seemed resolved to try how to torture me physically, and I concluded by the narrative of a dream I was supposed to have had, when I saw Lily reclining on a sofa, and as far as I could judge, enjoying the caress of an eager tongue. She was spending, and some hidden power held me back, and prevented me from rushing to her, or calling out her name. Yes, she was spending, and he murmured: "Enough! Enough!" All my lust seethed up in me; I felt I must approach her, and making one mighty effort, I awoke! I rose from my bed, to refresh my burning mouth and wipe away the trace of this "wet dream." Before returning to my weary couch, I gathered together some sheets of paper on which I had been taking some rough notes, before falling to sleep, and Lily must judge of my surprise when I found impressed upon a fragment of white paper the beloved features of my sweetheart in the act of enjoyment. I had felt inwardly during the vision, that I longed to possess her portrait as she thus appeared, and now some mighty, supernatural power had caused the dream-face to leave its impression on a leaf from the note-book of her lover and victim. I terminated with the humble wish that one day I might perhaps be allowed to produce her orgasm with my tongue.

Generally, according to Lily's old directions, I always addressed my envelopes in my disguised female hand, and posted them at a post-office a little way away from my dwelling. This time I did not disguise my writing, and posted the bulky missive, so that it bore the postmark of an office in the very next street to where I lived. I need hardly add that this was never mentioned to me later, but I noted it silently for my own satisfaction.

AUGUSTUS MALLANDYNE TO JACKY. (*Telegram.*)

Brussels. Friday, March 31st. 1899.

Commission executed, writing.

AUGUSTUS MALLANDYNE TO JACKY.

Brussels. March 31st. 1899.

Dear S...,

Yours to hand. I know the two Boomaens, Ghent people, brothers, who keep the Hôtel des Trois Pigeons. I saw the principal man. He very willingly gave me all particulars.

The couple took Room No. 4, composed of two rooms *en suite*, separated by a lobby, where you could hardly see. The front room, with

one or two windows, I forget now, but I think two, giving on the boulevard, is large, and with two beds.

Introduced the girl as daughter—several times—and also to gent in room when taken, who had not yet turned off. Boomaens tells me he would say, with pride: *Ma fille, monsieur!*

When the out-going lodger came down to the *bureau*, he said: "Funny father! I almost thought he wanted me to have his daughter. Seemed to be throwing her at my head!"

They had one room with a screen as shown by the drawing enclosed.

Out every evening, theatres, etc. Very gay, apparently happy. He recognised photo. They arrived on March 8, and registered as A . . . , *père et fille.* A . . . has been here before and is a client of the hotel, to a certain extent. I am well known there and they have a great respect for me, as I send them customers. Of course, I gave no name as to my principal. Boomaens knows I am acting professionally. *He seemed quite to understand that the mutual relations of the two visitors were assumed.*

They could have used the other room if they liked, but they never touched it. They used to get up late. It appears somebody in the hotel, one or more persons, used to slip into the dark passage between the two rooms and pry and listen. They heard noises of romping, laughing, sounds of slapping, and smothered, inarticulate sounds, as plainly demonstrative as they were incompatible with the declared relationship. The bedding was always in a very tumbled state, leaving no doubt as to what took place. Also, towels, stains, etc. I fancy from what I elicited that something peculiar had been seen.

I dared not ask for more details, as it might get to my wife's ears, and she might think I was spying for myself, but it was plain, those walls, could they have spoken, would have unfolded a tale of lust as seldom reaches the public ear.

Why not come yourself and stop a few days with us as you did before? I'll take you to Boomaens. Shall all be glad to see you.

This is a cheap, quiet hotel, very well conducted, and quite respectable. My wife and a lady friend came there only a month ago, in order to take an early train, next morning, to Italy.

A . . . coming there with a little Parisian prostitute, and registering her as his daughter caused a sort of excitement in the hotel. She was known as *la petite femme.*

Boomaens said A . . . was in some way connected with the Stock Exchange. I am quite sure that Boomaens is not likely to commit any indiscretion. He took me upstairs on his own invitation and explained the arrangements of No. 4, about the best in the hotel, on first floor.

The visitors' book was blank as to departure but I would not, in fact could not, wait while he turned up his accounts. I had a heap of business to attend to, but I managed your affair all the same.

I wired you this morning: "Commission executed, writing," which was intended to show you all was in train. Are you happy? Let her have it *hot*.

Yours truly,
A. M.

Very pleased to be of use to you—old friend!

I can find nothing better to write here than the well-known sentence: "Truth is stranger than fiction." Lilian and her mother's keeper had gone to a town together where lived my friend, who "understood things," and to whom I could write freely; and by a lucky chance, he happened to be on intimate terms with the proprietor of the hotel where they stopped. I am perfectly certain that many of my readers will smile increduously at what they will consider the artfulness of the author of this book, and the very strange coincidence which I point out will suffice to make them doubt my veracity, a contingency which I cannot prevent in the least.

I was satisfied with the result of my enquiry, which fitted in well with my suspicions, and I felt myself fully armed to meet my darling and see what would be her next move.

Is it not extraordinary that a man known to an innkeeper should register as *père et fille*, and remain from the 8th. to the 16th. in a double-bedded room? Apart from the question of vice, is it not madness? Sleep with your daughter or stepdaughter if you will, while on a trip, but is there not some other cleaner way of going about it for the sake of the young woman, whose reputation you are thus coolly damning, whose life you are wasting? As I write these lines, the hot blood rises to my face, I blush for shame to think that I should dare to judge this man; I, who had perhaps been as great an agent of corruption as he.

Arvel's behaviour in this instance was so monstrous that even Boomaens does not believe his companion can be his daughter, and Mallandyne, who is far from squeamish, has not guessed, and cannot guess at the truth. Perhaps that is why Arvel does it?—"If I do it openly, no one will believe it." Like the woman who goes up boldly to her husband and says: "Do you know, dear, that your friend has just had connection with me?" The newly made cuckold bursts out laughing at his wife's indecent fun, and the jesuitical adulteress joins in his mirth. Perhaps he tells the lover in covered terms of his wife's joke and they all roar together.

The great Mallandyne had returned me the photograph and my own letter, together with a sketch of the room at the Hôtel des Trois Pigeons, from which I have prepared the plan given in this volume.

If the reader has any doubts as to the fornication of Arvel and Lily, I must beg him or her to reflect a little on what a celebrated English judge, Mr. Barnes, said when directing the jury in the suit for divorce of Sprague v. Lihme, which was decided in the spring of 1899, in London. (*See Appendix C.*)

JACKY TO MALLANDYNE.

Paris, Monday, April 3, 1899.

My dear Mr. Mallandyne,

It is impossible for me unless I were to write eight pages, to thank you for the clever and prompt way in which you have behaved in rendering me this signal service.

It is strangely lucky that the only person I know in Brussels, should be the very one, almost the only one, who could see through things, and guess exactly what I wanted and do what was wanted. If you had read in a novel how a man possessed a friend in a strange city, who did for him what you have done, precisely when he required his aid, you would sneer at the barefaced lameness of the invention.

I remembered your many delightful stories of the law-courts and how you had taught me some of the tricks of spies and criminals, and that is why I took the great liberty of asking you to help me.

What I have done through you is not a very clean thing, I admit.

Spying is mean and I say so myself. My excuse: "All is fair in love and war."

I have no need to tell you the whole story. It would be too long and I see by your letter that you in your worldly wisdom have guessed everything.

No doubt we shall see each other before we die and have a nice, long "crack" together over a friendly glass. Then you will hear all. It is only of interest to me.

I don't think I shall give it to her "hot," though she deserves it; I shall tuck your information away in a pigeon-hole of my brain and await developments.

Perhaps one day, I shall ask her if she has ever read a novel by Conan Doyle, called: "The Sign of Four."

Thanks for your kind invitation, which I shall remind you of in July, if you are then in the Belgian capital and care to have me.

Please remember me to Mrs. Mallandyne.

With more thanks,

Yours very truly,
JOHN S...

END OF VOLUME II

III

1

GLORY. Look into my face. You must believe me in spite
of everything.

. . . .
STORM. What are you saying?
GLORY. I love you, I have always loved you, and you love
me—you know you do, you love me still.
STORM. For God's sake. Glory.
GLORY. Kiss me, John.

HALL CAINE.

ERIC ARVEL TO JACKY.

Sonis-sur-Marne, March 31st. 1899.

My dear Jacky,

Many thanks for all the papers you have sent me. I went to see
your uncle last Sunday week, and came away with a bad attack of
influenza, which I do not seem to be able to get rid of. I was in bed
three days last week and I feel as if I could put in the same time again.
Raoul is at home for his Easter holidays. If Wednesday suits you,
would you come down and taste the *cuisine* of "our boss." Raoul is
obliged to return on Thursday morning.

If you like Tuesday better than Wednesday—"tip me the griffin."
With every good wish for you and yours, believe me to remain,

Yours very truly,
ERIC ARVEL.

337

I was far from being cured of my grip, and ought not to have accepted this invitation, but I was dying to see my lying Lily. So I sent a postcard, on which I had printed my own photograph, with my cordial acceptation.

I felt very shaky on the morning of April 5th. and a peculiar accident happened to me, that troubled me still more.

I got into a fiacre to drive to the Eastern station, and the horse bolted in the Rue Lafayette, dashing on to the pavement, and breaking the shafts. I jumped out and looked at my watch. I had just time to catch my train. I called another cab, and I had not been in it five minutes, when this second horse bolted also, and shying at a handcart, which stood by the curb, went headlong into a shop-front, and stopped suddenly, pitching me forward, while the coachman flew bodily off his box, one of the front wheels passing over his ancle and hurting him seriously, if not dangerously. Luckily for me, directly I saw the horse become uncontrollable, I had let down all the windows of my closed conveyance, and as I fell forward, I heard the crush of glass down below in the hollow frames. No harm came to Jacky. I thought I bore a charmed life that day. I jumped out again and was confronted at once by some gentlemen who had witnessed my first accident. They defied me to get into another fiacre, but I did so, and caught my train with not a minute to spare.

Why I mention these strange narrow escapes—two bolting horses in ten minutes—is because they shook my nerves to a fearful extent, and I forgot all the calm resolutions I had made to myself. I had arranged not to mention my enquiry at Brussels, but to be quite cool and collected, and play the part of a lovesick, ignorant fool, sympathizing with a martyr. In my half-feverish state, under the effects of the influenza, these accidents made me quite unfit to struggle against the Arvels, or carry out my schemes with a view to the ulterior publication of my adventure as a novel, as I should have wished.

APRIL 5, 1899.

When I arrived, the father was alone in the garden cleaning the bicycles of Lily and his wife, and grumbling about the way they had neglected them during the winter. "If I object to their care-lessness, they say that *I* ought to look after them." Then he com-plained of Lily, who had been ill all the time in Brussels, where he had taken her on a little trip, he said. She would go out to a theatre every night, and never got up until noon. He had a bad corn and was evidently worried, haggard, sick and tired of every-thing. He was especially bitter against Lily's brother. Raoul wouldn't get up early. Raoul did not offer to help him to clean the bicycles. Raoul never opened his bedroom window when he got up. Raoul—he repeated an old story, I had heard from the women—once asked his mother in his presence to leave the house for ever. I enquired when that took place.

"Four years ago," he said, moodily.

"Then what does it matter, what a sixteen-year-old lad has said? He is not your flesh and blood."

I told him that I had brought up a boy, the nephew of my mistress, and that the lad had an awful temper. I went on to say that if children behaved honestly to the world, worked and got their own living, as Raoul did at the London wine firm, never got punished once at the regiment, don't thieve, drink, or get into debt, we ought to be satisfied and we do not want them to hang round our necks and pretend to love us. If children turn out to be respectable, that is about all we can expect. After this and a little more desultory talk, I went up to the house and saw the mother who told me to go upstairs and find Lily.

I saw her with Raoul in the best bedroom. She looked only tolerably well and was highly powdered.

I gave her the sixth volume of "Justine," where I had marked two paragraphs in pencil; one "Lily," and the other "Jacky," with the date: April, 1899 (see Appendix D); the first volume of "Gynecocracy," a most clever and obscene work on the subjection of man to woman; and the scarce novel *Césarée* (see Appendix E). The latter work I had told her about the last time I had seen her. I also had the Eau de Cologne for Raoul, more perfumes for Madame Arvel, and the quinine wine of my own manufacture for Lily, with papers and magazines for Papa; the arrears of a month.

Lily greeted me very coyly and strangely. She could not look me in the face and I think she had told Raoul to stop with her for a few moments.

I threw the books on the bed before her brother, and after the usual greetings, she kissed me in front of him, and gave him the volumes, which were fastened up in tissue paper, to go and hide for her.

When he had left the room I put the ring on her finger. She seemed highly pleased, and kissed me again very nicely, to my surprise showing me two others that were on her hand.

One was a sapphire, surrounded by brilliants, that Mr. Arvel had bought her in Brussels, and the other was a little pearl with a few roses. This last she refused to tell me who had given it to her, and I did not insist, as I really did not care, and I am pleased to say that I felt only friendly pleasure as I pressed my lips to hers, and I was very cool towards her.

I may declare at once that from this day forward I was able to sit at her side and feel the warmth of her body if she pressed against me, without that electric, instantaneous erection that I had always had in former days.

I praised the beauty of both her new rings, and said that mine was nothing beside them; but I can assure the reader that my gift was handsomer than any she had on her fingers, and she wore a lot of trumpery circlets on both her hands.

Lily said that Papa was in an awful temper, and that the house was topsy-turvy with quarrels, principally through his hatred of Raoul.

"You put him in this terrible state. It is all through you."

She did not reply. I looked round and saw that the door of communication between her mother's bedroom and hers had been put back in its place. She saw the direction of my glance and then I fastened my eyes on hers. She guessed the reason of my mute questioning gaze, and as if replying to the question that was in my mind, said:

"Yes, the door is closed now!"

More proofs of her connection with Papa. When she was only a child-toy for Arvel, Mamma let her come in and out of her bedroom, but now she was his second wife, so to speak, her mother in her first wrath, vexed by the pleasure trip, had caused the door to be fitted up, saying:

"You can have her if you like, since it is no use crying over spilt milk, but she shall not come into our sleeping apartment. Go and see her in her room, since it is to be so, and do all you desire with her, but do not let me see it. When you played with her just a little, under my eyes, before enjoying me, I did not mind, but at present, as you have her completely, it must not be in my presence."

It might also have meant that the connection of the three being no longer innocent; their guilty conscience smote them and they had put up this apparent barrier for servants and visitors, as there was nothing to prevent them opening it in the night; but Mamma would soon get used to these Mormon-like manners, and all three would pass the greater part of the night in one bed again. It was only a matter of time, and money from Papa.

Mademoiselle said she would go and show her Pa my ring, and so we went together.

"She has begged one of you too," grumbled he, "I could not get her out of the jeweller's shop, until she tore the sapphire out of me. You are a fool to listen to her."

Lily had bought a false ring for Raoul, out of her own money. She said: "Pa was furious."

We went in to lunch, and her mother feigned to be a little vexed that I had given the ring, but I think she was pleased all the same. Papa grumbled and quarrelled all the time of the meal. I showed my photographs and they were a great success. Raoul took them all.

Lily opened her eyes, when she saw the one where she was reclining on her brother's breast, and handed it over to Papa, saying:

"Why this is obscene, Pa!"

He took it, looked gloomily at it, and said nothing.

I talked about the Brussels trip and elicited that they had been nowhere and seen nothing. The shops, the streets, and theatres and music-halls, but not a museum, nor had they visited Antwerp, as I had recommended.

After lunch, I went and sat with the father, who still talked about Lily's laziness and Raoul's nonchalance. Apropos of nothing, he told me a story of how, when Lily was at Myrio's, a young chap, a bookkeeper there, came and asked to marry her. He said he answered:

"Yes. Lily will have a thousand pounds when her mother dies, but if you really want to marry her, no dangling about, but an early date for the marriage must be fixed at once. No doubt the chap only wanted to poke her (sic), as he never returned."

Why did he tell me all this? Did he think I was going to ask for her hand?

He spoke again against his stepson, and I explained that I asked for no gratitude from the boy I had brought up.

"What I have done is for my own conscience, not for the youth. I only want him to be able to get his own living, and he can then turn his back on me if he likes. I have done my duty."

I told him that the lad was the son of an officer or a priest, no one knew exactly, and then he suddenly burst into a great fit of anger, and to my amazement launched out into a long diatribe against all wearers of epaulettes. How he had changed in so short a time! And he showed great concern for the martyr Dreyfus, as he called him now, and from this day forward always spoke against the sword-dragging idols he had formerly revered. I immediately concluded that an officer had behaved badly to Lilian; having seduced and abandoned her? Probably the good-looking fellow who came to fetch the dog. And never more did Lily talk of officers, she who had always spoken about handsome military men.

The ladies now appeared, and asked Papa to come out for a walk, or all go on bicycles. He refused, alleging his corn, and we four: Mamma, Raoul, Lily and I, went for a ride to a neighbouring forest, leaving Papa seated in an arbour, in his garden all alone.

Lily and her mother asked me what I had got so excited about. They had heard my voice in the house, a most unusual thing for me. I replied that I had been explaining about bringing up children and had been taking Raoul's part by telling Mr. Arvel about my protégé. They were quite surprised, and I repeated my story.

"You never told me you had a boy to whom you were a father!" said Lily, astonished that I had never spoken of him before.

"I do not like to boast," was all I answered.

The mother walked with me in the forest, and told me long stories about the bad temper and jealousy of her husband. How good the children were. How he did naught but find fault, was tight-fisted, envious of everybody far and near, and above all, hated Raoul. I said it was very strange, but if he was jealous, it may have jarred upon him to find Lily perhaps a little too free in her manners with her brother? Mamma answered indignantly that if the children could not play together without restrictions, during the brief time that Raoul was on leave, they might as well be dead. I said it was very mysterious, and I put it down to illness or influenza. We now separated and I talked to Lily.

She, remembering my supposed desire to be a "slave," cut a twig in the forest and began to try and play her part,—poor girl— evidently wishing to curry favour with me, but I had lost all control over myself, trembling with the fever of my cold and quite unnerved, so I wrenched the impromptu whip from her hand, and before she guessed what I was about to do, I cut her severely across the shoulders.

She ran from me out of my reach, shrieking in pain, and came back to me rubbing her shoulders ruefully. Her eyes met mine and she was silent.

"*Et allez donc!*" I said.

"*C'est pas mon père!*" she retorted defiantly.

Raoul had approached us, and heard this last short colloquy. He did not speak, but smiled with the peculiar sardonic leer and scornful twist of his lips. As I had always thought, he was cognizant of his sister's secret of shame.

I must break off here to explain that the dramatic success of the year in Paris was an amusing farce, called *La Dame de chez Maxim*, which has since been played all over the world, and the catch-phrase of the cocotte-heroine is: *Et allez donc! T'es pas mon père!*—"Go on with you! You aren't my father!" This is about the best translation I can make of this colloquial French sentence, originating from the vocabulary of the *gamins* of the streets, who, when reproved for bad language, etc., by a stranger, call out this phrase, meaning that they do not care for their interlocutor, as he has no parental authority over them, nor can they feel shame before him.

Lily had used it well, guessing my thoughts by the first half I had let slip, and instead of answering: "You aren't my father!" she had said: " 'Tis not my father!" And I had started this vulgar "gag," because I knew the play was being performed in Brussels, and I felt sure she had been with her Papa to see it. I found afterwards that I was quite correct in my surmise.

I quite forgot all my determination to be cool and collected, and trembling with rage and fever, utterly unmanned, I honestly confess it; I told her I was convinced that she had slept with her father, and I did not mind that, as I had advised her to give way, she having gone so far with him, if she saw it served her interests. She was indignant and protested that it was not true.

"Then you are all the more infamous to excite him, lead him on, and not give way after all. You are equally guilty, if not worse. I am vexed with you, because you wrote me a most pitiful letter from Lille the morning after your first night out with him. It was the cry of a violated woman. And it was all lies, for you went on to Brussels and enjoyed yourself freely, although you wrote on returning how you had suffered, and had no pleasure. You are gay and happy and go to theatres and concerts every night."

"Oh! he did not spend much money," interrupted Lily, with an ungrateful sneer. "The theatres are cheap there. The stalls are only two or three francs. He bought me the ring you saw and a few German aprons that I took a fancy to. That's all."

"You never bought anything for me," I replied, "nothing would have pleased me more than that you should have brought me a sixpenny packet of tobacco, just to show you thought of me."

"He never left me a second to myself. I dared not do it. It was all I could do to buy a ring for Raoul for thirty-five francs. But I assure you, you are quite at fault in what you think about Papa and me."

"Nonsense! You pass eight days in one room with him, doing

all your dirt together, dressing and undressing, using the chamber pots before each other and you want me to believe you are a martyr. *I went to Brussels and I know everything.* Two beds in No. 4 room, with a screen between, on the first floor. The Boomaens brothers from Ghent are convinced that you are only a little whore he brought from Paris, and not his daughter at all, for what father would sleep in one room with his daughter for eight or nine nights?"

"But he is not my father!"

"All the worse. If he was really your father, people might still think his instinctive pudicity could cause him to restrain his passions."

"If Boomaens said this he shall repent it. Besides, Papa quarrelled with him before we left."

That was a lie, as I ascertained a month or two later.

"Don't stir up any mud, is my advice. Your Papa is a monstrous madman. He could have done things cleaner, by putting you in another room, or in another hotel, or something similar, and contenting himself in the daytime only. You are compromised for ever in Brussels as Arvel's little prostitute. You are a liar of the worst kind, with your lost letters and your conduct last winter. I have found out why you would not see me in November and December. You had the 'whites' and God knows what other female troubles."

I saw a look of intense surprise on her dark lowering countenance. She started. I had enough presence of mind to draw back and remember part of my original plan for the day, which was on no account to speak of the supposed virginity, or the menstrual irregularities of January. It would not do to put her too much on the defensive.

"That is nothing," I continued, "but instead of telling me the truth, you profited by your indisposition to try and torture me, instead of telling me honestly to wait until you were better. You have been home nearly a month and have not tried to come to me, who you adore! You are frightened lest I should see the marks on your bottom, where Papa has whipped you."

She did not answer me, but looked vacantly before her.

"He has always been your lover, more or less. He used to feel your backside and then go and have your mother."

Again she was silent. I went on:

"I feel it is all over between us and it will be for the best."

"No! no! Don't say that—don't say all is over between us. Don't say that!"

"Your life is free as far as I am concerned," I continued, "I have never told you a lie, or served you a dirty trick."

"That is true," she said, "you never have."

"You think of nothing else but lies, falsity, and trickery. I will not and cannot put up with such deceit, especially as my eyes are quite open. I may be a fool with you, but I know my own folly, so that I am only half a fool after all. Infidelity I don't care a straw for—there is plenty soap to be had, but I'll have your heart and brain all truthful as well as your body, or nothing at all."

I do not try to describe her tearful eyes, annoyance, denials, and general air of stupefaction. I think I was in a rage. I am certain this was the first time I ever was in a passion with her. I felt strangely weak and ill, and my legs seemed to go from under me— a sure sign of influenza. She begged me not to get into a passion, and seemed frightened of me, as she said that if I loved her, I ought to believe that nothing had taken place.

My answer always was:

"I am not jealous, as you know. I only complain of being made a fool of, by lying grief and mockery of martyrdom."

But she hated Arvel, she said.

"But you led him on. Remember the eve of Shrove Tuesday, when dressed as a Japanese girl, you said you would never marry, but live always with your Papa. You both talked of the story of incest in the day's paper; your hand passed over his privates, outside his pants, and then spent hours in the photographic dark-room with him, much to your mother's annoyance, and once before me you warmed your hands in his trousers' pockets."

"Why do you talk of that night of Shrovetide? I dressed up for you. All those caresses mean nothing. I never touched his privates. Such tickling touches mean nothing with a father. You do not know what you say when you talk of exciting a father. It is so horribly vile and repugnant to hear you say that. With you I would do anything, but *his* touch revolts me."

And then, with a groan and a kind of half-sob, as if to herself, she exclaimed: "Oh, that eve of Shrove Tuesday!"

"If I am wrong, why did you not get indignant with the carefully-veiled advice in the letter I sent you before you left, when I called you Mademoiselle Bismarck?"

"What letter?" she asked, with an air of affected ignorance.

"Go and look at it! You've got it still. You are a liar—that is all I can say."

"I am not a liar. But I confess appearances are against me. About the double-bedded room, I acted without thought of guilt. Mother knows we occupied one room all the time. A gentleman and his wife, who own some property near Brussels, came and visited us in our room and saw the two beds."

"What must they have thought!"

"There was no concealment on our part. I am innocent. How could I do it? I hate him so!"

"But it was to your interest, maybe?"

"What interest? Show me what good it would do me, if you can."

I made no answer, but only shrugged my shoulders.

"I owe you an explanation, I confess, and I will give it. I must clear myself in your eyes. I love you, Jacky, and you are too cruel to me."

"There is no explanation possible."

"Yes, there is."

"I defy you to give me one!"

"Hush! hush! Don't talk so loudly. Mother will hear us!"

She ran to her mother, being unable to carry on the argument, and we went home in a tramway. As we walked towards the starting point, I noticed that her face was blue, and her lips violet, as she talked eagerly to Raoul. She was telling him that I had spied on her in Belgium. During the ride, Lily was tearful and sulky. I chaffed her unmercifully and bitterly, asking her what was the date of the month.

"Yesterday was April 4, I believe?" With strong emphasis on

the word, "four," alluding of course, to the number of the room at the hotel of Brussels. I added that the figure four had a great influence in my life, and I asked her brother if he had read a novel by Conan Doyle, called, "The Sign of Four."

I made a lot of stupid jokes.

"How gay you are, Mr. S...!" said Adèle.

"I play the clown!" I replied. "This is but the forced gaiety of a broken heart, madam, as they say in the dramas. I am only a clown!"

And aside in English, for Lily and Raoul: "A damned old clown!"

Then to the mother: "Laugh and the world laughs with you; weep and you weep alone!"

"That is very pretty, Mr. S . . . , and quite true!"

Then we reached the house. The stepfather was descried on his bicycle! He had been out alone on it.

We had tea, and then I walked about with Raoul and Lily, both of them complaining of their mad stepfather. He had gone to the wine-merchants, when in London, and complained of Raoul to them, saying he was not trustworthy, etc., and one of the partners told Raoul that Arvel had been to them, but that he had taken his statements with a grain of salt. Raoul showed me a recent complimentary letter from his employers. Lily told me that Arvel had advised one of her best clients to go to a rival milliner's.

During this, Arvel went and sulked alone in his arbour. Lily said:

"Now you won't be invited here so often, because you are talking too much to us. He has been spending too much money on his house and garden, and he is miserable and unhappy. When Raoul's time is up in September, I am going to London to start bonnet-building there. Raoul will then earn about £4 a week in the wine business, and I will keep house for him. I shall get all the custom of the ladies of his employers and their families to start me. Papa wants me to stop with him. He will make me his secretary at £2 a week, and get me work for fashion papers. He gave me that article to translate that I sent you. I could not do it, but I did not want to refuse, as he would have sneered, and grumbled, and scolded, and said I knew nothing. So you did it for me. I typed it on the machine and gave it to him. It was beautifully done, but he found fault, saying there were too many French words left in it. When I am in London, you shall come and stop with me."

She said she had wondered how I got the "dream-face" on the lustful letter I had written, and I explained how I had done it. Then, being alone with me a few minutes, she gave me her lame explanation, which she had now had time to forge, and I, worn out and careless, really ill, sick of quarrelling, said nothing to it.

"During the winter, I had been ill, and had kept the house alone while my parents were away on the Riviera. The doctor advised change of air in the spring. So the journey was arranged. The morning we started, Mr. Arvel went away quarrelling with his wife and servants. He was overpoweringly attentive, and to my surprise took seats in a first-class coupé. I was not present (!) when he retained the room at Lille. Nothing strange took place until I got into bed, when he came round the screen, for there was a screen here at Lille the same as at Brussels, and tucked me up. Then he did what he had never done in his life before (!). He kissed me full on the mouth. At that moment, all you had said, Jacky dear, flashed across me, and I had an awful feeling of disgust come over me. He saw that and left me. If I had given way to him, why should I write that letter from Lille?"

"Because you are a woman, and women often cannot help confessing half the truth of what runs in their minds, without knowing why."

"There you are right. I know that weakness of my sex, but I wrote to you, because after feeling his vile hot lips on my mouth, I cried as I thought of my poor mother, who has lived twenty-five years with him, and I sickened at the idea of letting him touch me. And then I thought of you who I love, who had warned me, and who else could I write to, but you, for comfort? I could not write to you from Brussels. He never left me." (In spite of her disgust, she had eight more nights in the double-bedded room at Brussels.) "I could not let my mother's lover touch me, I swear it. Nothing else transpired during the trip, although he might perhaps have got excited at seeing me dress and undress."

How did she know that he got excited?

She protested greatly, and I said I did not care. I was sick and tired of it all.

I trembled with fever and emotion, and once more, I felt my knees give way. She ran from me into the house, glad to have got through her wretched story, and I think she went and talked to her parents, while I stopped in the garden with Raoul in the dark, for night had now come on.

He took me upstairs into the best bedroom to wash my hands before dinner, and Lily reappeared with a lamp, got me out a clean towel, and left me again.

While drying my hands, she came in, and Raoul discreetly left us.

Now she hung round me, begged me to believe her, caressed my hands and face, and made me suck her mouth, her eyes full of tears, saying that she only lived for one man in this world—me!— and that I had driven her mad by my proposal to let her become the cruel mistress, and I her slave. She said she would soon try it. She promised me a long letter of passion, detailing what she would like to do to me, for Saturday morning, and so she changed the subject, and gave me more luscious, tongueing kisses, so that I could not do otherwise than respond to her embraces, and clasp her tightly to me, and I murmured, as I kissed her, speaking with my lips on hers:

"Lily! My Lily! Oh, darling Lily!"

I was now full of lust. But they called me from below to come and dine, and she released me. I left her to go downstairs first, so as not to show that we had been together, and as I went towards the door, my head swam round, I staggered, and had I not caught hold of the top of the banisters, I should have fallen. I looked round and saw Lily standing watching me, the garish flare of a petroleum lamp full on her face, as she held it up to throw a light on the stairway.

If ever I saw a fiendish look of wicked triumph on the features of a living creature, it was then. She thought she had fooled me completely and I shall long recollect how I said to myself: "I am glad I am slightly indisposed. I have the influenza. I have not said so, and they will think I am mad with jealousy, and lovesick as a callow youth. I am glad I stumbled, and that Lily saw me staggering down the stairs."

At this moment, Papa, who was waiting for me to go down to dinner, stepped out of his little library, holding a parcel in his hand. It was my "Romance of Lust," neatly tied up. He thanked me for the loan of it, and said he enjoyed it immensely.

I took it, and now Lilian came down in her turn.

"What is that you are giving to Mr. S . . . ?" She said this in a strange, drawling tone, looking steadfastly at her Papa, the while.

"Only some books," was his reply, and the light died out of his eyes, and the same frowning, dull expression came into his face.

I took the packet, and we all went downstairs, but I thought of the same scene last summer, when Mr. Arvel returned me "The Horn Book," and I knew they had read "The Romance of Lust" together.

I purposely forgot to take away the volumes when I left that evening, just to see what would happen, and always hoping that perhaps it might furnish an incident for my book.

We dined in the workshop in the garden. Everybody was dull. Papa hardly spoke. Lily took cod liver oil before dinner. I could not eat. I told them the two carriage accidents of the morning had upset me, and I thought I had caught cold.

Then the father suddenly, coolly spoke of the Brussels trip, and how Lily had prevented him from sleeping, by clapping her lips together all night, like a baby suckling. The mother joined in the conversation, and plainly showed that she knew of the double-bedded room arrangement. Lily kicked me under the table, and said that anything is better than "snoring." She meant that for me, when I slept with her last summer, as she explained to me after the meal, when we were going to the station.

While this talk was going on, I looked closely at them all. We each spoke in turn, except Raoul, who held his head down, bending over his plate, his lip curled in a devilish grin, and it suddenly dawned upon me that this was all prearranged. Mamma looked defiantly at me, as if to say: "Now, sir, where is the harm you thought you knew of?"

Lily had told Papa before dinner that I had gone to Brussels to spy upon them, and that I knew about the sojourn at the Brussels hostelry. Papa had then said: "Let us talk about it openly at dinner, as if it was the usual thing, and no secret." It was a "bluff," and Papa only made his case worse in my eyes, as he had shown me that they were all in the secret of his amours with Lily; Mamma, and Raoul, the brother. Granny I never saw again. She had now been pensioned off. I suppose she was in the way, and perhaps knew too much, as she was very indiscreet.

After this joking about the double-bedded room, there was an awkward pause, and Lily rose to get a clean plate. She left her seat, walked behind Papa, and I distinctly saw her pass her hand behind his neck, caressingly. I pretended not to see.

After dinner, Lily, Raoul, and myself went for a short walk with the dogs, and during our stroll, Lily, when Raoul forged once ahead, asked me if I was still angry with her. I was worn out and answered indifferently.

"You are vexed with me."

"How can I help it, when I think of what you wrote to me. Oh! that letter from Lille!"

Hypocritically, I looked up at the moon, and imitating Lily, gave a kind of a sigh, which died away with a little moan. She caught my hand and pressed it convulsively.

I told her I had a girl waiting for me on my return to Paris.

"If I do not find her at home, I shall go to a brothel, and choose a thin, dark lass, as much like you as possible, and while I enjoy her, while she caresses me with patient hands, and submissive mouth, I'll call her Lily."

"If you do that, you'll not be a man at all, but simply a beast!"

But she said that coolly and did not seem to care. She had got tired and pale, her features were drawn. The powder, worn off, had not been renewed. She was sallow and careworn, and I felt thankful to be able to say to myself: "She looks ugly."

When we returned to the house, we found that Mamma had kicked out the servant, the only one they had. Papa grumbled. Lily sat down and fell to pieces, as it were.

"I'm not well and we shall have to do the housework to-morrow ourselves."

They were all dull and miserable. I said "good night!" and Raoul and his sister saw me to the station.

They both talked against Mamma's temper now, and how she was a "servant-hater."

I had noticed during lunch that Lily's dog Blackamoor had a nasty wound, a piece an inch long being torn out of his cheek, along the jaw, and I had said at table: "I suppose he has been fighting?" Nobody answered but Lily, who hurriedly replied: "Oh yes, it is nothing!"

She told me now that she was frightened lest I should insist on this topic, or take up the dog and examine it, etc., as the wound really came from a tremendous kick given to the poor brute by her Papa.

She once more alluded to the slavery mania, thinking perhaps to please me. I asked her what she would do to me.

"You must not ask me, as you are my slave. The very fact of you wanting to know would make me refuse to tell you. But I know what I want to do to you and I won't say."

"Not if I beg you most humbly to be good enough to let me know?"

"I will put it in the letter I'm going to send you. You must come and see Mamma and me and have a cup of tea, when she is certain that Papa is going to be in Paris all day. You can come on your bicycle. I will make it right with Mamma and let you know the day. Papa is not to know."

She had made friends with her mother apparently.

I got into the train and leant out of the carriage window to say a last "good-night!"

"He has been very rude to me all day," said Lily to her brother, looking at me.

"Rude, perhaps, but natural!" was my answer, and she nodded assent very prettily, with a kind smile, as the train moved out of the station.

The next few days, circumstances, which I shall not reveal here, added to some old suspicions and recent slips of Arvel's garrulous tongue, led me to discover the true reason of the wretched state of things at the villa.

What he earned as a financial reporter was not enough to pay for all he had been laying out lately, and he had other employment connected with his travels. This had been suddenly cut off, and not only did he feel the loss of these resources, but there was danger in the air. It was worse than a mere pecuniary loss; it was a catastrophe which I shall say no more about, except that the dark cloud passed over, but the money did not return.

I went and reconnoitred the road to Sonis on my bicycle, to get familiar with the route, and on April 8th. I received the following:

LILIAN TO JACKY.

April 7, 1899.

My naughtiest and best,

At last, I have found something! After all my seeking, here is a combination, which I believe will receive your sanction. Here it is: you and I will go to Belfort for the Whitsuntide holidays, if my brother does not get leave, which is highly probable.

I have already said at home here, that if my brother does not come, I should go myself to see him, and Mamma approves of my project.

Naturally, my parents think I go alone, and as to my brother, you will tell him that having heard of my journey, you wished to accompany me, as you wanted to see him, and he will find this quite natural. I will arrange with him.

Now, do not go and raise a lot of objections, for there are none to be made, and if you don't find my idea a wonderful one, I shall know you do not love me any more. What day can you manage to come on a bicycle? Find out when is the next settling day at the Bourse.

I love you,

LILY.

I answered "yes" for the journey to Belfort, as Whitsuntide was May 21st., and things might change by then. I arranged about the bicycle visit in a rather short, cool note addressed to "my naughtiest and worst," and had strange thoughts about Raoul and the collusion of this wonderful family.

Lily did not want to come to Paris to me, to undress before

me in the open daylight. She wanted to ward me off until she could get me into a bed with her in a month's time, and make me believe I had taken her virginity.

I felt that I had no longer any influence over her; she had no strong desire for me, as her Papa's daily caresses with mouth and fingers kept her sufficiently cool to be able to play with me at her own sweet will.

I felt rather amused to think that Lily could offer me nothing of herself until Whitsuntide; and the pleasures of slavery and the passionate letter appertaining thereto, which she had promised me, had dropped out of her erratic mind.

I thought it time to throw a bombshell into the camp, and I sent her the following terrible letter, which was a sort of *ultimatum*. I did not care if she answered it or not, or how she took it. My only care was to leave the question of her maidenhead and her *fausse couche* of January as much as possible in the background.

When I wrote it and the following letters, I always asked myself how they would look in print. I was now working more for the gallery than myself.

JACKY TO LILIAN.

Paris, Monday, April 10, 1899.

Since I last saw you, Lily dear, I have reflected a lot. I have been thinking of nothing but you, and I write to you this day calmly and deliberately. My health is much better. Sleep has returned to me. And without gall, without acrimony, and without temper, without feverishness, erotic or otherwise, I tell you that I am absolutely decided to break with you entirely, and therefore with all your family as well, unless you treat me with the entire frankness to which I have a right. I have chained myself to you, but I left you your liberty always. I am not jealous, nor in your way. I am greatly excited to think that men desire you. You are my adored little whore. I love you with all the strength of my soul. You are the last love of my life. And that is why I am leaving you.

When you went away on your journey, I did not ask you to write to me. On the contrary. See my letter which you received on the morning of your departure, wherein I called you: "Miss Bismarck." I wrote in the most delicate manner possible.

It has pleased you to invent a fairy tale, so stupid, that when you tell it, it comes on to rain, merely to make me wretched. Please note that I did not ask you for any details, or to tell me anything at all. You have accumulated lies upon lies in your weakness for lying. But even among lies an observer can unravel the truth, for lying women cannot always lie.

What is this idea you have for posing as a martyr before me, who can read your thoughts as if your brain was in the palm of my hand? Why play the black drama of the unfortunate girl persecuted by an infamous father?

I told you this winter that no power on earth can prevent a woman from communicating with the man she loves. I go farther:

NO POWER ON EARTH:

a) could have made you take this journey, if you did not like;

b) could have made you sleep in that room at Lille, if you did not like;

c) could have made him stop out of your bed that night. That is IMPOSSIBLE;

d) could have made you continue your connection in Brussels, if you did not like;

e) could have made you accept the ring he gave you as a reward for your kindness to him, if you did not like.

Your false allegations, your comedy of indignation disgust and sicken me!

The story of the lunch with Fontarcy and Clara—and his lordship, and all of us, are ready to begin again if you say the word—the story of my brother and his refusal to meet the unknown little brunette I proposed to him; all this proves that I am no vulgar, jealous fellow.

Suppose that I am infamously vicious—(you once called me a vicious man in front of your Papa)—perverted, depraved, a *sadique*, like Mr. Arvel, whether he be satisfied or not (?)—anything you like— but I never laid a trap for you. I have never lied to you up to now. I have showed myself to you as I am. You could have refused me, or driven me from your side.

I will not have your body, if I cannot have all your sensual confidence. I want to know all, down to the slightest detail. That will excite me enormously. If not, all is finished between us for ever. I want to be your accomplice, but not your dupe. Besides, I have never been your dupe for long.

Never more shall you bring tears to my eyes. I'll have no sadness coming from Lily. I will not let you make me suffer morally any more.

Since the month of October, I have found you out three times in flagrant lies; useless and dirty, stupid lies, and all told to me, who loves you, and who you say you love.

And you do love me, I am sure, for nothing forced you to continue your connection with your poor old Jacky.

You know pretty well all about the horrible sadness of my life; the daily sickening torture I undergo; the terrible fatality that pursues me, and 'tis you, my little Lily darling, who offer me as a supreme consolation, a mass of stupid artifice, that the greatest goose of a coquette would not dare to use towards a schoolboy. Such mockery is too much for me to bear.

I shall suffer from this breaking off of our connection, I confess. I do not play at being strong-minded with you.

But I must and will suffer alone. I am free to inflict upon myself what moral torture I like, but I refuse you the right to make me suffer, by lying manœuvres and stories, supported by lame reasoning.

In answer to this letter, I absolutely order you to send me a wire at once, no matter what other letters, etc. may be on the way. In this telegram you must tell me if you consent to the complete breaking-off, or send me a word of tenderness to make me understand that you give way to my reasoning.

If you desire no more of me, of my caresses, of my virility, of my mouth, of my inventions of passion, slavery and other exquisite follies, I want my ring back, and I can manage to get it without putting your honour in danger. In my poor eyes, burnt with the tears you have made me shed, that ring has a sacred character, and I will not allow it to remain on the fingers of a lying woman, such as you are.

I love you, and shall always love you whatever happens. I kiss you over and over again, perhaps for the last time.

JOHN S...

At the same time, I enclosed a sort of commentary of Lily's letters, from the one sent from Lille, down to that ordering the translation of the article on ladies' fashions.

I copied her letters, and the comments were made in red ink.

I do not repeat them here, as they were simply the criticisms that I have given already in the preceding chapter.

I began by saying that I wanted her to be as depraved as she liked, but with frankness with me.

I alluded to the villanous character of the Lille letter, and how I had wept on receiving it, and believed she was a martyr, until I reflected upon the cruelty of her postscript on her return, when she said she was free on that Sunday.

I pictured her drinking champagne with Papa, and I wanted to know why he should be jealous of the brother, when he loved the sister?

I told her I should have married her long ago, had I been rich enough, and I asked her if that infamous letter, written after her "first night," was not a vast mystification. I informed her that certain things had transpired between her and her mother's lover at Nice in 1898, and that they had both conspired in the past winter to cheat Charlotte out of marriage with Raoul. That they had read my bawdy books together.

I alluded to the falsity of one of her letters where she accepts my ring, and says not a word about the one Papa had given her in Brussels. How could you, I went on to say, since you talked of how he worried you with his open manifestations of passion, which do not prevent you accepting jewellery from him. And on April 5th., after speaking against him all day, you caress him furtively at dinner.

I made no copy of this strange document, but I have just discovered the last page in the rough, and so I give it here:

Then comes the article to be translated, and I write the ironical and erotic rubbish about the man who suffers from unsatisfied desire! The whining letter of Lille is forgotten, or is naught but a lie.

And so I depart for Brussels, thinking that Lily, her eyes open at last, had shut her door against him at night. I shall find that they have had two separate rooms when I make my little inquiry. I start off, like the idiot that I am, saying to myself that if everything has taken place as I fancy, the gift of my poor little ring may have a deeper meaning.

(Here I drew a rapid sketch of the famous No. 4 room.)

Why then this false story of martyrdom; why pose as a victim when it is she who causes pain, and wants to make all men suffer, or rather those who cannot save themselves by reasoning or common sense?

At Brussels, I am told of her gaiety; her happy life; she goes out every night and sleeps until noon. Why not? But why this eternal desire to lie?

Then there is the noise of her childish romping with Papa like puppies playing, as they were heard in the hotel; and the state of the bedding, the sly hints of the lookers-on about the little Parisian whore of Mr. Arvel, who pretends she is his daughter, and introduces her to the outgoing lodger, saying: "*Ma fille, monsieur!*"

All this is nothing to me. I knew it, pointed it all out, and prophesied it long ago; but why always this fearful craving for muddy lies to me, when I am so liberal in my ideas, and to whom Lily has spontaneously said ten times this year: "I love you?"

To my great surprise I got a reply by return of post, she having received my awful letter and "commentary" in the morning. She answered it at once, and I read the following at dinner time:

LILIAN TO JACKY.

Sonis-sur-Marne, April 11, 1899.

Your letter, as mean and as unworthy of you as it is of me, will nevertheless not make me confess a thing, which is even still more infamous than your conduct towards a woman, who has only one reproach to make herself, that she loves you. All the proofs that you seem to have accumulated against me, leave me absolutely full of disgust for the littleness of your principles and your judgments. I believed you had larger ideas, and I supposed that at your age, you had enough knowledge of the world to know that even when appearances are against a person, it does not always result therefore that she be guilty. But enough talk of this sort; all I could tell you would not convince you, since you seek a motive to break with me. Let us note by the way, that the one you have found is simply idiotic and won't hold water.

Certainly I will give you back your ring, but in a thousand fragments. Then you will have to work your brains, as you were obliged to do when you ordered this one, so as to have another made for your half-sister. Choose it of louder taste; this one would be too simple for the daughter of Madame X. It was useless to threaten me with means to make me give it back; do you think I would wear it now? I have no wish for it. But know that your threats do not frighten me. Now: adieu! Remain with the people who love you, and know not how to lie. Cherish such worthy folk, and above all do not neglect your half-sister. She may be useful to you.

LILY.

I was delighted at the success of my manœuvre. Her letter, with its allusions to the "accumulations of proofs," and her acknowledgement that "appearances were against a person," were precious, and constituted as near an approach to an avowal as anyone could expect from a perverted female of her class.

It will be noted that she calls herself a "woman." In her letters of the autumn and before, she always spoke of herself as a "young girl."

My mother had married again, and my half-sister by my late stepfather, was now a very handsome young girl. Mr. Arvel knew her, and had seen her often in Paris. So I am almost sure that he was reading all my letters now, and had helped Lily to write the foregoing one.

These allusions to a female member of my family; her vile show of jealousy, shows us how her brain had been warped when young. Incestuous herself, she doubtless believed with a faith cunningly fostered by Papa and Mamma for their own ends, and to stifle eventual remorse, repentance, or disgust in their daughter-prostitute, that promiscuous intercourse was a regular thing in all families.

I recollected too the story of Pa's hot kiss at Lille and compared it with what a woman had done to her, as the reader will note she told me when first we talked freely together. What a trumpery machine is a female's magic lantern of lies and how few are the slides!

JACKY TO LILIAN.

Paris, April 12, 1899.

Excuse me if I write to you again to-day, but I wish to rectify that part of my letter relating to the ring, which you were good enough to accept from me.

It was wrong on my part to have asked for it back. I ought not to have spoken about it. It was a gift: that was enough. I do not quite remember what I said that seemed to be threats, but in any case, believe me that nothing was farther from my thoughts.

For all words that might have wounded you, concerning my poor little ring, kindly accept my sincere apologies. Sincerely, I ask your pardon.

To show my good faith, *only on this head*, I beg you, not without a little emotion, to be amiable enough, on the contrary, to keep it always, as a *souvenir* of the few nice moments we passed together, trying to forget all bad ones.

Do not wear it unless you like; but keep it in a corner of your wardrobe, with the old letters, bits of ribbon, locks of hair, and other trifles that women hide jealously from all eyes. Now and then, the ring will come under your notice, and it will be very pleasant for me to suppose that you will then think of him, who was—not for long—your

JACKY.

Once more: I retract with frank regret all I said about the ring I gave you, which was made for you, which belongs to you, and no one else, and that you, ought—dare I say it?—that I order you, to keep for ever.

LILIAN TO JACKY.

Sonis-sur-Marne, April 13th. 1899.

No, a thousand times no, I'll not keep your ring. If all is to be at an end between us, it has no longer any value for me, and will only be a source of grief and regret. I have been frank with you, but I ought not to have been so. Please let me know, how I can send you the ring, as well as the books I now have of yours.

This Whitsuntide voyage, which seemed to please you, is the reason that caused you to seek a rupture, I am convinced. You dared not refuse me, and yet you did not wish to make this trip, for many reasons that I know as well as you. And I was building so joyously on the idea of passing a few delightful days all alone with you.

Indeed, when I reflect upon your conduct, I detest you.

LILY.

JACKY TO LILIAN.

Paris, April 14, 1899.

My Lily,

You say that my poor little ring would have no value for you and would be a source of grief and regret if all is to be over between us? As I do not wish anything coming from me to give you trouble and woe, I prefer to tell you at once, that nothing is over between us. There now! Are you pleased?

Tell me frankly that you are happy, and that you detest me. Write me at once a very long, very passionate letter, brimming over with love and hate. I understand that you detest me now. I have done all I could for that, it seems. I am "mean, unworthy, infamous; I disgust you by the littleness of my principles and my judgments. I threaten a poor woman, who has only one reproach to make herself—that she loves me—and I seek for enjoyment in incest!"

Chuck nothing more, please. There's no room for the rest! In spite of all these faults, in spite of Jacky being the most crapulous and cynical being; in spite of his having insulted, vilified, and dragged you in the mire; as no other woman has ever been mortified since the world has been a world, you still have the courage to want to travel and remain alone several days with this criminal; this scoundrel; this wretched insulter of women; this incestuous beast?

So be it, your perversity shall be satisfied. I swear to you, little Lily, that you shall take this journey with me, but I will make you cruelly expiate all the wrong you have done me, by the shameful erotic humiliations you will have to submit to, to make me spend, by all the ways I shall order, without troubling about your pleasure, and you shall hate me as much as you like. You will have to work hard all the same. I shall have a whip. You are warned. Don't come unless you decide to be the docile slave of a hard and severe master; as you were last summer my bitch, my slut, my toy.

I feel you love me and that you can't do without me. I won't let you be unhappy. If you only want my love and my caresses to be completely happy, come and I'll take you, sweet little monster.

Besides, why should I deprive myself of the soft pleasure that this connection gives me, because I believe that you like to juggle with my heart, excite my jealousy(?), and get up tricks for me generally! Since I see clearly through all your little manœuvres, your malice and finessing—what matters it to me, after all? Run along, my love, my passion, do as you like. You act on my flesh, and I excite you. Let us forget the rest.

But you are not going to let me long for your dirty little body up to Whitsuntide, I hope? Have you no longer any desire to strip naked before your master? I offer you my mouth, and a bottle of champagne when you choose. I'd like to lunch alone with you. I want to see you and quarrel with you, if you like. To bite your lips, spend in your mouth without the least shame, clutching your head until I hurt you, between my thighs, and saying roughly: "Go on—suck away!" And you would swallow all my disgusting spendings, so hot and thick, that I should spurt into the back of your throat. If you write me a nice long letter, very erotic, very loving and very dirty, I will tell you in my next, how I spent with a little trollop I met at the Eastern station, when I left you on the 5th.

Come quick, or arrange something. Keep me from spending with a lot of females who disgust me.

Shall I be your slave? If you care about it, you will remember that you owe me a long letter, where you said you would tell me how you would spend by the cruelty you would show to me, if I was at your disposal, resolved to obey you for an hour.

Write then. When you go to bed, take some paper and a pencil, and any book you like, to serve as a desk, and write to me at length and voluptuously—in bed.

Sunday, I made a reconnaissance to find a good road from here to your place on my bike. I find I can do it in about an hour. I was within three miles of you.

Take it and suck it.

JACKY.

Please lend me for a few days, that "commentary" I sent you—the extracts of your letters, with the red ink notes. I will give it back to you. I want to look at something.*

I lent an obscene work in four volumes to your Papa: "The Ro-

---

* I wished to make a fair copy of it for my book, and I also wanted to see if she dared to allude to the fearful exposure of her hollow lies. I had the same sort of motive for mentioning "The Romance of Lust." As I expected, she never referred to either of my questions. It amused me very much to set these trifling traps for her and her Papa. About this time, I used the type-written address, that I had saved from

mance of Lust." He made up a parcel to give it back to me. I forgot to take it. Will you open your eyes and see if the packet has not been lost or mislaid? The book is rare and worth a trifle.

The journey that I can easily take with you, has nothing to do with the motive of my breaking-off, I swear it.

Here is the true motive. I explain once more, although I believe I have already made you understand in my letter and the "commentary."

You write from Lille, that you are unhappy. I take that awfully to heart. At the end of the month: you back again, I begin to suspect that you are not unhappy at all, *on the contrary*, and that your story of martyrdom has only been imagined to torture me by jealousy (?) and malice aforethought. It didn't take, dear, because I'm never jealous. To find out the truth, I go to Brussels, where you have "suffered" from the "task," etc. I arrive and hear you have been going the whole hog.

What am I to believe? You say yourself "that appearances are against me." I won't insist. I only note that you possess a peculiar frame of mind, that I have not yet seen in any woman up to now, and I've known a few. You say to yourself: "I love him, what can I invent to teaze him?" Generally, when a woman loves, she says: "I love him, let me try to please him in every possible shape and way."

Now I know you. I shall finish up by laughing at your wickedness. I know all your tricks! !

JACKY.

LILIAN TO JACKY.

Undated (Received April 17, 1899.)

No sir, you shall not have a long and loving letter from your Lily, since when you felt inclined to be "naughty," you let the first "trollop" you meet, profit by it; a girl picked up I know not where. How clean and how appetising for me!

You are cynical with your ideas, and the cheek you have to tell me of your dirty pranks, me who you love and who loves you so madly,

---

her Pa's letter of January; cutting it off the old envelope and pasting it on another. She never spoke or wrote about this little joke, which must have been noticed at the villa, proving that her parents, or at any rate, Sir Giles Overreach-Arvel, knew what was going on; or pretty near, according to the muddled version that the daughter would give them, as my letters poured in.

so sincerely. I forbid you, do you hear, to tell me of all these horrors. You will make me believe that the love you feel for me is bestial. Please note that I wish also for that love, but as I am very greedy, I want the other love as well. You understand me, do you not, since you read all my thoughts so well?

It is evident that you cannot always burn yourself up with simple desire, but when you let yourself go, keep the news to yourself. I wish to fancy always that you only love me, in thought as well as otherwise. I am as one crazy at the idea of being able to be entirely alone with you for a few days, and above all a few nights.

I do not for a moment wish to make you languish until Whitsuntide, and I ruminate over a host of projects, so as to be able to slip off and lunch, and remain a few moments with you, but it is awfully difficult. Why don't you come down on your bicycle? At least, I should see you, and feel you near me, and then I have to make you expiate all the pain you have made me feel for the last fortnight.

You are not jealous, say you? So much the better for you. I am jealous enough for two, and I am very unhappy now and again, when I think that there are people who see you every day; who form an essential part of your life, whereas I? . . .

Come then next Thursday on your bicycle. It will seem quite natural. You will arrive after lunch, and you will certainly be invited to dinner. Is that settled?

If you have been well disinfected since April 5, I kiss you with a long, long kiss, as I should wish to do in reality.

LILY.

JACKY TO LILIAN.

Paris, Monday, April 17, 1899.

Little Lily,

Your nice letter, to hand this morning, only confirms what I have known for a long time, that you would be an exquisite woman, if you would only behave towards me with simplicity, truth, and straightforwardness, without your roguish manœuvres in such bad faith. Perhaps after all, it is better that you should be as you are for it is certain that if you added to your qualities of adorable prentice-whore, frankness and true faith in me, I should be madly, absolutely madly in love with you.

For the moment, I shall always feel this consolation, that if we were now separated, and it was nearly coming to that the other day—I should say to myself: "So much the worse, but after all, I'll not cry over my broken toys. Here lies Lily; she had an atrocious temper!"

What you say about the "other love," is exactly copied on what I have explained to you a thousand times, but—exquisite oddity!—you *have done all that a woman could imagine, to destroy in me that very love you describe!*

I'll not tell you of my orgies. If I "side-slip," I'll keep it to myself. But do you know that I should adore you to narrate to me your escapades. When you told me of the attempt of Gaston in the train, it produced an unimaginable effect upon me. When I saw you assailed by Lord Fontarcy, I was transported with lust; otherwise, why should I have done it?

And in other circumstances . . . in your house . . . how many times . . . I have seen . . . I have felt . . . it was lascivious . . . too nice . . . delicious!

You know what you have to do, if you wish to please me. Read between the lines, and for the love of God, and the love of Jacky, do not be a silly goose next Thursday.

Don't tell me that you are crazy at the thought of being alone with me for a few days, a few nights, for according to the loyal manner in which I have always treated you, and which I want to keep up, I feel that I should have a terrible desire to possess you properly. Oh! to stretch you wide, to rape you entirely, to feel myself inside you, burning, panting, bruised, wounded, crushed beneath me, and me buried in my Lily! . . .

No, I'll hurry to finish this letter. I'll only write a few lines in future.

Take all your precautions—beware of me—don't come if you are still a virgin; if you want to remain a virgin. Beware of a brutal embrace on my part.

Thanks for your plans for lunch with me. I hope you write in good faith; we'll talk it over.

I will come for certain on Thursday, if the weather is anything like fine. I must think of appearances. If the roads are not practicable— if it rains—what excuse could I make? I pray for fine weather.

I have no need to be disinfected.

I am curious to know what you will do to make me expiate all the harm I have done you for the last fortnight, in one single afternoon, and that in the rare intervals when I shall be alone with you! What saves me is that you know you are ugly when you sulk, or are in a bad temper.

I'll wind up this letter gaily with a little bit of English poetry. I'll no longer worry myself about you.

The first time I saw you in your Japanese costume, I began this little poem; at the table, openly, if you remember. I have been two months finishing it. That's a long time, but the result is extraordinary. 'Tis a masterpiece—sweet, charming and very dirty:

> Lily Arvel's a lewd little Jappy,
> Fond of Jacky—her poor silly chappie.
>> With her tongue she loves to lick,
>> His red sugar-stick;
> And when he comes in her mouth—she is happy!

(To be learnt by heart for Thursday.)
My sweet tongue in your dirty little pussy,

JACKY.

This day I have sent your Papa a big packet of English papers and magazines. There are three large fashion papers for you, with a band round them: *Pour Mdlle. Lili.* If you want them, look after them.

2

THURSDAY, APRIL 20, 1899.

I rode down on my bicycle, as arranged, arriving at 2:15, and
found the mother and stepfather in the garden. Mamma was neatly
dressed and tightly laced, not being in a dirty *peignoir*, and evidently expecting me. She wore a large pair of false pearl earrings,
which if real, would have been worth a thousand pounds. They
feigned surprise. Lily appeared at once, also neatly got-up. She wore
a bodice of black velvet, with large strass buttons; her black hair
nicely done, her face fully powdered, and her lips reddened. After
the usual compliments, inspection of my bicycle, which they had
never seen, etc., Lily took me away to show me a dress of which
she was superintending the making for her mother, who it will be
remembered, is a little, dark woman. It was a flaming red foulard

that they were having made at home, and Lily made game of it and her mother. Being in the workshop with her girls, Lily talked in English. It may be guessed that our conversation only ran on one topic—the so-called incestuous trip—and Lily, who I watched narrowly, flushed up deeply at each remark of mine.

She stood up, leaning over her work-table, and I sat beside her. I saw her only in profile and she did all she could not to let her eyes meet mine. At each remark I made, I noticed a red spot mount in her neck from the arteries, and spreading itself out from the band of her collarette, gradually rise until it gained her cheek and all her face. Then it would die away, and as surely come up again at any fresh remark I made concerning her Papa.

She refused to make anything like a confession, but when I plainly told her: "Whatever you do, I forbid you to 'put me away' with him," she suddenly turned round and looked me full in the face, her eyes dilated with a look of intense and horrified astonishment. She was quite dismayed and did not reply. "Do not force us to quarrel, or make bad blood between us." And as she turned her head away from me, without a word, I felt sure that she had done all she could to prevent us two men ever being friendly together again, as we were in February. She wanted to "work" each one separately, and I was now perfectly certain he knew all, or what was worse for me, Lily's pet version.

Mr. Arvel had to go up to Paris on business in the afternoon, as he did every Thursday, which accounted for me being invited that day, and I was practically alone all the time with Lily. I tried her all ways. My principal argument was: "I don't care what you do if you are good to me. I love you, but why tell such useless lies continually? Look at that letter I sent you in October. Why stick to the lie that you never got it?"

"You never sent it!" she answered with a scowl.

And then she kept putting forth her great love for me. At last, worn out, she said:

"To amuse you, I'll allow you to think that it is true, on the condition that you never talk about it."

I agreed, exclaiming: "Hurrah! That is a confession!" and she immediately started off again herself on the same subject. I sum up here our principal remarks as far as I can remember them:

JACKY. "If your disgust was true, you could not remain under the same roof with him."

LILY. "But I go to London in September."

JACKY. "He will never let you."

LILY. "I hate him and discourage him all I can. For the last fortnight, he has left me alone."

I guessed from this statement that he could manage to ejaculate about twice a month, and the rest of the time his mouth and hands would be kept busy.

JACKY. "Then why did you caress him on the sly at dinner on April 5th?"

LILY. "I did not."

JACKY. "If you say that, I'll never speak to you again, for I saw you do it with my own eyes."

LILY. "Then I did! Why should I not caress him if I like?"

I told her of a woman I had known who could never sulk with me, but when she thought she was vexed and met me, resolved to scold and be angry, she would laugh, and put her hands in mine, give me a kiss, and say: "I cannot quarrel with you!"

I explained the folly of lying to me, who knew as much about female mendacity as a male fool could. I added: "A woman like you has no chance with a man like me."

JACKY. "If you tell me all, I can advise you. All conversation between us is impossible now. Imagine a drunkard consulting a doctor, who would say to him: 'Don't drink!' The slave to alcohol replies indignantly: 'I never touch spirits.' And he expects the medical man to cure him." Lily liked that little allegory.

She spoke of the novel *Césarée*.

"I think it is a lovely book, but when I read it, I see myself with you; not with Mr. Arvel. I should like to do all that with you. I am always thinking of you. When a young man, named François G., who is always running after me, and who lives down here, is speaking to me, I keep thinking what you would say in his place and how you would look."

"I like your smell. People smell differently. I don't like the smell of my brother, nor of François."

LILY. "Why don't you leave me alone on *that* subject? You have lost half the day, instead of spooning nicely with me. You might have had lots of kisses, instead of talking like this to me. I won't kiss you now. You made me very ill on April 5th."

JACKY. "Well, I'll have pity. You have been on the gridiron long enough. You are cooked now." At the word "pity," she fired up dreadfully, and said:

LILY. "If we quarrel, it is because you don't see me often enough. Why don't you come down more frequently?"

JACKY. "Oh, Lily, how can you say that? You know I can't come here unless it is arranged beforehand."

LILY. "Oh yes, that is true, perhaps!"

She meant that if I would give money, I might come there when I liked.

She spoke of her maidenhead: "I am still a virgin and you may do as you like with me. I don't care a bit about it, but I have always seen that when a man 'has' a virgin, he soon leaves her afterwards. That is what I fear with you."

I made no answer, but I supposed that this is what had happened to her, and will account for her returning me the novel *L'Anneau* without a word.

She wanted me to be a "woman." In this way: I was to have a meal with her. She was to order what she liked, as a man, and I was to be a "virgin," very docile and obedient, eating and drinking as she directed. She wanted to treat me as if I were of the weaker sex. She would *perhaps* remain dressed, and I was to be naked. She would undress me herself, as it pleased her.

"I would fasten your hands with that strap you left in my room last summer. I have kept it carefully."

This struck me as being strange, but conclusive. Evidently,

she had been keeping off me, not being a virgin, and this scheme would prevent me finding out her condition.

I told her how Papa had given me the story of her suitor, "who only wanted to poke her."

JACKY. "Why did he speak so coarsely about you to me, who never mentions your name to him?"

LILY. "He doubtless wants to lower me in your eyes. He is little-minded. That is the story of Teddy, who was bookkeeper at Myrio's. I did not know you then, so I can tell you without making you jealous, that Teddy made great love to me and I used to get awfully wet. I did not know what that meant then, and it used to frighten me."

She forgot she once told me that I was the first man who produced that effect upon her. I never spoke a word, as she dashed another of my illusions to pieces.

I explained that if he was little-minded, she had become imbued with Pa's doctrines, as she was like the daughter of a pettifogging lawyer.

I asked her too, ironically, how she managed to restrain her passions, having nothing but flirtations to feed upon.

"Oh, I am waiting for you, and I manage to get on by masturbating myself now and again."

Her cool impudence made me laugh, and I felt sufficiently indifferent not to contradict her in any way.

"If you do that, you'll be sure to have the 'whites' again. Masturbation brings them on."

"I never had the 'whites'!"

"Not last winter, in January?"

"That was not the 'whites.'"

"Let us say the 'reds,' if you like!"

She gave a little false laugh, making no reply which caused me to be certain of the *fausse couche* that ushered in the New Year.

Alone with the mother, after tea, I asked her whose daughter Lily was. She did not seem astonished at my query and gave me the following story of her life.

"Mr. Arvel was my suitor as a young girl. I did not like him. I got married to please my family to a man I did not love. I had two children, a boy and a girl, Raoul and Lilian. My name is Adèle-Lilian and that is why the house is called Villa Lilian. Then Mr. Arvel turned up again and used to meet me out with the babies. He would run after Lilian when she was but two years old. My husband died. I was penniless. Arvel helped me with money, and then was intimate with me, and I began to get over my dislike to him out of gratitude. We have lived together ever since. He never touches me now. I don't care. I never loved him. It was only habit with me. His temper was always bad, and he is very difficult to get on with. He is jealous, and envious, and full of curiosity."

Lily now appeared.

"How happy he ought to be between you two, both devoted to him. You, the mother, superintending the 'tit-bits' of the table he likes so much, and Mademoiselle waiting on him hand and foot."

Adèle got cross at this remark of mine, and flushing, her eyes sparkling with rage, declared he was not to be envied at all!

While concluding this conversation, Lily stood bolt upright behind her mother's chair, staring at me, but without speaking.

I afterwards told her that I had been pumping Mamma about her past life. Miss Arvel made no reply. She never even asked what her mother had said. Mamma knew all, and Lily's position in the house was secure, so she did not care.

When washing my hands before dinner, I was alone, and Mamma came and sought me out, a thing she had never done before, and said:

"Lily is not happy. Her business is too limited here, that is why she is going to London with her brother. What will the two poor children do in that great town? Suppose she does not succeed? She is too proud ever to confess a failure and come back home, and what would become of my little girl then? I want to let this place, which costs too much to keep up, and all of us would go to Paris and set up a millinery business. I would help her, but Mr. Arvel won't leave the country, where he is so comfortable."

"But he could stop here," I replied, "and she could work up

a business in Paris, you being with her as much as possible. It only wants a little money. Mr. Arvel could advance it."

"He won't give a penny. He says she is to stop here at home, and he will look after her, if she likes to be his secretary."

"Alas!" I answered, "I know what it is to want money. Look at my position now. I am 47 and I have got to begin life all over again, as I have no money."

My frank confession of poverty put an end to our conversation, but the mother, and Lily, and even the father, shutting his eyes, wanted me to offer money to set her up in business.

At dinner, Lily spoke in English of a woman near them, who had just died. It was rumoured that her husband had beaten her to death.

"Perhaps she liked being beaten," I said.

Lily affected surprise, and Papa and I agreed that it did women good to be beaten. Pa finished up as usual by telling Lily he would try it on her. No doubt he used to slap her dear posteriors a little. We were interrupted by Mamma, or I had intended pushing on the topic. That was why he liked me to be with him and Lily. But Lily was too jealous ever to let things go too far. She will always be between two people to put them at loggerheads. No doubt that was how she got her brother away from Lolotte.

Mr. Arvel, chattering privately to me, said that Lolotte's breasts hung down to her waist. I suppose he had reasons to know. He also told me that Charlotte's virginity being too heavy for her, some few years ago, she went to an oyster bar where she was known, and asked the young man who opened the bivalves to open her, and he did so. He also wanted to know if it was possible that Raoul could marry a girl, who earned no money and who wore silk chemises and drawers to match? He forgot Lily's beautiful *batiste* shifts and knickers, that covered her slight frame and limbs when she was "on the job." At home, she wore a thick flannel-like material for her drawers. I have had my hands there many a time. Her mother must know that now and then she would put on her soft pants of the spidery material you could blow away. They wash at home.

Now the day wears on, and the mother gets colics, and Lily

and I go to the chemist, who orders paregoric elixir, *i.e.* tincture of opium. We also drop in at the post-office and Lily registers a letter. The postal clerk is old and keeps us waiting. I tell my sweet companion that old men are always rather long.

We return home and Mamma takes a dose of the medecine. She dines on top of it, which is foolish, with neat Bordeaux wine, and a small glass of rum to top up with. Lily tells her boldly to go to bed. She evidently wished to be alone with Papa and me, perhaps not forgetting what I had hinted in my letter, as to her behaviour with her stepfather-lover, but Adèle gets quite jolly and will not stir. We—Lily, Papa and I—are to take the dogs out for a walk, before I go to the station, when suddenly Mamma spins round like a top and faints away. Lily never turns a hair. She does not love her mother; she is only disgusted at not being able to go out with us. Pa don't care either—he goes out with me, leaving Lily with her sick mother half undressed on the sofa.

There was no real love or tenderness in that house, nothing but appetites—sensual longing, gluttony and cupidity, with quarrels between whiles. That was how they lived. The master of the house cared for two things only in this world: cooking and copulation.

I had explained in the afternoon to Lily that life was impossible without genuine affection. We cannot be always spending.

"Oh! how truly you talk! I am very unhappy!" she exclaimed.

"You must not say that!" I quickly retorted. "It is not true. It is very wicked to pretend to be unfortunate, so as to make me miserable, thinking you are not happy. That is wrong of you, Miss Clever."

"Oh, Jacky! I'm not clever! I am foolish in many ways!"

"Not so foolish but what you try all you can to make me jealous, although you see how you fail. I wish you had a hundred men, so as to know what I am worth."

She was obliged to laugh at this fatuous outburst of mine, but would not explain what she meant by saying she was foolish. I was getting fatigued at Sonis now. This continual fencing was not to my taste, and only the thought of my book made me think of returning there. The idea that I was living a future volume and building up my novel kept me buoyant.

This new experience tickled my fancy and I had no sensual longings for Miss Arvel now.

Papa and I go out. I advise cutting off his wife's two daily glasses of rum. He does not appear to listen to what I say, but starts off again talking against Raoul and Lily.

Raoul had said that he would not come to see his mother at Whitsuntide. (Pa probably knew that Lily would not let him, and Lily had told me that day that she had made it all right with her brother for our journey to Belfort.)

"If he don't come and see his mother, I've got influence with the military and I'll look after him. He shall come out from England next year and do his twenty-eight days—the second service of reserve men in France—although I can get him off if I choose. My arm is long enough. Because he earns £5 a week in the wine business, he thinks the world is his own. They only keep him on because they know I could make it hot for them, as they robbed me with some shares in their concern, but as I held my tongue and did not prosecute, they gave the lad the berth. He is lazy, and speaks English with a Whitechapel accent. He wouldn't help me to clean the bicycles! (*Again!*) Lily wants to go to England. She shall have no money of me. Let him keep her. She is lazy, and vain, and fond of new clothes and jewellery. All her profits go on her own back. She wants us to live in Paris and set her up as a *modiste*. She would never be in until midnight and I should soon be known as her *maquereau*. Not for me! She was very ill in Brussels, but directly I popped in with a theatre ticket, she was off all right again. I tried to get her to learn writing for English fashion papers. I gave her a French article to translate (*the one I arranged!*), but she did it dreadfully badly. She would want a lot of practice."

"It was full of mistakes, I suppose?"

"Yes, indeed!"

He must have known I did it. I put in sentences purposely which it was not possible she could ever have written. Spangles, I called: "dainty, little, dazzling discs." A grey cloth became: "a fabric of a cloudy, pearl white, akin to the greyish tint of a fleeting morning mist." He must have known she could not knock off that stuff. A doll's tea service, I worked up as follows: "Those tiny cups, lilliputian saucers and wee plates, etc." He also feigned intense hatred for Lily's pet dog, Blackamoor. But winding up, he said:

"One thing in her favour is that she is very intelligent."

All this was said for me. He did not intend to let her go to Belfort.

We returned; Mamma was in bed. I told Lily some bits of his conversation. She was not astonished and showed no curiosity, which convinced me of their complicity.

"He hates your mother!"

Lily pretended to be surprised.

"You watch it. He hates everybody and everything, but you, and for you he shows false scorn to me, feigns to despise you perhaps—for me to share that feeling."

I did not say: "You hate your mother too." And in point of fact, all hated or despised each other. Papa despises Lily for being his plaything, and yet wants her ever between his thighs to feel and kiss him. He scorns his mistress for having sold him her daughter and prizes her as a servant and cook. Raoul hates his mother's lover for having debauched him and his sister, and Lily has no respect for any of them, nor for herself.

She then kissed me deliriously, and at the end of a long drawn-out, sucking, tongueing bout, she exclaimed with a loud sigh: "Oh, sweetheart!" as she had done to her brother in my presence on the eve of Shrove Tuesday.

She felt my sign of manhood outside my trousers to see if I stiffened by dint of her ghoulish mouth, as she had been doing on and off all day.

Then we went to the station, she kissing me behind Papa's back all the way in the dark. She "took sights" at him, continually, behind his back. But that was only to please me, as she is very fond of him, I fancy. But is she fond of anybody? She showed intense passion for me. Too much of it, I thought. She protested too much. I was getting very cool.

I showed her a photograph of my half-sister, with "yours

lovingly, March 1899," on the back. She said nothing at the moment, but later on pretended to be angry at my having connection with women! Then she was rude about my half-sister.

"How your thoughts run on incest, Lily!" I replied, and that silenced her.

Before wishing them a cordial good night, Lily told me that she would very likely try and get to Paris Sunday evening and dine with me. A visit to Lolotte was to be the pretext. She was almost sure to be able to manage it.

I smelt a rat about this visit on a Sunday night to Paris, so the next day I wrote her a few lines, saying: "That if Sunday was to be for her dinner with me, I should not be at liberty until 8 P.M. But if that evening she was passing through Paris, I should be pleased to see her, if only for an hour."

That was a trap, as I thought that if she had an appointment in Paris, I might meet her and learn something.

I also said: "I have had a conversation with Papa concerning your brother and his Whitsuntide holidays, which I had not time to tell you the other night." I may say at once that she never recurred to this important topic, showing that she would ask Papa when I left: "What did you tell Mr. S . . . ?" And he answered and narrated what I had said to him. The fact of her evincing no curiosity when I put forward conversations I had with him plainly showed that they were as one to deceive me.

LILIAN TO JACKY.

Undated (Received Sunday morning, April 23, 1899.)

My Jacky,

For to-morrow night—impossible, therefore we are obliged to put off our meeting until a fortnight, or three weeks hence perhaps. I am very vexed about this, as I confess that I have a mad desire—oh! but really an extraordinary wish to have you all alone mine own for several hours; therefore—

(Here we come to the bottom of the page, and turning over, the letter changes agreeably)—if thou art free the day after to-morrow, Monday, April 24, say so, and be at the Square Montholon at 11:45.

I will come and fetch thee and we will go and lunch together. Then we will see.

Wilt thou come?

I adore thee,

LILY.

I answered and acepted. She would have got my letter by the first post on Monday morning. I wrote as if she were a man, and I was the woman. I had also been calling her in my recent writings, "my wife," or "all my little wifie." And all this scribbling, and my apparent stupidity and calm on my last visit had thrown all of them off their guard. I was a fool, madly in love with their daughter.

I could not understand that Papa would let her dine out one evening and not lunch at home the next day. It was too good to be true.

Sunday evening, during dinner, I got this wire:

LILIAN TO JACKY. (*Telegram.*)

To-night at the American bar, near the Opéra. Nine o'clock.

LILY.

I went and found my charmer in a new flaming dress, made entirely of vivid red cloth. She had white kid gloves, with a nice hat, and looked very well, being very red in the face too. She had with her the Lesbian Lolotte, ex-mistress and ex-betrothed of her brother Raoul. They were both very jolly. I had never seen Lolotte before, but she knew me by name from Lily. I chaff them about their sexless kisses when alone together, and want to know who is the man of the two. It is the stereotyped stuff that is always poured out to a tribadic couple. Lolotte is a pretty, plump blonde. She was very free and charming; about Lily's age, 22 or thereabouts. We are soon very comfortable together in the back saloon of the bar, where, it seems to me, Lily is well-known. It was near the Café de la Guerre, and she went there with her brother on Shrove Tuesday.

Directly I saw Lilian, I exclaimed: "Hullo, all up for our luncheon to-morrow!"

"How do you mean?"

"Why, you fetching me out in Paris to-night proves it is all off."

"But that would not prevent us lunching tomorrow, although I can't come for the following reasons. How strange you should have guessed it! I had to take some hats to a customer in Paris on Monday, so I profited by that to get to you. This morning comes a postcard, which Mother sees, to say that the lady prefers to come down to the country. So I can't get out to Paris. My excuse is destroyed. If it had been a letter, I could have suppressed it, and seen the lady to-day, so as to stop her coming down. Thus our lunch is knocked on the head!"

"Lies!" I thought, but I said nothing. I should have liked to have seen that postcard.

"I have finished Césarée," said Lily. "It is beautiful. You have marked it well, and scored the best bits, but you are all wrong in one instance."

"About the bedrooms at the Swiss hotel, I suppose?"

"Yes. You know you are quite mistaken in your ideas about me!" She said this slowly and dreamily, not looking straight at me.

"I am absolutely convinced of the truth of my conjectures and stick to every word I have ever said or written on the subject!" I say this firmly, loudly, and impressively.

Charlotte was listening to the conversation, and Lily spoke quite openly, showing that her fair friend knew the secrets of Sonis. I told her that Lily was a liar, and had an awful temper. She knew it, and replied that all women were liars, out of necessity.

Lily's friend talked about London and declared that she would like to go there during the season. I offered, jokingly, to take her. She replied with emphasis, that it would be very nice, and people would take her for a *daughter travelling with her Papa!*

And she looked fixedly and archly at me. I had enough presence of mind to pay no apparent heed to her bold words, but I felt I had scored again. She knew.

I said I was impotent. Lily cried out: "No, he isn't!"

Lolotte said she was sentimental, and Lily was not. Nevertheless, the blonde confessed that she liked something stiff and rather long. I could see by the way she spoke that Lily was now like herself; a common, ordinary, middle-class, half-and-half kind of whore, always on the look-out for a man with money, and had I told her the story of her friend's virginity, she would have been quite surprised. It was a great pity that I knew Lily's stepfather-lover and all his connections and history so well. Under ordinary circumstances, they would never have thought of hatching these intricate and silly plots against me.

I spoke of Raoul, but both the girls begged me never to tell him of the meeting of the two beauties in Paris at night.

Lily told us the story of her day:

"I got up at nine, had a bath, lunched; then went on my bicycle, came home, dressed again; came to Paris, fetched Charlotte, and we both went to Narkola's to dine, *us two girls alone* (!!). We had lots of nice things—*bisque* soup and fine wine."

"In a *cabinet particulier*, both alone together?"

"Oh no, in the public room!"

All lies, but I say nothing.

"How *dry* you must both be now!"

They roar with laughter, and whisper together, and giggle; and again our conversation about the sexes becomes lewd and stupid. They have two American drinks each. I have a soda and Scotch whisky. Lily amuses herself dropping her saliva in my half-emptied glass, making me drink her spittle mixed with my beverage. She tells me that Gaston taught her that clean manner of showing affection. Lolotte gets on well with me and wants me to take her to London more than ever.

To lull Lily into security I thank her for having sent for me, and she alludes to how I said she sickened me, when she sent me a sudden summons by wire last September. She also spoke of my birthday, and remembered the date well. I merely quote these two facts to show that her brain was clear on technical points, and although she was artful enough to give no sign, all I had ever written to her, all I had ever said, had always gone right home to the mark, and remained in her memory. No doubt she read my letters over and over again. Poor, miserable Lily!

The girls kiss and say good night. We put Charlotte in a cab, and off she goes to her home, somewhere beyond the Bastile. Lily has a little, jealous scene about my freedom with her friend, as Lolotte had taken off her glove and held my hand and tickled it. We go for a ride to the Eastern station, to catch the 10:30 to Sonis. I am not to get out of the cab at the station, so as not to be seen by the neighbours who might be taking this train, or anybody, or somebody.

"When shall we meet again?" I ask.

"I don't know. You are aware how difficult it is for me to get to Paris."

"It used to be difficult. It ought not to be difficult now."

No answer.

I tell her I shall masturbate her in the cab. We get in. We exchange hot and luscious kisses, as we have been doing all the evening, more or less. After a lot of resistance, with cries of: "People will see us! Oh! They are looking, etc.," I get my hand up her clothes. I pull down the blinds. She pulls them up. At last, I overcome her feigned resistance and begin to excite her with my finger.

She has on her best drawers, and to my surprise, her cleft, generally smelling strong of the wonderful odour peculiar to the sex, is quite inodorous. It has evidently been freshly washed after dinner. My fingers afterwards were entirely without any feminine perfume. I knew also that a virgin's vulva is always more fragrant than that of a woman used to coition. I remembered that when her people were at Nice at January, she had a dinner at Narkola's, with Madame Rosenblatt and her male relations, who had purposely sent a false telegram to her Granny. Of course that was a cock and a bull story. Here is Narkola's again! Had I chosen, I could have gone there the next day, and inquired about an imaginary earring dropped by the young lady in the red dress, but I really was now quite indifferent, and would not have walked twenty yards to find out anything about her. I had spied upon her in Brussels—that was enough.

Suddenly, while gently caressing her clitoris, I turned half round, so as to get almost facing her, and placing my right forearm under her chin, on her throat, I drive her backwards into her corner of the cab, and while she is thus pressed there, unable to move, I thrust the middle finger of my left hand as far up her vagina as I can, until it is stopped by the knuckles.

I measure my finger next day finding 2½ inches, and my hand is small.

The 2½ inches of medius go up easily. I move my finger about inside, with a slight corkscrew motion. Within all is soft and damp, but not wet from randiness, only from the drink. She has not left me to void her urine since 9 P.M. She shrieks loudly and says:

"You hurt me! You hurt me!"

She struggles, but I have her tightly jammed in the corner. I find that her grotto is strangely altered. The outer lips were always very fleshy, but inside all was small, and the skin tightly drawn together, as on a thin hand. Now it is very fat, mellow, and as I said, not wet, as she was not feeling "naughty." My finger went in as in butter, and she has now evidently what I should call a large, fat gap, which has been properly stroked, doubtless by big, manly tools. But then, having been used that evening, it might be a little puffed up, as women's parts are after connection.

I cried out: "You are no longer a virgin! No longer a maid! Now I shall be able to have complete intercourse with you!"

I took my finger out and released her. She made a wry face, as she put down her clothes, saying:

"Oh, you did hurt me! But I'm still a virgin. Your finger went in because it was not in the right place. You were between the two!"

Possibly meaning just under the clitoris and above the hymen. I need not stop to point out the absurdity of this anatomical statement.

"You are a virgin? Bosh!"

"I swear I am! On my mother's life, I swear I am still intact!"

I was so delighted at having attained my object, that I did not realise the contemptible horror of the situation. It was only afterwards, when I was alone, that I gauged the depths of Lilian's baseness. At the moment, curiously enough, I thought of how I should describe the scene in my book. I saw it all in print, and it seemed comic and unreal, as if it was happening to someone else, and I was but the spectator of my own disgusted self. But there was a glorious warmth of triumph thrilling through my veins. I felt like a detective, who after many months has run his man down, and at last got the handcuffs on a criminal. I do believe that if I had found she really was a virgin, I should have been disappointed to find a maidenhead. It would have seemed like a monstrosity. Never did a surgeon operating on some special case of hidden cancer, feel more awful, intense joy than I did at that critical juncture.

"Come," said I, laughing, "and I'll finish you gently."

She was now quiet and subdued, and expected likely enough a storm of reproaches. She kissed me and let me put my hand up her clothes without any show of revolt. I began again to manipulate her rosebud, but naturally enough, she had no enjoyment. Then I got very stiff, but not too much, as I had been indulging that afternoon, and I got it out and put her hand on it.

She caressed and agitated it a little. Seeing we were getting near the station and having a sudden desire for her hot mouth, which I knew would make me ejaculate in a jiffey, better than her awkward pulling at me with her gloved hand, I said:

"Give me your mouth, Lily!"

She shook her head, and kept on with the movements of her fingers. I take her hand away and say:

"I must have your lips and tongue, Lily!"

She sulks and turns her back to me, looking out of the window.

"Well, I'll masturbate myself!"

"Oh no, don't do that!"

"I will! I'll spend alone! And you can go to the man with no finger-nails!"

At this rude remark, which called up the vision of the hands of her mother's lover, to my astonishment she turns round and kisses me. She was so pleased to find I showed jealousy of the wrong person. She was waiting for a scene about the people she had dined with. Out comes her hand again. I push it away, and rub my member a little, like a schoolboy. She turns her head away again, and to give her a chance, I say:

"I suppose your stays prevent you stooping down?"

She, the fool, cannot take my handsome hint, but has turned her back once more entirely towards me, and does not answer.

So I, in despair, cover myself up and button my pants. At this moment, we are just nearing the station.

Seeing this, she is evidently delighted that all is over for the evening, and turning, draws me towards her, gently patting my cheek with her hand, her arm resting on my shoulder, as I had often seen her with her Papa. At this Judas-like caress, I confess that I felt myself boiling over with rage.

She has disdainfully refused me her lips, without a word of excuse, although I have not spent with her since the 1st. of March, and have not had her mouth since the 1st. of October.

If she had said: "I am tired. How can I suck you in my tight stays, new dress, jacket and hat?" I would willingly have excused her, especially as I was not very lustful just then. But she had not even taken off a glove. Her stroke on my cheek meant: "Now that it is too late to suck him, I'll make it up with the idiot."

My blood boiled at this thought, and I repulsed her, pushing her from me by the shoulder. She was on my right hand. I felt like a brute and behaved like one. I dashed out my right arm and caught her a fearful backhander on the lower part of the left cheek and jaw.

She gasped for breath, and said slowly and quietly in a low tone:

"How brutal!"

"I am mad," I replied, "go and spend when you get home."

This was foolish, as she had freely emitted in Paris, and was not ready for me after her dinner, frolic, and two American champagne mixtures. She had had her enjoyment, and was not yet whore enough to play the proper part with another man at two hours' interval. Besides, her temper would not allow her to do so.

She was on the proper side to leave the cab, as it was now stopped, so she stepped out without a word, and I saw her go slowly and shakily along the station frontage, not boldly entering the first door in front of her, as she ought to have done, but sneaking along slowly, evidently thinking I was going to come after

her, or perhaps tipsy, or crying, or mad with rage at being out-
witted. Or going to the ladies' W.C. at the end of the building.

I slowly paid the cabman, watching her the while. I dared
not follow her, for I knew that if I did—God help me!—I should
have struck her again. So I turned away and walked home. How I
got along and what streets I took, I do not know. I am surprised
I was not run over. I found myself in front of my door, that is all
I can say. It was about 11:30 or 11:45. I got into bed and smoked
until 2 A.M. I could not settle to read. I could only smoke and
stare at nothing. I was very much upset, although I had known
the truth all along by intuition.

Then I found that the knuckles of the second and third fingers
of my right hand were torn and bleeding. I did not think I could
have burst the skin with the force of the blow on her face. I do
not suppose I hurt her much, as I had no room to swing my arm
in the cab, and she did not put her hand up to her face after the
blow. I hoped that I had torn my knuckles on her brooch, or
neckpins, or earrings, or garters, or something of the same kind,
while struggling with her, and these slight abrasions were only
coincidences.

Strange to say, but it is the truth, I had no regret for having
struck her and feel none now. When I wrote her that insulting
letter about the Belgian trip, and sent the analysis of her own
letters, I felt strangely delighted, and was surprised when she was
silly enough to answer.

It was the first time in my life that I had ever lifted my hand
to a woman in anger.

The next day I was quite calm again, and hugely pleased to
find how well I had succeeded.

I had quite deceived the infamous Trinity at Sonis and I had
proved to Lily that I knew she was no longer a virgin.

I had set myself a threefold task: to prove that Lily was Papa's
mistress, by exposing the lies from Lille; that her maidenhead was
gone, despite her assertions to the contrary; and that they were
all in league to conspire against me.

All I had to do now was to bide my time to taunt her with
her complicity, and then I could go away.

I wrote and sent the following letter, but it was not meant specially for her. It was for Papa,—and a little for my book which was rapidly taking a practical form in my brain,—and I composed the details of the famous ride, just as I have given it here, and leisurely prepared notes for the rest.

When I posted the letter I now give, I thought she would not answer me, and that I should never see her more. Anyhow, I made up my mind that she would never come to my arms again. I did not see how she could.

JACKY TO LILIAN.

Paris, April 27, 1899.

You arrive with Charlotte Sunday night, and tell me that the appointment arranged for the next day has fallen through. I say nothing, but I find the story suspicious. I should like to see the postcard of Sunday. But I pass that over. I don't care.

I hear that the two young ladies have dined alone. I venture to say they are "dry." They laugh, not understanding that I am mocking them. Lolotte must think me stupid. I say nothing. I don't care.

I make the following remark: in January, Lily also went to dine at Narkola's with Madame Rosenblatt. Put the two things together. Had I curiosity, nothing would have been easier for me than to have gone on Monday to Narkola's to find out about the lady dressed in red. I have not done so. Neither shall I. What better proof can I give that I don't care?

We get in a cab. I discover that she is no longer a virgin, in spite of all the stuff she has recently told me. I had already my suspicions when I did *minette* to her in January. Then I found her parts absolutely changed beneath my tongue. When a maid, she was rather thin down there, the skin tight over the bones, as with all virgins. Now all is fat. It is soft, as if swollen, but she is rather large, I find. Evidently she has met a strong sexual partner. It is true that she had just been enjoyed by a man, and at such a moment, directly after connection, the parts are always a little puffy. But she is too fat in the lips for such a young woman and I repeat—rather vast. But my examination was necessarily superficial. Her "pussy" was excessively clean, without any special smell. Therefore, there had been private, recent ablutions. Injection? After dinner, I think. The men were all married, as she was not perfumed.

I pushed my finger in freely as if in butter—six centimeters. The entrance was easy, all being open. She was not excited by me. There was only a little moisture through the drinks. The reason is simple; she had just spent a lot. Nevertheless, she swore on her mother's life that she was still a virgin, and that I had put my finger "between the two." Comedy! I said nothing. I did not care.

She did not try to caress me. She never even took off her glove. I did not care. (She used to say: "To you I would do anything.")

I ask for her mouth. She turns away without a word. I did not care. I give her a hint, telling her that perhaps her stays were too tight. I wanted her to excuse herself prettily. She did not understand. I did not care.

Then a wonderful thing took place, that I really did care about. Seeing that we were nearing the station, she left off sulking, and turned round to me, caressing my cheek. This is how I understand this Judas-like caress: "Fortunately, we are at the station. He can't ask me for anything now, the idiot! I have eluded the task. Now to coax him to get away."

In a twinkling, I understood the horror of this idea, and I made you feel severely the weight of my opinion. I struck you in the face—movement of brutal impulse. But whose fault was it?

She has dragged me down to the level of the brute—or would like to do so.

Do I regret what I did? I do not believe so. I don't care.

But what I do care about are the rude words I uttered concerning a poor man, victim of Lily, who I pity with all my heart. How he must suffer! How he will regret having let himself be seduced—if he does not regret it already. I understand the kick given to the dog. I understand everything, and from the bottom of my heart I ask his pardon for the insults I addressed to him by insulting the infamous Lily. If I could only make him understand the compassion and sympathy I feel for him, victim of Lily!

I, at least, possess common sense; I can reason, and I finish by regaining full mastery over myself. Then again, I do not live with her. Sincerely, I pity him. What a sad existence she will make for him—she does make for him! Poor man!

Why, Lily, this accumulation of lies, to enable you to play continually and solely for me, this part of the perpetual virgin, letting no one touch her but me, and yet always in somebody's arms? You are immaculate, of course. Jacky and you masturbate, or suck six times a year, and that is all.

Are you mad? Do you take me for a madman? Or are we all mad, and you alone sane?

It is laughable. But I don't care. When in a rage we say: "I don't care a damn; what does it matter to me?" Generally we feel quite the contrary. I believe that I prove, and I have sufficiently proved lately, the appearance of a slight commencement of indifference. And if you do not believe me, I do not care.

A few guesses:

Lily was certainly a virgin in October last. January she was so no longer, nor in December either. ("Don't be silly, darling!")

When sucking her in the dining-room in January, I felt the difference. I ask to be allowed to try with my finger. She consented, and cunningly put me off: "It is so tender now I've come!"

When did she lose her maidenhead?

In London in October? I think not. I saw her at the beginning of November, when she forged the hideous lie of the lost letter. At that moment, she wanted to be my wife. I still believe in her relative honesty, and she would not have wished to marry me if she had not been physically intact. You see, Lily, that I have still a little illusion. You are surprised? I do not care.

I think that the thing happened in November. With whom? After November, there is no talk of marriage.

I have two ideas: Mr. Arvel, or a stranger. I put aside the first-named, I don't know why, and from some signs that I have no time to set out here—especially as all this is very vague in my brain; I grope in darkness now—I lean towards a stranger, who, either because he feared the consequences, or else because he tired of her after once or twice, has not set eyes on her since. Or he is perhaps absent momentarily. And I believe he is an officer.

I suppose he abandoned her. Out of spite, she threw herself into the arms of those who she thought she loved a little: Mr. Arvel, who, on second thoughts, I think she loves a great deal, who she seduced; and Jacky, who she don't much care about, except to make him suffer, and excite Mr. Arvel. Nevertheless, she is always telling Jacky and writing to him how she loves him. I do not speak of the *parties carrées* with her Lesbian Charlotte.

A woman who truly loves cannot live without the man she has chosen. She only knows one thing; to see him as often as possible, although she may have to dig up the earth with her nails to get to him. In a word—'tis love. And when she sees her lover, she only knows one other thing: to get into bed, to open her thighs, to give herself up, and let herself be taken, virgin or not. Does a woman really in love think of her virginity? She loves. That is all.

Lily the liar does nothing of this with me. She loves not, neither Jacky nor anybody. Mr. Arvel a little, and the remembrance of her first real lover—that is all. She loves nothing. She fetched me out Sunday night through vanity, to show Lolotte that after having copulated in her society, she had yet another man waiting for her. I do not care.

Excuse all faults of French of your old foreign snob. I have a copy of this letter. Shall I make a few extracts for Lolotte, or do you prefer to read this to her when you see her?

This is a calm and sensible letter, without empty phrases; without tears, flowers, birds, or music. You like novels. This is better—here you have a living romance, of which you are the heroine.

You love voluptuous letters that you can show. Show this one, I'm not ashamed of it. I set forth my weakness, I allow, but I've no vanity. I boast of nothing. The part of victim does not displease me. And to prove that I should not blush if it be shown to who you like, I write it on paper stamped with my die, and I sign my name in full,

JOHN S . . .

But I have wagered with myself that you will not answer me. You are in a tight corner.

What lying bubbles I have burst since you became a neat little Césarée! I kiss you, and conclude—at last!

From a sensible point of view, it doubtless seems a silly thing to have sent the foregoing letter. The reason why I did it was because I was afraid that Lilian, perhaps half tipsy—she must have been so, or she would never have opened her thighs so wide—would not, or could not see my motives. Also, that I did not wish to spare her; I felt a savage pleasure in rubbing her nose in her filth. I wanted to drive her to give me up herself. I wanted to see how far she would go; whether she had any pride left; whether she was utterly debased and abandoned or not; and lastly, I was now certain that Papa knew all our story, and had eagerly devoured my letters, just as Lily and he had read all my obscene books together. I told her so; I told her I found his big, black thumbmarks in one of them. She never answered; she never did, when I guessed rightly. I thought he was putting her up to most of her tricks. In their narrow-mindedness, they cannot believe that I have always been truthful, and in spite of all I have said, think I am a miser and that there is still something to be got out of me; never mind how little—it is all profit. They were trying to "work" me. Pa, Ma, and Lily were all conspiring. They were accomplices, more or less, and I was to be the fool. Where they were all wrong, was that according to my mad letters and my still madder talk and ideas, they suppose and hope that I am absolutely gone crazy on Lily and that she can do whatever she likes with me. Habitual liars are the easiest people in the world to deceive. They believe everybody. But you must never lie to them. Tell them the truth or nothing, and they will be as children in your hands.

I had now to make a most dreadful sacrifice, with only the voice of my conscience to applaud me—the sacrifice of my passion; of my sensual enjoyment; of my thirst for lust with Lily, which I could have still assuaged had I chosen to be a weak coward towards myself. This holocaust, perhaps I am too vain in saying so, seemed to elevate me in my own sight, and I felt like a hero, in thus conquering my concupiscence in solitude, between four walls, all alone with my thoughts.

3

. . . . Go, call my daughter;
And if she comes not, tell her that I come.—
What sufferings? I will drag her, step by step,
Through infamies unheard of among men,

. . . .
She shall become (for what she most abhors
Shall have a fascination to entrap
Her loathing will), to her own conscious self
All she appears to others.
. . . . I will make
Body and soul a monstrous lump of ruin.

SHELLEY.

ERIC ARVEL TO JACKY.

Sonis-sur-Marne, May 1st. 1899.

My dear Jacky,

If you have nothing better to do on Wednesday, will you bring down your bike and come for a ride? We will breakfast at 11:30, *sans façon*, and see you get home safely at night. Raoul has written, and desires to be kindly remembered to you. I was very much obliged to you for the papers you sent.

Hoping you are all well at home, believe me to remain,

Yours very truly,
ERIC ARVEL.

392

P.S.—Look at the enclosed photo, and tell us what you think about "Mount Calvary"?

WEDNESDAY, MAY 3, 1899.

This postscript and the photograph, representing Lily between her brother and myself—taken by Papa in February—confirmed me in my opinion that Papa knew all, and so did Lolotte, for Lily never troubled about my threat of writing to her Sapphic friend. I sent a wire, accepting the invitation, and went down on my bicycle; my hands full, as usual.

I had made up my mind to be calm, cool, collected and merry, and not to say a word to Lily on the subject of our secret (?) relations, unless she spoke first. I half expected she would not be there. How could it be possible that any woman, even the lowest of the low, could sit unmoved in front of the man who, in the right or in the wrong, had sent her such a vile, horrible, loathsome letter, without counting his brutal assault on her? But knowing her petty thoughts, I guessed she would say: "How he must love me to write such things! How vexed he is!" And she would be proud to think she had got me in such a mad state. So Pa and Lily invited me to gloat over my supposed sufferings and make me suffer more. The best reason of all was, perhaps, that Papa did not want to quarrel openly with me, as I knew now too much about him.

I arrive. The servant tells me that Madame has gone to Paris early, and Mademoiselle will receive me. Not a soul to be seen, which was most impolite in a villa, when you are expected as the only guest. When the garden gate shuts to, somebody should run out to meet you, I think. At least, such was always the case with me, but not this time. I am ushered into the house and am left to wait five minutes alone. A cool reception. Papa comes downstairs at last and we go out for a walk to meet his wife at the station. We return, all three of us, and he talks of his "Calvary" joke, while I see Lily, peering at me from the summer-house workshop.

"That was your invention," I reply, "because she is between two thieves?"

"No. She mentioned it first. Where is she? Lilian! Lilian!"

And he bawls out her name. She will not answer. She does not appear until lunch, fully an hour and a half after my arrival, and greets me coldly. I am, I am pleased to say, perfectly indifferent and quite self-possessed. She does not excite me as she used to do. She has on an old dress, and no powder, or red on her lips. The beauty spot on her cheek is gone.

We lunch. During the meal, she has to get up and pass behind my chair. She puts one hand heavily on my shoulder, near my neck, boldly in front of her two parents. The lunch is a poor one, compared to what they used generally to put on the table for me. They are all dull. The duller they get, the gayer I am. I actually go so far as to imitate Sarah Bernhardt!!

"You do well in mentioning the name of the actress," says Lily.

"I always do when I give an imitation. It avoids all discussion." Then I add: "To-day is an anniversary! Four years ago, in May, I forget the day exactly, I brought the little fox-terrier, Lili, here. That was the first time I ever came into this house. How time flies, and what changes take place in four years!"

This with a little emotion, half real, half feigned, but I felt I had acted it well. I don't think they liked the little speech. There was no response, except from Lily, who saucily but angrily, sniffing, snorting, replies:

"I thought you meant her birthday, when you said anniversary!"

I notice that Papa treats Lily with mock gravity, and calls her Madame, all through the meal. Ever since the return from Brussels there has never been any romping between the pair as in olden days, but they treat each other with great seriousness. They have no need to play with each other in the daytime now. Perhaps too, Mamma's susceptibilities have to be reckoned with.

When the coffee comes on, the beautiful porcelain cups and saucers, which Papa brought from China, are no longer put on the table, as they used to be for me. Lily asks me how I will have my coffee—in a cup or in a glass. I see no cups on the table, so I reply that I will have it in the same way as Mr. Arvel. She says that

Papa takes it in a glass, and she pours it in his, on top of the dregs of his white wine, and serves me in the same way.

It is impossible that Pa and Ma did not notice these little shades indicating my disgrace in their house, and they must also see the way Lily treated me. Their collusion was glaring.

While we are drinking the coffee, Mamma goes and has an awful row in the kitchen, and kicks out one of her two female servants. The same thing occurred on April 5th.

Papa and Lily remain at table with me unmoved, and I feel dreadfully ill at ease to hear Adèle shrieking in the kitchen and the vulgar howling of the domestic replying to her. My interesting pair tell me that Madame Arvel is mad and can't keep a servant. They are like husband and wife, and Mamma is the housekeeper: Lily sneers at the muffled sounds of the dispute, and Papa swears and growls.

Mamma returns, very red in the face, and apologises to me for her outburst of passion. She must tell servants all she thinks of them, and give them a bit of her mind. This one had been talking against her in the village.

"Dear Madam," I say, "why get in a passion with hired menials, and expect devotion from them, when you see so often in families that even blood relations betray each other. You expect too much of servants."

Of course, Adèle never answered, and the guilty couple was silent too.

Lily stuck with Papa and me. I followed Papa about all day like a little dog and would not be left alone with Lily. She now began to look wistfully at me. She could not make me out, and was waiting for some advance on my part. I noticed her in the glass.

She talked about a new photographic lens and said to her Papa:

"Papa, you must photograph me as a Japanese girl and in all sorts of costumes."

And she looked at him with her sweetest smile, and her nostrils quivered nervously.

"Papa, I am going up to Paris at 2:37."

But she did not go. She never left us hardly a minute.

"Here's the postman," says Lily, and she rushes down to the gate. She returns with a letter for Pa, and cries out: "One from *him!*"

As she ran back into the house, Pa tapped her posteriors, where her pocket was, and said to me:

"She has got it in her pocket!"

I made no remark.

"Lily is not going to London, in September to live with her brother," he suddenly broke out. "She has found out that she would probably have to keep him."

"What is she going to do then?" I say. This is the first and last time that I ever asked him anything about her.

"She will stop here with me."

Afterwards, he speaks very affectionately to her in front of me, as he has never done before, and while he is talking, I wink facetiously at Lily. I am certain that he is trying to teaze me on behalf of his stepdaughter and secret wife, even as a mother might do, who would be the procuress of her own girl.

Finally, she manages to get me alone and chaffs me about being too thin. I retort that I look after myself, as the doctors advise me that if I get too fat, I shall be in bed again with rheumatism.

"I do not spare myself," I say quietly. "You find fault with my personal appearance, because you have no longer any feeling of desire for me. *Qu'importe le flacon, pourvu qu'on ait l'ivresse!*"

She throws up her head and snorts, but says: "No! No!" as I stroll away from her, back to the side of Papa.

She makes us two men take her out for a walk. She does not try to go out alone with me and never does again. Surely Pa and Ma can see the change?

She chatters about a certain fashionable actor, and turns very red; crimson are her cheeks, as I tell her tales of his amours. She says she does not like him any more, as although he looked beautiful on the stage, she would prefer him to be less of a rake. Lily declares that actors and actresses have strange ideas, but she adds with a sigh that lots of other people have strange ideas too. Papa smokes in silence. I play the clown, and they are both obliged to laugh at my foolish antics.

I ask her if she is rich—if she has not a few hundred francs saved up in a corner of her wardrobe, under her clean drawers. She cannot help smiling as she wonders at my astuteness in feminine matters; that is exactly how her Mamma hides her money. Lily's pocket money is limited. She got one hundred francs for a pair of puppies, thanks to my advertisement. In spite of my advice, they did not advertise again, but the other three pups were given away—one to the officer; one to a friend of mine, the jeweller, who made the ring; and the last to a brother-journalist, a friend of Papa's.

Lily wore no rings that day. I never saw my poor ring on her hand again.

We return to tea. Then Lily stands in a doorway, waiting for me to speak to her. I repeat my movement of retreat, walking away in the garden, after Papa, and she looks so wild; frowning and black under the eyes, that I turn round, and thoroughly happy to feel myself so free in front of her—for perhaps I feared I might weaken—actually laugh outright at her. She goes in, but not at once. Then later, she complains of a headache. Alone with me, for I continually find her at my heels, I gravely advise castor-oil.

Papa and I go out for a ride on our bicycles. He is very slow, careful and nervous. He does nothing but talk of Lily and how well and fearlessly she rides. He confides to me that his member shrivels up on a bike, and asks me if mine does! What does he mean? Does he want me to ask to look at it? I answer that I have never noticed this phenomenon in myself.

When we return, Lily's head is worse. She has got a face as black as a negress. She comes to me and says:

"I have left all the books I have of you at the station. Here is the ticket!"

After my laugh, while we were out on our bicycles, she had evidently made up her parcel, and had gone to the cloakroom of the little station of Sonis.

Unmoved, I take it.

"Thank you," I reply. "I have got a couple of novels ready for you. One is on the same subject as *Césarée* but much stronger."

"Where are they? Have you brought them with you?"

"No, but I will leave them at the cloakroom of the Eastern station and send you the ticket."

That was all. She got more sulky, and I gayer than ever. She calls her Papa.

"Pa, will you come down to the cellar with me?"

I used to do that. Papa puts on his gloomy look and is delighted to go with her, while I, all alone, recline on the famous divan, where we sat at Shrovetide.

I think they exchanged notes down below. Papa sent her up alone, and kept out of the way, to give her an opportunity to make me say something.

She rushes through the room, on her way to the kitchen, where her mother is, and says to me, in a voice choked with passion:

"Rest yourself; take things easy!"

"Thank you, Mademoiselle."

"Make yourself at home, quite at home!" She flounces out. In a few minutes, she returns and sits down. After a pause, while I watch her frowning, she again complains of her head, and in answer to my coldly polite sympathy, hints that she often suffers in this way—every month. She wants me to talk.

"Sexual causes, I suppose, and not the stomach?" Another pause. Then I add:

"When I got home that Sunday night, I found my fingers torn and bleeding. How was that? Do you know?"

"Of course I do. It is not surprising!"

"How did I manage to tear my skin?"

"Let us talk of whatever you like, but not of that evening. I will not talk about it at all."

Aghast at her impudence, I hold my tongue, and a few seconds afterwards:

"I don't think I shall come here again."

"I don't force you to come," she replies quickly, black with rage.

"There is no question of force."

Then another long pause, as neither of us speak, until Papa arrives, and I am asked to go and wash my hands in the best bedroom as I always do. I have stated that Lily used to accompany me, get me hot water, a clean towel, and kiss me. This time Pa takes me, apologises for a black residue in the cold rain-water of the ewer, tells me to pick out any dirty towel off the horse, and sits on a sofa, while I wash my hands. He never did this before. I take a long while purposely, as I like to see him seated, waiting for me. He is leaning forward, his joined hands passed between his thighs. I cannot prevent myself comparing him to an old bawd, and there is something womanish about him, as I think that he has espoused the quarrels of Lily with a lover. The day has been instructive for me, and I ask myself who has been the most ridiculous of us all? I vote for Papa, and fancy he would look well with a double-bordered cap, à la Sairey Gamp.

We dine and he starts the Calvary story again.

"Has Mademoiselle really suffered so much?" say I. "This is the first time I hear of a female Christ."

"She has a crown of thorns," replies Papa.

"The crown of thorns of a young lady can only be tight boots and tight stays."

He still calls her Madame all through the meal, as he did at lunch, and says, looking at her and me:

"Bitter! Bitter!"

She seems very worried, and I exult, as I am so self-possessed. I can see that Papa is resolved to draw words out of me, and create some scene for his diversion, and the more he tries to teaze me the more jolly I get. Nothing could have vexed me that day, or caused me to lose my temper that night, and as I watched Lily's bluish lips and Papa's snarling grin, I thought of my little growing manuscript at home and wondered if the great masters of the art of novel-writing had ever lived their stories *in advance*.

I was aroused from my reverie by Papa's loud voice, saying:

"Pass the sauce, *Satan!*"

I do not even start at this new jibe, but say very quietly, with a pleasant smile:

"I did not quite catch what you said. Did you call me 'Satan'?"

"Oh! I meant that for Lily. I ought to have said 'satin.' "

I am satisfied with his retreat and say no more.

Lily now wakes up, and she talks of a new red dress she has—meaning the one she wore when she dined at Narkola's—and says it is too conspicuous, she will never wear it again.

"Wear it as a dinner dress," I answer. Pa knows she dined in it on Sunday.

"It is cloth and tailor-made," she explains.

She wants to know what are masks to be worn at night for the skin. I explain that they are pieces of kid with holes cut in them, smeared with creams for the complexion. And I add that women not only wear masks at night, but very often in the daytime as well. All our talk is in English. Mamma does not speak English. She is a cypher. Now and then she joins in and wants to know what we are talking about. So we change to French.

"Women are fools," says Lily, "to bother so much about their skins."

"There is no such thing as a foolish woman," I answer, "I have asked several and they all told me they were very clever."

I get a laugh for this, but Papa for the sixth time murmurs his catchword of the evening: "Bitter! Bitter!"

Lily says she has been suffering from a swollen nose, big and red. It is only just better. Can it have been my blow? No, she is anæmic, and strumous. I remember a disabled hand from the bite of a mosquito; a stye in the eye; an abcess in the mouth. She caught cold in Paris, coming out of the hot restaurant or bar, insufficiently clad in the courtesan's cambric underwear, after the thick and comfortable everyday Cinderella combinations.

"Mademoiselle has had what we call in English—a nose . . . gay!"*

---

* A certain analogy exists between the nose and the genital organs, since both of them (and the nipple as well) contain an erectile tissue. Congestion of the nose is often regularly produced at the period of menstruation and excesses of venereal enjoyment may provoke inflammation of its membrane.

The dinner is over. Mamma goes up to bed and leaves us three.

Arvel talks about the Dreyfus affair, being against the officers now, and I tell the story how an old Jew of 80 years of age, seeing the hetacomb of corrupt officers, had exclaimed:

"It is the justice of Jehovah! They tried to teaze Jehovah! Never teaze Jehovah!"

Lily asks what Jehovah means. Papa harshly interrupts her, telling her that she would not understand, and so I see how for years he has carefully diverted her understanding from all that was good and noble. Her life is wasted.

Her foot gently touches mine. I do not respond. Mr. Arvel asks me if I have ever been to Italy. I answer in the affirmative, and I tell how I took lessons, so as to acquire a little Italian before starting. To try my new knowledge, being in London, I went into a penny ice-shop, and said to a swarthy, moustachioed foreigner behind the counter:

"*Parlate Italiano, signor?*"

He lifted a cover off a zinc pail, and stirring up its contents with a wooden spoon, replied in a business-like way:

"Shtrawberry or cream-a?"

Lily laughed immoderately at this, until the tears came into her eyes.

"I am glad I have at last made you laugh, Mademoiselle, but I am sorry to inform you that this little story, which I am flattered to see has had the good fortune to so excite your mirth, is not true. I made it up myself. It is a lie, although as a rule, I do not tell lies. Do I, Mr. Arvel?"

And I turned to Papa. He smiled grimly, but did not answer, while Lily, perfectly black and sulky at hearing the word: "Lies!" seemingly very vexed, left the chair close to me on my right, on which she had been seated, and went off to recline on the divan with her dog, leaving Papa and me to cap each other's stories and smoke without her. She never took her eyes off me.

I make much of my bitch Lili, as I have been doing all day, and all my sentiment with the animal is met with icy coldness on their part.

Lily is in a complete fit of the sulks, seeing me so indifferent, and the time for my departure approaching, without my having said anything at all.

No doubt after my letter, which Lily never alluded to, from that day to this, they expected I should forget myself in some way, or show some wretched weakness. That is why they sent for me. The whole of the day, Papa never left me, and instead of doing photography, he walked round and round his garden, and took care to keep near the house. I followed him.

Lily, at one time, brought some work into the dining-room, so as to be near to us; but I made no sign, and they both circled round me as if watching an epileptic patient. I suppose they thought I might burst into tears, or faint away, or better than all, beg Lily's pardon and make a substantial peace-offering.

Do wicked women bleed foolish men's purses by excess of ill-treatment? Probably they do, or else Lily and her Pa would have behaved in a different manner.

I look at my watch. It is time to go.

"We'll take the dogs out, come back and fetch your bike, and take you to the station," said Papa.

Lily, who generally went with us, or alone with me, very dull and black, begs to be excused. She goes to Pa, says "good-night" to him, and putting up her face to be kissed, he salutes her on both cheeks. She never did this before. Papa looks surprised, and the light fades out of his eyes, as it always does when stirred by the power of his passion for Lily. It stirs me too, and I feel very lewd, as this is the first time I ever saw them kiss before me. I may say that I never saw Lily kiss her mother all the time I had known her, and it will be noted that Mamma was not present when Papa kissed Lily. She knew I liked to see her playing with Papa. Was she doing this to pander to my vile mania; or to excite my jealousy; or to please Mr. Arvel, by telling him that I was jealous of him?

I never knew. Had I been on good terms enough with Lilian to ask her, she would have only told me some lie, so when the pleasant quarter-of-an-erection sensation it created in me had worn off, I forgot all about it, and it is only as I strike the keys of my type-writer nearly a year afterwards that I see the girl and the old man kissing so chastely before me, both trying to get at the little brains and money I may have had. I bear no malice, as I led them on to believe I was malleable.

Lily says: "*Bonsoir, monsieur!*" to me very coldly. We go out. She goes with us into the hall, standing behind us, still hoping for a word, or a sly caress perhaps. I take off my hat and say very softly and nicely: "*Bonsoir, mademoiselle!*"

She answers, really hissing it through her teeth: "*Bonsoir!*" Quite curtly, and there is no "*monsieur!*" with it, which is very rude.

The sibilant sound of her last word betrayed the rage she felt, after a useless day of simulation in the face of my unfeigned indifference. And Papa would taunt her, and ask her what had become of the boasted power she had over me.

I go out with Papa, who must have noticed the change in his girl's manner to me.

He talks smut.

"Girls nowadays don't seem to care about real copulation—they like being 'messed about' better."

This was a bold thrust at me. I answer quite indifferently and insignificantly.

I let him keep up the conversation, and he gets on to sleep and sleeping draughts, in order to be able to say:

"Lilian sleeps well. When we were in Brussels, she would get to bed after the theatre at midnight, and never wake until eleven the next day. As she was away for her health, I never disturbed her, but let her have her sleep out. We had a fine, big, double-bedded room. There was a large screen and I rigged it up across the room, fixing it against the washstand."*

A month ago, he had told me that Lily was lazy and would

---

* "I think the washstand (one only), was against the outer wall, on the left of the fireplace and could not have been behind the screen. The room is about five or six yards square and the screen could not reach halfway across. It was the ordinary height of a large screen and one could only look over it by standing on a chair."—NOTE BY A. MALLANDYNE.

not get up. But that was nothing. He was a man who said just what came into his head, as it suited him. But what did he want me to reply that night? What was I to answer?

I felt inclined to be smutty, and chaff him about Lily, and her love for her Pa, and so on. But I would not take the trouble, and after all it might have been a trap. I simply said nothing. I expect he was pursuing his same old "bluffing" tactics. But there was an undercurrent of fear of me. He was too clever. It would have been much more simple to have said nothing, as I did in answer to him. There was now a very long silence between us, more significant than any reply I could have given. He broke it by talking of bawdy-houses. I explained that they were not much good. Some fellows, I said, liked to take a green girl there with them. But it is generally a bad move. He replied that possibly it was wrong to go with anybody you might care about. I put an end to this debate, by declaring that as a general rule it was not a wise thing to do.

He evidently had the idea of seeing Lily with him in a brothel, among its abandoned denizens, a favourite pastime among fast Parisians. Had she been with him; did he long to take her; or had she gone to one with a miché? This was the second time he had spoken to me of lupanars. He had got them prominently in his mind.

There is nothing new under the sun of sexuality, and nearly all old debauchees, when they get hold of a young woman, new to depravity, or who they fancy is not quite corrupt, feel a great delight in going to a brothel with her. Each one thinks he has been the first to be so diabolically lecherous. What fools we old voluptuaries are!

I thought he would have liked me to speak out and go about Paris with him and Lily. I hardly knew what to think. Lily had stopped all friendship between Arvel and Jacky, by her lies. It was a very difficult position for me to be in, especially as I got no help from the wretched young woman. Suppose I had begun to talk lightly about her to the father and he had turned round on me? So I said nothing. By this time, we had returned to the house.

A light was burning in Lily's room. Immediately, Arvel's head goes up, looking at the bright window like a boy of twenty. He puts up the dogs for the night, and conducts me to the station. He is very cordial and says he will soon have me down again. He wants me to go and visit some ground he has bought on the Western line. I promise him some special photographic printing paper—which I send him a day or two after—and we part.

I get my parcel of books at the station. There is Césarée; the first volume of "Gynecocracy," and volumes 2 to 6, inclusively, of "Justine."

In volume 6, I had marked the paragraph about the pleasure of seeing one's mistress in another man's arms. I had asked Lily if she had noticed and read it. She swore she had seen no marks. I attached no importance to this, thinking that perhaps after all I had pencilled some later volume that she had not seen yet.

That idea did not suit Lily's plans at this juncture, as she wanted me to become jealous, so she told this lie; as when she pretended to ignore the Mademoiselle Bismarck missive. How I discovered her prevarication again, was by looking through the books in the train, when I found, not only my underscoring and marginal lines, but the place in the sixth volume was marked with a long strip of orange photographic paper, such as I had seen plenty of at Sonis, but I possessed none of that kind. This made me more sure than ever that Papa had read the book, and that he would have been more free and geniune with me, shutting his eyes to my connection, had she not worked him against me, as he was, to a certain extent, a puppet in the hands of Lily and her Mamma. The two women can kill him by inches, if they choose. The mother has but to tempt him with her choice cooking, which he cannot resist, and Lily will follow suit with her cunning caresses. To regain fresh strength daily, he will eat heavily, and drink rich wines, followed by fiery, cheap whiskies. No man, especially at his age, can burn the candle at both ends with impunity.

I give here, out of curiosity, the odd notes I jotted down the day after my visit, just to show the state of my mind, with all my doubts and contradictions.

It is all over now. I cannot visit there again, unless Lily was to come forward and go down on her knees to me. This she will never do. She is too hard. I know her. What will the next move be? An invitation from Papa? If so, I shall probably decline it. I must do so. Besides, I am tired. If I go, it will only be to tell her of the fact which is now perfectly clear to my eyes: that every hand at Sonis is against me.

Papa behaved all day like an old procuress, trying to put two lovers together. I remember how silly he looked at her side, the day the officer arrived to see the puppies. Papa has spoken since about the two that were sold; and of that presented to his colleague; while Lilian has oft recurred to the fate of the one my jeweller had, but there has not been the slightest reference ever made to the animal that was given to the soft-eyed soldier, whose appearance and bearing pleased me so much. He was a man any woman would have been pleased to be seen with.

She cannot come near me now. Even her Whitsuntide journey must now be knocked on the head, if ever it was sincere, as Papa will not hear speak of the brother spending his holidays away from home, and she is going to live always at the villa now.

She depends on Papa for everything, even to her food, and I know he is very kind to her. She too, evidently likes him very much. He is not married to her mother, but he will have to do so now, so as to reward her for the sacrifice. The trio are firmly bound together by their material wants and pecuniary interests. Mamma's "courses" are leaving her, and she has no more feeling. She hinted as much to me. So what chance have I in such a household? With Lilian's obstinate lies and her desire for money against me too. She has spoilt everything, and I must retire.

I now know all I want. She is the mistress of her mother's old lover and her maidenhead has been gone some months.

She only cares for me for what she thinks she can tear out of me. If I was wrong in this surmise, she would simply try to see more of me, or work for me with her Papa, as she seemed to do so nicely before she left for Brussels with him.

MAY 3, 1899.

I took to the Eastern railway station, two novels, as I had promised, and left them in a parcel at the cloak-room, sending the ticket to Lily in an envelope, without a word. I wrote on the fly-leaf of one of them that I did not want them back, as they were of no value, except for reading.

One was *Suzanne*, by Léon A. Daudet (Paris, Charpentier, 1897), and the subject was the incest of a bad girl, a liar and a hypocrite, who glories in her wrongful lust for her own father. He takes her away on a trip to Spain; her health being the pretext, and both alone together, they put up at a hotel, when he gives her a ring, just as Papa did in Brussels. It is one of the most powerful works of the kind. I underscored all the erotic passages, with any remark which seemed to touch on Lily's case, and there were many.

The second novel was *La Femme et le Pantin*, by Pierre Louÿs (Paris, Société du Mercure de France, 1898), which is a pretty little story of a wicked woman and a weak man, who continually returns to his torturing mistress, in spite of her vile treatment of him.

I think that Lily was egged on me for marriage from the very first, and flirting was allowed, but perhaps her visits to me in Paris were added by herself? Or they knew she came to me, but she would tell them at home that I walked her about the parks and squares and sighed over her.

Another proof that Papa knows all, and had read my last disgusting letter, where I spoke of the kick to Blackamoor: this time, in front of me, he feigned to get in an awful rage with Lily's dog, and took a big stick, pretending to hit him. Lily seemed (?) distressed. Then he brought the cudgel softly down on the crouching body of the trembling pet and burst out laughing, caressing the animal. That was clearly an answer to my allusion to his cruelty to Blackamoor.

Papa had asked me if I knew the price of nickel saucepans in Paris, intending to replace all his kitchen utensils by that new metal. I got him some tariffs and catalogues of these goods, with the offer of a very large discount, on account of my efforts. But I soon suspected that he would have liked me to make him a present of these utensils, and when he spoke of a new photographic stand camera, as he only had a fine detective apparatus, or of chemicals and requisites, of which I got him some catalogues, it was only mendicity in disguise, and I was required as a dupe to feed them all.

Lily was contemptible. She was capable of everything that was bad, and why? For nothing, through that invincible force which drove her alternatively from good to evil, from evil to good, in the same irresponsible way.

Her absence of all moral sense was unimaginable. She had no idea of rectitude or honesty, nor of what was allowed or forbidden. She had no conscience of her acts. She felt she was despised, even by those she pleased, and those who were the most indulgent towards her, would judge her as eccentric and lacking brain equilibrium. She realised the impression she created, but did not try to overcome it. Subtle, loving, caressing, kind; full of curiosity; crafty, and above all perfidious; adoring intrigue; stopping at nothing; obstinate, bad-tempered, and sly. She was full of coquetry and false pride, with the low tastes and bad language of a prostitute, although not vulgar. Yet without animosity, I should be insane to take any interest in her, despite her evident perversity.

Lily belonged to the category of hysterical unfortunates. I am certain that she had a certain instinct of sincerity. She would have liked to have been loyal, but she could not. She lied, in spite of herself, without knowing it, and always for the sole reason that the one simple characteristic of hysteria is the madness of mendacity.

Like the tongue of the fable of Aesop, Lily was, or could be good or bad. Doing evil, as suggested by the stronger will of Papa, she loved good actions, and passed long hours teaching one of her illiterate workgirls to read and write. To another, she advanced money when in trouble and was never repaid, and I felt certain that if she obtained gold by her prostitution or her millinery, she would freely give her earnings for her family. Strange mixture of qualities leading to vices; of vices conducting to virtue; all these contradictions were united in her.

Perfidious, she was clumsy; cunning, she was credulous; courageous, she was cowardly; a young lady, she liked the company of paid hirelings; indefatigable, she was lazy; perverted, she was devoted; vain, she was humble; witty, she was silly; and ugly, she was very pretty at times.

She inspired disgust and excited desire; in a word she troubled the brain of whosoever took an interest in her.

4

ERIC ARVEL TO JACKY.

Sonis-sur-Marne, May 28, 1899.

My dear Jacky,

I have been so busy of late that I have had no time to call my own.
I had intended asking you down last Monday, as Raoul had got forty-
eight hours leave, but I am under the impression that you were in the
midst of a family fête, so I was afraid to disturb you.

I just had time to take a photograph of Lilian and Raoul, copy of
which I send you.

We still are as badly off as ever, as far as servants are concerned,
but if you will come down and take pot-luck, bicycle and all, with us
on Tuesday, we shall be very pleased indeed to see you, and do our best
to entertain you.

With kindest regards from all, believe me to remain,

Yours very truly,
Eric Arvel.

May 28, 1899.

I sent a polite wire in answer and some of my perfumery for the mother and daughter, and went on my bicycle, arriving in the morning.

The photograph represented Lilian in her Japanese costume, standing up, her head reclining on the left breast of her handsome brother, who is swathed in the Japanese robe I had once put on. His arm is round her waist; he holds one of her hands in his, and presses it on his shoulder, while his cheek touches her hair, and she looks out of the picture with a wicked smile on her naughty face. Raoul seems sly, sardonic, and serious, as was his wont.

This group had been shown to my brother at the Bourse a a few days before I got mine, much to his surprise. He asked Mr. Arvel what it meant.

"It is a brother and sister," was the answer. My brother found this very funny, as he thought it was slightly lewd.

When I got in, Papa was in his little, photographic dark-room near the garden gate, and he was evidently quite gone with admiration on this Japanese group. I extolled it, and said it was very voluptuous, giving an impression of indecency, by reason of the flowing drapery of the girl, as one could see she had no stays on.

"You mean the backside!" he replied, coarsely.

I said it was very beautiful, and continued:

"Why don't you get photographed with her? *I should like to see you two together.*"

He did not answer, but I saw the usual change in his face, and he began arranging some bottles.

He told me he would photograph me that afternoon with my bicycle, and I could take him, as I expressed the wish to have his likeness. I said I wanted *him*, as I had already got Lilian and Raoul, and he gave me some more copies of the Japanese couple on other papers, as there were several hanging up to dry.

I had brought a fancy little trick photograph, representing Lily as a ballet girl. They sell in Paris cards without heads to print photographs upon, and if you have a negative you can get your friends' faces on comic bodies. Arvel liked the joke.

After some conversation, Lilian appeared to invite us in to breakfast, and greeted me with marked and studied coolness, still playing a part for her Papa. She looked old, worn, and seemed to get uglier every time I saw her. Her skin was dark and sallow, and a moustache was coming. She was black under the eyes. She was dressed without any care, and had no powder, or lip colouring. There were no rings on her hands.

I was very gay and quite self-possessed. I chaffed her about the Japanese photograph. I told her that her brother looked sly and devilish: as satanic as myself.

"My brother says it is indecent. He has seen it. Your Papa showed it to him at the Bourse. He is now quite gone on the little Japanese girl."

"Pa," said she, "you are mad to have shown that at the Bourse. I suppose everybody has seen it?"

And I persuaded him to have it enlarged and coloured. We now went in to breakfast, and I told her quite loudly before her Papa, not to be sulky that day.

"Don't put on your black face, and show those ugly, violet, distorted lips. Last time I saw you, you looked like a Christy minstrel."

She walked rapidly away in front of me, turning her back to both of us, quite surprised, and he, of course, said nothing.

I had on for the first time at Sonis, bicycle breeches and Scotch stockings, and I began to make fun of my own calves, as we sat down to table. I said that all the ladies were in love with me, since my relations and my half-sister had forced me to put on cycling costume.

"Oh, your love! That must be very precious!" exclaimed Lilian, sneeringly and loudly, so that both her mother and father could not fail to hear her.

"Precious or not, once tasted, women always return for it," was my quick rejoinder.

She made no reply to this vain boast. The rest of the talk at *déjeuner*, although I made as many jokes as I could, and caused them all to laugh, does not concern our narrative.

I said that I had been to London just before Whitsuntide.

"I wish I had known," said Papa, "you could have brought me over a camera. There is no duty on it."

"I should have been very pleased to do so. I went to see some friends, had some clothes made, and I purchased this bicycle rig-out."

I said, which was perfectly true, that every Sunday, I had been coming to Sonis, to lunch in the pretty village, with a party of cycling friends, but that the weather had been too cold. They were astonished. I said I should come down next Sunday. They told me they were all going to the races in Paris. I expect Lily got me invited, after nearly a month's silence, to tell me she was going to the races. They evidently thought I should go too, and walk them about, give her and her Mamma drinks, and gamble a little for them. Instead of which, I said I was coming to Sonis with some ladies. I, of course, did not tell the principal lady of the party—no other than my Lilian at home—that the Arvels would all be absent on Sunday. So that was all smoothed over. And my artful puss of a "missus," who thought I dared not go to Sonis with her, was now thoroughly mystified. At the end of the lunch, Lily broke out with her old lie:

"I must go to Paris this afternoon to get some cottons, etc."

"You can't go now that Mr. S . . . is here!" said Papa.

This was her usual comedy. I said nothing, but it will be seen later in the afternoon, that it was only a fib to teaze me and hide the fact that my invitation had been deliberately planned by the pair.

Now comes a big parcel from the Louvre, with household goods, brooms, etc. Papa will not pay and flies into a passion. He does not pull out handfuls of gold, as he did in February.

Ma runs out in a huff. Lily chides Papa for getting in a rage, just as if he were a little boy: "Temper, Pa, temper!" she says.

"Let her go mad if she likes and tear her hair and grit her teeth, as she did the other day," snarls Arvel.

They must quarrel horribly at times.

"She has no money left," says Lily quietly, "and she will only send the things back. It is silly of you."

Papa reflects, and then relents, with a heavy sigh.

"Well, go and pay it out of your money."

Lily goes and gets the money upstairs and he is alone with me. He groans about the two women's extravagance.

The meal is finished and I am to go out on my bike with Papa. Lily refuses to accompany us. I do not ask her. She has customers coming. She also takes piano lessons now. She says she has a new bicycling costume.

Papa starts his parrot-cry again: "Bitter! Bitter!" And then he says, apropos of nothing:

"Raoul spells 'bitter' with one 't'." He chuckles at this.

"Ah, that makes 'biter,'" I reply. "The biter bit!"

His laugh stops suddenly and there is a pause, enabling me to add:

"Sometimes people try to trick you, but you see through them and they lose the game."

"In that case,"—and Papa spoke with some warmth—"the loser retires, and don't go into mourning for so little."

"How can people try to trick you, when there is not any interested motive to be seen?" broke in Lily, as she rolled up the napkins and put them in the drawer of the buffet.

"But if the motive is hidden?" quoth I.

No answer came, and Papa and I go and work at photography. He takes me in two positions. I take him in two others. He is a handsome man, or was. Lily comes now and again to see us at work, and once in a fit of rage, she tears up her photograph as the ballet-dancer, which has been shown to Mamma and all the work-girls. I could see that they had still some lingering idea that I was a jealous lover, full of agony at Lily's coldness, and she hated to see me so natural and undramatic.

I tell her in front of Papa that I am cleverer than he is.

"He does you, Mademoiselle, as a Japanese girl, because he has got you in front of him, but I transformed you into a ballet-girl without seeing you!"

I inform her that I have got her negative and shall make a dozen more dancing girls, and send her one every week. With her black face, she goes off in a huff to see her customers, who now arrive.

Papa remarks that Lilian has a devil's temper and he coolly adds that she is wicked, and a liar.

My photograph is now finished, and I say that I shall go and show it to Lily and dare her to tear it up. Arvel tells me to be careful, as she very likely will. She appears again, and I tell her that I will not show her my picture unless she kisses me. This is all before Papa. I never spoke so freely to her before in the presence of her parents. She is really quite surprised and is obliged to say:

"What is the matter with you to-day? I have never seen you like this!"

I now feel I am master of the situation, and I become more of a wag than ever. I chaff her about having a husband soon, and tell her that Papa will get her a nice little man and she shall have twins. They glance at each other. I continue to play the clown.

The negatives are now finished and dry, and I go and find Mamma in the kitchen to get a petroleum lamp for printing purposes.

I joke with her too, and tell her that my calves are such a success, that a lady in Paris makes me put on a pair of her black silk stockings every time I go to see her. Mamma says I am very gay. I ask her if her daughter always tries on hats and bonnets on her customers' heads down in the country, or sometimes goes to Paris to do so.

"I suppose now and again they countermand her by postcard, or so on?"

"I never saw a postcard countermanding anything," she answers, and then adds sadly:

"My daughter don't tell me everything!"

All mothers who know their daughters are foolish virgins pretend never to know what is going on under their noses. Adèle, I think, shuts her eyes to everything, puts up with anything, waiting for her old man to marry her. He told me again he would at the end of the year, Raoul having only one year's soldiering to do as the only son of a widow. If his mother was married, he would have to serve three years.

Back with my lamp. Lily says Papa is too fat. She makes me pinch his ribs. We talk of women's bellies. Lily says she has none and what little she has, she keeps down by wearing suspenders instead of garters. I say that a woman with a belly does not exist for me.

"Hush!" exclaims Lily, "Ma may hear you!"

Adèle was quite near, having come into the garden unobserved by us. Papa hears all this loose talk, but is dumb.

"You should be very nice to Mamma," says Lily to me, after she has left us. "You ought to try and make love to her."

What does she mean? I dare not guess. Papa is right beside us, but he is mute.

I now go after Lily alone in the garden, as the customers are gone and she has had her piano lesson besides. How about the visit to Paris now?

I ask her how she liked the novel of *Suzanne* I sent her. Not as much as *Césarée* it appears.

"That is because Césarée is a good little virgin and Suzanne is vile. How did you like *La Femme et le Pantin?*"

"Not at all!"

"No, because it shows up women like you. Come here, I want to talk to you for the sake of old times."

And we go away behind some trees, she looking very happy, thinking I am going to be very nice, from my opening words. As we walk together, I say to myself: is it really to be believed that by sheer strength of false letters and lies, the truth, the whole truth can be entombed? It cannot, shall not be. She has lied enough. It is impossible to lie more. The strength of lying is doubtless enormous, but it finishes by being exhausted. She has tried to build a very wall of falsehood round her house and fabricate with forged sentiment, supported by lies, a monstrous idol of seeming truth, before which I am, forsooth, to stupidly kneel.

Now I have been all round the circle of lies. I know, I understand, I judge, and that gave me the tone of authority which ought to have impressed her greatly, had she loved me.

I felt myself soaring above all humane consideration. I forgot my book. I was no longer myself. I was the impersonal mouth of truth, and the grandeur of the part I played gave me simple, strong, and luminous facility with which to speak; and ample demonstration gushed forth abundantly.

I told the facts and classified them, unrolling the chain link by link before my victim. I explained all, and showed all. Each hypothesis became a reality, accompanied by a procession of proofs, without any jesuitical insinuations, or sneaking blows in the back.

"I very much enjoyed my last visit here, when after that Sunday night in Paris, you thought I was going to come round again and humble myself. You waited all day for me to speak. I said nothing and have held my tongue for a month, until it pleased you to send for me. And I am not asking for anything now—not even a kiss—as you are the vilest creature that ever breathed. I am not the weak hero of "The Woman and the Puppet."

I pass over her denials, and her false laugh of scorn, which she puts on, trying to show me that she did not care what I said to her, but will continue with as much as I can remember of all I forced her to listen to. I was quite calm. She did not excite my lust as she once did, and I found a peculiar pleasure in insulting her and dragging her through the ordure she kept on shovelling up herself, until she should get tired of trying to drive me silly by her stupid wickedness. I think that is all she wanted to do. Did she really know what she was about?

"I gave you a turquoise ring. Strange, I have just found that 'turquoise' means November. I 'had' you first November 26th., 1897, and in November 1898, you got deflowered."

"It's a lie! I'm still a virgin! Oh, that month of November!" she added, with the half-groan, half-sob, that I had already heard when I taunted her with the remembrance of Shrovetide.

"A virgin of three inches of finger! I don't care if you are a virgin or not. What made me angry was your imposture, extending over three months, when you kept me from touching you between the thighs, as much as you could, and told me"—here I could not help sneering—"how you were keeping your maidenhead for Jacky, and how you would like me alone to have it."

She was silent. Her jerky, imitation laugh stopped, and she bent her head.

"You were free to do as you liked, but not to try and trick me who never did you any harm. You invented that lie about the unregistered letter; how you suffered at Lille and Brussels; and how you were always a poor, persecuted virgin, adoring me. You are worse than any woman I ever met. How much do you get, when you dine out with Lolotte? A hundred francs between you?"

"You talk to me as if I were a common prostitute. I want no money. I have plenty."

"You are lucky. I have none. I want to tell you that you have been trying to trick me, and I never was your marionette. You invented a cheating dodge that I never heard of before. You give a rendez-vous by letter, knowing you cannot keep it, and then you countermand it, and if reproached, say: 'But I meant to see you and could not. It is not my fault. Did I not make the appointment?' The last one made by you and stopped by a customer's postcard that your mother saw, was a fine cheating joke. You Ma has just told me that she never knows what you do. Your letter with the appointment for Mi-Carême was a lie. Your Papa, as a man of business, knew in advance the date of his departure. It was a slack time with him in Paris and the Carnival was on in Brussels. And your 'monthlies' were just over, for you went out cycling with me on the first of March."

I paused for a reply. None came, and even her spasmodic laugh was hushed.

"And I hear no more about your trip with me to Belfort. You knew it was impossible."

She turned her head from me. I could not see her face.

"I never went to Brussels. I sent there, and I have got a long report all about you and your Papa in the double-bedded room, in writing. That is better than if I had gone myself. All my letters since were got up to lead you on in your cheating lies. You have shown them all to your father, and both of you have been trying to work me, and exploit me, and trick me for some base and mercenary motive. You have both fallen into my traps. Your mother even knows all about the books I lent you, 'Justine.'"

She had been silent, but this last blow went home, and she

was mad with rage, as with flashing eyes and curling lips, showing her gleaming teeth, she exclaimed:

"How can you be so wicked? How can you imagine such horrors? Ma knows nothing. You think and think until you do not know where you are. You know nothing. You guess all wrong. I *am* a virgin. Pa has never touched me. Now let me tell you once for all that he knows nothing about all you and I have done together and he must never know. That I ask of your loyalty."

Not *all*, certainly, but as much as she had cooked up for him.

"Then why does he always talk dirt about you to me?"

"Perhaps he is jealous of you." She said this very slowly, and with averted gaze.

"I never answer him about you."

"That is good of you and quite right."

"No, no! you are accomplices here in this house to cheat and harm me!"

"Say that again, and I will never invite you here any more!"

"I don't want to come. You have always run after me. I still say you are all in league to play with me and against me, but you have not got the best of me yet. I am too clever for you. And you yourself are not cunning enough to beat me. That article I translated and the 'passionate' letter of lust, written by your order, were all for his amusement."

"You are awfully bad. You must be very wicked yourself, or else you could not imagine that such horrors could exist in others. I will go to Papa with you now and tell him all."

"Come on," I answered, and I stepped towards the studio. She did not move, but remained still, trying to laugh sarcastically at what she called my "stupid imagination."

"I don't care what you say," I continued, "I now know all I want to know about you. I could have gone to Narkola's and found out more. I could, if I chose, go and sleep with Charlotte."

"Why don't you?"

"Because I won't take the trouble. I know enough. You are a common whore, dining, and letting all men enjoy your body in *cabinets particuliers* for a few louis, and without the excuse of a poor prostitute who does it for bread. You have got all you want and your Papa as a lover. You dined at Narkola's regularly last winter with your subscribers."

She was not offended. She did not feel my insults. Never had I so insulted a woman. The hot blood comes in my face as I copy it out now, months afterwards, and she was able to find the following lie to clear herself. It is true that she had had three weeks to concoct it.

"I will explain about that," she now replied. "Lolotte was going to marry Raoul. We broke that off. Pa won't let her come here and I won't go to her place. She has a big brother, and I want to keep him from doing harm to mine. To talk with her we dined alone together at Narkola's. Papa must never know I went there, or that I was out with Charlotte. You must not betray me."

"You put on cambric drawers to dine alone with Lolotte?"

"I had no cambric drawers!"

"You had no drawers on at all perhaps? And where do you wash them? What does Ma say to you putting them on, when you go up to Paris alone at night? You are a nice, amusing, incestuous little viper!"

"Now let me be! Go away! I want to work! I won't listen to any more of your ravings."

"You must. You shall. I enjoy telling you all this. I have lots more to tell you."

She ran from me, but I followed her into the workshop, continuing my vile talk in English.

"I'll slap your face, if you say more!" cried Lily, through her clenched teeth.

"Do so!"

She slapped one side, half-angry, half-laughing. I offered the other cheek and she slapped it too. She did not hurt. This was in front of her workgirls, and she told them in French that I was teazing her and would not let her work.

"You can work." I speak now in English, as she takes up her needle and a hat. "See, your hand does not tremble; you don't make a stitch wrong. You don't care."

"I do. You hurt my feelings terribly. I never knew you were such a bad man. But now I will go and sleep with my Papa, although I have never done so yet, just to spite you."

"That lie I expected. I know that old trick—one lie to cover another! You will say: 'When I wrote to you from Lille, I resisted him. It was true what I wrote then, but now I am his mistress!' And as for being a virgin, you will declare: 'When I swore on my mother's life in the cab that I was a maid, the night you slapped my face, I told the truth, but I was so disgusted with you, for whom I was keeping my maidenhead, that I immediately went and gave myself up to somebody else!' You will have to invent some new lie.—Now tell me, Lily, who had it? Was it not in November, just when I wrote to you after your lie of the lost letter, in which I enclosed the fifty-franc note, that Lily was dead?"

"You never sent that letter."

"Then why, when I told you I had done so in November last, did you at once write back wanting to marry such a scoundrel?"

"Because I was very fond of you then, and would have done anything for you."

"Yes, because you thought I was rich. That night in the cab, you must have been tipsy, else you would never have opened your thighs as far as you did. In January and February, you always gripped them close together."

No reply came, so I tried the following little artifice upon her:

"Look here; I'll tell you something that will astonish you. If you will come with me to a doctor, not chosen by you, but somebody I'll take you to, and let him examine you; if he says you are a virgin, I declare, without swearing on mothers' lives that I'll marry you."

"I am a virgin and I'll go to any doctor you like, but I'll not marry you now!"

"Because you think I've got no money."

"I know you haven't. Pa always told me so."

Then, after a pause, as I take breath, turning her face from me; not daring to look at me, she says slowly, in a low and tremulous voice:

"I think you would marry me without caring if I was a virgin or not."

"No, I would not. After all, the least I could ask for as a huband, when I think over what passed between us last year, would be your virginity."

"Last year I had somebody else as well as you."

"What do I care?—Your Pa tells me you prefer feeling and sucking to proper coition."

She was too surprised to answer, and she waited for more. I had gathered this from his statement that modern girls preferred superficial caresses.

"How about the Mount Calvary? That proves he knows all."

"He only meant that I was between two thieves."

"Then why did he add a remark about your crown of thorns?"

She was strangely mute.

"He meant that you had suffered, going up the mountain. And why does he call me Satan? He will tell me all in time, if I like. I ought not to say so much to you, as you will now stop his mouth. I can imagine you talking to him, in your bedroom, just after I went away last time:

" 'Well, Pa, what did he say to you?'

" 'Nothing! But what did he say to you, Lilian?'

" 'Nothing, Pa!' What fun for me you both are! It is grand to be able to read you all here, wanting for nothing, caring for nothing, and telling you all I think of you. I am going to put our adventure into a novel. I have already written a lot of it. I shall call it 'Suburban Souls.' I shall alter the names and places."

"That is the least you can do!—Now, will you go away! Leave off, I say. You do not know what nonsense you are talking and how you are mistaken in every way."

"If I am wrong, I am an utter rogue. You have never yet called me a liar, because you know I am not one. But say so now; spit in my face, and tell me to go!"

She turned away without a word, and her mother appeared.

"Don't say any more, as Ma can catch up a few English words she may know," whispered Lily, hurriedly.

So I saluted the workgirls and retired.

It was always the same. She could not tell the truth. Driven in a corner, she covered up the first lie with a second one; then if wanted, placed a third one over them, and so on as long as necessary. It is true that she deceives no one, as she must always be detected sooner or later; but she gives herself the satisfaction of believing that she has blinded her victim for the nonce.

I went back to the dark-room. Papa was hard at work, finishing my second photograph, and his own. I help him a little, as it is too late to go out cycling.

I now make up my mind to do what I have never done before: to "work" *him* a little, and talk to him, as he has tried to talk to me. If he knows all, as I think, it will not matter, and if he does not—I shall see what comes of it. So I begin to talk smut. That soon draws him out, and I boldly tell him about virgins, and how girls swear you out that they have never been penetrated by a man.

"You can't tell," he says, looking at me with a puzzled expression.

"Can't you? You've only got to put your finger up."

"That is not a test, but still if you thrust in four inches or so, they can't be virgins. My fingers are no use. They are too short."

And he stared at me with increasing uneasiness.

"Then I am right. You agree with me. My experience has proved this."

"But then, there is no certainty. *The hymen gives!*"

What a splendid, strange remark for him to make! An elastic maidenhead! Surely he knew all, and was trying to make me believe that Lilian's membrane still closed up the vaginal passage, and was like a bit of india-rubber!

"You can't tell," he continues. "They can make a virgin cleft with alum water."

"That is no use against the medical exploration with the finger."

"Ah, you've never tried to get into an alum girl!"

I cannot help shrugging my shoulders disdainfully, and keep on:

"What is really difficult is not to have children. To get them is easy, but to enjoy a woman and not impregnate, is hard work."

"To get children," he answers, evading my proposition, "the best way is to have connection dog-fashion, and not let the woman empty her bladder for twenty-four hours afterwards."

I can hardly keep from laughing at this new cure for female sterility, and we prepare for a walk before dinner, when Lilian appears from the kitchen. She looks so ill—so black, dull, and rancorous—that even Papa notices it, and asks her what is the matter.

It is the effect of my talk, and she has been having a little explanation with her mother about what I had said. She chaffs me and I retaliate gaily, all before Papa. I tell her how rude she was, never to thank me for some English fashion papers I put in Papa's parcels. She curtsies down to the ground with ironical politeness, saying:

"I thank you, sir!—Are you satisfied now?"

"Hardly. You are not overpolite as a rule."

"I shan't take lessons from you."

"You might do worse."

She tells her Papa that she is going to Paris the next day, and she says:

"I must have a little cheque: fifty francs will do!"

And she pirouettes in front of us, lifting up her skirts slightly, but turning her head away. When in a fix, she hides her face. Papa does not answer, but looks at her with his most gloomy air, showing how strongly she stirred him then. This is also to vex me, and show me what money she can have of him! With this she runs in doors, still with averted face. Shortly afterwards, I am alone for a few moments, while Papa has gone up to his room, and I hand her the preface (see Appendix B), and the first eighty pages of "The Double Life," a rough proof; with all the incestuous passages marked, and some newspaper cuttings: "An Infamous Father" (see Appendix F) and "The Tête-à-tête" (see Appendix G). I give her to understand that I have arranged this preface. She seems very pleased and is evidently delighted that I do not sulk after the blowing-up. Her lips twitch, her eyes laugh, and her nostrils quiver, exactly as when she used to get "wet." Can she make her nostrils palpitate at will? Yes—women can do it.

"Don't spend!" I say, and she runs away laughing.

Papa and I go out with the dogs. We talk more smut and I tell him:

THE TALE OF TRIXIE.

A few years ago, I was carrying on an intrigue, to use a polite term, with a married lady, and she used to give me a *rendez-vous* somewhere in Paris, during the afternoon. Her lord and master was rather jealous and she was obliged to take great precautions, frequently changing the place of appointment. One quiet spot I had found out was the Terrasse de l'Orangerie, in the garden of the Tuileries, where one might have thought oneself to be in a dull provincial town, had it not been for the roar of the distant traffic. My sweet adulteress very often never appeared at all, as a whim of her master might stop her many a time from going out.

At least, so she told me. One fine day in June, I was at my post, under the trees, and I knew by the time I had been there that she would not come that day. I felt rather glad than otherwise, and was debating with myself whether it would not be better to give up such an unsatisfactory liaison altogether, as I lazily smoked a cigar, and fell to idly watching the movements of a trim-built little lady who was impatiently trotting up and down, all alone, with a bunch of roses stuck in her waistband. She was simply, but neatly dressed, and it was easy for a man used to the ways of a big city, to see that she was not a common wench, seeking the acquaintance of the first man who would accost her.

She passed in front of me, and went to the stone parapet that borders the terrace, and like Sister Ann, looked out afar, but nothing was to be seen. With a gesture of impatience, she tore the roses from her girdle and flung them away. Then she looked at a tiny watch and made as if to leave the garden. I got up and followed her, and although repulsed at first, I managed to make her conquest, and finally, after a deal of trouble, she told me that she was seeking an adventure, and had answered an advertisement in the Ruy Blas newspaper, where, under the cloak of matrimony, kindred souls poured out their desire to find fitting mates, and restless spirits sought for their affinities. Trixie, for thus I shall call my new friend, was fresh to Paris and its ways, and she had answered one of these announcements, when she had been directed to come to the Tuileries, with the bunch of roses as a signal, so as to make herself known. The correspondent had not kept his appointment and so she made my acquaintance.

I may say at once that, after two or three appointments, she let me do what I chose with her and I found her to be a most charming little woman, and possessing all the qualities that I always sought for in a mistress: strong sensuality and no squeamishness or false prudery.

Before giving way to me, she told me that she had already been seduced and abandoned by her lover. Her parents had got to know all about this intrigue, and although they let her live at home with them, they made her life very unhappy, reminding her daily of her fall, and she was naturally never allowed out after dinner. She was exceedingly well educated, and spoke English, French, German and Spanish, writing all the four languages without faults. She could play the piano and seemed domesticated. Trixie spoke vaguely about giving lessons to earn a little, albeit she confessed to not being in want of money.

She was not of a mercenary disposition and soon got to be very fond of me. Being of a passionate nature, she was delighted to fall across a man who was not jealous, and who taught her, or thought he taught her, a few new tricks and turns of vice. She dubbed me her "professor," and in truth she was an apt pupil in my hands.

Trixie was fond of her own sex, and frequently asked me to introduce her to some nice girl, promising me that I should join in the fun. We made up our minds we would try all sorts of strange games together, and taste of all the fruit that the orchard of passion could possibly contain.

I had not known her a month, and none of our projects of lust had as yet been put into practice, when one morning, the *Ruy Blas* contained an advertisement, stating that a young couple desired to meet with a lady and gentleman with a view to friendly intercourse.

I showed this to Trixie and asked if I should answer it. She demurred at first, but finally consented, and I entered into correspondence with a person who turned out to be a tall, handsome gentleman of about thirty years of age.

He came to a meeting that I gave him on the terrace of the Tuileries, and I saw he was perfectly sincere and acting as I was, without any base motive. He told me that he was married, and had taught his wife that the heart and the senses were two distinct things. He was far from being jealous and left her entire liberty, although he preferred that when she took a lover, she should do all with him and without concealment.

The idea of a *partie carrée* pleased him greatly, as I told him we were both perfectly free to keep our names to ourselves. I had no curiosity, and wanted nothing but pleasure.

I let him know at once that I was not married, but that I had a little mistress, named Trixie, whose story I told him, and it was agreed between us that the two ladies should meet. If they liked each other, as we two men did, we would arrange to dine or lunch together and change partners, besides letting our companions enjoy themselves in Lesbian fashion, as he confessed that his wife was not averse to playing the part generally ascribed to the poetess Sappho. This, I knew, would suit Trixie.

We arranged to tell our ladies of the result of our interview and I said it would be best for us all to meet on the terrace, and as soon as I could see Trixie, who could only come out in the afternoon, I would let him know.

The next time I enjoyed my new sweetheart, I told the story to her and drew a highly-coloured sketch of the cultured young married man I had met, but she did not seem enthusiastic. I was myself very hot on the scent of this honest rake's wife, as he had offered her to me in exchange for my Trixie, and no doubt he felt the same towards me.

At last, my lustful little woman promised to come to the Tuileries at three o'clock on a certain day, and after the exchange of a few notes and telegrams with the young husband, an appointment was made by me and accepted by Trixie, who was to meet her "Professor" in the public garden, where she and I would await the coming of the advertising couple, when the two men would introduce their brace of beauties to each other.

I was punctual, but Trixie did not turn up, which annoyed me not a little, as I thought that if the young fellow appeared with his spouse and found me alone, he might reasonably suppose that no Trixie existed and that I had invented my story with the sole object of getting to see his wife.

While fretting and fuming up and down the terrace, my new friend made his appearance and he too was alone.

I told him at once that Trixie had not come, in spite of her promise, and that I was very vexed. He replied that his wife had been taken ill just before getting dressed to go out with him, and had gone to bed, refusing to accompany him that afternoon to meet Trixie and myself, although he had told her everything, described me to her, and had extorted from his wife a promise to go on with the adventure.

I begged him to excuse me, and I could only say it was not my fault. Trixie had promised too and Trixie had not come to me.

We adjourned to a *café*, and he once more expounded his free-love doctrines. It suited me admirably to agree with him. I promised to let him know directly I heard from Trixie, as I did not possess her real address, but only wrote to her at a post-office, as I was doing with him, and he with me.

A few days later, I was called to London, and wrote to the disappointed gentleman that he should hear from me on my return. I dropped a line to Trixie too, giving an address where a friend would receive the answer for me, informing her that I had not met the young wife I ought to have seen, and I scolded her slightly for not having kept the important appointment.

I had not been a week in the British capital before I received a long letter from Trixie in reply, covering about eight sides of notepaper. She seemed to be in dire trouble lest I forgot her, or would be eventually disgusted with her, after what she considered it was her duty to write to me.

My Trixie and the free-love gentleman's wife were one and the same person!

He had drawn up the advertisement and put it in the paper, without consulting her, as she was in the habit of obeying his strangest behests.

When my letter arrived, she knew the writing, but kept her own counsel and let everything go on until the day came for the meeting of the two men and the two (!) women, and then she got out of it at the last minute, exactly as her husband had told me.

She concluded with a piteous appeal to her "Professor," not to abandon her, and added that if now, knowing all, I cared to see her naked in the arms of her husband, she would try and do it for me.

I had nothing to be offended about, and had I felt sore at her little trick, her frank avowal would have disarmed me entirely.

On my return to Paris, we met again and I tranquilised her. I informed her that I had no curiosity, nor any wish to see, or know her husband, and I was perfectly content to enjoy her, in any way she liked.

She was delighted at what she called my generous magnanimity and we became fast friends, as well as eager lovers.

Anything I wanted, she said she would always try to do for me, and would even consent to introduce me to her husband officially, but she plainly showed that she would not care for him to enjoy her in my presence. She would go with delight from my arms to those of any man I chose, but not her husband, unless I desired it, and would be resigned to any sacrifice of her body or her affections, sooner than lose me.

The idea of witnessing her conjugal copulation was not a tempting one for me, and I put her completely at her ease, by petting the poor little woman and informing her that she could do precisely as she chose.

Trixie had married very young, and had two children, a boy and a girl, although no one would have guessed it to look at her, with her clothes on or without.

She was *petite*, very slightly built, with no breasts to speak of. Pretty features; fine grey eyes; beautiful mouth and good teeth; long black hair, and every other charm in proportion.

Trixie was a woman among a thousand, as she was a perfect female rake, and at the same time perfectly honest, truthful, and sincere, ready to do anything and join me in any extraordinary caprice and freak of lasciviousness, whether men or women, or both were concerned.

Her husband had debauched her, soon after the birth of her second child. He had often propounded his theories of love and liberty on both sides, and that husband and wife should be partners in passion with mutual confidence, and no jealousy; but she had repulsed him with horror, having been brought up strictly, and married to him when in her teens, very soon after leaving school. Her parents were in trade, and her mother and father of different nationalities had lived in various countries, not being those they were born in, which accounts for her polyglot talents. Her husband was, like myself, an Englishman, who had passed his life on the continent.

He had made the acquaintance of a young cavalry officer, who I will call Achille. He was married too, and with his wife visited Trixie and her husband, and a slight cordial friendship sprung up between the two couples, with mutual pleasant intercourse; dinners out and at home; visits and return visits; theatre parties and so forth.

Achille and Trixie's lord and master seemed to be, strangely enough, of the same opinion as regards sexual liberty, and Madame Achille had given herself freely to the latter gentleman, with full permission of her husband, and the two men had been together in the same bed with her.

Trixie was quite unconscious of this trifling intrigue, and busy with her two pretty dolls of children, refused to listen to the theories of her spouse, which seemed loathsome to her.

But he was resolved to drag her down to his level and corrupt her entirely, for such was his mania, and a conspiracy was formed and carried out in the following cold-blooded way.

Achille and his wife came to dine with Trixie and her lord and master at the latter's house, and champagne was freely drank. After dinner, the conversation turned on the subject of female sexual inversion, or the love of women for women, and in front of the two men, Madame Achille made love to Trixie, as a man would have done. The young mother was horrified, and at last, out of patience at the bold advances of the half-tipsy officer's wife, who dared to approach her with audacious fumbling fingers and mannish kisses; disgusted with the applauding leer of her wine-flushed husband, and the brazen words that Achille, excited at the scene, let fall without restraint, she rose to leave the table, pretexting a headache, which she ascribed to the champagne.

Seeing the quarry about to escape, her husband rushed towards her, and seizing her hands, called to Achille to help him. In an instant, the military voluptuary full of lust, was upon her, and despite her struggles, shrieks of shame, and appeals for mercy, the two men bore her slight frame, as light as a feather, more like a pretty boy than a mother, to an armchair, and threw her backwards in it. Her husband held her hands and kept her seated against her will, while Achille on his knees, threw up her skirts, and roughly separated her well-built little legs.

She kicked about as well as she could, struggling and calling out, until she was quite exhausted, and Achille, with the consent of her husband, exhibited a magnificent weapon, which Trixie could not look at and closed her eyes not to see. Madame Achille now came forward, threw herself madly on the panting victim, and began to undress her, or rather undo her clothes as well as she could, considering the position she was in, held down in the chair. Achille, with coarse jokes and worse than rude remarks, clumsily assisted his wife, and between the two, they tore her garments off, and left her nothing but a few shreds of torn linen.

Achille's wife, telling her husband to pull the outraged mother's legs well apart, then applied her mouth to Trixie's secret spot, and despite her shame, notwithstanding the horror of her position, the tongue of the Lesbian was so cleverly worked, that finally she succumbed and emitted into the mouth of the sly, sucking woman. At first, the feeling that a strange woman's mouth was kissing that part of her body, which no one save her husband and a doctor had hitherto seen, filled her with disgust, and she so violently upbraided her treacherous female friend that Madame Achille seemed inclined to relinquish her purpose, had not Trixie's husband forced her to continue.

It was only by dint of sticking to her task that the continued lingual onanism of Madame Achille produced its effect, and when that was evident by the change that came over poor bruised and outraged Trixie, a roar of triumph was started by the two men, who relaxed their hold and left the young novice to be finished off by a last few rapid touches of the tricky tongue of the officer's wife.

She rolled to the ground exhausted, and Achille boldly plunged his perforator into the palpitating body of Trixie, and emitted freely in the vagina, all moist with his wife's saliva, while the father of her children gloated over what was for him a delightful spectacle—to see his wife ravished by his friend, after being outraged by a woman in his presence.

Directly he saw that Achille had finished and was forcing his tongue between Trixie's lips; he turned to Madame Achille, and she responded to his mute and significant appeal by boldly unbuttoning his trousers, and searching for the staff of life, which was as familiar to her as that of her husband.

She was soon riding over him, while Achille tried to pacify Trixie, who had begun to cry, and to the sound of Trixie's tears and sobs her husband ejaculated close to the neck of the greedy womb of his friend's wife.

Trixie recovered from the shock, and for the sake of peace, yielded now to her husband, and soon finding the forbidden, but juicy fruit, sufficiently palatable, she threw all scruples to the winds, with the idea that if she did not help her husband in his salacious pastimes, he would get other women to help him. Her passions being now thoroughly roused by the efforts of her husband, she plunged into the vortex of depravity, and fell into my hands, just as she was ripe for any devilment.

Puritans will shake their heads sadly as they read this story, and say that such a life could not last; that the laws of divorce would be called into play; and that such a lustful couple would soon separate, with talk of the mutual respect necessary between husband and wife. They are entirely wrong, as Trixie and her spouse lived perfectly happy together, devoted to each other, and bringing up their children with the utmost care.

Trixie visited all the secret haunts of Paris in my company, and the history of what this darling little woman did with her "Professor," would fill a stout volume.

Suffice it to say, that although she loved her husband more than anything in the world, she had a great deal of affection for me, and she proved it, because she never told me a lie. I mean that no doubt she may now and then have uttered a fib or two, but she did not invent mean or wicked falsehoods to teaze and worry me. On the contrary, she told me all about her lovers, always kept her appointments, and never quarrelled with me.

I was very fond of seeing her in the arms of another woman, and I gave her orders to entrap and entice young girls whenever she could, and we used to enjoy them together.

She was always ready to obey my bidding, and, my dear Mr. Arvel, if I had asked you to dine with her and me, and after the meal, had told her to go away with you, she would have done so cheerfully, if I had desired it. We had many *parties carrées* together, although I must confess I did not care about them. I liked to possess her with another woman.

The foregoing rapid sketch was an enormous success with Mr. Arvel. He constantly kept recurring to it. I told him I had lots more to tell him. I also consulted him about a married woman I was just then trying to get hold of, and I asked him if it was honest to try and debauch a friend's wife? My conscience pricked me. He advised me to get her if I could.

"If you don't, someone else will!"

"Alas!" I say, "there's no honesty when our desires are aroused!"

He concurs, and tells me some of his experiences. They are silly, schoolboy yarns. I continue to astonish him with some of my adventures. I want him to retail all this to Lily.

Then he talks of the books he likes. Miss Braddon is his favourite author. He does not like French novels, as a rule, but he wants to read that celebrated book on the vice of masturbation, *Charlot s'amuse*. I promise to get him a copy. He does not like "Fanny Hill." I tell him it is good, and written in good English too. He hates reading philosophy. He prefers "Tit-Bits" and "Answers." He has read the book I lent him—"The Romance of Lust"—twice since February! He is going to send it back to me. I shall then go through it and see why he liked it so much. He gossips anent flagellation, and tells me how much he likes books on that subject, especially "The Mysteries of Verbena House," which he had from me, and which I passed on to Lily.

I narrate to him some recollections of Trixie's birching experiences with me. I have never been like this before with him. He listens with open mouth, and his pipe goes out. I cannot now remember all I told him. A huge budget of stories of the same kind I unpacked for him after dinner.

I begged him never to sneer at novels, except very farfetched stories of travel and murder, because authors simply hear of strange doings in private life and write them up, when by practice we can, as we read, pick the truth even out of a mass of lies in a three-volume love-story.

I confide to him that a gentleman friend of mine had written a vile book, and having gone away travelling, had left me to correct the proofs. I promise him a copy when done, in a few months.

"What is it about?" he asks.

"I dare not tell you. It is so awful. You shall see it when finished."

"I should like a copy, but I must not keep it. I will return it when read, as I am frightened of the girl getting hold of it!"

Of course, I am alluding to "The Double Life," the proofs of which he got from Lily soon after I left his house, I expect.

We return to dinner; he still saying, as he opens the door:

"That story of Trixie is wonderful!"

I must remark that they had cut off the afternoon tea, and I have not washed my hands since the morning. It will be remembered that they used to take me into the best bedroom, which communicates with Lily's. Have they altered their sleeping arrangements? I walked behind my man, chuckling as we go in to the evening meal. Trixie has kept us out late. It is eight o'clock. Mamma and Lily are awaiting us impatiently. We sit down talking "dog," and I say:

"Mr. Arvel and myself disagree on one point. I will not allow that in-breeding is good. All your dogs will have faults, unless you get some outside cross."

He has just had another brother and sister put together. They are also by a brother and sister.

I notice that Lily and her Papa have not yet been able to meet that day. I have never left one or the other, so I know I can continue to try and talk to Papa again after dinner, before she has time to tell him that I have declared they are accomplices in every way against me. He is charming to me all through dinner and until I leave; quite different from last time, when he was probably under the influence of Lily's story to him of the little drama of the cab, told in her own way, of course, as she has a certain set of lies for him, no doubt. Perhaps he is glad I am no longer friends with her?

I am certain he is quite bewitched by her and she likes him very much. But still I fancy she has not yet found the man who can influence her. Will she ever? I think not.

How a young woman of 23 can allow a man to talk and write to her as I have done, surpasses my comprehension. And still she sends for me. The lowest street whore, or brothel wench, would have shown some little pride of some sort ere this; or would have fled from my awful talk; or shed one or two tears, if only of vexation. She must be hysterically mad. She is lustful, but cold-hearted, in spite of her heated centre of love, which is like a fire on an iceberg.

I am forced to come to the conclusion that she no longer cares for me—if she ever did—and I make up my mind that this shall be my last visit. I have a scheme for closing the doors of this House of Lies against myself, so as to guard against any future weakness on my own part.

We sit down to dinner. Lily gets up occasionally, and once she stands over her Papa, and plunges her eyes in his as if she was fascinating a dumb animal. He looks at her for a few seconds, and then, quite confused, unable to bear her glance any longer, drops his head sheepishly into his plate, like a boy sick with passion.

We talk of legs and calves again. Lily says she has no calves. Mine are false, I say. She determines to see if what I declare is true, and feels them under the table, finishing up with a sly pinch.

She passes me the salt, with the remark that she is helping me to sorrow.

"Dost hate me then so greatly?" I exclaim, in the exaggerated, gruff tone of the stage villain. She does not like that remark and says so.

There are asparagus which Mamma tells me Lily went and got specially for me. I ask her to mix me some sauce of oil and vinegar, as she is doing for herself. She consents, and when finished, puts her finger in it to taste it. Mamma chides her. I say I will be revenged, and when she is beginning to eat her asparagus, I put my finger in her plate and taste her sauce. She offers me more asparagus. I take some from her hand and say:

"Thank you, Madam,—Mademoiselle, I mean!"

At this, which I say loudly and boldly, her face shows true temper; the black cloud comes over her features, and her lips are blue and distorted.

"I hate being called madam!" she cries angrily. Both Mamma and Papa are curiously silent during my encounter with Lily.

We talk of types of character. I tell them that if the negatives of the photographs of the illustrious personage, who died in February in a woman's arms, of Papa, and of myself, were all superposed and drawn off together, the features would mix and melt into one face, as we were of the same race, tastes and temperament. No one replies to me. I do not think they understand, or else they have read my thoughts. I add that I really think my host is a Jew, and appeal to my hostess. She answers coolly: "I know he is not!"

"No one knows better than you, madam!"

She does not turn a hair, nor does Lilian. They make as if they did not know what I am talking about. Of course, Papa is silent.

Dinner is over. Papa leaves me alone with Mamma and Lily.

Mamma tells me about Raoul as a soldier. I had told him that if ever he got into trouble privately, and there was anything he did not want his mother or sister to know, he was to write to me. This I now told to his mother and she thanked me. An officer has taken a dislike to him and he is being persecuted. He is unhappy. I say that there is perhaps a petticoat in the case. They agree with me. Raoul has never been punished. Both the women say that it is thanks to the good advice I have given him. I do not quite understand. Lilian tells me that he never forgot how I instructed him to behave at the regiment last November, and if he has got on so well, it is all on account of my counsel. And that was eight months ago. She never told me this before. Ma informs me that Lilian is not going to London with her brother in September, but is going to give up bonnet-building, as her health will not permit her to remain the long necessary hours in the workroom, and that it is a fearful trade unless you have a very good connection. She requires plenty of exercise in the open air, and to live in a pure atmosphere, not inhaling the rebreathed air of the stifling workshop, with a stove in it.

Here Lily grips her lips with her hand and hides her mouth; her elbows resting on the table.

Mamma continues: "She is not going to take any fresh customers, but gradually drop the old ones. I want her to shut up at once, but she wishes to wait until September, when the season here is over. She will become her Papa's secretary (*I kick Lily under the table*), he will give her a salary (*a kick*), and teach her the business (*a kick*); so that she will become a lady journalist (*a kick*); and remain comfortably at home with her Papa!" (*Kick, kick, kick!*)

I agree heartily with Mamma. "Certainly, she cannot do better than always remain with her Papa!"

Lily holds her lips tight and does not move. Papa returns and says that she does not help him. She retorts that the other day she prepared a lot of newspaper cuttings. Papa says:

"You were to have worked a day with me, but you never turned up."

She takes some medecine, which I opine is for cramps of the stomach, a well-known symptom of poor-blooded hysteria, and the dogs come in.

One bitch licks my ears. Lilian pretends to be disgusted. Mamma not being present, I say that ear-licking is nice and that lovers lick each other's ears.

"When you are married, you will be glad to lick your husband's ears!"

"Horrible!" she exclaims. Papa smokes in silence.

Mamma returns and the talk turns on theatres. Lily tells Mamma to go to bed. Lily has a pleasant, cool way of saying curtly:

"Go to bed, Mamma!"

Her respectable parent refuses. Lily talks of the plays she saw in Brussels.

"You went to a theatre every night?"

"Not every night," answers Papa, "as she was ill part of the time. She caught cold during a drive in the Bois de la Cambre, and went to bed early.* I wanted to go out and leave her. She would not allow me to do so."

"No, certainly not!" protests Lily. "Pa wanted to see the Carnival. I wasn't going to let him gad about alone."

Mamma laughs and looks at me with sparkling, aggressive eyes.

"She only let me go from her side once the whole time we were there, and that was for ten minutes," said Papa.

And he then held down his head and looked quite silly and delighted. And so did Lily. They were really, without exaggeration, like a newly-married couple talking of their honeymoon. Mamma beamed on the guilty pair, and glared defiance at me, with glitter-

---

* More irregular menstruation!

ing glance, as if to show me that she was on guard, to defend the happiness of Papa and Lily against a wicked stranger. Poor foolish mother! She too, was trying to torture Jacky.

"How about taking the dogs out?" asks Papa.

"Lilian! Why don't you go out with Mr. Arvel and Mr. S . . . ?" says Mamma.

"I don't like three people walking together," retorts her daughter.

This was a hint for me, but I refused to take it.

Lilian thanks me for some of my own make of Eau de Cologne that I have brought her. She is going to be rubbed with it, as I have advised her. She says that Mamma does not know how to "friction" her. Ma declares that she is a bad nurse. Lilian replies freely before her mother that Pa alone knows how to rub her properly. Papa says he will come and wake her up early as usual, and rub her with Eau de Cologne. Lily answers that she will not be woke by him any more, and forbids him to come into her room in the morning. So Mamma goes to bed, looking at me with a triumphant air, and Papa and I go out together, leaving Lily alone. There is no more strolling for me alone with her. They are punishing me.

We walk and I talk. Again Papa recurs to Trixie. He asks what has become of her. I reply that she had a slight illness. That I lost sight of her, and during the Easter holidays I saw her husband in deep mourning with the children.

If a husband walks out in black at Easter with his little family and no mother, it is a sure sign that their Mamma is dead. I often caught sight of him since, but always in mourning, and never with Trixie. He cannot get over the fact of her having procured women for me. I explain to him that a woman who really adores a man will do almost anything, and suffer a martyrdom; or go through the most disgusting vicissitudes, enduring what seems sometimes beyond human strength. (He ought not to be surprised, for has not Adèle given him her daughter?) I quote wife-beaters, and how they refuse to charge their husbands. It is all love.

"Lust, you mean!" he adds, with a snarl of deep scorn. He is a man who despises women, and hates them because he cannot do without them in the kitchen and in bed.

We speak of jealousy. I tell him that Trixie was always ready to go with any man or woman I told her. Jealousy is a ridiculous feeling. He declares that he is jealous and that he could not care for a woman if he thought she had anybody else. He could not enjoy a *partie carrée*. This interesting talk takes up so much time that when we return, I have missed a train. There is none now until 12:20. He will sit with me another hour.

Lily is alone, reading one of my magazines. Papa leaves us.

"Well, what do you think of me?" I say. "You did not imagine I was so clever with women? I should like to have your frank opinion of Jacky."

"I think you are not clever. You are very bad. I could never have supposed you would have had such horrible thoughts of me."

I laugh disdainfully.

She then says, slowly and sadly, with a sigh:

"I am very wicked sometimes."

This is the nearest approach to remorse or regret that I have ever heard from her.

I do not reply, and a moment later, Papa returns, and she shortly afterwards touches his cheek with her lips, chastely, and he salutes her on both cheeks as on the occasion of my last visit, and she bids us both "good night." After this kissing comedy, she says "Good night," softly and kindly to me specially, and gives me her hand. She is sad. Still she does not go at once, but hovers round Papa and strokes him gently on the head with her book. At last, she goes, gliding away gravely, bidding me good night for the third time, gently and warmly, as if regretfully. I rise respectfully from my chair, touched in spite of myself by the misery of her tone, and return her good night as she goes by, and she begs me to be seated and not derange myself.

Thus she passes out of my life. I have heard her speak to me for the last time and her last words were: "I am very wicked sometimes!"

Could a novel-writer find a better exit for his heroine than that?

Papa and I are once more alone together. Still more bawdy chat. I say that I had a *demi-vierge* all the year before and that I respected her virginity. Did I do wrong or not? Am I not a fool?

"No," says Pa, "you acted properly."

"But she went afterwards and gave herself up to somebody else."

"You can't help that. You did your duty."

He would like to meet a woman with an elongated clitoris. I talk to him of hermaphroditism. I am getting tired and sleepy. I remember that in January, Lily was greatly struck by that character in "Justine," called Dorothée, who possessed a penis-like clitoris. Miss Arvel frequently mentioned it. The idea tickled her fancy. And now Papa talks of the same anomaly! How they must have enjoyed my bawdy books together!

Again he says that girls now-a-days prefer being "messed about" to honest coition.

"Ah! they tell you that to please you," I reply, "when you don't have connection with them nicely; or when they don't like you; or when you can't."

He pauses and reflects, and I think that masturbation and prolonged and unnatural caresses, when practised before the age of puberty, or shortly afterwards, at the dawn of woman's sexual career, lead to an aversion for normal coition in later life. In such cases, some abnormal stimulus trains the sensual desires to respond to an appeal which has nothing to do with the fascination normally excited by the opposite sex. Anything will therefore serve to produce the orgasm: man, woman, or child; an obscene book, or their own finger, without counting purely mechanical means. There is no warmth or tenderness: one man being as good as another to them. Indeed, once their venereal sluices opened and shut, the presence of the male, or the active agent, becomes more wearisome than otherwise, and they evince no desire to return in kind. The organs are quickly excited and as quickly dormant again. The private parts, thus so early brought into use, and subjected to such sudden strain, revolt against the repeated unnatural shocks, and becoming flaccid, lose their tone. All is soft, stretched, and open, and lovers are bewildered to find a young face on the body of a woman, whose soft flesh seems to be dropping from the bone, while they go away wondering how such a darling little chit should carry between her thighs the yawning gulf of an older mother of a family.

Love, in its essence, becomes distasteful, and the feeling of natural lust, engendered by real affection, being entirely foreign to their nature, all sentiment forms the object of their mockery; they fall back on the pleasures of the table, or think of nothing but money, jewellery, and dress.

But I do not take the trouble to tell him all this, so I explain succinctly how girls learn to practice onanism with the hand or the mouth, alone or with their lovers, in countries like France or North America, where conjugal frauds are practised. They learn such tricks from their mothers, who teach them early how to satisfy men without getting *enceinte*. All this, he pretends is new to him. I can see he is surprised to find me speaking so freely.

I tell him of some of my amours in tropical lands, for I have been round the world. I can see he is quite astonished. He tells me that all girls having Spanish blood in their veins are largely made; their private parts seem to spread out early in life. Here is another part of my last letter answered by Papa. But why does he systematically try to always lower Lily in my eyes?

It is time to go. I promise him more bawdy experiences for later on, and he sees me to the gate. He excuses himself for not accompanying me to the station. He does not talk of any future visit. He is evidently displeased at my free and easy attitude and is in a hurry to go and ask questions of Lily, and tell her my stories, and my hints and innuendoes. This is the first time I have been left to go to the railway alone. I know too, that I have kept them apart all day.

I cannot find my gloves. He promises them to me with the negatives of my photographs, so that I can print them off myself, and to return me "The Romance of Lust" shortly, and so I go away.

I should like to hear what Papa said to Lily as he went up to her room, after my departure, and how much of my scathing diatribes she retailed to Pa and Ma.

I am now heartily sick of the whole lot of them, and I resolve never to put my foot in Lily's house again. And there is my own smouldering weakness for Lilian Arvel to be guarded against. I have been patient, but can be so no longer, and have carried out my scheme to the bitter end. I now resolve to do what I think few men would be capable of. I am going to "put myself away" with the family, and at the same time calm my mistress's growing jealousy, and make a neat finish for my romance.

I really think that Papa and Mamma have been pushing Lily on to me for "the good of the house." In order to get anything out of me, it was necessary to forge these elaborate lies with Papa's help. If Lily confessed that she was merely the easy, satisfied mistress of her mother's lover, she could have no hold on me. If she tells the truth, she would be saying: "I want for nothing. Papa keeps me in idleness. I am no longer a virgin. You can possess me now without fear or remorse." There is no money hanging to the truth in her case.

SUNDAY, JUNE 4, 1899.

My mistress is tolerably well. I dress her up in her best, with all her diamonds and jewellery, and a friend and I go on our bicycles to Sonis, meeting my lady, who takes the train, at the restaurant I told Papa, Mamma and Lily I should choose, and we sit in the open air at a table on a low terrace giving on the road to Paris.

MENU.
Hors-d'œuvre.
Truite saumonnée, sauce verte.
Entrecôtes grillées, pommes sautées.
Poulet rôti.
Salade.
Fromage.
Fruits.
Café.
Liqueurs.

At 12:45, a hired victoria appears in sight. On the box, next to the coachman, is Pa, in a large Tyrolean straw hat. He frowns and looks straight before him. Ma, in the red foulard, turns her head away. I touch my cap. Lily looks up defiantly, tosses her head, and snorting, laughs scornfully. They roll by. They are silly. They should all have returned my salute, as the lady who is with me, for aught they knew to the contrary, might have been with my friend. They have never seen and do not know my mistress. I have never spoken about her to anybody except Lily. And if they had pulled up a moment and let me run and speak to them, it would have been cleverer still, and would have quite damped my rocket. It must also be noted that Lily's mother is not married either.

Ten minutes afterwards, one of the workgirls appears on the road, and inspects us carefully. Then she goes back again, having turned up her nose at us and sniffed, as if we were a parcel of bloaters. She had evidently been left a roving commission to go and see whether I was at the restaurant, and who I was with, as I might not have had a table giving on the road, and Lily might have gone to the races without seeing me. She must have given her orders before leaving.

After lunch, we stroll past the house. The workgirl is at the window. She sees us three. She glares.

At the window of a neighbouring villa is the sister of François. She visits at Mr. Arvel's and knows me well.

JUNE 6, 1899.

No doubt my offence is great. But my great desire for bringing about my own downfall is not yet satisfied. I want it to go home to the hilt. I want to show Lily that I have really done it purposely and that I do not want her any more. I write the following letter, so that it is impossible for any of them to fathom my conduct, and know whether I am a fool, a madman, or a cold-blooded joker.

The worst they can say is: "How he must be gone on Lily to take all this trouble!" Even that I do not mind. But I think the Queen of Liars cannot like it. And my poor mistress looked really very nice, being in one of her best days. Woman-like, she brightened up at the idea that she was playing a trick on two females she was jealous of. She is pleased, poor thing, at what I did. So I have killed two birds with one stone. My poor ailing girl! So devoted to me, really fond of me, rich or poor. If she could only have her health again! But that is impossible.

What I did, flaunting my mistress in front of the Arvels, was silly and bombastic, but it pleased her, and teazed Lily, for whom I have no more consideration.

Papa writes an article in a London magazine for June, and alludes to men touting English visitors on the boulevards for bawdy houses. It is very unusual and in very bad taste. (*See Appendix H.*) It shows what his mind was running on.

I post this letter to Lily, addressing the envelope boldly in my own handwriting, and underlining the word: "Mademoiselle."

JACKY TO LILIAN.

Paris, Tuesday, June 6, 1899.

I think, perhaps wrongly, that I owe you a slight explanation of my lunch at Sonis on Sunday. This hasty letter is useless, but I write it principally for my own self, for conscience sake.

The poor woman, formerly divinely handsome, who is my faithful, devoted, and disinterested mistress since 1880, has become very jealous and sour-tempered, knowing that she is suffering from a mortal malady which declared itself about four years ago. Her rare beauty is gone, and she feels that she no longer possesses any influence over me. She had long since asked to visit Sonis, where she had never been. That was out of jealousy. And then she has been "worked up." Of course, she believes herself to be in a position of inferiority, despised by my *friends* of Sonis, who she *knows* are legitimately married. She is only the mistress of a common Englishman, formerly a "runner" at the Bourse.

Envy, vanity, jealousy, curiosity—you know what I mean.

Is not life sad, with these terrible ironies? Is not all this petty and vile? Such is the punishment of social irregularity.

I constantly refused to take her to Sonis. But a month ago, in the face of the welcome of my last visit but one,—after the scene in the cab—I gave way, and granted the trip. I was happy to know you were all going to Paris. That is all the story. Must I excuse myself? I hardly know. Put yourself in my place. Should I show any delicacy or have any regard for you?

I have nothing more to say. It would be too easy to overwhelm the Japanese girl. I have had enough of rummaging in your heaped-up mass of disgusting lies. All this is adulteration, fabrication, sophistication. Anyhow, I have left the game easy for you to finish—Suzanne-Césarée, false virgin; falsely incestuous; falsely cunning. Your "Papa-lover" told me you were a liar and wicked. Strange woman! Must then all your lovers scorn and despise you? What will become of you in a few years? Soon you will tire of the unnatural life you lead. Will you become a Miss Pawle* or worse?

Here is your pretext for closing the doors of your house against me. A few words thrown out about the audacity of S . . . coming to your town with his whore, and you are all well rid of me. Am I not a good fellow? I take all the wrong-doing over to myself. Such is my last act of delicacy. Final coquetry of your ex-lover, the son of Satan. That devil Jacky!—one never knows if he is mocking or no.

So, adieu! Keep a good recollection of me. That should be easy for you, as I am the man to whom you gave the least. Do not hate me too much. You will never more help me to salt. Only say this to yourself:

"Of all my lovers, both beneath my roof and out of doors, this one never did me any harm."

With the remembrance of the last lingering kiss of your lying lips,

JACKY.

P.S.—I shall always send the papers to your "Papa," as I have done for years.

I enclosed two newspaper cuttings. They were, "Divorce Among the People," (See Appendix I.) and, "The Alleged Offence under the Criminal Law Amendment Act." (See Appendix J.)

JUNE 14, 1899.

Lily sends me back the two novels: Suzanne, and La Femme et le Pantin, together with the proofs of "The Double Life," and the newspaper cutting: "Tête-à-Tête," but she did not return the two paragraphs I had enclosed in my letter of rupture.

---

* Miss Pawle was an American girl, once very pretty. She wrote for the New York fashion papers, and was a well-known Lesbian and discreet whore. She had been "gay" about fifteen years in Paris. She was supposed to have supported her family by her prostitution.

I had expressly told her I did not want the books to be returned, and I had so written on the flyleaf of one of them. Nevertheless, she sent the whole lot by post. This was for me to write, I think, but I did not reply.

JUNE 20, 1899.

No acknowledgement being received by Lily, she consults Papa, I suppose; because I receive, six days after the novels, a parcel containing my gloves, the negatives of my likeness as a cyclist, in two positions, and all the books he had of mine, including "The Romance of Lust," which had been in his possession since February.

I examine this obscene work and find that the corners of several pages have been turned down, and one which has been so treated with very dirty fingers—page 72, vol. II. On that page is the description of a young woman named Lizzie, with a little clitoris sticking out like a boy's penis.

In January, Lily talks incessantly of the character in "Justine" with the elongated clitoris. In April and May, Papa mentions this deformity twice to me. He returns me "The Romance of Lust," marked at the page where such a thing is described. Comment is needless.

I do not acknowledge the parcel.

In my letter of adieu, as in all my others since the return from Brussels, I had not put everything that I exactly thought. I always tried to "keep a little bit up my sleeve," for a future time, or until I could find more evidence on certain points. It will be seen that I never alluded to her frolics with Raoul, nor did I ever write, or even speak about the visit of the officer.

I also pretended that I thought an officer had been the first to possess her entirely. It was prettier and more romantic. Whoever it might have been: Papa, or a man who paid, it is not of the slightest consequence, but the work was done before the 11th. of November 1899.

After the lunch with Lord Fontarcy, at the end of September,

I did not see her until that latter date, and then she was full of grief; denied receiving my letter, with the money in it; was behind-hand with her "courses," and had a fit of hysterical weeping. She then asked me to marry her for the last time, believing me to have more money than I actually possessed.

No doubt she was already hymenless at that juncture, and this was her last desperate move to regain her lost position. Had I accepted, she would have kept me from getting into a bed with her until after the ceremony, with the aid of Papa and Mamma, who would have taught her how to bring me an alum-made virginity on the wedding night. To fully cheat me, she wanted a night in a bedroom. It could not be done otherwise, and this accounts for her strange behaviour ever since, and her continual plans for travelling with me to London and Belfort. She feared the free play of the Rue de Leipzig, when she would fling herself unrestrainedly about, stark naked, outside a bed in the open light of day.

That is why she dared not confess the slightest thing to me, as the comparison of dates with what she had written, and which she hardly remembered herself, would have damned her in my eyes. At least, so she thought in her petty way, little knowing that a frank avowal at any period would have disarmed me at once. And so she had gone on from falsehood to falsehood, until she had piled up such a scaffolding of lies about her, that if she had made the slightest move towards the truth, the tottering fabric would have fallen down and crushed her.

When I lifted my mask of stupidity in her pretty garden, she had to choose between my love and her lies. She elected to remain rotting in her silly infamy, especially as I had plainly made her understand that my pockets were empty. That last thought would be her supreme consolation.

Finding that her daughter's young life was spoilt, her mother—poor, tactless, ignorant, avaricious creature—preferred her to become a prostitute at home, sooner than drive her out into the gutter. It was also to her advantage for Lilian to lend her body for her keeper's lusts.

There are many other strange little secrets in this peculiar and patriarchal family, but it would be useless to say all here, and I do

not wish to drag on the tiny stage of my theatre of living marionettes a variety of characters who were more sinned against than
sinning. The figures passing like frightened shadows through the
crude confessions of my worst passions and vices, are vile enough in
all conscience, including the wretched writer, but he has had
moments of remorse, and has not made many of his actors half as
bad as they really were. He has done penance publicly and without
stint, but he has handled his old friend Eric Arvel with comparative
discretion and tenderness, and has let him off easily, suppressing
much that he knows about him, because he sleeps with stepdaughter Lilian, who formerly played at being Jacky's incestuous,
half-virginal offspring.

5

Je l'ai forcée d'adorer mon mérite, j'ai pris mille
plaisirs avec elle, et je l'ai quittée en confondant son
amour-propre.

"Le Grelot," Londres, 1781.

And thus I clothe my naked villainy
With old odd ends, stol'n out of holy writ,
And seem a saint, when most I play the Devil.

Shakespeare.

I had no news of the Arvels, and carefully avoided Sonis-sur-Marne, devoting myself to my invalid mistress, whose health seemed to get worse and worse.

I still sent Papa his bundles of newspapers and magazines, and suddenly I got the following extraordinary note:

Eric Arvel to Jacky.

Sonis-sur-Marne, July 13, 1899.

My dear Jacky,

I have been going to write to you over and over again to thank you for all the papers which you have sent me, but I have been upon the shelf for nearly a month from the effects of some violent poisoning with bichloride of mercury.

You know what you gave me was put away in my *cartonnier*. It

449

got all over my papers, and when sorting them I got a full dose, and only just managed to scrape out with violent salivation.

I am going over to London to-morrow for a few days and then to Ireland for a change.

Can I do anything for you when in the little village?

With best wishes, in which all join, believe me to remain,

Yours very truly,
ERIC ARVEL.

I answered as follows:

JACKY TO ERIC ARVEL.

Paris, July 14, 1899.

Dear Mr. Arvel,

I am very sorry to hear you have been so ill. I hope you will soon pull round and will profit by your trip.

I ought to be away myself, for fear of fresh rheumatics next winter, but all my people have been ill. And so I stick in Paris.

I got the negatives quite safely, and the prints thereof have been a great success wherever shown. For which many thanks.

I am grateful for your offer to be of use to me in London, but I have nothing I can worry you with this journey.

Renewed health, pleasant journey and a happy return home,—that is all the harm I wish you.

Yours faithfully,
JACKY.

I was, rightly or wrongly, so disgusted at his letter, that I hesitated a few hours about answering it, and at last sent him the foregoing, out of common politeness, but I took good care not to mention Adèle or her daughter: his two concubines.

The story of the "violent salivation" seemed diabolically fantastic, if true.

Salivation by inhalation is possible, but rare. I feared to think that the shadow of syphilis was hovering over the villa of Sonis, and that my quandom host had simply been taking mercurial frictions, thus accounting for the malady of years ago.

Anyhow the lips of Lily, that I once thirsted for, were at the disposal of a salivated man. She was the mistress of her mother's old lover, with rotting gums and fetid breath; sore lips, and ulcerated mouth and tongue.

I prefer not to write more on this subject, and hope that his letter was strictly true.

Although he had only spoken of the British Isles in his letter, I heard afterwards that he was seen in Brussels. I did not verify the statement. I could have written to Mallandyne again, but I resolved to try and forget. I cared very little. I was a subscriber to a newspaper, where Arvel contributed articles regularly, and he would date them from different places he used to visit, so that would have been a slight indication of his movements, and the whereabouts of Lilian. My subscription was up, and I did not renew it.

This peculiar mania for writing half the truth to me suddenly and without cause or reason, betrayed a strange hysterical frame of mind in a man of his age, and made me think that most of Lilian's later letters, including the famous one from Lille, were suggested and dictated by him. It was not nice to say: "the bichloride you gave me." I got it at his request.

This poison story made me very angry and as I still continued to send Mr. Arvel his bundles of newspapers, I resolved to teaze him a little, as he was trying to do with me, and at the same time to offend him thoroughly.

I amused myself by marking with a red pencil all paragraphs that seemed to have a bearing on illicit connections between fathers and daughters, or brothers and sisters; and cuttings from periodicals, together with any matter that seemed to allude to my amours with Lilian.

I found a number of stories, scandals, policecases and gossip in society papers, which had a special meaning for him and me, but I will only mention a few of the most remarkable ones.

There was a small article in a number of "Answers," called: "That Wonderful Number Four," and I did not fail to frame it with crimson dashes.

In "Society," during this month, I marked a few lines about Napoleon the First. (See Appendix K.) I took the paper regularly and Papa had it as soon as I had read it.

JULY 28, 1899.

Here are a few specimens of what I sent him:

A prospectus of a new work on sexual anomalies, entitled: "The Ethnology of the Sixth Sense."

I wrote on the first page in pencil:

"I have a copy of this book, which I can lend you, if you like to say the word."

The second page gave a table of contents, and following the mention: "Monstrous clitores," I added:

"Compare with Dorothée. ('Justine.') Conversations in January.

"Compare conversations on the same topic in May.

"Compare 'Romance of Lust,' vol. II, p. 72: Lizzie."

What could he think of the month of January being mentioned by me? At that time he was away in the South, and the allusion was plain to the fact of Lilian and him being in complicity, by the mention of the two books, one lent to him, and one to her.

I also added two cuttings, one relating to the crime of Bordes, an incestuous murderer, and the other headed: "A Horrible Crime." (*See Appendix L. and M.*)

ERIC ARVEL TO JACKY.

Sonis-sur-Marne, August 2, 1899.

Dear Jacky,

If you have not anything better to do, will you come down to-morrow Thursday, and have lunch with us? We shall all be delighted to have you. Raoul is here just now, but is going back on Friday.

Hoping to see you and have a good chat with you,
I remain,

Yours very truly,
ERIC ARVEL.

I was greatly surprised at getting the above invitation, after the mercury missive and my selection of insulting paragraphs. What made me smile bitterly was that the invitation arrived Wednesday evening, August 2nd., and I was to go the next day.

Most of the letters from Sonis were type-written, and I could nearly always tell whether the father or the girl had used the machine to write to me, as there were slight differences in the writings.

It would be too long to describe how I arrived at the knowledge by comparison, but I was certain that the above had been composed and typed by Lily and signed by her Papa.

Besides, it was the beginning of the month and she would be under the influence of her "menses." Immediately before and immediately after the flow, there would be a heightening of actual desire and she would think of me, for such is the effect of menstruation on unbalanced individuals.

The time I saw her, after I searched for her maidenhead in the cab, was May 3rd., and she is complaining that she is about to be unwell.

She gets me invited again for May 28th. I am not sent for again until August 3rd.

I felt a little pity for her, as I thought of her monthly martyrdom, and I asked myself if she were not perhaps only a miserable victim of the workings of her womb.

When we think of the debased, mercenary whore, who counts upon the weakness of men to feather her nest, we must keep her image distinct from that of the normally healthy woman, with true equilibrium of the reasoning faculties, who has nothing in common with poor-blooded neuropaths hardly responsible for their actions every twenty-eight days, and who pass half their lives seated on a cold custard.

A woman to keep her secrets should never let her male victim know her diaper days.

During the menstrual period of these hysterical women, we find falsehood united to wickedness and craft; cowardly slander; calumnious denunciations; the setting of perfidious snares, and the invention of satanic fables and even robberies, while they cleverly arrange things, so that suspicions shall fall on innocent parties.

My reader has only to run through the dates set down in this book and he will see that all the principal events take place between the 20th. of one month and the 8th. of the next; except when there is an irregularity, as when Miss Arvel denied receiving the money I had sent her, and during the *fausse couche* of January.

No doubt all her life was controlled by her "flowers," being a hereditarily neurotic subject, and on such a morbid soil, early masturbation and the tantalizing practices peculiar to half-virgins, and women who refuse to have children, would produce neurasthenia with its manifest symptoms.

I made up my mind that if Lily wanted me, she would have to come forward herself, and I sent off the following telegram at once, so as to stop Mamma going to market and providing for me:

JACKY TO ARVEL. (*Telegram.*)

August 2, 1899.

Thanks for amiable invitation, but regret, impossible to leave Paris at present. Very busy.

So they had to pass the day without me. I suppose they thought I should appear at once at Lily's beck and call, with presents for the Mamma and girl, and cigars for the boy; papers, books, gossip, news and smut for Papa, and he and Lily could teaze me at their ease and so get him an erection for when I was gone.

And I should have had to play clown all day to make them laugh, when I was full of worry, and trouble and grief in Paris! Not that I mind acting a part in society; I am very good at it, and would go splendidly through it, if the girl had been sweet and tender and I knew a *rendez-vous* would follow the visit.

It must be remembered too that it was my birthday on the 19th. of July, and Lily knew it well. She had also made me send a wire to her Papa on his anniversary. I got nothing from them, and I wanted nothing, expected nothing; but why invite me suddenly?

Lilian Arvel would never forgive me this refusal to see her, as both Papa and Raoul would sneer at her, and her vanity would be wounded to find her power was gone.

AUGUST 16th., 1899.

In that lively London weekly, "Society," since the month of April a serial story had been running, entitled: "The Confessions of Nemesis Hunt," giving the history of a clergyman's daughter, who becomes an actress, going through the most extraordinary experiences and cynically talking of her various loves and lovers.

She becomes the mistress of an actor, who is a member of the same travelling troupe, and in the number of August 12, 1899, this tale took such a strange turn that I am certain Papa would think I had a hand in it to annoy him and Lilian. (See Appendix N.)

It was simply a strange coincidence. I also sent him a cutting relating to another incestuous father, condemned at Troyes. (See Appendix O.)

The prospectus of "The Double Life," which was now announced as soon ready, went to him as well, and I pencilled the following note on it.

JACKY TO ERIC ARVEL.

(Note.)

Dear Mr. Arvel,

This is the prospectus of the book of which you saw a few rough proofs in the early days of June.

I shall send you my own copy, as I have been foolish enough to subscribe, as soon as I get it, probably in September.

You will read it, enjoy it, just the same as the others I lent to the Villa Lilian, and return to

Yours faithfully,
JACKY.

I was now finishing the revision of "The Double Life," and I had inserted the two following paragraphs,—Vanderpunk did not know English,—and I do not think my additions spoilt that otherwise extraordinary work:

Page 237.—"Her nostrils quivered with fresh rising lust; her lips were moist. She clung to me, murmuring:

" 'Papa! Papa! Don't be silly, darling! F . . . me last. Just one little tiny spend of your poupée. Tiny! Tiny!' "

Page 419.—"I have a vision, papa! I dream that we are living in a pretty cottage in the country amid trees and flowers! We are happy there with poor dead mamma come to life again. All three we play together. Our bedrooms communicate. Sometimes you take me travelling alone with thee to foreign climes. I shall have a beautiful, tall brother. He shall have a sweetheart, and we will all enjoy her. He shall frig and suck with me, and thou shalt be jealous. Thou wilt make me cheat and deceive all men, and I will rob them for thee and mamma. And I will hoodwink them, telling that I am a virgin, and how papa teazes me with his infamous love, and they will take pity and give me gold for my dress and the house. And I will try and never get the pox, so as not to give it to my darling old papa sweetheart!"

It was sweet after having been something like a puppet to turn round and make a marionette of the showman.

It was rather bold to mention that "you saw a few rough proofs," especially as they had only been lent in secret to the girl, his daughter-mistress, and he always told me what wonderful precautions he took so that "the girl should not get hold of any book you may lend me."

I had picked up an original edition of *Charlot s'amuse*, which I sent him in a packet of magazines on the last day of August; and on September 5, a number of "The Illustrated Police Budget," containing the "Awful Story of a Daughter's Shame," heavily marked by me. (*See Appendix P.*)

On the 16th. of September, I forwarded to him by registered bookpost, a clean, fresh, and uncut copy of "The Double Life," which had arrived the same day from Rotterdam, and I received the following letter:

ERIC ARVEL TO JACKY.

Sonis-sur-Marne, September 18th., 1899.

My dear Jacky,

I am half ashamed to write to you. It is so long since I was "going to" do so. When I went away to Coblenz a month ago, I made up my mind I would write to you during my travels, but I have such a lot of work to do manipulating the promotions of these new Anglo-German companies for the English market when I am in Germany that I have hardly time to eat.

We went down the Rhine to Cologne, and then from Cologne by

train to Brussels, to Blankenberghe and Ostend, returning to Paris in time to spend Sunday, the 10th., quietly at home.

I cannot tell you how much I am obliged for all the papers I found waiting for me at the Rue Vissot, and also for the loan of *Charlot*, and of "The Double Life," both of which I am returning to you to-morrow with many thanks.

I think the last is very erotic reading, but there is nothing real about it, as there was about the four little volumes,—"The Romance of Lust,"—which you lent me previously.

They were really good as such things go, but what I should like to find would be a book written really by a woman, giving us the *contre-partie*, and probably convincing us that the act of copulation which plays such a large part among human pleasures is simply based on the vanity of men who "kid" to themselves, while the women are simply relieving themselves of a more or less troublesome itching, and simply regard the male as a *parfait jobard*.

This idea no doubt came to you when you were out in Samoa?

Can we ever think we hold a woman by her senses? I do not think so, and I have an idea that the mere act of copulation without a love which has been mutually ripened by long acquaintance is not worth "twopennorth of gin."

I have not had time to work at my photography, but I hope to get into full blast when some relations, who are going to stop with us, have concluded their visit.

I saw your brother at the Bourse yesterday. You never come there now.

I hope all your people are well.

I am very, very much obliged to you for all the papers, although I do not think much of "Nemesis Hunt," who is rather too much of a whale for my swallow.

Yours very truly,
Eric Arvel.

Jacky to Eric Arvel.

Paris, September 22, 1899.

My dear Mr. Arvel,

I am very pleased you like the papers I send you. All the magazines that come into the house are always put on my desk after perusal by the different members of our family, as they all know they go to you. And when the pile gets troublesome, I send it off. Therefore I deserve no thanks.

I am afraid you do not approach erotic tales in a proper spirit. Of course "Nemesis Hunt," and "The Double Life" are unreal, but still here and there are incidents relating to passions, natural and unnatural, which are such as take place every day. I prove my words by enclosed cutting. (*See Appendix Q.*)

Work up the amusements of Mademoiselle Vial into a little story, and everybody will say it is all lies, the outcome of the writer's diseased imagination.

Your idea about a woman writing her own double life is a very good one. But as there exist no really truthful autobiographies or confessions written by men, how can you expect women to have less vanity and more veracity than we have? Nevertheless, women are always confessing, if you only take the trouble to listen to them. They are so cunning and clever—not intelligent, for malice and craftiness do not betoken intelligence—that they continually overreach themselves, and if you coolly think over all a woman has said and written to you, you ought to get very near the truth. A man who can't do that, is of no use with women. But all are not daughters of Judas. There do exist loving, tender, truthful women. Sensible people know how rare they are. Their lives would be uninteresting, so we could only get revelations from wicked creatures.

A man need not take much trouble to "hold a woman by her senses," or otherwise. Be natural, straightforward, and patient, and if she loves you, she will hold you herself. But she must feel something with you which she feels with no other. She must prefer you.

I have a pet theory, although in these matters there are no hard and fast rules to be laid down. It is this: a man may love many times in his life; a woman loves but once. If you could get at a woman's heart, you would only find one name deeply engraved upon it, even though she may have had countless lovers. Some women meet that one man at the outset of their career, others later, and many never.

Some have come across the one man they could have loved and have kept their secret. They have never been "had" by him and he never knows how he was loved. If you have fallen across that genuine, disinterested tenderness during your life, you are all right. If not, you have never known the real love of a woman.

I am most happy to hear you have been enjoying good health and been taking pleasant journeys.

Since June we have left off subscribing to "The Stock Exchange

Review," so I do not see your articles, which I suppose you still contribute and send from the different continental towns you visit?

All my family, you will be pleased to hear, are very well indeed, "as it leaves me at present."

Yours faithfully,
JACKY.

P.S.—I didn't have "Nemesis Hunt" last week.

There was a slight *retard*. Not surprising when we think of what she gets up to,—and down to, as well.

It's a far cry indeed from "Mord Emly" to my sweetheart "Nimmy Hunt."

"The Double Life" got into Mr. Arvel's hands on the 17th. of September. On the 18th., he wrote the letter saying he would send me back the books "to-morrow."

It is a stout volume of 446 pages! He and Lilian were reading it together, no doubt, and he wanted to lead me to believe that he could get through it in two days! In point of fact, he sent it to me back a week afterwards, on the 24th., after he had received my answer to his letter. When he wrote on the 18th., prompted by Lily, they had not got to page 417, where I talked about the daughter hoodwinking men by pretending to be a virgin, whose Papa teazes her with his infamous love, while she gets money out of her lovers for her dress and the house and is masturbated by her own brother, etc.

All this, however, is only to lead up to this concluding and amusing result:

The book came back entirely cut open for reading, with but one exception: one page of the preface,—the one containing the lament over the daughter's death,—of which I had lent the proof to the girl only, in May, was not cut. This was a damning oversight.

OCTOBER 8, 1899.

During the whole of the month of August and the best part of September, my faithful mistress had been in the country and had not been well at all.

She returned about the 22nd. of September, and went to bed.

It was her last struggle. The doctors gave me no hope, and this morning she is gone from me, after suffering such agony that to stand by the bedside of a loved one, and see her hellishly racked, fighting for life, as each essential organ gave way, would make an atheist of the most fervent believer and he would ask himself as I did: Is this the work of the Almighty? Is God a cruel Chinese mandarin or a torturing Torquemada?

In repose at last, on a bright Sunday morning. How beautiful she looked! During her illness I could not recognize her as the handsome, strong lass who had footed it merrily with me over peak, crag, and glacier but a few short years before in Switzerland.

Many a time she would fatigue our guide and he would drag himself slowly from the valley, while I, in despair, would lie down panting by the side of the steep path and looking up, admire my devoted companion's perfect frame, profiled against the clear sky, as alpenstock in hand, she stood triumphantly perched on some projecting rock.

And now she is gone. After death, the pristine beauty came back to the loving face, as if the mocking devils who had torn at her poor heart for years with the red-hot pincers of disease, had relented, and pleased to have finished their horrible task at last, satiated with her sufferings, had allowed her to look her best to show us poor mortals what fragile, feeble shadows we are.

And so she sleeps. Her big, blue eyes will never more brighten at my footfall. I shall never see their laughing light again.

I kissed her still warm cheek passionately and lengthily. I could have kept my lips to her face for an hour, but my tears fell upon her and that I did not like.

I am sorry I did not send for a photographer. I thought of that too late.

And so she sleeps. For the first time in my life I have seen a cherished being die and gazed at my love after death.

Up to now, I think I must have feared the end of all things. At present, the skeleton may come with his scythe, because I saw on the peaceful features of the white figure on the bed, who had been my girlish sweetheart, my wife without the priests, my devoted woman who lived for me alone, that she was at rest, and I really grasp the fact that death is the only true release.

And so she sleeps.

OCTOBER 15, 1899.

My fair Lilian is dead. She knew of naught but her love for me. The black Lilian lives, and she hates me by now. She will never forgive me for having seen through her tricks and wiles, aided in her natural cunning by the artificial villany of her salacious step-father, and her selfish mother.

The fathers are generally responsible in these cases, but when the mothers are weak, and sacrifice their daughters to keep the man at home and get all his money for the house, we must pity the young lass whose flower of virginity is torn from her by those who should be its most vigilant sentinels.

Corruptio optimi pessima, the corruption of the best is the worst,—is not only true for the victim, but also for the seducer. Women who have been debauched in their teens, or earlier, under ordinary circumstances, often rise again. But those who have been led astray by their fathers, who have known a villanous priest, as it sometimes happens, never succeed in getting out of the mire. As criminals of olden days were marked with a branding iron, it would seem as if the defiling culprit seared his youthful living plaything with an indelible mark of shame.

At the same time, the unnatural parent, who may have shown an honest face up till then, acquires in his features an expression of savage hatred. He becomes quarrelsome and morose, and like Mr. Arvel, his soul torn by his unholy passions, knowing that the slightest whisper may render him a thing to be scorned by friends and neighbours, he hurries to snarl at everybody, as if preparing an everlasting defence of his conduct; as if he found an excuse for himself in vilifying his wife and speaking with scorn of the daughter-prostitute, whose caresses he would go and humbly beg for a moment after he had traduced her.

Women of infamy, like Lilian Arvel, are seldom perfect types of beauty. Our passions are printed on our features, and wicked thoughts make wicked faces.

Sensual women are sad, until aroused. Their development of breast is rudimentary, as was the case with Lily, who in male attire might have been easily taken for a young lad. Her maternal grandmother, I have already said was more than eccentric, and her mother flew into tremendous passions when put out, and was unreasonably jealous. Lily had always a very bad temper; she was a liar, vicious, and thought of nothing but men, jewellery and dresses. I fancy that she suffered from chronic inflammation of the intestines and that would account for the peculiar bluish tint that overspread her features whenever put out. But I am no doctor. Her menstruation was tolerably regular. There were nervous troubles, spasms, cramps of the stomach, stifling, but never a complete hysterical fit with me. Her nerves troubled her during her monthly derangements. She had been some time at a convent-school, and in answer to my inquiries told me that she had never witnessed, or been invited to take part in any acts of saphism. I remember on one occasion, before I was unduly intimate with her, that some young women from Myrio's dined at the villa while I was there. One of them was called "Mahogany," in allusion to the colour of her hair, and she was supposed to be married, but she had all the freedom of manner of the kept mistress. After the meal, Lily went and sat on a garden bench with her, and by the way in which she sprawled on her friend's shoulders, I felt sure they were all disciples of Sappho.

Lilian's conduct was lax and provoking with all the young men she met, and some elderly financiers, from the London Stock Exchange, who had been invited to dinner by Arvel, came away with the conviction that the daughter of their host was a dangerous flirt, if nothing worse. Four years ago, she ran away from home and took refuge with her grandmother.

Lilian Arvel is a neuropath, who has unfortunately not found in her dwelling, between her mother and her mother's lover, the advice and examples that might have had a happy influence, so as to modify any bad instincts she may have had within her. She has much false pride; extraordinary ambition; her tastes lead her towards dress and debauchery; she hates her mother, and she surely despises her Papa, although she accepts his caresses. He serves as a machine to calm her lust. But she can reason perfectly well on all subjects which have nothing to do with the satisfaction of her passions. The manner in which her mother lived, combined with the conversations of her customers, all professional harlots, adult-teresses or kept women, showed plainly that there was little chance of her moral sentiments being nurtured, or of her receiving the good advice and education which might have changed in some slight measure the disposition and tendencies of a young woman of uncontrollable imagination. She is endowed with very lively intelligence; her repartees are pointed and prompt; her memory is surprisingly precise. But I perceive a great change when I proceed to analyse her feelings and nature. Here I find enormous gaps, and I note the excessive development of egotistical feelings, vanity, and a yearning to be talked about and always play the principal part. If I call to mind her childhood, when she served as an aphrodisiacal plaything, in the bed of her mother; afterwards toying with her brother; then eagerly drinking in the bawdy chatter and risky songs of the milliner's workshop; her dangerous flirtations with Gaston, Ted, François, and all the others I know not of; her connection with Madame Rosenblatt and Charlotte; without counting officers, actors and myself, I can only reconstitute a type of character much more often to be met with than many people think. The principal characteristic of this style of person is the complete absence of all idea of morality. Such individuals are quite capable of saying what they ought or ought not to do, but all moral notions are abstract for them, and have no bearing on their determinations. Lusts, appetites and instincts predominate and their perverted impulses carry an intellectual activity, which is often intact, towards the goal of selfish satisfaction only. Acts entirely at variance with all moral and social laws do not excite their horror, but are quietly accepted by these curious unmoral people, who are as those suffering from colour-blindness.

They are afflicted with moral cecity, and do evil deeds with complete indifference. And as their intelligence, seemingly without a flaw, is only superficial; as the versatility of their feelings is as great as that of their ideas, they have no remorse. They may suffer slightly from an annoying obsession, when they cannot have their own way, but never from the remembrance of a bad action.

My poor dead Lilian had a great liking and esteem for the Arvels. She was proud to find that they invited me so often and delighted to know that her Jacky should be so sought after.

It proved her own good taste. She would see that I was well-dressed to go to Sonis and would wake me early so that I might not miss my train, after having chosen my cravat herself.

She had respect for them too and never thought of herself on the same footing, for were they not married, whereas she was but my concubine? I never deceived her. During the last year of her life, she began to get jealous of them all at Sonis and suspected me of being in love with one or the other of the women of the villa.

When I had been preparing a new chemical product in 1897, Lilian Arvel had done some type-writing for me. My poor girl knew of this and was always grateful to the young lady who was so kind to Jacky. She was sure the good wishes of a pure maiden would bring luck to my new invention.

On her deathbed, although her approaching end had been carefully concealed from her, she had forebodings and said to me:

"Jacky, I am dying. I know I am. You will marry Miss Arvel. You know,—the young lady who typed your prospectus two years ago. I am not jealous of her now. I can't be jealous if she loves you. Don't sleep with her in this bed. We two have passed every night in it for well-nigh fifteen years . . . You made fools of us both this summer."

NOVEMBER 8th., 1899.

In my packets of newspapers for Mr. Arvel towards the end of October I enclosed a curious cutting from the "Figaro" (see Appendix R) and an extract from Zola's latest novel that was just out (see Appendix S) copied on the type-writer, as, to change the current of my sad thoughts, I had bought a machine and was beginning to practise with it.

Then Papa wrote to me and the following correspondence took place. I was evasive and elusive. He was incomprehensible and bitter.

I only note a sort of rage and hate to think I had got to know his secrets, had read him and his daughter-whore through and through, and had walked away when I was tired of their intrigues.

If the girl was still at home, living quietly with him and Ma, and "getting her own living"—this was Arvel's pet phrase as applied to women—by carefully moulding the weak brains of moneyed lechers; there was no excuse for him to write as he did, and drag his own concubine in the mud, to "bluff" an ex-lover, trying to convince him that he had never played at the game of incest with her. Surely I should never believe that he would so vilify his own mistress?

If she had left him, disappointment might be a motive.

Be that as it may, his long and prosy letters did not trouble me much, as will be seen by my vague answers, and my mind was perfectly at rest as regarded the triumvirate of Sonis-sur-Marne. I never asked anybody about them. I knew nothing of their movements.

ERIC ARVEL TO JACKY.

Sonis-sur-Marne, November 7th., 1899.

My dear Jacky,

I ought to have written to you some time ago to thank you for your long and philosophical letter. I do not want to argue, or I could show you that you are sanguine on points, which picked to pieces, would show but a bare canvas, to be covered by the daydreams and fancies of the man who has forgotten the grand truth that all is vanity.

Women keep their secrets well, and they know how much they are pandering to the vanity of men, a knowledge which prevents them from disclosing the secrets of the charnel house. Men may write such tales as "Nemesis Hunt," and give spice to the commonplace adventures of a gay woman, by introducing the incestuous intercourse between her and the lover of her mother, supposed to be her father, for the amusement of those who are fond of gutter literature.

I must confess that the idea of any save platonic intercourse with the wife, or relation of any friend has always been very distasteful to me, and I have often thought, when running my eye over the legends in the Old Testament referring to the chronicles of the Jews, that the low system of enlightenment remarkable among whole colonies of Jews in Southern Russia, is fostered by those intermarriages, which to my mind, are as incestuous as the coupling up of Nemesis Hunt and Jean Messal.

Among the early Jews, and no doubt among many of the present day, incestuous connection is no crime and quite a matter of course.

I can understand that every one has his opinions on the subject, and I know that I had to pay very dearly once for expressing mine, when the son of a twin sister married the daughter of his mother's twin. I am told this was according to the Jewish rite. Naturally the object was to keep the money in the family.

I do not want to inflict any long sermon on you as to the virtues and vices of "Nemesis Hunt." The book will take, but it will not come up to my standard of "blue" books, according to the samples you have so kindly placed at my disposition from time to time, and while there may be some excuse for the lover, who was not sure the woman who offered him such rapturous embraces was in any way related to him, there was none for the woman who suspected the truth, from the time she met her father on the steamer.

I owe you so many thanks for the papers you send me with such charming regularity that I am ashamed to say I look forward to them as a right.

By the way, I was very much entertained with the volume: "The Scarlet City," which I will return to you next week, as I want to read it over again for the references it contains to men I have known.

I see you have taken to type-writing. I am sending off this by twilight, as I can only just see the letters on my machine. I am sure you will never feel inclined to take your pen up again, once you get into the swing of type-writing, and though you may often strike a wrong letter, the thing is so easy that you would never be persuaded to mess about with pen and ink for any consideration.

My dear Jacky, will you let me offer my most heartfelt sympathy for the loss you have so recently sustained. I only heard of it recently, and if you were thinking of the person whom it has pleased a higher power to remove from this earth when you last wrote to me, and so ably championed the affection of woman, then your loss must have been severe indeed, and I might say irreparable.

Yours very truly,
Eric Arvel.

Jacky to Eric Arvel.

Paris, November 9, 1899.

My dear Mr. Arvel,

I am always flattered and honoured to hear from you, but more so to-day, as I am deeply touched by your kindly expression of sympathy.

There were *lettres de faire part*. I did not send you one. I did not want anyone to see me that day, nor did I wish to see anybody.

I begin to think you are right in all you say. You have evidently had a greater and more varied experience with women than I. I see that I have been spoilt. I never had to make love . . . at least, not much.

Now, I suppose, I must swell the ranks of the *michés* (*Le Miché malgré lui*, Molière . . . slightly altered), or else go and "listen to the band," instead of joining the merry maze of mercenary, menstruating Messalinas!

Glad you like the papers and books. When you send back "The Scarlet City," I will lend you another of the same sort: "A Pelican and a Pink 'Un." Also, an "indigo" novelty: "Dolly Morton," the true (?) confessions of a lady fair. And lots more.

I have only taken to typing since the 26th. ult., *plus* two lessons with a fairy-fingered maiden. I had some work to do which necessitated it. I thought I would try myself and have hired a "Nonpareil" for a month. I am a rare cuckoo at it! (Sounds like a fable: "The Cuckoo and the Type-writer.") Thought I should save money with it, but am spending a small fortune in erasers. There the love of gold, from my Bourse education and frequenting the Jews, peeps out again!

And yet a lady-authoress told me the other evening that she "had never met such a sensitive Christian."

I should like to know how long it takes to get to real speed on this clattering monster? I must stop at home with it a night or two, and have a real tussle with it.

Faithfully yours,
Jacky.

ERIC ARVEL TO JACKY.

Sonis-sur-Marne, November 10th, 1899.

My dear Jacky,

Many thanks for your letter, but I am afraid you are a sad flatterer. I am finishing "The Scarlet City," for the second time, and I will send it to you on Monday. I shall be very pleased to read the "Pelican and the Pink 'Un," as also the "blue" volume, purporting to be the confessions of a lady fair, although I am afraid the mother of most of the ladies fair and frail was "Moll Flanders," and that the supposed petticoated authoress wore bluchers and smoked a short pipe. By the way, talking of what is "blue," you said you would lend me a "blue" book, the prospectus of which you sent me, relating to various mal-conformations of certain organs.

(*The rest of the letter was all about the art of type-writing.*)

About the 20th., I shall be going to England, where I shall remain possibly three weeks, trying to get something to do, as times have not been over brilliant with me of late, and the expenses of my Bourse telegrams have increased so much, that working for the financial press has become bare bread and cheese.

Whenever you have any idea of taking a lesson on your type-writer, think of me, and remember that I shall always be glad to have your news, which I hope will always be good and couched in your usual happy strain of mind.

Very faithfully yours,
ERIC ARVEL.

I wrote a very short note in answer to the above, thanking him for his kind offer of tuition on the type-writer, and announcing that I was sending him the books he asked for.

I noted that Papa did not bear malice, as he coolly demanded the volume of which I had annotated the prospectus in such a vile manner a few months before. This is the first time he alludes to any of what may be called, my obscene innuendoes. So he got "Dolly Morton," "The Pelican," and "The Ethnology of the Sixth Sense." This last work I took the liberty of marking here and there in the following manner:

"The first shape of the hymen, almost invariable in infancy, and which is sometimes prolonged beyond puberty, consists in a labial arrangement of the membrane, the edges of which, separated by a vertical opening and facing one another, make a projection at the entrance of the vagina, which it closes, if I may say so, like a fowl's anus." (P. 275.)

". . . we often see tall and strong women showing a small vulva, and a mount of Venus without hairs, while little dwarfs display a largely developed vulva, followed by a vagina capable of satisfying an enormous penis." (P. 291.)

". . . an abundance of hair under the armpits, and . . . a slight moustache on the lips. Most frequently brunettes alone have this advantage." (P. 292.)

"EXAGGERATED AMPLITUDE OF THE VAGINA."

"In certain women, the vagina may acquire a considerable amplitude. If it is congenital, and the woman is salacious, and indulges beyond measure in the pleasure of love with men who have a large member, her vagina may become a veritable gulf, in which a penis of ordinary dimensions finds itself quite lost. There is no remedy for this deformity, except to endeavour to palliate it with tonics and astringents within the limits of possibility." (P. 311.)

". . . If a woman has a small one, she makes no difficulty in showing it, and displaying the neatness of her receptacle. But if she has a large one, she never permits it to be seen, for fear of revealing her disgrace." (P. 313.)

It will be noticed that mention is made in this last letter of Mr. Arvel to the well-known romance of Daniel Defoe, "Moll Flanders."

Papa was always alluding to this book, which had evidently made a deep impression on him. It will be remembered that the heroine unwittingly marries her brother. So whichever way we turn with the master of the Villa Lilian, the incubus of incest must always seemingly oppress us.

There was now a desire to see me again at Sonis. The lessons of type-writing were a pretext, and there was the hint of his departure to London, showing that the coast was clear for me in his absence.

ERIC ARVEL TO JACKY.

Sonis-sur-Marne, November 21st., 1899.

My dear Jacky,

I am returning your three volumes, which I have read with much interest and I tender you my very best thanks for the loan of them.

The "indigo" one reads like a true story, as it might fall from the lips of a woman who had given herself up to circumstances, and set perhaps the correct value of a "jewel," which is simply a marketable commodity, appraised by the vanity of man, held up to him as a temptation to commit all kinds of follies, in the hopes of obtaining a *primeur* from a source, which has, in ninety-nine cases out of a hundred, been tapped in a moment of curiosity by the *demi-vierge*, who wanted to go one better, having learnt from friends of her own sex, that there is still a resource in the *sonde* of the angel purveyor.

The interesting young lady who relates her adventures, bears out my theory that the "Sixth Sense" does exist, not as the outcome of Love or Affection, but as that of lust, played on and developed by the art and wiles of woman, the past mistress in converting vain man to the worship of Priapus, whose altar reposes on a solid foundation of *rosserie*.

When some ten or fifteen years have passed over your head, and your shoulders get bowed with age, and your whitened hair cries out: "Ichabod!" to show that some of the glory of your house has departed, you will find that Youth looks on you with smiling eyes, and that the tempting morsels are offered you, with the hope that they will be as the Dead Sea fruit to you, and with the determination to give you nothing better than the husks which have fallen from the trough of the swine.

Go on the boulevards and see the *vieux marcheur*, who can but limp, and watch the play around him, as he stops at the shop of the *modiste* or the jeweller, and then exclaim with Hamlet: "To what base uses may we return!"

There are a few exceptions to the general rule, and the endeavour of the woman seems to be to compromise actually or morally the weak, vain mind of man.

The husband of "Mademoiselle Giraud" *would* marry, and the comedy she played to disarm the man who thought he was on the point of possessing the woman he had yearned for, has been copied over and over again. The woman often throws herself into the arms of a man, decided that he shall, even with a show of a complete abandonment of herself, enjoy no more than the *petites privautés*, into which she has been initiated by her comrades.

You see I am drifting into the zone of platonic friendships, and getting by experience to know how to discount that mendacious exclamation: *Je t'aime*, which seems to warm the cockles of our hearts. All is vanity. It is given to some of us to learn that woman is capable of pure devotion, and that at times she can abandon herself to a kindred soul, but as a rule, woman is the author of such a book of follies in a man, that as Bulwer said: "all the tears of angels could not blot them out."

Some of these days I must try and write my life, with all the follies I have committed "writ large," but perhaps before the idea is carried out, I may have gone over to the other side, and buried a long record in the silent grave, where the wicked cease from troubling and the weary are at rest.

Yours very truly,
ERIC ARVEL.

P.S.—Many thanks for the budget of papers, which have just been brought down to me and will accompany me to London to read on the way.

My address will be Potteton's Family Hotel, Trafalgar Square, W.C., for the next three weeks, so that if you want anything from London, you will know where a letter will find me.

At last, Papa began to show a little temper. He preached me a sermon to let me see what a silly man I was, and how badly the "half-virgin" had treated me.

I suppose the couple was annoyed at my indifference to their timid overtures, and the marked passages in the "Ethnology," to which book Papa took care not to allude, must have shown them sufficiently that I did not wish to renew with Lilian.

His position was a strange one between Lilian and me, her old lover, with whom he corresponded, never mentioning her name, and I never asked after her. And now he suddenly breaks out in the foregoing letter, to my great delight.

A few days afterwards I replied evasively. I was resolved not to say anything that would compromise me in any way, or enable him or her to have the least idea what my real feelings were.

As I read this over, correcting the proofs, I cannot help thinking from the outburst in the foregoing letter and the allusions to female vice and treachery in the following ones that Lily had gone away. The month of November was always a fatal one for her. It is not possible that a man could so write if the wretched girl was at his elbow, as in former days.

Not that the quarrels of such people mean anything. They may hurl the vilest insults at each other, and even come to blows, but like dogs, it does not prevent them licking each other afterwards.

Even had Lily departed, whenever she met Papa again she would be at his disposal, if he so willed it, until death should part them.

But in the meanwhile she had exhausted his two purses and was no longer at Sonis.

The unbreakable chain that united Lily and Eric was no heartfelt attachment. It was a double heavy yoke of dissimulated interests. Their *liaison* was a commercial partnership.

JACKY TO ERIC ARVEL.

Paris, November 29, 1899.

My dear Mr. Arvel,

I received the books and was glad to see you liked them. I too fancied that "Dolly Morton" sounded as if half true, perhaps in part told to a man who knew how to listen. I did not like to say so, for fear of being wrong.

I sent you to London, three newspapers that ought to have gone in the last bundle, and would have been too stale if kept three weeks longer. I shall collect your papers and not send any until three weeks, counting from the 21st.

I did not flatter you when I said that you had greater experience than I with the fair sex. Your letter of the 21st. proves it beyond a doubt, and what is more strange, you seem to have the power of reading my thoughts to a certain extent. I have not your knowledge. I am all theories, and that is not much good, I know. It would take me a long time to explain all I mean and to answer your clever and deep-thinking letter properly. In September and before, I could write; now I cannot.

So you must forgive me if I do not reply to you as you deserve. I will try later on if I can, but I shall never be able to discriminate and reckon things up as wonderfully as you do.

I have read your letter over and over again, each time with more absorbing interest.

I would be ungracious not to thank you for your offer to try and render me any little service in London, but I have absolutely nothing that I can ask you to do for me.

Before writing any of your erotic recollections, you must read the "Memoirs of Casanova."

If you have never done so, I will lend you the work in French or English.

Faithfully yours,
JACKY.

DECEMBER 8th., 1899.

I liked the above letter, because it was a masterpiece of empti-ness. I sent it to his hotel in London, but I knew he would not answer until he had seen Lilian. I fancied too, that Lilian had told him how I spoke about publishing the story of my intrigue with her, and that is why he wrote concerning his own autobiography. But I was not to be drawn.

I was musing on these things, on a dark evening about half-past five, as I was slowly going home, passing the St. Lazare rail-way station, when suddenly I thought I saw a ghost.

It was Trixie tripping gently along, her eyes bent on the ground.

She might not have been alone. Her husband, or a lover, might have been just behind her. I cared not; nothing could have stopped me from speaking to her just then.

I rushed towards her, and I refuse to write the sweet joy of our meeting.

Trixie cried a little, but I soon petted and soothed her, and we had a cup of tea together in a fashionable resort behind the Opéra.

And how she did talk and tell me all that had happened to her since I had last seen her!

Her husband and children had been in mourning for a near relation, and she herself had been in bed with pleurisy all through March and April; and afterwards, she had been away from Paris, during a long convalescence.

Achille was dying. His brain had given way under the strain he had put upon it, by his unnatural cravings and curious practices for years, and I began to think that we have to pay dearly for all our excesses in life; be it the bed, the bottle; or even common gluttony.

Over-indulgence with women and the searching after extraordinary pleasures and uncommon delights in the higher grades of sensuality, will lead us eventually to the padded room, while the masturbating Lesbian,—a menstruating fiend,—who makes such inordinate use of her tender organs; sucking, injecting, checking conception, washing with all kinds of lotions, teazing and tickling, without counting natural coition, must in due course fall beneath the surgeon's knife. The medical Jack the Ripper removes ovaries and the womb itself, and leaves a female eunuch, and thereby partly demented. Lucky will she be, if only the operation is needed and succeeds, and she does not have to sojourn for a short or long period in a private asylum; her plump arms hidden in a straight waistcoat and her luxuriant tresses ruthlessly cut off.

ERIC ARVEL TO JACKY.

Sonis-sur-Marne, December 22, 1899.

My dear Jacky,

When I was over in London, they sent me such a dreadful machine that I had no inclination to sit down and write. Otherwise it would have been my duty to thank you for the papers which followed me to London and your interesting letter of the 29th. ult. which afforded me pleasant reading. I have never read the "Memoirs of Casanova," in fact as you may hardly credit, the first obscene book in print ever read by me were the poems ascribed to the Earl of Rochester, among the State Papers in the British Museum, and then after perusing the *Ecole des Biches,* and "Fanny Hill," I have been permitted to fall back on your well-stocked library. Would the "Memoirs of Casanova" aid me in jotting down from the tablets of memory the old, old story of how man is caught in the snare, like the bird in the net of the fowler, and how neither experience nor age can prevent him imperilling all that he otherwise held most dear and sacred, for what? For what the veriest courtesan in the street can sell him for a mere song, as part of her daily business. Analyse the whole thing and the absolute sameness sickens one from a rational point of view. When the heart beats, and the innermost soul is moved, who can say that the feeling we conjure up under the name of love is reciprocated or exists in either the passionate woman, seeking relief from the heat of animal passion, or in the man who is offering a tribute to his *amour-propre* by taking possession of a woman, who draws her calculations from the vanity of the man to whom she offers herself, not with the unreserved franchise of the courtesan, but with the mock-modesty of the *demi-vierge* of the XIXth century, decided to take advantage of his weakness. What more can I say than others have said before me in writing their memoirs? I can plead that *plus ça change, plus c'est la même chose,* and the only difference is to be defined by the student of the sense of lust. That calculating philosophy and logic which makes a man in close contact with a woman recoil from actual sexual intercourse might be described by those who argue in favour of platonic love. The world taxes all such hesitation with a less polite term and Brown Sequard is advised. This may be correct when we are judged by the standard of youthful desire, but there are few of those over-ardent temperaments, who have not often wished afterwards that they had possessed the same dose of philosophy as the older man, who seeks out the courtesan, and opines that Love has very little to do with the mere connection of two bodies. I might write for a whole year without changing anything or without being able to fathom the depth of the feminine deceit. In woman there lies no truth at the bottom of the well. There are however, close friendships, and women have surrendered themselves to men to whom they have shown the deepest devotion, and for whom they are ready to give up their lives; and when you find such a one, tie her to you with every link a reciprocated affection can forge. Were I to write my "erotic" recollections, the cry of "Chestnuts" and "Rats" would be raised, as I wandered through the list of clergymen's daughters, and offspring of officers who have ministered to me carnally, and gradually come to more recent experiences, proving perhaps that "There's no fool like an old fool," and that however philosophically a man may be inclined, there is the old leaven of vanity which bright eyes, a smile, and youth know how to turn to advantage. Eve was the tempter, and her daughters have been armed to give battle successfully to man.

My dissertation is long and wearying, no doubt, so I will end it and turn to another theme more interesting, by wishing you and all yours a very merry Christmas, and renewed health and prosperity for the coming year, with plenty of health to enjoy everything Providence may send you.

Truly and sincerely yours,
Eric Arvel.

This letter contained a *lettre de faire part*, printed in silver, setting forth that Eric Arvel had married his mistress, Adèle, and he had written the word, "Private" upon it.

Jacky to Eric Arvel.

Paris, December 26th., 1899.

My dear Mr. Arvel,

That you should enclose in your last letter the announcement of your union, causes a variety of conflicting emotions in me; the principal being the thought that you consider me worthy of being apprised of such a delicate piece of news. I am vain enough to suppose therefore, that you count me among a privileged set of *intimes*, and if so, I fully appreciate the honour you do me. May I say you *both* do me? I have learnt by my own experience that a mere ceremony, or writing down of signatures, does not constitute a real marriage, and some of the unconsecrated associations are several degrees more perfect than the legitimate ones, because the man, if he is a man at all, tries by untiring devotion and continual solicitude, to make the woman he has chosen to share his joys and troubles, forget the loss of worldly consideration, which she sees vouchsafed to others, who are often wicked shrews or worse, but they are called "respectable" because they have gone through a legal process.

I should not dare to speak so freely and boldly on this matter, were it not that I look back ever so sadly, and see nineteen years—nearly half my life—of the same companionship. But I was not fated to find the rest and peace that you will now enjoy, combined with the sweet sense of gratitude, of which you will reap the benefit.

I always envied you, I confess that fault, every time I saw you in your pretty villa, and now I envy you still more, as I think of what might have been, and how I lived for years, trembling lest the secret confided to me by the doctors should reach the ears of my Lilian, and powerless to arrest the sure progress of a relentless malady.

Nobody ever knew. But I purposely cease writing on this subject, as I do not possess the necessary talent to describe my sad existence, and even if I did, I do not think I could summon up courage to put my thoughts on paper. And besides, why should I come and throw a shadow of gloom over your happy household just at this festive period of the year?

I thank you for your good wishes expressed for Xmas, and am deputed by all my family to wish you the same, continued far into the next century. To make us quits, I personally return your Xmas greetings with my best hopes for your felicity, good health and prosperity during the new year: "OO," which I hope will not turn out a "naughty" one for you. You terminated your beautiful letter by saying that you feared to weary me, but I wished it had been much longer, as I can learn from you. I have met no man knowing the wiles of women as you do, and you have also the power to set forth your ideas in polished style, which I try in vain to imitate.

You must not be offended if I now take the liberty to put a question to you; and I tell you frankly that I shall not mind if you do not answer it. Do as you think best; whatever you do will be well done.

You write that "your more recent experiences prove that there is no fool like an old fool," and I fully agree with you, taking the lesson for myself, and accepting it as I have accepted other deserved strictures, with the pleasant thought that you take a kindly, friendly interest in me and are writing to me for my good. But it seems to me, and perhaps I am wrong, that you reproach yourself, and one or two sentences are ambiguous and might apply to the writer as well as to the receiver.

To sum up: what are those recent experiences? That is my audacious question.

I now give you my humble opinion of erotic recollections in print, but I fear this letter is far too long. I must ask you, if you take in "Le

Journal," to cast your eye over the *feuilleton: Le Partage du Cœur,** where you will find a good model of psychological writing, where the author seeks to penetrate into the innermost souls of his sensual characters and show the motives, desires, jealousies, etc., that sway them. The adventures should be presented so as to demonstrate the peculiarities of passion, and the downright filthy part only becomes readable when it falls naturally into its place as the outcome of circumstances previously sketched, and which should be out of the common, as rapid sordid encounters and swiftly-ended *passades* with prostitutes are not of the slightest value. Mere meetings of men and women and descriptions of what they do, even if true, are of no use. Those who can throw a light upon the workings of the female mind, when under the influence of lust, real or feigned; or show us what a man feels, thinks, and does when "in the net of the fowler"; or becomes crafty, fights, escapes; or mayhap enjoys the humiliation of his captivity; will be rendering a service to all students of sexuality, surfeited with impossible tales of artificial amours, written to order.

I have just left at your *bureau*, Rue Vissot, a litre of my best Eau de Cologne, as a most trifling wedding present for Madame, and also to prove that whatever my faults, I possess, at least, the *reconnaissance de l'estomac.*

Faithfully yours,
JACKY.

ERIC ARVEL TO JACKY.

Sonis-sur-Marne, December 27, 1899.

My dear Jacky,

Many thanks for your nice long letter and for all the good wishes which I most heartily reciprocate. I hope that the year about to commence will be a happy and prosperous one for you and yours, and that the healing hand of time will efface from your memory all those pains and sorrows which weigh at the moment so heavily upon you.

Mrs. Grundy still holds a certain sway in society, and compelled us both to legitimise those ties which have bound us so close for many years past. Each act is weighed in a certain social balance, and though bell, candle and book were not required to cast any halo about a union

---

* Since issued in one volume: Paris, Fasquelle, 1900, 12mo.

based on mutual inclination, we thought it best to place things on their proper social footing, so that when I have passed over the river on to the other shore, what I may leave will rightly be claimed by the woman who gave herself to me. What I have done was due to the woman who gave up her fair name for me. I am deputed by Mrs. Arvel to offer you her sincere thanks for your present, and to tell you that she has no faults to bring to your door, save the one that you are more happy in the giving than in the getting.

Now to your "audacious query." I do not read any *feuilleton*. I lack the necessary patience to await the *suite à demain*. I told you that any attempt to write the biography of any man as you would have it with the heart laid bare, and the "Sixth Sense" analysed, would raise the cry of "Rats" and "Chestnuts." Every line written would come home to you, and the words inscribed upon the wall at the feast of Belshazzar would haunt your eye for ever more. The recent experiences I allude to are those of later years, the outcome of observation, and of the sayings and doings of those we find on every side, in a world where women discount the vanity and self-assurance of the man, who is about to double the cape of platonic affection. Surely you have analysed the furtive glances of the *trottin*, and the *frôlements* of the woman by your side as you gazed in the shop of jeweller and bonnet-maker? You have not been without knowing how with looks and implied promises the "Sixth Sense" has been cultivated to the highest degree of tension, and then how bitter has seemed the deception which has followed. You may have found the "Sixth Sense" so overstrung by doubts and apprehensions that even when the promised fruit falls ripe to your lips, you close them, not to give admission to the foul thing which will be more sorrowful to the heart and more bitter to the taste than the apple which drove Adam from Paradise. Is there anything new under the sun? Is it not always the old, old story, and what divine hands will ever weave the crown of golden myrtle, which shall adorn the head of the man who can conquer himself, who in the burst of youth can control his passions, and remember how Solomon warned us against the lips of the strange woman and that end which was bitter as wormwood and sharp as a two-edged sword? Have you never studied the philosophy in the old German ballad "Die Handschuh," where the knight courts death to please his lady-love, and then indignant at the peril he has been exposed to at the mere whim of a woman, refuses the reward the proud Cunegonde had in store for him.

"Have you been at the cockles?" Why do you see any stricture in what I write of past and present experience? You do not know what each year will bring forth, and how the human mind becomes more and more as an open book, as age creeps on and desire is fanned to sleep. The time will come for you when each day will bring its lesson, and then you will say with me, not from the experience of the hour, that there is "no fool like the old fool," but from the experience brought about by that spirit of comparison which never deserts us? Who has not been fooled has never sought. The seeking is mere lust; a simple satisfaction of the amour-propre, aroused by the wiles of woman, who is in her heart of hearts a much better judge of humanity than you or I are inclined to believe. How she delights in bringing out the weaknesses of the "idiot" who calls her "the weaker vessel," as though her capacity for giving pleasure did not long outlast that of the man for imparting it. The older the man the more susceptible he becomes to the charms of a sex, which has given him so many pleasant souvenirs in the store-room of his mind. He is easier beguiled; he thinks that Spring and Autumn can be linked together, and when the "Sixth Sense" has been roused, prudence and most of the other virtues are cast to the winds so that the passion of the hour may be indulged in.

"Have you been at the cockles?" Why try to fit the cap of generalities? Experience bitter as wormwood and sharper than a two-edged sword has taught me, not to-day but long since, how readily we embark on the journey to Cythera "as the bird hasteth to the snare knowing not that it is for his life." Will my experience benefit you? If so, you should have it, but the only experience of value is that bought with tears and lamentations, when in the solitude of our chamber we open our hearts and say: "I have sinned."

Recent experiences have I none. I have sunk to anchor in my haven of rest, with plenty of time for reflection, for examining the past, and making the general confession a man makes to himself, when he feels that the time is approaching for him to turn his face to the wall. I have not offered myself as a candidate for the crown of gold and myrtle, and I am as full of those faults and imperfections as any man who is human, and God alone knows if I can affect the same indifference as the good Saint Anthony, when the temptress comes across my path. Perhaps age will by that time have conquered the folie érotique which warps our best intentions, and I shall have sang-froid enough left to ask myself the why and the wherefore of the wiles of her who seeks to ensnare me. Possibly prudence and caution may cause me to ask myself why the appât has been so tempting, and Passion tempered with

Age will enable me to see through the plot made against happiness or honour. Many have succumbed, and if I follow their example I shall only be one of the few who have sacrificed so much to gain so little. Human resolves are as the words which are written on the sand of the sea-shore, and yet there are men cowardly enough to say with their first parent: "The woman who thou gavest to be with me she gave me of the tree and I did eat." When the cup comes to your lips, will you dash it aside and say that there was the warning in the words that "there's no fool like the old fool"? Believe me, it is hard even to aspire to friendships with the young, when a certain period of life is attained, and women have the instinctive desire, the unhealthy curiosity, to see how far they can arouse the old Adam. What are the peculiarities of Passion? Sordid motives on the one part, and vanity on the other. Passion is not devotion, and in my opinion Love only comes when the man has learnt to appreciate the sterling qualities of a woman, apart from the carnal pleasure she can afford him.

I hope my sermon has been long enough, and that you are convinced that when I wrote to you, there was no secret sorrow gnawing at my heart, and no desire to throw stones in the glass house inhabited by my neighbour. Age enables me to philosophise, and when I have time to sit quiet in my own room and review the past, analysing my own feelings, wondering whether I could withstand the smiling promises of the temptress, I am impressed with the wisdom of the man who said there was "no fool like the old fool."

Here on let me again thank you for all your kindness, and good wishes, and hope that the new year may bring you and yours the realisation of every wish.

Yours very truly,
Eric Arvel.

I wrote no more to Mr. Arvel, and ceased sending any papers. I gave no sign of life.

January 1, 1900.

As I awoke on the first morning of the New Year, I received the following from Trixie, and I cannot refrain from giving it here, as it is such a triumph for my theory of true love and affection, which Papa affects to sneer at.

TRIXIE TO JACKY.

Paris, December 31st., 1899.

My dearest friend,

For the last few days I have not had a moment to myself. I wish that all these holidays were passed; they do not amuse me.

Thank you for the pretty paper, it is quite in good taste, like everything that comes from you, and when I use it I shall often think of you, and that will prevent me from gathering my ideas together.

For the year 1900, I send you, with all my heart, my most sincere and best wishes. May it be luckier for you than the one that is gone. For myself, I ask you to keep me a little corner in your heart, for you know that I love you very much.

I want also to tell you once for all, that I will no longer let you put on your little sardonical look, when I say that I love you for yourself,—or, if you like, for myself,—without any desire for money.

I will not let you compare me to other women. I am almost happy that you are hard-up just now, as that gives me the opportunity to show you that I wish to abandon myself to you, entirely, for love, without any other thought than that of making you happy and so becoming myself at the same time the happiest of women.

I have been deprived of your caresses too long; you must never leave me again,—do you hear me, darling? Be good to me, dearest, and let me love you. I will overwhelm you with so many caresses; I will be for you such a perfect sweetheart, that you will be forced to succumb beneath the weight of evidence, and you, who are so straightforward, possessing such perfect common sense; knowing so well how to judge men and women, I want to force you to say to yourself and to me also, that if I have faults, as is only natural, I have no idea of lucre with you.

So see how I am dragged hither and thither: I would that you remain poor, so that you should have the proof that I love you for yourself alone, and at the same time I wish that you were rich and independent. I hope that you may become immensely rich, and yet if that was to happen, I should live under the eternal apprehension of seeing later on that you have the idea that I have only loved you in the hope of being enriched by you. After all, you are only a man. . . . Pardon me if I foresee that you may become like all other men.

To-morrow, on returning from your walk, come and wish me "Good morning," at the post-office, Place Victor Hugo, about 11 o'clock, if you can; I so much wish to see you.

Can you see us on our bicycles this weather? It would be a great success. And your dear muddy, dirty dog I was forgetting! I want to see him too.

A thousand tender things and as many clever and voluptuous kisses,

TRIXIE.

And now, Mr. Prompter, please ring down the curtain. This drama is finished.

The actors wash off their paint; the brown holland is put over the boxes. We go home, and all is dark until the next night.

So it is on the mimic stage, but in life there is no ending to the long succession of comedy and tragedy which is played out in many acts, and is never ended.

Death now and then calls at the stage-door, and one of the players: poor, painted, false villain, or roguish clown; tragedy queen, or meretricious dancing girl; is carried away in the black hearse, but the universal spectacle of love and hate goes on all the same.

Thus with my most vile story. I must break off here, but there is no finish to a real book, such as this is.

When the novel is a mere phantasy, it is easy to dispose of the characters. But this tale being a true one, I can only bow and go, making way for some fresh actor, who is waiting in the wings to caper in the light, when I shall have disappeared, whether I will or no; for I am, and so are you, Reader, in the hands of the Great Scene-Shifter.

JULY 1899.–JANUARY 1900.

END OF VOLUME III

Appendices

Appendix A

PLEASURES OF CRUELTY.

ACCOUNT OF A SCENE WITNESSED IN A WOOD, BY A GENTLEMAN, WHO
HAPPENED TO BE UNSEEN BY THE ACTORS
(EVIDENTLY FATHER AND DAUGHTER).

FATHER.—"Come, my dear, this is a beautifully quiet spot, let me look at your legs."

DAUGHTER.—"Oh! Papa! Papa! What do you mean, you can always see my feet and ankles?"

FATHER.—"That's nothing, I must see more, and teach you to obey me in everything I order; now, lift up your skirts."

DAUGHTER, all blushes.—"Well then, Papa; there's my legs," drawing up her clothes so as fully to expose beautiful well-filled stockings and the ends of finely embroidered drawers: "Is that what you require?"

FATHER.—"Only a little portion of what I want to see," handling her calves and putting his hand up her drawers, "you have sweetly proportioned legs and beautifully firm flesh, my dear; up higher with your skirts, please."

DAUGHTER, scarlet with shame.—"Oh! Oh! Papa! How can you; there, only a little higher, that's all I can do: it's so indelicate," drawing her skirts half-way up her thighs.

FATHER, in a rage.—"Do as I tell you, Miss, do you think I can't

487

examine my own child without her pretending to tell me it's improper!
I will look you all over if I choose to do so, and whip you soundly into
the bargain, Miss Prude!"

DAUGHTER, with tears of shame running down her crimson face.—
"Oh! Papa, Papa, pity me, I never showed so much to anyone before!"
lifting her clothes, so as now to show all her drawers, well up to her
waist, but she stands with her legs so close that nothing is visible.

FATHER.—"That's how you dress, is it? It's time I looked after your
underclothing a little, your chemise is too long," putting his hand between her legs and pulling out the tail of her undermost garment,
"what a pretty little pussey you have, my dear little Miss Bashful, I
suppose you won't let your husband even look at or touch that; why
how beautifully it's covered with this soft hair!" caressing and tickling
the pouting lips with his fingers; "and you're only just over sixteen, you
must have been rubbing your belly against something hairy."

DAUGHTER, in still greater confusion, turns away from him to hide
her mortification, sobbing hysterically.—"Oh! Oh! Papa, Papa. Have
mercy, how can you talk so?"

FATHER, taking out his knife.—"Stand still, Miss Prude, I'm going
to make this chemise the proper length, so as to be a pattern of what
you ought to wear." Then cuts a great piece off back and front so as to
leave her quite exposed where the drawers are a little open, as he purposely leaves them. "You have a fine plump bottom, is it tender? do
you feel that?" giving her a loud slap. "Oh! you can feel, can you; does
it hurt you much?" as she starts with the sudden smart.

DAUGHTER.—"Oh! Oh! Papa! Pray don't, you humiliate me so!"
bursting into fresh hysterical tones.

FATHER.—"Kneel down, and beg my pardon and own that all I do
is proper; there, this place will do very well."

DAUGHTER.—"But that's all mud, I can't kneel there!" (Sobbing.)

FATHER.—"Can't again; will you never do as you're told? Down on
your knees this instant, or I will kill you."

Daughter, in trembling confusion, kneels in the mud crying and
hiding her face in her hands.

FATHER.—"Now, get up, your drawers are only a little soiled,"
laughing at the great patch of mud on her knees; "take my knife and
cut me some of those nice long thin twigs, and ask me to correct you
with them."

She complies, being too frightened and confused not to obey; the
twigs are handed to her father, who ties them up into a nice little
switch; then orders her to kneel on the ground with her bottom towards

him; makes her, with her own hands, hold her drawers well open be-hind for him to inspect her posterior beauties, then makes her pin them back so as they will not close over the exposed rump.

FATHER.—"Now, my dear, you would like me to correct you, would you not, Miss Bashful?"

DAUGHTER.—"Oh! Oh! No. No. Box my ears, anything but that. I've done nothing!"

FATHER.—"You must be made to see your own conduct in the right light: ask me to whip you properly," switching her bottom smartly, and making long red marks at each stroke. "Tell me you wish it or I'll tickle you more and more with this."

DAUGHTER, screaming with pain.—"Oh! Oh! Ah! Papa! I can't bear it, indeed I can't. Oh! Oh! Yes, correct me properly, dear Papa. Oh! Oh! Have mercy," as he cuts harder and harder, drawing little drops of blood from the tender flesh.

FATHER.—"That's right, my dear, you are just beginning to take it in a proper spirit. Oh yes! you can bear it, shriek out, it will do you good," switching away vigorously, and enjoying the wriggling of her rosy-coloured bottom, as each stroke tells its tale: "Confound it! these twigs are not strong enough, they are all breaking to pieces; get up and cut me some better ones, mind you select them well; or I will punish you more and more for it."

The poor girl is almost ready to faint, her bottom smeared with blood from the broken weals; she wants to let down her clothes, but he makes her crawl just as she is to the bushes and cut another birch, en-joying every movement; then when she presents the twigs to him, he makes her kiss them, and tell him, "she hopes he will flog her well for his pleasure and her own good."

FATHER.—"That's right, my dear, I must cut that prudishness out of you; now open your legs well as you kneel, a little more dear," switching her gently at first: "It hurts me as much as it does you, poor dear," cutting harder and raising more weals on her devoted bum.

DAUGHTER.—"Oh! Oh! Papa. Have, have mercy: you're hurting me so! Oh! Oh! I shall die!" as he gives another harder switch, then, "Ah-r-r-r-re," as he cuts under between her legs.

FATHER.—"Does that hurt you so much, dear? I think you had bet-ter drop your drawers quite down. I must hurt you a little more, for your good; that's right, it will do you good," as she screams frantically for "Mercy, Mercy! Oh! Spare me now, Papa."

DAUGHTER, sobbing and crying in most humiliated distress.—"Oh,

Papa! Oh, Papa! I've done everything; you do hurt so, you are so cruel! Ah-r-r-r-re!" as he gives a sharp under-cut on her pussey.

FATHER.—"That's right; scream loudly; I couldn't help touching up your poor little pussey," cutting again and again, in the same place, and all over her poor naked bottom, till it is quite covered with weals and blood-stained all over.

The poor daughter writhes and wriggles with the pain, her sobs and cries get weaker, till at last she fairly faints.

The sight of her inanimate form seems to bring him back to his natural feeling, for he caresses and kisses her, calling her "his darling victim of a daughter, poor thing, poor thing," etc., and as soon as she revives a little, conducts her from the scene.

The Pleasures of Cruelty. Constantinople (London), 1896, 8vo.

Appendix B

THE DOUBLE LIFE.

(MY ADDITIONS TO THE PREFACE.)

. . . That I was an incestuous father, I admit, but I shall go to my grave happy in the knowledge that I made my daughter's life a happy one. Her last words of love were for her father. She died in my arms and when I lay down my pen in a few moments as the sun sets, I'll take my hat and stick, and slowly climb the hill that leads to the little shady churchyard where Innocent sleeps her last sweet childlike sleep.

I am very old and racked with pains of gout, but I'll rest myself upon a neighboring tomb and gaze at her grave until the light fails, and as I read and read her name cut in the stone, I feel once more as I do at each daily pilgrimage that our incest is forgiven because our great and veracious love had nothing base about it.

When I can no longer climb up to the restingplace of my child, my own daughter, my flesh and blood that was sweetheart, wife, concubine and devoted whore to me her father, I shall be ready to stand before my Maker who will pardon me in his infinite clemency. And you must fain forgive me, reader, for she forgave me long ago and felt no remorse or shame.

May I live to finish this book and join my girl for all eternity. Amen.

CUTHBERT COCKERTON,
Attorney-at-law.
Brighthelmston, July 1798.

Appendix C

SPRAGUE v. LIHME.

(DIVORCE CASE.) London, 1899.

Mr. Justice Barnes, in directing the jury, said that the case was a difficult one for them to determine, because of the relations which for many years had existed between the parties. It was for the petitioner to satisfy them that the case had been made out.

It was not necessary to give direct evidence of misconduct, because it was not often that the accused parties were caught in *flagrante delicto*; but if familiarity, opportunity, and other circumstances were shown, they might legitimately be asked to draw the inference that adultery had been committed.

They must not, however, act upon surmise or suspicion, but must have evidence upon which to draw their inference, at the same time considering the relationship of the parties which had existed for many years, because, had it not been for that earlier intimacy, the case might have assumed a very different aspect.

Appendix D

"In the infidelities that Saint-Fond allows, there is a feeling of debauchery. . . . Saint-Fond enjoys the idea of knowing that you are in the arms of another; he puts you there himself and has an erection so to see you; you multiply his delights by the extension you give to your own, and you will be always more loved by Saint-Fond, when you do to the utmost that which would arouse the hatred of another."

The heroine replies:

"Saint-Fond will like my tastes, my wit, my humour, and will not be jealous of my body! Oh! how that thought consoles me; for I confess to you, my friend, that continence would be impossible for me. My nature must be satiated at all costs; with my impetuous blood . . . with the imagination you know of, how can I resist these passions which are irritated and inflamed by everything!"—*La Nouvelle Justine ou les Malheurs de la vertu, suivie de l'Histoire de Juliette, sa sœur.* En Hollande, 1797. 10 vols. 18mo. (Pp. 82–83, Vol. 6.)

Appendix E

CESAREE.

This is the simple title of a novel by Edmond Tarbé, a successful author and journalist, turning upon the reciprocal passion of a father and daughter, as embodied in the diary of the former. It is carefully and delicately worked out and the style is perfect. The book was never published. While the first edition was in the press, in 1891, the publishers —the well-known house of Lévy, Paris,—were informed that the subject was one totally unsuited to their *clientèle*. The work of printing was put a stop to, and the author tore up his contract and took the few copies that were finished. These he gave away to his friends and none were ever sold. It is now very rare.

The daughter-heroine, Césarée, is twenty, and her father forty, when they go away on a little trip to Switzerland. They have never lived together, the father having left her when a baby.

The writer describes the pleasure the girl feels at being all alone with her adored father, when they are taken for husband and wife.

The first night they are alone together, they have two bedrooms, communicating, and Césarée begs her Pa to do his writing in her chamber, while she is in bed, reading. He obeys her, and when all is quiet, she gets up and forces him to let her read his diary, where she sees to her delight that he loves her madly. He declares that he fears his passion and she answers:

"There is a barrier which we must never pass. To break it down would be the signal of certain remorse and shame that neither you nor I could resign ourselves to support. But in front of this barrier, we find all liberty of love, and I invite you fearlessly to feasts where our hearts will find satisfactions, which are quite great enough. . . .

"*I am your daughter* . . . that is to say, you cannot renew with me the work that brought me into the world. I am your daughter! . . .

"But if, because I am your daughter, the consummation of our passion is forbidden to us both; on the other hand, because I am your daughter, I belong entirely to your sterile embraces. I am your thing, created by you, animated by you . . .

"Believe in that love and give yourself up to it, father, with complete joy, as I abandon myself to it, proudly and without remorse."

He takes her in his arms and thus describes what he does:

"With a single caress, my hands and my lips at the same time covered her shuddering flesh with one long kiss, embracing her whole soul at once. Passive and silent, as if nearly dead, she thus received in a few ardently-lived moments, the reward of her two years of secret adoration. From the moisture of her outstretched limbs, the perfume that I found twice more, mounted to my brain and penetrated it, in intoxicating emanations. Now I drank it, as it were."

After a variety of charming episodes, poor little Césarée commits suicide and dies a virgin.

Appendix F

AN INFAMOUS FATHER.

Victor Blanvillain, a workman, 38, living at Chatenay, 22, rue des Prés-Hauts, is the father of ten children, of which seven are girls. A few days ago, M. Cuvillier, commissary of police at Sceaux, received an anonymous letter informing him that Blanvillain had inflicted horrible treatment on five of his daughters, of the ages of sixteen, thirteen, twelve, ten, and nine.

After a rapid enquiry, which confirmed the accusation of the letter, the commissary informed the justices in Paris, who ordered a supplementary investigation and charged M. Joly, judge of instruction, to follow up the affair.

This magistrate, after hearing a certain number of witnesses, and having no longer the least doubt of the guilt of Blanvillain, who, besides, had made a partial confession, issued a warrant against the unworthy father.

The workman was at once arrested and taken to the Dépôt; but nevertheless his capture had been made as discreetly as possible, as it was feared that the indignant population of Chatenay might lynch the scoundrel.

Blanvillain's wife is mad with grief, and finds herself with her children in the most cruel position, having nothing to live on but the meagre earnings of her vile husband.

The wretched woman seems in despair and only the advice of the magistrates and the promise of assistance have given her a little energy.

Le Petit Journal, Paris, April 9, 1899.

Appendix G

TETE-A-TETE.

. . . One evening, Monsieur Le Hardeur, who up till then had shown himself almost like a father, frightened me and disgusted me with him to such an extent that I was very nearly calling for the help of the servant-girls of the restaurant where we were dining *tête-à-tête*; or else I should have foolishly jumped out of a window.

. . . It was fearfully hot. I had taken off my hat and slightly opened my surah blouse.

I forgot to eat or drink as I gazed upon the summer sky. . . . I must have been quite lost. I am sure I had the eyes of a little girl examining pretty coloured pictures, one by one.

And I perceived too late that my godfather had emptied two bottles of sparkling Asti, one after the other, and for the last few seconds had been examining me and looking me up and down with the fixed stare of a drunken horse-dealer.

"Hullo there! It's no fun to dine in front of one's napkin," cried he, suddenly. "Do you go in for the beauties of nature?"

I turned round in a fright and I thought he was going to have a fit.

With half-closed eyelids, his cheeks shining and pimply, he stammered out:

"You mustn't leave a poor man all by himself . . . a poor man who has never done anybody any harm; especially as,—as—"

He interrupted himself to breathe noisily, as if invisible hands had tightened his high, starched collar.

"Especially as you are superior to your mamma in every way. 'Pon my word, that madcap Fripette never had such a complexion. Roses in milk. And that head of hair! Silken rings, and so light, so golden, so well planted!"

I imitated in spite of myself his husky tone of voice, and replied with effrontery:

"And what's the next article, sir?"

He was not put out for so little.

"And she has already got hips, the little minx, and love-apples in her basket. First prize for beauty: Mademoiselle Jeannine Margelle? Ninette for her godfather, her excellent little godfather. Drop a nice curtsey to the gentleman, before you get your prize and a kiss."

He had jumped up and thrown himself on me so treacherously that I had not had time to avoid the odious embrace of his arms, and the caress of his wine-bedewed lips.

I struggled against him; I tried to scratch him; I insulted him; vexed, humiliated, trembling with rage and emotion, he let me go at last as if come back to his senses, and half-sobered, growled:

"Confound it! I'm only a juggins, a jay! The jay of jays, to put myself in this state for nothing at all. Yes, I say so, for nothing. Not that you are too young. After all, at seventeen, your confirmation has been over long ago. It's the age when you could take an excursion ticket without fear of accidents."

He took his seat at table again, threw himself back on the chair, quite cheerful, the thumbs in the armholes of his waistcoat of white piqué with blue spots.

"Oh, don't think I'm not inclined to start the game! Unfortunately, it's impossible—the danger signal is up; the line's blocked; I'm condemned for life. People would talk, and there would be too much gossip about the respectable Monsieur Le Hardeur. At the next elections, I should be left alone in my glory. And all that because a lot of people imagine that I worked at your existence; that you are probably my daughter. Yes, Ninette, my own offspring of the left hand. What silly tales get about! And yet there's not a word of truth in it all!"

I was leaning against the window sill, with the impression that I was listening to the ravings of a fool.

"I've compared dates, I've turned over dirty linen like a detective.

There were a pair of us, Flochet and I; two masters, each with the key, slippers and toothbrush. Flochet was only there for show. I had the best of it. But Fripette betrayed us both by the job, hour, day and week, with a fine soldier, an officer of the Cent Gardes, or the Empress's lancers, I don't remember exactly. How could a simple civilian fight, in those days, with the prestige of the sabre, or struggle against the points of waxed moustaches. *Ferrum est quod amant.* You don't understand? No matter, it's Latin for men. So I heard the cry of the cuckoo, and I was a cuckold, as no man has ever been before or since. I am sure of it; I'll show you the letters. Sad recollections; grief; wounds received in action. Q. E. D. that you are the daughter of the handsome soldier and not mine. If it was not that everybody thought the contrary at my club, the little business might have been brought off in the bosom of one's family, but Monsieur Le Hardeur does not possess the right to brave the world's opinion. That's as clear as clean water!"

I was silent; I felt more inclined to cry than to laugh.

Le Journal, Paris, May 17, 1899.

(This episode is from a novel by René Maizeroy, which was begun in the columns of the Parisian daily paper I have stated and was left unfinished.

It was the story of a "cocotte's" bastard daughter, who eventually is destined by her two fathers to practise for the stage and is introduced to a crowd of Lesbians and courtesans. The story broke off at that juncture but was afterwards published under the title of *Amuseuse*, Paris, Nilsonn, 1900, 12mo, illustrated with photographs.)

Appendix H

NOTES FROM THE GAY CITY, by Eric Arvel.

(Extract from "The London Stock Exchange Magazine," June 1899.)

". . . a steady tide of visitors sets in towards the 'City of Pleasure,' the Mecca of the man whose imagination has been fired by the songs and gestures of the Parisian singers and dancers, but who too often on his arrival at the goal of his desire finds everything as flat and dull as the proverbial ditch water, for I know no more prosaic place than Paris under the Republic. The old animation of the boulevards is like the ball at the Opéra during the Carnival—existing simply in the minds of those who have read the memoirs published by men prior to the days of Nestor Roqueplan. The Jardin de Paris, although Oller is always up to date in his attempts to cater for the visitors, is but a very modernised imitation of Cremorne, and the old Jardin Mabille, where Rigolboche and Finette preceded the ladies who delight in such names as 'Grille d'Egout.'

" 'Nini Patte en l'Air,' and 'La Goulue,' has disappeared for want of patronage. Tradition seems to impress English tourists with the legend of Paris; but small wonder that most of them declare on their return that they prefer London to Paris for everything: cooking, drinking, and all the comforts money should purchase when the Briton is on his travels or bound for enjoyment. The summer holidays are the harvest time of those shameless individuals: the touts for all that is bad and vile in a city where men avow deeds so carefully hidden by Pharisees on the other side of the Channel. The police are too busy hunting up small political conspirators to think of arresting thieves, much less these men, who are the purveyors of clandestine places resorted to by foreigners, who often carry their lives in their hands, and owe their safety to the generosity to which they are prompted by the surroundings."

Appendix I

DIVORCE AMONG THE PEOPLE.

". . . And now with regard to girls:

"You know in what conditions of deplorable promiscuity the little people of Paris live. The whole family sleeps in two beds, in the same room.

"As long as the real father is there, we may hope that some remains of instinctive shame will prevent him from showing his children certain sights, from which we turn away our thoughts.

"But what happens when the mother, who cannot live on her own earnings, has started house-keeping with a second husband or a lover? What examples do you think will then be given to the little girls?

"They may think themselves lucky if, one day when the mother has gone out to market, the drunkard, as yet bewildered by the debauch of the preceding evening, does not violate them.

"I know what I am talking about. In the very poor working classes, there is no physical virginity after the age of fourteen."—*Le Bilan du Divorce*, by Hugues Le Roux.

Le Figaro, Paris, April 28, 1899. (Since published in book form.)

Appendix J

THE ALLEGED OFFENCE.

UNDER THE CRIMINAL LAW AMENDMENT ACT.

At the Wimbledon Police-Court, a clerk, 33 years of age, now living at 132, Arngask Road, Catford, but formerly of 153, Hartfield Road, was charged on remand with unlawfully and carnally knowing his stepdaughter, Maud Frances Lacey, on various dates between March 1898 and March 1899.

Prisoner has been remanded from time to time for the appearance of his wife. That lady now appeared and denied that she had made any statement to the police beyond saying she was of a nervous and jealous disposition, and very much annoyed at certain things that had occurred between prisoner and her daughter. On many occasions she had caught the pair kissing, once surreptitiously, and this made her extremely jealous, as she thought the girl received attentions which ought to have been paid to herself, and actuated by this she communicated with the police with the idea of getting them separated. Witness gave a direct denial to the most essential points of the girl's evidence.

The girl also went into the box, and denied some of her previous evidence.

Mr. Matthews pointed out that no jury would convict on such evidence.

Mr. Meates said he did not feel disposed to take the responsibility on himself of allowing the case to drop through.

Mr. Matthews, after arguing the legal points of the case at some length, said there was absolutely no corroboration. Prisoner's wife was a jealous woman, who would not suffer her husband to kiss his step-daughter, and that jealousy was her motive for acting as she had was apparent from the fact that she had contradicted all the most vital points of the girl's evidence. If the case was sent for trial it would in-volve a repetition of a most unsavoury story, which must already have become indelibly impressed on the young girl's mind. Besides, no public advantage would be gained by such a course, and therefore, in the in-terests of public morality, he ventured to suggest that the case should be dismissed.

Mr. Meates said that a man in the position of father and husband, such as prisoner was, must be able to bring an enormous influence to bear on the witnesses, traces of which there had been all through the hearing. He must, therefore, adhere to what he had already said, and prisoner would be committed for trial at the Central Criminal Court.

"The Illustrated Police Budget," London, May 27, 1899.

Appendix K

"The Bonapartes have been very much in view lately on account of a book, recently published, consisting of reports of Louis XVIII's secret agents in Paris during the Consulate in 1802 and 1803. This period is one of the most interesting in French history. Napoleon was in the very prime of his vigour and genius. His power was felt by the whole of Europe, while at home he was rebuilding what the Revolution had over-thrown.

"Napoleon's private character is painted in the blackest colours, in a way that only certain pages of the press with regard to Dreyfus to-day can equal. Hortense Bonaparte, wife of Louis, and stepdaughter of Napoleon, forms the subject of a report, her child being said to be the son of her stepfather. Talleyrand's marriage is related very spiritedly."

"Society," July 22, 1899.

(See *Relation Secrète des Agents de Louis XVIII.*—Paris, Plon, 1899.)

Appendix L

CONDEMNED TO DEATH.

Montbrison, 18th June.

Bordes, a workman in a foundry, has been condemned to death by the assize-court of the Loire. He murdered his daughter aged ten, and his wife. Bordes had incestuous intimacy with the little girl and un-natural connection with his wife. The assassin lived sixty-five days alone with the corpses of his victims, and it has been plainly shown that he slept on the dead body of his daughter.

The culprit feigned not to know what impulse he had obeyed in killing his wife and child, but the medical testimony was unanimous as to his entire responsibility.

Les Droits de l'Homme, June 19, 1899.

(For the benefit of my readers I may add that this revolting crimi-nal was beheaded on the morning of August 7th., and he died with great courage. He asked for a mass to be performed; confessed his crimes; asked for pardon; had a cup of coffee; lit a cigar, and boldly ascended the scaffold of the guillotine.)

Appendix M

A HORRIBLE CRIME.

(From our own correspondent.)—Charleroi, July 3.

Charles Lechien, a tinker, living at Jumet, was the father of six children, three being girls.

For several years past he had indulged in criminal intimacy with the eldest of his daughters, Marie, nineteen years of age.

Yesterday Lechien met his daughter at the fair of Gesselies, in the company of a young man. This caused him to be terribly jealous.

Last night, all the family were asleep in three beds, in the same room.

Lechien got up and fired three shots of a revolver at his eldest daughter, wounding her in the temple. Marie was killed instantaneously in her sleep and died without making a movement.

Her mother and the other children jumped out of bed and tried to disarm the father, but Lechien had had the time to put two bullets in his head and he then shot his last cartridge at his wife, but missed her.

The pistol now being empty, the murderer, covered in blood, wished to force one of his sons to give him some more cartridges, but he, on the contrary, got the weapon away from him.

Lechien had strength enough left to take to flight; he went and threw himself in the canal of Sars-les-Moines. His corpse was recovered this morning.

Le Petit Journal, Paris, July 4, 1899.

Appendix N

"Jean had been a master at Rocton, my father's school; he had left suddenly, and rumour said because he had been over-attentive to my mother. Jean Messel, my lover, had been, according to the gossip, my mother's lover also. Possibly it was only an idle tale, but as I watched the urbane Mr. Osborne placidly smoking his cigarette, I could not think that he was the man to speak lightly and at random on so serious a subject. Then again, Jean's hitherto inexplicable terror of my father; everything seemed to fit in. It was all very horrible, and my brain reeled as the thoughts rushed through it. I tried hard to disbelieve, but more and more surely the conviction became strong in me that it was true, and that this man, whose kisses had been so sweet upon my lips, had, twenty years ago, kissed the lips of my mother, the mother whose remembrance I cherished, through all my wickedness, beyond anything else on earth. The image of Jean, smiling, debonnaire, and handsome, swam in the misty curtain that hung before my eyes, and a great loathing for him rose up in my heart.

"The vision of the old red schoolhouse at Rocton, and the sundial garden, with its carven hedges, where I used always to imagine my mother walking, was continually with me; but now there was another figure in the garden—Jean, as I imagined him to have been twenty years

ago, as handsome as a man could be. And then his arm came to be
about my mother's waist; but, oh! the picture was too dreadful, and I
ran about the room in despairing efforts to distract my mind."

"The Confessions of Nemesis Hunt."—
"SOCIETY," London, August 12, 1899.

Appendix O

At the assizes of Troyes, Carlier, for indecently assaulting his
daughter who he had forced to be his mistress for nearly six years was
condemned to twelve years penal servitude.

Le Journal, Paris, August 12, 1899.

Appendix P

AWFUL STORY OF
A DAUGHTER'S SHAME.

One of the most horrible stories of immorality that could possibly
be conceived was unfolded at the village of Cleasby, before Dr. J. S.
Walton, coroner, Northallerton. It appears that a young woman named
Margaret Eleanor Stott, aged 23, was delivered of twins a fortnight ago,
alleging the paternity of them to her father, a decrepit-looking old man
of 74 years. Whether they were born dead or alive was open to question,
but it seems that they didn't live long, for they were in the first instance placed in a box under the bed, then removed to an outhouse, and
finally the whole circumstances revealed owing to the mother going to
the vicar to ascertain if they could be properly buried in the churchyard. A sister, who should have proved an important witness as to the
disposal of the bodies, and in fact as to whether the children were born
alive, died the previous day. How it was the police were so long in obtaining information is rather strange, seeing that the affair has been the
common gossip of the village for nearly a fortnight; in fact, the strange

doings of the family have frequently been the cause of a good deal of gossip.

After briefly stating the facts to the jury, the coroner called:

Margaret Eleanor Stott, who stated that the children were hers by her father. They were born a fortnight ago that day, and at the birth the only person present was her sister Martha, who had died the day previously, and with whom she was sleeping. Witness had had another child two years ago, and it was still living, but the father of that was a young man at Darlington. Witness sent another sister for Mrs. Turnbull, but she was too busy to come, and no one else was sent for. This last sister referred to was but fourteen years of age, and she was sleeping with her father at the time. There were two rooms in the house, with beds in each of them. The occupants of the house were her father, herself, and two sisters and two boys. The sister who had died was nineteen, whilst the boys were aged four and two respectively. As the newly-born children did not move, her deceased sister picked them up, and put them in a little box under the bed, where they remained a day or two, after which her father buried them. Witness did not see him, but the sister who is dead told her. Witness dug them up last Monday night, and put them in a little house. In the afternoon of the same day Mrs. Smedley warned her that she would get wrong, and she then went to the vicar and asked if she could bury them in the churchyard. In reply to the coroner, she said she did not think the churchyard was the proper place at first. The boy in the house two years of age was hers, whilst the other boy belonged to an unmarried sister, Mary, aged 21.

The Rev. T. Churchyard, vicar of Cleasby, stated that the first witness came to him at seven o'clock last Monday evening, and wanted to bury a "still-born child." Witness asked her a few questions, as he had heard rumours in the village about the girl's father's conduct with her. He communicated with Dr. Johnson, of Darlington, who had attended the family, but he was from home. In the meantime he communicated with the guardian for the village, stating that he could not bury the child, and asked what he was to do. The guardian communicated with the police.

Dr. Walker, of Aldbrough, spoke to having seen the bodies that morning; but they were in such a decomposed state that he could not tell whether they had been born dead or alive.

After Jennie Stott, aged 14, had stated that she did not know the children were buried in the garden.

The jury expressed a desire to hear what the father had to say.

A police constable having requisitioned him, he replied, in answer to the Coroner, that he "knew nothing about 'em, but he was blamed for being the father of the children." Continuing, he said he first heard of it between ten and twelve o'clock on the day they were born. Martha, the deceased daughter, told him that Maggie was confined, and she said there were two children, both dead. He saw them the same morning, when they were put in a box in the bedroom where the daughter was. He next saw them in an outhouse three days afterwards, and in a callous, laughing manner, he exclaimed that he "took a look after them to see that the cats didn't get at them." They were taken through the garden into the house. He had nothing to do with them, and they were never buried by anyone. He certainly never saw anyone bury them. Again assuming a laughing air, he said: "I took blame for them myself; they might be mine. I am blamed for it, but don't know."

The Coroner, intervening, said he was not asking the witness what he was blamed for. He was a disgrace, and a good horsewhipping about his back would do him good. (Witness laughingly assented.) You are a disgrace to be their father, and your conduct here to-day is a disgrace also. I have done with you, you can go.

As the witness seemed in no hurry to go, he was removed from the court, the Coroner observing that the man had become such a sinner that he did not know what sin was.

The Foreman observed that it was generally understood in the village that all the children belonged to the old man.

The Coroner: For over forty years I have fulfilled the duties of coroner over this district, and during that time I have had many singular and serious cases in hand, but never during the whole course of my career have I heard of one to be compared with the rascality of that old villain. It is a wonder that the old women in the village did not take him and put him in the water. He added that he had intended to send a memorial to the Home Office on the subject, and it would be advisable for the jury to back him up. The old man was not worth talking to. He was nothing but a brute, and it was strange that in this country a man could seduce his own children without being punished, and there was no means of getting at him. A law for such offences did exist about 1650, but it had been repealed. He would write to the Home Secretary on the subject.

A verdict was then returned in accordance with the medical evidence to the effect that there was nothing to show whether the children had had a separate existence or not.

Subsequently the old man was brought back and severely lectured by the Coroner, who told him that in the whole course of his career he had never met with a bigger brute, or a more thorough old rascal. If the old women had tossed him into the Tees they would only have done their duty. (Applause.)

"The Illustrated Police Budget," London, August 26, 1899.

Appendix Q

INFAMOUS ACTS.

LA FERTÉ.—Recently we announced the arrest and condemnation of a young girl of fifteen, named Vial, living in the hamlet of Courcelles, charged with indecent exposure. It will be remembered that this girl had shown herself in a complete state of nudity.

The gendarmes, continuing their enquiry, have found against the girl Vial facts of such gravity and of such odious obscenity that we cannot give the details here.

The girl Vial and one of her friends, Jeanne Mahé, used two children nine years old to satisfy their mad passions; they had Lesbian habits, and the evidence of Louis Gabriel Vial and his sister Alice is frightful.

Gabriel Vial is own brother to the condemned girl!

Journal de Seine-et-Marne, September 14, 1899.

Appendix R

Monsieur Coudol has had a lucky escape! Monsieur Coudol, from Nantes, is fifty-six. In 1885, he got legitimately mated, but, inconstant and changeable, he soon abandoned his wife, who obtained a separation.

Monsieur Coudol then came to Paris. He was employed at the Montagnes Russes, then at the Moulin Rouge. Monsieur Coudol likes gaiety.

In this latter establishment lived a female dresser. Pretty? History is dumb on that point. Young? Still blooming, albeit she had a daughter of nineteen.

Monsieur Coudol fell in love with the dresser, madly in love. And when he learnt that the young girl had no father, he offered to legitimize her by marrying her mamma.

The household lived peaceably.

Nevertheless, one fine day, the dresser got tired. Her husband had become insupportable. And did she not engage her affections elsewhere too? But what pretext could be invented to obtain a fine divorce?

Allow me to draw a gauzy veil.

The dresser confided her wish to her daughter.

The daughter made it her duty to help her mother. Together, they organized the indispensable little *flagrant délit*. The legitimized girl consented to play the principal part.

Monsieur Coudol fell into the trap. Two coachmen, taken as witnesses, bore testimony to the affair.

A demand for divorce was registered by Madame Coudol, of Paris, and during the suit the discovery of Madame Coudol, of Nantes, was made.

The bigamist of the Moulin Rouge has just been tried. But he pleaded with such good faith his ignorance of the difference that exists between separation and divorce that he benefited by a verdict of acquittal.

He won't be caught again!

Le Figaro, Paris, October 21, 1899.

Appendix S

"As for the adventure of Mademoiselle Rosine, of whom I spoke to you and which I got from being intimate with Victoire, it is far from being funny. Imagine that she is the daughter of a very rich jeweller. Naturally, we do not know the name, nor even in which quarter is the shop.

"She is just turned eighteen, and the father is a man of forty-four. I tell you the age, you shall see why by and bye. Well then, the jeweller's wife dies and do you know how he arranged matters to replace her?

"Two months after the burial, one fine night, he goes and seeks his daughter Rosine. He quietly sleeps with her. That's a bit thick anyhow, isn't it? Such goings-on are not uncommon among poor people, I know more than one at Grenelle who has been through the same thing, but among middle-class folks who have got money enough to treat themselves to all the women they want! And what sticks in my gizzard more than anything is not that the fathers ask for it, but that the daughters consent to it.

"Now Mademoiselle is so sweet, so amiable, that doubtless she did not wish to let her Papa suffer. Never mind, here they are both nicely trapped. They have placed her here as if in a prison. Nobody comes to see her, and you may well think that orders are given to juggle the child away. A fine bastard who will be able to show off in society!"

Fécondité, by Emile Zola, Paris,
Fasquelle, 1899, 12mo. (P. 181).

Appendix T

The Yellow Room

TABLE OF CONTENTS

"There is nothing, I am convinced by several years' experience, so good for a girl as a thorough good flogging administered upon her bare bottom with an elastic birch, she having been compelled to take off her own drawers herself."

Extract from a letter of mrs. B. H***n.

CHAPTER I

SIMPLICITY SHOCKED.

"Come in," said Coupeau. "No one will eat you!"

—L'ASSOMMOIR.

When the widowed aunt of Miss Alice Darvell, with whom she had been living for several years in Yorkshire, died, her residence was transferred to her nearest relative and guardian's house in Suffolk. And the change from a small house in a bleak and lonely part of the West Riding to a baronet's establishment was hailed with rapture by the handsome and healthy girl of eighteen. The only, or at any rate, the principal, advantage gained by her life with her aunt was one she scarcely appreciated. The life, the bracing air, the country rambles, and the rigorous punctuality of the old lady had allowed Miss Darvell to fully develop all the physical charms which so distinguished her. And not only that, to the fresh complexion, the laughing brown eyes, and the magnificent contour of her form and of her limbs was added a distracting air of reckless ingenuousness, picked up no doubt in her moorland scampers. But become conscious of her charms, she sighed for the pomps and vanities of the world. They were held up to her by her aunt as perils of the deadliest description—a view regarded by Alice with sceptical curiosity. Her solitude increased her imaginative faculty, and the fascination it attached to balls, parties and life generally in the world was greater than their charm actually warrants, as Alice subsequently found out. The only disquiet she had experienced arose from a vague longing which was satisfied by none of the small events in her puritanical life. She was modest even to prudishness; had long worn dresses of such a length as to make them remarkable; had never in her life had a low one on; blushed at the mention of an ankle, and would have fainted at the sight of one. The matter of sex was a perpetual puzzle to her, but she was perfectly unembarrassed in her intercourse with men, and quite unconscious of the desires she excited in them. All she knew of Sir Edward Bosmere of Bosmere Hall was that he was her trustee and guardian; that he was a widower much older than herself, a cousin some degrees removed from her, but that, notwithstanding, she called him "Uncle."

Thither then she went. Sir Edward turned out to be a man of about fifty; very determined in his manner, powerfully built, and of a middle height. But what surprised Alice most was to find herself introduced to a tall, dark girl, who looked about two and twenty, as his housekeeper. She was dressed in exquisite fashion, but Alice thought most indecently, and she, too, called Sir Edward "Uncle."

The first few days were taken up in making acquaintance, but Alice was surprised one morning at breakfast to see Maud grow very pale when told by Sir Edward, that she was to go to the yellow room after breakfast, and that she was to go straight there. This direction was in consequence of some cutlets which were served at the meal being slightly overcooked; and when Alice again saw Maud she was flushed and excited, and appeared to have been crying her eyes out. In some consternation, she inquired what the yellow room was, and the only reply she obtained was that she would find out soon enough. On the same occasion, when Maud had left the breakfast-room, Sir Edward, who had by that time quite taken in Alice, told her he thought she dressed in a very dowdy fashion, and said he had given directions to their maid to provide a more suitable wardrobe for her. The girl was covered with blushes and confusion when he spoke of her dressing like Maud. Now Maud showed a great deal of leg and of other charms; so Alice tried to pull herself together and reply that she really could do no such thing. Sir Edward looked at her in a very peculiar way, and said he felt sure her present mode of dress hid the loveliest neck and limbs in the world. He went on to ask whether she did not admire Maud's style of dress, and if she had noticed her stockings and drawers.

"I have indeed, uncle; but I could never wear anything like them."

"And why not, pray?"

"I should be so ashamed."

"We will soon cure you of that. We punish prudish young women here by shortening their petticoats. How do you like the idea?"

"Not at all; and I will not have anything of the sort done to me."

"I am afraid, miss, you want a whipping."

"I should like" (defiantly) "to know who would dare such a thing."

Sir Edward again looked at her in a peculiar manner, but said nothing more on the subject. Simply observing that he thought it right that young women should learn how to manage a house before they had one of their own and did not know what to do with it, he said she and Maud were to take the management in turn weekly, and that a week from that day she would have to do so.

"In the meantime, my dear, you had better learn as much as you can from Maud; especially not to let them burn cutlets like these." Saying which, he left the room.

At this point the narrative can best be continued by Alice Darvell herself:

"*Wed., July* 3, 188***.—As soon as uncle had left the breakfast-table, I felt quite disturbed, but on the whole determined to go on as if nothing had happened. A message came a little later by our maid from Maud to say that she could not go out riding as we had arranged. What a terrible woman our "maid" is! Why on earth does uncle have a Scotch-woman of so terrible an aspect for us two girls? She makes you quake if she only looks at you. Well, I made up my mind to go alone; and rode off very soon after.

On my return I met Maud, very red, and looking as though she had been crying dreadfully. She would not tell me what had happened. The rest of the day passed in the usual way We drove out after lunch, paid some visits, received several at our kettle-drum, dressed for dinner; and while waiting for the gong to sound Maud came to me, and to my horror began talking upon precisely the same subject Sir Edward had been speaking to me about at breakfast.

"Uncle does not approve of your dresses, you little prude, and Janet (the Scotch maid) has another one for you."

"If Janet," said I, "has a dress for me like yours, showing my neck and breasts and back, and my feet, my ankles, my legs—I mean like yours—I declare flatly I won't wear it."

"Don't be a fool, dear. I am mistress this week; you will be next week, as uncle has explained to you, and if you do not get rid of your ridiculous shame you will be soundly punished. You may be thankful if you are only obliged to show your legs up to your knees and your bosom down to your breasts. That is all.'

"I do not care. I have never been punished."

"Very well," said Maud; "have your own way. You will soon know better."

When I got down, there were uncle and Maud, three or four young men, and some very handsome women in low dresses, every one; I was the only one in a high dress. Uncle said something to Maud, who whispered to me that I was to go with her. As soon as we got into the hall, she told me I was to be taken to the yellow room and that I was a goose. I asked her why; she only laughed. Arrived there, she said she was very sorry, but must obey orders. She then strapped my hands firmly behind my back. My struggles were useless in the end, but kept her so long that she said, "I shall take care that you shall have an extra half-dozen for this." I could not think what she meant. It got darker, and still no one came. The yellow room was in an out-of-the-way wing, and I heard the tower clock strike ten. My hands behind me began to hurt, and I began to lose my temper. I wondered how long I was to be kept there, and then who had the right to keep me; and supposed it was called the yellow room because the curtains of the windows, the valances, and the bed-curtains were all yellow damask, and then I wondered what the ottoman, such an enormous one, was doing here, in company with a heavy oak table, a bar swinging from the ceiling, and—what with vexation and impatience I went to sleep.

I was awakened about half-past eleven by carriages driving off. It was pitch dark, and the curtains had been drawn. I know it was about half-past eleven because about half-an-hour later midnight struck. There was a footstep in the corridor, and uncle came in. He said:—

"I am extremely surprised at your insubordination, miss, for which I am about to punish you." What followed I cannot write.

So much for that part of the diary. Later on, by way of penance, as the sequel will show, Miss Alice Darvell was compelled to write out the minutest description of her punishments and her sensations and secret thoughts.

What happened was this; Sir Edward Bosmere at once informed Alice that he would have no more prudish nonsense; that he was going to strip her and flog her soundly, when he had first obtained a promise from her to take off her own drawers—a very important humiliation to which to subject a proud young beauty. She protested in the most vehement manner.

"He had no right to whip her; she would not be whipped by any man or anyone else; he was at once to undo her hands; being kept all the evening in that room without any dinner was quite punishment enough; she did not know why she had been punished; she would not wear horrid dresses which only served to make nakedness conspicuous; and if she was going to be treated in this way, she would go away tomorrow." "As to promising to take off her own drawers, and before him, he must be mad to think of such a thing, and she would die first."

She looked lovely in her fury, and an alteration in the surface of Sir Edward's trousers showed his appreciation of her beauty. He longed to see her naked and all her charms revealed.

"I will not dispute with you, you saucy miss, and your face is too pretty to slap; I will settle accounts with your bottom—yes, your bottom, and a pretty plump white bottom I have no doubt it is. I can promise you, however, it won't be white long. Now lie across that ottoman on your face. What? you won't? Well, across my knee will do as well, and perhaps better."

Putting his arm round her waist, he dragged the girl with him to the sofa, telling her that her shrieks and struggles in that heavily-curtained and thickly carpeted room were of no avail; that even if they were heard no one would pay attention to them, and that the only result would be, if she went on, to double her punishment. He did not, however, at that moment wish to do more than examine the charms that were so jealously concealed, the magnificence of which might be easily guessed from the little that did appear of her figure. He walked her to the sofa and sat down upon it, still holding her by the waist, and then, putting her between his legs, pulled her down across his left one. Her power of resistance was very much lessened by her hands being strapped behehind her, but still she managed to slide down upon her knees in front of him instead of being laid across his lap. He then held her tightly between his knees and proceded to unfasten the neck of her dress, and as the buttons were at the back he was obliged to put his arms round her and draw her so close that he felt her warm pressure upon him. The passion he felt was intensified, and the girl then, for the first time, seemed in a hazy sort of wonder as to whether the treatment she was undergoing was altogether unpleasant, which occupied her to such an extent that she ceased her useless resistance. At length the buttons were all undone to the waist. The dress was pulled down in front as far as the strapped-back arms would allow; sufficient, however, to disclose a neck as white as snow and the upper surfaces of two swelling, firm globes. Sir Edward immediately, placing his left arm under his victim's armpit and round her shoulders, drew her closer to him, spreading his legs wider, and notwithstanding her pretty cries to him to desist, inserted his right hand in her bosom. At last, succeeding in loosening her corset, he was able to caress the scarlet centre of the lovely, palpitating breast whose owner lay in most bewitching disorder in his lap. Her hair had partly fallen; her bosom was exposed by the dress three parts down and the loose corset—her eyes swam, and her colour was heightened.

"Oh, stop! uncle; oh, do, do, do stop! I never felt like this before. Whatever will become of me? I cannot bear the sensation. You have no business to pull me about so."

"Do you not like the sensation, Alice?" asked he, stooping and putting his face into her bosom; "and being kissed like this, and this, and this? And is not this nice?"—taking her red teat between his lips and gently playing with it with his tongue.

"Oh! uncle! whatever are you doing to me?" said the girl, flushing crimson all over, and her eyes opening wide with amazement, while her knees fell wider apart, as she herself fell slightly back upon his right knee.

"Is it nice? Do you like it? Does it give you sensations anywhere else?" asked he, glancing at her waist—and then, a moment after, putting his hand down outside her dress, said, "here, for instance?"

Still a deeper blush of crimson shame, but there was a gleam of rapture after the momentary pressure, followed by the exclamation: "How dare you?"

"How dare I, miss? We shall see. Now you will please lie on your face across my knee. You can rest on the sofa."

"Oh, I suppose"—with some disappointment in the tone—"that you are now going to button up my dress."

"Am I?"

"Then what are you going to do?"

"Make you obey me, and without any more resistance, or you shall have double punishment. Lie down at once, miss."

"Oh, uncle, don't look at my legs! Oh, do not, do not strip me. Oh, if I am to be whipped, whip my hands or shoulders; not there."

"You are a very naughty, obstinate girl, with very much too much prudishness about you. But when you yourself have been forced to expose all you possess in the most unconcealed manner, and have been kept some days in short frocks with no drawers, there will no doubt be an improvement. And, as I said before, I shall flog your bare bottom soundly, Miss Alice; and pretty often if you do not mend. Lash your arms and shoulders, indeed. I shall lash your legs and thighs. Lie down this instant."

The poor girl, seeing resistance useless, said nothing; but the arm put round her back soon cured her inaction. She lay across her uncle's left leg and under his left arm, which he had well round her waist.

"Now," said he, tightening his grasp, "we shall see what we have all along so carefully hidden; eh, miss?" pulling up her dress behind, despite her struggles and reiterated prayers to him to desist.

"No use struggling, miss," he went on, slipping his hand up her legs and proceeding at once to that organ in front which woman delights to have touched.

"Oh, uncle! oh, leave off. How dare you? How dare you outrage me like this? Oh! take your hand away! Oh! oh! oh!"

"So you are a little wet," feeling the hairs moistened by the voluptuous sensations he had caused her by caressing her breasts; "and you hoped that no one would know, no doubt. Now just let me stroke these legs. What a nice" (turning the robe above her waist) "fine pair they are; and" (opening the drawers) "what a pretty, what a perfectly lovely bottom! What a crime to hide it from me. However, you will make amends for that by taking your drawers off presently.."

"Never! never while I live! You monster! you wretch! If ever I get out of this room alive I will expose you!"

"My dear, let me try a little gentle persuasion, a novel sensation. If that does not suffice, I can find some more striking argument."

And, again pressing her down upon him, he slipped his hand up, and putting his finger in her virgin orifice in front, he placed his thumb in the rear. Feeling his finger first, she jerked herself upwards, upon which in went his thumb; then, with a little scream, again bouncing forwards, his finger slid in as far as her maidenhead would admit—her hands were all the time still tied. He kept up a severe use of both his finger and thumb for some moments, and she was unable to contain herself, and ultimately obliged to abandon herself to the sensations he provoked. Her legs were stretched out and wide apart; her bottom rose and fell regularly; her lovely neck and shoulders, which were still exposed to his sight, increased his rapture and her dismay; and at last, when the crisis had arrived—pretty nearly at the same moment did it overtake them both—she lay panting and sobbing, almost dead with shame; but for that time subdued.

"Well, dear, how do you like your new experience?"

"Oh, uncle, it is awful, simply awful! I am beside myself."

"When you have rested a moment, will you stand up and take off your drawers before me?"

No answer.

"Answer directly, miss."

With a sudden revulsion of feeling, she bounced out:

"No; I won't! I won't, and you shall not."

Getting up, he went to a chest of drawers, and, opening one, took out a riding-whip. Silently, and notwithstanding her violent resistance, he again got the refractory girl over his knee, with his arm round her, her dress up, and her bottom as bare as her drawers would admit. Across the linen and the bare part he gave her a vigorous cut, making the whip whistle through the air. It fell, leaving a livid mark across the delicate white flesh, and caused a yell of pain. Again he raised it and brought it down—another yell and desperate contortions.

"Oh, uncle, don't! Oh! no more! no more! Oh! I can't bear it. I will be good. I will obey."

Sir Edward paid no attention, and raising the whip, made it whistle a third time through the air. A more piercing shriek.

"It is not enough for you to promise to obey; you must be punished, and cured of your obstinacy. And you called me a wretch and monster"—swish—swish—swish.

"Oh! oh! oh! oh! oh! oh! oh! don't! oh! don't! Oh, you are not!

I say you are not anything but what—oh! oh! put down that whip. Oh! please, dear uncle! You are not a wretch! or monster! I was very naughty to call you so, and I liked what you did to me, only was ashamed to say it. I will take my drawers off before you if you like! I will do *anything*, only don't whip me any more."

"You shall have your dozen, miss"—swish. "So you liked my tickling your clitoris, did you, better than"—swish—"tickling your bottom with this whip, eh?"—swish—swish. "You will expose me if you escape alive, will you?"—swish—swish.

"Oh, stop, stop! You have given me thirteen. For heaven's sake, stop!"

"I have given you a baker's dozen, and"—swish—"there is another because you complained."

Sir Edward was carried away by the passions excited by punishing this lovely girl, and her yell as the whip again cut into her delicate flesh he did not hear, so beside himself was he. Still holding her, he asked the sobbing girl whether she would be good.

"Yes. Indeed, indeed I will."

"There is a very satisfactory magic in this wand. Now, if I unfasten your hands, will you stand up and take your drawers off so that I may birch your bottom for refusing to wear a proper evening dress?"

"Oh, uncle, you have whipped me once, and punished me severely, too, by what you did to me. Why should I be put to more shame?"

"Shame! Nonsense. You should be proud of your charms and glad to show them. What I did should give you pleasure. Anyhow, will you take off your drawers?"

"Oh!" (flushing and in despair) "however can I? I should have to lift my dress quite up, and I should be all exposed. Besides, it is so humiliating."

"Precisely you yourself must bare all your hidden fascinations. And the humiliation is to chastise your prudishness. You must do it. You had much better be a good, obedient girl, as you promised you would be just now."

"Very well. I will then."

"That is a good girl. You shall have a kiss for reward," and, putting his lips on her beautiful mouth, Sir Edward gave her a long and thrilling kiss, and inserted his tongue until it came into contact with hers.

"What a delicious kiss," she said, shuddering with delight; and coyly added: "I shall not so much mind taking off my—my—my drawers" (in a hushed tone, her eyes averted from him) *"now"*

"That is right, dear. Now let me undo your hands. There. Now stand before that mirror and let me arrange the light so that it may fall full upon you. Now I shall sit here."

Miss Alice Darvell walked over to the mirror in a graceful and stately fashion, and started as she saw herself. She turned round and looked shyly at her master, but said nothing. Stooping down, she gathered up her gown and petticoats in her arms and slowly lifted them to her waist. The act revealed a slender and graceful pair of ankles and calves, but the knees were hidden by the garment she was about to remove. After some fumbling with the buttons about her waist—they increased her confusion by not readily unbuttoning, at which she, in a charming little rage, stamped angrily once or twice—the drawers tumbled down.

"Keep up your petticoats," cried Sir Edward," and step out of your drawers. Keep them up," said he, rising, "until I tell you you may let them down. What lovely thighs! what splendid hips! what a lovely, soft, round bottom! Look at it, Alice, in the glass."

"Oh," she said, simply," "I am so glad you think so. I have never looked at myself before."

At which he laughed, and stroked the satin skin with his hand, rubbing her limbs in front and behind and all over her bottom, until at last, when he had gradually stroked her all the way up, he put his hand between the cheeks of her back right through to her cunt, which, and the passage also, he kept gently stroking for some minutes, while she rested against him, uttering inarticulate sounds of delight.

"There," he said at length, "that will do for to-night. You may let your clothes down now. It is so late that the birching shall be postponed until the morning."

"May I take my drawers with me?"

"No, my dear; it will be some time before I shall allow you to wear them again."

"Oh, uncle!"

"Not as long as you are a maiden," added he, significantly.

"Oh, that will be years."

"Will it?" he inquired, innocently.

"Come," he went on, "I will take you to your room. You will in future occupy that one to which I am now going to take you, and not your old one."

"Why, uncle? All my things are in the old one."

"That does not matter, my dear. I must keep you under my eye until you are reduced to abject submission."

The room to which he took her was cheery and warm. Although the month was July, a fire had been lighted, and had evidently been recently stirred. And on a small table near the hearth stood a biscuit box and a small bottle of Dry Monopole. Alice would have preferred a sweeter wine, but was told that was better for her. It was quite plain that either uncle had told someone the precise hour at which he would bring her to the room, or that someone had been watching, for the wine was still frothing in the glass, and therefore must have been poured out but the moment before she entered. Terrible thought— Could anyone have been watching *her* and have seen her nakedness? Her uncle could not have know at what hour he would take her there. She was for an instant paralyzed at the notion; but the next moment, accidentally catching sight of a bare breast and arm, it caused her a certain voluptuous thrill to think she had been seen by someone besides Sir Edward. As she slowly undressed herself, her uncle having gone off and shut the door behind him, it struck her that she would herself, for her own satisfaction, have a peep at all she had been compelled to expose to him. She blushed at her own resolution, and commenced to feel what Miss Rosa Broughton describes as delightfully immoral, a sensation first taught her by her uncle's hands, and of which all her lifetime until then she had been wholly ignorant, although she had had at times a conviction that some such pleasure exists. She stood before one of the large glasses with several of which her room was furnished, and having let down her wealth of brown hair and divested herself of all but a single garment, she allowed that—her chemise—to slip off her shoulders and arms, and for an instant only gazed at herself in the glass. For an instant only, for, overcome by a flood of shame at her nakedness and at the sense of it, she hurriedly averted her eyes and looked about for her nightdress. That she could not find; and she then recollected that the room was not the same she had previously used, and supposed they must have forgotten to bring her things. No; here was her dressing-gown. She would put it on, and go to her old room for her night dress.

She went to the door, and to her utter amazement found that there was no handle inside. She was a prisoner. She looked about, but there was no other door anywhere to be seen.

"Very well," she said to herself; "I shall have to sleep in my chemise."

Taking off her dressing-gown when she was again naked to put on the chemise again made her feel immodest, and as it was cut low in the neck and left her arms bare, she felt more immodest still when she had got it on—a sensation renewed on several occasions when she awoke during the night and was reminded by her bare arms of her plight and of what she had undergone—and was to undergo later in the morning.

Before she got into bed she looked about for the article ladies generally use. There was nothing of the kind in the room, and there was no bell. Then it struck her that the deprivation of her nightdress and of the utensil referred to must have been done deliberately by Sir Edward, and the idea that he had thought of such things so intimately connected with her person gave her a fresh delightful glow of sensuality as she plunged into the cold, silky, linen sheets. The necessary effort to retain her urine, the sense that she was being punished by being made to retain it, and the knowledge that her uncle knew all about it and was so punishing her, excited her to such an extent that she went to bed a very naughty girl indeed.

Chapter II

INITIATION.

"Don't be afraid; a little bleeding does 'em good."

—L'Assommoir.

Awaking next morning about nine o'clock, she caught herself wondering what the whipping would be like, and how it would be administered, and was filled with a delightful sense of shame when she recollected the part of her body which would receive the castigation and the exposure it would inevitably entail. The thought or anticipation of this did not disturb her much. She even contemplated with pleasure the exposure there would be of her legs and thighs, and of that which she did not name to herself, considering the word immodest; but she did trust that her uncle would not flog her very severely.

As she lay thus occupied with these thought there was a tap at the door, and Janet came in with a cup of tea and some bread-and-butter and the announcement:—

"You have just an hour for dressing, miss, for breakfast will be served at half-past ten in the blue sitting-room—the one which overlooks the park. Miss Maud will come to show you where it is."

"Thank you, Janet," said Alice, keeping herself carefully covered. "There are several things I want from my old room—linen and a dress. Will you please bring them?"

"Yes, miss. I have the clothes you are to wear all ready, and will bring them to you."

521

"What do you mean, Janet?"

Janet did not reply. She grimly thought she would leave the girl to find out for herself.

She returned presently with an armful of clothing, which she deposited on a sofa.

In the meantime Alice had jumped up and donned the dressing-gown. She then again found it necessary to look about for that piece of furniture which is a feature in most bedrooms, but could not find it anywhere. She did not know, however, how to mention the matter to Janet, and while she was wondering how to accomplish it that amiable domestic had left the room. Alice had told her to return in about half an hour to do her hair, and the reply was that her hair was not to be done up that morning—a circumstance which, recalling what was before her, made her blush deeply. Then Janet departed, shutting the door, which only opened from the outside. Alice, consoling herself with the reflection that she could wait at any rate until she was on the way to breakfast, proceeded to wash. In the wall, close to the wash-hand-stand, was a black marble knob, with the word "Bath" upon it in gold letters. It was exactly what she wanted at the moment. Putting her hand upon it, she happened to press slightly, when the panel slid aside and showed a marble-floored room surrounded by looking-glasses, with several large slabs of cork for standing on, and a large bath of green Irish marble in the centre. Proceeding to it, she found that the same plan filled the bath with water as opened the room itself. She soon ascertained that not only was the water per-fumed, but deliciously softened. The champagne and the tea made her wish again that she could have got rid of the water she herself con-tained, but she could not make out how the water ran away or was made to run away from the bath—so that little idea was knocked on the head. While bathing, she caught sight of herself continually in the glasses about her, and fell in love with her round, plump limbs and frame, and wondered why she had never done so before. She also noticed with indignation the red marks across her bottom made by the cruel whip that night, and shuddered as she dried herself with the deliciously woolly and warmed towels, and remembered that she had a flogging to undergo. She came, however, to the conclusion that her disobedience deserved punishment; and felt naughty, as she confessed to herself that she "really deserved to be whipped for it."

Hardly had she so determined than she found her obedience again put to the test. Proceeding to dress, she found the clothes brought far worse than the dress she had refused to wear the evening before. They were fit for a girl of ten, and, indeed, unfit for even her. The chemise was abominably low behind and before, the petticoats were quite short. So was the dress. And the petticoats were so starched that instead of hiding her limbs they would display them. And there were no drawers. What was she to do? Sir Edward was rigid in exacting punctuality at meals and generally. If she waited till Maud came she would be too late, and probably receive a worse flogging; besides, in all probability, Maud would only again laugh at her. So, a little indignantly, she dressed herself in the white silk stockings, which reached just half-way up her thigh, tied them with the rose-coloured garters above her knee, put on the patent leather low-cut shoes, the black and yellow corset, and the white frock with a rose-coloured sash. She tied her hair with a ribbon of the same colour, and then looked at herself. She looked like a great, overgrown schoolgirl, but, she could not help owning to herself, a very lovely one. Her arms were bare, and the frock was so low that she noticed with horror it only just concealed her red teats, looking at her from straight in front, but that if you looked down from her shoulder they were quite visible. And the dress stopped at her knees; no effort could make it longer. And the petticoats would make it stick out so. The only comfort was her hair, which did help to hide her naked back. Dressed at last, but feeling worse than naked, she sat down to wait for Maud, and, to her horror, noticed in a glass opposite that the dress stuck out to such an extent that not only could her leg be seen to the top of the stocking, but that the rosy flesh beyond was quite visible; and after a trial or two she discovered that if she was not very careful how she sat, not only would the whole of both legs be displayed, but her cunt also. She wondered however she could go about, and whether she would have to; and at last the costume so excited her passions that she was compelled to walk up and down, and became so naughty that she did not know how to contain herself or the water she had been unable to get rid of. While fidgetting about the room in this state of agitation, Maud entered, and immediately exclaimed, in the most disingenuous manner:—

"How perfectly lovely you are, Alice, with that blush-rose flush! What a splendid bust! Good gracious! do let me look at them. What lovely straight beautifully-shaped legs" (catching hold of the skirt of the frock). "Oh, do let me see——"

"Oh! don't, Maud! Don't!"

"Very well, dear. But you have not done up your hair. That won't do."

"Janet told me I was not to."

"Yes; I know. But that was a mistake. It hides too much."

"That is just why I like it down."

"And just why I do not, dear. You must let me roll it up for you so that your back and nuque and shoulders may be fully shown. There; now you look a perfect darling. I thought I should find you quite cured of anxiety to hide any charm. Do you not wish now you had take my advice?"

"Yes."

"But," she went on, "it is not of much consequence; for if you had not rebelled, some other excuse would have been made for punishing you."

"Indeed?"

"Yes; and you deserved it, Alice."

As Alice had herself come to this conclusion, and felt her bare legs, she only blushed, and said:—

"Oh, Maud, do you know I have no drawers on; and that when I sit down my legs and all show? Shall I have to go about in this dress? and how long shall I have to wear it?"

"That depends upon how you take your punishment. While you wear it you will certainly have to go about in the house and grounds with it. I suppose you wish you had drawers on?"

"Indeed you may suppose so. Oh, Maud, however can I——"

"We must be going, Alice, or we shall be late."

"Oh, Maud, do tell me, does uncle whip very hard?"

"I should have thought," and Maud's eyes flashed, "you could have answered that question yourself."

"Yes. He hurt me dreadfully with the riding-whip. Have you been birched?"

"Yes. I have."

"Was it very bad?"

"In a few hours you wille be able to judge for yourself."

"How does he birch?"

"Here," said Maud, slyly putting her hand under Alice's petticoats upon her bare bottom.

"Oh, don't, Maud."

"Silly child, you should be obliged to me for the sensation. Do come along to breakfast."

"Oh, Maud, there is something I want to ask you; but how to do it I do not know. Perhaps" (with a deep blush) "the best way is to say they have forgotten to put something in my room."

"I know very well what you mean, Alice. You mean you have no po; and you want to pea. All I can say is that I hope you do not want to very badly, because it is not at all likely that you will be allowed to do so until after your flogging. But, of course, you can ask uncle."

"However could I ask him?" replied Alice, aghast and pale at the notion and the prospect of what she would have to endure. "Does he know?" remembering her thought of the night.

"Yes. Of course he knows; and he does it to punish you, and to help to make you feel naughty. Do you feel naughty, dear?" asked Maud, and, again putting her hand under Alice's petticoats, she began tickling her clitoris.

"Oh, don't! Maud. Oh, pray don't! Oh, you will make me wet myself if you do. Oh, can't you let me go to your room?"

"My dear girl, if I were to let you pea without permission, I should probably be forbidden to do so oftener than twice in the twenty-four hours for a week or a fortnight. And I advise you to say nothing about it to uncle, for if he finds out that you want to very badly, he will probably make you wait another hour. It is a very favourite punishment of his."

"Why?"

"Oh, I don't know; except that it is a severe one. And it is awfully humiliating to a girl to have to ask; but it certainly makes one feel naughty."

"Yes; it does. Do you know, I was nearly doing it in the bath?"

"Lucky for you that you did not. It would certainly have been found out, and you would have caught it. But, Alice, why do you say 'doing it' instead of 'peaing'? When you ask you will have to use plain language."

"Oh, Maud!"

"Yes; and very likely have to do it before uncle. If he finds out you squirm about saying things and calling them by their names, he will make you say the most outrageous things, and write them also. But there is half-past ten chiming. Come along."

When they got to the blue room—on the way to which they passed, to Alice's intense consternation, several servants who gazed immoveably at her—they found Sir Edward there in a velvet coat and kilt. He greeted them cheerily. The view across thu park, in the glades of which the fallow deer could be seen grazing, was, lovely; the sunshine was flooding the room, and the soft, warm summer air wafted in the perfume of the flowers from the beds below (the blue room was on the bedroom floor) through the windows, which were thrown wide open. Alice was so struck by the view that she for a moment forgot to notice how her uncle was gazing at her, until she felt the air on her legs, and it provoked a consciousness at which she blushed.

"How do you like your frock, my dear? It becomes you admirably."

"Does it, uncle?" Looking coyly at him. "I am glad you like it."

"I am glad to see you are a sensible girl after all. We shall make something of you."

"How long am I to wear it, uncle?"

"For a week."

"For a fortnight," struck in Maud, maliciously. "She is to be mistress next week."

Maud knew very well she would find it much worse to be dressed like that when giving orders, and that her orders would not be so well attended to. She revelled in the notion of getting Alice soundly punished.

Sir Edward noticed with a gleam of amusement how fidgetty Alice became towards the end of the meal, and Maud smiled gently to herself. Alice thought that after breakfast she would have a chance. She was disappointed. Sir Edward then said, in a severe tone: "I think, Miss Alice, we have a little business to settle together. Your disobedience cannot be overlooked. You must come with me. Your short skirts will punish your prudishness, but the birch is the best corrector of a bold, disobedient girl's bottom," She grew quite pale, and trembled all over, both with fright and at being spoken to so before Maud, who, reposing calmly in her chair, was steadily gazing at her.

She had got up. When her uncle had finished speaking, he came up to her and took hold of her left ear with his right hand, and saying, "Come along, miss, to be flogged," marched her off to the yellow room.

There, to her consternation, she saw straps and pillows on the oak table. In a perfect fright, she said: "Oh, pray do not strap me up, uncle; pray do not. I will submit."

"Undress yourself," he said, having closed the door; "leave on your stockings only."

"Oh, uncle!"

"You had better obey, miss, or you shall have a double dose. Take off your frock this instant."

"Now your petticoat bodice."

"Now your petticoats. Now your corset and chemise. Now, my proud young beauty, how do you feel?"

He had not seen her to such advantage the evening before. She had then had her long dress on the whole time, and while punishing her he had only uncovered a small portion of her legs. It is true she afterwards had been made to take off her drawers; but the skirt and petticoats gathered about her hips had still concealed much. Now she was naked from the crown of her head to her rose coloured garters Burning with shame, she put her hands up to her face, and remained standing and silent, while Sir Edward feasted his eyes upon the contemplation of every beautiful curve of the lovely little head poised so beautifully upon a perfect throat; of the dimpled back and beautifully rounded shoulders; of the arms; of the breasts and hips and thighs. It was the most lovely girl he had seen, he said to himself, and then, seating himself, he added aloud:—

"Come here, miss. Kneel down: there, between my knees; clasp your hands, and say after me:—

"Uncle, I have been."

"Uncle, I have been."

"A naughty, disobedient girl,"

"A naughty, disobedient girl."

"And deserve to be soundly birched."

"And deserve to be soundly birched."

"Please, therefore,"

"Please, therefore,"

"Strap me down"

"Oh, no! oh, no! Oh, please don't strap me down!"

"Say what I tell you at once, miss, or it will be worse for you."

"Strap me down"

"To the table,"

"Oh! oh! oh! To the table,"

"With my legs well apart,"

"Oh, dear! I can't. With—with—I can't—with my—oh, uncle!"

"An extra half-dozen for this."

"Oh, uncle!"

"Say at once: With my legs well apart."

"With my—my—oh!—legs" (and she shuddered deliciously and blushed bewilderingly) "well apart."

"And give me"

"And give me"

"Please,"

"Please,"

"Four and a half dozen"

"Oh, uncle! please not so much!" (recollecting the baker's dozen with the riding-whip.)

"You will have more if you do not say it at once."

"Four and a half dozen"

"On my bare bottom."

"Oh! that!—my—I can never say—"

"*You must.*"

"My bare——"

"You had better say it. Stop; I will improve it. You must say: On my girl's bare bottom."

"Oh, uncle!" she said, looking at him; and seeing his eyes gloating upon her and devouring her beauty, and the lust and fire in them, she immediately turned hers away.

"Now, Alice, 'On my girl's bare bottom.' "

"On my girl's bare bottom."

He moved as he said this, and Alice noticed he adjusted something under his kilt.

"Well laid on."

"Well laid on."

"Yes; I will, my dear. I will warm your bottom for you as well as ever any girl ever had her bottom warmed. I will set it on fire for you. You will curse the moment you were disobedient. I will cure you of disobedience and all your silly nonsense. Come along to the table. There, stand at that end"—Alice began to sob—"put the cushion before you, so. Now lie over it, right down on the table. No resistance" (as he fixed the strap round her shoulders she made a slight attempt at remonstrance). The strap went round her and the table, and when once it was buckled she could not, of course, get up. He then buckled on two wristlets, and with two other straps fastened her wrists to the right and left legs of the table; then another broad strap was put round the table and the small of her back. This was pretty tight, as were also those that at the knees and ankles fastened her legs, wide apart, to the legs of the table. She was like a spread eagle, and her bottom, the tender skin between its cheeks, her cunt, and her legs were most completely exposed.

"Now, my dear, you will remain in that position half an hour and contemplate your offences, and then you shall have as sound a flogging as I ever gave a girl."

"Oh, uncle, before you flog me, do let me do something. Maud told me I should have to tell you, but I do not know how to. I will come back directly and be strapped down again if you will only let me. And, oh! please do not leave me in this dreadful position for half an hour."

"You must say what it is that you want."

"Oh, uncle"—feeling it was neck or nothing—"do let me go and pea before I am flogged. I want to, oh, so dreadfully. I have not been able to all the morning, nor all night."

"So you want to very dreadfully, do you, miss?" and going up to her he put his hand between her legs from behind, and severely tickled the opening through which the stream was burning to rush. It was all that Alice could do to retain it.

"Oh, don't! Oh! If you do I shall wet myself. I shall not be able to help it. Oh, uncle, pray, pray don't! Oh, pray let me go!"

"No, miss, I certainly shall not. It is a part of your punishment. There was an unnatural coldness about these parts of yours which this will help to warm up. Have you not felt more naughty since you have had all that hot water inside you?"

"And you are beginning to see how ridiculous prudishness is. Now, just you think about your conduct and your disobedience until I return to whip you, and remember you owe your present shameful position to them."

Saying this, Sir Edward left the room. Poor Alice, left to herself, all naked save for her stockings; her arms stretched out above her head and tightly strapped; her legs divided and fastened wide apart; the most secret portions of her frame made the most conspicuous in order that they might be punished by a man—did feel her position acutely. She considered it and felt it to be most shameful. Her cheeks burned with a hot, red glow. But all concealment was absolutely impossible; the haughty beauty felt herself prostrate before and at the mercy of her master, and experienced again an exquisite sensual thrill at the thought that she really deserved to have her bottom whipped by her uncle.

Presently Maud came into the room in a low-necked dress, with a large bouquet.

"Well, Alice," she said, "I hope you enjoy your position and the prospect before you."

"Oh, Maud; go away. I can't bear you to see me in this position. I won't be punished before you."

"Silly goose! Young ladies strapped down naked, and stretched out for punishment like spread eagles, are not entitled to say shall or shan't. What a lovely skin and back, Alice. Alas! before long that pretty, plump, white bottom will present a very altered appearance. How many are you to have?"

"I was made to ask for four dozen and a half, well laid on."

"And you may depend upon it, you will have them, my dear, most mercilessly laid on"—stroking her legs and thighs, which caused Alice to catch her breath and to coo in a murmuring way from the pleasure Maud's hand gave her. Maud asked her whether she had tried to induce her uncle to let her go somewhere.

"Yes," replied Alice; "I did. But he would not."

"And I suppose you want to very badly," went on Maud, maliciously placing her fingers on the very spot.

"Yes; I do. Oh, don't, Maud, or you'll make me!"

"Now mind, Alice, whatever you do, hold out till your birching is over. If you do not I warn you that you will catch it."

"I think it is a very, very cruel, horrid punishment," said Alice, whimpering.

"It is severe, I know, and it is far better not to be prudish than to incur it. But here comes uncle."

"Now, you bold, disobedient girl, I hope you feel ashamed of yourself," said Sir Edward, entering the room and shutting the door. "Maud will witness your punishment as a warning to her what she will receive if she is disobedient."

Going up to the wardrobe, he selected three well-pickled birches, which had evidently never been used, for there were numbers of buds on them. They were elastic and well spread, and made a most ominous switching sound as, one by one, Sir Edward switched them through the air at which Alice shuddered and Maud's eyes gleamed.

"Oh, pray, pray, uncle, do not be very severe. Remember it is almost my first whipping. It is awful!"

Maud had changed the dress she had worn at breakfast and, as already mentioned, now had on one cut very low in the body; her arms were bare and her skirts short. Between her breasts was placed a bouquet of roses.

"Hold these," said Sir Edward, giving her the rods.

He then put his left arm round Alice, and said: "Now, you saucy, disobedient miss, your bottom will expiate your offences, and by way of preface"—smack, smack with his right hand, smack, smack, smack "Ah, it is already becoming a little rosy."

"Oh, uncle! Oh, how you hurt! Oh, how your hand stings! Oh! oh! oh!"

"Yes. A bold girl's bottom must be well stung. It teaches her obedience and submission"—smack—"what a lovely, soft bottom!"— smack, smack, smack.

Maud's eyes gleamed and her face flustered, as Alice, wriggling about as much as the straps allowed, cried softly to herself. When her uncle had warmed her sufficiently, he removed his arm and moved about two feet away from the girl, whose confusion at the invasion of her charms by the rough hand of a man increased her loveliness tenfold. Maud held one birch in her right hand. She, too, looked divine. Her dark eyes flashing, her lovely bosom heaving, she handed it, retaining the other two in her left hand, to her uncle. Alice could not see that as she gave him the birch, as soon as her hand was free she slipped it under her uncle's kilt from the back, and the instant increase of his passion and excitement left no doubt as to the use she was making of it. Sir Edward stood at the left side of his refractory ward. He drew the birch, lecturing her as he did so, three or four times upwards and downwards from back to front and from front to back between the cheeks of the girl's bottom, producing a voluptuous movement of the lovely thighs and little exclamations of delight.

"Oh! oh! oh! don't do that! Oh! oh! how dreadful! Oh, please, uncle!" trying to turn round, which, of course, the straps prevented. He next proceeded to birch her gently all over, the strokes increasing in vigour, but being always confined to the bottom.

"Oh, uncle, you hurt! Oh! how the horrid thing stings! Oh! it is worse than your hand! Oh! stop! Have I not had enough?"

"We will begin now, miss," said he, having given her a cut severe enough to provoke a slight cry of real pain; "and Maud will count."

Lifting up the rod at right angles to the table on which she was bound down, he brought it down with a tremendous swish through the air across the upper parts of her hips.

"One," said the mellow voice of Maud—her right hand and a portion of her arm hidden under her uncle's kilt, the movements of its muscles under the delicate skin and the wriggles of the Baronet showing that Maud had hold of and was kneading a sensitive portion of his frame. The bottom grew crimson where the stroke had fallen, and the culprit emitted a yell and gasped for breath. With the regularity of a steamhammer, he again raised the rod well above his shoulder, and again making it whistle through the air, he again gave her a very severe stroke.

"Two," said Maud quietly.

A shriek. "Oh! stop! Oh! stop! Oh! *stop!*"

Swish. "Three," calmly observed Maud.

"Oh! you will kill me. *Oh!* I can't—I can't——"

Swish. "Four, uncle."

"Oh, ah! Oh, I can't bear it! Oh, I will be good! Oh, Maud, ask him to stop——"

Swish. "Five"

Maud had given her uncle an extra pull when Alice had appealed to her, and this stroke was harder in consequence. Spots of blood began to appear where the ends of the birch and its buds fell, especially on the outside of the off thigh. The yell which followed number five was more piercing, and choking sobs ensued; but Sir Edward, merely observing that she would run a very good chance of extra punisment if she made so much noise, without heeding her tears or contortions or choking, mercelessly and relentlessly gave her six, seven, eight, and nine, each being counted by Maud's clear gentle voice.

"Now, miss, that you have had one-sixth of your punishment——"

"One-sixth! Oh! oh! oh! I can't bear more! Oh, I can't bear more! Oh, let me off! You will kill me! Oh, let me off! I will—I will I *will* indeed be good——"

"I suppose you begin to regret your disobedience."

"Oh, don't punish me any more," cried the girl, wriggling and struggling to get free—of course ineffectually, but looking perfectly lovely in her pain.

"Yes! You must receive the whole number. It is not enough to promise to obey now; you should have thought of this before. You are now having your bottom punished, not only to make you better in future, but for your past offences."

And Sir Edward walked round to the right side of his niece, and there, in the same place, but from right to left, gave her nine very severe cuts. Alice yelled and screamed and roared and rolled about as much as she possibly could, perfectly reckless as to what she showed.

The next nine were given lengthwise between her legs. Her bottom being well up, and the legs well apart, the strokes fell upon the tender skin between them, and the long, lithe ends of the rod curled round her cunt, causing her excruciating agony.

"There is nothing like a good birching for a girl." Swish.

"One," said Maud, moving voluptuously.

"Oh! oh! yah! Oh! my bottom! Oh! my legs! Oh! how it hurts! Oh! oh! oh!"

"They are all the better for the pain!" Swish.

"Two," said Maud.

"Oh! oh! oh! Oh, don't strike me there!" as the birch curled round her cunt.

"And the exposure. I do not think you will disobey." Swish.

"Three," said Maud, apparently beside herself, her eyes swimming.

"Oh! oh! oh! yah! Oh! I shall die! I shall *faint!* Oh! dear uncle! I will—please forgive me—I will never disobey. I will do *anything;* ANYTHING; ANYTHING!"

"I daresay you will, miss; but I shall not let you off;"—swish— "there's another for your cunt."

"Four," said Maud.

"Oh! Oh! not there! Oh! I am beside myself! I shall go *mad!* I shall *die* or go *mad!*"

"You will not do anything of the sort, and you must bear your punishment." Swiish.

"Five," counted Maud.

The cries gradually lessened, and the culprit seemed to become entranced, whereupon the uncle. at whom Maud looked significantly, directed the remaining four strokes to the insides of the thighs, leaving the palpitating red rose between them free from further blows, *for the present.*

Alice's moans were then succeeded by piercing shrieks, but her uncle, perfectly deaf to them, continued the flogging. When the third nine, given lengthwise, had been completed, Sir Edward put down the birch he had used and took a second from Maud. During the pause, his niece, with sobs and tears, earnestly implored him to let her off. For all reply, he again took up his station at her left side, and saying: "No, miss; I shall certainly not unstrap you; you have been far too naughty. I will punish you, and your lovely legs and bottom, to the fullest extent of the sentence, and teach you to be good, you bold hussey, and give you a lesson you will not forget in a hurry"—gave her nine more sound cuts; but this time, instead of their being administered on the upper part of her bottom, perpendicularly, they were given almost horizontally on its lower part, where it joins the thigh. Fresh yells and shrieks, all of no avail, were uttered by the unhappy girl, who in her agony lifted up her head, her shoulders being fastened down with the strap, and prayed her uncle, by heaven, to spare her. But the relentless rod still continued to cut into her tender and now bleeding flesh, as she was told "she would receive no mercy."

Maud's even voice continued to number the strokes, and Maud herself seemed aflame, and the sight of the agony her uncle was inflicting seemed to excite her sensuality in an extraordinary degree. Her lips were moist; her eyes swam; the eyelids drooped; and all the indications of a very lovesick girl appeared in her. The bleeding bottom, the tightly-strapped limbs, the piercing cries, and the relentlessly inflicted punishment excited her strongest passions. She could have torn Alice limb from limb; and she encouraged her uncle, by rolling his balls and pulling and squeezing his prick, to continue the punishment in the severest manner.

She gloated over the numbers as she called them out.

Sir Edward, too, seemed beside himself. His eyes were as two flames; he watched every motion of Alice's body; gloated upon all she displayed; could have made his teeth meet in her delicate flesh, which he lacerated with the rod yet more severly as his organ, already excited to an enormous size, was still further enlarged by Maud's hand.

At length, Alice's lower bottom having been well waled from right to left, as well as from left to right, there remained but the nine strokes to be given lengthwise.

For these, Sir Edward took the third birch from Maud, who by this time was standing with her legs wide apart, uttering little sounds and breathing little sighs of almost uncontrollable desire.

The unhappy culprit's yells had somewhat lessened, for the flowing blood had relieved the pain; and it had also been so severe that her sensitiveness to it had much diminished. But now, feeling the rod curling round her cunt, which, being all open and wet, was more than ever exposed, she yelled in a perfectly delirious manner.

After some few of these strokes had been given, her uncle asking her whether he was a wretch and a monster, as she had called him last night, she replied with vehement denials:—

"No! oh, no! oh! oh! oh! oh, no! Not a monster! Not a wretch! My own dear uncle, whom I love! Oh! oh! oh! My bottom burns! Oh! oh! It is on fire!"

"Will you be a good, obedient girl miss?"

"Yes! Yes! *Yes!* Oh! indeed—"

"And thank me for whipping you?"

"Yes; indeed I do."

"Whip well in, uncle," said Maud quietly, in her rich voice.

And he did so. Alice shrieked; flooded the floor with urine, and fainted!

Maud, beside herself, threw herself backwards on the long and broad divan—her breast, her legs (without drawers) wide extended. Sir

Edward, throwing down the birch, threw himself upon her with fury. He inserted his enormous affair into her burning cunt, and he fucked her so violently that she almost fainted from delight.

When Alice came round, Sir Edward rose from Maud's breast, and then Maud said, in clear tones:—

"Uncle, I told Alice yesterday evening, when she kept me so long before I could succeed in tying her hands, that I would take care it secured her an extra half-dozen."

"Oh, uncle! I beg Maud's pardon. Oh! after all I have gone through, let me off that half-dozen. Oh, *dear* Maud! do ask uncle to let me off. Oh, do! If I am birched any more I shall go mad! I shall —I shall indeed!"

Maud, still lying backwards on the couch, supported by a big, square pillow, said nothing. Her hands were clasped behind her head.

But Sir Edward said: "No miss; you can never be let off! You must have the half-dozen. It will be a lesson to you." And taking up the birch, he gave her six severe strokes, distributed evenly all over her bottom.

As they were being administered, Maud's left hand stole down to her waist and found its way between her legs.

While Alice was smothering her sobs and cries after her last half-dozen, Sir Edward again threw himself upon Maud and enjoyed her.

About ten minutes or a quarter of an hour later he proceeded to unstrap Alice.

She could not stand without Maud's help. The cushion and carpet were soaked with her urine and stained with her blood.

"You will to-morrow have a dozen on the trapeze, miss, for disgracing yourself in this beastly manner; you will write out fifty times, 'I pea'd like a mare before my uncle'; and for the next fortnight you will only pea twice in the twenty-four hours. And now come and kiss the rod and say: 'Thank you, my dear uncle, for the flogging you have given me.' "

Quite docilely she knelt down before him, kissed the rod he held to her lips, and repeated the words.

"Will you be a good, obedient girl in future?"

"Yes, dear uncle; indeed I will!"

"Tha's a good thing. There is, you see, nothing like a good, sound flogging for a girl. Were the rod more in use how very much better women we should have. Now go with Maud and get some refreshment. I have various engagements, and shall not be in till dinner. After lunch you had better have a sleep." And so saying, he packed the two girls off to Alice's room, shut the yellow room door, and ringing for a footman, gave orders that the estate steward and horses should be in attendance at the front door in half an hour.

Maud and Alice went to the latter's room. By Maud's advice, Alice, who was so sore that she could scarcely move, got into bed and had some strong broth and Burgundy, and presently fell asleep. Maud spent her afternoon at an open window reclining in a lounge chair, pretending to read a novel, but in reality revelling in the reminiscences of the morning and meditating upon its delights—and wondering when she would get whipped next herself—until she was disturbed by some afternoon visitors.

Chapter III

MYSTERY

"My passions, however, are very strong; but my Soul
and Body are hostile sisters, and the unhappy pair, like every
imaginable couple, lawful or unlawful, live in a perpetual
state of war."

—Mademoiselle de Maupin

Alice's slumbers were profound. For four or five hours she continued in the deepest sleep; but as consciousness gradually returned to
her she dreamt: and dreamt, as she had never done before, of love. Her
innocence was gone; and she would awake an experienced girl. Her
dreams were of the softest pleasures; they were prompted by that new
and wonderful sensation, under the influence of which she still was,
which had been roused once for all while she lay ignominiously extended under her uncle's eye and received the cruel lashes of the birch
upon the most secret and divine organ of her exquisite body. They,
it is true, profaned the Temple; but they summoned to life the Divin-
ity there enshrined. Her sexual instincts were aroused; she became
conscious of her femininity. She felt the influence of Man; and a
longing and insatiable desire to possess him. She now knew why she
was beautiful, and in her dreams she pictured herself with soft delight
—her velvety skin; her soft, plump, round arms; her throbbing bosom,
and the ravishing sinuosities of her back—as being embraced by her
uncle; she felt his weight on the front of her thighs; she imagined his

tongue again between her lips. Her body glowed; her charms ripened; her mind, casting away the prudish veils with which it had so long been encumbered, already contemplated life in another and rosier light, and prepared her to bloom into that lovely and beautiful woman she was so soon to become.

Innocence! (so called) and virginity! in you we do not believe. Flowers, not of virtue, but of a dunghill; the conceptions and impure fruit of Shame, begotten upon Superstition—this is the pedigree we give to you. Ye are fostered by those who fatten upon the fears of the ignorant and weak-minded. Poor human creature, trembling upon the threshold of nature's holiest of holies; terror-stricken at the revelation of her most tremendous mystery about to be made you; you are swooped upon by the priest and called upon to deny your own nature! Your young and budding desires are described to you as sin, such as will condemn you hereafter to endless flame! Impurity is imputed to passion the most natural and the chastest which can possess the soul! and, outraged by the obscene imputation, it recoils in horror upon itself; but if initiated, if forearmed with knowledge, it crushes and stamps the foul tempter under foot, exclaiming: "Monster! the obscenity is in thee. Avaunt!"

Yes; we would have it enacted that all young creatures who had not by one and twenty years of age become women should be made so by compulsory union with a lover; and as the measure could not have a retrospective effect, all old maids—incomplete human creatures, mentally and physically, that they are—should be given three months and the services gratuitously of the most energetic advertising agency in the matrimonial market, and if they did not within that period form some true union and become the fulfilment and completement of some man (for no man is perfect until he includes woman), and, moreover, produce to the court incontestable proofs of the destruction of their maidenhead, that they should perish ignominiously as unnatural deformities. And so infatuated are many of these old deformities that we believe some would perish, although no doubt most would prefer forcible violation; and therefore those who, at the end of the three months, failed to produce the required evidence in court should be given one more chance. They should be placed in charge of a robust curate or other officer of the court, and this charge should be called marriage; the union to endure during the joint lives of the parties; and if at the end of the year the husband swore that all his efforts to storm his old virgin's citadel had failed, the marriage should be declared null; the old woman transfixed by the usher with a weapon to be duly provided for the purpose, and fitted to carry it out, and then strangled; and the curate or other officer provided forthwith with another beauty.

You will say this marriage of yours is a punishment; and we reply, perhaps marriage always is, but in this case that it ought to be so, as the men concerned—all of them—should be those, and those only, who have been indicted and convicted before a court composed of young women, of not having found and enjoyed a mistress before the completion of their twenty-fifth year. We apprehend that the class would not be very numerous, and "marriage" would therefore receive a salutary limitation.

But listen! Alice is rubbing her eyes and puzzling herself with reasons why she should be so possessed by the idea of, and longing for, her uncle, who had used her so cruelly. His being somehow or other overshadowed her, and she seemed to long to be absorbed in it. The strictest analysis of her craving only reduced it as far as a wish that he should take her in his arms and do with her what he wished—what that would be she knew not, but instinctively felt it would be something tremendous, which would entirely alter her whole subjective existence. He had seen her naked; he had reduced her, naked, to absolute submission to his will; he had inflicted upon her the cruellest pain; and the direct medium of the infliction of this pain had been the most secret portion of her body. Yet she delighted in the notion that *he* had seen her (with the exception solely of her stockings) completely nude; she enjoyed the idea that his hand had inflicted the stripes of which she still felt the effects; her breath came more quickly and she trembled with joy when she called to mind that it was to him she had been compelled to display, with the greatest possible humiliation to her, the most intimate recesses of her person and her most jealously-concealed charms without any reserve whatsoever.

She was much puzzled, and her perplexity was accentuated as she moved and felt how tender and how sore her bottom still was.

"Shall I ever be able to sit down again?" she wondered.

Then she recollected the catastrophe that had taken place the moment before she had swooned in that inexplicable ecstasy, and her cheeks flushed and grew hot with shame. And they flushed again and grew still hotter the second time when she recollected that she had to write out fifty times, "I pea'd like a mare before my uncle."

What a little beast she was, and how well she deserved flogging! How just and proper it was that for the next fortnight she should be allowed to relieve herself but twice in the twentyfour hours. The inconvenience would be a very proper lesson for so naughty a girl as she was.

In the midst of these reflections, in came Maud with some egg-flip.

"I would not let them disturb you for luncheon, dear, as I am sure uncle would wish you to be fresh in the evening; and, besides, you must have needed the rest dreadfully. How did you like your whipping?"

"Oh, Maud, it was dreadful! How cruelly severe uncle is."

"I suppose it has made you hate him?"

"No; that is the strangest thing about it. Last night I thought my hatred of him could not be sufficiently intense; but I now feel that I am completely mastered by him, and find that I am glad that it is so!"

"Dear Alice, that was my own experience."

"Has he whipped you, Maud?"

"Yes, dear; and sometimes I purposely do something in order to get myself flogged."

"How curious! When did he whip you first?"

"Oh, long ago. I must give you a full account of it another time. Did you faint with pain?"

"No. I seemed in heaven."

"You do not seem very much exhausted; but you had better eat this cake and egg-flip—it is better for you than tea—and let me look at that poor bottom and see what can be done for it."

So Maud sat down upon the bed, and Alice, to her own astonishment, now nothing loth, laid on her face while Maud removed all the bedclothes from her waist downwards, and, as they chatted, gently anointed her bottom with Vinolia cream, and gave her many a pleasant sensation by the adroit use she made of her hands and fingers.

Alice explained that she now felt a much more experienced girl, and much surprised at a former coyness, which she thought must have appeared extremely ridiculous.

She wondered that anyone could be prudish.

"Yes," said Maud, "It is want of education"—smiling—"and as for modesty, I verily believe innocent girls are only just one little bit less nasty than the very British old maid herself," ended Maud, with a delicious laugh.

"And you, Alice," she went on, "how absurd you were when first you came, blushing at every second word, buttoning your dress up to your throat, wearing it on the ground, and almost screaming at the mere mention of an ankle."

"Oh, Maud, you do not know what I went through in the yellow room. When uncle turned up my petticoats and whipped me, and made me take off my own drawers before him—oh! oh! oh! the mere thought of it is fearful—and then when he put me across his knee and put his finger and thumb——"

"Where?" asked Maud.

"Oh, one in frond and the other behind"—hiding her face with her hands.

"Like that?" said Maud.

"Yes. Just like that. Oh, Maud! oh, how nice! Well, dear, the wonder is that I am alive."

"The sweetest has to come yet, Alice dear. You said you were glad that uncle had mastered you. Do you not long for him?"

"Oh, Maud, I cannot tell you how I do. In such a strange way. I feel I could devour him!"

"Well, dear, all in good time. At any rate, you will not wish to conceal your charms now."

"Oh, no. I take quite a healthy delight in displaying them. I think a long dress quite immodest, because it must be a sign of a mind itching with nasty thoughts."

"Unless, indeed," she continued, after a moment's thoughtfullness, "it is because the natural growth has been checked."

"Oh, Alice, I am so glad that you are such a sensible girl. What splendid times we shall have together. I was never before so fully convinced how right uncle is in his opinion that there is nothing like a sound flogging for a girl. But although we have such a good opinion of ourselves, there are heaps of people who would condemn us with faint praise, and say we were only engagingly immoral. Uncle told me once it was because we were free and emancipated and capable of freely enjoying pleasure which the silly geese—although it is such a *natural* pleasure—think they are bound to deny themselves. There, Alice dear," ceasing her rubbing, which she had so caressingly done; "is the poor bottom better?"

"Yes, thank you, Maud dear, ever so much. I feel so surprised at being able to lie so unconcernedly before you."

"You see, Alice, you are emancipated—almost. Now you had better have a warm bath, and mind that you use the soap scented with attar of roses. Make a good lather, and bathe yourself all over with it. And then, my dear, you are to put on a low chemise of black silk trimmed with yellow, a yellow corset, black silk petticoats, yellow stockings and shoes, and a net dress with great big yellow spots all over it. It won't come below your knees, dear," said Maud, significantly, at which Alice gave a joyous laugh. "In your bosom you are to place some yellow roses which the gardener has been ordered to bring in on purpose for you."

"And," went on Maud, interrupting Alice, "you are to have your hair twisted up in one great coil and fastened with this arrow, which, you see, is studded with cairn gorms; and round your throat," opening a casket on the dressing table, "you are to put this necklace" (a magnificent one of cairn gorms set in brilliants). "By the bye, you are to tie your stockings with black, not yellow garters, and mind that the first petticoat you put on is that which is lined with yellow silk. Now mind, Alice, and do not make a mistake."

"Oh! how lovely!" cried Alice. "How good you are to me, you dear Maud, to take such an interest in me. I shall be dressed all in black and yellow. Why? I wonder."

"Because," mockingly answered Maud, "black and yellow are the devil's colours, and you have his beauty."

"Now, Maud, you are laughing at me. I wonder what you will wear?"

"Oh, something not so striking, dear. You see, it is your turn to-night. You are to be the heroine of to-night. And before I go to dress, I must say goodbye to you, Alice, for I shall not have another opportunity of doing so during the evening, and to-morrow I shall not see you girl again."

"What on earth do you mean, Maud?" asked Alice, experiencing an unaccountable sensation of which she did not understand the significance. "You are not going away, surely?" in alarm.

"Oh, no, you dear goose," replied Maud. "I only meant that I should not see you a girl to-morrow because in all probability you will then be a woman," and the room rang with the musical and merry peal of laughter Maud gave.

"You speak in riddles, dear. I wish you would explain, and not tease me so."

"Not I," said Maud. "Write to Miss Ada Ballin, of the *Ladies' Pictorial*, duly enclosing a coupon, and she will tell you the difference between a girl and a woman; or, by the bye, as it is not the sort of matter the editor (who ought to be circumcised) would allow an explanation of publicly, you had better send her a fee for a private reply; or, better still," she went on maliciously, "ask her for the address of a medical man competent to set forth the mystery personally to you, and," said Maud, in shrieks of laughter at her own wit, "Miss Ada Ballin will certainly send it, if you enclose a stamped, addressed envelope so that it may be sent you privately, as it would be a violation of professional etiquette to publish it; and misses are said to hate violation of every sort. Come! Come! Alice," seeing that Alice began to pout, thinking that Maud was laughing at her, "do not be offended at my nonsense. You will know all about it by to-morrow yourself. Dear me, there's the dressing bell. Only an hour to dinner. Whoever would have thought it was so late?"

"Why not stop and dress here?"

"No; not to-night, dear. One word more, Alice. I heard that you are, for the next fortnight, only to go somewhere twice every day. Now, dear, take my advice and do it late as you can after dinner, and in the morning after you have left the yellow room, if you have to go there. And I know you have to to-morrow."

"Yes; I have; but I do not dread it so much. But I am not going to be birched; am I?"

"No, dear. You are going to have a dozen on the trapeze, which is in some respects worse. I can't stop to explain, though, because, if I do, I shall be late, and then I should be birched."

"Oh, Maud! Very well, dear, I will take your advice, with thanks."

"I am sure you will find it good. Here's Janet. I must run off."

"What? Miss Maud in here after the bell has rung. Get off to your room, miss, or ye'll have the tawse, and nae doot aboot it."

Then the old Scotch maid, without ado, stripped Alice stark naked and conducted her to her bath. Though she treated her like an infant, and gave her a pinch and a smack or two on the buttocks if she considered Alice was slow in obeying her directions, yet she washed and dressed her with tenderness and care, mingled with a certain amount of reverence for the girl's absolute loveliness.

"She's a bonnie bit lassie anyhow; but, gudeness guide us, what a lashing she has had about her puir body."

She would not, however, allow any nonsense on Alice's part. The yellow corset was laced as she thought proper. Alice's protests were unheeded, and her breasts were placed in what she still considered unnecessary prominence. The roses were placed between them. The magnificent hair, done up in one great coil, was rolled up on the top of her shapely little head and fixed with the arrow, which sparkled with the brilliants in the setting of the great cairn gorms. At last her toilette was complete, and, bewilderingly and bewitchingly beautiful, exciting not only her rugged Scotch attendant's admiration (who exclaimed: "It was not work thrown away to deck so bonnie a bairn as hersell"), but her own, she descended to the drawing-room with that gently undulating motion which adds so greatly to the fascinations even of those who may otherwise possess charms of the highest degree.

In the drawing-room she found Maud and Sir Edward; to her surprise, there was no one else. But Sir Edward was dressed "fin de siecle," and was gay with a yellow rose in his buttonhole. And Alice blushed with gratification when she noticed, as she did the instant she saw it was precisely the same kind of rose as those in her bosom and the single one in her hair. Maud looked demurely lovely, and, though dressed in the height of fashion, had somehow good-naturedly managed to efface herself so that she might not interfere with Alice's triumph.

Then they went to dinner, Alice, again to her surprise, on her uncle's arm and at the head of the table.

"Maud has abdicated in your favour to-night, my dear, although, it is true, it is not your week. But she has only surrendered the glories to you, so do not be disturbed about the responsibilities," her uncle added, kindly, noticing a slightly anxious expression appear.

The table groaned with summer fruits in chased gold dishes, and was decorated entirely with white roses. Never did soup taste more delicious or were its odours and flavours more appreciated; never did the chicken of the ocean, the twisted whiting, or the lordly salmon or the saintly sole meet, or were better qualified to meet, with heartier approval; never was the wine in better order—although Alice thought the Chablis (La Moutonne) a little too heavy. The champagne, iced to a nicety by the portly butler, was not on this occasion Dry Mono-pole, but a sweeter wine, which pleased Alice more. It soon added cordiality to a gay and merry scene. Sir Edward sent his compliments to the delighted *chef* upon the production by him of a work of art which had occupied that artist ever since he had received the neces-sary hint from Maud. It reminded her, said Alice, "of nothing so much as of a wedding cake," at which Maud covertly smiled. It was a representation in confectionery of Venus, her cupids, her doves, and her triumphs. The figure reminded Alice for a moment of her own. It was not until afterwards she discovered that in a panel of her bedroom was fixed a secret camera, and that while the night before she had stood for but a minute naked before her glass, Sir Edward had found time to take an instantaneous photograph of her, and that it was this photograph which, shown to the enraptured *chef* by Maud, had proved his inspiration. Sir Edward was enraptured, too, as he gazed, and the message for his cook was delivered with such warmth to his own valet that that functionary, immoveable although he appeared, was quite startled in reality. And his description of his master's earnest-ness pleased the genius of the kitchen quite as much as the jewel which Sir Edward had taken off his own finger and sent with the message. Monsieur Philippe felt that the ambition of a lifetime was to some extent attained, and thanked his gods that he possessed a master who could appreciate the efforts of genius.

After dinner was served that rare growth of Burgundy "Romance Conti," than which no Clos Vougeot or Chambertin or any other growth of the Côte d'or is more delicious. Château-Laffite, Château-La-Rose, Château-Margaux suggest, they do not equal it. And they are clarets. It is a wine which fills the veins with an elixir of life, and so Alice thought it. Why she was made so much of; why she was so petted, she could not understand. Was that courteous and gallant cavalier opposite her at the other end of the table, more like a lover in his addresses than her guardian, the same cruel and relentless uncle who had flogged her with such merciless severity in the morning, and who was, she recollected with wonder, again to punish her on the morrow? And then she called to mind herself. Was the laughing girl, full of joke and mirth; the beauty decked out in black and yellow, displaying with such artless coquetry her many charms, and giving herself in her high spirits so many winning airs, and feeling so much at ease, although she had no drawers on, as Maud and her uncle knew, and although her dress only barely came down to her knees, at all of which she was now rather more pleased than otherwise—the same Alice she had formerly known, dressed in a high-fitting, tight, dowdy brown garment, and expiring with shame at the sight of half an inch of leg? She laughed with joy to feel that she was becoming free from such ridiculous notions, and rejoiced at the growing sense of liberty to enjoy the possession of her charms, and to employ the power they gave her to the uttermost.

After dinner they went to a room upstairs, panelled with rose-coloured silk and hung with water-colours.

CHAPTER IV

MYSTERY UNVEILED.

"Away!" she cried, "grave face and solemn sighs;
   Kiss and be merry! Preach the sermon after.
Give me the careless dance and sparkling eyes;
   Let me be wooed with kisses, songs, and laughter!"

—THE MONKS OF THELEMA.

Then up he got and donned his clothes,
   And dupped the chamber door;
Let in the maid that out a maid
   Never departed more.

—OLD SONG: SHAKESPEARE.

It was a beautiful summer's night. The air was heavily laden with the sweet perfume of the flowers in the garden below the windows, which were thrown wide open. There were besides several china vases, or rather bowls, standing about the room, full of roses, of shades varying from the deepest crimson to the softest blush scarcely more than suggested upon the delicate petal. The only sounds were the gentle rustle of the summer zephyr amongst the trees and the weird hoot of the owls. The deeply-shaded lamps gave animation to the rosy tints of the boudoir They were emphasized by the yellow flame of the fire which, notwithstanding the season, crackled merrily in the grate.

548

(A fire upon a summer's night is an agreeable thing.) Between it and Alice there at once appeared to be something in common. She and the fire were the only two black and gold things in the rosy apartment. The fierce flame struck Alice as being a very adequate expression of the love she felt seething in her veins. She felt intoxicated with passion and desire, and capable of the most immoral deeds, the more shocking the better.

This naughty lust was soon to have at least some gratification. Maud had seated herself at the piano—an exquisite instrument in a Louis Seize case—and had played softly some snatches of Schubert's airs, and Alice had been reclining some minutes on a rose-coloured couch—a beautiful spot of black and yellow, kept in countenance by the fire—showing two long yellow legs, when Sir Edward noticed that every time she altered her position she endeavoured, with a slightly tinged cheek, to pull her frock down. Of course he had been gazing at the shapely limbs and trying to avail himself of every motion, which could not fail to disclose more—the frock being very short—to see above her knee. He thought once that he had succeeded in catching a glimpse of the pink flesh above the yellow stocking.

Alice, sensible of her uncle's steadfast observation, was more and more overwhelmed with the most bewitching confusion; her coy and timid glances, her fruitless efforts to hide herself, only serving to make her the more attractive.

Maud looked on with amusement from the music-stool, where she sat pouring liquid melody from her pretty fingers, and mutely wondering whatever had come over Alice, and whatever had become of the healthy delight in displaying her charms of which she had boasted before dinner. Maud felt very curious to know how it would end.

"Alice," at length said her uncle, with a movement of impatience, "have you begun to write out that sentence I told you to write out fifty times?"

"Oh, no, uncle! I have not."

"Well, my dear, you had better set to work. It will suggest wholesome reflections."

So Alice got up and got some ruled paper, an inkstand, and a quill pen; then, seating herself at a Chippendale table, began to fiddle with the pen and ink.

Her uncle continued to watch her intently. Maud had ceased to play, and had thrown herself carelessly on the couch which Alice had just left. Maud's dress, too, was quite low and very short; but in the most artless way she flung herself backwards upon the sofa and clasped her hands behind her head, thus showing her arms, neck, bust, and breast to the fullest advantage; and pulling her left foot up to her thigh, made a rest with the left knee for the right leg, which she placed across it, thus fully displaying her legs in their open-work stockings and her thighs encased in loose flesh-coloured silk drawers tied with crimson ribbons. Her attitude and abandon were not lost upon Sir Edward.

Alice's sensations were dreadful. How could she, there, under her uncle's eye, write that she had "pea'd"? And not only "pea'd", but with shame and anger she recollected the sentence ran, "like a mare!" —like an animal; like a beast; as she had seen them in the street. And all "before her uncle." Whatever would become of her if she had to write this terrible sentence; to put so awful a confession into her own handwriting; to confide such a secret fifty times over with her own hand to paper? If it was ever found out she would be ruined—her reputation would be gone—no one would have anything to say to her —she would have to fly to the mountains and the caves. She had not realized until it came to actually writing it out how difficult, how terrible, how impossible it was for her to do it. If her uncle knew, surely he would not insist. He could not wish her to humiliate herself to such an extent; to ruin and destroy herself with her own handwriting; neither could he have realized what it would be for her to write such a thing. While these thoughts were passing through her mind, she kept unconsciously pulling and dragging at her frock. If only she could cover herself up. So much of her legs showed; and the long yellow stockings made them so conspicuous under her black frock. Although they were above her knee, unless she kept her legs close together she could not help showing her black garters. And her arms and her neck and her breast were all bare. She began to feel almost sulky.

"Well, Alice," at length said her uncle; "when are you going to begin?"

"Oh, uncle! it is dreadful to have to say such a thing in my own handwriting—I am sure you have never thought how dreadful."

"You must chronicle in your own handwriting what you did, miss. Writing what you did is not so bad as doing it. And you will not only write it, but you shall sign it with your name, so that everyone may know what a naughty girl you were."

"Oh, uncle! oh, uncle! I can't. You will burn it when it is done; won't you?"

"No; certainly not. It shall be kept as a proof of how naughty you can be."

And as she kept tugging at her frock and not writing, her uncle said:—

"Maud, will you fetch the dress-suspender? It will keep her dress out of her way."

Maud discharged her errand with alacrity. In less than three minutes she had returned with a band of black silk, from which hung four long, black silk ribbons. Making Alice stand up, Maud slipped her arms under her petticoats and put the band round Alice's waist next her skin, buckling it behind, and edged it up as high as the corset, which Janet had not left loose, would allow. The four ribbons hung down far below the frock, two at the right and two at the left hip—one ribbon in front, the other at the back.

Maud then walked Alice over into the full blaze of the fire. Putting her arms round her and bending down, she took the ribbons at Alice's left side one in each hand, and then pulled them up and joined them on Alice's right shoulder in a bow. The effect, of course, was to bundle half Alice's petticoats and dress up about her waist, disclosing her left leg from the end of the stocking naked. Maud, with little ceremony, then turned her round, and, taking the ribbons at her right side, tied them across her left shoulder, thus removing the other half of Alice's covering and displaying the right leg. She then carefully arranged the frock and petticoats, smoothing them out, tightening the ribbons, and settling the bows. And by the time she had finished, from the black band round her waist nearly to her garters, Alice was in front and behind perfectly naked—her breast and arms and thighs and navel and buttocks. The lower petticoat was, it will be remembered, lined with yellow, and the inside was turned out. It and the stockings and the two black bands intensified her nakedness. She would sooner have been, she felt, stripped entirely of every shred of clothing than have had on those garments huddled about her waist, and those stockings, which, she instinctively knew, only heightened the exhibition of her form and directed the gaze to all she most wished to conceal.

"Now, miss," said her uncle, "this will save you the trouble of vain and silly efforts to conceal yourself."

"Oh, uncle! uncle! how can you disgrace me so?"

"Disgrace you, my dear? What nonsense! You are not deformed. You are perfectly exquisite. With," he continued, passing his hand over her, "a skin like satin."

Feeling his hand, Alice experienced a delicious thrill, which her uncle noticing, recommended her to sit down and write out her imposition—a task which was now a hundred times more difficult. However could she, seated in a garb which only displayed her nakedness in the most glaring manner, write such words?

"Alice," said he, "you are again becoming refractory."

Putting his arm round her, he sat down and put her face downwards across his left knee. "You must have your bottom smacked. That will bring you to your senses." (Smack—smack—smack—smack—smack—smack.)

"Oh, uncle! don't! Oh!"—struggling—"I will write anything!"—smack—"oh! how you sting!"—smack—smack—"oh! oh! oh! Your hand is so hard."

Then, slipping his hand between her legs, he tickled her clitoris until she cooed and declared she would take a delight in saying and writing and doing the "most shocking things."

"Very well, miss! Then go and write out what I told you; sign it; and bring it to me when it is finished."

So Alice seated herself—the straw seat of the chair pricking her bottom—resolved, however, to brazen out her nakedness, and wrote with a trembling hand: "I pea'd like a mare before my uncle; I pea'd like a mare before my uncle; I pea'd like a mare before my uncle." Before she had half completed her task, she was so excited and to such an extent under the influence of sensual and voluptuous feelings that she could not remain still; and she felt the delicate hair in front about her cunt grow moist Before she had completed the fiftieth line she was almost beside herself.

At last, for the fiftieth time, she wrote:—

"I pea'd like a mare before my uncle."

And with a shudder, signed it, "Alice Darvell."

During her task Maud had looked at what she was writing over her shoulder, and Alice glowed with shame. So had her uncle; but

Alice was surprised to find she rather liked his seeing her disgrace, and felt inclined to nestle close up to him.

Now Maud had gone to bed, and she was to take her task to her uncle.

He was seated in a great chair near the fire, looking very wide awake indeed. He might have been expected to have been dozing. But there was too lovely a girl in the room for that. He looked wide awake indeed, and there was a fierce sparkle in his eye as his beautiful ward, in her long yellow stockings and low dress, her petticoats turned up to her shoulders, and blushing deeply, approached him with her accomplished penance.

She handed it to him.

"So you did, Alice," said he, "so you did," sitting bolt upright, "pea like a mare before me, and here is, I see," turning over a page or two, "your own signature to the confession."

"Oh, uncle, it is true; but do not let anyone know. I know I disgraced myself and behaved like a beast; but I am so sorry."

"But you deserved your punishment."

"Yes; I know I did. Only too well."

He drew her down upon his knee, and placed his right arm round her waist, while he tickled her legs and her groin and her abdomen, and lastly her clitoris, with his hand and fingers.

He let her, when she was almost overcome by the violence of her sensations, slip down between his knees, and as she was seeking how most effectually to caress him, he directed her hands to his penis and his testicles. In a moment of frenzy she tore open his trousers, lifted his shirt, and saw the excited organ, the goal and Ultima Thule of feminine delight. He pressed down her head, and, despite the resistance she at first made, the inflamed and distended virility was very quickly placed between the burning lips of her mouth. Its taste and the transport she was in induced her to suck it violently. On her knees before her uncle, tickling, sucking, licking his penis, then looking in his face and recommencing, the sweet girl's hands again very quickly found their way to his balls.

At last, excited beyond his selfcontrol, gazing through his half-closed lids at the splendid form of his niece at his feet—her bare back and shoulders—the breast which, sloping downwards from her position, he yet could see—her bare arms—the hands twiddling and manipulating and kneading with affection and appreciation his balls; his legs far apart, himself thrown back gasping in his arm chair; his own most sensitive and highly excited organ in the dear girl's hot mouth, tickled with the tip of her dear tongue, and pinched with her dear, pretty, cruel ivory teeth—Sir Edward could contain himself no longer and, grasping Alice's head with both his hands, he pushed his weapon well into her mouth and spent down her throat. He lay back in a swoon of delight, and the girl, as wet as she could be, leant her head against his knee, almost choked by the violence of the delightful emission, and stunned by the mystery revealed to her. How she loved him! How she dandled that sweet fellow! How she fondled him! What surreptitious licks she gave him! She could have eaten her uncle.

In about twenty minutes he had recovered sufficiently to speak, and she sat with her head resting against the inside of his right leg, looking up into his face; her own legs stretched out underneath his left one—she was sitting on the floor.

"Alice, you bold, bad girl, to pea like a mare. I hope you feel punished now."

"Oh no, uncle, it was delightful. Does it give you pleasure? I will suck you again," taking his penis, to his great excitement, again in her warm little palm, "if you wish."

"My dear, do you want to pea?"

"Yes; before I go to bed."

"Then here is the key Run along and go to bed."

"Oh, I would rather stay with you."

"Although I have whipped you and birched you and smacked you and made you disgrace yourself?"

"Yes, dear uncle. It has done me good. Don't send me away."

"Go, Alice, to bed. I will come to you there."

"Oh, you dear uncle, how nice. Oh, do let down my things for me before I go. Some of the servants may see me."

"And," she continued, after an instant's pause, with a blush, and looking down, "I want to be for you alone."

Touched by her devotion, her uncle loosed the ribbons; let fall, as far as they would, her frock and petticoats; and giving her a kiss, and not forgetting to use his hand under her clothes in a manner which caused her again to cry out with delight, allowed her to trip off to her bedroom. But not without the remark that she had induced him to do that which did not add to her appearance; for the rich, full, and well-developed girlish form had been simply resplendent with loveliness in the garments huddled about her waist; the petticoat lining of yellow silk relieved by the black bands from her waist to her shoulder crossing each other, and bits of her black frock, with its large yellow spots, appearing here and there. And as the eye travelled downwards from the pink flesh of the swelling breasts to the smooth pink thighs, it noted with rapture that the clothes concealed only what needed not concealment, and revealed with the greatest effect what did; and, still descending, dwelt entranced upon the well-turned limbs, whose outlines and curves the tight stockings so clearly defined.

Sir Edward, who had made her stand facing him, and also with her back to him, was much puzzled, although so warm a devotee of the Venus Callipyge, whether he preferred the back view of her lovely legs, thighs, bottom, back, nuque, and queenly little head, with its suggestion of fierce and cruel delight; or the front, showing the mount and grotto of Venus, the tender breasts, the dimpled chin and sparkling eyes, with the imaginations of soft pleasures and melting trances which the sloping and divided thighs suggested and invited.

The first thing which Alice noticed upon reaching her room was the little supper-table laid for two; and the next that there were black silk sheets on her bed. The sight of the supper—the chocolate, the tempting cakes and biscuits, the rich wines in gold mounted jugs, the Nuremburg glasses, the bonbons, the crystallized fruit, the delicate omelette—delighted her; but the black sheets had a somewhat funereal and depressing effect.

"What can Maud have been thinking of, my dear, to put *black* sheets on the bed; and to-night of all nights in the year?" asked Sir Edward, angrily, the instant he entered the apartment, and hastily returning to the sitting-room, he rang and ordered Janet up. She was directed to send Miss Maud to "my niece's room, and in a quarter of an hour to put *pink* silk sheets on the bed there."

Then Sir Edward returned, and giving Alice some sparkling white wine, which with sweet biscuits she said she would like better than anything else, he helped himself to a bumper of red—standing—expecting Maud's appearance. Alice was seated in a cosy chair, toasting her toes.

Presently Maud arrived in a lovely déshabille, her rich dark hair tumbling about her shoulders, the dressing-gown not at all concealing the richly-embroidered robe de nuit beneath it, and the two garments clinging closely to her form, setting off her lovely svelte figure to perfection. Her little feet were encased in low scarlet slippers embroidered with gold, so low cut as to show the whole of the white instep.

Her manner was hurried and startled, but this pretty dismay increased her attractions.

"Maud," asked her uncle, "what do you mean by having had black sheets put on this bed, when I distinctly said they were to be pink?"

"Indeed, indeed, uncle, you said black."

"How dare you contradict me, miss, and so add to your offence? You have been of late very careless indeed. You shall be soundly punished. Go straight to the yellow room," he went on to the trembling girl. "I will follow you in a few moments and flog you in a way that you will recollect. Eighteen stripes with my riding-whip and a dozen with the cat-o'-nine-tails."

"Oh, uncle," she gasped.

"Go along, miss."

Alice, to her surprise, although she had some little feeling of distress for Maud, felt quite naughty at the idea of her punishment; and, noticing her uncle's excitement, concluded instinctively that he also felt similar sensations. She was, consequently, bold enough, without rising, to stretch out her hand and to press outside his clothes the gentleman underneath with whom she had already formed so intimate an acquaintance, asking as she did so whether he was going to be very severe.

"Yes," he replied, moving to and fro (notwithstanding which she kept her hand well pressed on him). "I shall lash her bottom until it bleeds and she yells for mercy."

"O, uncle!" said Alice, quivering with a strange thrill.

"Go to the room, Alice. I shall follow in a moment."

Poor Maud was in tears, and Alice, much affected at this sight, attempted to condole with her.

"The riding-whip is terribly severe; however I shall bear it I can't tell; and then that terrible cat afterwards; it will drive me mad."

"Oh, Maud, I am so sorry."

"And I made *no* mistake. He *said* black sheets. The fact is, your beauty has infuriated him, and he wants to tear me to pieces."

Sir Edward returned without trousers, wearing a kilt.

"Now come over here, you careless hussey," and indicating two rings in the floor quite three feet apart, he made her stretch her legs wide, so as to place her feet near the rings, to which Alice was made to strap them by the ankles. "I will cure you of your carelessness and inattention to orders. Your delicate flesh will feel this rod's cuts for days. Off with your dressing-gown; off with your night-dress." Alice was dazzled by her nakedness, the ripeness of her charms, the whiteness of her skin, the plump, soft, round bottom, across which Sir Edward laid a few playful cuts, making the girl call out, for, fixed as she was, she could not struggle.

Alice then, by her uncle's direction, placed before Maud a trestle, the top of which was stuffed and covered with leather, and which reached just to her middle. Across this she was made to lie, and two rings on the other side were drawn down and fixed her elbows, so that her head was almost on the floor, and her bottom, with its skin tight, well up in the air. Her legs, of course, were well apart. The cruelty of the attitude inflamed Alice.

"Give me the whip," said her uncle. As she handed the heavy weapon to him, he added, "stand close to me while I flog her, and," slipping his hand up her petticoats on to her inflamed and moist organ, "keep your hand upon me while I do so."

Alice gave a little spring as he touched her. Her own animal feelings told her what was required of her.

Maud was crying softly.

"Now, miss," as the whip cut through the air, "it is your turn" —swish—a great red wale across the bottom and a writhe of agony— "you careless"—swish—"wicked"—swish—"disobedient"—swish— "obstinate girl."

"Oh, uncle! oh! oh! oh! oh! I am sorry, oh, forgive———"—swish —"no, miss"—swish—"no forgiveness. Black sheets, indeed"—swish —swish—swish—"I will cure you, my beauty."

Maud did her best to stifle her groans, but it was clear that she was almost demented with the exquisite torture the whip caused her every time it cut with relentless vigour into her bleeding flesh. Sir

Edward did not spare her. The rod fell each time with unmitigated energy.

"Spare the rod and spoil you, miss. Better spoil your bold, big bottom than that," he observed, as he pursued the punishment. The more cruel it became the greater Alice found grew her uncle's and her own excitement, until at last she scarcely knew how to contain herself. At the ninth stripe, Sir Edward crossed over to Maud's right to give the remaining nine the other way across.

Swish—swish—swish—fell the heavy whip, the victim's moans and prayers absolutely unheeded.

"A girl must have her bare bottom whipped"—swish—"occasionally; there is nothing"—swish—"so excellent for her"—swish—"it teaches her to mind what is told her"—swish—"it knocks all false shame"—swish—"out of her; there is no mock modesty left about a young—lady after"—swish—"she has had her bottom under the lash."

Alice trembled when she saw the cat-o'-nine-tails, made of hard, tightly twisted whip-cords, each tail bearing several knots, and when she looked at the bleeding bottom she grew sick and pale. But when her uncle began to lecture Maud as he caressingly drew the terrible scourge through his fingers, and to tell her that for a hardened girl such as she was a whip was insufficient punishment, and that she must also be subjected to the cat's claws, Alice began to revive, and she noticed that, while Sir Edward again approached boiling point, Maud gave as much lascivious movement as her tight bonds permitted.

But the first three strokes, given from left to right, evoked piercing yells and shrieks; the next three, given across the other way, cries and howls of the wildest despair, followed by low sobs. The blood flowed freely and was spattered about the room. Alice felt some on her face and arms.

"You will not forget again, I know," said Sir Edward, as he wielded the terrible instrument. "You careless, naughty girl, how grateful you should be to me for taking the trouble to chastise you thus. The cat has quite irresistible arguments, has she not?"

The last six were given lengthwise, first along the legs, then round the bottom, and lastly on the cunt. Maud's roars and yells were redoubled; but in an ecstasy of delight she lost her senses at the last blow.

Alice, too, was mad with excitement. Rushing off, as directed, to her room, she, as her uncle had also bid her do, tore off all her clothing and dived into the pink sheets, rolling about with the passion the sight of the whipping had stimulated to an uncontrollable degree.

Sir Edward, having summoned Janet to attend Maud, hastened to follow Alice.

Divesting himself of all his clothing, he tore the bedclothes off the naked girl, who lay on her back, inviting him to her arms, and to the embrace of which she was still ignorant, by the posture nature dictated to her, and looking against the pink sheet a perfect rose of loveliness. Sir Edward sprang upon her in a rush and surge of passion which bore him onwards with the irresistible force a flowing sea. In a moment he, notwithstanding her cries, was between her already separated legs, clasping her to him, while he directed, with his one free hand, his inflamed and enormous penis to her virgin cunt. Already it had passed the lips and was forcing its way onwards, impelled, by the reiterated plunges of Sir Edward, before Alice could realize what was happening. At last she turns a little pale, and her eyes open wide and stare slightly in alarm, while, finding that her motion increases the assault and the slight stretching of her cunt, she remains still. But the next moment, remembering what had occurred when *it* was in her mouth, it struck her that the same throbbing and shooting and deliciously warm and wet emission might be repeated in the lower and more secret part of her body, and that if, as she hoped and prayed it might be, it was, she would expire of joy. These ideas caused a delightfull tremor and a few movements of the buttocks, which increased Sir Edward's pleasure and enabled him to make some progress. But at length the swelling of his organ and his march into the interior began to hurt, and she became almost anxious to withdraw from the amorous encounter. His arms, however, held her tight. She could not get him from between her legs, and she was being pierced in the tenderest portion of her body by a man's great thing, like a horse's. Oh, how naughty she felt! And yet how it hurt! How dreadful it was that he should be able to probe her with it and detect all her sensations by means of it, while on the other hand, she was made sensible *there,* and by means of *it,* of all he felt.

"Oh! uncle! Oh! dear, dear uncle! Oh! oh! oh! oh! Wait one minute! Oh! not so hard! Oh, dear, don't push any further—oh, it is so nice; but it hurts! Oh, do stop! don't press so hard! Oh! oh! oh! Oh! please don't! oh! it hurts! Oh! I shall die! You are tearing me open! you are indeed! Oh! oh! oh!"

"If you don't"—push—push—"hold me tight and push against me, Alice, I will—yes, that's better—flog your bottom until it bleeds and the blood runs down to your heels, you bold girl. No, you shan't get away. I will get right into you. Don't," said he, clawing her bottom with his hands and pinching its cheeks severely, "slip back. Push forward."

"Oh! I shall die! Oh! oh! oh!" as she felt she pinches, and jerked forward, enabling Sir Edward to make considerable advance, "Oh! I shall faint; I shall die! Oh, stop! Oh!" as she continued her involuntary motion upwards and downwards, "you hurt excruciatingly."

He folded her more closely to him, and, altogether disregarding her loud cries, proceeded to divest her of her maidenhead, telling her that if she did not fight bravely he would punish her till she thought she was being flayed alive; that he would tear her bottom for her with hooks; and he slipped a hand down behind her, and got the middle finger well into her arse.

After this, victory was assured. A few more shrieks and spasms of mingled pleasure and pain, when Sir Edward, who had forced himself up to the hymen and had made two or three shrewd thrusts at it, evoking loud gasps and cries from his lovely ward, drew a long sigh, and with a final determined push sunk down on her bosom, while she, emitting one sharp cry, found her suffering changed into a transport of delight. She clasped her uncle with frenzy to her breast, and throbbed and shook in perfect unison with him, while giving little cries of rapture and panting—with half-closed lids, from under which rolled a diamond tear or two—for the breath of which her ecstasy had robbed her.

Several moments pased, the silence interrupted only by inarticulate sounds of gratification. Sir Edward's mouth was glued to hers, and his tongue found its way between its ruby lips and sought hers. Overcoming her coyness, the lovely girl allowed him to find it, and no sooner had they touched than an electric thrill shot through her; Sir Edward's penis, which had never been removed, again began to swell; he recommenced his (and she her) upward and downward movements and again the delightful crisis occurred—this time without the intense pain Alice had at first experienced, and with very much greater appreciation of the shock, which thrilled her from head to foot and seemed to penetrate and permeate the innermost recesses of her being.

Never had she experienced, or even in her fondest moments conceived, the possibility of such transports. She had longed for the possession of her uncle; she had longed to eat him, to become absorbed in him; and she now found the appetite gratified to the fullest extent, in a manner incredibly sweet. To feel his weight upon the front of her thighs—to feel him between her legs, her legs making each of his a captive; the most secret and sensitive and essentially masculine organ of his body inside that part of hers of which she could not think without a blush; and the mutual excitement, the knowledge and consciousness each had of the other's most intimate sensations, threw her into an ecstasy. How delicious it was to be a girl; how she enjoyed the contemplation of her charms; how supremely, overpoweringly delightful it was to have a lover in her embrace to appreciate and enjoy them! How delicious was love!

Sir Edward, gratified at length, rose and congratulated Alice upon her newborn womanhood; kissed her, and thanked her for the intense pleasure she had given him.

After some refreshment, as he bade her good-night, the love-sick girl once more twined her arms about him, while slipping her legs on to the edge of the bed, she lay across it and managed to get him between them; then, drawing him down to her bosom, cried, "Once more, dear uncle; once more before you go."

"You naughty girl," he answered, slightly excited; "well, I will if you ask me."

"Oh, please, do, uncle. Please do it again."

"Do what again?"

"Oh! It. You know, What—what—what," hiding her face sweetly, "you have done to me twice already."

"Don't you know what it is called?"

"No. I haven't the slightest idea.'

"It is called 'fucking' Now, if you want it done again, you must ask to be fucked," said he, his instrument assuming giant proportions.

"Oh, dear, I do want it ever so; but however I can ask for it—

once more before you go?" and she lay back and extended her legs before him in the divinest fashion.

In a moment he was between them; his prick inserted; his lips again upon hers; and in a few moments more they were again simultaneously overcome by that ecstasy of supernatural exquisiteness of which unbridled passion has alone attempted to fathom the depths, and that without reaching them.

Exhausted mentally and physically by her experiences and the exercises of the evening, Alice, as she felt the lessening throbs of her uncle's engine, found she was losing herself and consciousness in drowsiness. Her uncle placed her in a comfortable posture upon the great pillow, and throwing the sheet over her, heard her murmured words of thanks and love as she fell asleep with a smile upon her face. Janet came and tucked her up comfortably. And she slept profoundly.

CHAPTER V

PUNISHMENT.

Whipping grown girls is a pastime rare
Few males, if called on, could refuse to share.

—ROMANCE OF CHASTISEMENT.

Alice lay awake next morning listening to the birds, in a sweet trance as the recollection on which she dwelt of what she had passed through the night before. She felt completely changed, and could she have seen the dark stains upon the crimson sheet under her, she would have known that she really was so.

She met Maud in the breakfast-room and was warmly greeted by her.

"Well, love; well, Alice?" cried she, clasping both her hands in her own and gazing into her face with a glance in which there was deep meaning.

"Oh, Maud!" ejaculated Alice, blushing, and then, to turn the subject, "how are you, dear, after that terrible flogging? I could almost have cried at what you suffered at one moment, and yet I could have made uncle tear you in pieces the next."

"Yes," said Maud; "I have experienced the feeling. The result was that you and your uncle enjoyed yourselves the more. Now, wasn't it?"

After breakfast Alice remembered that she had to go straight to the yellow room. She did so without much dread, feeling that she

563

could not have worse to go through than she had already suffered; although one or two chance expressions of Maud had made her doubtful of this conclusion; and the cold sternness of her uncle startled and alarmed her after his warmth and tenderness of the preceding evening. When he met her and wished her good morning in the breakfast-room he was apparently absolutely unconscious, and certainly totally forgetful, of what had passed.

Alice went with Maud arm-in-arm to the yellow room, wondering what the trapeze would be like.

Her uncle soon followed her and locked the door. He had a long carriage-whip and some sheets of paper which she recognised in his hand.

"You are Miss Alice Darvell, and this is your handwriting and signature?" asked he severely, showing the papers to her.

"Oh yes, uncle; they are," answered the girl, trembling with fright.

"You pea'd like a mare before your uncle, eh, miss?"

"I—I—I couldn't help it."

"Did you?"

"Y—ye—yes!"

"Well, you shall be flogged like a mare. Strip yourself."

"Oh, uncle!"

"Strip yourself absolutely naked, or," he said, raising the whip and lightly slashing it about her legs, for her frock only came down to her knees, "you shall have double."

She jumped as she felt the lash sting her calves, and drew up her legs one after another.

Then, seeing her uncle's arm again raised, she began to quickly undo her bodice and slip off her frock; her petticoats and corset soon followed, and, lastly, slipping off her chemise, she stood naked except for her long stockings, and covered with a most bewildering air of shame, not knowing whether to cover her face or not, or how to dispose of her hands and arms.

"Take off your shoes and stockings," said her uncle.

She had to do so seated in her nakedness, and the action added extremely to confusion.

Sir Edward then went to a bracket or flat piece of wood screwed on the wall, on which were two hooks fixed back to back and some distance apart; round them was fastened a thick crimson silk cord. As he unwound it, Alice saw that it communicated with a pulley in the ceiling over which it hung, and dangling from which was a bar of wood about two-and-a-half feet long—the cord dividing about three feet above it and being fastened to each of its ends.

"Now, Maud," said Sir Edward, "put her in position and fix her wrists."

Maud walked up to Alice and led her beneath the pulley. Sir Edward allowed the bar to descend to a level with the top of her shoulders. Maud then took the naked girl's right wrist and fastened it by a strap ready prepared to one end of the bar, so that the back of the hand was against it. And then she did the same with the left hand.

"Ready?" asked Sir Edward.

"Ready," answered Maud.

Whereupon he pulled the cord, availing himself of the hooks to get a purchase, until Alice's arms were stretched high above her head, and her whole body was well drawn up, the balls of her feet only resting on the floor.

"Oh, uncle! oh, uncle! oh, please! oh! not so high! oh! my arms will be dislocated! oh! it hurts my wrists!" and, involuntarily moving, she found very little would swing her off her feet.

Sir Edward, finding her sufficiently drawn up, fixed the cord, and, taking the whip in his right hand, played with the lash with his left as he gloated upon the exquisite naked girl—her extended arms, her shoulders, her breasts, her stomach, her navel, her abdomen, her back, her thighs, her buttocks, her legs, all displayed and glowing with shame and beauty.

At last, raising his whip, as he stood at her left, he said:—

"So we 'pea'd like a mare before uncle,' and are now going to be flogged like a mare."

Alice, in silent terror, drew up first one leg and then the other, showing off the exquisitely moulded limbs, and giving more than a glimpse of other charms.

"And," went on her uncle, "on the very part guilty of the offence." Whisp—whisple.

He had raised the whip, swinging out the lash, and brought it down with full force across the front of the girl's thighs, the lash striking her fair on the cunt. For a moment she was speechless, but the next emitted a piercing yell as she threw her head back and struggled to be free.

Sir Edward's arm was now across him.

Whisp, whisple went the whip as he gave the return stroke severely across her bottom, making her dance with anguish and leaving a red wale.

Whisp, whisple went the whip with merciless precision back again.

Alice's gymnastics were of the most frantic description. She jumped and threw out her legs and swung to and fro, showing every atom of her form, in utter recklessness of what she showed or of what she concealed.

When three strokes had been administered backwards and forwards from the left side, Sir Edward went round to the right—there her bottom received the forward and her front the back strokes, and well laid on they were. Sir Edward delighted in the infliction of a punishment which left his victim no reserve or concealment whatever, and he made the whip cut into the flesh.

Alice, almost suffocated with her cries and sobs, writhed for several minutes after the last stroke. At last her agony became less intense and her sobs fewer.

A high stool was then put before her and on it a po.

It was pushed close up to her, and Sir Edward inserted his hand from behind and tickled and frigged her cunt, saying:

"Yesterday you pea'd to please yourself. To-day you shall do so to please me."

Alice, beside herself, knew not what to do. She had not relieved herself since the night before. At last, with a shudder, a copious flood burst out, partly over her uncle's hand, and she gave a groan as she realized the manner in which she had been made to disgrace herself.

Her uncle then loosened the rope sufficiently to let her heels rest on the ground, and calling Maud to the sofa, which was immediately in front of Alice, he threw her back on it, while she quickly unfastened and pulled down his trousers, exposing his back view entirely to Alice. Maud, too, whose petticoats were up to her waist, threw wide her legs, and Sir Edward, prostrating himself upon her, fucked her violently before Alice.

Never was Alice so conscious of her nakedness as then.

Never, apparently, did Maud enjoy the pleasure of a good fucking more than she did in the presence of that naked and tied-up girl.

And never did Sir Edward acquit himself with greater prowess.

Alice's movements, as she saw her uncle's exertions in Maud's arms, and his strong, sinewy, bare and hairy legs, and his testicles hanging down, and heard his deep breathing and Maud's gasps and sighs—began again, but this time from pleasure instead of pain. She could not, however, as she longed to, get her hands to her cunt, and could only imitate the motions of the impassioned pair before her by a sympathetic movement to and fro—which expressed, but did not assuage her desires—and by little exclamations of longing.

At length the crisis was reached, and Sir Edward sank into Maud's embrace, while Alice could see, and imagined almost that she could *hear*, the throb, throb, throb that was sending thrill after thrill through Maud, and was causing her such a transport of delight that she seemed about to faint from it.

And then he untied her, and was about to leave them, when Alice said, in a most bewitching way:—

"Could you not 'fuck' (a deep blush) me—just once, dear uncle?"

Het half-closed eyes, her splendid form, her nakedness, reawakened her uncle's love and reinvigorated his bestowal of those sensible proofs of it in which ladies so delight. He replied:

"Maud has made me work pretty hard, my dear; but," putting one hand upon her shoulder as she faced him, "as you honour me with such a command, I should be but a *fainéant* and ungallant knight were I not to execute it—or at any rate to make an effort to do so," added he, leading the beautiful girl, nothing loth, to the couch whereon he had enjoyed Maud and gently pushing her backwards, amid her cries and exclamations and involuntary but pretty reluctance, inserted himself into her embrace. She inundated him once, and Maud, perceiving it, slipped her hand between his thighs. This help, good at need, soon worked the cavalier up to a proper appreciation of the situation in which he lay, and to a due expression of his sense of it; to the lady's intense gratification especially, as her forces were sufficient to enable her to, a second time—and this time at exactly the right instant—

> Tumble down,
> And break her crown

and, fortunately, *not* "come tumbling after" Jack, as Jill does in the story.

Although her uncle gave her these marks of affection, yet he did not relent in severity. She was kept without drawers the whole fortnight—a severe punishment! And the stiff white petticoats kept what skirts she had well off her legs, so that when she was seated could not fail to be seen.

And, indeed, after the lashing on the trapeze, she was not allowed to resume that day any garments at all.

She had been given a notebook in which she was compelled to make an entry of every fault and the punishment she was to receive for it.

In her room, on that particular day, aghast at her own nakedness, and thinking herself alone, she had taken up a pair of drawers which, by accident or design, were left there—she had gone to get ready for luncheon—and put them on, when suddenly Sir Edward entered the room.

"What do you mean, miss, by putting on those things? Did I not tell you you were to remain naked the whole of to-day?"

"I only put them on for a moment. I felt so ashamed of being naked."

"Take out your book and write:—For being ashamed of being naked, and for disobedience to my uncle, I am to ask him to give me two dozen with the tawse across his knee after supper this evening, and I am to remain stark naked for three days."

"Oh! oh! oh! Forgive me, dear uncle. I won't be ashamed any more. I won't disobey you any more. I won't indeed."

But it was no use.

At luncheon she had to sit down naked. All the afternoon she had to go about so. If only she might have had one scrap of clothing on! At dinner she could not dress, absolutely naked again; not even shoes or slippers permitted. And that to last three days more! All the evening naked; and as she thought of it she rolled over on to the pillow of the couch and hid her face; but, notwithstanding, felt naked still.

After supper came those terrible two dozen with the tawse. The tawse is a Scotch instrument of punishment, and in special favour with Scotch ladies, who know how to lay it on soundly. It is made of a hard and seasoned piece of leather about two feet long, narrow in the handle and at the other end about four inches broad, cut into narrow strips from about six to nine inches in length.

Alice had never seen, much less felt one.

She was commanded to bring it to her uncle, and had to go for it naked—not even a fan was allowed! How could she conceal the least of her emotions? Oh, this nakedness was an awful, awful thing!

She brought it, and opened her book and knelt down and said:

"Please, uncle, give me two dozen with the tawse for being ashamed and trying to cover my nakedness, and for my disobedience."

"Across my knee."

"Across—your—knee."

"Very well. Get up. Stand sideways close up to me. Now," taking the tawse in his right hand and putting his left arm round her waist, "lean right down, your head on the carpet, miss," and holding her legs with his left one, he slowly and deliberately laid on her sore bottom two dozen well-applied stripes. Then letting her go, she rolled sprawling on the carpet with pain and exhaustion.

The three days' nakedness were rigorously enforced.

They entirely overcame and quenched every spark of shame that was left about her, and she was much the more charming. Her silly simplicity, her country ignorance, were replaced by an artless coquetry and a self-possession which took away the breath and struck those in her presence with irresistible admiration.

Other punishments, too, she had to endure, some of them of a fantastic character.

The fortnight passed rapidly; but the last week, during which she was mistress, was a trying one for her. The servants scarcely heeded a baby in short frocks, with bare legs except for her long stockings, and became careless.

Many a smacking she received across her uncle's knee in the dining-room, or wherever they might happen to be, for some short-coming; often was she sent away hungry from the table and locked up in a black hole for hours because she had not ordered this or that, or someone had done what he disapproved of And after supper every evening, and all night if he was in the humour, she was required to be at his disposal and to give him pleasure in every form his endless ingenuity could invent.

At the end of the week, when her drawers were restored to her, she scarcely cared for them; but had not worn them long when the recollection of having been so much without them gave her the sweetest sense of shame possible.

CHAPTER VI

THE END

Quoth she, "Before you tumbled me
You promised me to wed."

—OLD SONG

So life continued for a long while at Bosmere Hall The summer ripened into autumn; winter followed, and then spring, when, on good authority, it is said the thoughts turn to love.

The hunting had delighted Alice, notwithstanding that she had been once or twice soundly birched by her uncle in the open air for some error of the *ménage*, and made to ride home without trousers.

She came, however, to like these punishments; but one day she thought she had seriously offended him, for he declared his intention of marrying her to his heir. She would have preferred him.

The heir and she met at a ball. He was a charming young man. Alice's bashfulness had long departed. She recognized some likeness to her uncle—she knew his wishes. She waltzed five or six times with her cousin, who was intoxicated with her beauty and her short dress, her openwork stockings with the clocks at the side, the tiny little dancing shoes; the rosy flesh, and the perfume of love in every breath she exhaled.

They went together to supper, and afterwards retired to a distant conservatory. Soon his arm was about her, while his other hand was busily engaged, to her delight, underneath her petticoats. The

honeyed phrases and sweet nothings that so please lovers followed, and
they were to be married in three months. The period rapidly passed.

On her wedding day her uncle presented her with a hundred
thousand pounds personal property of his own, which became her
own, apart from her husband and the inheritance and settlements, and
also with the famous cairn gorms.

Alice smiled and wept as brides will on her departure to spend
Easter with her husband at Rome.

She taught him much, and, on the other hand, learned one or two
things from him. But what surprised her most of all was that, whilst
she often thought with ridicule and contempt of the days spent with
her old aunt in Yorkshire, she always regarded with joy and satisfaction
those spent at Bosmere Hall with her uncle and Maud, and felt she
would ever consider them as the happiest of her life.

"The most secret parts of virgins have been submitted to the examination of ignorant matrons and prejudiced physicians, without dreaming that such an act of indecency is an offence against virginity; that the attempt to discover it is a rape in itself; that every shameful situation and every indecent condition at which a virgin is obliged to blush within, is a real defloration."

BUFFON.